James Crumley: The Collection

James Crumley was born in Three Rivers, Texas, and spent most of his childhood in South Texas. He currently teaches creative writing at the University of Texas at El Paso and summers in Missoula, Montana. His earlier work includes a novel of Vietnam, *One to Count Cadence*. Mr. Crumley is at work on a novel about Texas.

James Crumley
The Collection

THE WRONG CASE

•

THE LAST GOOD KISS

•

DANCING BEAR

PICADOR
Published by Pan Books

The Wrong Case first published 1975 by Random House, Inc. New York
The Last Good Kiss first published 1978 by Random House, Inc.
Dancing Bear first published 1983 by Random House, Inc.
All three books first published in Great Britain in this collection 1991
by Pan Books Ltd.,
Cavaye Place, London SW10 9PG
1 3 5 7 9 8 6 4 2
© James Crumley 1975, 1978, 1983
ISBN 0 330 32213 3

Printed and bound in Great Britain by
Billing and Sons Ltd, Worcester

Phototypeset by Intype, London

James Crumley
The Collection

Michelle –
Thanks for
the representation
in Paris.

James Crumley

CONTENTS

AN INTRODUCTION TO
THE ENGLISH EDITION OF
THE DETECTIVE NOVELS

It started in Mexico. In Guadalajara. In the aisles of the supermar-
cado bathed in that hot Mexican light. I remembered what the fat
man had said months before on a cold, bleary night up in Montana.
I glanced around, as furtive as a tourist priest destined to be sacrificed
to Montezuma's Revenge, cursed to dance the Aztec Two-Step
forever, then my fingers lunged in a frenzy . . . over to the nearest
garish novel on the paperback rack of over-priced American novels.

Well, sad to say, not all life imitates art.

The fat man was Richard Hugo – poet, raconteur, and friend –
and what he had said that winter evening was something like this:
'Goddammit, I wish I could write like Raymond Chandler.' Dick
was already on his way to becoming recognized as a major American
poet (and also a fine detective novelist, as he proved in *Death and
the Good Life* some years later). I had read all of Dick's poetry and,
completely ignorant of Chandler's work, couldn't understand why
this poet wanted to write like that. Of course, I was fresh out of
graduate school at the Writer's Workshop at the University of Iowa,
deep into the beginning of my first novel, a work, I hoped, of high
literary purpose. So I replied, with one of the many useless lines I
learned in graduate school: 'He just writes detective novels.' Dick
gave me a look Sidney Greenstreet would have admired.

As it often does, my ignorance came back to haunt me. The 'garish
paperback' I grabbed off the rack was one of the Ballentine reissues
of Chandler with the wonderful Tom Adams art deco covers. *The
Little Sister* I think it was, or perhaps *The Lady in the Lake*. I have

read all of Chandler so many times, I can't remember the order in which I first discovered those wonderful novels.

I was soundly hooked, but I didn't run back to the house on *Paseo de las Aguilas* that I shared with two other young writers and my first disintegrating marriage to start writing a detective novel. I was on the home stretch of my first novel, *One to Count Cadence*, and had no time for frivolities.

That was in the summer of 1967. Seven long years later, after my first novel had been published to confusingly mixed reviews and sold to the movies (my first but not last experience with Hollywood, the Holy Den of Thieves), after my second novel died in my hands like a pet armadillo, after five or six major cross-country moves, three children, three university jobs, two divorces, some other shit I prefer not to remember, and a long and serious encounter with the rest of Chandler and Ross MacDonald, I found myself in Colorado, laboring in the peachy groves of Academe again.

During the break between winter and spring quarters, I remembered a line my father once told me: 'If you don't like what you're doing, get the fuck out.' He was talking about college, which I was attending without purpose, and the South Texas oil fields, where he worked. After he had told me that line of such simple purity, I quit college and joined the Army, hoping that when I returned, I might have purpose. (As it turned out, *purpose* was a little more complex to discover, but I did have my first novel stuck in the distant recesses of my brain pan.) So I walked into the office of the department chair, told him I was going to quit, and move to Seattle to write a *new* novel.

(Who knows what I had in mind? As far as I can tell, I get bored with and won't finish a novel if I know what's going to happen next, or how it ends. I suspect I also refuse to live a life that, even though I know the ending, has a plot that isn't constantly changing as I live it.)

That was 1974, the last time I had a full-time teaching position. Before then, I lived to write. Now I had to learn to write to live. With the help and shelter of friends – Bill Kittredge, Gil Findley, and Peggy Culbert – I managed to finish a novel. Of course, the *new* novel turned out to be a detective novel, something to make a living and keep me at the typewriter while I waited to do something more important. The night after I walked out of the chair's office at

Colorado I wrote the first lines of *The Wrong Case*, began the invention of Milton Chester Milodragovitch, and nothing has been the same since then.

My experience with the detective novel, to say the least, has been ambiguous.

I wrote *The Wrong Case* with the hope that it would be mildly entertaining and discovered that I was mightily touched by Milo and his friends and enemies; I wrote the novel against the genre and found myself captured by it; I wrote it hoping some New York publisher might buy it, which with the help of my agent and old friend, Owen Laster, happened, even though detective novels weren't exactly hot that year.

The Last Good Kiss was a gift novel. The first paragraph only took two years from that moment outside Sonoma when I found the bulldog and the beer joint, both now sadly gone, but after that first paragraph the novel fell into my hands during a year of writing frenzy, a year during which I had to invent a new detective, change the character and focus, and rewrite like a mad monk. But still it was a gift. The novel got me out of Portland, Oregon, a sweet, even lovely city, but far too civilized for my taste. Some years later, the novel would make enough money to get me into tax trouble, a condition with which I am all too familiar.

Dancing Bear, which was written in one of my favorite American cities, El Paso, Texas, was more like work. Making the disparate images work – a couple who met in front of my house in Portland each Tuesday afternoon; a Willie Nelson song, 'Local Memory,' the original title of the book; an important book by Michael Brown, *Laying Waste: The Poisoning of America by Toxic Chemicals*; and a drunken moment with the Dumpp Family Singers while we delivered garbage to our local dump – it seemed to take years to put it all together. But with this novel, all the readers of the earlier novels seemed to come together to buy enough books to keep me from being embarrassed.

After all this time since *The Wrong Case*, seven or eight or ten cross-country moves, years of being broke, two more children, two more marriages and divorces, I still don't know why I write detective novels. The novels make a little more money now and they have gotten me work in Hollywood, so I'm not so broke so often anymore. My audience is still made of the best sort of folks – loyal, weird, funny, and more than willing to write or even call collect in the middle of the night – I never get tired of that part.

So if you've come with me this far, let us hope that spring will yet return to the mountains, that all our kisses will be good and lasting, our cases right, and our dancing, barefoot and mad with laughter.

Thanks.

Jim Crumley
Missoula, Montana
March 1991.

THE WRONG CASE

for Peggy

and with special thanks to Lee Nye
for the loan of his faces
and to Gil and Jean Findlay
who provided shelter

Never go to bed with a woman who has more troubles than you
do.

— Lew Archer

1

There's no accounting for laws. Or the changes wrought by men and time. For nearly eight years the only way to get a divorce in our state was to have your spouse convicted of a felony or caught in an act of adultery. Not even physical abuse or insanity counted. And in the ten years since I resigned as a county deputy, I had made a good living off those antiquated divorce laws. Then the state legislature, in a flurry of activity at the close of a special session, put me out of business by civilizing those divorce laws. Now we have dissolutions of marriage by reason of irreconcilable differences. Supporters and opponents were both shocked by the unexpected action of the lawmakers, but not as shocked as I was. I spent the next two days sulking in my office, drinking and enjoying the view, considering the prospects for my suddenly very dim future. The view looked considerably better than my prospects.

My office is on the fourth floor of the Milodragovitch Building. I inherited the building from my grandfather, but most of the profits go to a management corporation, my first ex-wife, and the estate of my second ex-wife. I'm left with cheap rent and a great view. At least on those days when the east wind doesn't inflict the pulp mill upon us or when an inversion layer doesn't cap the Meriwether Valley like a plug in a sulfurous well, I have a great view. From the north windows, I can see all the way up the Hell-Roaring drainage to the three thousand acres of timber, just below the low peaks of the Diablo Range, that my grandfather also left me. And from the west windows, if I ignore the junky western verge of Meriwether, the valley spreads out like a rich green carpet running between steep rocky ridges. On the north side of the valley, Sheba Peak rises grandly, holding snow until the heart of summer, as white and conical as the breast of a young woman, a woman conceived in the tired dreams of a dirty miner, a dream only gold or silver might buy.

Unlike my prospects, the view was worth toasting, which I did. Since I assumed dissolutions of marriage would arrange themselves without my professional assistance, my prospects were several and unseemly. I could take up repossession full time, taking back the used cars and cheap appliances so sweetly promised by the install-ment loan, pursuing bad debtors as if I were a hound from some financially responsible hell. I could do that; but I knew I wouldn't. No more than I could live on the forty-seven bucks and odd change left each month from my office leases, no more than I could cut my timber, or no more than I could convince the trustees of my father's estate to turn loose any of his fortune before my fifty-third birthday. At least I could have another drink out of the office bottle, another drink and another glance around my office to search for hidden assets.

The large old-fashioned safe in the corner, left from my grand-father's days as a banker, was empty, except for two thousand dollars of untaxed mad money. The three file cabinets were full of the records of failed marriages, not even worth anything to those unhappy folks recorded there. The portrait of my great grandfather had been painted by a famous Western artist and drunk, and might be worth something, but it seemed unkind to consider selling my great-grand-father. Surely, I should sell my timber first. Or the old desk and Oriental rug, which looked shabby enough to pass for antiques, scarred with cigarette burns and gritty with the detritus of grief and outrage that had scraped off all the husbands and wives who had trembled through my office. Age and sorrow, those were my only assets, my largest liabilities.

But like most men who drink too much, I had spent most of my life considering my dismal future, and it had stopped amusing me. So I had another drink and walked over to the north windows to look down on the happy, employed folk of Meriwether. Once, we Milodragovitches had been big stuff in this town, but now the only way I could look down on anybody was to climb up to my office, stare down from the windows. Lunch hour was done; people were hurrying about their business, driving back to office and store in air-conditioned cars, even though the air seemed more like spring than summer. I had never owned an air-conditioned car, so I could feel vaguely smug. Until August anyway.

Directly beneath me, a gray-haired woman, dressed in modern elegance, stepped out of the side entrance of the bank that leased the ground floor, and as she was fussing with her open purse a long-haired kid jerked the purse out of her hands and fled clumsily across the street, pumping his legs and swinging his elbows wildly, like a heavy bird longing for flight. He dodged the eastbound traffic on Main, gathering speed, but he ran into the side of a car as it slowed to make a right-hand turn north on Dottle; bouncing back, he turned, grinning dreamily like a man who has just had a final fix, then stepped into the westbound lane. The car that hit him never touched brake shoe to drum but drove right through him like a good solid punch. The kid rolled up the hood, throwing the old woman's purse straight up in the air. As the contents of the purse scattered in the air, the kid fell off the hood into the center of the intersection. Another old woman, who obviously hadn't seen any of this, turned her giant sedan illegally left on to Dottle and ran over the kid with the two right tires. He rolled, stuck beneath the rear bumper, and she dragged him half a block up the street before she could stop.

I had never realized that purse snatching was such a dangerous crime and I wondered what the kid needed badly enough to take up petty theft. Meriwether didn't have much street crime, perhaps because we still suffered from some frontier idea of justice: shoot first, apologize to the survivors. Whatever the kid had intended, he was obviously dead, crumpled under the rear of the car like a road-kill carcass at the end of a broad blood spoor. The old woman whose purse had been stolen was wandering around the intersection gathering up the debris from her purse, carefully checking each item. The man who had hit the kid was walking around his car, examining it for damage. Up the street, the other old woman was being helped from her car like an invalid.

It was a lovely summer day, smogless and fresh, and below me the flies struggled against their violent amber. But when the first siren split the air, they slipped free, went quickly about their business. Except for the kid, squashed into place, and one woman standing across the street from my building. She held her own small pink purse to her open mouth as if it were a secret message she'd devour before she'd divulge. From where I stood, she looked good. Nice

9

legs, a trim body. Red hair that seemed aflame above the pink dress. The sort of woman who stayed out of bars and away from the likes of me.

When the light changed, she stepped off the curb, stumbling slightly, breaking the spell. I went back to my desk, had another sip of whiskey, and opened a carton of blueberry yogurt. I watch my weight; I wouldn't want to look like a drunk.

As I ate I concentrated on the small decisions, letting the problem of my future take care of itself. I knew that if I had another drink I would probably get drunk instead of driving out to the university to play handball with my friend Dick Diamond, but I had another hit at the bottle just to prove that I could handle it. Have the drink, fight the drunk, play handball anyway. That was the plan. But somebody rapped timidly at my office door. Private investigators always have somebody rapping timidly at their doors, so I didn't leap out of my chair and spring into action. Back in the days when I still had a business, I would have hidden the bottle and the half-finished yogurt, slipped into my boots, and answered the door as if I knew what I was doing. But not this day. I left things as they were, didn't even answer until the light tapping resumed.

'Go away,' I said. But not loudly enough.

The lady in the pink dress opened the door and peeked around it like a kid who hopes the dentist is still out to lunch. But as she stepped into the office I could see that she wasn't a kid. A well-preserved thirty-five perhaps, maintained not by working at it but by saving it. And she'd saved it fairly well. A slim, firm body beneath the pink knit dress. Thick, dark red hair tucked away from a sweetly freckled face. Slightly myopic eyes that had that dreamy contact-lens blur about them. A mouth, daubed half-heartedly with a color that nearly matched the freckles, that seemed mobile and generous in spite of the prim way she pursed her lips.

'I'm sorry,' she said softly, as if she had failed to meet my standards, still standing at the door. I decided that the lipstick, which would have looked bad on any other woman, gave her just the right touch, as if she were still young enough to be foolish about a lipstick, choosing a color because she liked it, not because it went well with her face. 'I'm sorry,' she repeated, as if it were the password.

'So am I. The dentist's office is four doors down. We have the same name because we're cousins. I'm famous, but he's rich.'

10

'Oh, but I'm not – I wasn't looking for the dentist,' she said, flustered, then held the pink purse, which looked as if it had come in a set with the summer flats she wore, back to her mouth.

'Surely you aren't looking for me,' I said. 'Don't you read the papers? They don't have divorce in this state anymore. Just dissolutions of marriage. You can do it yourself. Thirty-four-fifty. I charge a hundred a day, plus expenses. A three-day minimum.'

'I'm from out of town,' she said, as if that explained everything. 'And I'm not married.'

'That's nice.'

'What?'

'That you're not married. Marriages can be messy. And expensive. I should know.'

'I'm sorry,' she said again. 'Do you mind if I sit down? I've just seen a terrible accident. In the street. Some poor young man was hit by a car. Then run over. It was awful. I'm quite shaken.'

'Certainly,' I answered, standing up, wishing I had put my boots on. 'Please sit down.'

She shut the door quietly, then walked over to the chair I was holding for her. She stepped on my foot, then nearly knocked the chair over as she sat in it.

'I'm sorry.'

'It's all right,' I said, retreating behind the desk to safety, slipping into my boots and sitting down. 'Well, what can I do for you?'

'I've interrupted your lunch, haven't I?'

'It's all right.'

'Please go ahead. I'll wait.'

Rather than argue with her, I had a spoonful of yogurt, then took out my note pad, asking her again what I could do for her.

'Well, an old friend of mine recommended you. Said you might be able to help me.'

'Who?' I asked, not telling her that she didn't look like the sort of woman who needed my sort of help.

'I'd rather not say, if you don't mind.'

'Why should I mind?'

'I don't know,' she answered, as literal as a child. .

'We're not getting anywhere, you know?'

'I guess not,' she said.

'Let's try the easy questions first, okay?'

11

'I'm sorry. I've been under quite a strain. And when I saw that young man – killed, I nearly went to pieces. I'm sorry. If you would just bear with me for a moment.'

'Certainly. Take your time. Would you like a drink?'

She shook her head quickly, as if she had a bad taste in her mouth. Feathers of red hair, tidily pinned back, began to drift across her face. She brushed them back, sighed, then changed her mind.

'Yes, I think I will. Perhaps it might help. And it *is* after lunch, isn't it? Do you think I could have a whiskey sour?' she asked shyly, then leaned back in her chair, fluffed her skirt, and stared at me expectantly, as if I were her favorite bartender. She looked at me silently, smiling so sweetly that I knew I must seek whiskey sours wherever they might be.

I had had some strange requests in my office. Husbands who wanted me to do obscene things to myself when they found out that their wives were exactly the sluts they supposed them to be. Or when they found out how expensive my services were. And wives had made their share of indecent requests too. Usually concerning my fee. They tried to take it out in trade, and sometimes became angry when they discovered I'd take it out but wouldn't trade it for anything. Some of the ideas that hurt and angry wives had in my office were damned strange. But I'd never been asked to whip up a whiskey sour.

'Okay,' I said, 'one whiskey sour coming up.' She smiled and crossed her legs, managing to kick my desk and expose a trim thigh at the same time.

I dialed Mahoney's, which is forty quick steps south of my office, and told Leo to whip up two whiskey sours in go cups and to send Simon up with them. Leo grumbled a bit, grousing about fancy drinks and my running tab, but he said he'd try to remember how to make a whiskey sour. Mahoney's is a wino bar, and anybody who asks for anything fancier than soda with their whiskey was either a sissy or a stranger.

'The drinks are on their way,' I said after Leo hung up on me.

'Is that legal?' she asked, concerned.

'Sure. This is the great American West. Where men came to get away from laws. Almost everything in this state is legal. And a lot of things that are illegal are done in spite of the law. You can order ten whiskey sours in go cups, then get into your car and fly up and down

12

the highways at whatever speed you can call reasonable and proper. You can murder your spouse and the lover in a fit, preferably of passion, and the maximum sentence is five years, and even that is usually suspended. And it's all legal. If you prefer gambling or drugs, which are still illegal, you can find any sort of game or machine you'd like within three blocks of my office, or buy all the drugs you want, except heroin, right on the street. So don't worry about two little drinks coming up the street.'

'All right,' she said. 'I won't worry. Please go ahead with your lunch.'

As I finished the remains of the yogurt, she tried very hard to sit still and look unworried. Her hands were clasped tightly around the small purse and crammed into her lap, but her fingers kept plucking at the ragged cuticles of her thumbs. At close range she seemed more girlish, nervous and giggly, like a teenaged girl on her first date. And scatterbrained and clumsy. The sort of woman who would need help to find her clothes afterward, who would always be losing things – gloves and glasses, hairpins and ribbons – then would prance around the room, smiling coyly as she looked in all the wrong places. I thought I might like that. It had been a long time since I had been with a woman who could seem innocent and vulnerable. Not that I mind strong, self-reliant women, but most of the women I knew were so tough they could chip flint hide-scrapers with their hearts. I decided that I liked this woman. Perhaps more than I should on such short notice. Whatever her problem, I intended to console her until she discovered that there wasn't much I could do to help her. Two drinks in the office as we discussed her problem, an early dinner at the Riverfront, martinis as we waited, brandies afterward as we watched the river flow into the setting sun, then home to my little log house by Hell-Roaring Creek to smoke a little dope and watch the long mountain dusk become night, to listen to the creek rumble in its rocky bed.

What the hell, I wasn't above taking advantage of a woman, running out the tired trappings of romance, even drugging them to have my way. We could make up the morality afterward in that sad time when passion has degenerated into a quick cigarette, a slow drink, silence.

'So what can I do for you?' I asked one more time, hand poised over my pad.

'I'm . . .'

13

'Wait a second,' I interrupted, reaching into the bottom desk drawer for the cassette recorder, which I'd bought from Muffin when I'd had to sell the fancy Ampex reel to reel. Muffin had assured me that the cassette recorder wasn't hot, but I didn't believe him for a moment.

'Do you mind?' I asked as I switched on the recorder. 'My secretary went to lunch and hasn't come back yet. I like to have a record of these things. I assure you that everything that passes between us will be strictly confidential.'

She hesitated, then nodded. I didn't tell her that my secretary had gone to lunch four years ago, and that the reason she hadn't come back was because she had run away with a dope dealer from Portland. It had been a successful match. They were living in Mazátlan now; she sunbathed, he financed dope deals.

'Where shall I begin?' she asked, a nervous tremor in her voice.

'How about name and address? That sort of stuff.'

'Oh,' she said, somehow surprised, as if she had expected to hire me without telling me her name. 'All right. My name is Helen Duffy, and I live with my parents,' she said, her voice unnaturally high and loud for the benefit of the recorder.

'Listen,' I said, 'just speak normally. You don't have to shout or anything.'

'Oh, I'm sorry. Those things make me nervous.'

'They make a lot of people nervous, but don't let it bother you. Just tell me where you live. More specifically than "with my parents," okay?'

'All right,' she whispered, then steeled herself to begin again. 'My name is Helen Duffy – '

'A little louder than that, please.'

' – and I live with my parents at Rural Route Number 4, Box 52B, Storm Lake, Iowa, Zip Code 50588, and I am an assistant professor of English at Buena Vista College in Storm Lake.'

'Isn't that where they had the massacre?'

'What? Oh, no, that was Spirit Lake. MacKinlay Kantor wrote a rather good novel about it.'

'Yeah,' I said. 'I read it a long time ago.' She looked so surprised that I added, 'I went to college too. Not very successfully but for a long time.' I didn't add that I went until my GI Bill ran out, along with the patience of the trustees of my father's estate.

'Where did you go?' she asked politely, her voice normal now, which was what I had been after.

'Here at Mountain States, Mexico City College, USC, a couple of junior colleges in California.'

'What did you major in?'

'Booze, broads, and various water sports,' I said, hoping to turn her back to the business at hand.

'Oh.'

'Who do you want me to find? Whom?'

'How did you know I wanted you to look for somebody?'

'Easy. You're not married, so you don't want a divorce. You don't look like the sort of woman who wants me to repossess a used car or a color television or hassle some guy for a gambling debt, so I assume you want me to find somebody. Let me guess,' I said, showing off. 'Your sister came out West – '

'Brother.'

'Younger?'

'Yes.'

'Okay, your younger brother came out West to work this summer and – '

'Two years ago. To work on his master's in history. Raymond always loved Western history,' she said, as if that too explained everything.

' – and dropped out of school into radical politics or into the drug scene – '

'To finish his research for his thesis on criminal justice on the Western frontier,' she corrected me.

' – and the family hasn't heard from him in several months, and you've come West on your summer vacation to find out what's wrong.'

'Three weeks. We – I had a letter three weeks ago.'

'Three weeks isn't very long,' I said, glad to be right about something.

'In his last letter, he seemed worried about something, under some sort of strain.'

'What about?'

'He didn't say,' she said primly.

'Then how did you know he was under a strain?'

'He's my brother,' she stated flatly.

'Sometimes parents don't even know their own children.'

15

'That isn't the case here.'

I managed to keep myself from saying, 'Well, what is the case, lady?' It was a beginning. In the book it says to let the client talk, to listen carefully and take copious notes, and making certain that when you do speak, to be sure to reveal your perception and intelligence, your deep understanding of human behavior, and that way the client will have the utmost confidence in your abilities, etc. But I always seemed to do it this other way: stagger them with wit, ply them with romance and whiskey sours, and convince them that I wouldn't be able to eat that night unless they paid me a large retainer. Sometimes it worked.

'Okay. Did the letter have a return address?'

'Yes. A hotel. But when I went there, it had burned down.'

'The Great Northern?'

She nodded sadly.

'What the hell was he doing living there?'

'It had something to do with his research, I think.'

'What was he researching? Cockroaches and bedbugs?'

She didn't bother to answer.

Once, the Great Northern had been a fine Western hotel, where prospectors who had hit it and ranchers who could afford it came to raise hell in Victorian splendor. Even after its heyday, it was a good hotel, somewhat run-down but still holding on to enough elegance to make a person feel comfortable. But an Eastern corporation had bought it, and in order to show a profit they had subdivided the rooms; made it into a flophouse for winos with a steady income and a hot-sheets home for Meriwether's few prostitutes. It had burned down about three weeks ago, burned down in about fifteen minutes because the sprinkler system was rusted shut.

'A terrible fire,' I said.

'You don't think . . .'

'No chance. I was there when they sifted the ashes. Everybody got out, except for two winos. Petey Martinez, who was deaf and wouldn't wear his hearing aid except on formal occasions, and the old man who started the fire, smoking in bed, drunk probably. Your brother wasn't in there. At least not when it burned down.'

She didn't seem relieved, so I tried another question.

'Was your brother – Raymond, isn't it? – into the drug scene or radical politics?'

16

'No.'

'Are you sure?'

'Of course I'm sure. He was a decent middle-class young man. Well-mannered, considerate, intelligent. Somewhat timid, I suppose, but then that seems to run in our family. He was opposed to the Vietnam war, of course, but he certainly wasn't a radical, and he wouldn't have had anything to do with drugs. He had hobbies.'

'Hobbies?' I guess I said it as if I wanted to know what they were. She took it that way.

'Yes. He was a fine horseman, and his gun collection was the finest in the state. He was also a regional fast-draw champion.'

'Some hobbies.'

'He enjoyed them, yes. He was kind to his horses and he never killed a living thing with his guns.'

'Okay,' I said, not knowing what else to say without making her defense of her little brother even stronger. I had the distinct feeling that her little brother wasn't quite the angel she had in mind, and I knew we wouldn't get anywhere if I told her that. So I changed tactics: 'Have you ever smoked marijuana?'

'Of course not. Why do you ask?'

'Just trying to see how reliable a source of information you are,' I said. 'Sometimes people who aren't familiar with drugs don't know when – '

But she burst into tears before I could finish. After all that had happened, she chose to fall apart over that.

'I – I may not know anything about – about drugs or radical politics or anything like that – but I do know my – my little brother,' she sputtered, trying to hold her face together. 'Know he wouldn't do – do anything awful.' The *awful* nearly became a scream. Her pain and worry was real, and it dangled between us like a frayed empty sleeve.

'Excuse me,' she blubbered, coughing to cover the tears. 'I – I have to take out my contacts . . . I haven't had them very long, I'm not used to them.' So she removed her contact paraphernalia from her purse and started prying at her eyes.

I switched off the recorder. Some things didn't need recording. As I watched her face tilt over her open palm, I tried to think about her missing brother. I almost told her that it was senseless for us to go on like this, since the chances of me finding her little brother were less than slim. Runaway children are almost impossible to find, even for people who are trained in missing-person work, which I wasn't, and the only lost children I'd ever found had been lost in the woods. But I didn't tell her. I still wanted her, so I didn't tell her. She seemed like a woman from a simpler, better time, a small-town time when sprinklers graced neat lawns and screen doors smelled like rain or dust instead of plastic, when the seasons changed as gracefully as scenes on greeting cards, when snow was never dirty, when fall leaves were never soggy and damp, and when children never cried, except for brief moments, and then were so gently comforted that they didn't mind crying at all. She did that to me, made me homesick for a childhood I'd never really had, the one I sometimes constructed in odd drunken moments to make me forget the real one. And she made me hope, something I hadn't done for years, made me believe in a better, cleaner world where a man and a woman could raise a family in peace. I decided then that she deserved better than my tired version of comfort; she deserved my help, such as it was.

So I didn't have another hit off the office bottle, but capped it and set it back in the bottom drawer, trying to think seriously about her little brother. But she dropped one of her contacts, and we spent the next few minutes crawling around the faded and scarred carpet, searching the charred spots for her contact. She had one eye closed, and I acted like I could really see after drinking most of the day. I cursed silently, cursed Simon and the missing drinks, which I knew he had slipped into an alley to drink, hating himself even as he drank them but already constructing the lie he would tell Leo to get two more and another free shot for his grief. And I cursed vanity: hers for the contacts, mine for refusing to wear my glasses. The longer we searched, the more it looked like she was going to need a drink. She snagged her panty hose twice; she bumped heads with me only once, but so hard that she sat back on the carpet, her knees folded under her, her hand to her forehead. For a moment it seemed as if she was going to wail like a hysterical child, but she caught herself when I found the lens in the chair. At least I found something. She put it away, took out the other without incident, and we went back to business.

As I switched the recorder back on, I said, 'I know this must be a strain, but if I don't ask hard questions, I'll never be able to help you. Okay?'

'I'm sorry,' she answered, slipping on rimless glasses that made her look more her age. 'I'm not usually this sensitive. But sometimes . . . sometimes, as my mother says, I'm a ninny. I never know when it's going to happen. Sometimes the tears just start. Sometimes when I lose things, I just can't . . .'

'That's all right. Don't worry.'

'How can I help but worry? I just know Raymond is in some sort of difficulty. Otherwise he would have been in touch. Raymond and I are very close.'

'Okay, I'll take your word for that. Let's start over. What sort of trouble do you think he might be in?'

'I don't know,' she said quickly.

'You won't even guess?'

'I thought you were supposed to do that.'

'Yeah. I guess so. Who referred you to me?'

'I told you I'd rather not say. If you don't mind,' she answered, folding her hands around the purse and arching her neck. Then she suddenly began to giggle and blushed very nicely, the warmth rising from her bare shoulders to her slim neck. I tried to blush back, but there are some things not even I can fake. After the giggles rattled away into the summer afternoon, she straightened her face and hair, then said, 'I'm afraid I lied a moment ago. I *have* smoked pot a few times. When I was in graduate school in the early sixties, but nothing happened.'

'What did you expect to happen?'

'Oh, something terribly sinful, I suppose. Don't look at me like that, please. I'm not as naïve as I may appear.'

'Whatever you say, lady,' I said, wondering where the blush and giggles had come from. 'But back to your little brother and his trouble.'

'Oh, I don't know that he's in trouble,' she said gaily, 'I mean I don't know it for sure. I think he's in trouble but I don't know it for a fact, and as my mother is always telling me, thinking isn't knowing. Perhaps he's just angry at the family and is staying out of touch to hurt us.'

'Why should he be angry with your family?'

'That's rather personal. I'd rather not go into it, if you don't mind,'

19

she said quietly, her gaze dropping back to her lap, where her fingers were busily mauling each other, her voice no longer gay at all.

'Why should I mind,' I said, but she missed the irony. *Family life*, I thought, *wonderful family life*. There ought to be a law against families, or, at the very least, children should be given a choice of families or colors of their Skinner Boxes. Families are always a mess: everybody always wants to fuck everybody else and usually finds a particularly vicious substitute. And love doesn't seem to matter either. Too much, not enough – somehow the same unhappy family life comes out. Her family was probably a nice middle-class, ordinary group. My family had been a nightmare. My father a rich, worthless drunk; my mother an insane drunk. So here was Helen Duffy coming to me for help, when I probably needed help more than she did. And her little brother probably wanted nothing more in the world than to be left alone by his family. But help I intended to give, and for that help I intended to be paid in kind. Long days looking for a kid who didn't want to be found, short nights with his big sister.

But as I thought about it, I suddenly didn't like myself very much. I'd never been really fond of myself anyway, but now I disliked myself so much it made me feel old and tired, deceitful and dirty, the drunk in the gutter unworthy to even touch the shoes of the passing lady.

'Miss Duffy – Helen. Do you mind if I call you Helen?'

She sighed rather than answering, keeping the nightwatch on her frantic fingers.

'Miss Duffy, I'll be frank with you, if you don't mind. I haven't been frank with anybody in years, not since I started this grimy racket. In the ten years or so since I started this crap, I've done almost nothing but divorce work. A little repossession work, but I don't like it. Every now and then somebody comes into my office wanting me to find somebody else – a runaway kid or a husband who decided to become somebody else – and what usually happens when I look for a runaway is that I find them really quick because I bribe some creep at the power company or the telephone office or the post office, which costs my client three bills plus the bribe and which makes me feel worse than the creeps I have to deal with. If that doesn't work, and a lot of times it doesn't, then I never find the runaway, and that costs my client a small fortune and makes me feel even worse than when I find somebody. It makes me feel like warmed-over shit, if you'll excuse the expression.

'And if I'm looking for a kid who has slipped into the street scene here, I never even get close. Not even the hometown freaks who've known me all their lives, who deal me dope, they won't help me find somebody in the street scene. They know that nobody wants to go home – that's why they ran away – so they won't talk to me, and I can't find my ass with either hand when people won't talk to me.

'So save your money. If you want somebody to look for your little brother, go to the police. The bastards are corrupt but they're cheap. I'm expensive and corrupt. And not very good at my job. I can find a naked woman in a dark room, but not if she runs – Shit,' I said, trying one of her sighs and discovering that I was standing up, leaning heavily on my desk, shaking slightly like a man who needed a drink more than he needed frankness. So I reached in the drawer and had one.

Her hands had fallen still, and she looked up at me blankly, then said quietly, 'You're rather a profane and unhappy man, aren't you?'

'Lady, I'm worse than that,' I said as I sat down.

She stared over my shoulder into the blue slopes of the Diablos, her clear blue eyes reflecting the peaks and the mountain sky.

'Oh, you're probably like most men,' she murmured, a sad authority in her voice as she looked past me, 'not nearly so terrible as you think. Men are always so hard on themselves. Morally, I mean. My friend, who recommended you, says you're a good man. Unhappy but good. And he warned me that you would be profane. I really don't mind. I just can't talk that way, you know, the words feel dirty in my mouth.' Then she giggled faintly but not happily. 'My friend said you knew – knew whenever anybody farted in Meriwether County –'

'His opinion is too high,' I said.

'And he said that if anybody could find Raymond, you could, and I'm so afraid that – that something awful has happened to him – he was such a lovely child, so kind and gentle. Not like other boys. And he left home too soon; he wasn't ready for the world just yet. But my mother – my mother . . .'

But she had stopped talking to me. Her words were directed somewhere else. Inside her perhaps, or into her past, or maybe off into the mountains where she saw herself living in a quiet, sheltered cabin, mate to a pious man who might help.

'And if you don't help me, I don't know where to turn. I'm so afraid – I must find him, you know.' The eyes she turned toward me were glazed with a fear approaching madness.

'What are you afraid of?'

'I beg your pardon?'

'What are you frightened of?' I asked again.

'That something awful has happened to Raymond, of course.' She picked at her cuticles again, digging at them so hard that I could hear the thrum as thumbnail ripped flesh, even over the sound of the afternoon traffic drifting up from the street below. She bit off a piece of cuticle as neatly as my grandmother used to snip thread with her store-bought teeth, then spit the skin sharply onto my carpet. I expected her to apologize, but she didn't seem to know that I was in the room. Her glazed eyes turned misty and sorry with some unexplained loss.

'Hey, let's start over,' I said.

'What?'

'Let's try again, okay?'

She touched her face with her hand, her fingers moving like a blind woman's across an unfamiliar face. Then she came back, saying, 'I must apologize for taking your time, Mr. Milodragovitch. You've been very kind and patient. But somehow I thought – thought it would be different somehow – '

'Like on television?'

'No. Easier somehow. I don't know. But I can see now that you can't help me, can see that this was a mistake from beginning to end, so if you'll just tell me how much I owe you for your time, I'll pay you and be on my way,' she said, her voice carefully controlled. Then she giggled again. 'Be on my merry way,' she said lightly, taking a sheaf of hundred-dollar traveler's checks, so thick that she couldn't fold them, out of her purse. In another time I might have thought, *Hey, this dame is loaded!* And since I'm an old-fashioned guy, that's exactly what I thought. She had come prepared to look long and hard for the little brother, had come burdened with the family hopes and fortune.

'Hey, put the money away,' I said, taking a quick hit off the whiskey, making myself talk without thinking. 'Hey, listen,' I began again, then had one more drink, that drink that frees the tongue. She neither looked at me nor stuffed the checks back in her purse; she sat there at my command like a child waiting to be punished.

'Hey, listen for a minute, will you? I'll make a deal with you. My life hasn't been too grand these past few years. Shit, my life was never grand. And the thing I liked best of all about divorce work was that I never had to see anybody whose life was any better off than mine. The people who came asking for my help convinced me that the world was just as stupid and filthy and cruel and corrupt as I thought it was. And maybe I still think that, I don't know. It doesn't matter what I think, I guess, because that part of my life is over. I'm out of business. The Robin Hood of the Divorce Courts has slung his cameras and mikes and dirty pictures behind him . . . and I've got nothing to show for those years but bad debts and grief, I've not done a single thing in all that time I could be proud of, so maybe here at the end I should do something nice for a change, something for free, and maybe this shitload of misery I call myself will feel better instead of worse for a change. Maybe.

'So I'll make a deal with you, okay? I'll make your little brother my last official act as a private creep, I'll look for your goddamned little brother in the daytime, if you'll . . .'

But when it came down to it, I didn't have the guts to say it.

'I'm not sure I understand,' she said into my pause, and she didn't sound as if she cared to understand either.

So I said it: 'I'll look for your brother in exchange for your nights . . . my days for your nights.'

So what if I was half in the bag, lonesome and dumb with self-pity, left with a life that had become all hangover and no drunk. I wanted to feel human again, and the only way I knew was with a woman, and the only women I knew were gay divorcees, stoned hippie chicks, and tired barmaids whose emotions were as badly mangled as mine, and I wanted more, wanted this squirrelly, oddly virginal English professor from some goddamned crossroads in Iowa, wanted her like I hadn't wanted anything in a long time, too long. So I said it again, 'My days for your nights.'

She glanced up coldly, her face composed and prim.

'I'm afraid I don't know what you mean.'

'Fuck it then,' I said, finding myself standing again. 'Just fuck it, okay?'

She didn't seem particularly angry. She just slipped the checks back into her purse, snapped it shut, then left my office without another word. As she walked she held her back very erectly, moving

23

her legs as if she had envied too many models. It was an exit, but she tripped over the sill, stumbled down the hall, leaving my office door open. I didn't feel much like laughing but I tried one anyway. It sounded like the croak of a crushed frog, so I turned back to my bottle and my northern view, shut off the recorder and sat there without thinking about anything.

A light haze shrouded the Diablos, not smog yet but the hot afternoon sun vaporizing the pine pitch, drawing moisture from the needles and the bark. When the trees were dry enough, lightning or a careless smoker would start the first fire, and my timber would finally burn all the way down. Again I considered selling it, maybe even selling the land to some rich tourist. Recreation land, they called it, better than gold or silver. I thought of selling and taking the money away with me to some foreign land where I could live cheaply until my fifty-third birthday made me a rich man, but even as I thought about it, I knew I wouldn't leave. Not yet.

Traffic north of Dottle Street was still stalled by a fire truck. Two firemen washed the blood off the street, leaving a larger, darker stain that steamed on the hot asphalt. The man with the hose worked very intently; his partner stood with his hands on his hips, his cap tilted back, the smile of an untroubled man wide across his face.

When I went to shut the door, the smell of her was thick in the cool air of my office, a fragrance of spring, flowery and untainted, then old Simon shuffled sheepishly through the open door, bringing the drinks and the smell of stale cigarettes and whiskey sweat with him.

'Sorry, sorry, Milo, sorry to be so long, sorry, but these two kids, Milo, these two kids took, sorry . . .' he babbled in his usual drunken manner as he sat the drinks on my desk. Then he began to pound his clothes so hard that dust puffed from his shoddy suit. 'Cigarette, Milo, sorry, Milo, cigarette, Milo, please, just one.'

'She's gone, you old fart, so you can act human again. The cigarettes are right where they always are.'

He filched a whole pack of Camels from the drawer where I kept them since I quit. After he lit two, he gave me one, then sucked on his so hard that he nearly choked to death. As soon as he caught his flimsy breath, he said, 'Thank you, Milo. You're a real gentleman.'

'Fuck you, old man,' I answered as I had the single drag I allowed

24

myself. I flipped the long butt out the window, hoping it landed on a tourist. 'What took so long with the drinks, huh?'

'You know how it is,' he said, not even bothering to lie. He was drunk but maintaining. He could still rub his hands together as if he were just about to freeze to death, could still revolve his cigarette in the corner of his mouth as he spoke, and he still spoke in a normal voice, which meant that he knew who I was and spared me the string of foolish chatter which he used like a shield against the sober world. 'Who was that lovely bit of fluff on the stairs, Milo?'

'Fuck you, Simon.'

'Since you don't care to confide in an old and trusted friend – who's saved your dumb ass more times than can be counted – perhaps you'll share these as yet untasted drinks with an old man in great need of a taste.'

'Weren't the first two enough? And the two shots?'

'Milo, my boy, there's never enough.'

'Yeah,' I said, stepping over to the desk to get the drinks, since Simon obviously wasn't going to. I handed him one, then looked at the recorder. I started to erase the tape, but the sound of her voice was there. I thought I might want to hear it sometime, might want to hear my own foolishness, so I took the cassette out and slipped it into my hip pocket. Then Simon and I snapped the lids off the Styrofoam cups, left the office and sipped the drinks as we strolled the forty easy steps down to Mahoney's, sauntering like lords through the summer afternoon buzz of shoppers and gaping tourists, down to Mahoney's Bar and Grill, where I had unlimited credit and willing friends, grease to ease the squeaking wheel of a summer afternoon.

'Did you hear about the tragic purse snatcher?' Simon asked. When he said it, it sounded like the first line of a dirty joke, but I told him I'd already heard it.

25

2

During his more lucid moments, Simon often said that when I grew old enough to become a full-time drunk, he and I would have a worthless contest, and he maintained that I would lose because I lacked the necessary character to forgo the last vestiges of middle-class morality. 'When I'm so soused that I defecate in my trousers,' he would confide in his rich, rolling, private voice, 'even in your deepest stupor, boy, you will turn away in disgust. However mild, still disgust. And the man who would truly discard his life lacks that fatal disgust. And prides himself upon that lack.'

Simon and I had been friends for years, ever since the night I had taken him home in my deputy sheriff's unit instead of heaving him into the county drunk tank, which had been filled with its usual Saturday-night complement of outraged Indians, collapsed winos, and downright mean drunks. I'd fed him bacon and eggs, coffee and whiskey, and talked to him, I guess, as if he were still a man, and we'd become friends. It had been on his advice that I'd become a private investigator after resigning from the sheriff's department. He told me that if I didn't have a job I'd drink myself to death before I really had time to enjoy it. He added that being a divorce detective was about all I was good for. Like most of his advice, it sounded good, so I took it. But in all those years, he never told me why, out of all the people in Meriwether's bars, he had chosen to allow only me behind his drunken mask. Perhaps he did it in memory of my father, who had been his friend and drinking companion too, or perhaps simply on a drunken whim. When I asked him why, he would only say lightly, 'Even the foulest drunk needs a friend. One dependable friend. Any more than one confuses the issue. When I die, I'm assured one mourner.' Then he would laugh until he choked, adding, 'And that's more than you can say, boy.' I never asked myself why I let him choose me.

Like me, Simon had been the scion of an old Meriwether family, and until he was in his early forties had been a damned successful criminal lawyer, perhaps the best in the mountain West, feared by prosecutors in seven states, beloved by assorted murderers, rapists and bank robbers. Then one spring day he lost it, lost his belief in the law, in justice, in the court system. He said that anything that easy to best couldn't be any good. So he closed his office and opened a bottle, drank from that bottle seriously for ten years, long enough for people to forget who he had been and to see only what he had become. With whiskey he destroyed their memories, then settled down to steady drinking, his thirst strong but not suicidal, and joined that fair brigade of peripatetic drunks that makes Meriwether such a fine and pleasant city, the best little town in the West, a small city that could boast of the highest per capita ratio of bars in America.

(It could but it doesn't. Instead it chooses to boast of mountain vistas, trout streams and the most highly speculative land values in the West. Sometimes I think the Chamber of Commerce and the tourist office should tout the bars: at least they aren't filled with strangers.)

Although he worked on it very hard, Simon didn't quite qualify for the honors of town drunk. They were reserved for a young man who had appeared in the local bars one day wearing an old Brooklyn Dodgers baseball cap and claiming to be able to repeat the radio broadcast of any Dodger game within the last twenty years. When he was sober, that is, which was never. Nonetheless, Simon was a character of some renown in his own right. He lived in the discarded clothing of other men, possessed nothing except those clothes, a pencil and a child's notebook for his letters, and whatever might lurk in the dusty pockets of other men's suits. Year round he slept where he fell or wherever people dragged him afterward. I never saw him buy a drink or a meal, although he had a small monthly income from his father's trust. Surely sometime during those years he must have bought a meal or a drink, but I never saw him do it. A matter of pride, he maintained. There were a few things that he wouldn't do for a drink, though. He wouldn't humor a fool, if he recognized the fool beforehand, and he wouldn't change his political opinions, which were dangerously violent and radical.

27

Periodically he was arrested for threatening the life of some political figure, and only because he was Simon Rome he spent two or three months drying out at the state mental hospital at Twin Forks instead of two or three years in a federal slammer. Almost daily, he wrote long, rambling letters of protest to Washington, letters that must have given many a sweet laugh to poor secretaries dulled by the Capitol atmosphere. During the days of antiwar protest marches, Simon could always be found at the head of the line, dancing and shouting the most vile threats against the government. The freaks and college students who came into Mahoney's at night, looking for a *real place*, loved Simon. They could cheer him on in his idiot act, buy him drinks just to hear him shout for presidential blood. Simon was our only radical wino and he played his role day and night. Except with me. With me he could be ordinary, normal, and even sad, if it suited his mood.

As Simon and I reached our favorite booth in Mahoney's, I waved at old Pierre, who was sitting like a stone at the back table next to the jukebox and the shuffleboard machine, watching each new customer as if he dared him to activate either electronic obscenity. I didn't offer Pierre a drink because his brain was so whiskey-soaked that he didn't bother to drink much anymore; he just sat around and thought about being drunk, which usually worked. Sometimes he would clutch his head and curse in his unintelligible French, squeezing his head as if that would put the taste of whiskey in his mouth. After he had awoken one morning to discover that he had completely forgotten the English language, he cut down his consumption, but he still spent his days in Mahoney's, watching the shuffleboard machine and grunting with a French accent. Sometimes, though, I suspected that like Simon's idiot babble this was the ruse with which old Pierre kept the world at bay. It certainly simplified life, and on certain days, such as this one, I envied that simplicity and wondered what sort of guise I would wear when I made that final retreat. When I waved at Pierre, he seemed to smile slyly.

When Leo brought the shots and beers, he mentioned that he had added four whiskey sours and two shots to my heavy tab.

'You mean you didn't buy Simon's story of robbery and near murder?' I asked, but Leo just sneered. The only person more cynical than a drunk is a reformed drunk.

After he left, Simon checked to see that nobody was close enough to hear his normal voice, then he asked, 'And what did that lovely lady want, lad? Not a divorce, I venture.' Then he cackled softly. The ruin of my business amused him greatly.

'I'm not sure what she wanted. A better man than me, I guess.'

'That wouldn't be hard to find,' Simon said, sipping slowly at his shot.

'Off my ass, old man. Let's get drunk and be somebody.'

Simon nodded sagely, sipped again, then started to say something, but Fat Freddy, whom Simon hated passionately, waddled slowly past our booth, picking his teeth and sucking the last juices from the debris of his Slumgullion lunch. Simon hated Freddy because he had been a corrupt cop, fired from the force of a large Midwestern city for running a string of whores. The passion came because Freddy had taught me to shadow by following Simon everywhere he went for three weeks. Simon had never seen us but he had felt us behind him somewhere, dogging his tracks like a pair of patient but lazy hounds. After a month or so, Simon had forgiven me but he had never forgiven Freddy.

'Good afternoon, Milo. And how are you today, Mr. Rome?' Freddy said as he loomed past our booth, presenting his enormous belly as if it were a treasure of great worth, a leg of lamb with mint jelly, perhaps, or a crown roast engulfed by oysters.

I nodded, but Simon went berserk, sputtering, 'Fa-fa-fat ba-ba-bastard bastard bastard.'

'Don't have a fit,' I said. 'Not at my table anyway.'

Simon hushed and Freddy moved on to dock next to Pierre, where they would wait out the afternoon, Pierre watching for the fool with a coin who would destroy his peace, Freddy plying his toothpick with a devotion my cousin the dentist would have admired.

When he finally settled down, Simon went back to the lady, saying, 'That was a truly fair maiden, boy. I would have thought that you would have done whatever she asked.'

'I tried.'

'A really lovely lady,' he whispered, pausing to stare into his shot glass. 'Something sweet and lovely about that lady. I remember the ladies. Vaguely . . .' Then he chuckled at his self-pity. Though there were rumors that Simon had been hell on the ladies in his youth, he had never married, but after the years of drinking, he had become

29

as sexless as an old woman. He didn't even indulge in the bitter, helpless comments of the other winos when they would appraise the body of a young woman in the bar. Just passing Helen Duffy on the stairs, he had been caught like me by the special nature of that woman. 'Lovely,' he repeated, as if the word would bring back the vision, then he smiled sadly, lifting his small red notebook and pencil from his coat pocket as carefully as if they were deadly weapons. He began to babble and scrawl, forgetting me completely.

He wasn't long for the world, I feared, wasn't going to survive many more winters. He would freeze in a dark doorway some night or stumble in front of another car or forget which role belonged to which time. He would die soon, I knew that, and dead, have a tiny gold star pasted into the corner of his portrait, which shared the walls of Mahoney's with those of his compatriots, the living and the dead and those still trapped in between. And that was nearly as sad as losing the lady.

Leo had been a hack photographer in upstate New York, shooting weddings and smarmy babies and beaming old couples whose bland lives had blurred their features into the same characterless mold, using his camera to support his painting and drinking. He had a good eye but no hand, so he gave up painting for drinking. His wife and family finally left him, and he couldn't find many customers who wanted their sentimental memories recorded by a drunk. He sold his business and equipment and fled into a long, down-spiraling drunk, heading West to die in a strange place where he wouldn't shame his family. But he didn't die; he broke the pattern and dried out. He didn't miss the drunks or the drinking, but had been at home in bars so long that he missed them – so he bought Mahoney's. I co-signed the note, putting up my timber land to secure it, and Leo made a success of the old bar. Then after he was sure he was going to stay dry and successful, he took up the camera again, seriously this time. His eye found the lost history in ruined cabins and old mines, the poetry in spare winter landscapes, and the dignity and pride in the battered faces of his patrons. He caught them in brave laughter and elegant sad loss and then hung the portraits on the walls of his bar, as if to remind them what they could be. The large pictures reminded us of hope, reminded us that we weren't social drinkers, and the gold stars in the corners of the dead were like medals.

Unfortunately, I hadn't been shot and hung yet. I meant to speak to Leo as soon as I finished my drink, to suggest that my time might have arrived.

But I never finished that drink. My friend Dick Diamond, my handball partner who taught English out at Mountain States University, came bounding into the tranquil and languid afternoon to harass me about missing another match.

'Thanks, old buddy. Had a great game. Really great. Played with two kids who were learning the game. Slowly. Only one was blind, though. And the other only slightly crippled. Both retarded, though. Don't have any idea how they ever passed the entrance exams. But thanks for the game, old buddy,' he said as he walked toward the table. Dick had never recovered from a strong dose of college basketball. He had been both too short and the only Jew on the team, but he made up for it by believing that death was preferable to losing. Sometimes I thought he only liked to play with me because he could beat me eighty percent of the time.

'You're welcome,' I said as he grabbed a chair and straddled it at the end of the booth.

'Know you're a busy man, Milo – dark corners and high transoms and all that – but can't you make it one time a week?'

I raised my shot glass at him, and he nodded. 'Understood, old buddy.'

'Is Marsha still mad at me?' I asked.

'Marsha?'

'Your loving, devoted, forgiving wife,' I said.

'Oh, you mean that woman who lives in my house, mothers my children, but who hasn't spoken to me in several weeks, not since my best friend ruined not only my marriage but also my career?'

'Yeah, her.'

'She forgives you, sure, she loves you more than your mother did, loves you because you're such a dear, lonesome man. But me? She hasn't gotten around to forgiving me. I've been sleeping in the study again, old buddy.'

'It wasn't my fault,' I said as Leo arrived with a mug of beer for Dick. 'I'm innocent.'

'Sure, man, innocent,' Dick said.

31

'Everything's your fault,' Leo said.

Simon nodded wisely.

'Couldn't you at least have found a fetid corner of the bathroom or gone out on the lawn like any self-respecting dog. Jesus H. Christ,' he said, then was silent long enough to drink half his beer.

'Want a divorce?'

'Wise ass.'

'Look, it wasn't my fault, how did I know . . .'

'Sure, man,' he said, 'she drug you into the wardrobe – Jesus, man, my antique cherrywood wardrobe – forced you in there at gunpoint, right?'

'I didn't know what she wanted in there,' I said, grinning at the memory of Hildy Ernst. 'I didn't know until it was too late. And what sort of gentleman would I be if I stopped in the midst of the act? Besides, it wasn't my fault the damned thing fell over. That's your fault for having unstable antiques.'

'Jesus, man,' Dick said, gunning the rest of his beer as if in a race. He waved to Leo for another round, but I told him to leave me out, since I still hadn't started yet.

'Who shouted "Earthquake!"?' I asked.

'Who do you think?'

'That's what Marsha's mad about, huh?'

'Right. Who gives a rat's ass? Sleeping in the study has certain advantages,' he said.

When the wardrobe hit the floor with Hildy and me engaged within and Dick shouted 'Earthquake!' the departmental chairman's wife was in the upstairs bathroom, drunk as a sow, and she believed it. She had fled down the stairs like an avalanche, her enormous white panties flapping about her feet like a small but very angry dog. After she had been laid to rest in the guest bedroom, six men lifted Hildy and me and the wardrobe off the floor, and we sauntered out the doors, grins on our faces and jism on our clothes like icing on the cake.

'Well, I'm glad you're happy about everything,' I said.

'Jesus. Every time I see the chairman, he harrumphs like a bull moose with terminal phlegm because his chubby, lovely wife has fled to Indiana and may never return,' Dick said, 'but I can't tell if he's happy or sad. And when I meet Hildy in the halls of Academe, she giggles like some monstrous child bride. I hope to hell it was worth it, Milo.'

'It was,' I said. 'It surely was.'

It had been one of those moments. Hildy and I had been talking politely about nothing. She looked at me, I leaned over and kissed her, and we fled into the wardrobe beside us. Wonderful. I didn't care. I had made a small career out of breaking up Dick and Marsha's parties, either by getting too drunk or fondling some faculty wife in the kitchen. Hildy had tenure, so she didn't care. We left the party hand in hand like young lovers, vowing loudly to do it again. Which we did, whenever and wherever we found the energy and room. It was a brief but athletic affair, fun while it lasted, but Hildy had an aversion to beds. Beds were for sleeping, she said, not balling. Which I found tiresome. Then she wanted to make the affair a crowd scene, so I moved aside, bowed out. But it had been fun.

'I wonder if all German ladies are like that?' I asked Dick. 'Have you ever been to Germany?'

'Are you kidding, man? Jesus.'

'Maybe I should go to Germany for these golden years while I await my fortune.'

'You'll be too old to ball by the time you're rich,' he said, grinning. 'Maybe that's what your sainted mother intended when she persuaded your old man to tie up the trust.'

'I think she had something else in mind,' I said.

'What?'

'To keep me from being a drunk like my old man. A heart as big as all outdoors and a liver as big as a salmon,' I said, raising my whiskey.

'Didn't work, did it,' Dick said, then casually added, 'Did Helen Duffy talk to you yet?'

I set the shot glass down without spilling a drop. 'Who?'

'Helen Duffy. She's, ah, an old friend of mine. From graduate school.' So I wouldn't mistake his meaning, he said, 'We were, ah, pretty close.' Sometimes we competed for women too, and part of his mock anger about Hildy was real because I had and he hadn't. But that didn't make up for Helen Duffy.

'She's lost her little brother, or something, and I told her you might be able to help,' he said. 'Told her you're great at finding lost people. Thought maybe you could use the business too.'

33

'Thanks,' I said, more shortly than I meant to.

'I didn't think he'd gotten too lost, maybe just a little misplaced, and you have enough contacts among freaks to handle that – don't you?'

'Sure.'

'No, man, seriously,' he said, then glanced at Simon, who seemed so busy with his bourbon and political complaint that he wouldn't have noticed an earthquake. 'Listen, man, we were really close for a long time. She's something special.'

'Wonderful.'

'No, really, man, I nearly left Marsha for her – '

'It's a good line, Richard, but don't waste it on me. Hell, man, I'm easy,' I said.

'What the hell's wrong with you, man?'

'Nothing, man.'

'Come on. So I fuck around, so what? Everybody fucks around. But this was different. It might have worked out. But Marsha caught us. She drove over to Helen's apartment one afternoon after somebody called her and told her what was going on, that there wasn't a Victorian seminar on Tuesday and Thursday afternoons. Marsha was six months pregnant, man, but she hammered the shit out of me. A terrible scene. Helen felt so bad about it that she left school right after that. Never even finished her degree.'

'How tragic,' I said.

'You saw her, huh? She does that to men, particularly the old and corrupt, the young and lonesome. How did you two get along?'

'Just great.'

'That bad, huh,' he said cheerfully. 'You couldn't help her, huh?'

'We couldn't agree on a fee.'

'That's strange. She's loaded, man. Her father sued the New York City Police Department a few years ago – false arrest and brutality, something like that – got over a hundred thousand in the settlement.'

'We weren't exactly bickering over money,' I said.

'You bastard. You propositioned her the first time you met her, didn't you? You bastard.'

'Didn't you?' I asked.

'Goddammit, Milo, sometimes you piss me off. You've got the moral fiber of a – a baboon.'

'Didn't you?' I repeated.

'All right, so what if I did?'

'Then get off my ass about "moral fiber." You know as much about morality as you do about baboons. So get off my case, man.'

'Okay,' he said, 'you're right. For a change. I'm sorry, but just talking to her on the phone brought it all back, man. She showed up at a bad time. Marsha is really pissed; I'm really sleeping in the study. No joke.'

'You know where she's staying?'

'She didn't say; I didn't ask.'

'Afraid?' I asked.

'You're damned right. That woman does things to me, man.'

'I know,' I muttered, remembering her face all over again, remembering the awkward walk and the torn hands. 'Say, man, if you hear from her, tell her . . . tell her I'm sorry. Tell her I was drunk or something, distraught over . . . over business failures. Tell her I'll seek her little brother all over the county, find him and put him safe and sound in her arms. And no fee. Okay?'

'Sure, man. If I hear from her.'

'You and Helen Duffy,' I said quietly, holding up the shot of pale Canadian whiskey, staring through it into the bars of afternoon sunlight that fell through Leo's front blinds. 'I can't get over it . . .'

'Say, man, I think Simon wants something,' Dick said.

Simon was rolling his eyes dramatically, flapping his tongue, and shaking his head like a palsy victim. He was so excited he couldn't talk. When I shook my head like a man who didn't want to be bothered, he nearly fell out of the booth, so I relented, got up and followed him into Leo's empty poker room. But that wasn't good enough for Simon; he wanted to go into my other office. We went into Leo's walk-in cooler, where he kept case and keg beer and enough smoked trout and whitefish to feed most of the drunks in the county, then I unlocked the door to my other office.

Unlike my regular office, a man could live in my other office. There was a double bed, a small table and chairs, a hot plate and sink, a fridge and shower, and a tiny Japanese color television, which was hot as a fresh muffin. All the comforts of home and as secure as a prison cell. It was my interest on Leo's note, my hiding place, except that everybody in town knew it was there. Drunks can't keep secrets. But Simon liked it; the room suited his sense of the melodramatic and made him feel as if we were as important as a

35

detective and his trusty sidekick in a movie. He wouldn't tell me anything he thought really important anyplace else. And as part of the cinematic ritual, he always made me pay him for the information.

He wanted to talk now so badly that he had to hop from foot to foot just to stay quiet, but still he rubbed his fingers rapidly together, his sign for money.

'Come on, Simon, I've been buying shit information from you for years and I'm in no mood for games today.'

'You wouldn't be nothing without me, boy, nothing. And this is something you really want to know, so come up with some scratch,' he said adamantly. 'Or find out for yourself.'

Since I didn't have any money in my pocket, I had to go back into the bar and borrow two dollars from Dick, who gave me a very odd look, then I carried the two bills back to Simon, who held them up as if they were scraps of used toilet paper.

'Goddamn, Milo, this is hot stuff and you come up with two lousy bucks. What sort of friend are you anyway?'

'A two-dollar friend, Simon. What the hell do you want?'

'Ah, what the hell. You really liked that lady, didn't you?'

'So?'

'Well, I know who her little brother is. You do too.'

'Who?' I asked.

'He's that kid who used to hang around with Willy Jones.'

'Who the hell is Willy Jones?'

'Ah, for Christ's sake, Milo. Willy Jones was that old fart who claimed to be Henry Plumber's son, the old man who burned up with the Great Northern. Remember?'

'Vaguely,' I lied.

'And this Duffy kid, he also hangs around with that large and ferocious faggot, Lawrence what's-his-name, the one that affects leather pants and purple eyeshadow.'

'Reese, Lawrence Reese. Shit, you mean the Duffy kid hangs around with that bastard? Jesus.'

'Absolutely,' Simon said. 'Absolutely.'

'I'll be damned.'

Nothing Helen Duffy had said prepared me for this. Reese was a bad dude, giant glitter queen of the Northwest. He dealt drugs and seduced young boys. Or maybe raped them. He was large enough, as big as a professional defensive end and probably even meaner.

When he found the heat oppressive, Reese also taught one of those esoteric, violent but dutifully spiritual Eastern combat arts. And he was hell on bare feet. Once in a northside bar, I'd seen him destroy three sawyers who made fun of his eyeshadow. Reese chopped tables and bit the necks off beer bottles between rounds as he waited for the sawyers to get up. When it was over, the sawyers went to the hospital, and when they got out of the hospital, they left town. And Raymond Duffy must have been his buddy, a tall, skinny kid in cowboy clothes leaning against the bar, watching the fight with what looked like a mad sexual excitement. He had a heavy black beard that grew high on his cheeks like a mask, and the eyes above the beard were as hard and opaque as marbles. If that was Raymond Duffy, Helen had a sick little brother. Really sick.

'This Duffy kid, Simon, tall, dressed in cowboy clothes, a black beard – '

'That's the one,' he said.

'He hangs around with nice people.'

'He's a creep, Milo.'

'But he shouldn't be hard to find.'

'Just hope you don't find Lawrence what's-his-name at the same time,' Simon said, shaking his head. He was so afraid of Reese that he wouldn't even stay in the same bar with him. Truth was, neither would I.

'But if you're really looking for the kid, I'd bet money that Muffin knows where Lawrence lives,' Simon said.

'Why?'

'They've had dealings in the past,' he muttered mysteriously.

'Well, I'll ask him,' I said. 'That should be a paternal right, right?'

'Hell, Milo, Muffin don't give anybody any rights.'

'I've noticed. Listen, thanks, Simon,' I told him as we walked out, but he didn't answer. He seemed worried about something. 'What's the matter, old man?'

'That kid, that Duffy kid. Milo, how could a lady like that have a brother like that . . .'

'I know what you mean,' I said, patting him on the shoulder as we stepped out of the cooler.

'Save your goddamned sympathy, Milo,' he said roughly, waving the two one-dollar bills. 'Two lousy bucks, Milo, two lousy bucks . . . Lemme alone. Needa taste.' He pushed past me and hurried toward

37

the booth for his drink, but somebody had drunk it while we were gone. Fat Freddy was grinning broadly when Simon looked at him, and Simon shouted at him, accusing him of all sorts of incoherent crimes. He made such a fuss that Leo came around the bar and ran both of them out of the bar.

'Dick said he had to go,' Leo said when he came back, still puffing with outrage. 'Goddamned drunks,' he sighed. 'Dick said he'd call if he found out where the lady was staying.'

'Thanks,' I said as I walked away from the booth.

'Hey, Milo, you didn't finish your drink,' Leo said.

'Yeah, well, give it to old Pierre.'

'Sure. Say, did you hear about the colonel?' he asked. The colonel was a retired mustang who lived upstairs in the Dottle Hotel, which catered to those members of the wino brigade who received monthly checks from the government.

'Nope.'

'Some crazy kid jumped him last night. Right in the hallway. Nearly killed him for six lousy bucks. He's in a critical condition. The kid threw him down the stairs. Broke some ribs. One punctured his lung. He ain't got a chance in hell. Six bucks. Christ.'

'They catch the kid?'

'Naw. All them long-haired kids look alike. Dynamite had a look at him but he couldn't catch him,' Leo said, looking like the sad father of too many wild children. 'Freddy said it was probably a junkie, but what the hell does he know.'

'Well,' I said, 'if he's seen one street junkie, he knows more than any of us.' There had always been lots of dope in Meriwether. It came in from the West Coast in large and frequent lots. But there had never been much heroin in town. The only addicts I knew were either doctors or nurses or rich old women. 'Maybe the kid was just freaking on speed or acid.'

'Maybe,' Leo said.

'Sorry about the colonel.'

'Yeah. Say, Milo, who's the lady?'

'What lady?'

'The one Dick said he'd call about.'

'Just a client,' I said.

'Sure, Milo, sure.'

'Cynic,' I said as I headed for the street.

38

'Fool,' he muttered behind me.

As I went out, thinking to drop by Muffin's, I found myself hoping that Helen Duffy would forgive me if I found her little brother, but I knew better than to think that she would fall into my arms in appreciation. Not many women like to feel beholden to a man. But at least it was a way to get to talk to her again, and I was sober and had nothing else to do, so I got my old Toyota four-wheel rig out of the bank parking lot and went looking for my adopted son, Muffin, who was the local electronic fence. As I drove across town, I tried to avoid being crushed by the summer horde of lumbering campers plying the hot streets like large, tired animals searching for a place to lie down.

3

'Don't ask me, man,' Muffin said for the tenth time. 'You don't need to know where that dude lives, man, you don't need that kinda trouble.'

'Muffin, you owe me.'

'What the hell I owe you, man? I don't owe you shit,' he muttered, stepping behind one of the four stereo color television consoles that divided his large one-room apartment. As he stood there glaring at me, his small black face nearly lost beneath the spread of his huge Afro, he looked like a gnome hiding under a giant black mushroom. He had a bottle of Ripple in one hand and a joint in the other and he took alternate hits of each, still trying to come down from two years of amphetamine frenzy, which had left his veins and nerves humming like wires in the wind. 'Don't owe you nothing, man,' he said.

'Four years' room and board, nearly three thousand in hospital bills, a shitload of grief – '

'Didn't ask for nonna that shit, man.'

'You took it, Muffin.'

'What the fuck, man. Just money. Shit, I got plenty a money. Pay you cash right now, man. Just tell me how much.'

'How much you reckon Terri's worth?' I asked. She was my second wife, who moved out when Muffin moved in. The marriage hadn't been made in heaven – she was a lady bartender, and I was her best customer – but it gave both of us somebody to drink and fight with. Three weeks and a day after the divorce decree was final, she and an airman from Nellis were killed in an automobile accident outside Tonopah, Nevada, leaving me the support payments for two children

40

of hers from a previous marriage. 'Come on, Muffin. How much you gonna pay for Terri?'

'That's low, man, mean.'

'You're the man with the money.'

'Yeah. What the hell you want with that Lawrence dude. Man, he's bad. And I don't mean good.'

'Business,' I said.

'You ain't got no business no more, Milo, and the only business that Lawrence got is dealing dope and handing dudes' asses to them. Which you looking for, man?' he asked, then skittered away through the maze of stereo gear.

'You owe me.'

'Fuck off, man.'

'Please,' I said.

'Damn, you must be getting old, Milo. Never heard you say no "please" before,' he said, then began to laugh and flap his arms. He stopped long enough to switch on one of his sound systems, the music blasting so loud that the walls of his apartment began to shake. Muffin hit the bottle, then the joint, dancing to ignore me.

It was more habit than anger that sent me after him, the habit of making people talk to me because they were somehow guilty, and I was somehow the law. I walked around the consoles, slapped the joint and the wine bottle out of his hands, grabbed his loose sweat shirt, and slammed him against the shelf of receivers and tape players and record changers until the music stopped.

'You owe me,' I said, then dropped him to the floor. Before he got kicked off the team for coming to practice stoned and started shooting speed, Muffin had been a first-string defensive halfback for the MSC Vandals, but now he neither weighed any more nor felt any stronger than he had when I'd jerked him out of a wrecked, stolen Corvette when he was fourteen. He hadn't touched the speed in nearly four years, but his body had never recovered. I felt as if I'd been roughing up a mummy, and the dust of decay tickled my throat.

'Go ahead, Milo,' Muffin said from the floor, 'you the man. You just ain't the bad man. You might hurt me but you ain't gonna kill nobody. That faggot'll kill me, man, if he finds out I had my mouth on him. So go ahead.'

41

JAMES CRUMLEY

For a moment my head filled with familial rage, and I started to kick him. But I stopped myself. I told him I was sorry.

'What's the matter with you, man?' he asked, standing up. 'You gone crazy? What the hell's wrong?'

'Nothing. I'm sorry. I'll see you around,' I said, starting for the door.

'You ain't gonna see my ass, man, you just stay off my case for good, you hear, off it.'

'Okay,' I said. 'I'm still sorry.'

'That's for sure, Milo. You one sorry mother,' he said to my back, then added, 'And one sorry father too.'

When I looked back from the door, he was grinning.

'See you around,' I said again, grinning too.

'Right,' he said. 'But don't be looking for my ass over on the north side, not on Lincoln Street, man, not two houses west of that abandoned church house.'

'Okay. I won't look there,' I said. 'Take care.'

'You take care, Milo. You the man with the trouble.'

'What's new,' I said, and he laughed.

Most of Meriwether's freaks, dopers, hippies and assorted young folk lived on the north side of town in an old blue-collar neighborhood, which the earlier residents had deserted in favor of tacky developments on the south side of town, but the neighborhood was still pleasant in a small-town way – inexpensive but fairly well-built houses that aged nicely, like a handsome woman, the yards shaded by old trees and overgrown with evergreen shrubbery and flowering bushes. Except for the psychedelic glare of an occasional headshop and the studied humility of several natural-food stores and the long hair and bright clothing, it could have been a working-class neighborhood of twenty or thirty years before. And in its own way, it was still working-class, since most of the freaks had manual-labor or service jobs, living quietly except for the occasional too-loud party or family fight, living peacefully with the few original residents who had stayed to grow old with the neighborhood.

In the past few years, as more houses with possibilities of elegant restoration came on the market, young professionals moved into the neighborhood, which made the police careful about hassling longhairs, so they patrolled it just like any other neighborhood, and unless

42

they saw somebody balling on the front porch or sm⟨ ⟩
the street, they left the young people alone to live wh⟨ ⟩
chose, as long as they lived it inside their houses.

After two years and three months as an infantryman i⟨ ⟩
War and ten years as a deputy sheriff, I knew how to b⟨ ⟩
took a long afternoon and about five whiskeys for me to fin⟨ ⟩
to go over to the north side to ask questions about the wher⟨ ⟩
one Raymond Duffy. I didn't have any foolish ideas tha⟨ ⟩ ⟨ ⟩uld
make Lawrence Reese talk to me if he didn't want to, which he
probably wouldn't, but along with the drinks, I took large doses of
the memory of the lady. The way her trim hips moved beneath the
knit dress, the sound of her hose as she crossed her legs, the eyes
so easily hurt. Then I drove over to the north side, just as afternoon
eased into dusk.

The house that Muffin said Reese lived in was slightly more
dilapidated than most of the others around it, and some former
tenant had added a large porch, which looked like a heavy afterthought about to collapse in the light of reason. On that porch,
Simon was standing, gesticulating madly at a slim, young girl wearing
cut-offs and a gray T-shirt that claimed to be the property of the
athletic department of the University of Connecticut. I didn't know
they had either a university or an athletic department, but then my
only vision of the East had come from the phony gentility of my
mother.

I parked my rig in front of the house, locked it, and set the alarm.
I always carried about a thousand dollars' worth of crap clattering
around in the back. Two rifles and a shotgun and a .38 revolver, a
tape deck and a toolbox, fishing rods and gear, a pint of brandy and
a partial lid of Mexican grass, and assorted junk. As ready as I'd
ever be, I turned around and walked up the buckled sidewalk.

'What the hell are you doing here?' I asked Simon as I stepped
onto the rickety porch and leaned against one of the fake frame
pillars.

'I live here, motherfucker. What the hell are you doing here?' the
young girl asked angrily, switching her hollow eyes across me like a
curse.

'Not you, honey,' I replied. 'Him.' And jerked my thumb at Simon,
who was locked in a paroxysm of flying arms and spittle.

Her anger passed as quickly as it had come, and she was stoned again, sinking gracefully to her rump on the wooden floor, where she sat, smiling happily and chipping the tired brown paint with her fingernails.

'Him?' she asked in a small, concerned voice. 'I don't know what he's doing here. He don't make much sense. I think he thinks he lives here, but I've been crashed here for weeks, and I don't think he lives here.' Then she giggled. 'But I don't know why not. Every other crazy mother in this creepy town thinks he lives here, so maybe he does. Who knows? You gotta cigarette?'

As I searched Simon for my pack, I whispered, 'What the hell are you doing here?' But he was trapped between roles, struggling like a man caught halfway into his pants and trying to explain to an angry husband why he was halfway out of them. He finally gave up, shrugged vaguely as he muttered to himself.

'Go away,' I said to Simon as I lit the girl's cigarette.

He didn't move, but she answered me again, pleasantly this time. 'Sorry, man, but I live here.'

'Not you, goddammit. Him.'

'Oh, him. He doesn't live here,' she reminded me, hitting the cigarette so hard that she flashed deeper into her stone.

'Does Raymond Duffy live here?' I asked quickly, hoping to catch her before she faded out of my reality.

'Who?' she asked, moving away.

'Raymond Duffy. A tall skinny kid. Black hair, big beard. Dresses like a gunslinger.'

'Oh, him. You mean El Creepo,' she answered, giggling again.

'Is he here?'

'Who?'

'Raymond Duffy.'

'Oh, him. Haven't seen El Creepo in a *long time*.' *Long time* sounded like forever.

'How long?'

'Who knows? Just a long time.'

'A week? Two weeks? A month?' I asked, leaning over her, pressing.

'Yeah.'

'Shit,' I said, standing back up. Simon looked like a man doing his income tax on his fingers. 'That long, huh?'

'Yeah,' she said, smiling up at me prettily. She had a narrow, ordinary face, but when she smiled she was pretty. 'Want to go inside? We're doing some bad hash, man.'

'No thanks,' I said, smiling back with a dry mouth. 'How do you know I'm not the man?' I asked, nearly giggling.

'I'm fucked up, man, but I ain't crazy,' she said by way of explanation, then touched me on the calf with her small hand as our smiles turned into grins. 'The man don't get contact highs,' she said, and we giggled.

'Is Lawrence Reese here?'

'Lawrence?'

'You know Lawrence?' I asked.

'Man, everybody knows Lawrence. It's his hash. Do you know Lawrence?'

'I'm afraid I haven't had the pleasure,' I said, grinning with her.

'It ain't always a pleasure,' a voice said through the screen door. Then Lawrence followed it outside, strolling across the porch, his bare, heavily callused feet gliding across the warped floorboards, his large body all muscle and fluid motion and threat.

'What's happening?' he asked the girl, ignoring whatever wisecrack I might have made.

But he was large enough to ignore anybody, broader and taller than I remembered, harder and older, nearer forty than thirty. His face seemed to hang off his skull in a hard, grainy mask, as if it were all scar tissue. The lavender eyeshadow didn't make his eyes look a bit feminine or soft. They just looked bruised and wary. Shoulders ax-handle-broad and arms like logs jutted out of his black leather vest, and in the tight leather pants his legs rippled and flexed as he raised his right foot, the toes pointed like a dancer's, to touch the girl's bare arm. His foot stroked her arm very lightly.

'What's happening, Mindy?' he asked again.

'Jesus,' she said, 'I don't know.' She stood up, wandered back to the front door, her slim hand drifting, intimately casual, across Lawrence's groin and hip.

As she slipped through the door I caught a glimpse of the Arabian nightmare within the room. Oriental rugs covered with plush pillows and slight bodies hid the floor, carelessly circled around a brass water pipe. The bodies were caught in the tender mold of pan-sexual adolescence, the faces blank, waiting to be formed out of youth, but the eyes were as dark and empty as burial caves etched into chalk bluffs. A ringlet of smoke curled slowly above the pipe, and the sharp, bittersweet stink of blond Lebanese hash hovered in the cool, heavy air.

'Having a party?' I asked, trying to be pleasant.

'Do I know you?' he asked in a slow, hard voice that went more with the ball-point pen and needle tattoo, which had faded into a blue smudge on his right forearm, than with the eyeshadow and the tailor-made leather clothes.

'Milton Milodragovitch,' I answered, holding my hand carefully toward him. 'I'm a private investigator and – '

'I know damn well I don't know you,' he said softly, disregarding my hand introduction. He spun slowly on the ball of his left foot toward Simon, who hadn't moved since Lawrence came outside. Lawrence lifted and cocked and extended his right leg so quickly that I only saw a black blur. The foot stopped so close to Simon's nose, quivering like an arrow shaft driven deeply into a tree, that Simon must have been able to smell it. Simon didn't have time to move, but his viscera flinched, and a loud fart escaped him, and the stench quickly filled the porch.

'Jesus Christ, that's disgusting,' Lawrence said, putting his foot down. 'Get outa here.' Simon went.

'Are you still here?' Lawrence asked.

'My name is Milton Milodragovitch,' I said, 'and I'm a – ' But I couldn't finish because I was stumbling down the porch steps. Lawrence's right hand had snaked out and shoved me lightly off the porch.

Though I carry fifteen or twenty pounds of whiskey flab, I don't look like the sort of guy most men would casually shove off their front porch, but Lawrence didn't seem too worried about it. As I got up off my butt, he sat down on the steps and began rolling a huge joint.

'Get your dander up, cunt?' he asked pleasantly, then licked the number and stuffed the makings back in his vest pocket.

'I think so,' I said, rubbing my hands together.

He lit the joint and took a hit off it large enough to paralyze an elephant. 'Flake off,' he said, holding the hit.

'Listen,' I said, 'I'm a private investigator and I'm looking – '

But he laughed so loudly that the smoke came roiling out of his lungs. 'Don't do that, man. Made me lose the hit. Just get the fuck outa here, okay?'

We stared at each other for a few seconds, then I looked around the yard for a big stick, relieved that I couldn't find one among the tangled high grass and blooming weeds. Lawrence smiled; I tried. In the house to the right, an old woman with gleaming white hair and a faded black lace dress stood at her side window, waving coyly at me. The dress belonged to another time, as did the neatly marcelled hair. Her cheeks bloomed hopefully with rouge, her mouth smiled beneath a contusion of dark red lipstick.

'Listen,' I repeated as I walked toward him. He stopped smiling.

'You want more, man. I got more than you can handle.'

'I've had plenty, thanks. You can throw me off your porch all night long, but it's no big deal. I just want to ask you a few questions about a friend of yours,' I said, still walking.

He kicked the inside of my right thigh, and when I turned sideways the foot hit me again, on the left shoulder, and I hit the sidewalk. I kept most of my face off the sidewalk by getting my hands in front of me, but the heels of my palms didn't feel too good about it.

'Hit the road, cunt.'

When I stood up, my left arm felt like it had been hit with a billy club, and there was blood and gravel in my hands.

'I never hit anybody wearing purple eyeshadow,' I said, picking at some of the smaller stones embedded in my flesh.

'Don't start now, friend,' he said, holding the joint in front of his mouth. 'Not now.'

We smiled at each other again, but I quit when my face started hurting.

'You're probably right,' I said.

'You know I'm right, cunt.'

'Don't go away,' I said. 'I'll be back.' But it was a weak and empty threat.

'I live here,' he answered as I walked away.

I wasn't mad, and the whole thing suddenly seemed a foolish waste of time better spent in a mellow bar hustling cocktail waitresses, so I was willing to leave it that way. But I forgot to switch off the alarm before I fumbled the key into the door lock, and the fancy air horns started blaring and the lights blinking wildly in the crepuscular air. And Lawrence laughed too loudly behind me. Enough is enough.

So I unlocked the door and reached into the back and unracked the twelve-gauge automatic, wishing it loaded with goose-loads but knowing they were just skeet-loads. It wouldn't matter, though, even loaded with rock salt, the three-inch magnum loads would blow down a house.

'All right,' I shouted over the horns as I walked back up the sidewalk, 'you cocksucker, we're going to talk now!'

He didn't even stand up, but I sensed rather than saw movement away from the living-room windows, small animals slipping off into the dusk. In an upstairs window, a faceless voice said 'Jesus' between the bleats of the horns.

'I don't think so,' Lawrence said. 'I don't talk to people who call me dirty names.'

'Either we talk, asshole, or you're going to be damned unhappy,' I said, keeping the shotgun barrel pointed at the ground.

'I'm already unhappy, cunt,' he said, flipping the joint away, the bright spark glittering as it arched toward the grass.

'Wonderful,' I said, 'I'm looking for a kid you used to hang around with –'

'I don't hang around with anybody.'

' – named Raymond Duffy.'

'Never heard of him.'

'Talk to me, you son of a bitch!' I shouted, raising the barrel at his face.

He looked at it, then at me. 'You're not going to kill anybody, cunt,' he said, then stood up and headed toward the door, his back toward me.

I'd never known that the ability to kill people was such a necessary asset in my business, but I didn't like being accused of it twice in one day, so I pulled the trigger. The left porch pillar exploded into a cloud of splinters and dust. A window crashed behind it. Lawrence flinched but he didn't run. He glanced up as the porch roof sagged toward him, creaking loudly.

'Missed,' he said, facing me. 'I'll send you the bill.'

So I blew up the other pillar, which turned into dust and splinters even more nicely than the first one. That made him mad. He started for me, and either I would have blown his leg off or he would have torn my head off, but the decision was taken out of our hands.

As the second pillar buckled, the porch roof creaked again, might-

48

ily, old nails squealing like lost souls and joists cracking like dry bones, as the porch roof swung down like a trap door, ripping off most of the front of the house and slamming shut on him. It knocked him right through the screen door. Suddenly, alert faces appeared in the void upstairs, then vanished. Two bare butts vacated the downstairs bedroom, bobbing and bounding away toward the back of the house. A disembodied voice tolled through the debris: 'Far fucking out.'

'Amen,' I said, grinning so hard that my cheeks cramped. The day hadn't been completely wasted.

4

By the time Reese recovered from the blow his porch roof had given him and began wading through the wreckage, the police had arrived, and, considering the reception he had given me, he was amazingly polite to them, which made me certain that he was an ex-con. I had thrown the shotgun on the grass as soon as I saw the flashing lights, raised my hands and tried to stop grinning. One patrolman cuffed me while the other put the shotgun in their unit and called Lieutenant Jamison, who I knew would be glad to hear that I was under arrest. Because the patrolman knew who I was, he cuffed my hands in front, but he still locked me in the back seat of the unit. Then he kept the crowd of spectators moving down the sidewalk, and his partner questioned Reese, who was busy dusting his clothes and combing splinters out of his long blond hair. Once he glanced over at me, shook his head and seemed to grin. The patrolman moving the crowd paused long enough to open the hood of my rig and rip off the horn wires. In his absence, the people bunched like cattle in a storm until he came back and prodded them along.

Even though Meriwether is a city of nearly fifty thousand, it often seems like a small town. Almost every face that passed was familiar, and I could put names to most of those. There were a few long-haired kids I had never seen before and one retired brakeman whom I had known by sight for years but whose name I'd never learned. Most of the crowd knew my face, too, and some my name, but only the strangers were crass enough to stare at me, cuffed like a killer, in the back seat of the police car. One came back several times, glancing covertly into the car as if to make sure that it was really me. His face was mostly hidden behind a thick black beard and dark glasses, but in spite of the shoulder-length black hair he was obviously middle-aged and too well dressed to be a working-class hippie. He smiled once, I thought, and seemed vaguely familiar, perhaps a professor from the college I'd met at Dick's, drunk, or an undercover policeman working narcotics. But before I could hang a name to the oddly familiar face, Jamison pulled in behind the patrol unit.

Jamison and I, as they say, go way back. We had been raised in Meriwether – same age, same grade in school, all that – and even when we were children, I had been his project: he intended to make me a better person, no matter what. And for years I'd paid him back with small nips and little jokes at the expense of his implacable seriousness, his elevated sense of morality. Small but mean things. Wintergreen in his jock the night he was supposed to lead the homecoming queen onto the football field before the game. His socks wrapped in condoms and soap in his rifle barrel our first inspection in basic training at Fort Lewis. He owed me lots of small pain, and one big one. He had married my ex-wife, and she made more money off my settlement and child support than he brought home at the end of the month.

But instead of being amused at my predicament, he seemed damned serious as he tugged me out of the back seat and trundled me back up the sidewalk. Lawrence was slapping shoulders and explaining that he didn't want to press charges because it had been as much his fault as mine.

'I'll decide that,' Jamison said grimly. 'What happened here?'

One of the patrolmen started to tell him, but Jamison hushed him and repeated his question to Reese.

'A private beef,' Reese said.

'How would you like to take an obstruction fall, Mr. Reese? Or maybe have me walk into your house to search for injured occupants?' Jamison asked.

'Okay,' he answered. 'It's no skin off my ass.'

'Thanks, Lawrence honey,' I said. 'I thought we were buddies.'

'Shut up, Milo,' Jamison said, and I did. 'What happened?'

'This dude,' Reese said, pointing a thumb as big as a shotgun barrel at me, 'came around looking for somebody – '

'Who?' Jamison asked, taking out his notebook.

'He didn't say.'

'Who?' Directed at me.

'A kid named Raymond Duffy,' I said.

51

'Runaway?'

'Nope. His family just hasn't heard from him in a while,' I answered.

'How long?'

'Three weeks.'

'Then what's the fuss about?' he asked. I shrugged, then he asked Reese if he knew the Duffy kid.

'I knew him. He used to hang around the house. Crashed here for a while – '

'How long?' Jamison asked.

'Who keeps track?' Reese answered.

'How long?'

'I don't know. Five, maybe six months.'

'And where did he crash-land after he flew away from here, Mr. Reese?'

'The Great Northern Hotel. He was shacked up with an old faggot, Willy Jones.'

'What's the matter, Reese? The kid leave you for a better piece?'

'No, sir. I asked him to split,' Reese said softly.

'What's the matter? Too butch for you?' Unlike me, Jamison didn't seem frightened of Lawrence Reese.

'No, sir. I got tired of him. I get tired of people, you know. Some people quicker than others.' Reese didn't like being pushed around, either.

'I hope you don't mean me, Mr. Reese. I hope you aren't getting tired of me.'

'Lieutenant, sir, I been tired of the man all my life but I ain't ever been able to do anything about it,' Reese said, almost sadly.

'Just don't forget that I'm the man, Mr. Reese. Don't forget that.'

'I'm sure I won't.'

'Good. What happened after you wouldn't talk to this creep here?'

'I asked him to leave, he wouldn't leave, so I helped him. He came back, so I helped him harder. I guess I pissed him off,' Reese said, smiling. 'He got a shotgun and offed my front porch.'

'Did he threaten you with the shotgun at any time?' Jamison wanted to know.

Reese glanced at me then smirked. 'No, sir,' he said. 'If he'd threatened me, I'd have gotten pissed off.'

52

'And what would you have done, Mr. Reese, if pissed off?' Jamison asked sweetly.

'Stuck it up his ass and pulled the trigger,' Reese said flatly.

'Too bad you didn't. Two creeps with one shot,' Jamison said as if he meant it. 'Uncuff him,' he added, and the patrolman did. 'Behind.'

'Thanks,' I said to the patrolman as he tugged my arms behind my back and snapped the cuffs. 'I was thinking of escaping and I'm glad you took the idea out of my head.'

'Shut up,' Jamison said. 'Mr. Reese, if you don't mind, I'd like you to come down to the station in the morning. Let's say nine o'clock. We'll find somebody to take your statement.'

'You're the man,' Reese said.

'Let's go,' he said to me, jerking on my arm so the cuffs could grind merrily against my wrists.

'Where?' I asked, smiling.

'Duck Valley,' he said. 'Two to five maybe, you dumb son of a bitch.'

'I've been needing a vacation,' I said.

'Ah, Lieutenant,' one of the patrolmen said behind us. 'Ah, we didn't read him his rights.'

'That's all right,' Jamison said. He read them to me on the way to the car. I didn't have any.

Jamison had forgiven me for years, had even gone to the trouble to make up excuses for all the things about me that he couldn't understand. Like not having school spirit and not playing for the team. He forgave me because I thought both silly. And in Korea, when he discovered that I didn't think night patrols or frontal assaults on Communist-held ridges were life or death matters, he thought I was joking, and he kept volunteering the two of us. While I was tending to important matters, like staying alive and keeping warm and hustling booze, he tried to kill us. No matter how much I goofed off, he kept believing in me. The only time I'd ever known him to lie or even slightly bend a rule, he covered for me one night when I was too drunk to go on patrol, reported me present when I was three miles behind our lines, passed out in the back of a wrecked ambulance.

In college after the war, I got away from him because we lived in different worlds. He was at the heart of things, an honor student

working his way through school, student body president and all that.
I was usually in a fraternity house, drinking beer and watching
television, or drinking beer and reading, or drinking beer and playing
poker. And I thought he had given up on me, but the day I joined
the sheriff's department, Jamison showed up at my house with all
sorts of great affectionate ambition. Together, arm in arm, city and
county, we would make Meriwether a decent place to live. I told him
that I'd become a deputy because the sheriff was an old crony of my
father's and I sort of liked the idea of tooling around the county in
a three-quarter-ton four-wheel-drive pickup and carrying a gun.

'Listen, Milo,' he had said, 'being a law enforcement officer will
get into your blood, just like it has mine. You'll love it.'

'You see too many movies,' I said.

'Hell, I've been so busy that I haven't seen more than two or three
movies since I joined the force,' he answered, his pride slightly
damaged.

'That's too many,' I said, but he laughed and slapped me on the
shoulder.

I don't know which was harder for Jamison: finding out that
Meriwether didn't care to be a decent place to live, or discovering
that I was on the take, like every other deputy in the county, from
the local boys who controlled the electronic slots, the pinball
machines and punchboards, and the sports pools. Whichever, he
never forgave me. And he nearly worked himself to death trying to
clean up Meriwether.

Sometimes I felt sorry for him. He had boy scout ideals in an
adult world, and after it became clear to him that there were certain
laws that were never going to be enforced, he began to look slightly
dazed – like a Thermopylae freak without a pass – then old and
tired. He had become, like most policemen, adept at selective
enforcement of the law, but not corrupt. He couldn't be bought for
love or money. I didn't have either anyway.

'How's Evelyn?' I asked from the back seat as we drove downtown.
'And the kids?' One mine, two his.

'What the hell do you care?' he answered without turning around.

'It costs me a lot of money every month to run your household.
The least you can do is give me an occasional report,' I said, knowing

he was willing to live like a pauper to stay out of my money – but Evelyn wasn't.

'You're a real bastard, you know that.'

'At least I don't gloat about my old friends doing time,' I said. Maybe he'd feel sorry for me.

'You'll be back on the street in an hour,' he said, then laughed. 'But it will do my heart good just to see you behind bars for a little while.'

'Glad I could help.'

'Who's this Duffy?'

'College dropout,' I said.

'Look, Milo, I'm tired and I'm busy and I got no time for your bullshit.'

'That's straight. The kid was a graduate student out at the college, and he dropped out of sight.'

'For how long?' Jamison asked.

'I told you once: three weeks.'

'Right. Got other things on my mind, Milo. What the hell's he doing hanging around with scum like Reese?'

'Love at first sight, I guess,' I said. 'Criminals and ex-cops are a heavy trip this year.'

'Did it ever occur to you not to be a smart-ass?'

'I don't think so,' I said.

'The kid ever been in trouble?'

'As far as the family knows, he's an angel.'

'I'll bet he is,' Jamison said. 'I'll just bet he is.'

At the station I was booked and relieved of my personal effects and allowed my telephone call. Everything polite and perfect, by the book all the way. I called Dick, but Marsha told me that Simon had already called and Dick was on his way down to bail me out. On the way to my cell, I waved at all my old buddies in the drunk tank, and those who could still see waved back gaily.

'Well, you look okay, old buddy,' Dick said as the desk sergeant gave me back my effects, 'but you ought to see Simon.'

'What's the matter?'

'He's sober.'

'Must be a frightening experience,' I said, checking the manila envelope, but the tape cassette wasn't there. 'Goddammit,' I said. 'Back in a minute.'

Jamison didn't complain when I didn't knock on his office door. He just looked up from the recorder on his desk and shook his balding head.

'Enjoy yourself?' I asked.

'If you weren't so sad, you'd be funny,' he said as he snapped out the cassette and flipped it to me. 'And you're gonna be sadder.'

'What's that supposed to mean?'

'Get out. Drop by and see your son sometime. He's a nice kid, in spite of you. That ought to make you feel better,' Jamison said, tilting his chair back and rubbing his eyes.

'He's not my kid,' I said. 'He's been around you too long – his head's too big for his halo.' Jamison was right, though. He was a nice kid, but his face was already pinched with the same sad serious-ness that crumpled Jamison's. I don't know which was more painful: for me to see my innocent face on the kid, or for the kid to see his face old and corrupt on me. Whichever, we stayed away from each other. 'Hell, he's even wearing your name.'

'That's something, Milo. You ain't got nothing.'

'I got a case,' I said, and for some reason that made me feel better.

'You ain't got nothing,' he said as I went out the door. 'You poor sad fucker.'

Simon was a pitiful sight. Sober, yes, but trembling wildly, and he seemed to have aged ten years. Somewhere he had found an ill-fitting sleazy suit, an iridescent gray that shimmered like an oil slick beneath the mercury vapor lights, cheap colors rippling across the fabric as his skinny old frame quivered. His face was so pale and hollow that he might have been dressed for a burial.

'What the hell were you doing at Lawrence's house?' I asked. 'And where the hell did you get that suit?'

'Don't, don't be mad, Milo, Milo, don't – I just – asked around . . . that's all.' Without whiskey, his voice seemed as thin as his suit.

'What the hell are you doing here?'

He flinched, ducked his head and, muttering, backed away from me as if I'd slapped him.

'What?'

'Advice, Milo, legal advice. I've been – disbarred, but I can – can still give legal advice,' he whispered into the gutter.

'Oh, for Christ's sake, go have a drink and stop this crap,' I said. 'You look terrible.'

'Yes,' he answered vaguely, 'yes . . .' Then he turned and drifted slowly down the street like a scrap of wrapping paper in a night wind, lurching and hitching the hip that had been broken the year before when he stumbled into the path of a pickup. I started to shout after him, but sober he was just too pitiful, so I let him go.

'What's wrong with him?' Dick asked as we got in his van.

'He just needs a drink.'

Being nasty to Simon had ruined the good feeling I had when I decided to find the Duffy kid, and the arm and the buttock that Reese had kicked were beginning to throb. Not even the sight of the ill-fated house cheered me. It had been deserted, and in the dim streetlight looked as if it had been bombed.

'Did a job on it, huh?' Dick said, but I didn't bother to answer. 'Remind me not to piss you off, old buddy.'

'I wasn't even irritated. It just happened.'

'And what happens now?'

'You find out where Helen Duffy is staying?'

'No. Why?'

'Because I'm going to find her goddamned little brother.'

'Good luck,' he murmured, not sounding too happy.

'Don't worry,' I said. 'I'm not after anything. I'm just going to find the little bastard, that's all.'

'It's none of my business,' he said lightly.

'Don't try to shit your friends, Richard.'

'Okay. Like I said, good luck. You going to stop for a taste?'

'Don't I always?' I said.

'See you at Mahoney's,' he said, then drove away as I stepped out of the van.

I started toward the rig, but the lights were still on in the old woman's house next door, and she was standing at the front door looking out. Thinking she might be the sort of Nosy Parker who might have seen the Duffy kid, I cut through the brambles and weeds and climbed up on her porch, but she wouldn't open the door. She just stood there, smiling and waving through the glass as if we were on opposite sides of the street. When I knocked on the door, a large,

57

angry woman came to the door, looked at me, shook her head, and took the old woman away before I could explain that I wasn't selling anything.

When I got to my rig, I discovered that I had been, as the kids say, ripped off. Everything was gone but the seats. Everything.

'You forgot the fucking seats!' I shouted at the silent, dark houses, then drove back down to the police station to report the theft in the hope that I could collect the insurance. If the premiums were paid.

Publicly I bemoaned my lack of desire to hunt animals and blamed it on the Army and the Korean War, but the truth was that I'd never really liked to hunt. It seemed a great deal of hard work, both before and after the quick excitement of making a good shot. But I liked guns, so I took up skeet and target shooting and promised my friends that I'd go hunting next year for sure. Driving down to Mahoney's, the inside of my rig as empty as a church on Saturday night, I thought about hunting low-life bastards, the sort who would steal a man's guns.

When I got there, Dick had already left. I had a quick drink by the door, then shoved my way through the frenzied melee of freaks toward the back and my other office. They didn't seem like happy flower children that night; their fragrance was that of the unwashed, and they were no nicer drunks than any other type of people. I bounced off a tall girl, made her spill her beer, and she snapped at me, her long, pointed breasts rearing like the muzzles of two Afghans. I shouted at the night bartender helping Leo, told him to give the bitch a beer on me. She ran her fingers through her kinky blond hair and asked me why in the hell I had done that. I replied that I was afraid she would bite my head off, then walked away, into the quiet sanctuary of my other office, grabbing a can of beer as I passed through the door.

Inside, I switched on the television, flipped around the cable stations until I found a movie on a Salt Lake station. I sat down to watch it while I loaded clips for my Browning 9-mm automatic pistol. Harry Carey and Ben Johnson were riding Roman style, standing on two horses each, as they circled the parade field. John Wayne had a mustache and a cavalry officer's uniform. His face twitched, as if the mustache made his face itch. Victor McLaglen looked as if he had a hangover, and Maureen O'Hara like a good Irish girl who needed a drink. I remembered the title, *Rio Grande*, but couldn't remember the actor's name who played John Wayne's son by Maureen O'Hara. He was riding with Harry Carey and Ben Johnson – that is, his stunt man was riding. Also, I couldn't remember who got killed in the movie.

'The old fart looks good in a mustache,' Leo said as he came into the office.

'Did you see Gregory Peck in *The Gunfighter*?'

'Think so. Why?'

'He had a mustache. Remember?'

'Oh, yeah.'

'He looked really good. You think I ought to grow a mustache, Leo?'

He laughed for a moment, then stopped and said, 'I just came from the hospital. The colonel just died.'

'That's too bad,' I said, filling my mouth with empty words.

'The old fart survived two wars and some goddamned punk pushes him down the stairs and kills him. What the hell kinda life is that?'

'I don't know, Leo. The kind we have, I guess. I don't know.'

'The kind a fella needs a drink just to survive,' Leo said, his hand holding his little gray beard. His mouth moved silently, as if pleading for a drink. 'I don't know if I can handle that mad-house tonight. Why don't you lock me in on your way out?'

'Why don't you just go home?'

'Can't be a success staying at home, Milo.'

'You want me to stay with you?'

'Ah, hell, you wouldn't be any help, Milo,' he said, then glanced at me. Maybe he thought he had hurt my feelings because he added quickly, 'I didn't mean that. You'd just get drunk, then I'd have to tend to you.'

'Might keep you busy.'

'I ain't up to tending drunks tonight, Milo. Not even myself.'

He left slowly, unable to face the business of his life, but going anyway. I turned off the television without looking to see what John Wayne was doing. From the old trunk beneath the bed, I took a .41 double-barreled derringer and a handful of rounds, then a shoulder holster for the automatic, and stuffed my armaments into a paper sack. I needed a quiet bar and a slow drink, a large sandwich and a telephone, more than I needed the guns, but they were important too.

*

59

Occasionally, in my line of business, I had to cause a small scene at a local motel to obtain evidence for divorces. As a result, I wasn't too popular with motel management. If a switchboard operator or night clerk recognized my voice on the telephone, they wouldn't give me the correct time, but by the time I started calling around I was so tired that nobody knew my voice. I found Helen Duffy registered at the Holiday Inn, and just after midnight had the switchboard ring her room. She answered on the first ring, sounded expectant instead of sleepy, almost cheerful, but I broke the connection, and leaving the remains of my coffee and cheeseburger, drove out to the east side of town, where the better motels lined the highway – large buildings discreetly lighted, looking like a government installation or the campus of a shoddy junior college.

When I knocked, she came quickly to the door, asking who. I told her. She opened the door abruptly, warm and flushed from her bath. Streaks of dark-red hair lay across her cheeks and forehead like smears of dried blood, and her eyes, reflecting the dark green of the velour robe, were wide and empty, like the eyes of an accident victim. She fell against me, throwing her arms around me as if she had been waiting for me all day, her shoulder banging heavily into my sore arm. But the groan came from somewhere deeper inside. I held her, wondering how she could cry when I was so happy.

As she cried, she scattered tissues about the room, and they seemed to surround us like a flock of little pink animals. Between her sobs, she told me that her little brother was dead. He had been found in the Willomot Hill Bar men's room, an Indian bar north of town, and the deputy had told Helen that it looked like a drug overdose. Raymond Duffy had been found with a shoelace around his biceps and the needle still hanging from the bend of his elbow. Helen had gone down to the morgue and identified the body. Her grief, seeking a safe object for displacement, had centered upon her little brother's hair and beard; she accused the morgue attendant of cutting his hair short and shaving off his thick black beard.

'I didn't believe it,' she murmured, dabbing her eyes, 'not even when I saw the body, and I didn't cry until you came. I've been taking showers, one after another. I used all the hot water in the motel . . .' She began to giggle faintly, but they quickly changed to sobs. This time she fell into a chair, out of my arms.

'But now I've accepted it,' she said, drawing a deep breath, seeming almost calm. 'However, I do not believe he – he died of a drug overdose. The young deputy seemed to think that Raymond was an addict; he didn't come right out and say it, but I could tell.'

'How did they find you?'

'Who?'

'The sheriff's department.'

'Oh – I don't know . . . they – didn't say,' she said brokenly. 'I didn't ask.'

'I'll ask,' I said, taking a pad and pen out of my pocket.

'I'm sure it isn't important,' she said, so I put the pad back.

'Did they mention the autopsy?'

'No. They can't do that . . . Can they? I mean I didn't sign anything. I can't – couldn't bear – that.'

'I'm sorry,' I said, 'but in a case like this, they don't need your permission.'

'Oh my God,' she wailed, the sobbing about to begin.

'If you don't believe he died of an overdose,' I said, reaching out to touch her shoulder, 'then an autopsy will prove it.' My fingers stayed a second on the warm, damp cloth of her robe, my thumb gently kneading her fragile collarbone.

'I'm sorry,' she said softly, moving away from my hand. 'I'm just not thinking – the shock, I guess . . . you're absolutely right.'

'Just don't think about it,' I said, which, of course, made her think about nothing else.

'How . . . He looked so frail – lying there – like a child – so young . . . innocent . . .'

'You must have been awfully close to your little brother,' I said, hoping she might remember happier times, and in the memory ease the grief.

She glanced up at me, staring for a long moment, then in a very calm voice said, 'Yes.'

'That's unusual,' I said. 'The age difference – ' I stopped because she seemed angry. Her eyes, abraded by tears, flashed a hard green and fired with anger. Then, as if heavy shutters had fallen inside her, the eyes became opaque with control.

'My father,' she said, 'is a wonderful man but somewhat – distracted and not the outdoors type at all. My mother – works. Raymond and I were very close.'

61

'Have you called your parents?' I asked, and for the second time said exactly the wrong thing.

'Oh my God,' she whispered, her hand flying to her mouth, her eyes suddenly frightened. 'Oh my God.' Sobs jerked her body, and she jammed her fist into her open mouth as if she could hold them back with physical force.

I reached for her, but she jumped out of the chair, stumbled across the room and threw herself across the bed, moaning about kindness and suffering, youth and innocence, and dreadful grief, both hands holding her face. She cried so hard that I almost envied her the grief. Nothing had ever touched me that hard, not since my father's death years before. She wept among the disarray of hurried packing or unpacking, slips and brightly colored dresses and dark hose scattered as if by the wind across the bedspread. An empty suitcase, wide open like a hysterical mouth, leaned against the headboard. As she sobbed and rocked, like a mother thrown across the body of her child, a cosmetics case slipped off the side of the bed and emptied itself on the carpet, glass and metal clinking, a heavy gold chain slithering out of its niche like a sigh. But she heard none of it.

Beside her now, I pressed my hand into the small of her back, finding in the raw palm another bit of tiny, sharp gravel, and I rubbed her back until she finally fell asleep, whimpering and flinching in the uneasy sleep. I cleaned off the bed, folding her soft scraps of clothing, then covered her with the blanket from the other bed, my fingers caressing once more the slim reach of her waist, then, knowing that my comfort wouldn't be enough, I called Dick.

'Did I wake you?'

'Of course not, old buddy. I'm never asleep at – one in the morning. Especially when I have an eight o'clock freshman comp class. Christ, I can explain illiteracy to the little bastards in my sleep –'

'Helen Duffy's little brother is dead,' I said, stopping him.

'What?'

'Helen Duffy – her little brother is dead.'

'Jesus Christ, what happened?'

'Doesn't matter. Can you come over?'

'Jesus, Milo, I don't know.'

'She's in pretty bad shape.'

'Okay. Be there as soon as I get my pants on. Where?'

'Room 217. Holiday Inn.'

I hung up before I could overhear the beginnings of Dick's excuse to Marsha, then went back to the bed to tug the blanket higher about Helen's shoulders. I nearly pulled it over the top of her head. An old habit from the days when most of the bodies I covered with blankets were growing cold beside steaming, mangled automobiles, hunks of meat quivering in the pulse of red lights. Sometimes I thought that the accidents had finally driven me out of a deputy's uniform and into the wreckage of the divorce courts. I slipped the blanket back from her neck, felt lightly for the pulse in her warm, soft throat. She groaned slightly, turning, but the blood ticked merrily along beneath my fingertips.

Our bodies betray us constantly. In grief and confusion that should still its beat, the heart murmurs on about its business. Cells wither like ash with every beat, but never from sorrow. And desire remains. As I held a handful of her thick hair, as I leaned over and buried my face in the smell of her, clean and unscented, my body, ignoring my pleas, wanted her, a fierce unbidden desire rising. I wanted her then, wanted to lie next to her, to stroke that bare damp skin beneath the green robe, to bury myself in her.

But I moved away, picked up the room, putting things in their proper places, until Dick rapped softly at the door.

While he sat with her, I went down to the lobby and called Jamison at home. Evelyn answered but wouldn't wake him.

'He's tired, Milo, damned tired. He works too hard,' she said quietly, sounding much older than I remembered her.

'If you don't wake him, babe, I'll come over and kick the goddamned door down.'

'You bastard,' she hissed, but she went to wake him. We hadn't lived together in years, but she remembered.

'What the hell do you want?' Jamison grumbled. He didn't sound sleepy, just tired.

'You knew about the Duffy kid, didn't you?'

'Yeah,' he sighed, 'I knew. I didn't know you were gonna wake me up in the middle of the night to tell me what I already knew.'

'Why didn't you tell me?'

'It wasn't any of your business, Milo. She wasn't your client anyway.'

'I'm going to take this personally,' I said.

63

'Thought you might. The Duffy lady – is she taking it hard?'

'That's none of your business.'

'Ah, get the fuck outa my life, Milo,' he said, then hung up, banging the telephone.

Dick and I spent the night watching over her, drinking coffee and talking about nothing in whispers, as she started and muttered through her restless dreams. Once she sat up, her wild eyes staring through us, then she laughed in short, hard barks. Before either of us could rise, she fell back on the bed, tumbled back into her dreams. Just after sunrise, she woke, sat up again, rubbing her eyes as if she were trying to gouge them out. Then she remembered and let her hands fall into her lap. Her robe gaped open, revealing small, freckled breasts with dark, heavy nipples. I looked away. She saw Dick, and with a moan that sounded as if it had been wrenched from her chest with a steel hook, she launched herself at him, nearly knocking his chair over. She wept against his shoulder. He glanced at me over the top of her head, his arms away from her body, his palms open as if in explanation or making a plea, his face drawn and confused.

I left, walked out into the summer morning, into birdsong and air as light and pleasant as children's laughter. The sun came up, as they say, like thunder, topping the eastern ridges, raining golden fire into the valley. It was a morning for youth and rosy cheeks, but I was old and tired and needed a shave, so I went home, up to my log house on the bank of Hell-Roaring Creek, on the northern verge of Milodragovitch Park, which had been the family estate and my front yard until my father died and my mother gave the land to the city, cut the family mansion into sections, had it moved east of town to be reassembled as a country club house.

The sun wasn't high enough over the east ridge to reach the creek or the house, but the tops of my tall blue spruces shimmered like blue flames above the cool, shaded air. Inside, I drew the drapes to capture the shaded morning. My father had solved his life with whiskey and the full-choke barrel of an LC Smith hammerless double. The police had my shotgun, but I still had his. And a case of Canadian whiskey. I switched the telephone to the answering service, then laughed and jerked it out of the wall, sat down at the kitchen table to work on my own suicidal drunk.

5

Since I've never been what they call a thoughtful man, I didn't spend much time worrying about why I only had one drink that morning. One drink and an omelette, then a shower and to bed. Maybe I was just bored with being drunk. Not that I tried anything quite so drastic as quitting. I drank; I didn't get drunk. For a change. Living very peacefully, working out at the gym and playing handball every morning, fishing in the afternoons but without ambition, watching the light ripple across distant mountains without thinking of it as scenery. In court, I pleaded nolo contendere, and paid small fines for disturbing the peace and discharging a firearm within the city limits. I persuaded the judge not to suspend my license, though what I needed it for wasn't clear, but failed to convince the telephone company that vandals had destroyed their property. I paid cash for that damage but had to sign a note to the real estate agency that owned Lawrence Reese's former house. And I thought about Helen Duffy more often than I meant to.

After the inquest, which attributed Raymond Duffy's death to a misadventure with drugs, she flew the body back to Iowa for burial. Dick went with her on the next plane. Whatever he told Marsha, she accepted it more gracefully than I did. Simon fell hard into the bottle again, going on a binge that put him back in the hospital. Muffin went to the Coast for a few days and drove a rented truck back loaded with thirty thousand dollars' worth of hot stereo gear and televisions. Fat Freddy was on his way to the hospital to harass Simon when he was mugged by two kids. They flattened him with a piece of pipe for four bucks and change. Freddy ended up in the bed next to Simon in the charity ward, and Simon recovered immediately.

65

Freddy's mugging was only one in a rash of petty street crime that began to plague Meriwether. Our mayor, who was running hard for Congress, attributed the crime wave to the heat wave, which had socked Meriwether in a frenzy of 100-degree heat and blinding smog. He began orating about the long, hot summer of Meriwether, finding urban problems and previously invisible ghettos primed for a riot, by which he meant the local Indians, freaks and winos. Perhaps he had visions of them attacking City Hall to demand free whiskey, cheap dope and a thirty-day party. The mayor might have been a fool, but this new street crime had made the citizens edgy. The streets emptied at night. Except for Indians, freaks and winos. The mayor made speeches about Meriwether making the transition from town to city – with a city's problems, a city's pride to solve them.

He was an ass and an idiot, but only corrupted by ambition. And he had a point. Meriwether had problems, problems that had existed even when it was smaller. Perhaps it was the hard, long winters, months of Canadian fronts falling upon the valley like wolves, howling winds sharp with ice and snow; or maybe the sort of rootless people who drifted into the valley from the urban East or Great Plains, looking for paradise and mad as hell when they didn't find it; or perhaps it was Meriwether's vision of itself as still part of the wild and woolly West, the last, lawless frontier. Whatever the cause, Meriwether had divorce, suicide and alcoholism rates that embarrassed the national average. And the dope, which for years had just been another way to get high, had become serious. The kids had moved away from marijuana and had begun to kill themselves with pills and speed. After four eighth-graders died from horse tranquilizers, the police shook down the junior high lockers and found a wealth of pills, speed and needles. Grass wasn't very profitable to deal anymore, so dealers turned to other, more profitable drugs. Even the police department became involved when two officers lifted twelve thousand ten-grain dextroamphetamine whites out of the evidence locker, then dealt them to a wholesaler right in Meriwether. They were fired but never indicted.

Some of the people who had either been raised in Meriwether or had lived there for years were beginning to drift on, seeking that place they remembered, trying to find it again in British Columbia or Alaska or Australia. I wished them well but stayed on, sitting in my office a few hours each afternoon, enjoying what I could see of the view through the smog, but not answering the telephone, watching my prospects become dimmer. And it seemed a fine way to live. Until Dick and Helen came back from Iowa after two long weeks.

They found me in the other office, stoned out of my mind and sharing the last of my smoked whitefish with the lady with the fuzzy hair and the pointed breasts. We had come to terms the night before, both of us showing up late on Saturday night, both being sober and bored by the party drunks. The next morning we got stoned again and attacked the whitefish. Somebody had been pounding on the office door for what seemed like hours, long enough to convince me that Leo had given my position away, so I answered it.

'What the hell you want?' I shouted through the door.

'It's me, goddammit!' Dick shouted back. 'Open the goddamned door! It's freezing out here!'

'Go get your own girl,' I said as I opened the door, grinning because Dick had maintained that the girl was too mean to bed. 'Oh, you've got one,' I added, then tried to act as if I'd spent most of my life naked in front of Helen Duffy. She blushed, glanced over my shoulder, then excused herself.

Dick wasn't amused; guilt and love had driven the amusement right out of his life.

'What's happening, man?' I asked, cheerfully blasted but not amused either.

'Don't you have any decency at all?'

His face flushed with anger when I laughed. I stopped to ask him what he wanted.

'Business,' he said curtly.

'Go find somebody decent to do business with.'

'She wanted you. For some reason,' Dick said.

'Fine. Tell her I have a business office.'

'What do you call this?'

'Go to hell.'

'Sure,' he said, leaving. He came back before I could close the door, and muttered unhappily, 'She wants to talk to you.'

'Today?'

'Today.'

'All right.'

'How long will it take you to straighten up?' he asked.

'There must be forty wisecracks in that answer,' I said.

67

'Try to resist them, old buddy, if you can,' he said bluntly.

'Don't hard-ass me,' I said, feeling very foolishly naked.

'How long, old buddy?'

'Couple of hours. In my office.'

He nodded, then left again. Friendship hadn't survived love. I went back to the table and the nude lady, who was carefully licking her greasy fingers with the happy greed of a child.

'Who was it?' she asked, as if she didn't really care.

'Adulterers. Fornicators. Lovers. Fools.'

'Jesus, what a crowd.'

'Yeah.'

'What'd they want?'

'Me to straighten up.'

'What an outa-sight idea. Where'd they get it?'

'Who the hell knows?' I said.

Now that I wasn't stoned anymore, the girl had nice breasts and a splatter of freckles across her shoulders, but her feet were dirty and her hair smelled of smoke.

Two hours later, with I spent alternating between the steam room and the sauna at the Elks Club, with occasional forays into the whirlpool and the bar, I made it to the office, slightly tipsy but functional, red as a boiled lobster. The dark glasses I'd borrowed from the Elks Club bartender felt silly. I left them on my desk, then wandered down the hall to harass my cousin the dentist for a heavy vitamin shot. He wasn't there. That's how I found out it was Sunday. I was back in the office, hitting the bottle, when Helen came in the open door.

'Lady, I get double-time on Sundays and national holidays,' I said, 'and it started forty-five minutes ago.'

'I'm sorry,' she said softly, 'I was – was occupied.' She shut the door and came over and sat down without turning over the chair.

'Where's your boyfriend?'

'Dick went home. I think.'

Except for her muted gray suit and her hands, which looked as if she had been forming concrete for the past two weeks, she didn't seem to show any signs of heavy grief. Her slim neck might have been a bit loose on her shoulders, and she shifted uneasily in the chair when I stared at her, but I thought the cause was guilt, not grief.

I switched on the recorder without asking her permission, and asked her what she wanted. After a long pause, she answered in a slow, measured voice.

'I would like to engage your services – employ you to look into the details of my brother's death.'

'Why?'

'Is that important?'

'This time I'll decide what's important.'

'I see,' she said, watching her hands. Then she folded them, sat up straight in the chair, saying, 'I'm not satisfied with the coroner's verdict. I suspect something must have happened.'

'You or your parents?'

'My father doesn't know how Raymond died. He hasn't been well for some time.'

'What does your mother think?'

'Oh, she agrees with me.'

'Or you with her?' I asked, thinking that the grief-stricken mother had sent Helen back out West.

'I suppose you could say that,' she answered slowly.

'And what is it you and your mother suspect?'

'Some sort of – foul play.' The old-fashioned phrase seemed proper in her mouth.

'Murder?'

'Something – like that.'

'What does Dick think?' I asked.

'Does it matter what he thinks?'

'He knows you better than I do,' I said, 'and he's a pretty bright guy. I'd like to know what he thinks. If you don't mind.'

'You're awfully sarcastic today.'

'I don't feel well. What's he think?'

'He thinks I'm a fool,' she said calmly. 'What do you think?'

After a moment's stammering, I managed to sound fairly sincere when I answered, 'I would guess that you're a fairly sensible young woman, but between your grief and certain sorts of family pressures, you didn't have any choice but to come back. But then, I'm not paid to think.'

69

'And I'm not so young, either,' she said, smiling pertly. 'Will you look into his death?'

'I don't know that I should,' I answered. 'I'd like to help, but right now I'm not too popular with the police. Your brother died in the county, but he lived in town, and that's where I'd have to ask questions. They might not like that.'

'Aren't you an ex-policeman?'

'Ex-deputy. But that doesn't buy me anything. I don't have any sort of working arrangement or good buddies on the force. There are a lot of guys over there who don't care for me, and a few who hate my guts. So there may not be much I can do. Why not try to get them to open the case?'

'I tried,' she said, trying not to smile, 'but they refused. The state police and the sheriff's department too. Everybody refused.'

'And I'm your last resort?'

'Yes,' she admitted, letting the smile come.

'It's nice to be in demand,' I said, the anger gone now, my face distorted in a goddamned boyish grin. 'I'm not busy now, so if you want me to poke around for a few days, I will. But you should know up front that I don't have much experience with this sort of thing.'

'I understand,' she said, staring over my shoulder.

'Better than nothing, huh?'

'What? Oh, I wouldn't have said that.'

'Thanks. What do you see out there?'

'I'm not sure. I thought I saw lightning in the mountains, but the smog . . .'

'Let's hope not,' I said, 'I've got some property up there. How long do you want me to look into this?'

'As long as necessary.'

'Lady, I charge a hundred a day. Plus expenses. That can cost.'

'I remembered your fee; I can afford it.'

'It's your money. I'll look until I dead-end, okay?'

'That will be fine. I'll trust your judgment.'

'Okay, but this time you answer all my questions.'

That was harder than the money, and her answer didn't come so quickly.

'I'll try,' she said, bowing her head.

'That's not good enough.'

'All right,' she said, 'but please understand that – that sometimes it's difficult – painful . . .' She settled herself into the chair as if I were about to extract her wisdom teeth. 'I'll do my best.'

'I guess that will have to do. I suppose Dick mentioned your little brother's living arrangements prior to moving to the Great Northern?'

'Yes,' she answered, sighing so deeply that I thought she might faint.

'You knew he was a homosexual?'

'It wasn't – his fault.'

'You knew?'

'Yes.'

'Since when?'

'I don't know exactly. I suspected it for some time, then found out for sure when he was a senior in college.'

'How?'

'Raymond was a dormitory counselor at Buena Vista, and he and another boy were caught smoking marijuana in a dorm room. During the interrogation, the younger boy claimed that Raymond had seduced him.'

'What happened?'

'The other boy was expelled. Raymond was allowed to graduate *in absentia*. As a personal favor to my father and me.'

'Your father teaches there too?'

'He did. For nearly twenty years. Until his accident – '

'Accident?'

'I suppose you'd call it that. He was beaten and robbed in New York City some years ago, as he was returning to his hotel after reading a paper at a conference of English professors. Two young men, drug addicts probably, beat him rather severely, then left him in the gutter. He lay there for some time in the cold and snow, and the people who walked past him must have assumed he was drunk. He's absent-minded about some things, like clothes. Mother packed his good suit, but he forgot to wear it, so he was dressed rather shabbily. Anyone who looked carefully would have realized that he wasn't a drunken bum. But no one cared. Not even the police. His identification was gone, he was incoherent and smelled of the single drink he had with an old friend after he read his Twain paper . . .

'So the police threw him into a drunk tank, where he was beaten again, where he stayed without assistance until he began to vomit blood the next afternoon. He never mentioned it, but I think he was

71

also – molested somehow – sexually . . . Oh, this is so sordid . . . I'm sorry – I can't seem to stop . . .'

She cried quietly for a few minutes. I let her, remembering how badly I'd comforted her the night Raymond died. Then she stopped, saying, 'I told you it would – would be hard.'

'There's no other way.'

'I guess not. After he got out of the hospital, my mother sued the city of New York. They settled out of court for a rather large sum of money, but by then it didn't matter. My father never recovered. After all that had happened, this was just too much. I had to quit graduate school to go home, and the college hired me to replace him. I suppose I've been replacing him ever since – '

'You said, "after all that had happened"?'

'Oh,' she sighed. 'From the outside, on the surface, we look like such an ordinary middle-class family, but so much has happened . . . We had no luck . . .' Her fingers were scrambling at each other now, and she was gazing out the window. 'We were happy – once, but we had no luck . . .'

The tears came back, flooding out of her open eyes and coursing down her cheeks. I handed her the box of tissues I kept in the desk for despondent wives, and she grabbed them and fled into my bathroom.

I didn't follow her. I did the necessary things. Erased the tape, switched off the recorder. Had a drink. Thought about families and luck.

When I lived in a family in the big house with overgrown grounds, we hadn't had much luck either. My father had blown his head off with a shotgun, but nobody ever discovered if it was an accident or a suicide or bad luck. He and my mother had been drunk, fighting as usual, breaking things to show their disgust for each other and their lives. Since I seemed somehow the center of their anger, I tried to listen, usually, but that night, had fallen to sleep. The two springer spaniels woke me, barking excitedly downstairs, as if they were ready for the hunt. When I walked to my window to see if it was near dawn, the night sky was black, except for a slice of the moon. In the verdant spring air, I smelled a skunk, then heard the shotgun go off downstairs.

My mother never told me why he was going for the shotgun. Her or the skunk or himself. Perhaps she really didn't know. Perhaps it doesn't matter. When he reached into the hall closet and pulled out the shotgun, the trigger caught on the open bolt of a Remington .30–06 rifle, and the full choke barrel discharged a load of number four shot just under his chin.

I remember the stink of the skunk, the dogs yapping in circles, my mother still shouting at the body, his heels rattling on the hard-wood floor. I was ten.

When I was twenty, during the long and stupid truce in Korea, the Red Cross informed me that my mother had died in a fancy alcoholic retreat in Arizona and her body had already been shipped back East to her family for burial. They offered me a leave, but I didn't need it. After the war, I found out that she had hanged herself with a nylon hose, but by then it was too late to feel anything, to do anything except curse the bad luck.

Helen came back from the bathroom, the make-up scheme of her face washed away, her skin pale and eroded with sorrow. She apologized quickly, then continued: 'We moved to Storm Lake when – '

'Let's skip the family history, okay? Concentrate on Raymond.'

I had confused her again.

'But – but how can you understand about Raymond, that he couldn't have – caused his own death?'

'Wouldn't it be better for me to have an open mind about it?'

'I'm not sure. You don't believe me either, do you?'

'You're not paying me to believe you,' I said, 'you're paying me to find out what happened. Right?'

'I guess so,' she said, her mind working at it. She seemed to be having her first doubts, to begin to consider that perhaps her little brother had died by his own hand, either accidentally or on purpose. But the concept was too hard. She shook her head like a dog with a mouthful of porcupine quills, then spit the idea out. 'He couldn't have killed himself!'

'Maybe it was an accident,' I said, not asking her why not suicide.

That seemed more repugnant. She continued to shake her head, a silent *no* falling from her lips each time her face reached the apex of its denials.

'Look, you want me to find out what happened? Or console you with lies?'

73

'Find out what happened, of course,' she said primly, but neither of us believed her.

'Okay. Let's start over. Why did he come out West?'

'What?'

'Why did he come to Meriwether?'

'I told you before,' she said, irritated now. 'To take a degree in Western history. He was quite a good student. He had finished his course work and was a graduate teaching assistant; he was writing his thesis when he dropped out of school. I know because I checked.'

'Did you think he might have been lying?'

'I doubted him, yes, but I shouldn't have. Raymond would never lie to me. Not even about the money – oh . . .'

'What money?' It was normal; my clients usually lied as often and as badly as politicians.

'What money?' she echoed.

'Come on, lady.'

'Oh, all right. The last time he wrote, he asked me for money . . .'

'Why not your parents?'

'Because I was sending him to school.'

'Why?' I asked, knowing we were back into family history.

'After the trouble in his senior year, my mother threw him out of the house. His clothes, his books, his guns, everything. Told him to never come back. She sold his horse and tack, she drove him away from the front door. She – she can be a hard woman. She didn't mean to be cruel; she just couldn't stand any more – any more grief and trouble. She even said she regretted adopting him. That was the – cruelest thing of all . . . she regretted being his – mother.'

'Raymond was adopted? I didn't know.'

'There's no need to be nasty. After the other boys had – had died, my parents adopted Raymond.'

'Others? How many?'

'Three.'

'I'm sorry. How?'

'One of the twins was killed in an automobile accident when he was four. My father hit a bridge abutment on the way to Chicago. My mother miscarried with a male child in the wreck. The next baby choked to death on a button. The other twin drowned in our pond when he was nine,' she said so matter-of-factly that I expected her to count them off on her raw fingers, but her eyes had found their

74

way to my north view again, hoping perhaps to see lightning in the hills.

'I am sorry. I didn't need to know that.'

'It doesn't matter.'

'Let's go back to Raymond. You were sending him to school. But he wasn't in school, yet he wrote asking for more money?'

'Yes. He did that sometimes. Unexpected expenses,' she said.

'What was it this time?'

'He wanted to buy – some papers – or something . . .'

'What?'

'Some historical papers, letters and diaries that some old man had. I think he was one of those who died in the hotel fire. Raymond had become his friend, and the old man told him that he wasn't really the son of the outlaw he said he was . . . Something . . . The old man claimed in public to be the bastard son of that bandit the vigilante hanged in Montana, the leader – '

'Henry Plummer?'

'That's the one,' she said hurriedly. 'But it wasn't true, it was just a way to get people to buy him drinks. He was really the son of a less famous bandit, here in this state, a Dalton – something-or-other. I'm sorry. I've forgotten the name.'

'Dalton Kimbrough.'

'That's it. Raymond said nothing had been published on this Kimbrough and that anything he did with the old man's papers would surely be published. Publication is very important in an academic career.'

'How much did he ask for?'

'Five thousand dollars. Two thousand for the papers, three to live on while he checked their authenticity and worked on the thesis.'

'Did you send it?'

'Yes, of course.'

'Where did you get that sort of money?'

Her face said that was none of my business, but then she remembered and answered, 'I have quite a bit in savings – I live at home.'

'And you believed this story?'

'Absolutely. I told you: Raymond wouldn't lie to me.'

'Maybe he needed the money to support his drug habit? Or maybe for a deal? Sometimes addicts deal too?'

'He was not a heroin addict,' she said.

There didn't seem to be any room for argument, so I paused, then said, 'You see that old bastard in the Cossack uniform hanging there on the wall?'

She turned so quickly that her chair nearly fell over, as if she expected to see a man swinging from a gibbet.

'That's my great-grandfather. He's the man who killed Dalton Kimbrough.'

'Oh, really,' she said. She didn't seem to share her little brother's interest in outlaws.

How fleeting is fame, I thought, laughing to myself. My great-grandfather had parlayed the death of Dalton Kimbrough into a fortune, and if he hadn't started wearing that damned phony Cossack uniform and carrying a knout, he would have been the first governor of the state. I knew how quickly they forget too, how fleet the foot of fame, how easily it tramples. Five months after I became a deputy sheriff, I had become momentarily famous. I captured a mass-mur-derer. A soft, fat honor student who had killed his mother, his grandmother, his aunt, and the four other women in the beauty shop his mother owned. All the law enforcement officers in Meriwether County surrounded the shop with shotguns and bull horns. I knew the kid and thought he had probably killed all the people he wanted to. Besides, I wasn't a woman. So I went through the rear of the house, through the jungle of doilies and knickknacks, and brought him out the front of the shop, cuffed and leaning heavily on my shoulder. The picture made the wire services and newsmagazines: intrepid young deputy captures mad-dog killer. *Time* even mentioned my splendid combat record.

What nobody knew except the two of us was that when I'd walked into the shop, he had stamped his foot petulantly, chunked his .22 pistol to the tile floor, then burst into tears. He nearly knocked me down, trying to get his head on my shoulder. I cuffed his wrists while they were around my neck. By the time we went outside, my shirt was wet with his tears. In the news photo, it looked like a bloodstain. The angry crowd outside was much more dangerous than the sad, fat kid. My great-grandfather had made a fortune off the hero role, but I didn't even get a raise.

'Really,' I said to Helen Duffy. 'He killed Dalton Kimbrough with a rock in the winter of 1866.'

'What?'

'Nothing. What made you come looking for your brother after only three weeks without word?'

'I'm not sure – I just felt that he might be in trouble . . .'

I had let her sit too long while my mind dabbled in my own past, so I said, 'It's been fun talking to you, Miss Duffy.'

'What's that mean?'

'It means that if you won't talk to me, there's no sense in going on. Save your money, I won't find out anything. Hell, I can't even find out anything from you.'

'Well – dammit, it's hard answering all these questions. Can't you understand that?' Grief had become anger; I was glad.

'Sure. But that doesn't tell me where to begin.'

'You're supposed to know that.'

'I do. I begin with you. Why did you come looking for him?'

'Oh – because – because my mother made me,' she answered impatiently, throwing her head back like an angry little girl. 'That's why. She found out I'd sent him that much money and she insisted that I come out to see what he was doing with it. She didn't believe him, she didn't believe me, and she made me come, and when I got here the damned old hotel was burned down. Can't you understand how frightened I was? I walked down the street checking numbers and looking for the sign and there was this gaping hole full of scorched bricks and twisted pipe and I didn't know what had happened or what to do . . . So I called Dick because he's the only person I know in this whole damned state and he suggested that you might help.'

'Okay. Take it easy.'

'Sometimes – sometimes I get damned tired of taking it easy.'

'Okay.'

'Well, I do.'

'Okay.'

'Raymond had been in that trouble before, and it hurt him so, and I was afraid he was in trouble again, this time with nobody to help him, and I was afraid to go to the police – '

'Why?'

'You know – how they treat – people like Raymond.'

'Did your mother make you come back?'

'What?' She was the most beautifully confused woman I had ever seen. 'What?'

77

'Your mother. Did she make you come back this time?'

'No.'

'Then why?'

'You've never loved anybody, have you?'

'What the hell difference does that make?' I asked.

'Then you wouldn't understand what I felt when I saw Raymond's face, when that man pulled back the sheet and showed me Raymond's face . . . Oh, I know you don't believe me, I know you had a fight with that terrible man Raymond was – seeing, I know you don't believe me, but it's all true . . . When I saw his face . . .' She paused, then gave me a helpless look. 'Why did they have to cut his hair and shave his beard? Why? He had such lovely black hair, and his beard was so full and fine, and in the sunlight sometimes it would look almost red, sometimes I could – '

'Almost believe that he was your natural brother?'

'What?'

'The red in his beard – it made you think he was your natural brother.'

'Oh, I don't know. He was such a lovely child, such a fine young man. Nobody knew him like I did. Nobody.'

'Okay,' I said. 'I understand.'

'No you don't.'

'Okay, I don't.'

'Then don't say you do.'

'Jesus Christ, all right!' I shouted. It took two tries to get the cork out of the bottle, but I made it and had me a long drink.

'Is that really necessary?' she asked, as snottily as she could.

'Asking you questions is hard,' I said. 'Can't you understand that?'

'I'm sorry,' she said quietly.

I reached across the desk, placed my hand against her cheek. She leaned her face into my hand, holding it against her shoulder. Her skin was warm and slightly damp. With forgiveness instead of grief.

'You're a troublesome woman.'

'I don't mean to be. Besides, you're a troublesome man.'

'I know.'

'But you don't mean to be,' she said. In that soft way that good mothers forgive their children, letting them know that they are better children than they know. 'Dick told me all about you. He's really fond of you, you know?'

'We were good friends,' I said, withdrawing my hand.

'Were? And now you won't be anymore? Because of me?'

'It doesn't matter.'

'I am truly sorry,' she said gently, then reached and took my hand back. And I understood what I had only sensed before. The woman behind the fluster, the dread and sorrow, the fog of tears and pink tissues – the woman that Dick had called something special – bloomed, blossomed forth like a nightflower under the new moon. The compassion, fine and lovely; the forgiveness, eternal. A woman so strong that she could believe in hope and trust and families and love, a woman who had survived without luck.

'I can understand,' she whispered, 'how you could think Raymond was on drugs, why you think he might have killed himself, but believe me, he didn't. And if you can find out anything at all about his death, I would greatly appreciate it.'

'I'll do what I can.'

'Thank you.' She had become as placid as a night pond, patient and calm. She needed to care as much as I needed to be cared for. 'Thank you very much.' Then she released my hand and took out the sheaf of traveler's checks.

'That's not necessary,' I said as she began signing them.

'Don't you want a retainer?'

'You watch too much television.'

'There isn't much else to do in Storm Lake,' she said lightly, scribbling at the checks. 'And if your other offer is still open, I'd like to take you up on that.'

'What's that?'

'Oh, you know,' she answered, perky now.

'No.'

'Your days in exchange for my nights,' she said, very businesslike about it, then she ripped out five one-hundred-dollar checks and laid them on the desk. 'Is that enough?'

'Why?'

'Why what?'

'Don't be coy.'

'Sometimes it's fun.'

'Not now. Please.'

'Oh, all right. I need to get over Dick. I've needed to get over Dick for an awfully long time. I must have been mad to let it start

79

again. Although I've ended it – that's why he was so angry earlier – I'm not over it. If I hadn't been so frightened the first time, I would have taken your offer then. You did look so desperate, and I was such a . . . so nasty to ignore you completely, and I know it's terribly unkind to ask – to use you like this, but I think you're probably a kind man, and perhaps as frightened of all this as I am. Well?'

Her smile was only partially strained, the rest happy and willing, and her face was solidly determined. She was serious. She wasn't exactly desperate, but she would do it. But I wouldn't. Or couldn't. And I didn't think about why.

'I'll work day and night.'

'Oh,' she said, the smile limned with white as she held it gaily on her face. 'You mean no, don't you?'

'I'm sorry.'

'See? I told you that you were a kind man, that you weren't as bad as you thought.'

'Who is?'

'Oh, anybody who really wants to be,' she answered, chattering as brightly as a hysterical squirrel, lonesome upon the high limb where I had left her. She didn't hate me for the rejection, but she didn't like the rejection either. We were back to business again.

'Do you have a picture of your little brother?'

'Yes,' she said, dipping back into the purse. 'I had these made up the first time I came out here.' She handed me a stack of three-by-fives. 'They're copies of his graduation pictures.'

The young man in the photograph had a narrow face with sullen eyes and full lips arched in a sly smile, longish hair but not to his shoulders, and the beard was only a shadowy potential. He didn't look like a young outlaw, but there were hints of arrogance and bravado about the eyes and mouth; my great-grandfather might have called him a back-shooter, but to me he looked like an unhappy punk.

'Of course he didn't look like that when he was living here,' she said.

'I know.'

'You know?'

'I saw him around the bars a few times.'

'You did? Why didn't you . . .' But she didn't finish. Whatever it was that I had failed to do, she blamed me for it now.

'Did he look like this when he came to Meriwether?'

'Yes – no.'

'Which?' I asked.

'Yes.'

'Then how did you know about the long hair and the beard?' I asked, not interrogating, just curious in an aimless way.

'I didn't,' she blurted out, then covered her mouth with both hands and her purse. 'I did . . . I don't know anymore.'

'How did you know about the long hair and the beard, lady?'

'I – ah – Raymond sent a picture.' The lie stood between us like a wall.

'And don't tell me you'd rather not say if I don't goddamned mind.'

'Oh.'

I handed her back the checks. As she stared at them blankly I had another drink, this one more necessary than the last, the whiskey doing its job, flowing in, washing out the bad taste of my life.

'He did,' she said meekly.

'Don't fucking lie to me.'

She stood up, tried to look shocked as she grabbed the checks and headed for the door. There she paused, slapped the checks against her thigh, then came back, hissing: 'All right. I came out last summer too. I live at home, and nothing ever happens at home, nothing. My mother still switches on the floodlights when a man brings me home, and nothing ever happens. So I came out last summer to see Raymond, and to see Dick, I hoped I'd see Dick, and, oh, damn you and your questions. Are you happy now?'

'Damn right. What happened last summer?'

She slammed the checks on the desk.

'What happened?'

'Nothing that has anything to do with this.'

'I'll decide that.'

'Really,' she pleaded, 'nothing.'

'What?'

'Oh, damn, if you must know. Raymond was living with a young history professor, who had left his wife for Raymond, and she kept coming around, dropping by or calling at all hours, threatening to *sic the law* on Raymond, and it was just awful. I never had a chance to call Dick. Really. And one afternoon she caught me coming

81

out of the apartment and followed me down the street, screaming obscenities at me, holding this tiny baby out at me like a club and shouting about who was going to provide for her children, and suggesting that – that I was somehow involved, somehow to blame – sexually involved – and she got right in my face and screamed that she was going to take a needle and thread and fix my – faggot brother so he couldn't – couldn't – I can't say it.'

'You want me to?'

'No! Damn you, no!'

'What do you want?'

'I don't know!' she screamed, then fled the office, her shoes ringing down the hall, all the way down the stairs, oddly confident in flight.

I didn't know what I was mad about. Her handwriting on the checks was as sorry as mine. I needed the name of the errant history professor and of Helen Duffy's motel, but that I could handle without her. Unlike my life. I needed Simon to drift into the office to tell me what a fool I was. I had a drink instead, toasting the heroic form of my great-grandfather. His dark eyes glittered above his large, defiant nose; his huge mustache shadowed what must have been an arrogant mouth. He seemed to be smiling, but I didn't like it.

6

The lady was gone, but the money was still on my desk. Thinking the money small recompense and wondering what I thought I was doing, I endorsed the checks and filled out a deposit slip. She hadn't signed a contract, but money had changed hands, so I had a client. I started a file and an expense sheet. My expenses were already immense but, unfortunately, unclaimable: my auto insurance had lapsed, so all the gear stolen out of my rig was just another lost cause; the two bruises Reese gave me had faded into large yellow stains, but the indignity hadn't eased at all; I'd lost an old friend and handball partner; and I had a feeling that Helen Duffy wasn't going to be a fond memory. I left the expense sheet blank and printed her brother's name at the top of a new legal pad, but the information I had about him was both vague and confusing. Praying that ignorance wasn't going to be a fatal handicap, I left the legal pad blank too.

As I pushed away from my incipient failure, I glanced into the Diablos. Summer thunder showers lurked about the peaks, shot with hairs of lightning and trailing transparent veils of rain too light to dampen the vigor of a lightning fire. By morning there would be fires, but not enough rain, and the valley smog would fill with the odor of pine pitch and smoke. On the ridges and timbered slopes, gray clouds would rise, writhing with flames, the animals would move nervously downhill, and in Meriwether the people would look into the hills, some hoping for small things – hoping the fires wouldn't frighten the tourists or ruin the fishing – others hoping that the fires might grow too large for the Forest Service crews so that civilian crews would have to be hired, hoping for a few days of work in hell to buy a few drunk nights. Since some of that timber was my last ace in a deep and empty hole, I hoped for a front off the northwest coast, for long steady rain, easy showers without lightning, clouds to cut the sun, cool air to slake the heat, and a long slow rain.

Some hopes aren't foolish, some prayers are answered. Just as I had decided to write off my timber, the shades on the western windows, lowered against the afternoon sun, darkened and rattled in a rising wind. I raised them; the front waited just behind Sheba Peak – a broad thick blanket of blue clouds heavy with rain, already lapping at the late afternoon sky behind the peak. Even as I watched, the gray cone of Sheba fell prey to the vaporous arms. Once again, by the grace of those infamous gods, who tend to fools and drunks, the long bitter summer was eased.

The wind kicked up a notch, rattling the shades in a dry brittle clamor that sounded like a soothsayer's bones being cast. And the wind moaned in the hollow Sunday streets below me, lifting cheap cowboy hats off the sun-baked heads of tourists, tilting the random shirt, hurrying the pedestrian on his way. I lifted my head into the wind, tilted my face.

Simon, who sensed rain and cool air in his bones, who could forecast the weather better than ants or barn swallows, was heading north over the Dottle Bridge, scurrying and scuttling and limping like a sorely wounded crab intent on the safety of his hole – wrapped loosely in a tweed overcoat, surely purchased only moments before from the Salvation Army store south of the river.

So he has it now, I thought. The overcoat. It had been my father's, a heavy Harris tweed overcoat, purchased in Winnipeg on a binge, a coat he loved and wore at the slightest excuse, as a woman might a new mink. Ensconced within the coat, his thick unruly black hair set above like a fur cap, my father was prepared to weather any storm. At home he used it in preference to whatever robe my mother might buy him. Outdoors it became his shield, his cloak against the world's expectant daggers. Sometimes, wearing the coat, if his hair hadn't yet been tangled by the wind or his thick fingers, if his whiskey flush still resembled a tan, sometimes he might have been taken for a successful businessman instead of a rich drunk. After his death, I stayed wrapped in it, unafraid in the solid odor of wool and sweat and whiskey, curled like a sleeping pup on the study couch, until my mother took it away, gave it away, along with all his other clothes, to the Salvation Army.

So the drunks and bums could have them, she said, so the whole

84

town could know for certain and remember forever what a drunken bum he had been. I didn't even know how to protest, how to stand before her hate and rage, which poured off her like heat from a burning house. I did ask why she had married him, and she answered '*Because of you!*' so vehemently that I flinched. But I didn't understand what she meant until I was older, and after I understood, I became very nervous when people talked about abortions upon demand.

I grew up as my mother meant for me to, watching my father's clothing parade up and down the streets of Meriwether, warming the backs of whatever dispossessed came into them. A retired NP engineer had been buried in his favorite tweed suit. His Russell snakeboots wore to greasy decrepitude on the feet of a local garbage man. Once I saw his Malone hunting pants on a drunken Willomot squaw, dirty and worn, the fly broken and a scrap of pink panties bulging out like a coil of gut. As I grew up, I saw my father sodden in doorways, urine snaking across the sidewalk toward the gutter, saw last rounds poured into him like *coups de grâce*, then saw the stumbling body disgorged like a walking corpse from two o'clock bars, saw brains and eggs shoveled into his toothless mouth, saw a brigade of fallen men falling to their death in his clothes.

Over the years I bought up what I could, haggling my allowance away to the Salvation Army, the Goodwill store, the second-hand dealers of Meriwether. On the streets and in the bars and skid-row hotels, I sought his clothes, bought and burned them. Once the winos found me out, I bought more clothing than my father had owned in his life, and if I had had enough money, the winos of our fair city would have been rich but naked.

But in the haggling, I learned that they were men also, that they had had lives full of chances too, not all of which had gone begging. And they still had dreams, dreams and lies enough to live with them. Unlike my mother, they were honest drunks, not too often ashamed. In their odd moments, drunk or sober, they knew who and what they were; they had looked at the world for a long steady moment, and found it wanting. As they took on individual faces and histories, I began to see them, both in the bars and at work – many did work, shoveled Meriwether's shit like white niggers – and the more I saw them, the more I preferred them to sober citizens. And I understood the defiance in the pathetic motto: I ain't no alcoholic, Jack, I don't

85

go to no fucking meetings. And they needed no army for their salvation.

Just before I went to Korea, I thought I had found all the clothes except the overcoat, which I assumed had been garnered on the sly by a tall, portly professor or trundled out of town on the warm back of a railroad bum. When I came back from the war, it was back on the street, but I didn't care anymore. The war taught me that I wasn't the heroic type, and my childish notion of slaking my grief by burning his clothes had always seemed vaguely heroic. So I stopped. When I saw the overcoat around town, I tipped my hat and said hello, let it cover whatever back needed warming. It had endured so long, I knew it wasn't about to wear out in my lifetime, thought it might outlive us all.

Once later, I thought I had found his red felt crusher hunting hat on the head of a dead Assiniboin buck who was in a carload of breeds that had missed the last curve coming down Willomot Hill. Even in the ragged light of my unit, I saw the name inked into the felt, black as blood through the sweat and grease of countless men. But it was my childish scrawl on the name, not his firm hand, darkly smeared where the buck had tried, like a cowboy in a B Western, to wear his hat all the way through the fight.

That was when I cried for my father. Or perhaps for myself. And I quit the sheriff's department. No more car wrecks, no more bar fights, no more lost children whimpering at the dark mouths of canyons, no more family disturbances. No overcoats, no hats.

And now the overcoat had passed from deathbed to second-hand store to Simon. The coat wasn't an omen of death but of life; Simon had been dying for years. I leaned out the window into the deepening dusk, shouted and waved at him in the rising wind as the first splatters of rain shattered against my face. He didn't hear me; he turned into Mahoney's as if it were home.

My past exhumed and worn ragged, I gave it up and went back to work. I called Dick, hoping he could tell me where Helen was staying and what history professor had had the delight of living with her little brother, but one of his little girls answered the telephone. Usually children are death on telephone conversations, but Marsha, with her infinite patience, had taught their children to cope, and the child went obediently to fetch her father.

She came back shortly, saying carefully, 'He's busy, sir, and can't come to the telephone. Can I – may I take a message?'

'Honey, would you please go back and tell him that it's Milo and that it's important.'

After a longer wait, she returned, her small voice full of wonder and apology, 'Hello?'

'Yes.'

'I told him – but he didn't say anything.'

'Well, thank you, honey,' I said, but before I could hang up, I heard a clatter of footsteps and Dick's muffled voice, but I couldn't make out what he was saying.

'What the hell do you want?' he asked.

'Two things, old buddy. Helen's motel and the name of the guy in the history department who lived with her little brother last summer. Okay?'

He paused, his breathing harsh against the mouthpiece, then said, 'Why don't you do your own fucking work for a change?'

Behind him, in her shocked stage whisper, I heard Marsha saying, 'Richard! Not in front –'

But then the line went dead. I hung up, then dialed the first two digits of Dick's number, thinking to mend fences, but then I realized that I didn't know what to say, so I hung up again. Then I picked it back up and called Hildy Ernst.

The telephone rang until my ear started to ache, but she finally answered breathlessly, as if she had just run up the stairs to her apartment.

'Hello,' she said. Hildy had one of those voices that rub women the wrong way and men the right. My knees were suddenly weak. But there were odd noises behind her, grunts and groans and thumps. It sounded as if she was holding the NCAA wrestling championships in her living room.

'Hildy. This is Milo.'

'How nice. Where have you been, love?'

'Recovering. How have you been?'

'*Comme ci, comme ça.* You know how boring summer can be, darling.'

'Right.'

'Then why haven't you called me, you terrible man?'

'I meant to. But every time I tried, my hands shook so badly, I couldn't dial.'

'You're sweet, Milo.' There was a thud, then cheering.

'What the hell is going on?'

'Oh, some friends dropped by. We're playing charades, darling. You want to come over?'

'No, thanks,' I said. 'Crowds make me nervous. Besides, I'm working. But I need some information. Last summer a history professor left his wife to live with one of his male students – '

'How tragic.'

' – and I wondered if you knew who it was.'

'Of course.'

'Who?'

'If I tell you, will you stop by?'

'Some other time?'

'Promise?'

'Sure, Hildy.'

'I don't believe you, darling, but his name is Elton Crider. He's one of those hillbilly types, all bone and Adam's apple. You will stop by soon?'

'Sure.'

'You bastard, Milo.'

'Say, Hildy.'

'Yes?'

'What did you ever see in me?'

'I get bored with younger men, Milo. They all expect me to be grateful,' she said, then laughed in her husky voice.

'Thanks,' I said, then hung up, laughing. Hildy was the sort of woman an older man could fall in love with – if he could keep up. I couldn't.

Elton Crider wasn't listed in the telephone book, and when I drove over to the address listed in the university directory, another family lived there. They had no idea where the Criders had moved, except that it was somewhere in the country. So I called my telephone-company creep, and for fifty bucks, his weekend price, he went down to the office and got me the unlisted number and the new address.

At ten o'clock and fourteen miles up the Meriwether River, I found a dark house and an empty garage. I rang the bell anyway, standing close to the door under the narrow eaves of the tacky new house, trying to stay out of the soft rain. The door flew open so quickly that I nearly toppled into the dark hole of the doorway.

'You son of a bitch,' a shrill voice rasped from the darkness. Then an angry hand whipped back and forth across my face as the voice cursed me with each swing. I backed off the low concrete stoop, but the hand followed me.

'Hey, lady, I give up,' I said, trying to hold my hands in front of my face.

'Elton?' she asked, her raised hand somewhere above my hot face.

'No, ma'am.'

She stepped back to switch on the porch light. In the yellow glow of a bug lamp, we considered each other. She was a tall woman wrapped in a faded pink chenille robe. An angular face with a broad mouth and a large straight nose and a sharp chin jutted out at me. She might have been a handsome woman once, but the softness had been eroded from her face, and the yellow light wasn't flattering. Sallow skin stretched tightly over her facial bones. Then she giggled slightly, and her face softened.

'Ah'm sorry, mister. Ah thought you's my husband,' she said in a Southern voice that twanged like an out of tune E-string, which was an improvement over her shout, which sounded like a ripsaw in a pine knot.

'You always wait in ambush for your husband?' I asked, but she didn't answer, so I rubbed my cheek, playing for sympathy. 'I guess I'm glad I'm not him. You nearly took my head off.'

'Ah didn't even double up my fist,' she said, smiling as if she had made a joke. The fist she held out to me was large, heavy, with knuckles like stones.

'I'm glad,' I said, shrugging and smiling.

'Well, Ah'm sorry Ah hit you,' she said, wrapping her long arms around her spare chest. 'What was it you wanted?'

'To begin with, you could let me out of the rain.'

'This'll do fine,' she said quietly.

It was late on a dark rainy night and the nearest house was five hundred yards away, but she wasn't a bit frightened. She was a hell of a woman.

'Is your husband home?' I asked, then remembered that he wasn't. 'Sorry. Silly question,' I said, rubbing my cheek. 'My name's Milo-

89

dragovitch. I'm a private investigator.' I showed her my photostat. 'I'd like to talk to your husband. Do you know where I might find him?'

'Why?'

'Business.'

'In the middle of a Sunday night?'

'I work strange hours,' I said. 'I've got to catch an early flight tomorrow morning, so I thought I'd try to catch your husband tonight.'

'What's Elton got business with a private investigator for?' she asked in a hard voice, as if I were the law.

'I'm looking for a missing student, and somebody told me that your husband knew her quite well.'

'Who?'

'Elaine Strickland,' I answered quickly. Elaine had been my childhood sweetheart; she had beaten me half to death with a rag doll in the third grade.

'Never heard of her. Who says Elton knew her?'

'Ah, her parents. She mentioned Professor Crider in several of her letters.'

'What did she say?'

'That she'd had several classes under him, that he had helped her with some research. That sort of thing.'

'Oh. Why don't you leave a number, and Ah'll have Elton call you tomorrow or the next day.'

'I won't be in town for a week or so. I'm flying to Seattle to follow another lead,' I said importantly. 'If I could talk to him tonight, I'd really appreciate it. If you know where he is.'

'Ah damn sure know where he ain't. Ah'd have to guess where he was.'

'A good guess is better than nothing.'

'Yeah. Lemme see that thing again.' I handed her my license. She examined it carefully as I stood in the rain. 'Milodragovitch, huh?' she said as she gave it back to me. 'Ain't that the name of that park in Hell-Roarin' Canyon?'

'Yes.'

'Kin a yours?'

'Used to be my front yard.'

'That so?'

90

'Yes.'

'Ah'll be damned. What happened?'

'Family fell on hard times,' I replied.

'Some folks don't never have no good times to fall onto hard from,' she said, her voice shifting closer to the rhythms of the Southern hills, full of hardscrabble farms and lost chances, failed crops and good hounds ruined by mean coons. She stared into the rain over my head as if she could see all the way back there to the dim hollows flanked by steep, sharp ridges.

'Kentucky?' I asked. 'Tennessee?'

'Don't matter none,' she answered. 'Don't live there now.' She shook herself like a lanky dog just awake, brought herself back to this new place of young mountains and old strangers. 'Elton is probably drinkin' at the Riverfront. He hangs out there some. We had a little fuss, and sometimes he goes there to sip whiskey and gnaw on his liver. You might find him there.'

'Thank you very much, Mrs. Crider,' I said. 'I'm sorry for the trouble.'

'Me too,' she whispered, 'sorry as hell.' Then as if the apology made her feel better, she brightened and smiled. 'Ah've been impolite to make you stand in the rain. Why don't y'all come on in? Coffee's on the stove. Warm yourself up.' Then she paused and added, 'May be that Elton will come on home 'fore the bars close this once.'

We looked at each other, both knowing he wouldn't. I didn't know what the invitation meant, and I decided that I didn't want to know, so I declined.

'Thanks, but I've got to be going. Thanks for your help,' I said, then turned to trudge out to my rig.

'Take care,' she said, her voice warm and vibrant through the easy fall of the rain.

After the divorce business went bankrupt, I thought I was finished with the long signs of dead marriages, but as I backed out of the driveway, she stood framed in the saffron glow, a tall woman, her long hair growing lank in the damp air, her strong hands strangling her waist with the cord of the ragged robe.

With the rush of affluent tourists in the 1960s, the mountain West had suffered a blight of shoddy motels, built, like mining camp saloons and whorehouses, strictly for profit. Cheap and fragile lodg-

91

ings, buildings just waiting for the rumor of another strike to collapse into permanent vacancy and decrepitude, instant ghost towns, as frail as dead neon signs.

But the Riverfront Motor Inn had obviously been designed in protest, in the vague hope of permanent opulence. The carpets were thicker and the furnishings ached to be tasteful, but the cedar shakes and natural wood and stone trim covered the same old plywood and profit motive. When credit cards slipped through their imprinters, they came out shaved, like crooked dice. The dining room had an elegant menu; the bar, fancy drinks; but the food was tasteless and the liquor spurted niggardly from a speed gun. They did a fine business in tourists, but the local people, except for lovers on an illicit tryst, stayed away.

Rumors persisted, too, that the Riverfront had been built with Syndicate money and was used to wash money skimmed from the gaming tables of Nevada, rumors aided and abetted by the fact that a local Italian, Nickie DeGrumo, had returned from World War II with an Italian bride from New Jersey, an ugly, hawk-faced woman who came West with money from unidentified sources, money that had started him in the bar business that had culminated in the Riverfront Motor Inn complex. This in spite of the fact that everybody in town knew him to be the worst sort of fool about business, the sort who leapt into each new venture at exactly the wrong time and wrong way. He built a drive-in movie just in time to be ruined by television, a pizza place that lasted a year before the franchised pizza companies moved into town, and a putt-putt golf course so easy that even the children were bored with it. He bought a fleet of soft-icecream trucks before the machinery was perfected, and he only missed an Edsel dealership because his wife refused him the money.

It became apparent that she and a series of cousins from the East ran the business, that Nickie was just a name on the liquor license, a local front tethered by a small allowance like a child. He was the only bar owner in town who never set up a round of drinks when he visited other bars, and his the only bar in Meriwether that never bought its regular patrons a drink. Like Simon, Nickie always seemed to have a drink in his hand that somebody else had bought. Around town he was known for being slow with his wallet but quick with his mouth. 'I'll get the next round, boys,' he'd say, but he so seldom did that the drinkers around town tagged him Old Next Round, and called him so behind his back and to his carefully smiling face.

Just after midnight, I parked in the nearly empty lot next to the dining room and bar, then poked around the few cars until I found one with an MSC faculty sticker, a battered blue Ford station wagon, paint so faded that it didn't even glisten in the rain, looking more abandoned than parked, listing on ruined springs like a tired horse, but it was registered to Elton and Martha Crider, so I opened the hood and lifted the rotor out of the distributor, slipped it into my pocket, then wandered into the Riverfront lobby – tired, lonesome, sodden as a drowned cat.

The building was fairly new but badly maintained. The ornate metal handles of the double doors showed the effects of pushing hands, the red carpet the marks of passing feet, and the night clerk, in spite of his razor cut and nifty gold blazer, had the sharp feral face of a cornered rat. His beady eyes, which checked the empty lobby around me, weren't happy; he had lost his last job because I had bribed a look at his guest register, then made a large fuss when I kicked down a room door to take pictures.

'I'm sorry, sir, but all our rooms are taken,' he said in a new voice, warm and rich, the split ends trimmed. Then he glanced around the lobby once more, and added in his old voice, 'Get the fuck outa here, Milo.'

I bared my fangs; he subsided into a whine.

'Any trouble, man, I call the law.'

I had stopped to consider what sort of trouble to give him, when Nickie came bouncing out of the darkened dining room. Nickie bounced because he affected expensive cowboy boots, but even with low walking heels, his heels bounced and his soles flapped against the carpet. On a hard surfaced floor, Nickie's walk sounded like slow ironic applause.

'Milo, Milo,' he greeted me, glad hand extended and inane smile pasted on his face. 'How's the boy, Milo? How you been? It's been too long. What's happening? You're looking great. Haven't seen you in a coon's age.'

I shook his hand and mumbled something before he flayed me with clichés.

'Business or pleasure? Business or pleasure?' he asked, pumping

93

my hand. His sun-lamp tan failed to cover the drinker's flush of his face, just as the expensively tailored Western jacket refused to drape his paunch. His thick black hair hadn't grayed, but it looked painted on his round head.

'A drink,' I answered, trying to move away from him, but he followed me toward the bar.

'Let me buy you the first one,' he said.

'That's okay, Nickie. You got the last one. I'll get this one.'

'Sure, Milo,' he said, clapping to a halt. 'I'll get the next one.' His face colored – anger, perhaps, or shame – then he looked very tired and gray when the flush faded, standing in his wife's lobby like a clown whose antics have failed to cheer the crowd, and rubbing his chest beneath his string tie.

'Sure,' he said again, trying to smile.

'Vonda Kay tending bar?' I asked.

'Huh?'

'Is Vonda Kay tending bar?'

'Oh, yeah.'

'I'll tell her the first one is on you,' I said.

'Sure,' he said. 'You do that.' A hard nervous edge sharpened his voice, as if he wanted to pick a fight with me, which would have been funny if it hadn't been sad.

'Thanks,' I said, ignoring his uneasiness, then walked into the dimly lighted bar.

Like the parking lot, it was nearly empty. Sunday night was for hard-core drinkers, and they didn't care for the California cocktail lounge décor of the Riverfront. The prices were too high for the serious drinker anyway. Their clientele that night was made up of occasional drinkers and refugees from love. In a corner booth, a drunken foursome mauled each other at random, two middle-aged men waxing prosperous, two middle-aged women waning, chipping and putting and hacking at lust, replacing divots in their chests. Another couple sat at the rear of the lounge, holding hands across the table and whispering seriously above the watery drinks – a younger couple, who, when they troubled to glance around the empty room, did so with lovers' disdain.

Vonda Kay, who had the biggest breasts and the sweetest disposition west of the Big Muddy, stood behind the bar as peacefully as a saint, working slowly at her nails, a serene smile lighting her face.

Her only bar customer sat hunched on a stool, as lonely and wasted as a man who has just discovered how bleak the shank of his evening. When he raised his glass to his mouth, his Adam's apple rose, then fell with the trickle of whiskey.

Elton Crider, I guessed – taller but as angular as his wife. He might have been her brother, but her bones were hickory, his rubber.

When I stepped up to the bar and ordered a Canadian ditch from Vonda Kay, the tall man turned toward me with a bright smile as phony as that of a trained horse, a forced grin so desperate that it went beyond the sexual domain, into that desert where any sort of human contact – the touching of fingers over coins, shoulders briefly wedged in a doorway – stood like a distant, shimmering oasis, the burning green toward which he loped, dry and sore-footed.

He should have been looking at Vonda Kay, who, if she was between boyfriends and if she felt sorry for a man, was the most comfortable one-night stand in town, as warm as freshly baked bread, as loving as a puppy. But it seemed obvious that he wanted something more, something spiritual and clean as a blue flame. An undying love, perhaps, a consummation of souls. Feeling sadder than I wanted to be, I remembered his wife framed in the wan light, twisting the frayed cord.

Vonda Kay handed me the drink and heaved her breasts on the edge of the bar like a man loading sacked feed. She took my hand in hers, said kindly, 'Long time no see, lover.'

When it rains, it pours, just like they say. I wished there were a mirror over the bar so I could look at my face to see if it was bright with love or lust or desperation. But there was no mirror, just Vonda Kay's shining eyes.

'How're you doing, lady?'

'Without, Milo, without,' she murmured. 'I've just worn out another occupation.'

'What this time?'

'Rock-'n'-roll singers.'

'Where the hell did you find a rock-'n'-roll singer?'

'Where the hell do I find anybody?' she said, glancing around the bar.

'What's next?'

'Old friends, I hope.'

'All right,' I said. Even a man of stone can be tempted to get out of the rain. 'You're on, lady.' As we laughed together the tall man down the bar coughed loudly. 'Who's your customer?' I asked.

'Don't really know, Milo. Comes in now and again and drinks till closing time. Never says much. What happened to your face? Looks like somebody slapped you good. Now, who would do a thing like that?' she said, teasing, touching my cheek with her hand.

'A chance encounter,' I said, 'in a dark alley.'

'Sure.'

'What's he do?' I asked, nodding toward her customer.

'Don't know. Somebody said he teaches at the college.'

'Sure,' I said loudly, 'I thought I knew him.' Then turning down the bar: 'Aren't you Professor Crider?'

He nodded hesitantly, as if he didn't want me to know, then grinned so widely that I thought he was about to whinny.

'I'm sorry,' he said. 'I don't seem to remember your name.'

'Milodragovitch. We met at a party a few years back,' I said. He looked confused, like a man who had good reason to remember every party. 'Can't remember where, though. I remember talking to you. Aren't you from the South?'

'Tennessee,' he offered slowly.

'Right. Didn't we talk about Nashville and the Opry? I told you about the time when I was stationed at Fort Bragg and a bunch of us drove over to see the Opry but got so drunk in the Orchid Lounge or whatever that place is called that we never made the show.'

'You did?' he asked, wanting to believe, to establish contact even with my lie. 'Must have blanked it. I did go to school in Nashville – Vanderbilt – but we never went to Ryman except to watch the rednecks queue up in the afternoon...'

· 'Right,' I interrupted. 'You told me about the Jesus Christ fans and the women standing there in flats, holding their high-heels in one hand and a drumstick in the other.'

'That's right. How did you know that?'

'You told me, remember?' Actually, it came from my second wife's first husband.

'Oh... yes... I seem to have some faint memory... certainly. It was at Frank Lathrop's spring bash two summers ago. Of course. Oh, Lord, was I loaded that day. That punch he made, my God,' he wailed, gleefully recalling the day, locking the false memory into his mind so tightly that I'd have trouble convincing him it was a lie.

'That's right,' I said, wondering who Frank Lathrop might be.

'Oh, Lord, Ryman Hall. I haven't thought about it in years. Of course, I never cared much for hillbilly music, or Country and Western, or whatever silly name it goes by today. Always seemed too shrill to me. And distressingly mawkish . . .'

He went on about Country music, now that we had shared experiences, occasionally shifting his hips on the red stool as if he were about to slide gracefully across the three that separated such good old friends. His accent was Southern-educated, genteel and effete, so languid that he might have brushed his teeth with sorghum molasses, but beneath it rang the sharp bite of a nasal hill accent, so much like his wife's that he sounded like her echo, and it crept under his assumed accent like a whining hound beneath a ratty porch. He was so damned snobbish about Country music, holding it up in such contempt, wrinkling his long nose as if he held a dirty diaper, that even though I wanted to pump him about Raymond Duffy, I nearly started to argue with him. So I bought a round of drinks instead, invited him to the stool next to me, hoping he would stop. He didn't.

'Say,' I said, breaking into his spiel, 'don't you teach history?'

'What? Yes, I do. Why?'

'I used to have a good buddy who was a graduate student in the history department and I haven't seen him in a long time. Maybe you knew him? Raymond Duffy?'

His eyes narrowed, and he looked at me in a frankly sexual way, thinking perhaps he had found a kindred soul, but he couldn't make himself believe it.

'No, I don't believe I know the name,' he said carefully. 'I don't teach graduate courses very often. Would you excuse me?' he said, pushing away from the bar.

'Hey, buddy,' I said. 'You haven't finished your drink.'

'I'll be right back. I'm just going – to the john,' he answered, pawing at the carpet with a scuffed loafer.

'Hope everything comes out all right,' I said heartily as he reared past me, blushing so hard that tears came to his eyes.

'Okay, Milo, what's going on?' Vonda Kay asked as Crider lurched toward the rest rooms.

'Working, love, working.'

'We don't need that kinda business in here, Milo.'

'Don't worry,' I said, standing up to go after him. I had gotten coy and lost him, so we would have to talk in the john. He looked as if he might have some experience with toilet communications.

'This is a good job, Milo. I don't need trouble.'

'No trouble, love, no trouble at all.' I gunned my second drink and went after Crider.

The rest room looked more like an operating room – white porcelain, beige tile and a soft green carpet. Crider was manfully trying to make water and ignore me. Thanks to modern technology, there was a hot-air blower instead of paper towels, so I jammed the swinging door with my handkerchief. Nobody was going to come in, and Crider wasn't going to get out quickly. He had a tall man's reach and thick wrists, and I wanted to immobilize him quickly. I stepped behind him and jerked his faded windbreaker over his shoulders to pin his arms. He reacted violently, not to get at me but at his fly to zip it up, and the London Fog gave up the ghost, splitting right up the middle of the back.

Zipped up, he spun around, anxious and confused, his teeth chattering and his lower lip trembling. 'Hey,' he stammered, 'hey, what's, what's happening, whatcha do that for?' He held up the two halves of his windbreaker. They dangled from his wrists like distress flags. 'Dammit, I've had this jacket since college, dammit, why, what . . .'

'It seemed like a good plan,' I said calmly.

'What?'

'I didn't want you to get excited. See? You're excited now.'

'What?'

'Now, don't get excited. I want to talk to you about Raymond Duffy.'

His eyes grew wide and wild, but I didn't hit him because they also filled with tears. I knew I could handle him, and he knew it. After the brief spurt of anger, his shoulders slumped like a man ready to take a beating. He looked as badly used by life as his wife, and somebody was huffing outside the door, so I shouldered the door and jerked my handkerchief out. Nickie, red-faced and breathing hard, came rushing into the rest room, saying, 'Goddamned door. Hi, Milo. Wonder what the hell's wrong with that door? You have any idea what those goddamned things cost?'

'No, Nickie, I don't,' I said, then walked out, went back to the bar to have another drink.

98

'What was that all about?' Vonda Kay asked as she handed me the drink.

'I don't know. Did you send Nickie back to the john?'

'Are you kidding, Milo? I don't send Nickie anywhere. He's useless as tits on a boar hog. Anytime there's trouble, I holler for one of the bar managers, then there's no more trouble.'

'Hard-asses, huh?'

'Nope. Just quiet and mean as hell. They even scare me,' she said, then laughed as if she weren't really afraid at all.

'See you later,' I said as I finished the drink.

'Want one to go?'

'Sure. Why not.'

She made one in a go cup, then said, 'See you about two?'

'If I can make it.'

'It's too cold for maybe's, Milo.'

'Best I can do, babe. I'm working.'

'Then come back some night when you aren't.'

'You know me, love, I work twenty-five hours a day.'

'That's not what I hear,' she said, but I didn't laugh.

Outside the rain had eased to mist, which shifted dully across the black gleaming asphalt and the empty cars. Elton Crider was hunched over his engine, busy with a flashlight. I walked up behind him, took the rotor out of my pocket, and said his name. He didn't hear me, so I said it louder.

His head whanged against the open hood as he stood up and dropped the flashlight. The lens broke and the light went out when it hit. It rolled across the asphalt, and I stooped and picked it up. He rubbed the back of his head and moaned.

'Is it broken?' he asked. He had taken off the pieces of his jacket and disposed of them somewhere. His shirt was soaked, and he looked so pitiful that I almost offered him my jacket.

'Looks like it,' I said.

'Damn. That was a new bulb too. Damn. What the hell have you got against me,' he groaned. 'What do you want?' Beneath the thin white shirt, his bones thrust out of his flesh like those of a concentration camp prisoner. 'What do you want?'

'To talk to you about Raymond Duffy.'

99

'He's dead. Don't you know that? It was in the papers. He's dead.' Then he began to blubber.

'I know he's dead. I want to know why. I want to know whatever you know about him.'

'No,' he moaned, 'no.'

I handed him his broken flashlight, but he flinched, falling back against his car, whimpering. 'Go ahead and kill me. I don't care, I just don't care anymore. He was the only person I ever loved and he's dead and I just don't care anymore.'

I shoved the flashlight into his hands, and he crumpled to the asphalt, wailing and cuddling his flashlight, rocking back and forth. A car full of drunks hissed over the Ripley Avenue bridge and down the ramp above us, fleeing through the night down black and wet streets, heading home or to another gaily lighted bar rife with music and dancing and sweaty women with bright eyes and lips like faded rose petals. As the driver down-shifted, the exhaust belched, the tires snickered across the slick pavement, a girl's shrill laughter flew out, abandoned like an empty beer can in the skid. The colored lights from the discreet Riverfront sign reflected off the dark asphalt, wavering as the wind sifted the rain, glowing distantly like the lights of a city beneath a black sea. I replaced Crider's rotor and slammed the hood, listening to his mewling, then squatted beside him, offered him my drink and handkerchief. He sniffled and took both; he snorted into the cloth, sipped at the drink, then asked, 'Why do you want to know about Ray and me?'

'His sister is in town – '

'His sister?'

'Right.'

'She's a nice lady. I was concerned when Ray asked her to stay with us last summer, but she was very nice, never judged us, never complained about – Ray and me – living together. She mothered Ray a bit, you know, and he didn't like that very much, but she didn't smother him. Say, why is she in town?'

'She doesn't believe that Raymond's death was a suicide – '

'Well, of course it wasn't,' he interrupted.

' – and she asked me to look into it.'

'Why didn't you say so?' he asked, wide-eyed again.

'Habit,' I said. 'People don't usually tell me what I want if I tell them what I want.'

100

'Oh.'

'Why don't you think he could have committed suicide?'

'Oh, Ray just wasn't the type. He had come to terms with his . . . his predilections. And though he was a wild man sometimes, he had enough sense not to mess around with heroin. That's what it was, wasn't it?'

'So I heard.'

'Well, Ray just wouldn't have. He was happy, in his own way. He thought he was bad, you know, tough, but he wasn't really. Just shy and quiet, a really sweet boy beneath his wildness.'

'So I keep hearing,' I said, thinking perhaps that I should begin to believe it. He offered me the drink, but I shook my head. 'You have a cigarette?' I asked. He shook his head sadly, his eyes shining with trust. He patted me on the leg; we were old buddies now. He told me about his love affair with Raymond Duffy, and it was properly sad, but nothing seemed to have anything to do with those cruel blank eyes I had seen glowering above the beard as Lawrence Reese destroyed the three sawyers, nothing to do with a kid dead on a toilet seat, the nail locked into the fatal vein. Nothing.

'What about friends? Who were his friends?' I asked, stopping Crider before he mourned his lost love into hearts and flowers.

'We didn't have any friends. We didn't need them,' he declared proudly.

'What about Lawrence Reese? Or Willy Jones?'

'Who are they?' he asked, gazing into my eyes with absolute innocence.

'Willy Jones is a dead drunk and Lawrence Reese is the world's largest faggot, complete with leather pants and purple eyeshadow,' I said, not hiding my disgust.

'Oh, I've heard of him.'

'Who?'

'The giant glitter queen.'

'From the Duffy kid?'

'Oh, no. Ray wouldn't have anything to do with trash like that,' he said.

'They were shacked up.'

'I can't believe that. But then . . .' He stopped, licked the rain off his lips, shaking his head.

'But then what?'

101

'Nothing.'

'What?'

'Oh, well, I guess it doesn't matter. I don't like to criticize the dead, but Ray did have one problem.'

'What was that?'

'He really was quiet and shy, you have to believe that, but he also wanted to be – an aggressive gay. A mean faggot, as he used to say. He used to stalk around the apartment, flashing his guns – his sister told you about the guns? – and threatening the straight world. He had the idea that he was going to be the last great faggot gunfighter or something – I mean, for God's sake, whoever heard of a faggot gunfighter in this day and age, and Ray was determined that nobody was ever going to make fun of him for being gay.'

'I thought you said he was happy with his life.'

'Oh, he was. Very happy. Very manic and almost never depressed, except around other people. Sometimes, you know . . .' He paused.

'Sometimes what?'

'Well, frankly, sometimes he scared me when he was happy. He liked to do that Yul Brynner trick from *The Magnificent Seven*, you know – draw and pull the trigger of his pistol before you could clap your hands. He had won all sorts of prizes in quick-draw contests, or whatever they're called, you know – '

'I know,' I said. Crider wasn't any help at all; his image of the Duffy kid was as confused as mine had become. Maybe it was true love and blindness, the old routine. So I changed directions. 'When did you see him last?'

'Several months ago.'

'What did you talk about?'

'Oh, we haven't talked since – since we split up last summer. We took a vow,' he said, bowing his head. Then he added apologetically, 'I've got a family. But every time I saw him on campus, it was so hard, you know, not to run over – '

'I know,' I said, patting his shoulder, wondering what warm bed Helen Duffy slept in while I hunkered in the cold rain. 'Do you know anybody who might have talked to him lately?'

'No. I don't know. Maybe.'

'Could you ask around?'

'I guess so. Around the department.'

'I wasn't exactly thinking about academic friends.'

'Oh. Well, I don't see those people much anymore, you know.'

I knew, but I didn't think he wanted to hear about it. I stood up, my old legs quivering under me, and wiped the rain out of my face. I said, 'Could I, ah, pay for your jacket?'

'Oh, that's not necessary.'

'I'm sorry.'

'Oh, it's not important, you know,' he said, clambering awkwardly to his large feet. He handed me my wet handkerchief and the empty plastic cup. 'Not important . . .'

'I, ah, fixed your car,' I said.

'Oh, thanks.'

'Take care,' I said, remembering his wife's voice and wishing them a better life than they had had so far, then I climbed into my rig, my wet pants sticking to the seat as I settled behind the wheel.

'So long,' he shouted as I drove away. I glanced back to wave. He was standing hesitantly at the door of his station wagon, staring back toward the bar, like a man who had left something behind. He shut his car door and walked back toward the lighted lobby.

I cruised the motels on the east side with no real purpose in mind – just an aimless, habitual shifting about – thinking perhaps I'd find Helen Duffy to tell her not to waste her money. These transient rooms were my haunts. Bribed night clerks and bugged rooms. The muttering plaints of illicit love, the refrain of muffled springs. Startled faces and scurrying bodies frozen in the explosion of the flash. Penises as flaccid as ruined breasts. Then the dull courthouse routine: professional testimony, shamed faces.

Tired of myself, I made one last swing through the Riverfront lot, hoping to see Vonda Kay venturing out into the rain. We could go home, have breakfast, smoke a little dope, and sleep comforted by the sound of the creek, the soft brush of the spruce needles, the placid warmth of two old veterans, our nerves ruined in the front lines of love and failure. But she walked out of the bar with another man.

As I drove away, my headlights swept across the line of cars stalled in front of the rooms. Dick's van was there. The lights of 103 were still on; dark upright figures hovered behind the drapes, measuring the room with strides and outflung arms – shadows that merged, then flew apart. At least I knew her room number now. I drove home to my empty log house, where the creek complained and the spruce needles rattled harshly against my windows.

7

By morning the rain had moved on, and at nine o'clock, when I knocked on Helen Duffy's motel room door, the puddles were retreating before the hot glare of a summer sun, the cool, damp respite destroyed with a vengeance. I was dry again, and Dick's van was gone.

She came to the door, keeping the safety chain fastened, but she peeped through the open crack as if she didn't feel safe at all. The same green robe, clutched to her neck, glowed at me, her red hair draped across her shoulders, and the same horde of pink tissues huddled about the carpet. But she was different this time; she didn't seem to know who I was.

'Remember me?' I said. 'I'm the one who loves you.'

'Wonderful,' she muttered. 'Can I go back to sleep now? I've had rather a long night.'

'Sure,' I said, full of cheer and energy. 'I just wanted to be sure I was still working for you before I deposited your checks.'

'I don't seem to have any other choices.'

'I'll take that as a vote of confidence. Are you going to stay here?'

'Yes,' she answered, daubing at her galled nose with a scrap of toilet paper. 'Why?'

'If you want me to call you, when and if I find out anything, you'd better leave word at the desk.'

'Whatever for?'

'They aren't very fond of me here.'

'I can imagine that,' she said. I couldn't tell if she was smiling. She blew her nose fiercely. Her face, pillow-wrinkled, and her hair, ruffled by the toils of sleep, hadn't spent the night cradled by any fond lovers, which is why I felt so good. 'Why aren't they fond of you?'

'This is a classy motel. They don't want no second-rate peepers or transom-sneakers to bother their guests.' Or breaking down doors and snipping safety chains with bolt cutters to take dirty pictures either.

'I see. All right, I'll inform them. Have you found out anything yet?'

'I've only had one night, but I'm still working on it.'

'Wonderful,' she said again, pursing her soft, tired mouth.

'You look like a woman who needs a good-morning kiss,' I said brightly, but she had already closed the door in my face.

A family of tourists filed past, glancing at me from the corners of sleep-swollen eyes – vacationers escaped from some suburban hell – the leading demon festooned in electric-blue curlers, the imps draped with pistols and leather vests, and the poor devil caught between, sagging toward a lower, more ulcerated circle. And they were no more startled than I was, when the door opened again and a vision of swift red and green slipped out and blessed me with those soft, tired lips, then flew back inside before my arms could encircle her.

'Don't gawk, Leonard,' the witch growled, but Leonard gawked his heart away.

'Who are those guys, Leonard?' I asked the little boy. But he didn't know either, so he drew and fired, shooting now but facing years of questions later, his cap pistol flashing with smoke and flame. I clutched my chest, reeled against a parked car, groaning, 'Ya got me, Leonard.'

He grinned like little boys should: ear-to-ear toothless gaps. It was probably the high point of his vacation until his mother jerked him away, whipping him along behind her like a banner, grunting, 'Come on, Leonard.'

'Hey, lady,' I shouted from the sidewalk. 'What kind of world is it, when the only fun left for little boys is shooting old men?'

'Drunk,' she hissed at me, then scurried down the sidewalk toward a well-deserved breakfast.

'Fucking-A!' I shouted, laughing. Leonard grinned as he disappeared, and the poor devil tried gamely not to.

I rose, still laughing, the gentle kiss still warm on my mouth, not having to fake my morning cheer anymore. Thirty-nine wasn't too late to begin. So I went to work. Just as if I knew what I was doing.

The county coroner, Amos Swift, had been a long-time friend of my father's, and he owed me four hundred dollars from a poker game so far in the past that neither of us really remembered the circumstances. Amos tried to like me, but he never made any bones about how he felt about my divorce work. I'd never had occasion to ask him a professional question, so I had no idea how he might react. But he owed me money, and if I couldn't make sense out of the Duffy kid's life, maybe I could of his death.

'How the hell are you, Milo?' he grumbled happily as I walked into his office. 'Say, I haven't forgotten the markers, lad, but I'm just a little short right now. If you're strapped, I can let you have some of it, but if you're not, I can sure make better use of it. Some of us are heading for Reno this weekend, and you know how it is, you can't win without playing.'

Amos was one of those fat, jolly pathologists, who acted as if violent death was a chance everybody took, as if the song of the bone saw caused him shivers of delight. But he and I both knew that he smoked cigars to keep away the antiseptic stink of the morgue, that he had become county coroner because he preferred to take his chances with the dead rather than the dying. He was a better autopsist than Meriwether County needed or deserved.

'But, lad, if you're down on your luck, I'll do my damnedest to come up with some of it, and, hell, I know you're having hard times but, dammit, it's hard times everywhere nowadays.'

'Let me have a cigar, Amos,' I said, sitting down, 'so I can stand yours.'

He did, but with great reluctance, as if it were money.

'Treat it sweetly, lad, that's a real Havana. And, say, if you run into Muffin, let him know I'm down to my last two boxes and smoking slow. Don't know where that boy finds them, and don't want to know, but it saves me a trip to Canada and maybe a bust. God, this is a sweet berth, lad, and I sure as hell hate to lose it next election for smuggling Communist cigars.'

'I'll tell him,' I said, starting to bite off the end of the long cigar.

'Goddammit, boy, don't bite it,' he huffed, handing me his clippers. 'Look at that,' he added, waving his fuming cigar at me, the end of it as immaculate as when it had left the wrapper. 'Be gentle, dammit. Hate to see a man mangle a good cigar. How much do you need?'

'Don't worry about the money,' I said, drawing smoke and blowing it toward his relieved face. 'I'm here on business.'

'What business could we have, boy? You ain't dead and I'm already divorced.'

'I'd like some information about an autopsy you did a few weeks ago.'

'Has the inquest been held?'

'Yes,' I said.

'Then it's a matter of public record.'

'I know,' I said. 'I looked at the record before I came downstairs, but it didn't tell me what I want to know. I want to know what you think, not what went into the record.'

'Who was it?'

'A kid named Raymond Duffy. An OD up at the Willomot Bar.'

'I remember,' he said, waving his thick hand through a cloud of smoke. 'A clear overdose.'

'Of what?'

'Well, hell, as I remember, everything. Alcohol, barbiturates and heroin.'

'Suicide or accident?'

'Who the hell knows? Some of both. The kid probably tried to settle down while he was waiting for a fix, then got hold of better junk than he was used to. We called it accident, but an insurance company would make suicide out of it, and who knows what really happened?'

'No marks of foul play?'

'Depends what you call foul play. He had a recent contusion on his right shoulder, which looked like a hickie, and there was evidence of anal intercourse recently, plus a sore throat.'

'A sore throat?'

'A dose of the clap, Milo. The kid was a fruit.'

'So I hear,' I said. 'How long had he been an addict?'

'Just guessing, I'd say around a month. Certainly not much longer.'

'Any other interesting facts?'

'Not that I can remember. I can dig up the report, if you want to see it.'

108

'That's okay,' I said. 'Thanks.'

'Sure. Say, what was that last hand anyway?'

'You tried to run four spades at a pair of sevens.'

'That's right, kid. I remember now. Dammit, boy, what kind of fool stays in against a broke man, four spades, and a four-hundred-dollar bet?' he asked, pinching his nose.

'You pinch your damn nose sometimes when you run a bluff, Amos.'

'I'll be goddamned,' he exclaimed, sitting up and staring at his thumb and index finger. 'Who knows about that?'

'Everybody in town, Amos.'

'I'll just be damned. Thanks, boy, I'll remember that. By God, you might be as good a player as your old man, and that son of a bitch was so good drunk that I wouldn't even play with him sober.'

'No sweat,' I said, 'he wasn't ever sober.'

'That's for damn sure.'

'Besides, he didn't have to worry about losing money.'

'That's for sure. Say, boy, don't forget to tell Muffin about those cigars.'

'Sure,' I said from the door. 'Say, one more thing. Why did you have his hair cut and his beard shaved?'

'Wasn't us, lad. When he came in, he was slicker than a preacher's kid. Say, Milo, what's this all about?'

'The sister doesn't believe the death was either suicide or accident.'

'Well, I'm sorry for her,' Amos said quietly. 'Damn sorry. Either she's blind or crazy.'

'Neither,' I said.

'Hell, boy,' he said, rising and walking around the desk to pat me on the shoulder, 'if you believe that, you're both. Sorry I wasn't much help.'

'Join the crowd,' I said, handing him back the dead cigar. 'Throw that away for me, will you?' I left him staring down at the cigar as if it were the corpse of a favorite son.

'Goddammit, boy,' he said as I closed the door.

I stopped at my office to check the calls and think about what Amos had said. The trouble was, though, that I believed Amos. The Duffy kid had either died of an accident or a suicide, died by his own unhappy hand. I didn't want to tell Helen Duffy just that. I thought perhaps I could shed some light on why, but Reese wouldn't talk to me and Willy Jones was dead. As I pondered that, Simon wandered in, still draped in the overcoat, stooped as if the burden might collapse his spine, his secondhand wing-tip cordovans ruffling the hem of the coat as it flittered behind him, almost touching the floor. I held up my hand so he would wait quietly while I returned the single call the answering service had given me. It was from Nickie DeGrumo. As I dialed I wondered what he wanted. But only briefly. I really wondered if Helen Duffy would kiss me again when I told her about her little brother.

When I asked the Riverfront switchboard operator for Nickie, she rang the bar, but Mama D. answered the telephone. Even though she had been out West for years, her accent was still thickly East Coast Italian. If she was a daughter of the family, I assumed that she had had a very protected youth, and I wondered how Nickie had managed to ferret her out of her father's house. Her papa mustache accent wasn't endemic, though, since her cousins all sounded like television announcers. Over the telephone, I could hear her heavy breathing, then Nickie's distant voice saying that he would take the call in his office. Instead of saying 'Hello' when she picked up the telephone, he told Mama to hang up, which she did after a long silence.

'Milo,' I said. 'What's happening, Nickie?'

'How's the boy, Milo, how's the boy?'

'Fine,' I sighed. 'What can I do for you?'

'Oh, drop around for a drink,' he said, trying to sound cheerful, but his voice still had an edge to it. 'On me, Milo, on me.'

'Okay. I'll drop in sometime.'

'Now would be better, Milo. Right now if you can make it.'

'I'm on my way to lunch, Nickie.'

'Listen, Milo, this is important. I'll spring for the lunch.'

'What do you want, Nickie?' He must be desperate to offer a free lunch.

'Got a job for you.'

'What sort of a job?'

'Can't discuss it over the phone, Milo. But hell, boy, I know you can use the business, and this might be worth two or three grand.'

'Who do you want me to kill?'

110

'Huh?'

'Just a joke. What's the job?'

'Not over the phone,' he said melodramatically. 'Just come on out.'

'I don't know, Nickie.'

'Hell, Milo, I'll pay for your time even if you don't take the job. How's that, huh? Pay you for the day.'

'That's expensive.'

'Ah, how much?'

'Hundred and a half,' I said, raising my fee for Nickie.

'Christ, Milo, I didn't know . . . What the hell, it's only money. Come on out. That's fine if you come out now.'

I didn't like to be pushed, but for that sort of money I guessed I could stand having lunch with Nickie, so I said I'd see him shortly.

'And, Milo . . .'

'Yeah?'

'If you could act like you just dropped in for lunch, I'd appreciate it. Understand?'

'You don't want Mama D. to know, right?'

'Oh, no, nothing like that. It's just that . . .'

'I understand,' I interrupted. 'See you in ten minutes.'

'Great,' he said, trying on the happy voice again, but I hung up before he could get started again.

'I wonder what he wants?' I asked myself, but loudly enough for Simon to hear.

'Who?' he asked, pausing in midshuffle.

'Nickie DeGrumo.'

'Whatever it is, boy, don't take a check from that cheap asshole.'

'Yes, sir,' I said.

'You going out there?'

'I guess so.'

'Can I go?' he asked, his weathered face cocked. 'Just for the ride. This is one of those goddamned boring days, so why don't you take me along?'

'I'll meet you at Mahoney's when I come back. Tell you all about it. How's that?'

'Goddammit, boy, you ain't got no respect for me, do you? You're so smart. Think I'm just an old drunk, don't you? Well, just g-go on out there and make a fool of yourself. See if anybody gives a shit.'

'Easy, you old fart. You'll have a stroke. I got something else going too. Maybe you can help.'

'Don't patronize me, boy,' he said grandly, then shuffled out the door.

'Stay sober,' I said, but Simon didn't look back.

Nickie met me in the lobby with a barrage of greetings, which I ignored, asking him what he wanted.

'All business and no pleasure, huh, Milo? Makes for a hard life,' he said, squeezing my arm. If it hadn't been Nickie, I might have thought he was being condescending.

'That's right,' I said. 'What's the job?'

'Come on, I'll buy you a drink,' he said.

I followed him into the nearly empty bar, to the booth in the corner occupied by the sensual foursome the night before. As I waited for Nickie to order the drinks from the day manager, I found myself checking between the vinyl cushions for change, a habit left over from following my father through the bars. I expected to find a used condom or a pecker track, but discovered sixty cents in change and a bobby pin.

'CC ditch, brandy soda no ice,' I heard Nickie tell the guy behind the bar. Somebody had told Nickie once that cold drinks caused stomach cancer. No ice in his drinks was Nickie's single gesture toward good health. At the other end of the bar, where she perched eternally, Mama D. rang the drinks, and the register obediently coughed up the ticket.

'Sign it for me, will you, Mama?' Nickie asked.

Without stirring her obese body, she turned her head toward him, her fat face haughty with aquiline disdain, her eyes like obsidian chips. A slight smile, like a knife mark in fresh dough, cut her face, and I expected cachinnations, but she answered in an oddly pleasant voice, 'You sign, Nickie. The books.'

And he signed. Walked all the way down the bar and signed the ticket. Her pudgy hand caught his, patted it once, then turned him loose. He carried the drinks over to the booth, unable to hide the disgust on his face from me, but Mama D. smiled like a happy mother as she watched him walk away from her.

'Listen,' he said, handing me my drink. 'I need a big favor, Milo, really big.'

'I thought you said a job.'

'Oh, yeah, it is. The favor is – to start right away, this afternoon.'

'Doing what?'

'Well, listen, this is kind of complicated, Milo,' he said, patting his dyed hair carefully, as if he didn't want to dirty his smooth hands. 'I, ah, got this friend, Milo, you know, and this, ah, friend has a friend, a lady, you understand, kinda like a practice wife.' He smiled at his own joke. 'And he had to leave town suddenlike, you know, and he sort of wants to know what his lady friend does. While he's not around, you understand. And my friend is a very important man, you know, ah, can't afford to have lady friends who – who mess around, you know.'

'I know, Nickie. That's how I made my living,' I said.

'Right, right. That's why I called you, Milo boy. You're a professional,' he said, smiling broadly. 'Listen, money's no object, so my friend wants you to handle this, you know. Twenty-four hours a day.'

'Nickie, I have to sleep sometimes.'

'Oh, yeah, I understand. But full time, you know, whatever you usually do – in a case like this.'

'Sure,' I said, already thinking that I could hire Freddy and Dynamite, charge the rented car and mobile phone to Nickie, and still make a nice price without turning a finger. 'How long?'

'Two, maybe three weeks. Till my friend gets back, you know.'

'That's going to cost a pretty penny,' I said.

'Like I said, Milo boy, money's no object.'

'Must be nice.'

'What's that?'

'For money not to be an object.'

'Oh, yeah,' he said, smiling again. 'Yeah, I'll bet it is.' Then he finished his drink in one gulp. 'Another?'

'No, thanks,' I said, but he had already gone toward the bar. While he was gone, I dumped the change into the ash tray for the waitress next on duty. When he came back, I said, 'Thanks. I'll go out to the rig and get a contract.'

'Oh, no, Milo,' he said quickly, then lifted his drink, gunned half of it. 'Nothing written down, boy-o.' Then he rubbed his chest and muttered, 'Goddamned soda.'

'What?'

113

'Goddamned soda give me indigestion.' His smile was gone, his face old and tired again. 'But, listen, no contract, huh? You understand? Nothing written down. My friend wouldn't like that, you know.'

'I don't like that, Nickie. If there's any trouble, my ass is left hanging out.'

'Trouble? What sort of trouble?'

'You never can tell, Nickie, not with a deal like this. Suppose the lady sees me following her and decides to call the cops –'

'Don't worry about that, Milo, she ain't the type.'

'Okay, what if I catch her in the sack with some dude, and your friend decides not to pay?'

'Don't worry about that,' he said.

'It happens.'

'Listen, I'll – I'll guarantee your fee, Milo, you know. You trust me, don't you?'

How do you tell a guy you don't trust him?

'It's just not good business, Nickie. You understand?'

'Yeah.'

'So either sign a contract or pay me up front.'

'How much?' he asked hesitantly, looking very unhappy.

'Let's see, two weeks, say twenty-five hundred.'

'Christ, Milo, I can't . . .'

'Then let's forget it, Nickie,' I said, standing up to leave.

'Okay,' he said, grabbing my arm. 'Okay. Just wait a minute, let me think a minute, you know.' Thinking involved finishing his drink and rubbing his belly to ease the indigestion. 'All right, Milo, all right. Be right back.'

As he walked away I watched him. Unlike his wife, I didn't have any fond glances for him. Nickie walked like a scared man, lost in his own house. His friend must be big stuff, I thought, if Nickie was going to front twenty-five hundred bucks. Then I began to worry. What if Nickie only came back with part of the money? What if he wanted to give me a check? But before I could worry too much, he came back to the table and slipped a white envelope out of his inside coat pocket.

'It's all there,' he said, handing it to me. 'No need to count it.'

'Sure,' I said, not counting it but peeking. Nickie's money was as old and worn-out as he was. I thought he must have hit his mad-money stash. 'Want a receipt?'

He wanted one but shook his head. 'Nothing written down, right? You don't even write down reports, you understand. You come tell me, you know, casual like. Okay? I trust you, Milo boy.' Being that close to money seemed to restore some of Nickie's lost confidence, so I tried for icing on the cake.

'Listen, Nickie, for an extra three bills a week, I can put a mike in her telephone that will pick up a fart in the next room.'

'My God, Milo, no bugs. Jesus, my friend . . . he wouldn't like that at all. Jesus,' Nickie blurted, scared again.

'Okay. I'll just tail her, watch the house. No more.'

'Perfect,' he said, touching my arm. 'Just right.'

'Okay. Who's the lady? Where's she live?'

'Huh?'

'What's the poop on the lady?'

'Huh? Oh, the poop. Christ, Milo, I haven't heard that since the war. God, that seems like a long time ago.'

'It was.'

'Yeah. Remember what this town was like then? A good town, Milo, a goddamned good town. Not so many tourists, no fucking hippies or dope or any of that crap. Kinda makes me glad I . . . we never had kids, you know.'

I nodded politely. For that sort of money, Nickie could tell me his life story, and I'd even act interested.

'Yeah, but, Christ, I used to really like kids, you know. Remember when I had those goddamned icecream trucks? I used to follow them around sometimes. At first I was just checking to see how much the drivers were screwing me, but later it was just to watch the kids. Damn, it was great to see them scooting out of their houses when they heard those goddamned bells. And when I lost my ass, I put in that little golf course, you know. Everybody told me it was easy, but, goddammit, the kids loved it. Everything doesn't have to be hard, does it? I mean, for Christ's sake, things don't have to be so hard.'

I nodded again, wondering if I should offer him my handkerchief, but he had something better. He went for two more drinks. It was strange to see Nickie boozing harder than me.

'Who's the lady? Where's she live?' I asked again, reminding him of business when he came back with the drinks.

115

Nickie stared at me for a moment, swallowed air and belched quietly, then said, 'Goddamned soda.'

'Yeah.'

'Back to business, huh, Milo?'

'Right.'

'Okay. Her name is Wanda.'

'Wanda what?'

'Oh, Wanda – Smith.' He waited for me to object, but I didn't care if her name was Smith. 'My friend has a house on the slope south of town, in that new development, Wildflower Estates, the last house on the circle at the end of Wild Rose Lane.'

'What's the number?'

'Christ, Milo, that's such a classy development that they have names instead of numbers, you know. Wish to hell I could afford a place like that, but I got every loose penny tied up in this place,' he said sadly.

Not every penny, I thought, and none of them his.

'What's the name, then?'

'I'll be damned,' he said, looking very confused. 'I . . . my friend told me the name, but damned if I can remember it. You can't miss it, it's the last house on the street.'

'Okay,' I said. 'I guess I can find it. What's the lady look like?'

'Oh, Milo, she's something else. A real looker. A real lady,' he answered, his eyes glassy with the vision.

'That's a little abstract, Nickie.'

'Huh?'

'What color's her hair?'

'Kinda blond, strawberry blond, I think they call it.'

'How old?'

'Oh, Milo, just right. Not too young, not too old, you know. Just right.'

'Okay, Nickie, I'll handle it from there,' I said. It didn't matter to me what she looked like. I wasn't going to tell some Mafia fat cat that his lady was messing around, not even if I caught her giving head to the grocery boy. 'Just leave everything to me.'

'Huh?'

'I'll take care of everything.'

'Great. Great.'

'And won't write down a word.'

116

'Huh? Oh, yeah, right. And listen, Milo boy – my friend, he likes the people who work for him,' Nickie said carefully, 'he likes them to just work for him, you know. So if you got anything else going, maybe you ought to – to think about dropping it. I think I can get my friend to cover what it costs you.'

'I don't have anything going.'

'Huh?'

'I said I'm free. Say, Nickie, are you going deaf?'

'No, of course not. Why?'

'Because you don't seem to hear me too well.'

'Yeah, well, I've got this goddamned ringing in my ears, you know. Been working too hard, I guess, need a vacation, you know. Maybe I can – get away soon . . . Goddamned soda,' he said, belching again.

'How's business?' I asked, tired of Nickie's friend and his practice wife.

'Huh?'

'Business. How is it?'

'Oh, couldn't be better,' he said, glowing now. 'I'm making so much money that it's making me feel young again, you know.' He paused for effect, then winked. 'Maybe I'll get me one of those practice wives, huh.'

What a pathetic creep. Of course business was great. Illegal whiskey, hijacked beef, and dirty money. I had never liked Nickie very much, just pitied him occasionally, but now that I was working for him, I gave up even the pity.

'This friend, Nickie. Is he family?' I returned his wink.

'Oh, no, he's . . .' Then he realized what the wink meant. 'Christ, Milo, don't do that. Why the hell does everybody think I'm – I'm in the Mafia or something, some kind of goddamned gangster, just – just because I'm – I'm Italian,' he sputtered, his face red and hurt. 'I mean, Christ, Milo, don't kid me about that.'

'Sorry, Nickie,' I said, no longer angry at him, just sorry again, almost sorry enough to tell him why everybody thought he was family. 'People see too many movies, I guess.'

'Christ, Milo, you don't know how much – how much I hate those goddamned slick East Coast bastards. I'd like to fix those bastards, you know, those bastards,' he muttered pathetically, a child's threat. Then he stood up, adding, 'Stay on this thing, okay, Milo?'

'I said I would.'

'Huh?'

'I got it, Nickie.'

'Yeah,' he said, then loosed a short bark of laughter. 'Yeah, you got it.'

'Sure,' I said, holding back the renewed anger. Once again, I had the feeling that Nickie was condescending to me, that there was some sort of antagonism seeping out of him. But I had always known that Nickie was unhappy behind all his smiles and gladhands. As he stood up, trying to look calm and self-assured, his shoulders slumped beneath the weight of his coat, his neck bowed under the weight of his dyed hair, and his fingers kneaded belches out of his sunken chest. He couldn't hide the fatigue of a long life of being nobody, a fatigue I understood more than I wanted to. To be childlike might keep a man young, but to be treated like a child makes him old too soon.

'Say, Nickie?'

'Huh?'

'Want some free advice?'

'What's that?' he asked, not wanting any advice from me at all.

'This afternoon, call up Meriwether Vending and order a couple of punchboards. They'll even tell you which cops to pay off.'

'That's illegal,' he said righteously.

'No shit. But you've always had the only bar in town without at least one punchboard. Makes the local people nervous. They think you're up to something really illegal, if you're afraid to have a few punchboards.'

'I'll be damned. I wonder how come Ma – how come I never thought of that?'

'Because she's still a stranger here,' I said quietly.

'Huh?' But he had heard me.

'Nothing.'

'Keep in touch, Milo,' he said, then walked away, muttering to himself, his boots slapping the carpet.

When I finished the first drink, I remembered the lunch that Nickie had beat me out of. It could go on the expense sheet. I left the other drinks untouched. As I walked through the lobby, Nickie was engaged in a serious conversation with an expensively dressed man. The motel manager, I thought, Another of Mama D.'s inevitable cousins. He listened politely to Nickie, nodding his head without interest, as if he were being told a very boring story by a child. He was listening to Nickie but he was watching me.

On the way back to the office, I drove by Wild Flower Estates, down to the end of Wild Rose Lane. Wanda wasn't visible, but there was a new Mustang parked in the garage. Poppy-red or something like that. I wrote the licence number down, then poked around the neighborhood, looking for a place to stake out the house. On the next street up-slope, a house was under construction. I knew the builder, so Freddy and Dynamite could hang out there without calling attention to themselves.

Back in the office, I called the builder, and after I reminded him that he had borrowed the money for his first house from my father, he agreed that he could use an extra hand in the daytime and a free nightwatchman. Then I started to make out another deposit slip, my second in two days, which didn't happen too often. I stopped, looked at the roll, thought about the IRS. The money was mostly twenties and fifties, with only a few hundreds, and the bills looked like they had been carried around in a wino's pockets, stuffed hither and yon, then ripped out at a wild moment and scattered across a damp bar. I wondered if Nickie had taken to rolling winos, but he was such a coward that the idea was ludicrous. Nearly as comical as the idea of paying taxes on unrecorded cash.

I took out five hundred and put the rest into the large safe in the corner which said CATTLEMAN'S BANK AND TRUST, MERIWETHER COUNTY, MILTON CHESTER MILODRAGOVITCH, PRESIDENT. That had been my grandfather. My great-grandfather wanted his son to have an American name. There was also a sign hanging from the handle which claimed that the safe was an antique and asked prospective safecrackers not to use dynamite or a crowbar or acid. A combination was printed at the bottom of the card. The wrong combination. It wasn't much of a joke, but then it wasn't much of a safe either.

When I leaned out the window to see the bank clock, it was only eleven, but I thought I'd have lunch anyway. On Nickie.

8

So Nickie had a friend who had plenty of money and a practice wife. Nickie, with his little boy's allowance and too real wife, must have been furious with envy. Perhaps that explained the odd flashes of hostility. But it was too lovely a day to worry about it.

As I strolled down to Mahoney's, careful not to jostle the tourists who clotted the sidewalks as if they owned both the streets and the summer morning, I begrudged them the day. But I only lived there; they were the paying customers, rubbernecking and crowing and snapping endless color slides of the cobalt sky and the peaks – white hot with new snow above the dark cool reaches of pine – and the lower slopes, which blazed with new grass, bright yet tender, yellow-green beneath the clean rush of sunlight.

I wondered if Nickie's friend was among the vacationers, out West for two weeks of expensive fun. Somehow, I'd never thought of gangsters on vacation, thinking perhaps that they enjoyed their work more than some poor slob condemned to an eternal salesman's smile, more grimace than grin, or spot-welded next to an assembly line, slapping door handles on Gremlins as they trundled endlessly past in mechanical cortege. But perhaps not. What did I know about the rigors of organized crime? The nearest I had been to it was an occasional hard look from one of Mama D.'s cousins when my voice was too loud or my tip too small. Maybe organized crime was hard work – all that corruption and graft and worry, the discreet violence undertaken with an air of urbane toughness. Hell, I had been corrupted on the local level, and the paltry payoffs I had received to overlook the punchboards and electronic slots were so small that they seemed almost moral in a world that made folk heroes out of airline hijackers and box-office successes out of Mafia dons, with

120

never a mention of the Mafia to avoid legal action; a world where politicians were for sale but overpriced; where giant corporations shouted the ideals of capitalism, then fixed prices; where even the President shaved without looking in the mirror.

Maybe I shouldn't have been so smug, not when I was walking down the street with a pocketful of dirty money, money I had lied to obtain and would lie to keep and would spend without a single twinge of conscience. But then, that's one of the great things about living in America: moral superiority is so damned cheap.

So I could saunter into Mahoney's, out of the sunlight and the dark clusters of vacationers, a smile on my face, no guilt in mind, and wish Nickie's friend a grand time out West, lots of fun and summer adventures and jerky home movies. Shots of him feeding candy to a surly sow bear with cubs. Or walking into a swollen creek in brand-new chestwaders. Or traversing a glacier in sparkling white sneakers. Or roasting his weenie in Old Faithful.

But in the cool shade of Mahoney's, the regulars were always on vacation, patiently waiting for their turn at that great trout stream in the sky, where the fish are always rising from deep clear pools to take the fly snugly in their mouths, where the women wait quietly on the banks, lovely and kind, where the nearest bar is only a cast away, and when you go in, your friends greet you with fond jokes and the bartender never mentions your tab.

'By God, boys, this is the life,' I exclaimed to three of the best as I joined them. Simon, Fat Freddy, and Stonefaced Pierre. They greeted me in dulcet tones – a belch, a grunt, a soft murmuring babble.

'Where did you get the goddamned fish, boys?' I asked, pointing at the mound of bones, as clean and white as cat's teeth, heaped in the center of the table.

Freddy leaned back, intent upon his toothpick. Simon tilted forward into his open notebook. Pierre glared at me with marbled eyes. They ignored, as if it were a corpse, the remains of the last of the smoked steelhead, which Leo and I had brought back from Idaho and which, all things considered, only cost thirty or forty dollars a pound to catch.

'Well, hell, boys, if it was one of mine, I hope you enjoyed it,' I said, then waved at Leo for a round of drinks, circling my finger in the still air. A torpid fly tried to land on it, but missed and buzzed

121

aimlessly away. Leo brought the shots and beers with a sheepish grin, so I knew who had divided the fish among the loafers. I handed him a twenty anyway, told him to put the change against my tab. He muttered something snide about the change being only a drop in some cosmic bucket. I told him to set them up for the house. On my tab.

When he rang the bell behind the bar, three sleeping winos rose from their stools, grinning, and two slipped in from the street. A small band of long-haired kids drifted toward the bar like calves at milking time. Everybody waved at me as if I were a movie star – one of them was the slim girl from Reese's front porch – then fell upon their drinks eagerly, ignoring me.

Once things had settled down, I gave Freddy a handful of Nickie's bills and told him to round up Dynamite, a rental car and a mobile telephone, setting my wino hounds loose on Wanda of Wild Rose Lane. I had used them before; they made a great team, cheap and carefully sober when working for me and oddly invisible. They were both local characters, recognized winos, and downtown they faded before the eyes of the good, sober folk. In the suburban developments, they used part-time jobs for cover, and looked like winos drying out or working a few days to support another binge. Their obvious failure to deal with life was a more effective means to cloud men's minds than any secret of the East.

Freddy was so happy to be working again that he discarded his frayed toothpick, replacing it with a brand-new one that smelled faintly of mint, then he rose and strode out of the bar, his shoulders back, his spine mightily erect, his stomach as rigid as a barrel. Pierre also rose, but more slowly, like a statue coming reluctantly to life, and headed for the john at a furious totter, where he would lean against the wall and wait for his tired bladder to empty, staring at everybody who came in, waiting until somebody, usually Leo, helped him rebutton his pants. Simon, who had overheard my talk with Freddy, scribbled madly in his red notebook.

'Bastard,' he muttered when he glanced up.

'What?'

'Let that fat bastard work for you, Milo. You must be crazy.'

'Hush, Simon.'

'I could have done it, I could have.'

'Simon, you can't drive a car.'

'That doesn't make any difference,' he said, then stared at me for a minute. 'I hear the lady is back in town.'

'What lady?'

'Don't be a wise ass, Milo. What's she doing back in town?'

I told him.

'What have you found out?' he asked.

I told him that too.

'What are you going to do now?'

'Well, goddammit, Simon, I don't know, but when I get through, I'll give you a written report.'

'I don't like the smell of this whole thing, Milo,' he said, disregarding the irony. 'Let me help.'

'Why don't you take that goddamned overcoat off before you have a heat stroke?'

'Hell, boy, it's cold.'

'That was yesterday, Simon.'

'It's always yesterday in here, boy.'

'It's at least a day behind, but I'm not sure if you have the right yesterday.'

'This was your old man's coat, wasn't it?'

'Looks like one he used to have.'

'Looks like it, hell. It is.'

'Okay, so what?'

'Wanna buy it, boy,' he said slyly, then grinned. 'Make you a good deal.'

'You old fart.'

'If you're going to sit there and call me names, boy, you have to buy me a drink.'

I waved at Leo, and he brought the drinks.

'To your old man,' Simon said, raising his shot glass. We drank, then he asked, 'So what's in your mind?'

'She paid for three days, so I'll give her three days. Try to find somebody who knew him, I guess, and ask some more stupid questions.'

'Reese knew him,' Simon said, smirking. 'Ask him.' Then he giggled like an old woman.

'Maybe I'll just do that,' I said, but my threats were as empty as Nickie's. Simon laughed so hard that I thought he would choke. To death, I hoped. 'What's so funny?'

123

'You, boy, you.'

'Thanks.'

'Anything for a friend. Want some help?'

'What did you have in mind? Fart and hope he faints?'

'That's not funny, Milo,' he grumbled, falling into a sulk. 'God-damned faggot.'

'Yeah, but don't tell him,' I said.

'Maybe if you took Jamison along,' Simon said thoughtfully, 'Reese might behave.'

'Jamison wouldn't help me across the street if I was an old lady. Besides, I don't know where lovely Lawrence lives now. His old house is empty,' I said. 'And the neighborhood kids are tearing it down, stick by stick.'

'I'll bet Jamison knows where Reese is holed up.'

'Probably does,' I said, meaning to walk over to the police station to ask him just as soon as I finished my drink.

'Want me to help? I could ask around. Like before. I found him before you did,' he said.

'I don't know, old man, you might get hurt,' I answered, which made Simon so mad he lost his small connection with reality, spitting and sputtering curses. He became a foolish, tired old drunk, unruly gray hair and liver spots, his horny fingers knotted so tightly around the pencil stub that it seemed the lead must squirt out, spraying like ash across the empty glasses and fish bones.

'All right,' I said, 'you can help.'

'Thanks,' he managed to say. But not as if he meant it.

'Anything for a friend.'

'Sure.'

'You remember the old lady in the window? Next door to Reese's?'

'Yeah, sure. Why?'

'Why don't you go by and talk to her. See if you can get a description of some of the people who were living there. Maybe it will give us somebody to talk to who won't try to kill us.'

Simon nodded his head so furiously that he banged his chin on the rim of his beer mug, then held his mouth as if he had a rock under his lower plate.

'I'll do it,' he mumbled, pounding his notebook as if he intended to make notes in iron. 'You can count on it.'

124

'All right. But promise me you won't go anywhere else. And stay sober.'

He nodded again, lifting his beer in agreement, but when he felt it in his hand, he set it down quickly, grinning.

'I'll finish my letter, Milo, then go see her before it rains.'

'It's not going to rain, you old fart.'

'Wanna bet?'

'Not with you about rain, old man.'

'What are you going to do?'

'Try to find Reese.'

'Be careful, boy.'

'You be careful, old man.'

'Sure,' he said. 'You care if the kid died on purpose or by accident?'

'Not really.'

'You got no curiosity, boy,' he said, turning back to his letter. 'And you don't care about nothing but the lady, huh?'

'Who are you writing to?'

He glanced up in disgust.

'What are you complaining about now?'

'Somebody ripped off my Social Security check. Right out of the mailbox.'

'What the hell can the government do?'

'Replace the son of a bitch!'

'You don't need the money.'

'What the hell difference does that make? I deserve it!' he shouted. And maybe he did.

'Take care,' I said, standing and patting his shoulder. Beneath the heavy tweed, his body felt as feeble as an old woman's. Stringy flesh on the verge of corruption, bones nearly dust. But he didn't look up, busy now with his protest, flailing at the political system with scrawled words. In the tranquil bar, among the wrinkled faces on the walls, secure from time, his nattering murmur was as peacefully eternal as a creek's plaint to stones, a hushed and wisely gentle sound, a finer silence, as much a part of my life as the rising and falling cycle of Hell-Roaring Creek. I ruffled his hair for luck, touched the parchment scalp, the fragile skull, making my amends, then I left him there in his repose.

On the way out, I glanced at the girl, Mindy, thinking to ask her about Reese, but she and a young boy were watching a fly circle the

125

inside of a foam-encrusted beer mug, watching it with the vapid concentration of the perpetually stoned, so I left her alone. Outside, in the brilliant summer noon, among the creep of traffic and bedizened tourists, I realized that I hadn't had a vacation in years. They seemed too tiring to chance another. But I wondered if Helen Duffy needed a vacation, wondered where we might go, how tired we might be when we came back, and I smiled benignly at the frantic tourists.

As I walked over to the police station, I thought about what Simon had said about the Duffy kid. He was right about one thing. I didn't care about the kid. What little I'd seen of him around the bars hadn't filled my heart with joy, and what I'd learned about him hadn't convinced me that my first impression was wrong. He might have been confused and unhappy, but he was still a bad kid. But I didn't think I'd tell Helen Duffy that.

I took a shortcut through an alley to avoid the crowded sidewalks, and at the far end a freak walked up to a large man dressed in logging clothes. The kid held his hand out shyly, as if he were panhandling, but the man hit the kid in the face, knocked him across the alley into a pile of garbage cans. I ran up, grabbing the man from behind as he advanced on the fallen kid to work him over with his boots. The kid didn't move, except to touch his swelling eye and brush away yesterday's garbage.

'Police!' the man shouted. 'Police!' He struggled in my grasp, swinging and kicking backwards with his high-heeled boots, catching my right shin. I changed holds and threw him against the wall, then hobbled over and kicked the fight out of him.

'Okay,' he groaned, clutching his gut as he rolled out of the garbage, lettuce pasted to his hair with Thousand Island dressing.

'Take the goddamned money,' he grunted, then tossed his wallet at my feet. 'You guys leave me alone, okay?'

'You guys? What the hell were you picking on the kid for?'

The kid tried to stand up, but slipped in the slops, falling to his hands and knees. I stepped over to see how he was, and the man lurched to his feet and ran down the alley, his heavy boots thudding, shreds of lettuce scattered behind him like dollar bills. I picked up his wallet and started after him, shouting, then the kid stood up again and ran off in the opposite direction, leaving me the alley and the wallet.

'Town's getting too goddamned nervous to live in,' I said.

*

126

The desk sergeant who accepted the wallet and my explanation looked vaguely familiar, but behind the bulletproof glass and his professionally calm policeman face, I couldn't place him. On the wall behind him, a platoon of riot helmets hung in rows, their dark plastic visors gleaming like the eyes of some fearful machine, and below them rows of gas masks sagged like empty faces. After the first protest march in the late sixties, during which only marchers were hurt, our local police officers had been hurriedly trained and equipped to handle riots up to the size of small wars, but nobody had been able to arrange one for them. The smoked plastic of the visors looked expectant, though, and as lethal as the racked shotguns.

When he had finished his report, I asked the distant, barricaded face if Jamison was in.

'Yes, sir,' came the metallic voice. Then he shut off the outside speaker and called Jamison's office over the intercom.

'He wants to know what you want?'

'To talk to his exalted lieutenancy,' I said. My shin was throbbing, and I wished I had kicked the logger one more time.

'About what?'

'Oh, goddammit, lad, just tell him I need to talk to him.'

'About what?'

'I want to report a crime.'

'What sort?'

'Against nature.'

'What?'

'Down on Main Street there's a pig fucking a goat.'

'Aren't you ever going to grow up?' Jamison asked after the boys in blue had conducted me to his office. Before I could answer, he asked, 'What the hell do you want? I'm busy and tired.'

He looked it, his clothes wrinkled and limp, his tie tangled at his throat. I didn't look like Cary Grant approaching forty, but Jamison looked ten years older than me.

'Yeah, well, you look tired,' I said, trying my best old-buddy smile. 'And, hey, I'm sorry about the trouble, but some of your help is a little arrogant. It was nice to see that dignified face get mad.'

'What do you want?' he repeated, having neither the smile nor the conversation.

'A favor.'

127

'You gotta be kidding.'

'Might help us both.'

'Get out. Get outa my life, Milo. Get outa town. Just get out.'

'Just listen a minute, okay? You owe me that.'

'I don't owe you the time of day,' he said.

'How many muggings and petty thefts you had in the last month?' I asked, playing it by ear.

'Read the papers, creep.'

'How many? How many kids arrested hooked on smack?'

'None of your business,' he said, but I knew I had guessed right for a change.

'Just go with me to see Lawrence Reese so I can ask him about the Duffy kid without getting killed, and maybe I can help you find out who's dealing smack in our fair city.'

He lowered his head as if thinking about what I said. His bald pate was damp and furrowed, his pudgy hands wrinkled with sweat. I nearly felt sorry for him. Being a cop is no fun, but Jamison looked as if he had never had any fun. Then he told me what he had been thinking, and I wiped the pity away like cold sweat.

'Milo, I've known you all my life, and you're a chickenshit, corrupt scumbag, and I'm goddamned tired of knowing you. Get your ass out of my office.' He spoke quietly, which was worse than shouting, which gave me a glimpse of the depth of his disgust. Then he added, 'I'm sorry.'

I seldom get angry, but that did it – the pity and condescension in his apology.

'Let's drive out in the country, motherfucker, and talk about it,' I said as quietly as I could. 'Right now.'

Jamison stood up swiftly, then grunted and sank back into his chair, saying, 'You don't know how much I'd like that, Milo, but I don't have time for your kids' games. Just get out. I've got work to do.'

He went back to the reports on his desk. More sad than angry, I left.

'What's going on?' the desk sergeant asked. He had been waiting just outside the door.

'No charge,' I said. 'The lieutenant is too busy to mess with scum like me.'

'How is he?' the kid inquired softly, as if we were standing outside a hospital room.

'Working too hard, but what's new.'

'That's for sure. Some goddamned crazy guy stopped two twelve-year-old boys on the Dottle bridge just after the movie let out last night. They didn't have any money, so he assaulted them. One's in the hospital; the other's in the river. They haven't found the body yet.'

'Catch the guy yet?'

'Nope.'

'Was it a junkie?'

'Probably, but who knows. They're sure making a mess out of my social life. We been on double shifts for a week now.'

'Yeah.'

'Say, Milo, how come you said that about the pig and the goat, huh? You were a law enforcement officer once.' The kid sounded honestly hurt.

'That was in another country,' I said.

'Yeah, it sure was. If things keep up like this, I'm moving to British Columbia.'

'Not a bad idea,' I said, moving around him.

'Hey, we recovered your property.'

'Great. How?'

'Two kids showed up at Deacon's store with all of it loaded in a wheelbarrow, and they got nervous when Deke started to check the hot sheet. When they ran, he pulled down on them with that .44 magnum he keeps below the counter.'

'Hit them?'

'Naw, they stopped too soon. Hell, even the wheelbarrow was hot. Kids had gall but no guts.'

'Yeah. Guess I ought to read the newspaper more often. When did all this happen?'

'Oh, a couple of days after you reported it. Hell, it wasn't even on the hot sheet yet.'

'How come it took so long to notify me?'

'Well, you know how paperwork is,' he drawled, scuffling the tile floor with his polished boot. 'We misplaced your complaint.' Then he grinned like a man who had more important things on his mind than paperwork. But I couldn't tell if it was Canada or crime.

129

When I opened the iron door between the administrative area and the front desk, my logger friend was standing there, examining his wallet, counting his money and checking his credit cards. I shut the door quietly and left by the back door. Out of the fluorescent gloom of the station and into the sunny afternoon. It should have been night. Or raining. Or something to account for the sudden lethargy of my legs.

9

Youth and strength might fail me and my sense of purpose be altered, but I knew how to get some of it back. I had a bag of whites in my other office; speed wasn't a good alternative, but it helped sometimes. I always had an odd notion that if amphetamines had been in vogue when I tried to play college football, I would have been an all-American guard instead of a bum. Speed reached inside me somehow, released the angry energy from its hiding place. It made me mean, but in my business that was sometimes necessary.

In Mahoney's, I ordered a plastic sandwich from Leo, then called my answering service, hoping Helen Duffy had called to take me off the case. But she hadn't. Mrs. Elton Crider had called and left word to call back, and Muffin had left a message, a song title: 'This is my year for Mexico.' I didn't know what it meant, so I returned Mrs. Crider's call. We had a brief conversation. Her husband hadn't come home the night before, but I didn't know where he was and told her so.

'Doesn't he ever stay out all night?' I asked, the fatigue making me more cruel than I meant to be.

'Sometimes,' she answered, 'but he usually goes to work.' She hung up curtly.

I sat down at the bar, since Simon had already left our booth, and had a beer with the packaged sandwich, wondering what Muffin had meant by his cryptic message.

'You shouldn't eat this kinda crap,' Leo said when he brought me the sandwich.

'You shouldn't sell it.'

'*Caveat emptor*, Milo,' he answered. But he didn't charge me for the sandwich.

131

I finished half of it, half a beer, then left the mess on the bar. When I came out of the cooler with enough whites in my pocket to start a small riot, Pierre was watching a long-haired kid and his little boy playing the shuffleboard machine, laughing and banging the chrome puck against the back of the machine. They were happy; Pierre wasn't. As I walked past him, I laid a hand on his shoulder, telling him not to worry, but I might as well have stroked a brick wall. His terrible glower had found focus. I waved at the freak and his kid, their matching ponytails bobbing with glee, and wished them love and luck.

In our state, children are allowed in bars. It's one of the few laws of which I approve. My warmest childhood memories were forged in bars. Not in zoos or camps, not on family outings or at church picnics, not with gracious gray-haired lady English teachers helping me love Shelley and Keats. All those things happened, but the bars counted more. Country bars with bowling machines and little balls that seemed to fit my hand and an endless supply of quarters. Cowboy bars, where all the men wore boots, and all the boots had stirrup scuffs. Darkened cocktail lounges and hushed conversations that had to be important. That's what I remembered fondly. And an old man, over eighty, whose withered arms were still strong from the years of farming, strong enough for me to chin myself on one of them. And a retired lady trick rider who taught me how to spin a loop, how to dance in and out. And all the stories, the bars and the drunks, and my father carrying me through them as if I were his good-luck charm, his familiar, his pride and joy.

After his death, I missed the bars just as hard as any alcoholic drying out. Perhaps my long quest after his discarded clothing was just an excuse to hang around the bars. Whatever, I guess I'm glad that children can be in bars here. It keeps them off the street, keeps the family together, and shows the children a world where the natural accidents of life can be forgiven with a shrug and an 'Oh, hell, he was just drunk.'

As I watched the father and son plumb the depths of Pierre's infernal machine, scattering lights and mechanical noises across the afternoon like golden coins on a table, I felt happy. But confused too. I'd seen the other side. I hoped nobody ever had to cover their torn bodies with a gray blanket or explain to a befuddled drunk driver that he had just killed somebody's son. Maybe there should be laws against automobiles, not drunks, but . . .

And the confusion stayed with me, a fierce muddle of mixed emotions and memories that gave me absolutely contradictory propositions. I wondered if only the simple-minded could keep one thing in mind, the simple-minded and the purposeful. To hell with it. I went to the bar for a whiskey. My hand trembled slightly as I raised it.

'How did you get to be a drunk, Leo?'

'Oh, Christ, Milo,' he answered, then stomped away on the duck-boards as if he couldn't stand the sight of me.

I glanced at my tired face in the old muddy mirror behind the back bar. I didn't like it any more than Leo did, but I watched it, working on my drink, trying to think through things. It was difficult. I'd never spent much time thinking, depending usually on action akin to instinct – act instead of think. But now I was out of my depth; action wasn't enough. I needed a theory about Raymond Duffy, right, and a plan, a plan of action, right. Wasn't that how the world was conquered? With plans and theories, right? Decisions arrived at after due consideration of relevant data, right? But I didn't even know what constituted relevant data. I could, however, turn around to see Mindy, who was watching a brigade of flies march through dried beer foam.

'Mindy,' I said rather loudly. She looked up. 'Mindy, do you know where Lawrence Reese is living now?'

'Sure, man. He's crashed up at the Holy Light Hog Farm,' she answered quickly, not so stoned anymore. The Holy Light Hog Farm was a capitalist commune up in the Stone River Valley about forty miles north of Meriwether – a real, live, working hog farm, where pigs lived as daintily as princesses on acres of immaculate concrete. 'You going up to see him? Can we catch a ride?' she asked, nodding toward the boy sharing her table.

I wanted to talk to the girl and didn't need the boy along, but then I wondered if he knew Reese.

'Does he know Reese?'

'Naw, man, he's new in town.'

'Then he can't go,' I said. They shrugged and accepted it without a moment's rancor, just as if it had been a command from their guru. I wondered how far I could carry it.

133

Mindy stood up, I finished my drink, and we left. It wasn't a theory or a plan, but it was movement. Out of the bars and into the real world.

'You gonna kill him?' she asked calmly as she lit a joint on the outskirts of town.

'Hadn't planned to,' I answered, chuckling like a jovial insurance salesman. 'I just want to talk to him, that's all.'

'Well, don't ask him no questions, man,' she said, holding the hit and passing the joint to me. 'He ain't a bad dude, really, but he don't like questions worth a shit.'

I looked at the joint, then took it, had a small hit, just to relax. I could stop at the Willomot Hill Bar for beer, wash down two whites, smoke some more grass, and dope my way into courage. A noble American tradition.

We smoked the number silently, then I asked her if she lived at the Pig Farm.

'Hog Farm,' she corrected. 'No, man. I thought I'd crash up there for a few days, get some meals, then hit the road.'

'Where you headed?'

'Just on the road, man, outa this crazy place. The freaks out here are weird, man. Everybody into speed and pills and smack and pure damn meanness. I been lotsa places, man, but I ain't never been no place like this. There ain't no grass in town but homegrown, all the acid is cut with speed, and I ain't seen so many smack freaks since I left the East Coast.'

'Yeah,' I mused, either stoned or drunk, trying to be casual. 'Does Lawrence Reese deal smack?'

'Man, he'd deal pigshit if you could get off on it,' she answered, giggling. 'And there's loads of pigshit up there. I went up with Lawrence, but the dude who runs the place wanted me to work, and I told him I didn't leave the farm to end up shoveling pigshit for some goddamned hayseed freak.' She giggled again. 'Burned the hair right off his ass – he got mean around the eyes just like my old man, and I thought he was going to try to whip me, but he just threw me off his wonderful fucking farm, right off, no dope and just the clothes on my back, but then, that's the way I showed up. I used to travel with a lot of shit, man, back when I first split, but now, man, I don't carry nothing but the clothes on my back – '

134

'I've got a friend like that,' I said, hoping to slow her babble. It didn't work.

'Hey, man, I kinda like Lawrence, and I wouldn't want to give him any grief. I ain't scared of him, or anything like that, but I wouldn't like it if you were going to shoot him or something,' she jabbered, twisting on the seat to face me, the white rims of her thighs above the tan slipping out of the legs of her cut-offs. She had an inflamed mosquito bite on the inside of her right thigh and she scratched at it with a dirty, broken fingernail. 'He's sorta silly some- times, but he ain't a bad dude. Just unhappy a lot, man. He's so goddamned big and strong, sometimes it's hard to remember he's got feelings just like anybody else, man. He's an ex-con, you know. That's where he got hooked on dudes. He says he can't get off too good no other way, and what the hell, man, I don't mind dudes getting it on, if that's what they like – like they say, different strokes for different folks – but I don't think it makes Lawrence happy, you know, not very happy. That's why he got into that glitter crap, I bet, and started hanging around with creeps – that must be amazing, man, balling in make-up. I ain't had make-up on since I was eleven, that's weird, man. I balled him a few times, and he kept wanting to do silly things, you know, tie me up and make me give him head, which is okay, I guess, if you like that sort of crap, but my wrists always started to hurt and I like to move around some, man.' She bounced up and down on the seat to illustrate movement, the nipples of her small breasts scribbling around her T-shirt nicely.

'Yeah,' I said, no longer hoping that she would stop, just wishing she would slow down, but she went right on, rattling like a loose pebble in a hubcap.

'But he's all right, man, and I hope you don't shoot him or anything, but you can shoot that goddamned hayseed freak if you want to.' She grinned, pleased at the idea. 'You can blow his fucking head off for all I care, except let me know and I'll split because dead people are a hassle. I was at a party once, somewhere in the Midwest, and one of the dudes fell out of a tree – we were all wrecked and sitting in this big old tree, and this guy fell out and killed himself, broke his neck or something, and the pigs came and busted all of us, but I jumped bail and I'll never go that way again, man, if I can remember where the fuck it happened.' She wailed laughter, pound- ing the seat and my arm, bouncing and pounding and laughing harder

135

and harder. 'What the hell,' she coughed, coming down, 'maybe I saw it in a movie, man, that happens to me sometimes, that's why I had to quit going to the movies, man, I had to give up dope or movies, man, I couldn't handle both, so I gave up movies.'

I looked at her. She was grinning widely.

'You're okay for an old man, you know. Lawrence is an old man too, maybe older than you, but sometimes he's a kick in the ass. Are you a kick in the ass, old man?'

'Right now, baby, I'm so stoned that I don't know,' I said, feeling as if I had been standing in a strong wind for hours. 'I just don't know.'

'Well, don't you go hurting Lawrence, old man, 'cause he's a kick in the ass.' She loved that, barely able to hold back the spurts of laughter. 'Sometimes.'

I sighed and promised that I wouldn't, under any circumstances, hurt a kick in the ass, which set her off again.

'You ain't all that bad looking for an old kick in the ass,' she said when she came back. 'Hey, man, you ever find old El Creepo?'

'Yeah, I found him,' I lied. 'But he was dead.'

'That's too bad, man, dead people – '

'Are a hassle,' I finished for her.

She sighed deeply, as if her wind was spent. She curled up on the seat, her legs drawn under her, her narrow head resting on the seat back, her face hidden in lank hair.

'Must be sad dying,' she whispered as I headed up Willomot Hill.

'Some people say that living is the sad part.'

'Well, that's silly,' she said, sitting up and brushing the hair out of her face. 'What the fuck is that?'

'Tourists,' I said.

A caravan of identical aluminum travel trailers occupied the right-hand lane, strung out up the hill like metallic sausages. I down-shifted the rig and roared around the laboring automobiles and their gleaming burdens in the passing lane.

'Goddamned tourists.'

'Be nice,' she said, shifting roles, flitting from stoned child to bemused adult as easily as I changed gears. 'I'm a goddamned tourist, man, into sightseeing and all that crap, I'm a tourist everywhere I go.' But the role slipped and the giggles came back. 'Let's give the bastards a sight,' she said, slipping out of her cut-offs. She hopped up on the seat and propped her naked butt out the window. But the slow trek of the trailers proceeded smoothly, the eyes in the cars fixed on some more distant and photogenic vista. Mindy was happy, though, grinning wildly, her eyes bright beneath spare brows.

'Put your clothes on,' I said at the top of the hill as I slowed to turn into the parking lot of the Willomot Hill Bar. 'I'm gonna get some beer. You want something?'

'Sure, man, a Coke and all the goddamned candy bars in the world,' she said, tugging up her cut-offs. A flash of white around the sparse pubic hair made me weak. But then I could always be tempted.

'Right,' I said, parking the car.

The bar was in a low building, windowless on both long sides, and it seemed to have been hacked out of the side hill behind it, then skidded down to rest slightly askew beside the highway. Blunt and unfriendly outside, it was like a cave inside, the lair of feral humans, dark and dank, the low walls lined with the mounted heads of deer and elk and mountain sheep and goats and bears, more like totems than trophies. At the very back of the long, low room stood an erect grizzly bear, dim and shaggy, frighteningly shapeless in the deep shadows, its glass eyes glowing like two embers. At night, filled with smoky yellow light and sullen drunks off the reservation, the bar seemed like some primeval ruin, a temple where human sacrifices had just been offered to the hirsute demon-god lurking at the back, an offering refused by the beast. I knew what it looked like at night because I had gone in too many times officially as peacemaker or arrester of vicious movements – roles the owner, Jonas, objected to. At night it looked like the sort of place Raymond Duffy might choose to die in, and in the day, empty except for the silent Indian woman behind the bar, it was no better.

'Jonas around?' I asked the woman bartender, whose face was so impassive and eyes so glassy that she might have been another trophy hanging behind the bar. I thought Jonas might remember the Duffy kid, but the Indian woman shook her head slowly, silently.

'Is he coming back today?' My voice sounded oddly reverent in the hushed bar. The woman shrugged, then nodded, then shrugged again. I didn't know what she meant, but it didn't matter. Jonas was easy to find: just look for the meanest, loudest, toughest runt in the county, and it had to be Jonas. I ordered a six-pack of beer, two

Cokes, but she didn't have any candy bars. I took a package of potato chips instead, hoping they would suffice.

On the way to the door, I thought of bringing Helen Duffy up to see the place where her little brother had died. Perhaps it might explain something to her, then she could explain it to me. But there was no need to kid myself. If Helen walked into the Willomot Bar, she would only see a dingy, depressing bar, sadly degenerate, and even worse, she would be able to tell that I was right at home in the bar. I made foolish noises to myself about being disgusted by the Willomot and I didn't hang out there too often, but I seldom drove past without stopping in, and in an odd way I was fond of the bar. It was a Kamikaze bar, pledged to a divine destruction.

Outside, back under the rational glare of sunlight, the vault of blue sky resisted the advance of another front, Simon's rain, a reef of bruised clouds stealing in from the west. Over a ridge directly north, the stone peaks of the Cathedral Mountains spired, as clear as chimes in the summer air. The column of trailers still trundled slowly past, metallic worms on a fatal migration. And sweet Mindy sat cross-legged and naked as a jay bird on the roof of my rig, waving gaily at the tourists.

'What's happening?' I asked, trying not to let her know how delighted I was with her.

'Nothing, man, absolutely nothing,' she answered over her shoulder. As she twisted, the muscles of her narrow waist shimmered in the sunlight. 'I haven't caused a single wreck.'

'Too bad,' I said. 'Come on down. I've got work to do.'

'It's too nice a day to work,' she said, waving at a logging truck driver as he pulled his truck back across the road, just missing the last of the shining trailers.

'It's gonna rain,' I said, pointing behind us at the relentless gray front, from which thunder showers were breaking off like reckless children, slipping ahead of the clouds, splashing rain and cool wind down the mountain valleys. 'Soon.'

'You can work after it starts to rain,' she said.

'It's supposed to be the other way around.'

'That's silly,' she grumbled, but she climbed down as I watched. She was so casually naked that there didn't seem to be any point in looking the other way. Her legs were long and slim, her perky rump firm, and her breasts were small but looked as hard as green apples.

Once in the rig, she tossed her clothes on the floor and sat with her head hanging out the window, her hair fluttering in the wind. Then she faced me again, shaking out the wind tangles, and popped the top of a Coke can.

'Thanks,' she said. 'They didn't have any candy bars?'

'Nope.'

'Good. They still make my face break out, man, and that's my last shred of middle-class vanity.'

'Got some potato chips, though.'

'Yuk,' she grunted. 'Fried in animal fats, man. Yuk.'

She was so smug that I had a handful even though I didn't want them. She was wrong. They had been fried in used crankcase oil.

'Hey,' she said, poking me in the ribs. 'You wanna ball?' she asked, not faking the casual nature of the question. 'I could use a little bread for the road, man. A little bread lets you choose who you have to ball for meals,' she added, grinning broadly as if she hoped to shock me. When I didn't answer, she said, 'Well, if you're in such a hurry to see old Kick-in-the-ass, I could give you some head while we're driving. I'm kinda skinny and don't have any tits to speak of, but I move around a lot to compensate, man, and I could use the bread.'

I wanted to ask her who she had been traveling with and how she had come up with the routine, but I asked her how much instead.

'I don't care, man, spare change or twenty bucks, it don't matter.'

'What if I just give you twenty bucks?'

'Outa sight. What if I ball you for nothing?' she answered quickly.

'I don't know,' I said, laughing. 'How old are you?'

'Who cares,' she said, reaching for my fly.

'I do,' I said, stopping her busy little fingers. 'I never ball a chick without a personal history.'

'That's weird, man. I ain't got the clap, so whatcha afraid of?'

'Balling strangers, I guess.'

'Everybody's a stranger, dummy, and you're puttin' me on,' she said, her fingers working again. 'So find a flat spot.'

'How old are you?'

'Nineteen going on forty, man, just like the rest of the world.'

She took my silence as criticism, which it wasn't. I had a momentary rush of sadness, but I didn't know if it was for me or her.

'Don't worry about me, man, I've been on the road since I was

139

thirteen. My old man wouldn't let me go to Woodstock, so I split and I ain't been back. You grow up quick on the road, man, and I'm about as old as I'll ever be,' she said, defending herself against the years between us.

'How old will you be at forty?'

'Who cares. To get old, man, you have to remember things, and I don't even remember this morning. My old man told me all the time that I'd have to grow up someday when I got out in the real world,' she said, moving closer as she talked. Her fingers had opened my shirt, and her hands were stroking my chest. Her breath was hot against my face. 'Well, I'm all grown up and this is the real world, man.'

'Right,' I said. 'Let's find a sylvan glade.' Helen Duffy wouldn't understand, but my father would have.

'What's that?'

'A nice flat spot.'

Afterwards, we exchanged the polite and breathless compliments by which casual lovers maintain their dignity. Consideration touches more deeply and longer than passion. We began with spontaneous passion but finished with consideration, which surprised both of us pleasantly. And after the surprise came the sadness. She rose after a few still moments of holding each other and wandered aimlessly over to the small creek that stuttered past our flat spot. She eased her slim foot into the cold water, muttered a complaint, then rambled on to a large, smooth rock which lay partially in the water, where she lay down to sun. I walked over and sat beside her.

'A while ago I asked you if Reese was dealing smack, but you never got around to answering me,' I said softly, rubbing her firm thigh with the back of my hand.

'Working, huh?'

'Yes.'

'You make a lot of money?' she asked.

'I used to. But I spent a lot too, so it evened out.'

'I never balled a private eye, man.'

'Neither have I.'

She grinned and held my hand tightly for a second, then said, 'Lawrence used to deal, man, but I don't think he ever dealt smack. That's what he took his fall for, so he was kinda afraid of it.'

'Dealing smack?'

'No, man, smuggling it across the Mexican border. I think that he asked El Creepo to move out when he got hooked. I heard that. But I didn't hear it from Lawrence, so who knows if it's true.'

'How long ago was that?'

'I don't know, man. I didn't spend much time keeping up with that crap.'

'How well did you know the Duffy kid?'

'As well as I wanted to, man. He was a prime creep. I knew that the first time I saw him strutting around with his goddamned guns, quick-drawing and snapping the trigger in people's faces. Man, after that I wouldn't even stay in the same room with him, and I told him that if he ever did that to me, he damn well better have a bullet in his goddamned gun because I was gonna knock his fucking head off. And I'd have done it too, man, I ain't no goddamned pacifistic flower child or nothing like that.'

'Was he around a lot?'

'El Creepo? Naw, he paid the rent, man, but he wasn't around all that much. But he was around enough so that some people wouldn't even crash there for free.'

'It wasn't Lawrence's house?'

'Naw, man. He never has any bread. El Creepo paid all the bills.'

'Was he dealing?'

'I don't know, man. He always had dope and money.'

Dope and money, the trappings of new wealth, I thought as I gathered my clothes and dressed, cursing myself for quitting cigarettes, needing that blue swirl of thoughtful smoke. Dressed, I walked back to the rock and held her tightly for another moment, not thinking at all.

'Hey, man,' she breathed against my neck.

'Yeah.'

'Hey, man,' she repeated, leaning back to stare at me with her soft brown eyes, light brown like her hair, dry and shaken clean in the wind.

'Yes,' I said into her silence, the silence of the young, which ran like an underground river beneath the dope babbles and inarticulate riffs of their private language, the silence of frustration and anxious grief for nameless losses.

'Hey, man, don't be sad, okay? Sometimes older guys, you know, they get down afterwards. I don't like to make guys sad when I ball them,' she said, sounding as lonesome as easy rain among stolid pines. 'Okay?'

'You don't make me sad,' I said, not telling her that youth was sometimes sadder than middle age, not telling her that she made me feel old, older than the mountains, more ruined than the gulleys jagged on sunburnt slopes. 'It's been too nice a day to be sad.'

'Great,' she said sadly.

And I lifted her in my arms, as light as a bundle of dry wood. She smelled of sunlight and stone, her limbs as smooth and limber as green sticks, and her mouth on mine, sun-warm and gentle, as soft as down, drove a stake into my tired heart. I wanted to break the spell, to heave her into the creek, to shout and splash water happily, to find some quick irony with which to resist, but the spell held.

'You're crying, you old fart,' she whispered sweetly, forgiving me, almost happy.

'I must be drunk.'

'You're crying.'

'Yeah, but I'm not sad.'

10

The Holy Light Hog Farm was one of those visions of paradise nurtured by dirt farmers going bust on the Great Plains – their faces implacable, sunburnt, wind-furrowed – a vision for which they would have gladly sold their souls. Lacking a market for souls, they did the next hardest thing: rose up from behind their plows and dragged their suffering families west out of that great bitter sea of harsh land that stretched to the bleak horizon in all directions, heading west to the promised land, rich wet valleys where the mountains broke the sharp thrust of the winter winds, land so fertile that fence posts took root overnight and cattle fattened like hogs. Not very many found their Edens, but the man who first owned the land and built the house now occupied by the Hog Farm did.

The house was yellow and square, three stories high, softened by a gabled roof and a broad veranda on three sides, and set on a shallow hillside at the foot of the Cathedral Mountains, which rise as grandly as the Tetons, overlooking the wide, fecund valley of the Stone River. Large and stately trees grew around the house, providing shade and dignity, and a deep lawn, broken randomly by flowering shrubs, flowed down the hillside from the house to the edge of the fields and meadows. It was a lovely place, a proper seat for a baron, an old man, tall and weather-honed lean, wrapped in faded, starched khaki, his collar buttoned loosely around his thin, stiff neck. So it was a shock to drive up and see a naked, pregnant woman stretched on the thick grass to catch the last of the sun and a bearded freak sitting on the veranda steps rolling a joint, to hear the dull thud of hard rock music rippling like thunder from the broad windows.

The young man who owned the place didn't have any illusions about the community of man. His land was posted, and nobody

143

stayed at the farm unless he worked. He grew his own hog feed organically, so the fifteen or twenty young people living there had plenty of work. Since I have the average older American's theoretical attachment to work, I approved of his concept, but I had been up to the farm on business – once to bring back a runaway teenage girl and twice to verify that runaway wives were living in sin – and I didn't completely approve of the people. Not that they were bad people. They were suspicious of strangers and too damned self-righteously superior about their modern morality to suit me. But they didn't bother anybody and they worked. Probably harder than I did. And because of my previous visits, they didn't like me at all.

'You wait in the car,' Mindy said, patting me on the thigh. She had made me promise once more not to give Reese any grief, and she reminded me of the promise as she climbed out of the rig and trotted across the lawn toward the front door, pausing to say hello to the pregnant lady.

The kid on the veranda obviously didn't know me because he waved and smiled and shouted, 'What's happening, man?' but the pregnant lady recognized me. She rose, eased into a loose shift and walked over to my rig. A tall blond lady, as beautifully healthy as some expectant mothers are, she was the ex-wife of a real estate salesman in Meriwether. In my own small way, I'd been responsible for the paucity of her divorce settlement.

'My ex-husband send you up here to spy on me?' she asked in a hard, flat voice.

'Don't be paranoid, lady,' I said. 'You'll hurt the baby.'

'Fuck off. Did he?'

'No, ma'am.'

'Then get your ass off the property.'

'Oh, go to hell,' I said, not knowing if my irritation was from my memory or the two whites I'd taken when Mindy and I left the creek. The tall woman left, striding across the lawn so strongly that she could have pulled a plow. It had been a lovely divorce. The dude she was shacked up with had taken a swing at me when I came up to verify her living arrangement, and then I had to sue her ex-husband for my fee. But the woman looked so good walking away from me that I was sorry she didn't like me.

'Occupational hazard,' I said to myself, sipping beer and wondering what I was going to do if Reese didn't show up. Or if he did. I reached under the seat for the Browning automatic, looked at it, checked the clip and made sure there was a round in the chamber, then put it back under the seat. I wasn't going to shoot anybody. The whole idea was silly. I had learned the hard way that if you pull a gun on a man, you damn well better be ready to shoot him. Otherwise, he might get mad. I had pulled my service revolver on a huge gypo logger once, and he broke my wrist taking it away from me. Then he knocked me cold, stuffed me in the back of my unit, and drove himself to the county jail. It felt nice to have the 9-mm pistol under the seat, but that's where it should remain.

Mindy bounced out of the side door, her lean legs flashing as the sunlight failed and the front settled over the valley. She threw a wave my way, then ran toward the barn, kicking her legs like a child. The air tingled with ozone and the hammer of distant thunder. A light mist dappled my windshield. I wished I were as happy about seeing Lawrence Reese again as she was.

I thought about other weapons, the leather sap hidden in the crack of the front seat, a flat sap with a spring steel handle and a lead disk in the head. It worked really well on drunks and fighting families when you could get behind them, but I couldn't see Reese letting me behind him. I also had a good knife, a large Buck folding knife, razor-sharp, but I didn't think Reese would roll over and play dead if I jerked it out and shaved all the hair off my forearm. That left my intelligence and his generosity, neither very dependable weapons.

Just as I had almost decided to forget about the whole thing and get drunk, Reese came shambling out of the barn door, Mindy at his side talking earnestly. Country living seemed to have changed him. His swagger had become a country-boy barefoot shuffle, his face was slightly sunburnt, and his hair had been cropped so short that his pink scalp glowed through his thinning hair. But he hadn't gotten any smaller; he was still a horse. His faded overalls would have fit a grizzly bear, his neck and shoulders done credit to a fighting bull.

I got out of the rig anyway, leaned against the fender, my arms crossed peacefully. I tried to look pleasant but unafraid. Reese stopped about three feet from me, his large hands hidden in his pockets, his bare feet scratching at the skim of dampness over the dust. We looked at each other without greetings. In the soft light, without the

145

purple eye shadow, his eyes were pale blue and dim, almost watery, no longer arrogant. Mindy paused beside him, then hurried to my side, hooking her arm in mine. Her smile had gone ragged at the edges, but she wore it bravely, and she held my arm protectively. In the damp, cool air, her slim body began to tremble, but mine had become oddly still.

'I'm not too happy to see you, man,' he said quietly, almost apologetically. And I started feeling cocky. As he spoke, the veranda filled with people coming out of the house and barn, most wearing worried grimaces, but others aglow with happy expectancy. The tall blond lady especially; she wanted to see me hurt.

'I didn't come to make you happy,' I said. 'I still want to ask some questions about Raymond Duffy.'

'Why don't you just go away,' he said.

'Not this time.'

'This time ain't gonna be any different.'

'It won't be as easy,' I said. Reese took his hands out of his pockets, flexed them, then jammed them back into his pockets. Something I didn't know about was holding him back.

'Listen, man,' he said in a harsh whisper, 'I don't need any trouble. Just go away. These people don't like you, man, and they don't like trouble.'

'Just answer a few questions, and there won't be any trouble.'

He thought about it, shaking his head, glancing once over his shoulder, then he mumbled, almost pleading, 'Just go away, man.'

There it was. In the ashen light of a rainy afternoon, no dragon, just a large, tired man on the wrong side of forty, punch-drunk from his life. His pale eyes were afraid, not of me, but of his future. I might not think too much of the Hog Farm, but he wanted to live there so badly that he might do anything, even talk to me.

'Hey, man,' I said, 'let's go have a drink of whiskey.'

Reese smiled, as if he meant to say yes, and I shrugged my right arm out of Mindy's clasped hands, but he shook his head, saying, 'No way, man.'

He could have ducked the punch, or dodged, or tried to block; instead, he let me have a free one, leaving his hands pocketed. I assumed that if it was free, it had better be good, so I aimed a straight right hand at his throat. But he lowered his jaw and took it

in the mouth. It split his upper lip and knocked him down but didn't
knock any teeth out or make his eyes glassy even for a second.

'I guess that means trouble,' I said lamely.

Reese glanced over his shoulder again, and a thin-faced young
man with a long beard nodded from the veranda, then Reese got up.

Afterwards, vaguely conscious but unable to stand up again, I
remained where I had fallen.

'Enough,' I said, hoping he believed me.

Mindy ran over, knelt and held my head against her bare thigh.
A long smear of blood and dirt stained her leg when I lifted my
head, but I couldn't tell where the blood was coming from.

'Are you okay?' she asked.

'I don't think I'm dead,' I said, tottering to my hands and knees,
'but I'm not sure.' My tongue took a roll call of teeth and came up
with a familiar number, and when I felt my nose, it seemed intact.
I dreaded a broken nose as much as a dentist, so I couldn't complain
too much. My eyes worked, if I concentrated on focusing them, and
I could breathe without fainting, which meant that even if I had
broken ribs, at least they weren't sticking into a lung. I tried standing,
which worked, then tried not to weave, which didn't. The crowd was
still arranged on the veranda, smiling gravely, as if for a family
portrait. The light mist fell coolly on my tired face.

'Why didn't you make him promise not to hurt me?' I asked Mindy,
trying to smile to let her know it was all right.

'She did, man,' Reese muttered from the edge of the lawn. 'You're
not hurt, man, not permanently.'

'Could've fooled me,' I said, my hand following the blood up my
left cheek to a gash three fingers wide in my left eyebrow.

'Sorry about that,' he said pleasantly, 'but you bobbed when you
should've weaved.'

'Someday I'm gonna get beat up by a guy who doesn't want to be
my goddamned buddy afterwards.'

'Hell, man, I'm hurt worse than you,' he said, smiling broadly, as
if he was happy about the injury, and holding up his right hand. The
middle knuckle had been jammed halfway back to the wrist.

'You're a hard-headed son of a bitch,' he added, as if it were a
compliment.

'You don't know just how hard-headed, buddy,' I said, then walked

147

over to my rig and took the automatic from under the seat, keeping my body between the gun and the crowd. I went the rest of the way around the rig and stood behind the hood. 'Okay, Reese,' I said quietly, 'I don't want to scare your friends, so I won't show this automatic pistol to them, but I want you to know that it's here, and that no matter how hard you try, you can't get to me before I put a large and painful hole somewhere in your large and painful body.'

'Get it on, man. I been to the hard place where the real bad dudes hang out, and you ain't nothing. And that's what you get, nothing.'

'Does this mean we're not buddies anymore?'

'You guessed it, man,' he said, moving a slow step closer to the rig.

'Think about it, now, before you do something foolish. Whatever happens when I pull this trigger, it's all bad, it means the man has to come out here to disturb this bucolic tranquillity.'

'You won't pull that trigger, man.'

'You can find out the hard way.'

The crowd on the veranda began to mill about, craning their necks to see why Mindy had her hand over her mouth. I smiled pleasantly, Reese shuffled his feet and jammed his sore hands behind the bib of his overalls, and Mindy stood absolutely still.

'What do you want?' he asked.

'Let's go have that drink.'

'Okay.'

I climbed in the passenger door and replaced the pistol under the seat. Reese walked toward the rig, moving reluctantly.

'Where you guys going?' Mindy asked, taking her hand out of her mouth.

'Get a goddamned drink,' Reese said, 'before that crazy bastard kills somebody.'

'Can I go?' she asked, looking at me. I looked at Reese.

'It's your party, man,' he said, shrugging.

So I nodded at Mindy, and she slipped in the door in front of Reese and settled between us.

'You dudes are crazy,' she said. She sounded happy about it.

'Just him,' Reese answered. When I glanced over at him, he wasn't smiling. But he looked as if he wanted to.

'Violence makes strange bedfellows,' I said, 'but then you guys know all about that.'

148

Mindy elbowed me in the ribs, her hand trying to hold back the giggles, and if I hadn't known better, I would have sworn that Reese blushed. At least he grinned. And we drove away through the shifting rain as cozy as a newly-wed *ménage à trois*.

At the small infirmary in the town of Stone River, a clumsy doctor put ten stitches in my right eyebrow, then let a nurse clean the rest of the scrapes and scratches while he checked the X-rays and set Reese's hand.

'You guys have a fight?' he asked as he wound Reese's hand with an elastic bandage.

'That's right,' I answered.

'Who won?' he asked.

'You charge extra for jokes?' I asked, but he didn't answer. At least they weren't listed on the bill, which I paid.

'My treat,' I said to Reese.

'That's right.'

The bar in Stone River was just a bar, the only bar in town. Two old farmers, excusing themselves from the fields because of the light rain, stroked lazily at a ritual pool game in the rear of the bar, bitching patiently at each other like a couple married much too long. The resident drunk aimed his blind grin at us when we came into the bar, but we didn't offer greetings or whiskey, so he staggered past us to the door to watch the rain. At the bar, I ordered a shot and a beer, and Reese had the same, but Mindy took too long to make up her mind, and the bartender asked for her ID. Except for lint, her pockets were empty, so she had another Coke.

'I hate that crap, man,' she groused.

'You can't have civilization without laws,' I said.

'Oh, Jesus Christ,' she groaned, then took my change and walked over to the pinball machine. She played the first few balls without using the flippers or touching the sides of the machine, just letting the balls roll wherever they might, but soon she had her fingers locked to the flipper buttons, and she was hammering and twisting, fighting gravity and the stainless-steel balls.

Reese and I drank silently, watching her battle. When we finished the shots, I ordered two more.

'I'm flat, man, I can't buy back,' he said.

149

'No sweat.'

'It's your money, man.'

'Not exactly,' I said.

'After all the trouble you caused me, man, the least you could do is buy the drinks with your own money.'

'Trouble?' I asked.

'Trouble,' he said, smiling. 'Blew up my porch, man, hit me in the mouth, broke my hand, and got the man on my ass.'

'Jamison?'

'You guessed it, man.'

'Give you a hard time?'

'No shit. Daddy, that's one uptight man. I can't afford any felony hassles, but that dude scared me so bad, I nearly busted him and run. He may think he's a boy scout but he's as bad as any cop I've ever seen. And I seen a few.'

'He takes his work seriously,' I said.

'He's crazy. All you goddamned hick cops are crazy. In the cities, man, the cops are usually just dudes doing a job of work, and some of them like it and some don't, some are good, some bad. But none of them think they're gonna save the world from evil. Hick cops always think they're John Wayne making the frontier safe for decent, God-fearing folk. That's why we're having this drink, man, 'cause you're a crazy cowboy.'

'I'm not the man and haven't been for years,' I said, feeling some need to defend myself.

'But you think you are, man. It's all over you.'

I didn't ask him what that meant because I didn't want to know. Or maybe I knew but didn't like it.

'You mind answering some questions?'

'Of course I mind, man. Didn't you get that impression from me yet?'

'Sure.'

'But you're just hard-headed enough to keep after me, huh?'

'You guessed it,' I said.

'What's in this for you?'

'You want the truth?'

'Why not?

'Maybe nothing. Maybe a lady.'

'The sister?'

'Maybe.'

'I told you you were crazy, man. Hell, if you want a lady, take that one home,' he said, nodding toward Mindy. 'Feed her a few meals and wash her back every now and then, and she'll follow you around like a puppy dog. For a while.'

'Maybe that's the problem,' I said.

'Christ, not true love, man. Not that. Yeah, that's it. I can see it now. Well, daddy, if she's anything like her little brother, you're in one hell of a mess.'

'She's not,' I said. 'The kid was adopted.'

Reese looked at me for a moment, rolling the shot glass between his thumb and forefinger so smoothly that it was hard to think of his hand as broken. Then he shook his head, saying, 'He never told me that.'

'Maybe he was ashamed of it,' I said. 'Some adopted kids are.'

'Not the Duff, man. Whatever he was ashamed of, he threw it right in people's faces. Like the homosexual thing. To compensate for the guilt with aggression.'

'You learn that in prison?'

'Man, they got more shrinks than cons in the joint. Group therapy on every floor.'

'Must be fun.'

'It's a scam, man, a way to get out. You ever see a crib sheet for the Rorschach test?'

'That's where my tax money goes, huh?'

'You probably cheat on the returns,' he said.

'That's right. But don't tell anybody.'

'Man, I never tell anybody anything.'

'So I gathered. Which puts us right back at the beginning,' I said.

'Wrong, man, this is the end. You wanted to buy me a drink, you bought me a drink, we chatted, and that's it.'

'Three drinks,' I said, motioning to the bartender. 'And either we have more conversation or round two.'

'You're serious, huh?'

'You better believe it,' I said.

'This time you might get hurt.'

'Reese, old buddy, I think you're afraid to hurt me. How many falls have you taken? Two? Three? How many more before you take a habitual rap? So you can't afford to hurt me.'

151

'You're real smart, man, aren't you? A real bad-ass, right? Well, just swing away, old buddy. I won't raise a hand to stop you, and when you get tired, man, I still won't have nothing to say.'

'I guess you got me then,' I said. 'To hell with it. Enjoy your drink.' Then I picked up my beer and started over to watch Mindy.

'Hey, man,' he said behind me.

'What?'

'Come here. What the hell does the sister want to know?'

'She doesn't believe that her little brother committed suicide or died by accident. Of course, she can't believe that he was hooked on smack either.'

'Well, he was, man,' Reese said sadly.

'I know. But not too long, right? A month or so.'

'Whatever the coroner says, man,' he answered, his face going blank again. 'You tell the sister that the Duff killed himself, man.'

'And if she asks how I know?'

'Come on, man, get off my ass.'

'No way,' I said. 'You asked me to come back, Reese. You got something you want to say, I want to hear it, so let's quit farting around.'

'Okay, man, but let me tell you something first. I ain't never been straight. As soon as I could walk, I was boosting shit outa the corner grocery store, and I been in and out of every kinda joint there is, but I ain't never talked to the man. Never. And I pulled some hard time for it, man, but I never been a snitch. And that's a hard habit to break. Just like being bent. But when that crazy bastard Jamison had me in interrogation, man, I got scared. I don't want another trip to the joint. No more bars, man. I couldn't handle it. And if I tell you what I know about the Duff and you tell the lady, and she makes a fuss, then Jamison is going to want to know how you know. He'll turn the screws on your ass, you'll babble, and I'll go back to the slammer for one final engagement.'

'Nope. Won't happen like that,' I said.

'What?'

'I won't give Jamison the time of day.'

'You won't take an obstruction fall for me, man.'

'Of course I would.'

'Why?'

'I don't know. Maybe I just like you,' I said, then finished my whiskey.

Reese was silent a second, then he burst out laughing. He slapped me on the back and said, 'That's pretty damn slim, man, but what the hell. Why not?'

'So give,' I said, ordering another round.

'None for me, man.'

'I'll drink it.'

'It's your money.'

'It's your turn,' I said.

'Right,' he said, almost sounding happy. 'Sure. Absolutely, man. What do you want?'

'Everything.'

'You ain't gonna like it. The lady ain't gonna like it, so you still gotta come up with a good lie, man,' he said.

'I'll worry about that.'

'Okay, man, it's your life. Or the Duff's. He was a kid looking to die, man, he was a real crazy. Makes — Made you and I look like saints. He was so crazy, even I was afraid of him. Then he started sticking that nail in his arm, and he was dead.'

'Who turned him on to smack?'

'Whoever he was dealing for.'

'He was dealing smack?'

'That's right, man.'

'Jesus,' I said. 'How long?'

'A couple of months.'

'Who for?'

'Don't know, man. Didn't want to know.'

'How'd he get started?'

'You gonna love this, man. He borrowed five grand from his sister.'

'I can't tell her that,' I said, gunning my shot.

'Don't tell me, man.'

'Christ. Where was he getting his goods?'

'He didn't say, but I can guess.'

'Guess.'

'From a cop, man. He was dealing high-grade junk, French probably, certainly not Mexican, and there ain't been nothing but Mexican junk coming through for over a year. So find the last big bust around

153

here before they bought off the poppy farmers and look in the evidence locker and you'll probably find milk sugar instead of junk.'

'That's lovely. What's dealing have to do with killing himself?' I asked.

'Probably nothing. Just a nice way to go out.'

'You don't think there's any chance that whoever he was dealing for might have helped him? Maybe they started worrying that the kid was too crazy to deal with. Something like that.'

'Doesn't sound right, man. Whoever's controlling the junk is strictly amateur, small potatoes all the way. And this is just a one-shot operation. As soon as the supply runs out, that's the end of the junkie plague in Meriwether.'

'Jamison would be happy to know that,' I said.

'He'd be happy to know lots of things, man, that he ain't ever gonna know.'

'Just kidding,' I said.

'Not funny, man.'

'Anything else I should know?'

'How should I know,' he said, looking away from me.

'Did you see him any that last week?'

'A few times.'

'What sort of shape was he in?'

'Terrible. He took that old man's death really hard, man – I mean, he was down, way down, and really freaky at the same time. Cut his hair and shaved off his beard, threw away all his guns and cowboy clothes. He and that old man musta been tight.'

'I wonder what that means,' I said, more to myself than Reese, but he answered anyway.

'Who knows, man, and who cares. They're both dead.'

'You're a real joy, Reese,' I said. 'I'm gonna go piss and think about it.'

'You one of those guys who thinks best with his pecker in his hand?'

'You guessed it.'

When I came back from the john, all I had was an inventory of aches and pains, and all I knew was what I read on the walls. Some ambitious soul in Stone River desired sexual congress with a broad spectrum of humankind. Jews, niggers, hippies and other long-haired and/or hairy apes and freaks. A-rabs, Chinks, congressmen, the former governor of our state, and the past four Presidents. Russians, commies and, for reasons undeclared, people from North Dakota. But the writer lacked the courage of his convictions: he didn't leave a telephone number.

Mindy had finally been conquered by the machine and stood beside Reese at the bar. He didn't look as happy as he had when I left.

'What did you find out, man?' he asked.

'That I hurt all over.'

'Me too. Let's split.'

'I need a drink,' I said.

'Have mine, man,' he said, and I did.

11

On the way back to the farm, we were silent, Mindy coming off her high and Reese sunk into his own thoughts. I didn't have anything to say because I didn't know what to think. The new role I had to think of the Duffy kid playing, a heroin dealer, made it difficult to keep the various pictures of him together. The whiskey and the small whimpers of pain echoing about my body didn't help. I touched Mindy's thigh, and she leaned her head against my shoulder, falling asleep quickly. Reese glanced at her, then at me, shaking his head.

'Take what you got, man, and forget the rest,' he said as we pulled into the driveway, but I didn't answer.

In the distance, muffled by the thick cloud cover, thunder grumbled, and the rain fell steadily now on the green fields and meadows. The lower slopes of the mountains, vaguely visible through the rain, seemed massive, hinting at the weight of the peaks hidden in the clouds, and the landscape seemed fallow and patient in the sodden air, ready to burst with growth when the sun returned.

'Tell your friends I'm sorry for the trouble,' I told Reese as we parked in front of the farm house.

'Yeah. Don't worry about it, man.'

'Thanks for the information.'

'Thanks for the drinks.'

'Sure. Next time you're in town . . .' I said without finishing.

Reese nodded vaguely, lifted his hand but didn't wave, making no commitments, except to the new life before him. As he walked slowly toward the house, his head bowed against the rain and his injured hand slung into the bib of his overalls, I wondered how many new lives a man could stand.

'How'd it go?' Mindy asked shyly.

'Terrible.'

'You mean, after all that, he didn't – '

'He told me lots of things,' I interrupted, 'none of which I wanted to hear.'

'Sorry, man,' she sighed. 'How you doin'?'

'Okay. There's no need to be sorry.'

'I am anyway,' she said. She flattened her palm against my thigh and rubbed it with long, slow strokes, back and forth, as if she were polishing my pants. 'That was an awful fight.'

'Right,' I muttered. 'I lost.'

'Whatcha gonna do now?' she asked, watching her hand on my leg.

'I don't know,' I said frankly. 'Go back to town maybe. Find a new life. Who knows.'

'Maybe you oughta hit the road, man. That's good sometimes.'

'I guess I'd better go back to town,' I said, thinking about obligations I neither wanted nor understood.

'I could go with you,' she said in a bright and casual voice. 'I don't eat much.'

When I looked at her, she was grinning. I buried my face against her; she smelled of rain and stones glistening damply in a pine grove, of moss and pitch, of easy silence. I closed my eyes tightly, held her, trying. But in the dim light of my waking dream, Helen stood there, her red hair glowing like an exotic flower in a rain forest, her naked body shimmering like a white-hot flame in the faint daylight.

'I could go with you,' she repeated, her small hand holding my neck, the fingers pressing warmly into tired muscles.

'Thanks,' I said, pulling away. 'You're a sweet lady, and we had a nice afternoon, and I guess I owe you – '

'Nobody owes anybody anything,' she said quietly.

'Yeah, I guess not. Whatever, I've still got too damn many things to do.'

'Start by sleeping off this drunk,' she said, smiling.

'I'm not – ' I started to say, then realized I *was* drunk.

'Hey, man, I didn't mean to bum you out.'

'That's okay. It doesn't matter.'

'Yeah, well, if I don't see you again, old man, have a nice life,' she said, then pressed her lips to mine.

'Hey, you still need some money?'

157

'Naw, I guess not. Maybe I'll crash up here for a few days. Guess it won't kill me to step in pigshit, huh.' She smiled once more, touched my thigh with the back of her hand. 'Take care, huh.'

'You too,' I said.

She slipped out the door and ran quickly through the rain. In the middle of the lawn, she stopped, turned back, pointing her finger directly into the murky sky.

'It's raining, old man,' she shouted gaily, 'go to work!' A broad and happy smile lighted her face, as if she were immensely proud of remembering what she had said earlier.

But as I drove away I remembered what she had said about remembering and getting old.

Driving back toward Meriwether through the gray rain, I did another white and cracked another beer, cursing myself for a fool. The memory of Mindy's body, as smooth and clean as an ax handle, took its place among the other bruises and scrapes. It might not have lasted too long – one day she would have gone for a walk in the park and never come back – but it might have been peaceful while it lasted. For an instant, I resented Helen Duffy almost as if she were a wife, a frumpy duty between me and the fleeting pleasures of young girls. But that wasn't fair. I had made my choice when I took the case. But I didn't want to tell her that her little brother had borrowed money from her to set himself up as a heroin dealer. I didn't mind lying, but I wished I had a shot of whiskey to prop up the beer – that might make the lie more imaginative.

That was the first thing I had to do, I thought as I sipped beer and dodged traffic on the rain-slick highway. And there were other things, too, irons in various fires. Bills to pay, my bar tab especially, and Simon to feed, and queues of winos who depended on me for an occasional drink. I had to make a living somehow, which meant I had to check with Freddy and Dynamite so I could fake it with Nickie. So much to do. It seemed years since I had sweated honestly or slept without being drunk; my body seemed to have already forgotten the three-week interlude of sobriety. That was another duty, to dry out again. And fences to mend. Dick Diamond. And I had promised Hildy Ernst I would drop by, at least to say hello and good-bye, maybe, and I should find out what Muffin wanted with his odd message.

I cracked another beer, confident now. I could handle it, damn right, whatever happened, even without a shot of whiskey. Helen Duffy wasn't the only woman in the world, not by a long sight – no, there was whiskey to drink and women to love, a world of both, enough for weeks, maybe even years, maybe even thirteen years until my father's trust fell finally to me, then I could sprawl in the silken laps of luxury, loll grandly about foreign beaches finally, dawdle with expensive whores, droves of exotic dusky women, maidens with conical breasts and wide, happy mouths, and there were tall, cool drinks I'd never had, a life to live like a king, so much to wait for, so much to do, yes, and . . .

But the first thing on my new agenda was to sober up. And quickly. Find a normal voice and steady eye with which to confront the highway patrolman who was following me, his harsh blue lights whipping through the gloomy late-afternoon light. Either sober up quickly or hope I knew him.

As we both climbed out of our cars, I saw that he was a guy I had worked with in the sheriff's department some years before. I seemed to remember that he didn't actively dislike me. Once before, he had found me sleeping in my rig, parked in the inter-state highway median, stinking of whiskey and vomit, and he had let me drive home without a ticket. But as he strode toward me his face seemed angry beneath the brim of his campaign hat.

'Are you drunk again, Milo? I thought you were going to drive all the way to town before you saw my lights. I was afraid to hit the siren, didn't want to wake you up or anything.'

'Sorry,' I said. 'I was thinking.'

'Well, next time drink less before you start thinking,' he said, a small smile moving about his face, so I knew I would be all right. 'Say, I just got a call. They want you in town.'

'Who?'

'Jamison.'

'What the hell's he want?'

'Well,' he said, then paused, his face suddenly still and blank, a look I remembered too well the feel of. *Dead*, his face said. 'Bad news.'

'Who?'

'Simon. I'm sorry, Milo.'

159

'Shit.' That was the only thing I could think to say as the blessed numbness that precedes grief settled into my guts. 'Shit.'

'Yeah.'

'Where?' I asked, thinking the old fart must have wandered in front of another car. 'When?'

'The call came in about ten minutes ago. Some address over on Lincoln, I don't remember the number, but I've got it written down,' he said, heading back to his unit.

'That's okay. I know where it is.'

'I'm sorry I had to be the one,' he said, shifting about in the rain.

'I know the feeling. Forget it.'

'Hey, I'm going the other way, but you take it easy on the way to town, okay?'

'Sure,' I answered. I tried, but it didn't help. The corpse driving my rig had a heavy foot, and we went to town like a blizzard wind, coldly cursing the old fart every step of the way.

Four uniformed policemen kept the curious crowd of old folks and long-haired kids at bay, but they nodded me through. The open front of the house looked like a stage, the curtain raised for the first act, the actors waiting for the star's entrance. Two lab men bustled about their work, moving like energetic cleaning women. Jamison and a plain-clothes cop I didn't know stood next to Amos Swift in a small arc about the body, the cloud of blue smoke from Amos's cigar hanging over them.

Simon lay on his side on the living-room floor near the stairs, lay on his side, his knotted and feeble hands still clutching the four-foot splinter of banister that skewered his body front to back. It had entered just below the sternum and exited beneath the right scapula. The heavy tweed overcoat humped over his back, a short stub, black with blood, exposed. In front, on the pale, varnished wood, long bloody scrawls marked his hands' futile struggle to extract the splinter. His eyes were open, his lower lip bitten through, and his shoes had left curved scrapes on the floorboards. Because of the damp, heavy air, the stench of blood and urine and feces hung in the air like dark smoke. Simon was right: I turned my head away.

Out the side window, I saw the old woman next door standing at her side window. She caught my eye, waved coyly, white fingers wriggling like grubs. In the ashen light, her gaudy mouth glowed like a neon sign. I couldn't look at her either.

'What happened?' I asked. I had wanted to be sober; now I was.

Nobody answered. A long silence flooded the room, perfected by the small crowd noises and the quiet sweep of rain. Amos mangled his cigar, his teeth loudly crushing the tobacco. He muttered something, but Jamison remained silent, not looking at me but watching the lab crew, his thumb rubbing at a short, gnawed stub of a pencil. It looked like Simon's, but Jamison stuffed it into his shirt pocket as if it was his. I looked for the red notebook, but it wasn't visible.

Finally, the other detective broke the silence.

'Looks like he was drunk, maybe looking for a dry place to sleep it off, and . . .'

Then he saw Jamison glaring at him with the hardened face he usually reserved for me and his voice ran down like a tired toy.

'Dammit, Milo, I'm sorry,' Jamison said. 'Right now it looks like an accident, but we'll make sure what it was before we say.'

'Don't make any promises you aren't smart enough to keep,' I said. He gave me a hard look too, but didn't say anything. We both knew how much time and money would go into the investigation of a wino's death unless it was clearly homicide.

'You stay out of this, Milo,' he said.

'Out of what? An accident? Sure.'

'I mean it.'

'Great,' I said. 'I mean it too.'

'What was he doing here? Was he helping you with the Duffy thing?'

'Simon was just an old drunk, Lieutenant. The last I saw of him was in Mahoney's. He was writing a letter and drinking.'

'Don't try to shit me, Milo. If I find out he was here helping you, I'll have your ass. I mean it. Don't lie to me.'

'Why should I lie?'

'Because you think you're smarter than me,' he said. It sounded like an old complaint, but this was the first time I had heard it.

'I just have more time, Jamison. That's all.'

'Milo, if you put your face into police business or withhold evidence, you won't have any time at all.'

'I'm scared to death.'

'Aw, dammit, Milo,' he muttered, too tired to hassle me. 'This won't get you anything but trouble.'

'What's new?'

'Nothing, nothing's ever new.'

'What have you got so far?' I asked.

'Not much. If it wasn't an accident, the only person I know strong enough to do that is Reese, so we've got an APB out for him. For questioning.'

'Pull it in,' I said. 'I spent the afternoon with him.'

'That what happened to your eye?'

'Sorta.'

'Told you he was a hard one.'

'You were right.'

'Did he give you anything?' he asked.

'No. What have you got here? Besides a wasted APB.'

'Where the hell do you get off asking me that? Who the hell do you think you are?' he asked, angry again, his voice booming, his face red. The two lab men glanced at him. 'Goddammit, Milo, someday –'

'Someday's ass. Either tell me what you've got so far, or I'll go down to the station and buy it, and you damn well know it.'

'Hey,' the other cop said, moving toward me, but Jamison looked at him again, and he shut up and stopped.

'Okay. It isn't much anyway,' he said, rubbing his pale face. 'No signs that the body was moved, no prints on the banister worth a damn, no evidence that anybody else was in here with him, except half the neighborhood.'

'Who found the body?'

'Two kids. Boy and girl. Said they came in to get out of the rain, but I'd guess they needed some lumber or maybe a quiet place to smoke dope and ball. At least they called it in, which is amazing. They were really scared, Milo, and still are, so I believe them.'

'They see anybody?'

He gave me a disgusted look, and I gave it back.

'All right. No. Not in the house. They said there was another longhair on the sidewalk. Maybe he came out of the house, maybe he didn't.'

'Get a description?'

'Sure. Long black hair and beard,' he said. 'How many people you know fit that description, Milo?'

'No details, no guesses?'

'Might have been an older guy. The girl said he walked like an older dude. No, she said he didn't walk like a kid.'

'Clothes?' I asked.

'Who knows? He wasn't naked; they might have noticed that. The girl said she had a feeling as they passed him that he was a narc.'

'Why?'

'Let's see,' Jamison said, consulting his little notebook. 'She said, "Too neat to be a freak," whatever that means.'

'What about the old woman next door?' I asked.

'That's the best part of all,' he said, smiling tiredly. 'She's not only crazy or senile, she's also an illegal alien from Poland. She doesn't speak a word of English, she's been in the country forty or fifty years but she still can't speak the language. Christ. And we can't rustle up anybody who speaks Polish.'

'She lives alone?'

'No, she has a spinster daughter. The daughter used to speak some Polish, but she and the mother haven't spoken in thirty or forty years, so she forgot what she knew. Can you believe that?'

'Family life,' I said.

'Yeah. And if that wasn't enough, the daughter was drunk as a sow, and when we went to the door, she went into hysterics. Seems she thought we'd come to take her mother back to the old country.'

'Where's the daughter now?'

'Either swilling apricot brandy or passed out. Who knows? Christ, sometimes I love this town, Milo, goddamned love it.'

'Everybody's got to live someplace,' I said.

'Yeah, but they could die someplace else,' he said, then paused and took my arm, leading me over to the wall. 'And there's this other problem.'

'What?'

'You know a prof out at the college named Elton Crider?'

'I met him last night,' I said.

'So I hear. At the Riverfront. I understand that you two had a small discussion.'

'So?'

'So they fished his car out of the river this afternoon. He was in it. He was drunk but not too drunk, and there weren't any skid marks. You want to tell me what you two talked about?'

'Raymond Duffy.'

'And?'

'And that's it. He hadn't had anything to do with the Duffy kid in months, almost a year, and didn't know anything. I drove away and he went back into the bar. That's the last I saw of him.'

'That's what Vonda Kay says too, but I don't like it,' Jamison said.

'Don't like what?'

'Don't like your version, don't like the blood-alcohol count, don't like the missing skid marks. But it's in the county.' By which he meant that nothing more would come of the investigation. In our state the county sheriff is an elected official, and in our county the sheriff knew a great deal about getting elected but little else. 'Anyway, you should stop in the sheriff's office and give a statement tomorrow. Then stop in to see me.'

'Why?'

'Because I want to know what you tell them.'

'Why?'

'Because I don't like it.'

'Neither do I,' I said. Already numb about Simon, I didn't have any room to think about Elton Crider and his sad life. 'But it's none of my business.'

'And Simon is?'

'I didn't say that.'

'You didn't have to.'

We both turned to look at the body again, neither of us mentioning the missing notebook or Simon's pencil in Jamison's pocket. I knew how careful Simon had been about stairs since his accident with the pickup; his hip hurt when he climbed stairs, and he was afraid of falling down them, so he clung tightly to banisters and climbed only one step at a time. And he had been sober, I was sure, just as sure as I was that somebody had pushed Simon off the stairs, that I would find out who, and that I would kill him. And it would be easier for me if Jamison thought accident instead of homicide.

'Hey, Jamison, maybe Simon thought he was helping me. He knew I was going up to Stone River to see Reese, maybe he thought he could find something here, something about the Duffy kid. I don't know. You know how he was when he was drunk.'

'Yeah,' Jamison said, but I couldn't tell if he bought it, so I gave him some more.

'Look, I know that's Simon's pencil in your shirt pocket, and that you are wondering about his notebook,' I said, but Jamison looked blank. 'He was just about finished with his notebook, man, and maybe the letter took up the rest of the pages. Don't make more of it than necessary.'

'Yeah,' he said, but I'd blown it, talked too much, and he didn't believe me. 'Sure.' But he wanted me to think he did.

'Goddamned old drunk,' I muttered, covering my eyes as the lab boys closed their cases and the boys from the ambulance carried their stretcher in.

'Yeah.'

The attendants had trouble fitting Simon and his splinter on the stretcher.

'Hey, Jamison,' one said, 'can we pull this thing out?'

Jamison gave them his hard, disgusted glare, which they ignored. 'Well, can we?'

'Only if you want it shoved up your ass.'

'Okay, man, you don't have to get huffy. Christ, I was just asking.'

'I'm not huffy,' Jamison said softly.

'Oh,' the guy said after a long awkward moment looking at Jamison's unhappy face. 'Okay. Whatever you say, Lieutenant.'

Simon would have loved it. He stunk so badly that even the attendants turned their faces as they lifted him onto the stretcher. They put him too far to one side, and his body fell off. They cursed and put the body back on, strapping it down this time. But then they couldn't fit him into the ambulance door. They sat the load down in the rain, scratching their heads and discussing the project like two furniture movers stuck with a piano larger than the doorway.

'Get him outa here!' Jamison shouted.

They had to unstrap the body, tilt it so the splinter would fit diagonally through the door, then strap it again. There was a loud tearing noise as the wood ripped the headliner when they lifted him in.

'Watch the headliner, man,' one complained.

'Go to hell,' the other answered.

'Jesus Christ,' Jamison muttered.

Amos followed them, patting my arm and muttering around his

cigar that he intended to do one hell of a good job on Simon's autopsy, then he waddled into the rainy dusk. Somewhere behind the clouds the sun found the horizon, and the long summer afternoon finally ended, night falling gently on the wet, shining streets of Meriwether.

'When the hell does summer start?' Jamison grumbled.

'Last month,' I said.

'Ain't it the truth,' he commented, then after a long pause he said, 'Say, Milo, I got some bad news for you.'

'So what's new?'

'But listen, you gotta promise me you'll stay outa this, Milo.'

'I don't have to promise you anything.'

'That's right, smart guy, you don't have to promise me anything. I just hate to see your kid grow up with a con for a father. How do you think he'll feel about that?'

'How does he feel about having a cop for a father?' I asked.

Jamison shrugged and smiled like a man about to tell the truth.

'Like every other punk in this country,' he said. 'I'm the enemy, Milo, and you're his hero.'

'I didn't know,' I said, thinking that a man shouldn't be ashamed that his son thought of him as a hero, wondering what I was ashamed of.

'You haven't been by in too long. You ought to spend some time with him, let him see what you're really like.'

'Is that your bad news?' I asked. It had already been a long day, but the look on Jamison's face told me it was about to get longer.

'There's a warrant for Muffin,' he said.

'So?'

'Illegal possession. Two packets of heroin. Do you know where he is?'

'Goddammit. When it rains, it pours,' I said. 'How the hell did that happen?'

'Anonymous telephone call.'

'And you got a search warrant with that?'

'Milo, this town is so crazy with junkies right now that I could get a search warrant on a hunch.'

'You know Muffin never dealt smack.'

'I don't know anything anymore. Do you know where he is? Have you heard from him?'

166

'No,' I said. Now I understood Muffin's message and knew where he had gone to ground. 'Not for a couple of weeks.'

'If you bullshit me, Milo, you're gonna take a fall. I promise you that.'

'Okay. This afternoon he left a message with my service that he had split for Mexico.'

'Yeah,' he grumbled, 'I got that too. What's it mean?'

'If it doesn't mean that he's gone to Mexico, or wants you to think that, then I don't know. We don't have any Captain Midnight secret codes, Jamison. I can't blame him for running. He wouldn't deal smack because it's too hard a fall and he wasn't hooked. He's not that kind.'

'I didn't tell you to adopt the kid,' Jamison said.

'You thought it was a good idea at the time.'

'Maybe I was wrong.'

'No chance of that,' I said. 'Do you think somebody might be trying to lay a bum rap on him?'

'That only happens in the movies, Milo.'

'Just like being right all the time, huh?'

'Yeah. Guess so.'

'Good thing he wasn't there when you showed up,' I said. 'I hope his luck holds.'

'Luck, hell. Whoever he owns over in robbery tipped him,' Jamison complained. 'I'll get that son of a bitch one day, and when he gets to Duck Valley, the cons'll eat him alive.'

'Good luck.'

'Fuck you.'

'How did you ever get to be a cop, Jamison? Your ideals are too high.'

'It was so long ago that I don't even remember,' he muttered.

'Remember what you said the night you found out I was on the take?'

'I remember cussing a lot,' he said, shaking his head.

'You gave me a long lecture about corruption, how it was like cancer. First, it took the man, then the police force, then the whole community.'

'That was a long time ago,' he said.

'Don't be so hard on yourself.'

'Don't be so easy,' he answered.

167

As we stood there, alone now, the lab boys gone, the crowd fed and dispersed, Simon's body off to the morgue to be butchered and probed, Jamison and I were nearly friends again, forgiving the distance between our lives. He reached over and squeezed my shoulder.

'I know how you felt about Simon, I'm really sorry.'

'Just another old drunk,' I said, sorry too now, trying to cover the tears.

'Reese give you anything interesting?' he asked, kneading his damp scalp.

'Lumps and pain.'

'Yeah, he's a hard one. He wouldn't give me anything either, but I got the feeling that he knew more than he was telling.'

'I thought so, too, at first, but now I don't know. He really looked like a man who wants to go straight, looked really tired of his life,' I said.

'Aren't we all,' Jamison said, patting his thin hair carefully back across his baldness. 'See you tomorrow.'

'Sure,' I said, then walked away, not bothering to look back at him standing confused among the ruined house. The wreckage didn't amuse me anymore.

I could accept Elton Crider's death as a coincidence. He had been depressed and drinking; coincidences do happen. And from what Reese had told me, the Duffy kid had good reasons for an accidentally-on-purpose way out of his dismaying life. But nobody was going to convince me that Simon's death had been an accident. He had found out something somebody thought worth killing for, and they had pushed the old man down the stairs and taken his notebook. Not a very bright somebody, either. A smart man would have ripped out the pages with notes and left the rest of the notebook; a smart man would have known that I would take the old man's death personally. Of course, if I were a smart man, I would know how to go about finding the not-so-bright somebody who had killed Simon and set up Muffin.

The only thing I knew to do was to find a junkie and sweat him until he gave me his pusher, then sweat the pusher and work my way to the top of the dung heap. Whoever I found there was standing in shit. That was the plan.

But as I drove to Mahoney's to pick up a pair of handcuffs from my other office, I discovered that I needed Simon to talk to. Without him I wasn't sure. I could hear his gruff voice telling me what a silly bastard I was. We both knew that I wasn't mean enough to follow through. Not that I couldn't be mean when it seemed necessary at the moment, but that I lacked that abstract edge that makes violence calm and controlled, a tool for justice or vengeance. I would either get sick and quit or kill somebody before they could tell me what I needed to know.

'Dumb-ass,' the old voice said. 'Think.'

I tried, but found only confusion compounded by grief. I needed a drink. Nearly as badly as I needed the old man.

When I got to Mahoney's, Simon's wake had already taken the bar by storm, filling it with so many local drunks that they stood in line outside to get in the door. I parked in the loading zone, put the automatic and the sap and the derringer into the paper sack, then got out and tried to buck the crooked line at the door. Somebody was buying the drinks. I hoped it wasn't me.

The first wino I nudged didn't know me, so he pushed back, muttering that I should wait my turn. I picked him up by the nape of his neck and his britches, meaning to just set him aside. But I had had too much, speed or death, and I threw the old man into a parked car. He fell into the gutter, mewling curses, but he looked at me and didn't get up. If he had, I think I might have killed him. *He* thought so, scuttling away quickly. The others outside the door either knew me or had been convinced that I wanted through. Everybody either left or stood silently aside. The silence spread into the bar as I walked in, and they all stood aside.

Leo was sitting on the bar, waving his hands over his disciples, swaying gently, an amazed, drunken grin on his face. I knew who had been buying drinks.

'Fell off the wagon,' he confided happily to me. 'God, it feels great. Makes me remember why I drank.' But then he saw my worried face and added, 'But by God, I'll be sober tomorrow, Milo, sober as a judge. Man can't stay drunk all his life, right?'

'Right,' I said.

'Goddamned old Simon,' he muttered, unhappy again. He lifted one clenched fist, nearly falling backwards behind the bar, and handed me the tiny gold star clutched in his sweaty palm. I had to

peel it off, didn't have to lick it when I pasted it in the corner of
Simon's picture, couldn't look at the smiling face behind the glass.
Some decent soul had unplugged the jukebox as I walked over
to the wall, and standing on the chair above the quietly drunken
crowd, I felt as if I should give a speech, so I turned around and
said, 'Fuck it.'

And they cheered.

When I walked into the cooler, they were still shouting. Somebody
had plugged the jukebox back in and turned it up so loud that I
could feel the bass notes thumping the floorboards, but I couldn't
hear the music over the roar of the wake.

Freddy followed me into the other office and watched silently as
I slipped into the shoulder holster and checked the automatic, holstered it and put the extra clips in my back pocket.

'You fixing to kill somebody?' he asked.

'If I get the chance,' I said, putting the sap into the back pocket
with the extra clips.

'That ain't hardly the rig,' he said. 'It's too slow. And you ain't
hardly the type.'

'It's as fast as I am,' I said, settling my arms back into the damp
windbreaker. The blood from my eyebrow had stained the left
shoulder with dull brown spots and the rain had smeared them. 'And
killers don't come in types.'

'Who you going after?'

'I don't know yet,' I said as I rummaged through drawers looking
for the cuffs.

'You best hope he's slow on the draw, Milo. I tell you that shoulder
rig with an automatic ain't for – '

But before he could finish, I had spun, drawn and cocked the
pistol, and faced him in the combat stance.

'Jesus Christ,' he said, ducking. 'I'll shut up.'

'I used to practice some,' I said, finding the cuffs and hooking
them over the back of my belt.

'You ever kill a man with that?' he asked, not shutting up at all.
Sometimes I thought that I had to either play father or son to every
drunk in town. 'Did you?'

'No.'

'Have you ever killed a man?'

'Not since the war. Haven't fired a shot in anger in nearly twenty years.'

'Hick cops,' he muttered, talking around his toothpick.

'What?'

'Milo, I killed four men and one woman. I got more time in front of review boards than you got on the crapper,' he said, taking out the toothpick and smiling. 'Why don't you let me do it?'

I looked at him. He was grinning, mean as hell, his pudgy face no longer a joke.

'No, thanks,' I said.

He shrugged, then asked, 'What about the twist I've been tailing? Want me to stay with it?'

'Oh, hell, I'd forgotten about that. Yeah, stay on it,' I said, not really caring, knowing Freddy liked the work. 'What did she do today?'

'Went shopping. Spent loads of somebody's money. Made five phone calls from public booths.'

'Catch any numbers?'

'Couldn't get that close. I can try tomorrow, if you want.'

'No, just tail her.'

'Whose hooker is she?' he asked.

'What?'

'Who does she belong to? She's a hooker, Milo. Didn't you know?'

'I should've guessed.'

'Big-city girl too. Maybe she's on vacation or something, maybe she's retired, but I know hookers, and she ain't done it for free in a long time.'

'Is she pretty?' I asked, wondering about Nickie's friend, why he had money to keep an eye on her but not enough money to come up with anything but a whore.

'She used to be. She'd turn your head till you got a good look.'

'Ain't it the truth,' I said. 'Stay with it.'

'That's some eye you've got. What happened?'

'Ran into a wall,' I said, and we grinned. 'And say, why don't you keep an eye on Leo tonight. I'll pay for the time.'

'Been watching him already,' he said, sighing bravely, a man who could hold his liquor, who could kill. 'But it's my time.

'Thanks.'

'It's nothing. Say, you carrying a backup gun?'

171

'No. Why?'

'When you're hunting a man, Milo, always carry a backup gun. Anybody who would kill a worthless old fart like Simon is liable to be looking for his friends. You still got that derringer?'

'Sure,' I said, lifting it out of the sack on the table.

'Strap it to your leg or stuff it in your shorts.'

'I'd feel silly.'

'Better silly than dead.'

'Okay,' I muttered, looking for some tape, thinking I would rather have a loaded gun on my leg than in my shorts. I found some electrical tape and strapped the derringer to my left calf. 'How's that?'

'It looks okay.'

'Hell, I don't know what I'd do without all these drunk advisers,' I said as I straightened up, grinning at Freddy.

'I don't either,' he said without a trace of a smile. 'Watch yourself, Milo.'

I nodded and followed him out into the throng of mourners.

Out in the bar, it looked as if Meriwether was finally going to have a riot. A geriatrics ward had gone insane – an old folks' home in revolt, or maybe the faces had climbed down off the wall, grown flushed and grossly swollen, shedding dignity and good humor like old clothes. The air stunk of smoke and rotten teeth, cheap whiskey and thin sweat, wine puke. Lorrie – resident hooker to all the old men whose erections hadn't completely retired, a short fat old woman, nearly bald beneath her gray curls – was dancing, her skirt lifted to expose thighs once meant to drive men mad, fish-belly white, pitted, jiggling thighs rising and falling to the rock beat. The crowd made room for her dance, not to watch but to protect themselves. A shrunken Indian, wrinkled and weathered in bars, joined her in the cleared space, dancing the dance of his grandfathers, his toothless mouth wide with lost songs.

And there was Billy the dummy and Arch the railroad engineer, and Duke Meadows who had once been hairdresser to the stars, and his constant companion, Buddy Wells, who had almost been a cowboy star at Republic. And a brace of retired supply sergeants loading Army crap on Skipper, the retired bosun's mate who hadn't made chief in thirty years. And Olinger, the failed mortician who watched with a professional eye as if he still had a business. And there was

Alf the swamper, who swept bars for drinks, and his ex-wife Doty who had divorced him but hadn't left yet. And they were all there but the dead, who were hanging on the walls, smiling in approval and looking like they wanted a drink.

But that was the pretty part.

As I pushed through the crowd and the grabbing hands, which offered consolation or begged for drinks to bear their sorrow, the drunken arguments and fights had already begun. Classic wino fisti-cuffs at the bar: one punch every five minutes until one opponent or the other could no longer rise from his stool to totter into the ring. And classic wino arguments: political discussions over men who had long since left office and died, personal grievances twenty years past. Rivers of angry tears. Leo was stretched out on the bar, sleeping and grinning like a man who meant to rise again. The drunk I had heaved into the parked car held his head at Leo's feet. A puddle of vomit, flecked with blood, blocked the doorway. As I stepped over it, a long-haired kid who was peering into the bar said, 'Them old farts is weird.' I hit him on the shoulders with the heels of my palms, and he stumbled down the street, inquiring what was wrong with me. But I couldn't tell him.

Armed and advised and ready, I headed north on Dottle searching for a junkie, until I realized that I didn't know what a junkie looked like, so I went back to the office to call Muffin to see if he knew anybody who was hooked. I thought I might need some more of Nickie's money too, just in case there was trouble. The front doors were always locked at night, so I went down the alley to the side door, all the steel hanging off my body feeling suddenly heavy and foolish.

12

They must have been waiting outside Mahoney's because they followed me into the alley and took me just as I stepped out of the light into the shadows. I must have heard something, a sole scraping on brick, perhaps, or a grunt as the one in front raised the length of two-by-four. I ducked and went to the left and back, trying to get inside the swing. The board missed my head, but his forearms caught my neck at the shoulder and knocked me into the building wall. The force took the board out of his hands, or everything would have ended right there, but I heard the wood skipping off the paving bricks with loud, flat smacks and I shoved off the wall, trying to stay close to them until I had room to run. I got one with an elbow, but the other caught me with a kidney punch, and I bounced off the wall again. The fight went on, but I had already lost; all the butting and scratching and biting afterwards just made them mad. Except for falling down, it was over quickly, as quickly as they let me fall down, which took a long time.

When I came to, they were still there, standing about five feet from me. One was counting my cash, the other wondering painfully if his nose was broken. I didn't have his problem: my nose was all over my right cheek. The one counting money paused, telling the other that there was supposed to be more money, but the other was more interested in his nose, so his partner stepped over to examine it. I watched their silhouettes against the lighted street, watched them as best I could from where I lay curled against the wall. The automatic wasn't beneath my left arm, but I didn't mind. The derringer was still on my leg, but I didn't think I could reach it. That didn't bother me either. All I wanted to do was lie very still and hope they weren't going to kill me. If they hadn't already.

174

'I reckon it's busted, Bubba,' I heard one say to the other, and Bubba began to breathe hard and sob, saying, 'I'm gonna kill the motherfucker.' I edged into a tighter ball, my hand reaching for my leg. 'No, Bubba,' the other said, but Bubba pushed against his outstretched arm. 'We ain't supposed to kill him,' the first one argued, but then he added gleefully, 'but we can damn sure put him in the hospital for a long time, break his goddamned leg or something.' Bubba agreed happily, but when the first one reached into the shadows to pull me out, he found the nickel-plated glint of the derringer in his face.

'Freeze,' I whispered. Maybe he heard me, maybe not. He tried to back up, to stand up and grab an automatic out of his belt. But he didn't make it. At two feet, even half blind and whipped senseless, I couldn't miss. I blew his face off.

The muzzle blast knocked him over, splashed blood and flesh all over me, blinded and deafened me for a moment. When I looked for Bubba, he was twenty yards away, streaking for the street, but I pulled off the other barrel anyway. Brick dust bloomed in his wake as he turned the corner, and the large lead slug flattened, singing across the street. A department store window exploded and fell into the display. Mannequins tumbled from their studied repose, hanging upon each other like the victims of a natural disaster. The store's alarm bell began gonging, deep and unhurried, as patiently regular as a fog horn. In the distance, sirens answered. A timid crowd formed at the window, peering inside then all around, trying to understand what had happened. Then a bolder soul moved, and within seconds, winos and freaks were fleeing down the streets with the display clothing and furniture, two wildly ambitious drunks staggering off with a wicker couch.

I knew better than to leave a gun in the hands of a dead man, since sometimes they only look dead, so I crawled over to the body, wrenching my bloody money out of his hand, jerked the automatic out of his waistband, trying not to look at what remained of his face. But I did. When the police came to answer the store alarm, they found us eventually, heaped like garbage in the alley.

'You oughta see your face,' Jamison said when the doctor finished.

'You oughta feel it,' I mumbled.

Jamison grinned, then followed the doctor out of the emergency room. Through the open door, I could hear them arguing over where I should spend the rest of the night, the doctor insisting on the hospital, Jamison on a cell. My face didn't feel too bad, not nearly as bad as it would the next day when the Novocaine wore off. When I sat up on the table, my head was light and my taped ribs sparked with slivers of pain, but I didn't faint. I could see fairly well, out of my right eye, around the tape on my nose and cheeks and forehead, and I thought I could walk. Actually, I was fond of the pain; it kept me from thinking about the dead guy in the alley.

'He should check in for observation,' the doctor maintained loudly.

'He should check into a home,' Jamison said, 'but he's going to jail.'

'You have to clear it with the supervisor,' the doctor answered, and I heard their footsteps echo down the hall.

I didn't want to spend the night either place, so I tried standing, then walking. My shirt was too much of a mess to wear. I tossed it into the trash and wrestled into the bloodstained windbreaker, picked up the empty shoulder holster and left. Jamison wanted to charge me with carrying a concealed weapon and first-degree manslaughter, neither of which he could make stick. He just wanted me in jail so he could talk to me while I was in no condition to resist. I needed a lawyer and some sleep, and Jamison wouldn't let me have either until it was too late. I didn't think he'd be too angry if I split, particularly if I could stay away from him for a few days. And I knew just where I wanted to lie down.

Outside, Amos was waiting for Jamison, and rubbing his hands together briskly, as if he wanted to wash them again.

'Jamison in there?' he asked.

'No, he left a half-hour or so ago. Said he was going home to get some sleep.'

'He probably needs it. You look terrible too. You ought to be in the hospital, boy.'

'I been in twice today, Amos, and it didn't help.'

'I know how you feel, boy,' he answered as if he really did. 'I guess I'll go on home and catch him tomorrow.'

'Do the autopsy yet?'

'No. We're going to wait until tomorrow. I got everything ready, but I just couldn't handle it tonight. That's what I wanted to tell Jamison. But I guess it can wait.'

'Sure,' I said. 'Say, can you give me a lift to Mahoney's?'

'You don't need a drink, boy.'

'Just want to pick up my car and go home.'

'Can you drive?'

'I can walk, can't I?'

'Not too well,' he said, then helped me around the corner to his car. 'They give you anything for the pain, boy?'

'No.'

'Here,' he said, rummaging in his bag and handing me a small bottle. 'Take two every four hours, son, and you won't feel anything.'

'Thanks. I don't feel anything now.'

'Wait, boy, just wait,' he muttered as he pulled out into the traffic. He dropped me beside my rig and drove away jerkily, like a man who wasn't going to sleep much that night.

Inside the rig, I sat behind the wheel trying to sort out things in my mind, listening to that unfamiliar voice in the alley saying, '*We ain't supposed to kill him,*' and wondering what it meant. If they meant to take me out of action, they had succeeded. I was through. Helen Duffy would have to live with what I knew about her little brother, and although I was fairly certain I had killed the wrong man, that was going to have to pass for vengeance this year. If Simon couldn't rest easy with that, then that was his problem, because I was tired and old and not nearly as tough as I thought I was, and I was through. As I drove away through the bursts of pain that came in bright flashes, I could see his laughing face, but his voice was still.

Maybe she heard my rig bounce off the curb or the sound of the slamming door. Maybe she heard me stumble, cursing the rain as I stepped across the curb and sidewalk. Or maybe she had just come to the door to check the weather. When I knocked she opened the door so quickly that she must have been standing behind it, waiting. Fresh from another bath, warm and flushed and sweetly damp, she seemed draped in steam, which seeped from her body through the green robe. Curls of wet hair looped against the freckled skin of her neck. In the pale light, her scrubbed face glowed, and her mouth was slightly open, as if in passion, or grief.

'You spend more time in the water than a fish,' I said, trying to joke so she would know I was still among the living.

'Oh my God!' she breathed. 'What happened to you?'

177

'Hard night,' I said. But the smile I managed cracked, and I fell, tilting toward her like a falling tree.

Her arms caught me, strong arms held me upright, clutched the blood and filth to her body, her hands smooth and rubbing and holding me beneath the damp windbreaker, her lips murmuring questions and concern.

'Easy,' I said as she found a bruise beneath the tape.

'What happened?'

'Lie down,' I mumbled. 'I've got to lie down.' As I moved into the room, she still held me, her hands on my neck tugging my ruined face to the soft curve of her neck, her gentle shoulder, bumping my left ear with her chin. She felt the stiff spines of the stitches and jerked away before I could complain. 'Got to lie down.'

'Oh, no,' she moaned, 'no.'

Thinking that she meant to deny the damage, I moved against her again, heading into the room, but she pushed back.

'You can't,' she whispered. 'Oh dammit, I'm sorry but you can't. Oh God, why do things have to be like this.'

'What?' I asked, stepping back to look at her.

'My mother – she's here.' Behind her, the splash of the shower echoed from the bathroom.

'What's she doing here?'

'I don't know.'

'Oh, hell, tell her it's all right, tell her we're going to get married – my God, tell her anything. I've got to lie down.'

'Oh, I can't. Now now. Not like this.'

'Like what?' I propped my hands on her shoulders and squeezed until she flinched. 'Like what?'

'Oh, I don't know,' she whispered, her face seeming to break into painful fragments. 'Drunk and beat up.'

'Lady, I'm always drunk and beat up. That's why I need you,' I said as clearly as I could.

She looked at me for a long moment, poised in that space between our lives, hovering like a hummingbird, the breath of her confusion and compassion so strong it blew kindly on my hot, tattered face.

'It will be all right,' I said.

'Oh no. Nothing is ever all right. You don't know her,' she said, sobs laboring like stones from her heaving chest.

'I'll tell her we're in love,' I said, brushing her cheek with my thumb, wiping away tears and a freckle of dried blood.

'Not now.'

'Now's all we got, babe.'

She groaned, brushed my puffy lips with hers, whispering 'Later,' pushing at my chest with small fists as the bathroom noises gathered to some conclusion that only she understood, murmuring 'Later, I'll come later,' and she gently shoved me out the door, closed it in my face.

'Someone at the door?' I heard a strong, vibrant voice ask.

'No. Yes, Mother. They had the wrong room,' Helen answered, her voice muffled as if she was leaning against the door.

'I guess so,' I said to myself and let my raised fist fall to my side. Then I walked toward the motel lobby and the bar beyond, letting the rain wash my face.

The urbane type who had been talking to Nickie that morning noticed the sudden hush of his customers and he came around the front desk quickly, inquiring in a carefully polite voice – the sort of voice that owns things and tells people what to do and how to do it – if he might be of assistance, but I walked right through him. Nickie was behind the desk too, but he hadn't moved, his face white and his eyes wide, and he didn't move until the polite voice said his name, then Nickie rushed around the desk. As I slowed, the man behind me grabbed my arm. The tourists and dinner customers hummed with confusion, moving away from the scene. But not so far that they couldn't watch.

'Nickie, tell this fucking bellhop to get his hand off me,' I said, 'before I tear it off.'

'Jesus Christ,' Nickie pleaded, and his friend held my arm tighter.

'Look, man, I need a drink real quick and real bad, then I'll split,' I said. 'I'll even go out the back door so I don't scare the tourists.' Then I turned to the man holding my arm, but he wasn't scared, and I didn't think I could survive another fight, so I ignored him.

Nickie looked at him, his mouth moving without sound, and the man said, 'All right. In a go cup.' Then he turned my arm loose, adding, 'And I don't ever want to see you in here again.'

'Sure,' I said, shrugging, out of snappy lines and empty threats.

The man smiled blandly, as if there had been no question, a

179

confident glaze over his face, an arrogantly arched eyebrow, but I couldn't even rise to that. If I didn't get a drink in this bar, I wouldn't make it to the next one. I let Nickie hustle me down a side hallway and through the kitchen to the back door.

'What about the drink?' I huffed; his flapping trot had worn me out, made the top of my head ache.

'I'll get it, I'll get it,' he grunted, sounding nearly as tired as I was. 'Wait there,' he said, pushing me next to the huge steel garbage hamper, 'I'll be right back.' I waited, slumped against the cold, wet metal, my hands quivering, my throat hot with sobs held back. 'Wha-what happened?' he stammered when he returned with a Styrofoam cup filled with ice and blessed whiskey, which I poured down my throat, over my chin and chest. 'You, you all right?' he asked as I gagged. The son of a bitch felt sorry for me; that kept the drink down.

'Another one,' I said.

'Huh?'

'Get me another drink, goddammit!'

'Okay, okay, right back,' he said, then left at his pounding trot.

While he was gone, I gobbled two of Amos's pills, then two more. As I waited I let my fingers finally take inventory of my face. The doctor had gotten the top half of my left ear back on my face but he suggested plastic surgery. When I touched it, it throbbed so painfully that I decided to leave it alone. The star-shaped gash at my hairline, which I had probably gotten giving a head butt, hadn't started swelling yet, so I could feel the dent and the forest of stitches. It felt as if this doctor had done a better job when he restitched my eyebrow than the first one. I didn't bother to check my nose; the doctor had set it but told me that if I wanted to breathe out of it, they would have to operate, adding that he hoped I had good medical insurance. Jamison laughed, so I didn't have to answer that.

When Nickie came back, I spit a mouthful of bloody ice cubes on the ground. He seemed to have more control over his face and voice, but his hand went back to the middle of his chest as soon as he handed me the drink.

'Wha-wha happened, Milo? Goddamn, you look terrible. Shouldn't you be in the hospital?'

'I just came from there,' I said, 'and look what happened.'

'Huh?'

'Nothing.'

'What happened? You wreck your car?'

'No,' I said, sipping the drink and rattling the ice. 'I got mugged. Right here in our fair city, Nickie, I got mugged.'

'Wha-who-wha –'

'Two guys jumped me in the alley next to the bank,' I said, not waiting for his question.

'They get away?'

'One did, yeah.'

'What about the other – one?'

'He's dead,' I said, making myself say it.

'How – Wha-what happened?'

'I shot him in the face.'

'Jesus Christ,' he groaned, looking sick, bending at the waist and belching.

'You all right?'

'Huh?'

'Are you going to be all right, Nickie?'

'Oh, yeah. Just haven't eaten yet. Goddamned business keeps me jumping, Milo, and my goddamn stomach, you know.'

'Might be an ulcer,' I said. 'You should have it checked.'

'Huh? Oh, yeah. Maybe so.'

'Nickie, I'm gonna have to take a couple of days off, but I've got somebody to cover your friend's lady friend. Is that okay?'

'Don't worry about it, you know. Take however long, you know, my friend will understand, you know.'

'I already got it covered, Nickie.'

'Okay, whatever you say, it's okay,' he mumbled. 'Hey, Milo, I heard about Simon, you know, and goddamn, I'm sorry.'

'You know what they say, Nickie?'

'Huh?'

'Nobody lives forever.'

'Oh, yeah,' he said, looking shocked. Maybe nobody had ever told him about it. 'But I'm – I'm really sorry.'

'Right,' I said. 'Check with you later.'

As I walked away he muttered something I didn't hear. A little bit of Nickie's pity and commiseration went a long way. I was too tired to stand around listening to him, so I went back to my rig and drove toward Mahoney's like a shot.

13

Two long drunken days later, after the coroner's jury had ruled Simon's death accidental, the body was released to me. Thanks to Jamison, I was free to bury the body. He must have felt sorry for me because, even though the coroner's jury hadn't ruled on the man's death in the alley, I hadn't been charged with anything. It wasn't because he couldn't find me, either, since I spent the whole time in Mahoney's, drunker than I'd been for years, too drunk to change clothes or even begin to understand the haze of pain around my head.

So I buried Simon – alone to mourn him, just as he said it would be. Leo had come along, but he was collapsed behind a nearby gravestone, too drunk to know where he was or why. Simon and I were dressed for the occasion, he in my father's overcoat, me in the bloody windbreaker. The rain had passed on, the sun returned, and the afternoon was as fresh as spring, the sky azure and cloudless, the air warm in the sun and cool in the shade. In the poplars along the road, a light breeze flashed among the crisp leaves, and the muted hum of traffic from the interstate highway buzzed like lazy bees in clover. Simon Rome had no service, no tedious eulogy at the graveside. Just the sound of Leo retching. No ceremony. I had brought a bottle of Wild Turkey to place in the grave with him, but Leo and I had drunk and spilled most of it on the drive out. I shared the rest with the two trustees from the county jail, then tossed the empty bottle into the open grave, gathered the sack of wasted flesh that contained Leo, and went back to town.

'You win, you old fart,' I whispered as I left the cemetery, 'but you cheated.'

*

182

On the way back to the bar, I dumped Leo at the hospital, glad he could afford a private room. The charity ward had been filled with drunks who had nearly killed themselves with Leo's free whiskey. Leo had fallen off the wagon, but I had fallen apart, withdrawn until I was as insensate as a stone just to hold the pieces together. The pain remained, as did the grief, as constant as a cloud of black flies. I drank, was drunk without being drunk, locked into that terrible and curious lucidity where the world has no more meaning than a movie, the colors vivid but the lighting too harsh, the focus so precise that the world seems cornered by sharp edges. So I walked into Mahoney's, shouting for whiskey and blurred definition, for drunken sleep, forsaking vengeance, forgiving love.

Later, afternoon threatening dusk, Dick Diamond woke me from the black hole of a dreamless sleep, his hand gently shaking my shoulder.

'Hey, old buddy, let's go home,' he said.

'Have a drink,' I mumbled, raising my head from the table.

'No, thanks.'

'For me, man, for me.'

'You've had enough,' he replied. 'There's no need to kill yourself.'

'Get my own goddamned whiskey,' I said, rising. When he reached for me, I swung at him blindly, but he ducked my fist, caught my arm over his shoulders, and carried me out into the neon-smudged dusk, carried me toward home and sleep, struggling uphill all the way.

In the confusion of sleep, she finally came to me, on wings in a cool throbbing wind, on her belly sinuous, angel and snake, her hair fire, her hair blood flower blooming, her hands cold, fingers ice, tears hot, her hands holding me again, to her soft breast, rocking and singing, small moans and the sound of a child weeping, hold me, held my face, my head cracked like a fallen egg . . .

And when I rose up from sleep, she came with the pain, forgiving, unlike the pain unforgiving that filled my body and burst out around the spike driven between my eyes, a pain more fierce than the thirst.

'How do you feel?' she asked.

'Whiskey,' somebody answered.

'No,' she sighed, 'no.'

'Yes I know yes what I'm doing I've been drunk before I need whiskey now and again to stand this,' I pleaded, crying finally, not for Simon or myself or loves lost, but for whiskey against this thirst.

She brought a bottle and a glass; foolishly, I held the bottle, my teeth rattling against the glass, and poured it into the fire inside, my stomach pleading for another, which I had, and another again. But when it came up, I couldn't find the toilet, couldn't hide the blood from her, couldn't find my hands to cover.

'Shouldn't he be in the hospital?' she asked somebody vague in the distance.

'He wouldn't like it,' a voice answered.

I croaked approval, then fell asleep. Or something akin.

'Hi,' she said when next I woke. 'How are you now?'

'Hi,' I answered, twisting in the fog, awake enough to appreciate the pain.

'You feel better, love?' she asked, gathering my hand in hers.

'Worse – but that's an improvement.'

'How so?'

'I'd have to get better to die.'

'There's a number by the phone, a doctor, call him, tell him – I've been drinking . . . but I'm sober now and need a boost . . . he'll understand . . . and next time I . . . wake up . . . food . . . love . . .'

When it seemed that the toast and tea were going to stay down, I started on the soup, but the spoon clattered against the side of the bowl.

'Let me help,' she said.

'Nope. Recovery is a matter of will. These small things count,' I said, but had to abandon the spoon in favor of drinking from the bowl. 'I used to go with a Chinese girl.'

'Really.'

'And she made the best egg-drop soup in the world.'

'I'm sure.'

'And if I had some now, I'd be up and about in a flash.'

'You just stay in bed, mister.'

'Oh, lady, I intend to. If I'd known it took all this to get you into my bedroom, I would have done it sooner. I know how, you know.'

'Just hush,' she murmured. 'And don't be silly.' But her smile glowed like a sunrise.

As I wiped the mist from the mirror, I asked the graybeard therein if he might be me, but she answered from the bedroom.

'I certainly hope not.'

'Me too.'

'You need some help?' she asked from the bathroom doorway.

'Take off your clothes and leap right in,' I said, smoothing lather over the lumps and bruises.

'It would probably kill you.'

'Braggart.'

'You'll see,' she smirked.

'I damn sure hope so,' I said, but there were sudden serious lines around her eyes, so I added lightly, 'When are we going to get married?'

'After you join the AA.'

'I don't want to hang around with a bunch of fucking drunks.'

'I just fell apart, that's all. Too much happening at once. It's cheaper than a breakdown. And if it doesn't kill you, easier to recover from. My father was a drunk, my mother was a drunk and a suicide, and my life hasn't been very pretty. I have neither character nor morals, no religion, no purpose in life, except as Simon said, to get by, so is it any wonder that I drink?'

'No.'

'At least I don't have to go to meetings.'

'No?'

'My name is Milton Chester Milodragovitch, the third, and I'm a drunk. Thank God.'

'No.'

When it became obvious that I had survived myself once again, we went out into the backyard to sun and listen to the creek as it constructed a rushing silence. We rattled our way through the weight of Sunday's paper, sipping tea and chattering as foolishly as two slightly mad squirrels. Beside her firm body, clad in a pink bikini, I felt like a suit of old clothes left in the alley for the garbage truck. But the sun worked on me, drawing a quick sweat, a greasy skim, like that of a chronic invalid, slimy with waste, odorous with my body's disgust. I went in and showered it off. The second sweat, when it came, was better, still rancid and bitter, so I repeated the shower.

'You spend more time in the water than a fish,' she commented when I came back out, then she rolled over on her stomach slowly, stretching languidly.

'Smart ass,' I said.

'Dirty mouth.'

This time, as I lay beneath the sun, my body seemed to become flesh again instead of a sack of vile, tepid fluid, my skin tightening as old muscle rose to meet the warmth. My face still felt as hard as dried mud, and as comfortable to carry, but my limbs began to rejoice about survival. When I seemed whole, I rose and knelt beside her lounge chair, ran my hand down the small of her back, across the heated skin soft with oil and clean sweat.

'Yes?' she breathed.

'Thanks.'

'For what?'

'For coming.'

'You're welcome, but it seemed the least I could do under the circumstances. This whole thing is my fault, and I wouldn't blame you for hating me – I mean, after leaving you outside my motel room when you were half dead, I wouldn't blame you.'

'No,' I said, 'it's not your fault at all. I walked into this with my eyes open, or at least they were both open at the time, and whatever happened, it was my fault.'

'You mean you forgive me?'

'There's nothing to forgive. Just so you hang around for a while, till I get well, then maybe – '

'Don't,' she groaned, rising from under my hand, turning away with a sob. 'Don't say that.' Then she covered her face with her hands and ran across the yard to the edge of the creek.

The hand that had held her was still there, as if measuring the height of a child, and it trembled. I never knew what to do when a woman ran away, could never tell if they wanted to be alone or if they wanted me to follow. I had tried both ways, but neither worked.

'Hey,' I said, and she turned. 'What the hell am I supposed to do?'

Whatever she said was inaudible against the noise of the creek.

186

'What?'

'What the hell am I supposed to do!' she shouted, stomping her foot angrily, her fists wiping roughly at the tears. But she was smiling, so I went to her, held her against me.

'I can't have this happen,' she said. 'I have a job – '

'You better hang on to it,' I said, 'because I don't have one.'

'And I don't know what to tell my mother.'

'Tell her our children will have red hair and Cossack tempers.'

'That's not funny,' she whimpered.

'Then tell her we'll be happy because we're both too old to be unkind.'

'Don't say things like that unless you mean them, unless you're serious.'

'I've been serious from the beginning.'

'Oh God, I don't know, it's all so confusing,' she said. 'I don't know – what to say – to anybody – anymore . . .'

'Don't worry,' I said, holding her tightly, so tightly that I felt her breath sigh out. 'It will be all right,' I said, staring over her shoulder into the sun-dappled shade on the creek. Inside my chest, the stone I had placed there crumbled into white dust, and now I could cry for Simon and love for myself. Only my face was hard, scabs and scars and lumps, the tape over my nose making it seem that I saw the world from a cage or through the narrow slit in a cell door.

'I'm not what I seem,' she said softly.

'Nobody ever is,' I said, thinking of her little brother in spite of myself. 'Don't worry about it.'

'I can't help it,' she whispered. 'You don't understand – about me.'

'Do I have to understand you to love you?'

'I don't know. I don't know if anybody has ever loved me.'

'I do,' I said. And it wasn't hard at all.

She nodded, gazing into the distance, then tucked her head against my chest, and we stood there, sun-flushed skin, heated flesh, hands slowly touching each other's backs.

'Let's go inside,' I said.

'If you want,' she answered in an oddly small voice, as if she had no say in the matter, no will with which to either resist or comply.

'I need you, love,' I said, and she followed me into the house.

*

187

Against our flesh, fired in the sun, the sheets were cool, and we were as timid as children, shy and clumsy, graceless, banging noses and clicking teeth, giggling among the aching moans. Once inside her, though, I found that lovely compliance, her hips tilting toward my need, and as I knelt above her, watched her face lose focus, her eyes widen, her tiny teeth nipping at her lower lip between sighs and moans, as I waited, still, unmoving, all the sorrow emptied from me into her.

'You're lovely,' I said, 'absolutely beautiful.'

She focused her eyes, smiled slowly, saying, 'And you're the ugliest man I've ever met.'

'It wasn't very good, was it?'

'It was kind. That's enough. We're not children, we'll learn.'

'Are you sure?'

'Absolutely.'

'I didn't hurt your face?'

'Who could hurt a face like this?'

'Someone surely tried.'

It was an easy Sunday, small talk and gentle love, weak drinks dissolving, cigarette smoke captured by bars of sunlight. The delight of a new body, the tracing of design among freckles. An afternoon of touching. Waking to the pleasure of a new love.

But once when I woke, she was gone. I found her at the back door, wrapped in the bedspread against the evening chill, watching the stars perforate the sunset sky.

'Hey, what's wrong?' I asked.

'Nothing,' she answered mournfully.

'Come on.'

'Well, okay, it's Raymond.'

'What about him?'

'Every time I start to feel happy again, I think of him – and the man – whoever killed him.'

'What makes you so sure that somebody killed him?' I asked as gently as I could.

'You still don't believe me, do you?' she asked as she turned around. Her face was shadowed, but I could see her eyes, which were oddly blank. 'Do you?'

'It could have been an accident,' I suggested mildly.

'How many times do I have to tell you that Raymond was not a drug addict,' she said, her voice as empty as her eyes.

'Love, you may have to face the fact that he was.'

'Never,' she whispered. 'And even if he was, it was because somebody forced him, and that's the same as killing him. Isn't it?'

'I guess so,' I said, not wanting to argue with her stony grief.

'You know something you're not telling me,' she said, her voice trembling.

'No.'

'No what?'

'I'll tell you someday,' I said.

'When?'

'When you feel – when you don't feel so strongly about his death,' I said.

'People never understand,' she murmured.

'What?'

'How I felt about Raymond. If you understood, you'd tell me what it is that you know.'

'It's sort of – incomplete,' I said, feeling myself being pulled back into the case. 'When I know all of it, I'll tell you.'

'When?'

'Tomorrow maybe, the next day. I don't know. I'll go back to work tomorrow or the next day.'

'I'm sorry about your friend,' she said as she brushed her lips across my cheek. 'Truly sorry. Do you think there's any connection?'

'No,' I lied. 'I don't think so.'

'Dick told me his name, but I've forgotten.'

'Simon,' I said, 'Simon Rome.' Buried at county expense, his grave unmarked, his death unavenged.

And with his name, my safe world ended, my castle came tumbling down into the stagnant waters of the moat, and in confusion it began all over again, all the questions, those with no answers, those with too many.

The next morning I woke early, showered and shaved, then tried to eat, but my appetite failed me. The bacon smelled like dead pork and the eggs accused me with their fierce yellow glare. I had a piece of toast and a shot of whiskey in my coffee, drank the coffee and smoked a cigarette in the bedroom doorway, watched the lady sleep, wondered where to begin, how to keep the lady in my bed on a more permanent basis.

But I didn't know where to begin.

What would Simon say, I wondered, thinking he'd probably say *Have another drink and forget about it, dumb ass*, which sounded good to me. For a moment. Then I realized how much I missed the old fart already. At least I was smart enough to know that. And what else did I know? The man in the alley saying I wasn't supposed to be killed, which meant that somebody didn't want me poking around. But around what? The Duffy kid's death? Simon's? Elton Crider's? Muffin's frame? Then I remembered that I hadn't returned Muffin's call, which I promised myself I would do just as soon as I passed a pay telephone.

The kid's death had to be the beginning, but I couldn't make myself believe that it had been anything other than the old accidentally-on-purpose death. Any other thing was too complicated a way to kill the Duffy kid. If somebody wanted him dead, there were much more certain ways. Still, somebody wanted me in the hospital and out of the way. Somebody had gone to the trouble to shove Simon down those stairs and steal his notebook. Maybe Jamison had the notebook, though. Then why did he hide the pencil from me? No, somebody had taken the notebook. A not-so-smart somebody. As it had occurred to me before, a smart man would have taken just the pages with notes and not the whole thing, so he had to be either dumb or excited, an amateur. And what had Reese said about the heroin dealer? An amateur. Just like me. But why couldn't Jamison come up with the dealer? Just for that reason. Which meant I was going to have the same problem.

So have another drink and forget about it.

But standing there in the doorway, watching the lady sleep, I knew I couldn't get enough drinks in my stomach to make my mind forget about it at all. My major problem, of course, was going to be the fact that I had neither training nor experience as a detective, no matter what it said on my license. For God's sake, I didn't even read mystery novels because they always seemed too complicated. As a minion of justice or vengeance, I just didn't make it. But I remembered something Muffin had told me once as I tried to convince him he should live the straight life. He told me that if I wasn't a cop, I'd be a crook, which I knew immediately to be the truth. I wasn't about to sell things or clerk in a store or teach children not to suck eggs or even bartend. But knowing that didn't help either.

Another drink, forget it.

I was just about to get mad when I heard tires crunching down the gravel of my driveway. I went to the door before whoever it was could ring the doorbell and wake Helen. When I opened the door, I saw Dick's van stopped in the driveway. He sat behind the seat, peering through the windshield toward the house. I waved at him, and he got out. We met in the middle of the lawn and shook hands gravely, then he smiled.

'You look terrible, old buddy. Happy but terrible,' he said, which sounded strange, since I didn't feel happy at all.

'Yeah.'

'You survived, huh?'

'Looks like it. Hey, man, thanks.'

'For what?'

'Bringing me home. Calling her.'

'She called me, man.'

'Thanks anyway.'

'It's nothing,' he said, looking away. 'How's it going?'

'What?'

'You know. Everything. The two of you.'

'All right, I guess. Nothing's settled,' I said, thinking that it might be a long time before anything was. 'We haven't talked about it much.'

'Yeah, I understand,' he said, watching his feet. 'Say, man, I'm sorry as hell about – about Simon.'

'It happens,' I said, wondering why I was so cold about it.

'Yeah. I thought it was going to happen to you, old buddy. When you started puking blood, I thought it was all over. Never seen you that far gone, man.'

'Never been that far gone,' I admitted.

'What happened?' he asked casually.

Something was wrong. I didn't know what it was for a moment, then I realized that I was suspicious of Dick without knowing what the hell for. I glanced at his van. It was new and expensive, and I wondered how much he'd paid for it, where he'd gotten the money. Then I thought, *Don't be silly.* My God, the next thing would be me

191

suspecting Jamison of being the policeman Reese thought probably had provided the heroin from an evidence locker. I couldn't go around suspecting everybody. That would be crazy.

'Well, you don't have to tell me, man. It's not any of my business,' Dick said.

'Sorry, man, but I'm not all here yet. I don't know what happened. Maybe Simon, maybe the beating . . .' Maybe Helen closing her motel door in my face. 'I don't know.'

'Feel pretty bad about the dude in the alley, huh?' he asked, a sly and nervous edge to his voice. There it was. He wanted to know what it felt like to kill a man. They always do. And it would be a long time before he could look at me without thinking about that.

'No, man, I don't feel bad at all,' I said.

'Oh.'

'I was full of whiskey and speed and had just seen Simon spitted and had just had the living shit beat out of me, so I didn't feel anything, man, it's like it happened to somebody else,' I said.

'Yeah, I guess so,' he said, not believing a word of it. 'Say, man, I want to apologize for blowing up at you – when you called me. I'm sorry. Helen – she had – '

'That's all right,' I interrupted. 'Forget about it.'

'Well, I don't know.'

'Have a drink and forget about it,' I said, smiling.

'Sure,' he said, then glanced at me, returned the smile. 'Hey, man, let's play handball sometime after – Hey, good morning!' he added, shouting over my shoulder.

Helen had come to the front door, the green robe shining darkly in the morning shade. She squinted, then waved. Watching the two of them, I waited for a rush of jealousy and anger. But only a trickle of irritation came.

'She's a good lady, man. I'm sorry for confusing things and I want to wish you two the best,' he said, almost formally.

'Thanks.'

'And, hey, I'll see you on the courts, okay?'

'Sure.'

'Take care, man,' he said, then went back to his van and drove quickly away. I guess I didn't like the exit.

'What did he want?' Helen asked as I walked up the steps.

'I don't know. Maybe he was looking for the back door.'

'What's that supposed to mean?'

'Nothing,' I said, the irritation quickly spent. 'It was a cheap shot. I'm sorry.'

'No, you're not,' she said, angry now.

'Yes, I am sorry.'

'Then why'd you say that?'

'I don't know. Hell, I don't know why I do anything. But I am sorry.'

'Well, you should be.'

'Don't do this,' I said.

'I didn't start it,' she said, then left me at the door.

When I got to the bedroom, she had hidden beneath a tangled heap of bedclothes.

'Are you going to be here when I get back?' I asked as I picked up the bloody windbreaker.

'Where are you going?' she asked, rising suddenly from the covers.

'To work.'

'In that thing?'

'It matches my face, lady. Are you going to be here when I get back?'

'I don't know,' she answered, a petty whine in her voice. 'How long will you be gone?'

'Until I get back.'

'What's that mean?' she asked.

'I don't know.'

'Then why'd you say it?'

'Oh, goddammit, I don't know!'

'Well, you don't have to shout at me,' she wailed, then fell sobbing among the sheets.

'I'm sorry!' I shouted. 'And goddammit, don't tell me I'm not!'

She looked up as if she was going to tell me just that, but the doorbell chimes rang like tin thunder.

'Goddammit,' I muttered and went to answer the door. The other plain-clothes detective stood on my porch, his thumbs hooked into his belt. He didn't look any better than I felt. 'What the hell do you want?'

'Hey, man, take it easy.'

'Sorry. What do you want?'

'Jamison asked me to drop by. He's been calling you but he don't

193

get nothing but your answering service. He'd like to talk to you. This morning.'

'What's he want?'

'Are you kidding? He never tells me nothing,' the detective muttered. 'He thinks I'm dumb.'

'Yeah, me too,' I said, and we grinned at each other.

'He's one hard son of a bitch to work for.'

'That's what I heard.'

'I'm going down to the station, man, if you want to ride along.'

'That's okay,' I said. 'I'll take my car. I'm headed downtown anyway.'

'Whatever.'

'Hey, I'm sorry – about – I guess it's called being rude.'

'No sweat. You having a fight with your wife?'

'Something like that,' I said.

'Figures. That's the way I'm gonna get it, man, one of these days. I'll knock on a door in the middle of a family altercation and some goddamned woman'll blow me away.'

'It happens. I got flattened with a cast-iron skillet once. Some broad called to complain that her boyfriend was beating on her head, but when I got there, they had made up. I arrested him anyway, but she got behind me. Took ten stitches in the back of my head.'

'Lucky she didn't kill you, man,' he answered sadly.

'Yeah. Hey, did you guys ever find that old man's notebook?'

'Naw. Goddamned Jamison had me sifting garbage for three days, but we never turned it up,' he said.

'Great job, huh?'

'Don't you know it. Garbage and puke.'

'Huh?'

'Aw, we found some puke at the top of the stairs, and I had to scrape up a sample to compare it with the contents of the old man's stomach.'

'Was it his?' I asked, trying not to act as if I cared.

'Naw. Belonged to some other wino. Nothing but brandy and gastric juices.'

'They make a brand on it?' I asked, but that pushed him over the line from shoptalk to nosiness.

'Ask Jamison, man. We closed the book on it.'

'Okay,' I said. 'Thanks.'

'Don't mention it. I loved being pumped,' he said, then looked worried. 'Hey, you won't say anything about this to Jamison, willya?'

'I hardly ever say anything to him.'

14

'That's a great line-up you've got there,' I said to Jamison, 'but a smart lawyer could hurt you with it.'

'What?'

'I know everybody in the line-up but the kid with the busted nose, and I'd bet money I'm supposed to know him,' I said, nodding at the line of cops and drunks. 'So even if I recognized him, it wouldn't hold up. You blew it, Jamison.'

'I'm tired,' he grunted, 'and I was in a hurry. Goddamned, smart-ass lawyers.'

'That's the legal system,' I said. 'Who's the kid?'

'Cousin of the dude you blew up. Albert Lucian Swartz. They call him Bubba.'

'Makes sense.'

'Yeah, well, he and his cousin are buddies, and they were seen together earlier in the evening. They both had five hundred dollars and some change in their pockets, which is too much for unemployed construction workers. Bubba's got the broken nose, bruises and scrapes on his hands, and a bad bite on his shoulder, so we figure he was with his cousin when they jumped you.'

'Well, maybe he was, but I couldn't tell you if he was or not.'

'Or wouldn't, huh?'

'It was dark, they were behind me, and I was on the ground most of the time –'

'You stood up long enough to bite the dude, Milo. You oughta see it. I've seen some bad bites, but this one, Milo, it's terrible.'

'I wish I could remember doing it but I don't.'

'You don't recognize him at all, huh?'

'No.'

'You wouldn't lie to me, would you, Milo? Try to make this a private beef?'

'Do I look like I need a beef, private or otherwise?'

'No, you don't,' he said, sounding almost happy. 'But if you can't identify the kid, we can't go into court with it, and some people are going to be upset about that.'

'I can't help that.'

'No. You probably can't at that. That's the way it goes,' he mused, slapping me on the shoulder. 'Say, are you gonna be in your office for the next hour or so?'

'I don't know. Why?'

'I might want to get in touch with you.'

'Why?'

'Just be there, Milo. In your private office. And don't ask me why, okay?'

So I went to the other office and had another installment on breakfast, a beer and tomato juice, as I waited for Jamison. I didn't like his mood. I couldn't think of anything that would make Jamison happy that wouldn't make me unhappy. I also couldn't imagine why he wanted to meet in the other office, but as I thought about it I liked it. We could talk about things. Brandy, for instance, and vomit.

'You want a beer?' I asked him as he came in without knocking. 'Or coffee?'

'Coffee,' he said as he sat down heavily at the table. 'Black.'

'Coming right up, sir,' I said and went out to the bar and brought him back a cup of coffee. 'Why are we, ah, meeting here?'

'I don't trust you, Milo, you and your goddamned tape recorders and bugs and whatnot.'

'I'm hurt,' I said, and he smiled an odd little smile.

'Yeah.'

'What did you want?'

'Huh? Oh, to tell you that your property has been released. You can pick it up anytime. And here's your automatic, too,' he said, then took the pistol out of his belt and handed it to me. 'Be careful, it's loaded.'

'Thanks. But why didn't you tell me at the station?'

'I forgot,' he said innocently.

'Then why not call me?'

197

'You said you were coming over here, and I knew you didn't have a phone back here, so I walked over.' He talked like a man setting up an alibi.

'You're covering your ass, Jamison. Why?'

'No, I really forgot. I'm getting old and tired.'

'Maybe you ought to look for an easier job.'

'Yeah,' he said, watching his coffee, 'that's true. I got an offer, you know, a birdnest on the ground. A small town in Idaho. Four patrolmen and a dispatcher who doubles as jailer on each shift. I'd be the chief, Milo. Good money, an easy life. All the violence there takes place in the home.'

'You gonna take it?'

'I don't know yet. There are a few complications.'

'What's that?' I asked.

'Well, the kid's only got one more year of high school and he'd sorta like to finish here, and I'd like to get this heroin dealer busted before I leave town. So I don't know if I'll take it or not.'

'Sounds good,' I said, 'but you ain't here for my advice about your employment.'

'That's right.'

'So what do you want?'

'I wanted to talk to you, Milo. Unofficially, you understand. I want to know what you know about the Duffy kid and Simon's death and anything else that might help, such as why you lied about not recognizing the Swartz kid.'

'You got it all wrong. I don't know anything you don't.'

'Now, don't fuck me around on this, Milo,' he said, serious now. 'I've seen more dead bodies in the past few weeks than I usually see in a year and that makes me unhappy, you understand. How long's it been since you've had to watch a kid pulled out of the river with grappling hooks, huh? I didn't like watching that, Milo, and I don't want to have to think about it. It doesn't make me happy. And, Milo, I want the man who brought smack into my town. I'm giving you a break; you can tell me here, and I won't say a word about withholding evidence or obstruction, but if we go down to the station and you continue to bullshit me, you're gonna take a fall. A bad one. You're in over your head, Milo, caught between the rock and the hard place, and I'm giving you an easy way out. So you better take it.'

'What sorta crap is this?'

'Now, goddammit, listen to me. I've never broken a law in my life, not even when we were kids. I believe in the law, Milo, and the system and all that goes with it. I don't make busts outside the law, I don't make deals, but I want this dealer and I want him fast. The goddamned mayor has asked for state help, and I don't like that, bringing state boys into my town.'

'It's not your town, Jamison,' I said, and a burst of anger flashed across his face, but it ended nearly as quickly as it began, turning into what looked like resigned sadness.

'You're right. But it used to be.'

'Sometimes I think you're crazier than me, Jamison.'

'Sometimes I think so too.'

'Then maybe you can understand my side. I don't give a shit about the law.'

'What sort of world would it be, Milo, without law? Can't you – '

'Don't you understand,' I interrupted. 'I don't care about the world, man, about the law. That shit takes place on television, man, not in my life. The World. The Law. That doesn't have anything to do with my life, man, and Simon died in my life. I want the smack dealer too, but when I find him, I'm gonna blow his fucking head off and then call the Law. Understand?'

'I thought you might feel that way,' he said, coming up with that odd smile again. 'I guess I just wanted to be sure.'

'What?'

'I don't want this one to go to court, Milo, it's too goddamned important, but if I turn up the guy, I'll have to arrest him. Same with the state boys. But you might just blow him up, and if you've got a good story, you might get away with it.'

'I'm not sure I believe you, Jamison.'

'I don't blame you. I don't even know if I believe myself, but we won't know for sure unless we try. Will we?'

'That's damned slim,' I said, remembering Reese's line, 'but what the hell. Why not?'

'So give.'

'Okay. You were wrong about the Duffy kid. He wasn't just hooked, he was dealing.'

'I knew that,' he said tiredly.

'Then why bullshit me?'

'Because I thought he was the main man and that the supply would dry up with him dead. But either he was in with somebody else or they picked up when he died. Either way, there's still junk all over town. I just can't figure why he killed himself.'

'Maybe he didn't,' I said, not really believing myself. 'Somebody got pretty excited when I started poking around. Simon got killed, Muffin got framed, and I got the shit kicked out of me.'

'Are you sure about the Swartz cousins?'

'Yeah. The one with a broken nose wanted to kill me, but the other told him that they weren't supposed to.'

'That figures. And there's this other thing. Remember the vague description of the longhair maybe coming out of Reese's house?'

'Sure.'

'Well, the Swartz cousins were seen talking to a guy who might fit that description, and – '

'And you've been turning the town upside down looking for him but can't come up with him,' I said.

'That's what I can't understand, Milo. This town ain't that big. I've busted a couple of street pushers, but they didn't know anything.'

'What kinda smack?'

'That's another problem. It ain't Mexican.'

'That's what Reese said.'

'Oh, he talked to you, huh?'

'Yeah,' I said, 'he forgave me for being a hick cop.'

'What else did he say?'

'Two things. That this was strictly amateur stuff, and that the smack probably came out of a police locker.'

'That's what I thought too, but we've checked every police force in the Northwest, and came up empty.'

'Check again.'

'We are.'

'Did you make a brand on the brandy in the vomit on the stairs?'

'How'd you know about that?'

'Where you getting your help nowadays, Jamison?'

'Huh? Okay, I see. Outa Cracker Jack boxes, I guess. But, no, we haven't made a brand yet. We sent it to the police lab in Twin Forks, but they haven't called back. Identified the soda, though. Came from the local distributor. He delivers to every bar in town that has a speed gun. You know how many bars that is?'

'No.'

'Twenty.'

'So that's probably dead, huh?'

'Yeah,' he grunted. 'And, hell, the vomit could have belonged to anybody.'

'Or it could have come from our long-haired friend. Maybe he has a weak stomach?'

'Like an amateur?'

'Right. So what else do we have?' I said. Jamison noticed the *we* and smiled.

'Well, I didn't bring my notes, Milo. I didn't know I was gonna need them. I didn't know if I'd have the nerve to do this.'

'I don't want to make you worry, man, but I don't know if I'll have the nerve to finish it,' I admitted.

'You did all right with the dude in the alley.'

'That was different.'

'Yeah, I guess so. I guess we'll just have to see what happens, huh?'

'Right.'

'So let's get after it,' he said, standing up.

'What's this, a race?'

'Sure. I'm gonna work like a son of a bitch. Just as soon as I get back from this little fishing trip.'

'You may be crazy, Jamison.'

'Yeah. You know what I was thinking about on the way over here?'

'No,' I said, expecting nostalgia.

'Evie has this cat book and she told me once what the Turks used to do with adulterous wives.'

'What's that?'

'They'd sew them up in a canvas sack with a cannonball and two live cats, then heave it into the sea,' he said pleasantly.

'Goddamn.'

'Yeah,' he said calmly. 'Cover your ass, Milo.'

'With both hands,' I said as he walked to the door. 'You sure we got the right man?' I asked, hoping I didn't sound as uneasy as I felt holding Jamison's hunting license.

'Oh, yeah. You should've seen the money the Swartz cousins were carrying. It was junkie money, Milo, ragged and dirty, stinking with filth,' he answered, his voice filled with disgust.

'If you say so. Say, what about Muffin?'

'What about him?'

'How about pulling in the warrant?'

'Let's wait till it's over, okay? It'll look better.'

'I hope that your boys don't decide to get trigger-happy if they arrest him.'

'Tell him not to run.'

'If I see him.'

'Right,' Jamison said. 'Good hunting.'

There didn't seem to be anything for me to say, so I nodded as he went out the door.

The trouble with sudden changes in people is that it's difficult to know if the change is real or just a moment's whim. I didn't know if I should believe Jamison. Maybe he was just playing some sort of game, using me to find the dealer. But like he said: we wouldn't know unless we tried.

I still didn't know where to begin, but I left anyway. As I passed the pay phone in the bar, I remembered Muffin, but when I went to make the call, I couldn't remember the number, so I had to go up to the office. When I got there, I called the answering service. Muffin hadn't called again, but Mrs. Crider had. Several times, each message more urgent than the one before. The last one threatened physical harm if I didn't see her right away. I called her, but she insisted on seeing me, so I promised to run out before lunch. Freddy had called too, and I called him back on the mobile unit.

'What's up?'

'We got some kinda trouble, Milo. The lady slipped the tail.'

'How?'

'Went into a café and ordered a big breakfast, then left her sweater at the table and went to the john – I thought. But she went out the back door. This lady's been around.'

'Are you still at the café?'

'No. She came back about thirty minutes later in a cab, paid for the meal, got her sweater, and went home.'

'Check the cab company, see where they picked her up.'

'Already did. The driver picked her up at a pay phone next to that tourist information booth east of town.'

'Well, hell, if she was only gone thirty minutes she didn't have time to do much, so don't worry about it.'

202

'That's not what I'm worried about, Milo. I want to know who dropped her off at the phone. Why don't you check the girl in the information booth.'

'Why not.'

'How you doing?'

'I'm alive.'

'Thanks to the backup piece, Milo.'

'Right, Freddy, thanks for that.'

'Well, watch yourself.'

'All right,' I said and hung up before he could give me any more advice.

I didn't care who Wanda of Wild Rose Lane balled in her spare time, but I knew Freddy would hound me for days if I didn't stop and ask a few questions. It was on the way to the Crider house anyway. And right next to a pay phone. I had a belt from the office bottle and found the telephone number of the hunting camp owned by the fence Muffin worked for. The fence was a Charlie Pride freak, and the jukebox in the camp bar didn't have any other singers on it. If Jamison only knew, I thought, how smart Muffin and I really were. At least Muffin.

The young girl behind the counter of the tourist information kiosk looked like she had been chosen for the job to make a good impression on the tourists. She had one of those lovely model faces that shouted Fresh, Clean, and Cheerful, that sells toothpaste or gives head with the same wooden sincerity. But the girl didn't go with the face: she was working stoned out of her mind, blown away and happy about it.

'Yes, sir, what can I do for you today?' she inquired as I stepped up to the counter.

'Let's fuck.'

'Wow,' she wailed, then broke out in giggles. 'Outa sight. But what would the Chamber of Commerce say?'

'What do they say about you coming to work stoned?'

'Nothing, man, my daddy is the president.'

'Great. Say, you see that pay phone over there?'

'Outa sight, man.'

'Slow down, babe. Did you see a cab pick up a woman there about an hour ago?'

203

'You some kinda cop, man?'
'A private investigator.'
'Wow.'
'Did you see the cab?'
'You gotta be kidding, man.'
'Yeah. Have a nice day.'
'You too, man,' she said, smiling prettily.

As I walked away, two women who looked like physical education teachers, burdened with cameras and maps, strode up to the booth to ask about the most scenic route to Canada.

'Walking, driving, flying, or by bicycle?' the girl asked cheerfully.

The counterculture revolution had done something for America: it let a lot of young people handle idiot jobs by getting stoned. As I got in the rig and stuffed the automatic under the seat, I wondered why I wasn't stoned myself.

As I drove east up the valley of the Meriwether River, past the golf course where my family home had come to rest, the morning sun exploded in my face, shattering my windshield with light. The undulations of the river, as it wound through the willowed flats, sparkled like liquid silver. An old man, distinguished and gray, outfitted out of an Eddie Bauer catalog, stood thigh-deep at the verge of a dark, shaded pool, his waders sturdy against the rushing water that thrust upon them, then divided in picturesque wakes. He stood in the shade below the cut bank, but his fly line looped and whistled in the sunshine like a burning wire. I wished him good fishing. Until I saw his station wagon beside the highway, his out-of-state plates. Then I wished him gone. And a fence built around the state.

You don't fish anymore, Simon's ragged voice nagged inside my head. *You haven't fished in years.*

Leo and I went to Idaho for steelhead last year, I complained.

Fucking tourist.

When I knocked on the front door, Mrs. Crider met me carrying a large baby straddled on her cocked hip. Over her shoulder I could see two more children and their playful debris, their faces long and sad like their father's, their eyes shining with the same lonesome hope. But Mrs. Crider's eyes were blank, clouded with anger or grief, like the sky before a snowstorm.

'I'm here,' I said lamely, after a long silence made unbearable by her eyes.

'Should Ah lead a cheer? Ah been callin' you for a long time.'

'I know. I'm sorry. I've been – busy.'

'Looks like you been damn near killed,' she said quietly, her hand brushing an errant strand of hair from her face. Then she gave it back to the child, gave him a raw, bony knuckle on which to teethe.

'That's what they say.'

'How's the other fella look?'

'I'm afraid he's dead.'

'That's what Ah hear,' she said. 'And Ah also hear you found Elton that night you lied to me.'

'I'm sorry about the lie, but lies seem to be an occupational hazard in my business.'

'That so? Like your face?'

I nodded.

'Maybe you're in the wrong business.'

'I've thought about that.'

She didn't reply, but in the silence, examined my face with her hard, black eyes. I had been so busy feeling responsible for Simon's death that I had neglected the guilt festered around Elton Crider's. Her eyes took care of that, though. I doubted that his death had anything to do with the Duffy kid's, except for his grief, but under those eyes I became responsible. Before I could apologize again, the two thin boys in the living room began to argue loudly about some vague rule in their children's game, their voices rising shrilly. She turned and spat a single nasal command as sharp as the slap of stove wood against bare thighs, a flat, inchoate sound, which they obeyed instantly, falling as silent as stones, the gravely pale eyes swinging toward their mother, then away, like the eyes of small animals fleeing the rush of headlights on a nighttime country road.

''Scuse me,' she said, then stepped back into the hall. She came back with a black folder that held a slim packet of paper and handed it to me.

'What's this?'

'Ah'm not sure 'xactly. It belonged to that Duffy trash. Ah found it when Ah cleaned out Elton's desk,' she said as she moved out the door and shut it behind her. 'Let's walk a bit.' She led me across the patchy lawn; I followed like a whipped child. She wore a gray

sweat shirt, clean but stained with the bleached remains of oil and
grease, and a pair of faded blue pedal pushers left over from another
time. Beneath the thin fabric, the muscles of her legs rippled strongly.
Her bare feet had seen rough use, suffered badly fitted shoes and
rocky trails, but when they touched the grass and earth, they seemed
elegant in their confidence and strength, as certain of their power as
were her swaying hips. And she carried her head proudly, as if she
were a valuable gift. I felt a terrible pity, not for her, but for the
confusions of sex.

'I'm sorry. About your husband,' I said to her back.

'Seems only right,' she answered without turning.

'What?'

'Since it was your fault,' she said, stopping and facing me.

'I – I understood it was an accident.'

'Mister, Ah may not have a fancy education but Ah ain't dumb.
Elton wouldn't have it known for the world but he was pure country,
and he could drive when he couldn't walk. He didn't go in that river
without some kinda help. That's why Ah called you.'

'Why?' I asked, afraid of the answer, unable to lift my heavy face
to meet her eyes.

'To hire you to find out who done it –'

'Oh no. I'm – busy – I haven't recovered from the beating,' I said,
but the look on her long face disagreed.

'And when you find out who, Ah want you to kill them. Ah don't
know how much money you'd want, but Elton had some insurance
at the college, and that oughta –'

'Mrs. Crider, what makes you think you can hire me to kill somebody?'

'You owe me,' she said, then walked away into the shaded pine
trees beyond the lawn, the sleeping baby riding easily on her hip.

'What?' I asked as I caught up to her and grabbed her elbow. She
glanced at my hand, and I turned her loose. 'What?'

'The lie.'

'No,' I said, but she paid no attention, unwinding her fingers from
the baby's fist and reaching up to touch my damaged ear.

'That there ear ain't never gonna heal right,' she said, her fingers
easy and smooth on my ear as she stroked it lightly, almost as if she
thought her hand could heal. 'Never. My Uncle Ab on my mother's
side had an ear like that. Some fella came up side his head with a

beer bottle 'cause Ab was messin' with his wife. Ab stuck his pocket knife in the other fella. Killed him dead. Ab got this funny-lookin' ear and a striped suit. He gets a letter near every week from this fella's widow.'

'No,' I said again, moving her hand away from my ear.

Bars of sunlight fell across the carpet of pine needles. Glints of red sparked off her black hair. The child stirred in the silence, his hands and mouth searching blindly for the gnawed, chapped knuckle. She let him take it, and he was quiet.

'You owe me,' she said.

'Lady, you're crazy,' I said, which made her smile benignly.

'When it's over, y'all come on out and tell me all 'bout it. Ah like mysteries, watch 'em on TV all the time.'

'There aren't any mysteries.'

'Ah'll be a-lookin' for you,' she said, then walked back toward the house. As I followed, banging the folder against my leg, I wondered if she had learned that walk on television too, or in some more elemental place, and I wondered how Elton Crider ever got up the nerve to leave her. She stopped at the front door to watch me walk to my rig.

'Y'all come back, yah hear,' she said, mocking herself. Then added in a hard voice, the accent lost beneath the mixture of command and promise. 'When it's done.'

The words felt like a rough hand on my shoulder, shoving me into the front seat, reminding me of all the sore spots. I drove away, afraid to look back.

'Look, man, don't give me no bullshit,' Muffin said after I had explained that the smack charges were sure to be dropped. 'Just come up with the bread.'

So I explained everything again, sorry now that I had stopped at the open telephone booth next to the tourist information kiosk. I had chosen that pay phone because the girl behind the counter had been the only pleasant thing that had happened to me all morning. But it had been a mistake. She was busy with the tourists, who stood around the kiosk as if they were waiting for a tour bus. Only one couple, a gray-haired man and his wife, wanted to use the telephone and they had the decency to stand far enough away so they couldn't overhear me. There were a number of small children who lacked any decency at all. I guess it was the face, but I wished that they were frightened instead of curious. It seems to take something really terrible to frighten children today, and it seemed that I was curious instead of terrible because I couldn't make them go away. I couldn't make Muffin believe me either.

'Milo, you've been a wonderful father, and I thank you, but, man, I need that mad money of yours. I'm good for it, man, you know that.'

'What is it? Don't you believe me? Don't you trust me? You think – '

'I think you're gonna fuck it up, man,' he interrupted, and I couldn't blame him for thinking that.

'Just hang on for a few more days, okay?'

'No, man, this dude up here is getting real nervous having me around, and he ain't nervous at all compared to me. I know what the slammer looks like from the outside, and that's all I want to know, man, that's all. Hell, I was counting on you for the bread, but if you ain't got it – '

'I got it,' I said, 'I'll bring it up this afternoon. Okay?'

'That's so fine, man, I can't tell you. And, hey.'

'What?'

'Don't let anybody tail you, huh?'

'Oh, shit, Muffin, shut up,' I said and hung up.

'My mother says it isn't polite to say "Shut up," ' I was informed by a little girl standing beside me.

'Tell her I said I'm sorry, okay?' I told her, ruffling her hair. She smiled as if she fully intended to.

When I glanced at the girl behind the counter, her smile was harried but undaunted, reminding me of Mindy. The Holy Light Hog Farm was a few miles out of the way but in the same general direction as the north-fork hunting camp where Muffin was waiting for my money. I thought about dropping by to say hello to Mindy and Reese. But when I climbed into my rig, I saw the black folder and remembered that I was supposed to be working, so I headed back to the office for mad money and a drink.

15

After I filled my wallet with my two thousand, I added a thousand of Nickie's and hoped I could cover it somehow. Then I sat down at the desk to have a drink and take a quick look at the folder Mrs. Crider had given me. But I thought about her instead. She was a hell of a woman. She had asked me to kill without even flinching. I liked that, but it also scared me. We weren't even on first-name terms yet, but she assumed because I had lied to her that I owed her a murder. Just as Jamison assumed that I owed Simon one too. Unfortunately, I didn't know who was owed what. And I began to wonder about their judgment of my character. So I opened the folder. It was the beginning of his thesis on Dalton Kimbrough and Western justice. As I had told Helen Duffy, my great-grandfather made his way into law enforcement and capital gains by killing Dalton Kimbrough, so I had always been interested.

But the thesis wasn't a simple history of Dalton Kimbrough or an estimation of Western justice. It was an examination of the difference between myth and reality in the Western hero and villain. The Duffy kid began with the distance between the Wyatt Earp created by Ned Buntline and the often too human lawman, then passed on through the careers of Billy the Kid, Joaquin Murieta, Jack Slade, et al. – the easy research – and on to the life and hard times of that infamous outlaw, highwayman and killer, Dalton Kimbrough. As it turned out, Dalton was a man ahead of his times: he handled his own public relations. The first thing he did was change his name from Ernest Ledbetter to the more heroic Dalton Kimbrough, then out of a spotty criminal career that included one arrest and one gunfight he made a name for himself throughout the gold fields of the post-Civil War West.

His solitary arrest record was for shoplifting in St. Joe, Missouri, where he had been raised. The shopkeeper had collared Dalton with a pocketful of .44 rounds and an old Navy Colt under his coat. The revolver was a paperweight with no firing pin. Dalton did his thirty days, then headed west for a life of crime and excitement in the gold camps. Dalton drank, tried mining, and probably hung around the bars more than he should have, looking for trouble. One winter, over in Montana, in a log-cabin bar just large enough for a four-foot plank bar, one table and two bunks on the opposite wall, Dalton finally found a gunfight in the midst of a poker game.

When the gunfire ended, everybody's revolver empty, there was a great deal of smoke and powder burns, but nobody had been hit. Except the bartender's dog, which had been killed by a single round through the lungs. The game resumed peacefully amid smoke and the good feelings that come with survival, only to be disturbed again. This time by odd groans from a miner sleeping off a drunk in the lower bunk. When they turned him over to tell him to shut up, they found a large puddle of blood beneath his body from a round that had passed through his thigh. He groaned once more, then died from the loss of blood. Dalton, ever ready for fame, claimed both killings as his very own, and nobody bothered to dispute his claim.

Dalton also boasted of numerous stage holdups and bank robberies, all of which either never took place in recorded history or were committed by other men, who had never heard of Dalton Kimbrough. As far as anybody knows, Dalton took part in only one stage holdup, his last one. Perhaps the gunfight in the bar went to his head. Later the same winter, he and two men stopped the Salt Lake stage as it topped the south pass into the Meriwether Valley, the stage carrying my great-grandfather to his new home, an Army wife with her young son, and a strongbox.

As the horses were blowing at the top of the pass, three armed men appeared on horseback, demanding the strongbox, which was bolted to the coach floor. Dalton fired five rounds at the lock, but it didn't open. So he went after the passengers. My great-grandfather couldn't speak English but he could count, and he was often courageously surly. When Dalton tried to open his coat to see if he carried a money belt, he met an unhappy Russian, who grabbed him in a clumsy hug. As they struggled, one of the mounted outlaws pulled off a round. Right through Dalton Kimbrough's kidneys. He fired once more from his wildly bucking horse, hitting the frightened stagecoach driver in the chin, then his horse pitched him off. When he hit the frozen ground, he went out cold. The third outlaw, who finally decided to take control, also began to fire, but for reasons unrecorded – probably either wet or forgotten percussion caps – his revolver wouldn't fire. He cocked the hammer and pulled the trigger several times, then rode away in disgust, never to be heard of again.

After being shot through the kidneys, Dalton lost his taste for holdups and fights. He fell to the ground in my great-grandfather's embrace, where his skull was crushed by a large stone in a Russian peasant's burly hand. When the snow had settled, my great-grandfather trussed the unconscious outlaw like a pig and tossed him into the boot with Dalton's body, bound the driver's face, helped the lady back into the stage, then drove into history. As soon as his English was passable, he was hired as Meriwether's constable, then elected sheriff, and nearly appointed territorial governor. In death, Dalton Kimbrough's public relations paid off. For my great-grandfather.

And in a less obvious way, for the stagecoach driver too. He stayed around town for years, wearing a scarf over his missing chin, becoming a local curiosity and drunk. The Army wife found her husband shacked up with a Willomot squaw, which she might have forgiven if he hadn't been cashiered too, so she went back East, where people were civilized. Dalton Kimbrough's body was hung next to his partner's, the good folk of Meriwether deciding that stringing him up dead was nearly as good an example to potential outlaws as hanging him if he had been alive.

As the years passed in the usual manner, the story bloomed into heroics with the aid of imaginative newspaper editors and my great-grandfather's whiskey. According to Duffy's thesis, my great-grandfather encouraged the Kimbrough myth to further his own political ambitions, which was probably true. At the end of the typed pages, he scrawled a sour note: *A fucking klutz.* I got the impression that although he believed his thesis, he didn't especially like it, preferring myth to reality even as he cast the terrible light of a debunking truth across the years of Dalton Kimbrough's petty life.

All this was twice as sad because the truth about Kimbrough and my great-grandfather had been known for years before Raymond Duffy found Willy Jones and his papers. Even the B Western filmed in the early fifties had to invent a hero: the chinless stage driver. In the movie, he knows the truth of the Milodragovitch pose and the puniness of Kimbrough's villainy, but is unable to tell anybody. Until he is taught to write by a gentle schoolmarm from Philadelphia. Then he is able to expose the character of my great-grandfather as a cowardly and overbearing sham. In the last scene, the actor playing Milodragovitch lies sprawled in the middle of a dusty, back-lot street, the victim of unfounded pride and drunkenness. As the camera draws back, the sober, upright storekeeper, who has shotgunned the mad Russian and his knouted hand, is seen advancing like a cartoon hunter clutching a hammerless double-barreled shotgun. Then the frame widens to include the chinless hero, his eyes above the scarf suggesting a triumphant but sad smile, his hand on the schoolmarm's delicate arm. She is smiling too, but in a rather pinched way, as if the chinless wonder needs a bath. They do not embrace. Music rises. Dissolve to list of cast.

Just to set the record straight: my great-grandfather died quite bitterly sober in an old folks' home.

There is a quaintly modern notion that information will eventually equal knowledge, which is neatly balanced by the cliché that the more one learns, the less one knows. Both ideas are probably more or less accurate, but neither is particularly useful in dealing with the human animal.

As I thought of Raymond Duffy, nothing came to mind. An image remembered from a bar, his eyes as black as gun barrels glistening with pleasure above his pale cheeks. They were murderous, not suicidal. And even though Reese had said that the kid was very depressed over the death of Willy Jones, I couldn't see him killing himself. *Maybe it was an accident, pure and simple, dumb ass, a mistake.* But I still needed a reason, if not for his death, then at least for his depression beforehand. If I knew what caused the depression, then I would be able to justify accidental death. Mistakes do happen. Like my father's death, which I had always thought of as an accident caused by the mistake of leaving the bolt open on his deer rifle, of not looking at the shotgun as he lifted it out of the closet, of not checking the safety when he put it away . . .

But as I thought of these things, an odd feeling came over me. I was missing something. And suddenly I knew and was damned sorry that I did. I remembered his first lecture about guns: Always keep them loaded, a full magazine and a round in the chamber, and you'll

212

never be killed by an empty gun; keep the safety on, check that always, but keep them loaded. Drunk or sober, he had never made a mistake with a gun; he put them away loaded, the safety on. But I remembered as clearly as I remembered the bloody stain on the hallway ceiling that the bolt of the deer rifle was open, the chamber empty. I wondered how long he had planned it, that accident planted in the hall closet like a bomb.

I had a sip of whiskey, which seemed proper, but I was too tired and sore to feel any real grief. If that was the way he had wanted it, then I wasn't about to disagree with him. I wondered if my mother knew, and decided that she did. Some knowledge rises out of information, disorganized but nonetheless true. If he couldn't kill himself with a whiskey bottle, my father had to make do with guns, which made me wonder why the Duffy kid had chosen drugs instead of his pistols . . .

'Bingo,' I said to myself and sat up straight in my chair.

Even though it seemed that my father's death wasn't caused by a mistake after all, I'd bet good, or bad, money that Willy Jones's had been. If you play with guns long enough, my father had told me, eventually you'll kill somebody. And I saw the Duffy kid, drug-crazed, playing with guns, drawing and snapping the trigger in the old drunk's face, saw the round left in the cylinder by mistake, saw the old man's face explode, the back of his head hit the far wall, skull fragments and blood and brain matter all over the room. Hollywood, and quick-draw contests; that would drive him over the edge. When he saw what firearms are meant to do, when he saw the effect of an unjacketed lead round fired into a human face, that would make him throw his pistols away, cut his hair and discard his gunfighter's clothes. I knew. At that range, when a bullet enters the human head, the hydrostatic pressure blows the face up like a cheap balloon; the eardrums burst, the eyes pop out, and the head seems to dissolve in a shower of blood. Oh God, did I know, and not want to at all.

Assuming that I had had a hard day that morning, I had a long drink, then another before I called Amos Swift. He agreed that he might have missed powder burns and a gunshot wound in Willy Jones's head because the body had been so badly burnt. But he bet money that he wouldn't miss it a second time. If I could come up with something solid enough to convince a judge to sign an exhumation order. I told him I hoped it wouldn't be necessary, then hung up.

What a mess, I thought, what a hard day. I called Helen just to hear her voice, to remind myself why I was doing all this. She came to the telephone on the ninth ring, answered it breathlessly, timidly.

'Hello?'

'It's nice to know you're still there,' I said.

'Oh. I'm still here. I just – didn't know if I should answer your telephone – I was in the backyard – and I tripped coming in the back door.'

'Are you all right?'

'Oh yes – I'm fine. How are you?'

'I'm not in jail, anyway. I'm in pain,' I said lightly, 'but free.'

'Oh – I'm glad.'

'Are you going to be there when I get back?'

'Are you – coming home – right now? I didn't know . . . when you were coming back.'

'Well,' I said, thinking about the trip up the north fork with Muffin's money, 'I've got a few things to do yet. It'll take three or four hours, but I'll be home to take you out to dinner. If you don't mind being seen in public with me.'

'Of course not,' she answered, sounding happy instead of confused. 'It's a date.'

'Okay,' I said. 'Hey, you know it's nice to call my house and have you answer the phone.'

'Oh – oh – I'm sorry about – this morning.'

'So am I, but let's forget about it.'

'Okay – if you want . . . I'll – see you tonight.'

'Take care,' I said.

'You too,' she answered hesitantly, then we both hung up.

Whatever I'd expected out of the call to make me feel better hadn't been there, but telephones had always had some sort of curse on me anyway, so I didn't worry about it. I started to take the office bottle with me but decided to put it back in the drawer. By the time I reached the top of Willomot Hill the weight of the morning made me regret my decision. I turned into the empty parking lot of the Willomot Bar, thinking to get a couple of drinks in go cups and maybe have an unfriendly chat with the owner, Jonas. I could depend on him not to change character, not to confuse me. He had hated my guts for years, and there was something reassuring about that.

Jonas was sitting at the first table inside the door, leaning back in a chair, his tiny boots crossed on the battered tabletop, his narrow eyes watching the tourist traffic avoid his place like the plague, watching the rectangle of sunlight retreat across his dirty floor toward the doorway. Standing in the bright doorway, I assumed I must have been an anonymous shade because Jonas smiled as I stepped in. I guess the smile was too much. I lifted my foot and shoved his table. He went over backwards, thumping his head solidly against the cement floor.

Jonas was small, but stout as a stump and meaner than a sow bear, with quick hands and agile feet. He wasn't a big man but he was damn sure a handful of trouble. I had taken him before, three or four times, but that had been in the line of duty, sort of, and I had used the sap or a billy. I had a frozen moment to remember my face and all the aches and pains, especially my nose, and to regret most of my life. Two middle-aged bucks sat over shot glasses at the end of the bar, working on their hangovers, and the thick-faced barmaid stood across from them. The three heads swiveled toward the crashing sound of Jonas and furniture. One buck banked toward the back door past the dark shadow of the bear, but the other raised his glass, either toasting me or trying to hustle a drink. The barmaid simply looked away in boredom.

But Jonas wasn't bored. He rolled once, came up ready, his feet spread, his short thick arms cocked, his head bobbing and weaving like that of a punch-drunk fighter, then he saw me and broke out in a mean grin.

'What the hell's happening, Milo?' he asked happily. 'You drunk 'fore noon, you old son of a bitch? What the hell happened to your face? Hey, man, I heard 'bout poor ol' Simon. What a fuckin' shame. He usta be a hell of a man. Did I ever tell you 'bout the time he got my old man off a manslaughter bust? The old man found two goddamned tourists cleanin' a cow elk up in that timber on the other side a the ridge and he cut down on the dumb-asses, and . . .'

As he rattled on with his favorite Simon story, he came around the table, kicking chairs out of the way with an absent-minded violence that amazed me all over again. He grabbed my arm and led

215

me to the bar, shouting for shots and beers, shaking my hand over and over, pausing only long enough to gun his shot and half the beer chaser. By the time he finished his story, he had forgotten why he was telling it to me.

'Oh yeah. Simon. Goddamned old drunk. Goddammit, I'm sorry 'bout him. That's a nasty way to go, man, ugly. I seen a bum one time when I was a kid been hit by a train, and that was bad as I ever wanna see, but when I heard 'bout how Simon got it, man, I nearly got sick,' he prattled. 'And goddammit, Milo, you know nothing makes me sick.' Then he laughed happily.

'Wish I could say the same,' I said, but he didn't hear me through the laughter. Then an odd thing happened: I almost liked the little bastard, even after all the trouble. Of course, it had been at least ten years since we had tangled, but those times didn't count the nights when he had been drunk enough to argue with me about who to arrest but sober enough to remember that I had fifty pounds and a badge on him. When he stopped laughing, I said, 'You know it's a goddamned sorry day when I can't even pick a fight with you, Jonas.'

That made him laugh so hard that he blew beer foam all over the bar and his dark face. As he wiped his face, he said fondly, 'Goddamn, we usta have some dandy times, didn't we. Seems like ever other night you'd come in here and put knots on my head a goddamned goat couldn't climb. Hey, you still got that little flat sap?'

'Yeah, I think so,' I said, trying to remember where it had gone to. 'No, I think the police have it. Hell, I don't know.'

'I tell you, Milo, that thing was mean,' he said, as if that was the nicest compliment he knew. 'Goddamn, those were some times. Shit, somma the boys up on the reservation are still 'bout half afraid of you. You see that ol' boy take off when you come in?'

'Yeah.'

'Well, that was his older brother knocked you cold that time and drove you down to the jailhouse. Half-brother, I think it was. Anyway, he ain't near as mean. That's why he took off when you come in.'

'That was a long time ago, Jonas.'

'You tellin' me – shit, we're too old for rough and tumble, Milo, and hell, you already sewed up and taped together like a busted watermelon. Hell, you look so bad a fella'd be afraid to give you a good shot. Might kill you,' he said, and as if to prove his point, he thumped me in the ribs with a short, affectionate punch that nearly knocked me down.

'Not in the ribs, Jonas,' I grunted, trying to breathe.

'Sorry 'bout that. Heard you took a hell of a beatin'. Got that one son of a bitch, huh? Blew his fuckin' head right off, huh. That'll teach them goddamned hippies not to mess around with home folks, huh.'

'He was a construction worker, Jonas,' I explained, knowing it wouldn't make any difference.

'Yeah, whatever, he ain't gonna mess with nobody no more, right?' he said, lifting a new shot.

'Right.'

He waited for me to lift my shot, but I didn't know if it would stay down behind the memories, the new and bitter knowledge of the morning. It did but it didn't want to.

'So how's business?' Jonas asked, thumping me again.

'Not so good,' I said. 'Say, were you in here the night the kid OD'd in your john? About a month ago?'

'Don't remind me of it, Milo. The goddamn Liquor Control Board tried to take my license, but hell, that's nothing new,' he said, then laughed again. 'Why?'

'That's what I'm working on now.'

'Who for?' he asked, his eyes squinting with suspicion.

'The family. They weren't too happy with the sheriff's investigation.'

'What investigation? That old bastard can't find his ass with either hand. Hell, there wasn't anything to investigate anyway.'

'They just wanted to know what happened.'

'Nothing happened, Milo. The kid comes in, orders a drink, then goes into the john. A couple hours later somebody complains that they can't take a crap because the stall door is locked, so I climb over and find him dead, sittin' there like he's passed out, but when I seen that needle in his arm I figured he was dead. That's funny, he didn't look the type.'

'Had he ever been in before that night?'

'Hell, Milo, they come and go. I don't know. But probably not. He was such a clean-cut-lookin' kid, not like that bunch a mangy goddamned hippies in town, that I'd probably remember. He didn't look the type to be on that dope.'

217

'That's what I hear,' I said. 'Did he come in with anybody?'

'Well, Milo, I was busier than a one-legged man at an ass-kicking contest and I was a hair drunk, so I don't know.'

'What was he drinking?'

'A draw,' Jonas answered quickly. He had a bartender's memory for faces and drinks. 'And there wasn't nobody with him, 'cause that's all I got was the one beer.'

'Where did he sit?'

'All the way down at the end of the bar.'

'Anybody sitting next to him?'

'Shit, Milo, I don't know,' he answered, sorry that he couldn't help.

'That's okay,' I said, 'it's not really important.' Then I thought about the guy with long black hair and a beard. 'Hey, there didn't happen to be a hippie in here that night, a guy with black hair and a beard?'

'I'll be damned. There sure was. Sittin' right next to the kid. I remember 'cause they ain't welcome here and they figure that out real quick, so we don't get many. Yeah, and 'cause he was a little old to be runnin' around like a goddamned hairy ape. He had on sunglasses too, but hell, I could tell he wasn't no kid.'

'You remember what he was wearing?'

'Milo, I could shut my eyes right now,' Jonas said, 'and I wouldn't be able to tell you what you was wearing.'

'What was he drinking?' I asked, sipping at my beer.

'Brandy and soda, no ice,' he answered quick as a shot, then motioned for another round.

Bingo. Goddammit, how could I be so dumb? Goddamned Nickie. Jesus.

'Help?' he asked.

'I don't know,' I said, forcing the thoughts and feelings out of me, retreating to hide the fear. 'Lots of people drink brandy and soda.'

'Yeah,' he said as he raised his glass. 'Sorry I don't remember more.'

'Thanks anyway, Jonas. Next time you're in town, stop by. The drinks are on me,' I said, then had a sip of beer and started to leave, but Jonas grabbed my arm.

'Wanna do me a favor, Milo?' he asked in a conspiratorial whisper so I would know it was an illegal favor. I shrugged, and Jonas took that as an affirmative answer. 'You seen Muffin lately? I got this friend on the other side of the mountains, and he's buildin' this motel. One big son of a bitch, two hundred units. But he's kinda strapped for capital right now, goddamned inflation, and he ain't got the bread for the color TV's and he can't come up with no credit he can afford. You know what I mean?'

'I'll act like I don't, Jonas. Muffin's out of business anyway.'

'That's too bad. There's a pretty penny in this deal, Milo. How 'bout puttin' me in touch with somebody else?'

'I don't know anybody, sorry.'

'Don't shit me, Milo,' he said, grinning like a small animal.

I wanted to grin back, but couldn't. Just like I wanted to rub my tired, hot face. Jonas was mean and crooked and slightly dumb, but the face he turned toward me was warm with affection. That has to count for something.

'Okay,' I said.

'How big a piece you want?'

'Nothing. I owe you, Jonas.'

'What?'

'Hell, I don't know. Maybe all those lumps on your head. I don't know.'

He grinned again, his tiny yellowed teeth nearly as dark as his Indian face, and started to poke me in the ribs. But he remembered not to.

'That don't matter none, Milo, not at all. Those were good times. Hell, you never tried to shake me down or run me in for some petty shit. You were fair, Milo, and I could count on you,' he said. 'Hey, by God, next time I'm in town, let's you an' me just get drunker than pigs in shit, then go down to them hippie bars and just kick the shit outa somebody. Anybody messes with us, we'll blow their fuckin' heads off. How 'bout it? Be like the old days, 'cept we'll be on the same side.'

'We've probably been on the same side all along and just didn't know it, Jonas, but I damn sure don't want to kill anybody . . .'

'Hey, you all right?' he asked as I headed for the john to heave it all up.

All drunks have theories, endlessly tedious arguments, both vocal and silent, with which to justify their drinking. They drink to forget or remember, to see more clearly or discover blindness, they drink

219

out of fear of success or failure, drink to find a home and love or drink to get away. Their lives revolve around drink. Some of the theories may well be true, but because drunks lie so much, it's difficult to divide the sharp perceptions from the sorry rationalizations. Once, my father talked to me about drinking and drunks, and in my memory it sounds not at all sorry. Just sad.

I was a boy, but old enough to have already realized that even the simplest life was too complex, that my parents lived together without very much love, that I was both curse and prize in their battles; old enough to love my father without thinking that I had anything for which to forgive him. It was then, when I was old enough to be sad, that one afternoon my father and I had gone fishing. As it usually happened, we lodged in a country bar to wet our whistles before we wet our lines, and as usual, we stayed in the bar, letting the trout, as my father said, grow one more day. 'Tomorrow, son,' he'd say, 'they'll be just the right size.' Tomorrow. And every time we caught a trout, he'd hold it up and tell me, 'See, son, just right.'

But this afternoon we stayed in the bar, and sometime during the long hours of drinking, he disappeared into the john and stayed much longer than usual. I was a child among strangers, a youth to be regaled with the hopes they no longer possessed because I had a future and they had only pasts. Slightly frightened by all this weight, I went to look for my father.

He was kneeling at the toilet, his eyes fearfully shot with blood from the efforts of his retching. A long string of glutinous spittle looped heavily from his trembling lips to the stained toilet bowl.

He spit and asked how I was doing; knowing I was frightened, he was calm. 'Don't worry about me, son,' he said, 'I'm all right. I been bellied up to this trough a time or two before. You go on out and wait for me, okay? I'll be out in a minute.' As I went out the door, I tried not to hear the convulsive, heaving rasp, tried not to be disgusted by the only person in the world I loved.

But I heard and was disgusted. I went all the way outside the bar to the porch, where I watched the afternoon steal across green hayfields and pastures, the shadows of the mountain ridges reaping light, sowing darkness. After the dank, torpid air inside the bar, air more like smoke, the air outside seemed as fresh and clean as spring water, and I filled my lungs with gasp after gasp, sucking down the sobs, vowing as seriously as only a frightened child can that I would grow up and never drink, ignoring the fact that I already sipped from my father's glass whenever I pleased. I vowed, promised in innocence already lost.

He came out behind me, a huge dark man smiling tiredly, a glass of neat whiskey in his large hand. With the first swallow, he rinsed out his mouth, then spit off the porch into the dust that rimmed the parking lot. The second, he drank, emptying the glass. Then he patted me on the head, perhaps sensing what I felt. Even at his drunkest, he was kind and perceptive, at least around me. As he held my head in his great hand, I was warm in the lingering sunset chill.

'Son,' he said without preamble, 'never trust a man who doesn't drink because he's probably a self-righteous sort, a man who thinks he knows right from wrong all the time. Some of them are good men, but in the name of goodness, they cause most of the suffering in the world. They're the judges, the meddlers. And, son, never trust a man who drinks but refuses to get drunk. They're usually afraid of something deep down inside, either that they're a coward or a fool or mean and violent. You can't trust a man who's afraid of himself. But sometimes, son, you can trust a man who occasionally kneels before a toilet. The chances are that he is learning something about humility and his natural human foolishness, about how to survive himself. It's damned hard for a man to take himself too seriously when he's heaving his guts into a dirty toilet bowl.'

Then he paused for a long minute and added, 'And, son, never trust a drunk except when he's on his knees.'

When I glanced up, he was smiling an oddly distant smile, like a man who can see his own future and accepts it without complaint.

If he had left it at that, I might not have understood, but he raised his empty glass and pointed at the vista. The fields, a lush, verdant green, grew dark with shadows, nearly as dark as the pine-thick ridges, but the sky above still glowed a bright, daylight blue. A single streak of clouds, like a long trail of smoke, angled away from the horizon, flaming a violent crimson at the far end as if it had been dipped in blood. But the middle was light pink, and the end nearest us was an ashen gray.

'A lovely view, isn't it, son?'

'Yes, sir.'

'But it's not enough,' he said, smiling, then he walked back into the bar, laughing and shouting for whiskey, love and laughter, leaving me suspended in the pellucid air.

Vomiting into the toilet of the Willomot Bar, not from the drink but from the knowledge and the dying, I felt my father's hand holding my head. He had left me this legacy of humility, and I accepted it. Where her little brother lost his life, I found mine, and understood that I wasn't going to kill anybody, except myself, and not myself for a long time yet. I remembered Simon telling me to slow down, not to drink myself to death before I had time to enjoy it. When I finished puking, I went back into the bar to wash out my mouth with whiskey.

16

When I woke the next morning, Jonas's bar resembled the field where the spirits of animals had done wild and lengthy battle with demons and ghosts, and triumphed. At least their eyes seemed glassy with victory, and their teeth bared in sneers of conquest as their heads surveyed the wreckage.

Tables and chairs had been upended, some reduced to splinters and kindling wood. Rags of clothing huddled about, some draped over the inert bodies of the slain. The floor was carpeted with fragments of glass and cigarette butts that didn't cover the drying whiskey stains. An improbably large brassiere dangled between the antlers of a bull elk, covering his eyes like a pair of cute Hollywood sunglasses. The only body I recognized in the dim morning light was Jonas's sprawled at the feet of his grizzly bear. I had been sleeping with my face in an ash tray, and when I brushed away the ashes, I wished I hadn't. My face hadn't healed during the long night. Fresh blood had dripped from my ear onto the front of my windbreaker, and when I checked it, it felt damn funny, hot and swollen, but intact. I didn't have any scrapes on my knuckles, so if I had had a fight, I had lost quickly.

I rose carefully, checking my wallet and limbs, found them, then lurched behind the bar for a cold beer, which I drank before moving on, taking one for the road. When I walked outside into a splendid sunrise, even though I hadn't taken Muffin his money or called Helen to tell her I wasn't coming home that night, I felt absolutely great. I was still drunk as a lord.

I only hoped I could hang on to it long enough to do something about Nickie.

*

223

Helen had the front door on the chain, so I had to hammer on the chimes until she came, haggard and perplexed. She opened the door on a bare toe, and as she bent over to comfort it, she hit me in the ribs with her head. We stood around a few minutes, checking our wounds, but she recovered before I did.

'Where in the name of Christ have you been?' she growled, brushing her hair away from her face, blocking the doorway. 'Just where the hell have you been?'

'Drunk.'

'How could you do that to me?' she wailed, covering her face with her hands.

'I did it to myself, lady.'

'I think I could learn to hate you,' she said, opening her hands. Her eyes were sparkling green in the shadow. When I didn't answer, she stomped her foot and grunted, 'I could!'

'Lady, I've been playing this scene in doorways all my fucking life, and I don't have the time this morning to – '

But when I cursed, a soft ululation quivered from her throat, and she shoved me out of the way and slammed the door in my face.

'It's my goddamned house!' I shouted. After a long pause, she opened the door, smiling.

'Nobody's perfect,' she said, giggling, and we fell into each other's arms, laughing and crying and kissing, ignoring my face, trying to fill our hopelessly hungry mouths with each other, her green robe open, my pants down, we fell to the carpet like leaves circling in a light wind, leaves falling into water.

'See,' I said afterwards as our breath still gushed into the morning air. 'I told you it would be all right.'

'Ohhh,' she groaned, sighing and snuggling closer. 'Jesus, I don't – think – it's ever been – that sudden. My God – I never knew – before – why the Victorian poets – called it dying.'

'You forgive me for staying out all night, huh?'

'Right now – I'll forgive you – for anything – whewww – if you'll close – the front door.' Then she giggled happily.

'It's too late,' I said. 'I heard the paper boy fall off his bike.'

'That'll teach him – to spy on people,' she murmured, then we held each other, crushing our bodies together, as if one couldn't live without the presence of the other.

'We're gonna be all right,' I said, and felt her head nodding against my chest.

But we couldn't lounge on the hall carpet forever. Eventually, I kicked the door shut, pulled up my pants, and we hobbled into the bedroom like two old people to lose the morning in sleep. I meant to know what to do when I awoke, but it didn't work that way. When I woke, it was in the confusion of a hangover worse than a beating, with a foul mouth and a numbing depression. That old familiar feeling.

After a long hot shower, two hits of speed and two of Amos's pain pills, and a cold beer, I managed to eat a piece of toast left over from the morning before. Afterwards, I walked out to the rig to get the pistol and the shoulder holster, then went back inside to finish dressing.

'Hey,' I said, shaking her beneath the covers, 'I'm going to town. This time I will be back.'

'Where are you going?' she asked, sitting up with a wonderfully sleepy and pleased smile.

'To work.'

'Not today,' she said, pulling me toward her, 'not now.' Then she felt the pistol. 'What's that?' The smile fled.

'A pistol.'

'What's it for?'

'Sometimes I carry it,' I answered as lightly as I could. 'It makes me feel better when I've got a hangover.'

'You know,' she whispered, covering her open mouth with her hand. 'I'm scared.'

'There's nothing to be afraid of.'

'You know – who killed Raymond.'

'I think so, yes, but I'm not sure.'

'Are you going to kill them?' she asked, no longer afraid, her eyes narrow and mean.

'No.'

'Who is it?'

'Nobody you know.'

'Kill them,' she demanded, her teeth clenched tightly. 'Kill him.'

'Don't be silly,' I said. 'I can't go around killing people.'

'Don't say that to me – my mother says that. I'm not silly – kill him.'

225

'Love, I can't.'

'Then give me the gun,' she said, eyes blazing madly, 'give me the gun.' She tried to reach beneath my windbreaker, but I grabbed her arms. 'Turn me loose.'

'Hey, lady, settle down.'

'Do it!'

I released her hands, and she reached for the pistol again.

'Do it! For me!' she screamed, the words seeming to open the wounds in my face stitch by stitch, to pound like a stake into the center of my face, between my eyes. 'For me!'

I shook her shoulders until she stopped, fighting off her hands, which clawed at my face and chest. The back of her hand brushed my nose, bringing tears. I pushed her down on the bed, shaking her harder, shoving her against the bed until the screams became sobs, until she stopped fighting.

'Hey, I'll be back in a little while, okay?' I told her, but she ignored me, so I left her there, sobbing.

But as I opened the front door she screamed, 'I won't be here unless you do it!'

As I walked out to the rig I couldn't tell why I was crying.

Not knowing what to think, I went to Mahoney's and had another drink, trying again to forget it. But I couldn't. I still saw those wild eyes, oddly familiar, that fractured face. I told myself I just didn't understand her grief, that she would be all right by the time I went back. I did understand that I still felt terrible, so I cranked another hit of speed into my system, another pain pill, and another drink. A deep breath, then I was ready. I called Freddy from the pay phone in the bar, told him to go down to the house on Wild Rose Lane and tell Wanda that the game was over, that she had better head out.

'What's this all about?' he asked.

'Don't ask, Freddy. Just for once do what I tell you without asking, okay?'

'What the hell's wrong with you, Milo? You sound like death warmed over.'

'Apt description, fat man. Just tell her and don't answer any questions, then go back up the hill to see what she does. Okay?'

'You're the boss,' he said, and for once I believed him.

226

I hung up and called the hunting camp to apologize to Muffin, to tell him that I had the man.

'Let me speak to your urban representative,' I told Muffin's boss.

'Buddy, we don't have no urban representative.'

'Goddammit, this is Milo. Let me talk to Muffin.'

'Nobody here by that name.'

'What's wrong? They got a tap on your line?'

'No, Milo. I pay a creep like you good money to make sure, but I don't know about your line.'

'I'm at a pay phone.'

'Why didn't you say so?'

'I don't know. Just let me talk to Muffin.'

'Can't, man, he split last night.'

'Did he say where he was going?'

'Don't be stupid all your life, Milo.'

'Okay. Did he leave a message.'

'Yeah, lemme see, here it is. *Orphans have to adopt themselves eventually*. What the hell's that mean?'

'I don't know,' I said. 'Probably means I should have never sent him to college.'

'Huh?'

'Nothing.'

'Say, Milo, there's a problem.'

'What's that?'

'Expenses. I fronted him a grand, he said you'd cover it. Familial duty, he called it, or something like that.'

'Okay,' I said, 'it's covered.'

'When?'

'As soon as I get up there.'

'Make it sooner, okay?'

'Fuck off.'

'Don't talk to me like that, Milo,' he said pleasantly, 'or I'll have your legs broken.'

'I got the money in my pocket, but it'll take me a couple of days to get loose down here.'

'Tomorrow will be fine.'

'The day after. Hey, I gotta deal for you.'

'What?'

'Two hundred television sets, color.'

'I don't deal black-and-white, man, there ain't no percentage in that. Where?'

'I want Muffin's piece of the action.'

'Only if you deliver the sets, Milo.'

'No way.'

'Then twenty-five percent of what Muffin would have made.'

'No deal.'

'Fine,' he said and hung up before I could disagree.

As I walked back to the bar I wondered if I'd ever hear from Muffin, then decided that I probably would. I wished I had told him before he left that he and my natural son were equal heirs in my will, but then I thought better. No sense in passing on my mother's unhappiness. I leaned on the bar and ordered a beer to sip while I waited for Freddy to call back, and I saw my face in the mirror. It wasn't the face of a hero – no character, no dignity. Just the face of another drunk who had bitten off more than he could ever hope to chew, a face so battered and unhappy and bloated that not even Leo could save it with his camera.

'How's Leo?' I asked the bartender.

'They moved him over to Duck Valley two days ago. Didn't you know?' The state mental hospital was in the same valley as the prison. 'He was in bad shape.'

'Did they say how long he had to stay?'

'Six months, a year maybe. Didn't you see him?'

'No,' I said. 'I've been busy.'

'Looks like it,' he said, handing me my beer, then going to answer the phone.

It was Freddy. Wanda had split from Wild Rose Lane without looking back. I didn't want it to be Nickie, but it was, and the only thing I could find to be angry about was that he thought I would quit after a beating, and I guess I was only angry about that because he was right. Maybe that's why I intended to go after him instead of calling Jamison. I told Freddy to come on and have a drink on me.

Waiting at the end of the bar for Nickie to walk through, I sat over a slow drink, but when he came in, he didn't look surprised. Just tired and gray and drawn.

'How's the boy, Milo? Feeling better?'

'Not too bad. How's yourself?'

'Fine, fine,' he said, rubbing his stomach and mouthing a silent belch. 'Let me buy you a drink. It's a little early for me, but maybe I'll have one too.' The bartender was busy at the other end, so Nickie went behind the bar and mixed the drinks. Mine was almost all whiskey. Mama DeGrumo watched him carefully from her perch, nodding once as our eyes met.

'What is it, Nickie?' she asked.

'A Canadian and water.'

'A double?'

'No, Mama. It's on me anyway,' he answered, and her register chugged through a ticket.

'What's happening?' he asked as he slid onto the stool beside me.

'Trouble.'

'Huh? Oh, yeah, trouble everywhere these days, Milo. Sometimes I think the whole world's gone crazy, you know. Even this town. This used to be a good town, you know, I can't understand – '

'This is a different sort of trouble, Nickie. More specific.'

'Huh?' he asked, belching. 'What's that?'

'This lady you've had me tailing.'

'What's the matter? I thought you – were gonna take a few days off,' he said, then pulled hard at his drink, swallowed air and burped. 'Goddamned soda.'

'I went back to work sooner than I thought I would,' I said, 'and let me tell you, Nickie, I haven't caught this broad in the act yet, but I know she's fucking around.'

'How – how do you know?'

'It's my business, Nickie. I've been tailing horny broads all my life and I can smell it. Hell, Nickie, you've seen her, you can tell. All those bitches fuck around,' I said, trying to keep my voice sly and grimy, but having trouble controlling the speed rush that had just kicked into my nervous system, having trouble keeping from blowing his head off.

'You don't – who – Did you catch her?' he stammered.

'Naw, I haven't caught her yet, I told you that, but I will. She's been giving me the slip, but I put a beeper on her car. I'll catch her, I promise.'

'How many times did you see her?' he asked, like a man who didn't want to know.

229

'Five, maybe six times. Once this morning, then just a few minutes ago. This broad's slick, Nickie, she's been around.'

'She gave you the slip just now?' He finished his drink and went around the bar. 'Want another?'

'No, thanks,' I said. 'Yeah, she took off five, maybe ten minutes ago. But like I said, I got a beeper on her car.'

'What's that?'

'A transmitter. It sends out a signal so I can find her car.'

'I – I don't understand – why . . .' He couldn't finish. His hand went back to his stomach, then away, as if he could ignore the pain. 'Goddamned soda.'

'Listen, we can catch her in the act. Right now. But I need some more money.'

'Huh?'

'Money, Nickie. This electronic crap is expensive to rent. I need five bills for a deposit and another one for the rent.'

'Five hundred dollars?'

'You'll get that back. You said your friend didn't care about the money, so what the hell do you care?'

'A few minutes ago, huh?' he asked, trying to hold his face together.

'Right. Just get the money, Nickie, and we got her ass-cold.'

'I – I gotta check – be right back,' he said, then walked away toward his office, his hand worrying his stomach, his boots slapping dully on the carpet.

I wanted Nickie in my rig, wanted to see his face when I told him that I knew. I thought about what Jamison had told me about Turkish wives and cats; the image of Nickie clawed into a puddle of flesh and blood by drowning cats didn't bother me at all. I asked the bartender for another drink. He brought it with the sneer of the sober.

'It's on Nickie,' I said.

He looked at me but didn't speak.

'Are you deaf, asshole?' I asked, trembling again. He didn't answer or change expressions, he just walked away when Nickie came back carrying a long white envelope in his quivering hand.

'Okay,' he said, 'damn right. Bitch.' Then he moved close to me, shielding himself from Mama D. I wondered how he'd feel if he thought his wife had been unfaithful instead of his mistress. 'Fucking

230

whore,' he whispered. 'How much you need?' He scratched his chest violently.

'Give it all to me.'

'Huh?'

'All of it, Nickie. You don't need it.'

'Huh?'

'You're dead, you fucking creep, dead,' I hissed and jerked the envelope out of his hand. His mouth opened, lips moving vaguely like undersea weeds caught in a current. 'I'm dumb, Nickie, I'm so dumb that it's taken me this long to come up with you. The only person in town who's dumber than me is you, and you're dead.'

I guess I'll never know if I would have killed him. When I reached under my windbreaker for the automatic, Nickie's face swelled up like a frog's and his arms laced across his chest, his fingers ripping his shirt as they tried to get to the pain wired around his chest, his body leaning toward me, his face in mine, his breath shallow and hot against my skin. Then he straightened up, turned as if he was going to walk calmly away, and fell forward on his face with a thud that silenced the idle conversation in the bar.

I leaned over him, grabbed his jacket and flipped him over, shook him, telling him that he couldn't die on me. But he did. Judging from the look on his relaxed face, he wasn't all that unhappy about it.

I stood up to look around the bar. Two tourists were craning their necks from their bar stools, but they didn't get up. The bartender had come to the end of the bar and was walking toward me, not looking at Nickie. I pointed my finger at him, but he didn't stop, so I pointed the pistol, and he did. But Mama D. didn't stop for anything. She was coming like a truck, I got out of her way, she fell upon Nickie's body, screaming incoherently in Italian, holding Nickie's face and covering it with kisses. I told the bartender to stay just where he was, then holstered the piece and walked out through the crowded lobby, bucking the people who were moving toward the bar to see what all the screaming was about. As I walked out, I could hear Mama D.'s moans bursting like bombs. I understood how she felt.

I was almost to my rig when I heard the first gunshot and the crash of plate glass falling to the sidewalk. I turned, like a fool, and saw Mama D. plowing through the lobby, waving a snub-nosed revolver and shedding people like wastepaper. Her first shot had taken out one of the lobby windows. As I watched she ran into the double doors like a fullback, flinging them aside, and waddled toward me as fast as she could, the revolver held unsteadily before her. I don't think I'd ever seen her off her stool before, and certainly never in the sunlight. She was much shorter and fatter than I had realized, her mustache much darker. I didn't think I was in much danger unless she got close enough to poke the revolver into my belly and pull the trigger. I wasn't going to shoot back, so I climbed into my rig and drove away as she emptied the revolver in my direction.

She missed me, but she played hell with the tourist trade with those last five shots. She put bullets into a pickup camper and a station wagon in the parking lot and hit another station wagon in the radiator as it turned into the lot. Her fifth shot disappeared up Hell-Roaring Canyon, but her sixth found a human target – a fisherman from Schenectady, New York – in a pay phone booth half a block away on Main as he was telling his wife how good the fishing was out West.

As I drove around the stalled station wagon, I glanced into my rear-view mirror. Mama D. hadn't given up, her chubby arms pumping as she tried to run, her right hand squeezing the empty revolver again and again as she chased me out of the parking lot and into the street. Her screaming mouth looked like a large black hole in her face. She had loved the poor bastard.

Later, I heard that she had followed me three blocks west on Main before the police finally caught her. She broke one patrolman's jaw with the empty revolver, and the other had to use his billy to handle her.

17

Without thinking about it, I went downtown to the office, not to Mahoney's, not home. I wanted to be alone, and nobody would look for me in the office. I wanted some time before I had to deal with Jamison. Without counting it, I put Nickie's money in the safe along with that I had taken out for Muffin. Then I got the office bottle, propped my feet in the open north window, and stared up into the Diablos, trying to decide what I felt.

Nothing. Empty, tired, ill-used. Hung over. Slightly nervous from all the drugs rattling around in my system. But oddly peaceful too. It was over, all over but the shouting. And when that was over, I wanted to go away for a long time. I didn't care where, just out of town, away with my lady. Just like Nickie.

Poor Nickie. He hadn't wanted much. Pocket money and a smattering of respect, to be able to buy a round of drinks, to have a woman that didn't look like a hawk perched on a pig's ass. Not too much for a man to ask. But what a way to go about it. Briefly, I wondered where in hell he had gotten the idea, how he had managed to buy the heroin. But that was Jamison's worry, not mine.

I stood up and leaned out the window to see the bank clock. It had been a busy morning; it was barely noon. I sat back down, sipping whiskey, sliding gracefully into a calm sulk. Goddamned Nickie, Next Round Nickie wouldn't be promising the drinks anymore. But there wasn't too much pity for him. He hadn't meant to, but he had released about five weeks of real madness in the town he loved. And he must have been terrified the whole time, skulking about Meriwether in a false beard and a wig and wrap-around sunglasses, frightened but feeling damned important, a real gangster loose on our streets. I guessed I'd never know if he had overloaded

233

Raymond Duffy's last fix, never know exactly how or why the kid died. Poor goddamned Nickie. Gathered up enough courage to shove a drunk old man down a stairway, then puking up his guts when he saw the result of that shove. I wondered, too, how he had gotten Elton Crider into the river. But that was Jamison's worry. For the life of me, I couldn't imagine Nickie killing anybody. He hadn't the heart for it. Any more than I did. Poor dumb Nickie. It had never occurred to me, wouldn't have in a thousand years, that he was hiring me just to get me out of the way. I believed him. But, of course, he believed me too. I didn't know what that meant. He had handled everybody else on his own, but had hired help to handle me. I didn't know if that meant he was afraid of me or thought me dumber than him. He wasn't going to rise from the grave to explain it either. Sad Nickie. I imagined him honestly amazed and disgusted when the junkies he had fathered took up crime to feed their habits. Junkies in *his* town. And dead men stacked like logs. I counted them on my fingers. It took both hands. Nine dead men. Or eight men and one twelve-year-old boy. All, except for Nickie and the Duffy kid, innocent bystanders. Jesus, I thought, never underestimate a klutz.

When the telephone rang, I expected it to be Jamison, but it was Mama D.'s resident cousin. He seemed to think that we had mutual interests to discuss. He wanted to come to my office, but I told him that I only discussed business at Mahoney's, and he agreed to meet me there in fifteen minutes. Thinking about Nickie, I had forgotten that Mama D.'s cousins were probably going to be interested in what had happened, and they weren't amateurs. I didn't think they would want a lot of trouble in a clean town, but I didn't know what they called trouble. The motel manager wasn't scared of me, so I thought perhaps I should be of him. And I imagined that organized criminals, like small-town sheriffs who have visions of being John Wayne, probably believed their own myths. That's why Mahoney's seemed like a much better place to meet than my office.

I leaned out the window to check the time again and saw the black Cadillac parked at the curb and Mama D.'s cousin, followed by the daytime bartender, walking into the bank's office entrance. They were early and at the wrong place. I checked the automatic, then locked the office door on my way to hide in the john at the end of the hallway just past the door of my cousin the dentist's office.

I peeked through a crack in the door and watched them get out of the elevator, the executive-type in front, the bartender flanking him. He had changed out of his uniform and into a leather suit with a short jacket and bell-bottom pants, a floral print shirt and low platform shoes. He looked like a Hollywood bit player looking for work. They didn't bother to knock on my office door, but the bit player lifted a leather tool case out of his hip pocket.

'Excuse me, fellas,' I said as I stepped out of the john, 'but that door is wired into the bank's alarm system, and if you open it, you're gonna cause one hell of a fuss, and those nifty tool kits are a mandatory two-year fall.'

They stepped back cautiously, then the older one started toward me, his hand extended, his smile sincerely abashed.

'Mr. Milodragovitch,' he said, 'we just thought – '

'You want to stop right there?' I didn't want to make him angry, but I didn't want him next to me either.

'Certainly,' he answered, as if he didn't mind at all. 'It isn't necessary to be quite so nervous.'

'I'm always nervous when plans are suddenly changed without me knowing about it. So let's just meet in the bar like we planned.'

'Certainly,' he said, nodding pleasantly.

'And leave your associate in the car.'

'Whatever for?' he asked, seeming genuinely perplexed.

'Just leave him outside,' I said. My heart felt like a rabbit running wildly around inside my rib cage. Too much excitement for one day. Or one hit too many of the little white pills. The older guy looked like that was all right with him, but the guy in the leather suit didn't look too happy about being left out. 'I didn't mean to hurt your feelings, asshole,' I said to him. That was twice in one day. He started to move toward me.

'Arnold,' the older guy said.

'Arnold,' I jeered, and he took another step. 'Arnold! Wow!' I mocked, and a wonderfully violent speed rush blew into me. 'Come on, creep,' I said as his hand moved toward the pistol under his arm. 'Come on! Go for it! It's just like in the movies, mother, I'm the fastest gun in this shithole town, so go for it!'

Arnold didn't believe me, but it didn't matter. His boss didn't want to be caught in our cross fire. He was reaching out for Arnold's gun hand just as my cousin the dentist opened his office door on his way to lunch.

That did it. Luckily, the executive had a good hold on Arnold's arm. Otherwise, he and I would have blown large hunks of my cousin and him all over the hallway.

'At Mahoney's,' the older guy said, tugging Arnold down the hallway.

'Right,' I said, feeling as wasted as an old, discarded condom.

'What's happening, Milo?' my cousin said, looking the scene over with round eyes. He was as big as a pro tackle but he had never played football.

'You just stepped right in the middle of a gunfight,' I told him.

'You're a card,' he said jovially, laughing and slapping me on the arm hard enough to bounce me into the wall. 'Listen, let's go to lunch, okay? And you can tell me if all that crap I read in the newspaper is true.'

'Working,' I muttered as I headed for the backstairs, and he laughed even louder.

I went in the back door of Mahoney's and took my usual booth. The older guy came in the front, moving through the early afternoon drinkers with a politely restrained force. Arnold was sitting in the Caddy in the loading zone, carefully not looking into the bar.

'Hello,' the older guy said, extending his hand again. This time I took it. 'I assume this is your usual table?' I nodded. 'Perhaps we might be more comfortable elsewhere, say, at that back table,' he said, then without waiting for my answer, he led the way past Pierre and the shuffleboard machine to a table between the silent jukebox and the shuffleboard.

'Well,' he said, offering me the chair that faced the front door so I could watch Arnold, 'I must apologize for the intrusion attempted upon your office. Events have transpired so quickly this morning, and we have never had occasion to do business with you, so at the time it seemed a necessary intrusion. I do hope you will accept my apology.'

'Sure,' I said, still standing.

'And for Arnold's unforgivable behavior also. He had been in the hinterlands too long, I fear – grown stale. I think perhaps he has much too much spare time to watch television. He is a professional, you know, and quite good, but perhaps he takes his rather limited function too seriously,' he said, his manicured hands moving like those of a well-trained lecturer to make small but significant points that I might have missed in his urbane voice. 'Won't you sit down?'

'After you,' I said. Being around him was like being around somebody who was stoned: contagious. 'Please.'

But he waited with his hand on the chair, the index finger of his other hand touching his cheek as if he was trying to think of the best way to say something mildly unpleasant.

'I hope you won't take this personally,' he said, 'but you are a private investigator and as such have access to sophisticated listening and recording devices.'

'When I can afford them, sure. A man has to keep up with technology.'

'Yes, I understand. I hope you will understand my necessary sensitivity about such devices and won't object to some sort of mechanical noise to cover our conversation – '

'Excuse me,' I said as I caught the bartender's eye. 'Would you like something to drink?'

'Thank you, nothing for me,' he said.

'You were talking about noise,' I said, nodding to the bartender when he held up a beer mug, shaking my head when he held up a shot glass.

'You wouldn't object if I were to play the jukebox?' he asked, stepping toward it.

'Of course not,' I said.

'Ah, this is rather embarrassing,' he said, turning toward me. 'Do you perhaps have some change?'

'Sure,' I said, digging into my pocket, then handing him two quarters. He found the coin slot, fed the quarters into the machine, then touched his soft fingers to the buttons, ranging across them like a piano player, playing songs at random. As he stepped back to the table he cocked his head, checking the noise level.

'That isn't quite loud enough, is it?'

'I don't know,' I said, then to the bartender as he brought my beer: 'Turn up the jukebox.'

'Go to hell, Milo,' he said as he walked away.

The nifty hood raised his eyebrow like an old maid. Nobody ever told him to go to hell.

'You make me wish I was bugged,' I said. 'Put some money in that shuffleboard machine there. No bug in the world can get past that sort of interference.' I didn't know if that was true, but he bought it.

'Really,' he said, walking over to the machine, his hands folded before him like a monk's.

'Really,' I echoed as I followed him and gave him another quarter. Like most drunks, I had a pocketful of drinking change.

'I feel I must apologize again,' he murmured softly, 'for the haphazard nature of these proceedings. Ordinarily, we have more time to plan for electronic countermeasures, but we were completely unprepared for the events of this morning. However, I hope you won't judge our organization too quickly. We really are quite efficient.' His voice was quiet, but the threat was clear.

'It isn't necessary to threaten me,' I said, just giving advice, not irritated by the threat.

'I wasn't,' he said, and that brought a small flash of anger.

'My ass is covered.'

'We assumed that, of course, but please don't overestimate the seriousness of this affair. We have a very nice business here, but quite limited in terms of our corporate structure, or, as you might say, the larger picture. I happen to be a corporate officer, you see, and I am authorized to deal with you in whatever manner I choose. It was pure chance that I happened to be in Meriwether, a sort of working vacation, you might say. I had a small coronary accident last spring and – '

'Runs in the family?' I interrupted.

'I beg your pardon? Oh, yes. Quite humorous. As I was saying, our business here certainly isn't of major importance. In fact, our major interest is familial – '

'So I've heard.'

'But haven't understood at all. Please don't interrupt unless it is absolutely necessary,' he said, chiding me as one would a child. 'Our major interest in this affair is to avoid any embarrassment to either Mrs. DeGrumo's father or uncle, who are large stockholders in our franchise operation, and if you can assist us in any way and if you are neither too expensive nor too inconvenient, we are quite willing to settle this matter with you. Otherwise, we will seek other means.'

'I've had some hard times out of this – '

'I can well imagine, judging by the damage to your face. I understand that a broken nose is quite painful,' he said, but I couldn't tell if he was commiserating with me or threatening to punch me in the nose.

'My stake in this is personal,' I said, 'and I might be willing to be damned inconvenient rather than eat shit.'

'But you can be bought.'

'Rented.'

'Semantics. Quibbling over a word – '

'Don't condescend to me,' I said.

We looked at each other. His tanned face was impassive, but his hand moved up to touch his wide silk tie as if it were some sort of talisman.

'Of course. Please accept my apology. It is often difficult for those of us from other sections of the country to remember that the West has been quite civilized for some time. I do apologize,' he said, his voice rich with humility, cultured and phony as a tin dollar. I wanted to break his jaw, but that would have brought sweet Arnold a-running and caused more trouble than I wanted. 'Would you like to play while we talk?' he asked, holding up the stainless-steel puck.

'No thanks. I like my hands where they are.'

'I see. Arnold isn't the only victim of the media. It isn't at all necessary for you to be quite so nervous, but I suppose it is to be expected. Evil times and bad public relations, wouldn't you say?' he said, an amused smile fluttering about his calm mouth. 'Now, how does one operate this machine?'

He put the quarter into the slot, and I hit the button, and the machine clattered into life. Pierre turned his head slowly, like a large stone tilting, cast his glare across me, shaking his fist and grimacing.

'Now what does one do? What is the purpose of all those lights? Oh, I see. These are the strike zones, and one should hit the strike zones as the flashing lights cross, and that elicits the highest score. Am I correct?'

I nodded, and he began playing with some intensity, like a serious amateur golfer, talking to me as he watched the blinking lights stutter across the board and his scores register in anxious clicks, pausing occasionally to dust his hands and the cuffs of his expensive suit coat.

'You might begin by giving me some insight into what might have

239

caused Nickie's coronary this morning,' he said, his tongue confident as it formed *coronary*. He wasn't afraid. But his hand slipped up to touch his tie again. 'And to what purpose were you carrying a weapon?'

'I told Nickie that I was going to kill him, but he collapsed before I could do anything about it.'

'Did you really intend to shoot him down right there in the bar?'

'I don't know. I don't think so,' I admitted.

'I suppose not. Why did you threaten him?'

'He killed a friend of mine.'

'Are you sure?'

'Pretty sure before, absolutely certain now.'

'He is dead, yes, so you must have been correct. But how did poor dumb Nickie ever come to kill somebody?'

'This friend of mine found out that Nickie was dealing heroin.'

'Are you absolutely sure about that?' he asked.

'Yes.'

'Amazing. We've been interested in that problem, of course, because the merchandise was of such a high quality, but we certainly never suspected Nickie. I mean, he was so *dumb*. But it begins to fit now,' he said, reaching into his coat pocket and taking out a page torn from *Time*. He glanced at it, then shook his head and handed it to me. 'We found this in his effects this morning, in a scrapbook of schemes for instant wealth – Brazilian farmland, Alaskan oil, soy bean futures, that sort of thing. He was such a fool,' he added, so much disgust in his voice that I had an odd impulse to defend Nickie.

But the clipping was sad and foolish. It explained how the Mafia was cashing in on the counterculture by cornering the supply of soft drugs and holding them off the market so that the young would move on to harder and more lucrative drugs.

'Pure nonsense, of course. Demand always exceeds supply,' he said, like a man who knew. Then he added casually, 'You wouldn't know where Nickie was getting his merchandise, would you?'

'Police evidence locker somewhere,' I said.

'Unfortunate corruption among law enforcement officers,' he intoned, smiling. 'You wouldn't know where Nickie had his merchandise hidden?'

'I can guess, but the police are going to be very interested in me as soon as they find me, and I have to have something to trade. Nickie's goods are my ticket.'

'Perhaps we could arrange something with the local authorities.'

'Too much heat right now.'

'I suppose you're right.'

'Besides, this was a one-shot deal. Nickie just wanted enough money to split, so he couldn't have much smack left in his stash.'

'You're right, of course,' he said sadly. 'Do you have any idea what Mrs. DeGrumo had in mind when she went after you with the pistol?'

'She just went berserk, as far as I know. Overcome by grief, you might say.'

'Yes, it certainly seems that way,' he said as he finished the game. 'A rather amusing device. Is that a respectable score for a novice?' he asked as the counters clicked merrily toward some mystic number beyond the ken of men.

'I wouldn't know,' I said.

'One of these might be just the thing for my family room. Do you know where I might purchase one?'

'Try Meriwether Vending.'

'Of course. Why is that old gentleman glowering at me?' he asked, nodding toward Pierre.

'He isn't too fond of the machine.'

'I see. Quite an interesting face, isn't it. And all those on the walls too. I assume those are the faces of the regular clientele?'

'Yes.'

'I don't seem to see yours among them.'

'That's right.'

'Yes. And the gold stars indicate those who are deceased?'

'That's right.'

'Very interesting. I wish I had the time to examine them more closely. I'm an amateur photographer myself, you know. But business calls. This wouldn't be quite so messy if Mrs. DeGrumo hadn't wounded that chap in the telephone booth – I take it you didn't know about that.'

'No.'

'Yes. One of her wilder shots hit a tourist in a telephone booth. He is in critical condition. It would be quite inconvenient.'

'Hell, they don't care if you shoot an occasional tourist out here.

Plead her temporarily insane. She'll spend six months in Duck Valley, then get out,' I said, giving advice again.

'We have a quite competent legal staff,' he said.

'Get a local lawyer.'

'Good point. Interesting. You're the person who told Nickie that the bar needed a brace of illegal punchboards, aren't you?'

'Yes.'

'You seem to have a rather sharp mind behind all that tape and damage. What are you going to tell the police when they, as you said, become interested in you?'

'The truth. Nickie put the dope deal together, I stumbled into it, and when I braced him to make sure, he died. Simple. Easy. Assuming Nickie was really in business for himself.'

'Oh, for heaven's sake, yes. Perhaps we misjudged him, but certainly we wouldn't have allowed him to handle anything of this nature. Perhaps we should have given him some sort of added responsibility. But, of course, every time we did, he made such a terrible mess of things. Well, you know Nickie.'

'Knew him.'

'Quite,' he said, holding the puck between his hands. He set it down. 'I suppose this is the point in the negotiations where I offer you financial remuneration, a rental fee as you called it, for your cooperation in this matter. To make sure that neither Mrs. DeGrumo nor the business is connected in any way with Nickie's lurid affairs.'

'I have to tell the truth about this whether you pay me or not.'

'I quite understand, but we would rather pay you something for your time.'

'Okay,' I said, knowing exactly what I was doing but not liking it. 'If you insist.'

'Oh, I do. We don't have a very large budget for this sort of thing, but I think I can offer you a reasonable sum,' he said, amused with himself and the way he had beaten me as easily as he had the shuffleboard machine. He took an envelope from his inside coat pocket and handed it to me, saying, 'Shall we say, a thousand now – earnest money, so to speak – and another when this situation works out satisfactorily.'

I took the envelope, folded it and stuck it in my hip pocket, and told him, 'That's not much.'

'Oh, but that's all there is, Mr. Milodragovitch. We will, of course, expect results,' he said, his hand rising to flick a speck of dried blood off my jacket. 'If this works out, we might be able to find a place for you in our local business. Provided you were neither greedy nor stupid, which I'm certain you aren't.' He smiled broadly, his eyebrow cocked again, his plump fingers finding another spot of loose blood. 'Think about it.'

'I will,' I said, thinking about it for a second, remembering what Muffin had said about me, wondering how Helen Duffy would take it if I went to work for their organization, and I found myself smiling. 'Sure, I'll think about it. Changing sides might change my luck.'

'Really,' he said, his hand reaching up to pat my cheek gently. 'You don't seem to be terribly concerned about the insidious tendrils of organized crime choking your hometown.'

'That's true,' I said, my hands moving up to straighten his tie. 'I just hate arrogant assholes.' Then I tugged on the short end of the tie, tugged hard. His smile had faded, his handsome face bloomed wonderfully florid. Then I jerked the tie, saying, 'I told you not to condescend to me.' Then I pulled the tie harder. He struggled for air, his mouth gasping loosely, his arms flapping as if they weren't connected to his shoulders.

I swung him around like a ball on a string, knocking over Pierre's table and slamming the guy into the jukebox, which went silent with a long scratchy burr, then leading him like a dog on a leash, I ran him at the shuffleboard machine and threw him down the board. His head banged into the plastic cover, then buried among the plastic pins with a fine crash.

That was too much for Pierre. He rose from his chair, walked around the overturned table and stood beside the nifty hood, raising his gnarled thick hands and bringing them down on his back, slamming heavily against the guy as he struggled to get his tie loosened and his head out of the machine. Pierre grunted like a man splitting firewood until the hood's struggles ceased.

As I looked toward the front door, remembering Arnold, heads and bodies were aimed toward the back until they heard Arnold's platform shoes banging on the wooden floor. I stepped into the aisle between the booths and the bar, and shouted 'Freeze!' at him.

He meant to, I think, but the moment seemed too perfect: the showdown between the handsome young stranger and the tired old drunk, the shared celluloid moment. He stopped, nearly falling down, but the roles had been written too long for him to change them now, and his hand went for his piece. It was still under his jacket, and he had a long instant to realize that the dying was going to be real, when I pulled the trigger. He was the wrong man, but it wasn't my fault.

18

After it was over and the echoes of the gunfire stilled, the bar emptied quickly, the afternoon drinkers fleeing into the sunshine, careful not to touch the blood-splattered doorframe or step on the fragments of bone and flesh scattered all the way out the door and across the sidewalk to the side of their Cadillac, which was spotted with bullet holes and human debris. The four jacketed rounds had gone through and into the door of their car. Arnold had managed to get his revolver out after the second time I hit him, but he didn't have the strength to pull the trigger. At least it was in his outflung hand.

'Nice shooting,' Freddy said as he walked up behind me.

'Goddammit, Freddy, shut up,' I muttered as I walked away from him around behind the bar to pour a drink. The bartender still huddled behind the bar, crouched like a whipped dog.

'It's over?' he asked, holding a bloody nose with his hand. He had banged it on the cooler trying to get down. I nodded at him, and he fled outside too, away from the stink.

Freddy checked Arnold's body, covering the entrance wounds with his hand, shaking his head like a man who couldn't believe it. Then he went to take Pierre off the other hood, sat him down, and tugged the guy out of the machine. He seemed to be alive, breathing shallowly but lying very still on the board, like a man laid out for a wake. Freddy walked over to the bar, moved my automatic out of the way, and I poured us a drink. We toasted something. When Jamison came charging into the bar in front of a squad of patrolmen, he found me hanging over a glass of whiskey, grieving and sick of the scene, acting as tired as Gregory Peck or Glenn Ford. And Jamison played the lawman well: confused.

*

Eventually he worked it out, though. By late afternoon he had arrested and impounded and searched to his heart's content. His boys found Nickie's heroin stash inside a water softener in the basement of the house on Wild Rose Lane. Wanda had been arrested at the airport, and when the police rushed in, the secretary in the police department who had faked the records about the destruction of a kilo of heroin went into hysterics and confessed to everything. As it turned out, she had been seduced by the Duffy kid, that gem of a young man. I was allowed to leave the police station on a personal recognizance bond, but I had to walk to the bank parking lot to get my rig. And when I got home, it was nearly sunset and the lady's mother was there.

She sat in the backyard on one of my lounge chairs, her trim legs crossed, her strong face inclined toward the setting sun, her neck arched gracefully. Helen sat on the back steps in the shade, hugging her knees and humming to herself. She heard me at the back door, rose quickly and came inside, hugging me fiercely, brushing her lips across my face, touching the stiff sutures with her soft mouth, murmuring, 'Oh, darling, I heard. How terrible, how awful, you poor darling.'

Then she tucked her face against my chest, her arms tight around my body as she swayed and hummed childlike in the still afternoon air.

'It will be all right. I have some time to spend in court, but then we can go away. Everything will be all right.'

'Oh, no,' she whispered, stepping back from me, looking up but not in my eyes. 'She knows. She's here and she knows.'

'What?'

'Everything,' she crooned, 'she's here and she knows everything.'

'What?'

'She does that to me, you know. She insists, she always does that, you know, insists on knowing everything. I hate – hate it when she makes me tell, you won't be angry – '

'I won't be angry,' I said, silencing her against my chest, too tired to think, too wasted to really care.

'Helen.'

At the sound of the voice, her head rose and she moved away from me, her hand wiping her nose.

'Yes, Mother,' she answered the voice.

'Bring your friend outside, please. I'm sure he's quite tired, and we must hurry. Perhaps you might make the two of us a drink.' The voice was as soft and melodious as the ramble of the creek – as insistent too. 'Please.'

Helen stepped around me into the kitchen, her shoulders hunched, her hands cupped before her. She walked around the kitchen in small aimless steps, muttering, 'Damn damn damn damn . . .' Then she looked at me. 'Whadda ya wanna drink?'

'A beer. That's all. Are you all right?'

'Are you kiddin'? With that old bitch here? How can anybody be all right? She ruins everything, you know that – everything.'

'Mr. Milodragovitch,' the voice intruded. 'Please come outside. Helen is quite capable of preparing the drinks.'

'Are you sure you're all right?' I asked again.

'Oh, go outside. *She* wants to talk to you.'

As I stepped out the door, Mrs. Duffy rose to greet me, lifted herself out of the lounge chair as gracefully as if she had been borne on silver wires, and she stood there, as tall and cool and slim as the frosted glass she held lightly in her firm hand.

'I'm quite pleased to meet you,' she said, taking my hand, holding it in a dry, muscular clasp. 'Finally.'

I nodded and took back my hand.

'I meant to come much sooner, but Helen had told me that you were indisposed. From what I hear, though, not completely helpless. I'm afraid Helen exaggerated your condition. She painted a portrait of you either mewling like a baby or dying of age. I suppose I should have recognized the symptoms – '

'Symptoms?'

'Of the lying.'

'Lying?'

'I thought you knew. But I can see that you didn't.'

'Didn't know what?'

'I simply assumed that Mr. Diamond had told you that Helen is a pathological liar.'

'Oh, yeah, he did, but I thought he was lying,' I said, waving my hand vaguely.

'Really,' she said as we looked each other over like a couple of dogs about to fight.

She was slightly shorter than Helen, but slimmer, and so poised

247

and held herself so erectly, she seemed much taller than her daughter. Her hands were aging but well tended, the nails glossy and tapered under a coat of clear polish, and the fingers that held the glass were as motionless as ice. She, too, had red hair but streaked with an arrogant gray, as if by some spell she had reversed the process by which steel was destroyed by rust. The blue of her eyes was steady, a deep violet, confident and cool. Her face might have been marked by age, like her hands, but the years didn't show beneath the smooth matte finish that covered the bevels and planes and angles of her face. Not a wrinkle marred her skin, which she hadn't exposed deliberately, not a hint of freckles. Beneath the soft sweep of her simple gray dress, her body looked as strong and supple as a willow switch.

'Have you surveyed me sufficiently?' she asked, her eyes locked on my face.

'Yeah,' I grunted.

'And what do you think?' she asked, tilting her head just enough for the sunlight to glisten off her firm jaw line, waiting with the first quivers of a confident smile for my compliment.

'Frankly?' I asked, puzzled by all this.

'Of course,' she said, straightening her head, letting the warm glow of light stray gently across her face. 'I admire frankness in a man.'

'Well, frankly, lady, I wouldn't want to meet you in a dark alley.'

She laughed. Not loudly, not throwing her head back, but laughed, deep and husky, the sort of laugh that insinuates itself through a noisy cocktail party like visiting royalty, making the women feel quite shabby and dated, making the men surreptitiously check their flies before edging toward the fount of that precious mirth.

'Well put,' she said. 'I like a man who can see beneath the surface.' Amusement wrinkled her eyes, and they sparkled wisely. Shafts of sunlight drifted within the blue and inviting depths of her eyes. 'Men are too often fooled, too easily impressed by the physical appearance of a woman, by the outer beauty. It's the cause of much grief, I'm sad to say – beauty and the inability of some men to see beyond it.'

She had confused me. At first, I had thought she was talking about herself, but at the end she seemed to mean Helen. I glanced toward the house, wishing Helen would bring the beer, come out and help me with her mother.

248

'Helen,' Mrs. Duffy said sharply, 'please bring the drinks.'

She must have been waiting just behind the screen door because she came out before her mother finished the command. She brought her mother another tall frosted drink, took the empty glass, then handed me a can of beer. She stood in front of us, her feet together, her hands held tightly at her waist, her head bowed.

'Perhaps Mr. Milodragovitch would like a glass, Helen.'

'Oh, no,' I said quickly.

'Then if you'll excuse us for a moment, Helen. Your friend and I have several things to discuss.' I reached for Helen to keep her with us, but she moved away from my arm, crossed the yard and hunkered on a large stone on the creek bank, doodling with a twig in a hand's span of dirt between the stones. 'Why don't we sit down,' Mrs. Duffy suggested firmly, sitting as easily as she had stood, so I took the other chair, slumping all the way into it. 'I understand from Helen that you have asked her to marry you,' she said, the tone of her voice letting me know how difficult it was to believe poor Helen. She sat on the very edge of her lounge chair, her knees together, her body and face posed as if for a portrait sitting. When I didn't answer, she asked, 'Or was that just sugar to blow in her ear?'

'No. I was serious.'

'Was?'

'Am serious.'

'Then I feel it is my responsibility as Helen's mother to acquaint you with several matters of some importance. I know that you must be quite fatigued, so I won't impose on your hospitality any longer than necessary.'

'Okay.'

'Are you a good man, Mr. Milodragovitch?'

'I don't even know what that means.'

'Are you a man with many virtues? Aside from the obvious one of endurance, which I judge by the condition of your face. A lesser man would have found a way to quit a long time ago. But do you have any other virtues?'

'Lady, I don't know,' I grumbled, irritated, wanting to take a hot shower and lie down next to my lady.

'I hope you do. I sincerely hope so. Particularly the virtue of forgiveness, because you have a great deal to forgive.'

249

'Can I get another beer first?' I asked. Somehow my beer was already empty. 'I always forgive better when I've got a beer.'

'How quaint. Don't bother to get up. Helen can get it. Helen! Another beer for your friend, please.'

Helen rose obediently from her stone and shuffled across the lawn, her gnawed hands stealing toward her mouth.

'Don't bite your nails, child.'

'Yes, Mother.'

We were silent as we waited. She sat as still as a bird sleeping on a limb, but I shifted constantly in my chair, finding a new sore spot each time I moved.

'You may stay if you like,' Mrs. Duffy said to Helen when she brought me the beer. But she went back to her stone. 'I understand that you've had quite a hard time of it since Helen first came to your office.'

'At least I'm alive,' I said. 'Some people aren't.'

'Yes, so I understand,' she said, nodding her head in a brief sympathetic dismissal. 'But I must go on. We have a flight to catch – '

'Goddammit, lady, slow down. All this crap got started, all this, a lot of people are dead, all because of your goddamned son, so don't tell me you've got a flight to catch, that – '

'Not my son,' she said bluntly. 'Hers.'

'What?'

'Raymond was her illegitimate son.'

'Come on – she's not old enough to – '

'Don't be silly. She's quite old enough. She seduced her high school band director when she was barely thirteen. I think she had had two periods before she became pregnant. I see you're having difficulty believing me. The women in my family have always been sexually precocious. We mature at an early age. Helen was a love child. I gave birth to her three weeks to the day after my fifteenth birthday. Unfortunately, unlike me, she had seduced a married man, which I could understand if not forgive, but I made the mistake of trying to atone for her mistake by adopting her son. Perhaps if she had never told Raymond of their relationship, he might have been a different sort of young man. Who knows? As it was, she told him and spoiled him terribly, and he grew up weak and effeminate, a vicious and greedy boy, full of senseless violence and hate. I tried,

God knows I tried, but each time I corrected the boy, he ran to her for protection – '

'Hey, wait a minute,' I said, flat in my chair like a man who hadn't rolled with the last punch. 'This is all very interesting, but I don't see what it has to do with me.'

Her slender legs crossed with a nylon hiss, she sipped at her drink, then she looked at me with her smoothly amused smile. She said, 'As you can see by Helen's face, this has a great deal to do with you.'

When I looked at Helen, her eyes were wild again, her hands held up like a mask, and I recalled why her eyes were familiar. They were Raymond's eyes without the hate.

'I still don't see – '

'I must apologize,' Mrs. Duffy interrupted quietly, 'for waiting so long to interject myself into this affair, but my husband is an invalid while I am still a healthy woman, with, as my mother used to say, my own special needs, and I admit that I've been occupied fulfilling them. Otherwise, none of this might have happened. You see, I've been in the habit of allowing Helen to spend her summers as she chooses as long as they are spent away from home. She is quite childish about some things and she lacks my discretion. In the past she has caused me considerable embarrassment in Storm Lake, which is, after all, a small town. I had no idea that she had used this freedom to come out here to see Raymond – I'd expressly forbidden it – until after his death, and I had no idea that she had come back to hire you to investigate the death until it was too late.'

'So?'

'So this afternoon, I caught her in rather a compromising lie, and made her tell me the truth. It's a rather dreadful story, but I'm quite certain that it is the truth.'

'And?'

'Well, it seems that Helen knew from the beginning that Raymond intended to use her money for his nefarious scheme. She didn't approve, of course, but she was, as usual, unable to resist his demands. And when he telephoned her, suicidally despondent because he had caused the death of one of his vile friends – '

'One Willy Jones,' I said. 'Raymond shot him accidentally.'

'Whatever you say.'

'And burned down the hotel to cover it up.'

251

'That seems quite possible, yes. After his telephone call, Helen rushed out here to prevent his suicide, but she wasn't in time, and I suspect her guilt about that caused her to return to try to find some indication, however slight, that her precious son hadn't committed suicide.'

'He didn't,' Helen moaned, 'he didn't, he called me, he was coming to me, he wouldn't have, somebody killed him.' She hammered her thighs with her fists and the ground with her feet.

'Stop that nonsense this instant!'

'It may not be nonsense, Mrs. Duffy. The kid was suicidal, but somebody helped him.'

'But you don't know for sure.'

'No. And now I'll never know.'

'You don't seem angry?'

'I'm long past that,' I said, watching Helen weep with her head on her knees. Behind her the sun broke into silver ripples in the creek. In a moment, as soon as my legs recovered, I would rise and go to her. That was how it would be. 'Long past anger.'

'It is a pleasure to meet a man with your equanimity. How many men did you say have died?'

'I didn't say.'

'How many?'

'Nine men, I think, including one twelve-year-old boy. But she didn't kill any of them.'

'How many did you kill?'

'It doesn't matter.'

'My current lover is a retired military man. He says that a man never forgets the faces of the men he killed. Is that true?' she asked, boring in with a quiet intensity that made Jamison seem like a piker. 'How did you feel?'

'I can take it or leave it.'

'Don't be glib with me, young man.'

'I haven't been young in a long time, lady, and killing men makes me feel disgusted and terribly sad, but it doesn't have anything to do with Helen.'

'You don't feel betrayed? You can forgive everything? Marry in love and live happily ever after?' she asked.

'Lady, I'm more interested in being forgiven myself and having a

252

soft place to lay my head,' I answered, and it made me feel good again, feel like things would work out. 'That's all.'

'Perhaps you are really the rarest of men, a forgiving man,' she mused, then sipped at her drink.

We watched each other again, our eyes working at each other. She smiled, but when I tried, my face was too stiff.

'Was there something else?' I asked.

'Why do you ask?'

'That shit-eatin' grin on your face.'

'You can be rather tiresome when you choose, can't you?'

'Lady, that's just the beginning.'

'Yes, well, there was one other thing,' she said, glancing pointedly at her silver watch.

'Spit it out.'

'Certainly, if you insist. I'm just afraid that you might find this additional fact rather burdensome, and I do hate to be so blunt, but – '

'I can tell.'

'Yes, well, are you aware of the fact that while you've been out doing whatever it is you do, even while you were recovering from the terrible beating you received from those thugs, that Helen and your friend, Mr. Diamond, have been, shall we say, dallying in your house – were you aware of that? Even this afternoon while you were killing that poor man?'

She allowed me a few moments of silence, allowed me to look at Helen's face, stricken with the truth, her wide frightened eyes, her fist knuckled into her open mouth.

'Strike home?' she inquired politely as I looked at Helen, my lady, my love. I found that smile.

'Fuck you, lady, and your fucking facts,' I said softly. 'Just get your shit and get your ass outa my house and my town, and take your . . .' I paused. 'Take your shit-eatin' grin with you.'

'That's clever.'

'Thanks,' I said, feeling all right now. I wasn't clever but I had endurance.

'Come, Helen, we're going.'

'She stays.'

'Oh, I'm afraid I couldn't allow it.'

'You can't prevent it,' I said.

'Oh, you poor foolish man. Helen agreed to go home with me several hours ago,' she said, smiling lightly as she stood up. 'Come, Helen, it's time to go.'

'Then what the hell was this all about?' I asked, looking around me as if I could find the answer in the thick grass of the lawn. 'What the hell . . .'

Helen rose again from her stone, discarded her twig, and scuffled toward her mother, her hands tearing at each other under the watch of her lowered eyes, walking slowly across the lawn out of the setting sun.

'What the hell – was this all about?'

'Oh,' she answered, her smile widening. 'It seemed the thing to do at the time.' She paused, then added, 'Say good-bye to your friend, Helen.'

My lady raised her face, her pale freckled face framed by the warm red hair that flamed in the sunshine like a halo of blood and fire, but the eyes that met mine briefly were as opaque as last winter's ice, 'as cold and dim. I stood up, she nodded once, then followed her mother to the back door of my house.

As I stood there, the blunt shadow of the western ridge advanced darkly to the verge of the creek. I sat down, heard the sound of a car driving away, I drank my beer, and forgave her.

THE LAST GOOD
KISS

for Dick Hugo,
grand old detective of the heart

You might come here Sunday on a whim.
Say your life broke down. The last good kiss
you had was years ago. You walk these streets
laid out by the insane, past hotels
that didn't last, bars that did, the tortured try
of local drivers to accelerate their lives.
Only churches are kept up. The jail
turned 70 this year. The only prisoner
is always in, not knowing what he's done . . .

– Richard Hugo, *Degrees of Gray in Philipsburg*

1

When I finally caught up with Abraham Trahearne, he was drinking beer with an alcoholic bulldog named Fireball Roberts in a ramshackle joint just outside of Sonoma, California, drinking the heart right out of a fine spring afternoon.

Trahearne had been on this wandering binge for nearly three weeks, and the big man, dressed in rumpled khakis, looked like an old soldier after a long campaign, sipping slow beers to wash the taste of death out of his mouth. The dog slumped on the stool beside him like a tired little buddy, only raising his head occasionally for a taste of beer from a dirty ashtray set on the bar.

Neither of them bothered to glance at me as I slipped onto a stool between the bulldog and the only other two customers in the place, two out-of-work shade-tree mechanics who were discussing their lost unemployment checks, their latest DWI conviction, and the probable location of a 1957 Chevy timing chain. Their knotty faces and nasal accents belonged to another time, another place. The dust bowl '30s and a rattletrap, homemade Model T truck heading into the setting sun. As I sat down, they glanced at me with the narrow eyes of country people, looking me over carefully as if I were an abandoned wreck they planned to cannibalize for spare parts. I nodded blithely to let them know that I might be a wreck but I hadn't been totaled yet. They returned my silent greeting with blank eyes and thoughtful nods that seemed to suggest that accidents could be arranged.

Already whipped by too many miles on the wrong roads, I let them think whatever they might. As I ordered a beer from the middle-aged barmaid, she slipped out of her daydreams and into a sleepy grin. When she opened the bottle, the bulldog came out of his drunken nap, belched like a dragon, then heaved his narrow haunches upright and waddled across three rickety stools through the musty cloud of stale beer and bulldog breath to trade me a wet, stringy kiss for a hit off my beer. I didn't offer him any, so he upped the ante by drooling all over my sunburnt elbow. Trahearne barked a sharp command and splashed a measure of beer into the ashtray. The bulldog gave me a mournful stare, sighed, then ambled back to a sure thing.

As I wiped the dogspit off my arm with a damp bar rag that had been used too lately and too often for the same chore, I asked the barmaid about a pay telephone. She pointed silently toward the gray dusty reaches beyond the pool table, where a black telephone hung from ashen shadows.

As I passed Trahearne, he had his heavy arm draped over the bulldog's wrinkled shoulders and recited poetry into the stubby ear: 'The bluff we face is cracking up ... before this green Pacific wind ... this ... The whale's briny stink ... ah, Christ ... dogged we were, old friend, doggerel we became, and dogshit we too shall be ...' Then he chuckled aimlessly, like an old man searching for his spectacles.

I didn't mind if he talked to himself. I had been talking to myself for a long time too.

That was what I had been doing the afternoon Trahearne's ex-wife had called me – sitting in my little tin office in Meriwether, Montana, staring across the alley at the overflowing Dempster Dumpster behind the discount store, and telling myself that I didn't mind if business was slow, that I liked it in fact. Then the telephone buzzed. Trahearne's ex-wife was all business. In less than a minute, she had explained that her ex-husband's health and drinking habits were both bad and that she wanted me to find him, to track him down on his running binge before he drank himself into an early grave. I suggested that we talk about the job face to face, but she wanted me on the road immediately, no time wasted driving the three hours up to Cauldron Springs. To save time, she had already hired an air-taxi out of Kalispell, which was at this very moment winging its way south toward Meriwether with a cashier's check for a retainer, a list of Trahearne's favorite bars around the West – particularly those bars about which he had written poems after other binges – and a dust-jacket photo off his last novel.

'What if I don't want the job?' I asked.

'After you see the size of the retainer, you'll want the job,' she answered coolly, then hung up.

When I picked up the large manila folder at the Meriwether Airport, I glanced at the check and decided to take the job even before I studied the photograph. Trahearne looked like a big man, a retired longshoreman maybe, as he leaned against a pillar on the front porch of the Cauldron Springs Hotel, a drink shining in one hand, a cigar smoking in the other. His age showed, even through his boyish grin, but he clearly hadn't gone to Cauldron Springs for the waters. Behind him, through the broad darkened doorway, two arthritic ghosts in matching plaid bathrobes shuffled toward the sunlight. Their ancient faces seemed to be smiling in anticipation of dipping their brittle bones into the hot mineral waters.

In the years that I had spent looking for lost husbands, wives, and children, I had learned not to think that I could stare into a one-dimensional face and see the person behind the photograph, but the big man looked like the sort who would cut a wide swath and leave an easy trail.

At first, it was too easy. Back at my office, I called five or six of the bars and caught the old man up in Ovando, Montana, at a great little bar called Trixi's Antler Bar. Trahearne had left, though, by the time I drove the eighty miles, telling the bartender that he was off to Two Dot to check out the beer-can collection in one of Two Dot's two bars. I chased him across Montana but when I reached Two Dot, Trahearne had gone on to the 666 in Miles City. From there, he headed south to Buffalo, Wyoming, to write an epic poem about the Johnson County War. Or so he told the barmaid. As it turned out, Trahearne never made a move without discussing it with everybody in the bar. Which made him easy to follow but impossible to catch.

We covered the West, touring the bars, seeing the sights. The Chugwater Hotel down in Wyoming, the Mayflower in Cheyenne, the Stockman's in Rawlins, a barbed-wire collection in the Sacajawea Hotel Bar in Three Forks, Montana, rocks in Fossil, Oregon, drunken Mormons all over northern Utah and southern Idaho – circling, wandering in an aimless drift. Twice I hired private planes to get ahead of the old man, and twice he failed to show up until after I had left. I liked his taste in bars but I was in and out of so many that they all began to seem like the same endless bar. By the middle of the second week, my expenses were beginning to embarrass even me, so I called the former Mrs. Trahearne to ask how much money she wanted to pour down the rolling rathole. 'Whatever is necessary,' she answered, sounding irritated that I had bothered to ask.

So I settled back into the bucket seat of my fancy El Camino pickup for a long siege of moving on, following Trahearne from bar to bar, down whatever roads suited his fancy, covering the ground like an excited redbone pup just to keep from losing him, following him as he drifted on, his tail turned into some blizzard wind only he felt, his ear cocked to hear the strains of some distant song only he heard.

By the middle of the second week, I had that same high lonesome keen whistling in my chest, and if I hadn't needed the money so badly, I might have said to hell with Abraham Trahearne, stuck some Willie Nelson into my tape deck, and tried to drown in a whiskey river of my own. Taking up moving on again. But I get paid for finding folks, not for losing myself, so I held on his trail like an old hound after his last coon.

And it made me even crazier than Trahearne. I found myself chasing ghosts across gray mountain passes, then down through green valleys riddled with the snows of late spring. I took to sleeping in the same motel beds he had, trying to dream him up, took to getting drunk in the same bars, hoping for a whiskey vision. They came all right, those bleak motel dreams, those whiskey visions, but they were out of my own drifting past. As for Trahearne, I didn't have a clue.

Once I even humped the same sad young whore in a trailer-house complex out on the Nevada desert. She was a frail, skinny little bit out of Cincinnati, and she had brought her gold mine out West, thinking perhaps it might assay better, but her shaft had collapsed, her veins petered out, and the tracks on her thin arms looked as if they had been dug with a rusty pick. After I had slaked too many nights of aimless barstool lust amid her bones, I asked her again about Trahearne. She didn't say anything at first, she just lay on her crushed bed-sheets, hitting on a joint and gazing beyond the aluminum ceiling into the cold desert night.

'You reckon they actually went up there on the moon?' she asked seriously.

'I don't know,' I admitted.

'Me neither,' she whispered into the smoke.

I buttoned up my Levis and fled into the desert, into a landscape blasted by moonlight and shadow.

Then in Reno I lost the trail, had to circle the city in ever-widening loops, talking to bartenders and service-station attendants until I found a pump jockey in Truckee who remembered the big man in his Caddy convertible asking about the mud baths in Calistoga. The mud was still warm when I got there, but his trail was as cold as the eyes of the old folks dying around the hot baths.

When I called Trahearne's ex-wife to admit failure, she told me that she had received a postcard from him, a picture of the Golden Gate and a cryptic couplet. *Dogs, they say, are man's best friend, but their pants have no pockets, their thirst no end.* 'Trahearne has this odd affinity for bar dogs,' she told me, 'particularly those who drink as well as do tricks. Once he spent three weeks in Frenchtown, Montana, drinking with a mutt who wore a tiny crushed officer's cap, sunglasses, and a corncob pipe. Trahearne said they discussed the Pacific campaign over shots of blackberry brandy.' I told her that it was her money and that if she wanted me to wander around the Bay Area looking for a drinking bar dog, I would surely comply. That's what she wanted, so I hooked it up, headed for San Francisco, a fancy detective hot on the trail of a drinking bar dog, a fool on her errand.

I should have guessed that the city of lights would be rife with bar dogs – dancing dogs and singing dogs, even hallucinating hounds – so it wasn't until three days later, drinking gimlets with a pink poodle in Sausalito, that I heard about the beer-drinking bulldog over by Sonoma.

The battered frame building was set fifty yards off the Petaluma road, and Trahearne's red Cadillac convertible was parked in front. In the days when the old highway had been new, back before it had been rebuilt along more efficient lines, the beer joint had been a service station. The faded ghost of a flying red horse still haunted the weathered clapboard walls of the building. A small herd of abandoned cars, ranging from a russet Henry J to a fairly new but badly wrecked black Dodge Charger, stood hock deep in the dusty Johnson grass and weeds, the empty sockets of their headlights dreaming of Pegasus and asphalt flight. The place didn't even have a name, just a faded sign wanly promising BEER as it swung from the canted portico. The old glass-tanked pumps were long gone – probably off to Sausalito to open an antique shop – but the rusted bolts of their bases still dangled upward from the concrete-like finger bones from a shallow grave.

I parked beside Trahearne's Caddy, got out to stretch the miles out of my legs, then walked out of the spring sunshine into the dusty shade of the joint, my boot heels rocking gently on the warped floorboards, my sigh relieved in the darkened air. This was the place, the place I would have come on my own wandering binge, come here and lodged like a marble in a crack, this place, a haven for California Okies and exiled Texans, a home for country folk lately dispossessed, their eyes so empty of hope that they reflect hot, windy plains, spare, almost Biblical sweeps of horizon broken only by the spines of an orphaned rocking chair, and beyond this, clouded with rage, the reflections of orange groves and ax handles. This could just as easily have been my place, a home where a man could drink in boredom and repent in violence and be forgiven for the price of a beer.

After I had thought about it, I stuck my dime back in my pocket, walked back to the bar for another beer. I had found bits and pieces of Trahearne all along the way and I felt like an old friend. It seemed a shame not to enjoy him, not to have a few beers with him before I called his ex-wife and ended the party. Whenever I found anybody, I always suspected that I deserved more than money in payment. This was the saddest moment of the chase, the silent wait for the apologetic parents or the angry spouse or the laws. The process was fine, but the finished product was always ugly. In my business, you need a moral certitude that I no longer even claimed to possess, and every time when I came to the end of the chase, I wanted to walk away.

But not yet, not this time. I leaned against the bar and ordered another bottle of beer. When the barmaid sat it down, a large black tomcat drifted down the bar to nose the moisture on the long neck.

'The cat drink beer too?' I asked the barmaid.

266

'Not anymore,' she answered with a grin as she flicked the sodden bar rag at the cat's butt. He gave her a dirty look, then wandered down the bar past the bulldog and Trahearne, his tail brushing across Trahearne's stolid face. 'Sumbitch usta drink like a fish but he got to be too much trouble. He's like ol' Lester there,' she said, nodding toward the shade-tree mechanic with the most teeth. 'He can't handle it. He'd get so low-down, dirty-belly, knee-walkin' drunk, he'd start up tom-cattin' in all the wrong damn places.'

The barmaid gave ol' Lester a hard, knowing glance, then broke into a happy cackle. As he tried to grin, ol' Lester showed me the rest of his teeth. They weren't any prettier than the ones I had already seen. 'One night that crazy black bastard started up a-humpin' ever'thing in sight – pool-table legs, cues, folks' legs, anything that didn't move fast enough – and then he did somethin' nasty on a lady's slacks and somebody laughed and damned if we didn't have the biggest fistfight I ever seen. Ever'body who wasn't in the hospital ended up in jail, and they took my license for six weeks.' She laughed, then added, 'So I had that scutter cut off. Right at the source. He ain't wanted a drink since.'

'Is that Lester or the tomcat?' I asked

The barmaid cackled merrily again, the other mechanic brayed, but ol' Lester just sat there and looked like his teeth hurt.

'Naw,' she answered when she stopped laughing. 'Ol' Lester there, he don't cause no trouble in here. He's plumb terrified of my bulldog there.'

'Looks like a plain old bulldog to me,' I said, then leaned back and waited for the story.

'Plain,' Lester squealed. 'Plain mean. And I mean *mean*. Hell, mister, one mornin' last summer I come in here peaceful as could be, just mindin' my own business, and I made the mistake of steppin' on that sumbitch's foot when he had a hangover, and damn if he didn't like to tore my leg plumb off.' Lester leaned over to lift his pants' leg and exhibit a set of dog-bite scars that looked like chicken scratches. 'Took fifty-seven stitches,' he claimed proudly. 'Ol' Oney here, he had to hit that sucker with a pool cue to get him off'n my leg.'

'Broke that damned cue right smack in two,' Oney quickly added.

'Plain old bulldog, my ass,' Lester said. 'That sumbitch's meaner'n a snake. You tell him, Rosie.'

'Listen, mister,' the barmaid said as she leaned across the bar, 'I've seen that old bastard Fireball Roberts come outa dead drunks and blind hangovers and just pure-dee tear the britches off many a damn fool who thought he'd make trouble for a poor woman all alone in the world.' When she said *alone*, Rosie propped one finger under her chin and smiled coyly at me. I glanced over her shoulder into the ruined mirror to see if my hair had turned gray on the trip. An old ghost with black hair grinned back like a coyote. Rosie added, 'He don't just knock 'em down, mister, he drags 'em out by the seat of their britches, and they're usually damn glad to go.'

'Well, I'll be damned,' I said, properly impressed, then I glanced at the bulldog, who was sleeping quietly curled on his stool. Trahearne caught my eye with a glare, as if he thought I meant to impugn the courage of the dog, but his eyes lost their angry focus and seemed to drift independently apart.

"Course now, if'n Fireball can't handle all 'em by his own damn self,' Lester continued in a high, excited voice, 'ol' Rosie there, she ain't no slouch herself. You get her tail up, mister, she's just as liable to shoot your eyes out as look at you.'

I nodded and Rosie blushed sweetly.

'Show him that there *pistole*,' Lester demanded.

Rosie added a dash of bashful reluctance to her blush, and for an instant the face of a younger, prettier woman blurred her wrinkles. She patted her gray curls, then reached under the bar and came up with a nickel-plated .380 Spanish automatic pistol so ancient and ill-used that the plate had peeled away like cheap paint.

'Don't look like much,' Lester admitted gamely, 'but she's got the trigger sear filed down to a nubbin, and that sumbitch is just as liable to shoot nine times as once.' He turned to point across the bar to a cluster of unmended bulletholes between two windows above a ratty booth. 'She ain't had to touch it off but one damn time, mister, but I swear when she reaches under the bar, things do tend to get downright peaceful in here.'

'Like a church,' I said.

'More like a graveyard,' Lester amended. 'Ain't no singin' at all, just a buncha silent prayers.' Then he laughed wildly, and I toasted his mirth.

Rosie held the pistol in her rough hands for a moment more, then she sat it back under the bar with a thump.

268

''Course I got me a real pistol at home,' Lester said smugly.

'A German Luger,' I said without thinking.

'How'd you know?' he asked suspiciously.

The real answer was that I had spent my life in bars listening to war stories and assorted lies, but I lied and told Lester that my daddy had brought one back from the war.

'Got mine off'n a Kraut captain at Omaha Beach,' he said, his nose tilted upward as if my daddy had won his in a crap game. 'Normandy invasion,' he added.

'You must have been pretty young,' I said, then wished I hadn't. People like Lester might tell a windy tale now and again, but only a damn fool would bring it to their attention.

Lester stared at me a long time to see if I meant to call him a liar, then with practiced nonchalance he said, 'Lied about my age.' Then he asked, 'You ever been in the service?'

'No, sir,' I lied. 'Flat feet.'

'4-F, huh,' he said, trying not to sound too superior. 'Oney here, he's 4-F too, but it weren't his feet, it was his head.'

'Ain't going off to no damn Army,' Oney said seriously, then he glanced around as if the draft board might still be on his trail.

'Ain't even no draft no more,' Lester said, then snorted at Oney's ignorance.

'Yeah,' Oney said sadly. 'By god, they oughta go over there to San Francisco and draft up about a hunnert thousand a them goddamned hairy hippies.'

'Now, that's the god's truth,' Lester said, and turned to me. 'Ain't it?' His eyes narrowed at the three-day stubble on my chin as if it were an incipient beard.

For a change, I kept my mouth shut and nodded. But not emphatically enough to suit Lester. He started to say something, but I interrupted him as I excused myself and walked over toward Trahearne. Behind me, Lester muttered something about *goddamned gold-brickin' 4-F hippies*, but I acted as if I hadn't heard. I reached over and tapped Trahearne on the shoulder, and his great bald head swiveled slowly, as if it were as heavy as lead. He raised an eyebrow, wriggled a pleasant little smile onto his face, shrugged, then toppled backward off the bar stool. I caught a handful of his shirt, but it didn't even slow him down. He landed flat on his back, hard, like a two-hundred-fifty-pound sack of cement. Rafters and window lights

269

rattled, spurts of ancient dust billowed from between the floorboards, and the balls on the pool table danced merrily across the battered felt.

As I stood there stupidly with a handful of dirty khaki in my right hand, Lester leaped off his stool and shouted, 'What the hell did you do that for?'

'Do what?'

'Hit that old man like that,' Lester said, his Adam's apple rippling up and down his skinny throat like a crazed mouse. 'I ain't never seen nothin' as chickenshit as that.'

'I didn't hit him,' I said.

'Hell, man, I seen you.'

'I'm sorry, but you must have been mistaken,' I said, trying to be calm and rational, which is almost always a mistake in situations like this.

'You callin' me a liar?' Lester asked as he doubled his fists.

'Not at all,' I said, then I made another mistake as I stepped back to the bar for my beer: I tried to explain things. 'Listen, I'm a private investigator, and this gentleman's ex-wife hired me to . . .'

'What's the matter,' Lester sneered, 'he behind in his goddamned al-i-mony, huh? I know your kind, buddy. A rotten, sneaky sumbitch just like you tracked me all the way down to my mama's place in Barstow just 'cause I's a few months behind paying that whore I married, and let me tell you I kicked his ass then, and I got half a mind to kick yours right here and now.'

'Let's just calm down, huh,' I said. 'Let me buy you boys a beer and I'll tell you all about it. Okay?'

'You ain't gonna tell me shit, buddy,' Lester said, and as if that weren't enough, he added, 'and I don't drink with no trash.'

'I don't want no trouble in here,' Rosie interjected quietly.

'No trouble,' I said. Lester and Oney might have comic faces, funny accents, and bad teeth, but they also had wrists as thick as cedar fence-posts, knuckled, work-hardened hands as lumpy as socks full of rocks, and a lifetime of rage and resentment. I grew up with folks like this and I knew better than to have any serious disagreements with them. 'No trouble at all,' I said. 'I'll just leave.'

'That ain't near good enough,' Lester grunted as he took two steps toward me and a wild swing at my face.

I ducked, then backhanded him upside the head with the half-full beer bottle. His right ear disappeared in a shower of bloody foam, and he fell sideways, scrabbled across the floor, cupping his ear and cursing. Oney stood up, then sat back down when he saw the broken bottle in my hand.

'Is that good enough?' I asked.

Oney agreed with a nervous nod, but Lester had just peeked into his palm and found bits and pieces of his ear.

In a high, thin voice, he shouted, 'Goddammit, Oney, get the gun!'

Behind me, I heard Trahearne stand up and dreamily wonder what the hell had happened. But nobody answered him. Oney and Rosie and I were locked into long silent stares. Then we all moved at once. Rosie dashed down the bar toward the automatic as Oney scrambled over it. I glanced at the bulldog, who still slept like a rock, then I lit out for open country. I would have made it, too, but good ol' Lester rolled over and hooked a shoulder into my right knee. We went down in a heap. Right on his ruined ear. He whimpered but held on. Even after I stood up and jerked out a handful of his dirty hair.

Behind the bar, Rosie and Oney still struggled for the pistol. Trahearne had sobered up enough to see it, but as he tried to run, he crashed into the pool table, then tried to scramble under it just as Oney jerked the pistol out of Rosie's hands and shoved her away. As she fell, she screamed, 'Fireball!' I gave up and raised my hands, resigned myself to an afternoon of fun and games in payment for Lester's ear. But as Oney lifted the pistol and thumbed the safety, Fireball came out of a dead sleep and cleared the bar in a single bound like a flash of fat gray light. Still in midair, he locked his stubby yellow teeth into Oney's back at that tender spot just below the short ribs and above the kidney. Oney grunted like a man hit with a baseball bat, dropped his arms, and blanched so deeply that ancient acne scars glowed like live coals across his face. He grunted again, sobbed briefly, then jerked the trigger.

The first round blew off a significant portion of his right foot, the second wreaked a foamy havoc in the cooler, and the third slammed through the flimsy beaverboard face of the bar and slapped Mr. Abraham Trahearne right in his famous ass. The fourth powdered the fourteen ball, the fifth knocked out a window light, and the rest ventilated the roof.

When the clip finally emptied, Oney sank slowly behind the bar,

271

the automatic still clutched in his upraised hand, and Fireball still locked to his back like a fat gray leech. During the rash of gunfire, the tomcat had come out of nowhere and shot out the front door like a streak of black lightning, while Lester had hugged my knees like a frightened child. Or a man whose war stories had finally come true.

'Goddammit, Lester,' I said when the echoes had stopped rattling the old beams, 'you're bleeding all over my britches.'

'I'm sorry,' he said quietly as if he meant it, then turned me loose.

As I handed him my handkerchief for his ear, Fireball came trotting around the end of the bar, his drooping jowls rimmed with blood. He scrambled onto the platform bar rail, a stool, then up on the bar. He worked his way along, tilting bottles, catching them in his muzzle, and drinking them dry. Then he lapped his ashtray empty, belched, then hopped down to the floor the same way he had gotten up. With a weary waddle that seemed to sigh with every step, he wandered over to the doorway and stretched out in a patch of sunlight, asleep before his belly hit the floor, small delicate snores rippling the dust motes around him.

'I don't believe I've ever seen anything quite like that,' I told Lester.

'Goddamned sumbitchin' dog,' Lester growled as he walked over to a booth to sit down.

I went behind the bar to check on Oney and Rosie. He had fainted and she lay on the duckboards like a corpse. Except that her hands were clasped to her ears instead of crossed on her chest.

'Anybody dead?' she asked without opening her eyes.

'Some walking wounded,' I said, 'but no dead ones.'

'If you'd wait till I get my wits about me before you call the law,' she said, 'I'd surely appreciate it. We got to figure some way to explain all this crap.'

'Right,' I agreed. 'You got any whiskey?'

She nodded toward a cabinet, where I found a half-empty quart of Old Crow. I did what I could for Oney's foot, took off his work shoe and cotton sock and poured some whiskey on the nubbins of flesh where his two middle toes had been, then wrapped the foot in a clean bar towel. After I washed out the dog bite with bar soap, I went over to help Lester clean slivers of glass out of the side of his head and tattered ear.

272

'Ain't no ladies gonna slip their tongues in that ear no more,' I joked.

'Never much cared for that anyway,' he said primly. 'How's ol' Oney?'

'Blew off a couple of toes,' I said.

'Big 'uns or little 'uns?'

'Medium sized,' I answered.

'Hell, that ain't nothin',' Lester said as he gently touched his ear. 'How 'bout Rosie?'

'I think she's taking a little nap.'

'Looks like the big fella is, too,' Lester said with a nod.

I thought it unkind to point out that 'the old man' had somehow become 'the big fella,' so I went over to see why Trahearne still huddled under the pool table.

'Are you all right, Mr. Trahearne?' I asked as I knelt to peer under the table.

'Actually, I think I've caught a round,' he answered calmly.

I didn't see any blood, so I asked where.

'Right in the ass, my friend,' he said, 'right in the ass.' Then he opened his eyes, saw the bottle, and took it away from me. 'You drink this pig swill?'

I didn't, or at least hadn't, but he didn't have any trouble getting his mouth around the neck of the bottle. Not as much as I had trying to get his pants and a pair of sail-sized boxer shorts down so I could see the wound. The jacketed round had left a neat blue hole, marked with a watery trickle of blood, just below his left buttock. I had no way of knowing if the bullet had struck a bone or an artery, but Trahearne's color and pulse were good, and I could see the lead nestled like a little blue turd just beneath the skin below the hump of fatty tissue hanging over his right hip.

'What's it look like?' he asked between sips.

'Looks like your ass, old man.'

'I always knew I'd die a comic death,' he said gravely.

'Not today, old man. Just a minor flesh wound.'

'That's easy for you to say, son, it's not your flesh.'

'In a few days, you won't have nothing but a bad memory and a sore ass,' I said.

'Thank you,' he said, 'but I seem to have both those already.' He

273

paused for a sip of whiskey. 'How is it that you know my name, young man?'

'Why, hell, you're a famous man, Mr. Trahearne.'

'Not that famous, unfortunately.'

'Yeah, well, your ex-wife was worried about your health,' I said.

'And she hired you to shoot me in the ass,' he said, 'so I couldn't sit a bar stool.'

'I didn't shoot you,' I said.

'Maybe not,' he said, 'but you're going to get the blame anyway.' Then he sucked on the bourbon until he curled around the empty bottle, adding his gravelly snore to Fireball's quiet drone.

2

As the official caravan, two ambulances, and a deputy sheriff's unit swept out of Rosie's parking lot in a cloud of dust, they all hit their sirens at once and wailed into the distance. From where Rosie and I sat on the front steps, it sounded like the beginning of the end of the world.

'Them boys sure do favor them sirens,' she said quietly.

'It's just about the only fun they get out of life,' I said.

'You speakin' from experience?' she asked with narrow eyes.

'I've ridden in the back seats of a few police cars,' I said, and she nodded as if she had too.

As she and I had cleaned up the mess inside the bar, moved the wounded outside, and concocted a wildly improbable but accidental version of the shooting, Rosie and I had become friends. Now we were also bound by our mutual lies to the authorities. Lester and Oney would have lied for free, just to be contrary, but I doled out a generous portion of cash to help with medical expenses. Lester pocketed the money, then told me that he and Oney, by virtue of several trips to the drunk farm, were medical wards of the state of California. The middle-aged deputy who questioned us seemed to know we were shucking him but he didn't seem to care. He was more interested in ragging Oney about shooting himself in the foot. As he left, though, he mentioned that I should drop by the courthouse the next morning to sign a statement, and he and I both knew what that meant.

As soon as the sirens had faded away, Rosie said, 'Reckon we should have us a beer.'

'Whiskey,' I said, then went over to my pickup for the road pint in the glove box. When I got back to the steps, Rosie had found two

275

whole bottles of beer for chasers. After we drank silently for a bit, I said, 'Sorry for the trouble.'

'Wasn't your fault,' she answered, waving with a tired hand. 'It was that damned worthless Lester. Truth is, when that there private detective caught him down in Barstow, Lester smart-mouthed him, and that boy proceeded to whip the living daylights outa Lester right there in his momma's front yard, whipped him till Lester just begged to pay some back child-support.'

'Thought it might be something like that,' I said.

'How come you were after that big fella, anyway?' she asked. Then she quickly added, "Course you don't have to tell me if it ain't none of my business.'

'I was supposed to find him before he drank himself into the hospital,' I said. 'Or into the grave.'

'That's a fool's errand,' Rosie said with authority.

'I was just supposed to find him,' I said, 'not take the bottle out of his hands.'

'Is that what you do for a living?' she asked. 'Find folks?'

'Sometimes,' I said. 'Other times I just look.'

'You do okay?'

'Fair to middling,' I admitted, 'but it ain't steady. I end up tending bar about half the time.'

'How come?'

'Beats the hell out of standing around Monkey Wards watching out for sixteen-year-old shoplifters.'

'I reckon so,' she said, then laughed and hit the pint. 'How long you been trackin' the big fella?'

'Right at three weeks,' I answered.

'Get paid by the day, huh?'

'Usually.'

'This job oughta do you nicely,' she said.

'Hope so,' I said. 'They might feel unkindly, since the old man got shot, and decide that I'm overpriced, unworthy of my hire.'

'Sue 'em.'

'Ever try to sue rich folks?' I asked.

'Hell, boy, I don't even know any rich folks,' she said, then paused to stare at the ground. 'What you reckon that old boy was runnin' from?'

'Maybe he just needed a high lonesome,' I said, 'or a running binge. I don't really know.' And I didn't. Usually, after I had been after somebody for a few days, I had some idea of what they had in mind. But not with Trahearne. During some of my less lucid moments, I had the odd feeling that the old man was running from me, running so I would chase him. 'Maybe he just wanted to see what was over the next hill,' I added.

'He musta got tired of lookin',' Rosie said quietly, ''cause he holed up here like a chick come to roost.'

'Well, if he's only half as tired as I am, he's plenty damn tired,' I said, ''cause I'm worn to a frazzle. I could sleep for a week.'

'But you probably won't, will you?'

'Probably not.'

'What are you gonna do?' she asked, too casually to suit me.

'Hang around the hospital until he gets out,' I said.

'How long would that be?'

'A week or so,' I said. 'Depends.'

For a few minutes we sat silently again, watching the soft spring sunshine spark green fire across the shallow hills, listening to the distant hum of traffic.

'Hey,' she said suddenly, as if the idea had just come to her. 'It might be that I could put you on to a piece of work while you're hangin' around. No sense in sittin' idle.'

'I usually work one thing at a time,' I said quickly. 'That's my only advantage over the big outfits.' When she didn't say anything, I asked, 'What do you have? A bundle of bad checks?'

'Enough to paper a wall,' she said, 'but that ain't the problem.' When I didn't ask her what the problem was, she continued. 'It's my baby girl. She run off on me, and I thought maybe you might spend a few days – whatever time you got – lookin' around.'

'Well, I don't know . . .'

'I know this place don't look like much,' she interrupted, 'but it's free and clear and it turns a dollar now and again–'

'It's not that,' I interrupted her. 'I just need some time off the road.'

'You wait right here,' she said as if she hadn't heard me, then flounced back into the bar.

As I waited, what had earlier seemed a fine spring haze clearly became Bay Area smog, which reminded me that this wasn't some country beer joint down in Texas on a spring afternoon in the '50s.

The maze of San Francisco lay just across the bay, a haven for runaways, and although the '60s were dead and gone too, young girls still ran there to hide. That hadn't changed, though everything else had. The flower children had gone sour and commercial or middle class, and even the enemy was tired and broken, exiled to San Clemente. I didn't want to hear what Rosie had to tell me – I didn't want to stare at another picture of a lost child. Whichever wise Greek said that you can't step into the same river twice was right, even though he forgot to mention that nine times out of ten, you'll get your feet wet. Change is the rule. You can't go home again even if you stay there, and now that everyplace is the same, there's no place to run. But that doesn't keep some of them from trying. And that didn't stop Rosie either.

'Here,' she said as she sat down and handed me a photograph. 'Look here.'

I glanced at the picture just long enough to see that it was a wallet-sized school photograph of a fairly pretty girl. Then I looked back and saw the dates: 1964–65.

'She was a pretty girl,' I said as I tried to hand the picture back to Rosie.

'Smart as a whip, too,' she answered, holding her hands between her knees.

I had to look at the picture again. It could have been a picture from my high school days in the '50s. The face was pleasant, no more, though she seemed to have good bones beneath a soft layer of baby fat. The wide mouth seemed pinched, almost sullen, and the thick cascade of blond hair looked fake. The nose was straight but slightly too bulbous at the end to be pretty. Only the eyes were striking, darkly fired with anger and resentment, a redneck rage more suited to a thinner face. She wore an old-fashioned, high-collared lace blouse with a black ribbon threaded through the collar to hold a small cameo to her throat. As I looked at the face again, the blouse seemed oddly defiant, the face so determined not to be laughed at that it seemed sad, too sad.

I knew the story: a nearly pretty girl, but without the money for the right clothes or braces or confidence, the sort of young girl who either lurked about the fringes of the richer, more popular girls, and was thought pushy for her efforts, or who stood alone and avoided the high school crowd, and for her lonely troubles was thought stuck-

278

up, stuck on herself without good reason. Ah, the sad machinations of high school. As I stared at the picture, I was once again pleased that I had missed most of those troubles. I lived in the country and worked, and although I hadn't exactly planned it that way, I had joined the Army three weeks before I was supposed to graduate. Somehow the GED I had earned in the Army seemed cleaner than a high school degree. Less sad, somehow.

'How long ago did she take off?' I asked Rosie, the photograph dangling from my fingers like a slice of dead skin.

'Ten years ago come May,' she answered as calmly as if she had said *a week ago come Sunday.*

'And you haven't heard from her since?' I asked.

'Not a single solitary word.'

'Ten years is too long,' I said, still trying not to sound shocked. 'Even a year is usually too long, but ten years is forever.'

Once again, though, Rosie acted as if she hadn't heard me. 'She went over to San Francisco one Saturday afternoon with this boy friend of hers, and he said she just stepped out of the car at a red light and walked off without sayin' a word or even lookin' back. Just walked away. That's what he said.'

'Any reason to think he might have lied?'

'No reason,' Rosie said. 'I've known him all his life, and his momma's a friend of mine. She's been fixin' my hair once a week for nearly twenty years. And Albert, he was torn up by it something terrible. He kept lookin' for Betty Sue for years after I give up. His momma says he still asks about her every time she sees him.'

'Did you report it to the police?' I asked.

'Well of course I did,' Rosie answered angrily, her wrinkled eyes finding an old spark. 'What kinda mother would I be if I hadn't? You think I'd let a seventeen-year-old girl wander around that damned city fulla niggers and dope fiends and queers? Of course I told the police. Half a dozen times.' Then in a softer voice, she added, 'Not that they did diddley-squat about it. I even went over there my own damned self. Twenty, maybe thirty times. Walked up and down them hills till I wore out my shoes, and showed pictures of her till I wore them out. But nobody had seen her. Not a soul.' She paused again. 'I just hate that damned city over there, you know. Wish it would have another earthquake and fall right into the sea. I just hate it. I was raised Church of Christ, you understand, and I

279

know I ain't got no right to judge, runnin' a beer joint like I do, but I swear if there's a Sodom and Gomorrah in this wicked, sinful world, it's a-sittin' over there across the bay,' she said, then pointed a finger like a curse across the hills. When she saw an amused grin on my face, she stopped and glared down her sharp nose at me. 'You probably like it over there, don't you? You probably think it's all right, don't you, all that crap over there?'

'You don't have to get mad at me,' I answered.

'I'm sorry,' she said quickly, then looked away.

'That's all right.'

'No, it ain't all right, dammit. Here I am askin' a favor of you and hollerin' at the same time. I'm sorry.'

'It's okay,' I said. 'I understand.'

'You got any children of your own?'

'No,' I said. 'I've never been married.'

'Then you don't understand at all. Not even a little bit.'

'All right.'

'And don't go around pretending to, either,' she said, hitting me on the knees with her reddened knuckles.

'All right.'

'And goddammit, I'm sorry.'

'Okay.'

'Oh hell, it ain't a bit okay,' she complained, then stood up and rubbed her palms on her dusty slacks. 'God damn it to hell,' she muttered, then turned around and gave Fireball a fierce boot in the butt, which knocked the sleeping dog off the steps into the skim of dust on the concrete. 'Goddamned useless dog,' she said. 'Get outa my sight.'

Fireball must have been accustomed to Rosie's outbursts. He slunk away without glancing back, not hurrying exactly, but not waiting around either. At the corner of the building, he stumbled over the black tomcat, who was curled asleep in the deep grass below the eaves, and they had a brief but decisive and probably familiar encounter, then went their separate ways, the cat beneath the building, and Fireball right back to his place in the sunshine warming the steps. As he lay down, he gave Rosie one slow glance, then shut his eyes, sighing like an old husband saddled with a mad wife. But Rosie was watching the breeze weave through the hillside grass.

'How about another beer?' I asked.

'I'd like that just fine,' she answered without turning. Sadness softened her nasal twang, that ubiquitous accent that had drifted out of the Appalachian hills and hollows, across the southern plains, across the southwestern deserts, insinuating itself all the way to the golden hills of California. But somewhere along the way, Rosie had picked up a gentler accent too, a fragrant voice more suited to whisper throaty, romantic words like *wisteria*, or humid phrases like *honeysuckle vine*, her voice for gentlemen callers. 'Just fine,' she repeated. Even little displaced Okie girls grow up longing to be gone with some far better wind than that hot, cutting, dusty bite that's blowing their daddy's crops to hell and gone. I went to get her a beer, wishing it could be something finer.

'It was the damndest thing,' she said when I came back, 'when I was looking for Betty Sue over there.' Rosie still stood upright, her wrists cocked on her hips, still stared southwest across the gently rounded hills toward the cold, foggy waters of the Bay. 'I never had no idea they'd be so many folks lookin' for their kids. Musta been a hundred or more walkin' up and down too, holding out their pictures to any dirty hippie that would look at it. Some of the nicest folks you'd ever hope to meet, too, some of them really well off. But, you know, not a single one of them had the slightest idea how come their kids run off. Not a one. And the kids we asked *why*, they didn't seem to know either. Oh, they had a buncha crap to say, but it sounded like television to me. They didn't even know what they were doing there. Damndest mess I ever did see, you know.'

'I know,' I said.

And in my own way I did, even though I had no children to run away. In the late '60s, when I came back from Vietnam in irons, in order to stay out of Leavenworth I spent the last two years of my enlistment as a domestic spy for the Army, sneaking around the radical meetings in Boulder, Colorado, and when I got out, after a brief tour as a sports reporter, I headed for San Francisco to enjoy the dope and the good times on my own time. But I was too late, too tired to leave, too lazy to work, too old and mean to be a flower child. I found a profession, of a sort, though, finding runaways. For a few years, Haight-Ashbury was a gold mine, until I found one I couldn't bear. A fourteen-year-old boy decomposing into the floorboards of a crash pad off Castro Street, forty-seven stab wounds in his face, hands, and chest. The television crew beat the police to the body, and none of it was any fun at all. Not anymore. I knew. I had seen Rosie in her best double-knit slack suit and pair of scuffed flats wandering those hills, staring into each dirty face that came down the street, then back into the photograph in her hand, just to be sure that it wasn't her baby girl hiding behind lank hair, love beads, a bruised mouth, and broken eyes.

'It's been so long,' I said to Rosie, 'so long. Why start looking again now?'

'She's all I got left, son,' she answered softly. 'The last child, the only one I ain't seen in a coffin. Lonnie got blown up in Vietnam right after she run off, and Buddy, he got run over by a dune buggy down at Pismo Beach last summer. Betty Sue's all I got left, you see.'

'Where's their daddy?' I asked, then wished I hadn't.

'Their daddy? Their wonderful, handsome, talented daddy?' she said, giving me another hard, accusing look. 'Last I heard he was down in Bakersfield sellin' aluminum cookware on time to widow-wimmen.' She let that stand for a moment, then added, 'I run the worthless bastard off when Betty Sue was a junior in high school.'

'You mind if I ask why?'

'He thought he was Johnny Cash,' she said, and stopped as if that explained it all. 'Damn fool.'

'I'm not sure I understand.'

'Ever' other year, he'd get drunk and clean out the bank account and take off for Nashville to find out if he could make the big time as a singing star. Only thing the damned fool ever found out was how long my money would last, then he'd drag-ass home, grinnin' like an egg-suckin' dog. Last time he done that, he showed up and found himself divorced and slapped in jail for non-support. That's the last I seen of him,' she said with a grin. 'He was sure enough a good-lookin' devil, but like my daddy told me when I married him, he's as worthless as tits on a boar hog.'

'He's never heard from Betty Sue either?'

'Not that I know of,' Rosie said. 'Betty Sue was always stuck on her daddy, but Jimmy Joe was stuck on himself and he didn't favor the boys too much, so I don't know if she ever forgave him for that, but I think he'd told me if he heard from her. He knows I been lookin' for her, and he's plumb scared I'll dun him for all that back support, so I think he'd mention it.' Then she paused and looked down at me. 'So what do you think?'

'You want the truth?'

'Not a bit of it, son. I want you to spend a few days lookin' for my baby girl,' she said, then handed me a wad of bills that had been clutched in her fist all this time. 'Just till the big fella gets out of the hospital, that's all.'

'It's a waste of my time,' I said, trying to hand the sodden bills back to her, 'and your money.'

'It's my money,' she said pertly. 'Ain't it good enough to buy your time?'

'What if she doesn't want to be found?'

'Did that big fella ask you to come huntin' for him?' she asked.

'She might be dead, you know,' I said, ignoring the point she had made. 'Have you thought of that?'

'Not a day goes by, son, that I don't think of that,' she answered. 'But I'm her mother and in my heart I know she's alive somewhere.'

Since I had never found any way to argue with maternal mysticism, I shook my head and went over to the El Camino for my note- and receipt books, carrying the wad of bills carefully, as if the money were a bomb. Then I went back, asked questions, took notes, and counted the money – eighty-seven dollars.

Rosie gave me the name of the boy friend, who was a lawyer over in Petaluma now, Betty Sue's favorite high school teacher, who still taught drama in Sonoma, and her best girl friend, who had married a boy from Santa Rosa named Whitfield, divorced him and married a Jewish boy from Los Gatos, named Greenburg or Goldstein, Rosie wasn't sure, divorced him, and was supposed to be going to graduate school down at Stanford. Details, details, details. Then I asked what sort of girl Betty Sue had been.

'You'll see,' she answered cryptically, 'when you talk to folks. I'll let you find out for yourself.'

'Fair enough,' I said. 'Why did she run away?'

After a few moments' thought, Rosie said, 'For a long time I blamed myself, but I don't now.'

'For what?'

'I live in a trailer house behind here,' she said, 'and one time after I divorced Jimmy Joe, Betty Sue found me in bed with a man. She took it pretty hard, but I don't think that's why she run off anymore.

And sometimes I used to think she run off because she thought she was too good to live behind a beer joint.'

'Did the two of you have a fight before she left?'

'We didn't have fights,' Rosie said proudly. 'Nothin' to fight about. Betty Sue did as she pleased, ever since she was a little girl, and I let her 'cause she was such a good little girl.'

'Could she have been pregnant?'

'She could have. But I don't think she would have run away for that,' Rosie said. 'But then, I don't know.' Then, in a shamed voice, she added, 'We weren't close. Not like I was to my momma. I had to run the place 'cause Jimmy Joe wouldn't, most of the time, and when he did, he'd give away more beer than he sold. Somebody had to make a living, to run things.' Then she paused again. 'I guess I still blame myself but I don't know what for anymore. Maybe I blame her too, still. She always wanted more than we had. She never said anything – she was a sweet child – but I could tell she wanted more. I just never knew what it was she wanted more of. If you find her, maybe she'll be able to tell me.'

'If I find her,' I said, then handed her a receipt for the eighty-seven dollars.

'Is that enough?' Rosie asked. 'I didn't get a chance to count it.'

'That's plenty.'

'You give me a bill if it's more, you hear,' she commanded.

'It's already too much,' I said. 'I'll talk to this Albert Griffith over in Petaluma and this Mr. Gleeson here, and see if I can get in touch with Peggy Bain, then I'll bring back your change. But I'm telling you up front, it's a waste of money.'

'Fair enough,' she said, then glanced at the receipt again. 'What's that name? Sughrue?'

'Right.'

'My momma had some cousins back in Oklahoma, lived down around Altus, I think, name of Sughrue,' she said. 'You got any kin down that way?'

'I got kin all over Texas, Oklahoma, and Arkansas,' I admitted.

'Hell, we're probably cousins,' she said, then stuck out her hand.

'Could be,' I said, then shook her firm, friendly hand.

'Folks don't understand about kinfolks anymore,' she said.

'World's too big for that,' I said. 'I guess I'd best head for town to see if my other client is still alive and kicking.'

'Want a road beer?'

'Sure,' I said, then went to the john to make room for it.

When I came back, she leaned over the bar to hand me the beer and said, 'You're a drinking man yourself.'

'Not like I used to be.'

'How come?'

'Woke up one morning in Elko, Nevada, emptying ashtrays and swabbing toilets.'

'But you didn't quit,' she said.

'Slowed down before I had to quit,' I said. 'Now I try to stay two drinks ahead of reality and three behind a drunk.' She smiled with some sort of superior knowledge, as if she knew that the idea of having to quit drinking scared me so badly that I couldn't even think about it. 'Would you keep an eye on Mr. Trahearne's Cadillac?' I asked.

'Get the rotor,' she said, 'and I'll let Fireball sleep in it after I close nights.' After I removed the rotor from the distributor and closed the hood, Rosie nodded at my Montana plates and asked, 'Don't it get cold up there?'

'When it does, I just drift south,' I said.

'Must be nice.'

'What's that?'

'Goin' where you want to,' she said softly. 'I ain't been more'n ten miles from this damned place since I went to my momma's funeral down in Fresno eleven years ago.'

'Footloose and fancy-free ain't always all it's cracked up to be,' I confessed.

'Neither's stayin' home,' she said, then smiled, the wrinkles etched into her face softened and smoothed, some of the years of hard living fell away like happy tears. 'You take care, you hear.'

'You too,' I said. 'See you the first of next week.'

As I climbed into my El Camino, a carload of construction workers in dirty overalls and bright yellow hardhats skidded into a rolling stop beside me, the transmission clanking loudly as the driver jammed it into park. The men scrambled out, laughing and shouting at Rosie, goosing each other in the butts, happy in the wild freedom of quitting-time beers, and they charged into Rosie's open arms like a flock of baby chicks.

I knew the men were probably terrible people who whistled at pretty girls, treated their wives like servants, and voted for Nixon every chance they got, but as far as I was concerned, they beat the hell out of a Volvo-load of liberals for hard work and good times.

3

When I arrived at his hospital room, Trahearne had been sedated into a deep rumbling sleep from which it would have been a crime to awaken him. I found the emergency-room doctor who had treated him, and the doctor suggested that Trahearne would live in spite of himself. He wasn't as sure about Oney and Lester, though. After their wounds had been cleaned and bandaged, they had split, heading back to Rosie's for another beer or two. As the doctor walked up the hallway, shaking his head, I finally used my dime to call the former Mrs. Trahearne collect. As usual, she sounded distantly reluctant to accept the charges.

'Well,' I said more brightly than I meant to – I blamed it on the whiskey – 'I finally ran the old devil to the ground.'

'Finally,' she said coldly. 'In San Francisco?'

'No, ma'am,' I said. 'In a great little beer joint outside of Sonoma.'

'Isn't that quaint,' she murmured. 'In what condition did you find him?'

'Drunk,' I said, not specifying which of us.

'I assumed that, Mr. Sughrue,' she said sharply. 'What is his physical condition?'

'Right.'

'Yes?'

'Yes, ma'am,' I stalled. 'He's fine, he's all right, he should be out of the hospital in three or four days, and he'll be as good as new.'

'It may seem presumptuous of me to ask,' she said smoothly, 'but if he is in such wonderful shape, why then is he in the hospital?'

'It's a long story,' I said.

'Isn't it always?' she said.

'Yes, ma'am.'

'You're being unnecessarily obtuse, Mr. Sughrue,' she said. Her voice sounded pleasant and refined, but accustomed to command.

'Yes, ma'am.'

'So?'

'Well, he had a little accident.'

'Yes?'

'He fell off a barstool and strained his back,' I said quickly.

'How absolutely delightful,' she said. 'Perhaps that will teach him a much-needed lesson.' Then she laughed, deep and elegant, like the rich susurruses of a mink coat being casually dragged down a marble staircase. 'But nothing too serious, I hope.'

'A minor sprain,' I said.

'I'm glad to hear that,' she said. 'I expect you to remain by his side until he is released from the hospital, and then stay with him during his postmortality binge.'

'Ma'am?'

'Violated flesh will insist upon wallowing in flesh,' she said. 'Particularly in Trahearne's case.'

'Ma'am?'

'He will insist on a drunken debauch as soon as he is released from the hospital,' she said. 'You know – wine, women, and song – expensive whiskey, high-class hookers, and finally the same old song of regret. I expect you to take care of him during those few days.'

'I'll do my best,' I said.

'I'm sure you will,' she said. 'And when he is ready to return home to lick his wounds, I expect you to see that he does so.'

'Yes, ma'am,' I said, hoping Trahearne was supposed to lick his wounds only figuratively.

'Perhaps if you inform him that his beloved Melinda is once again in the fold, throwing pots or whatever it is she does all through the night, then he may want to cut his debauch short.'

'Yes, ma'am,' I said, though I didn't have any idea who or what she was talking about. I didn't have any idea what Trahearne would think about my presence after his accident. Or my accident. The accident.

'Also, I'll expect a full report upon your arrival,' she said. 'Thank you and good night.'

'A report of what?' I asked. But she had already hung up the

288

telephone. 'Only a crazy man works for crazy people,' I told the dead wire, and a harried nurse hurrying past agreed with a quick nod.

Since it wasn't my money, and since I knew where I would probably spend the next night, I checked into the best motel in Sonoma, ordered a huge steak and some of that expensive whiskey the former Mrs. Trahearne had mentioned. Then I drove back out to Rosie's, got stupid drunk with Lester and Oney, and slept on the pool table.

'Where in the hell have you been?' Trahearne growled as I stepped into his room at ten o'clock two mornings later.

'A guest of the county,' I said.

'Huh?'

'Jail.'

'Why?'

'After the sheriff took my statement yesterday, he held me as a material witness. Just to see if I had a different version of the shooting after a night in a cell,' I said.

'Can they do that?'

'No,' I said. 'But if I had complained or called a lawyer, they would have found some minor crap to charge me with.'

'Bastards.'

'It's okay, I've been in jail before.' Jails are jails, and there's never much to talk about when you get out.

'Well, now that you're here,' he said, 'you can run some errands for me.' I reached into my hip pocket and pulled out a half-pint of vodka. 'Oh my God,' he whispered as he took the bottle from me. 'You're a saint, my friend, an absolute saint.' But before he could break the seal, a tall, nicely rounded nurse came briskly through the door.

'That will not do,' she said as she snatched the bottle from his huge, trembling hands. 'This will be returned upon your release.'

'Now, see there, Mr. Trahearne,' I said quickly. 'I told you they didn't allow drinking in the hospital.' Then to the nurse: 'I'm really sorry, ma'am, I told him I shouldn't do it, but you know how it is, since I'm just a hired hand.' Trahearne's face glowed red and greasy with sweat, and his chest rose half out of bed. He looked like a man intent on murder.

'Just so it doesn't happen again,' the nurse said.

'No, ma'am, it won't,' I said as I touched her lightly on the arm.

289

'And if he gives you any trouble, just give me a call. I'm at the Sonoma Lodge.' She smiled, nodded, and thanked me again, then carried her nicely moulded hips out the door with quick, efficient steps. 'Anytime,' I said to her back.

'Son, I don't mind you making time, but not on my time and not at my expense,' Trahearne grumbled. I lifted another half-pint out of my windbreaker pocket and handed it to him. 'You're not a saint, boy, you're prepared for emergencies,' he whispered, then had a quick snort. 'My God, it's even chilled,' he said, and had another. 'You may be worth all the money you're costing me.'

'I was under the impression I was working for your ex-wife.'

'It's all the same pocket, boy,' he said, staring at the clear liquor. 'One a day?'

'Two.'

'Yes, sir.'

'You certainly don't look like any of the others,' he said as he looked me over.

'Others?'

'They all looked like unsuccessful pimps,' he said, 'pastel leisure suits and zircon pinkie rings. You look like a saddle tramp.'

'I see you've had dealings with other members of my profession,' I said.

'You're the first one who ever found me before I wanted to be found,' he said. 'How'd you do it?'

'Professional secret.'

'The damned postcard, huh?'

'You have no idea how many dogs hang out in bars,' I said, and he grinned.

'You mind if I ask you a personal question?'

'What's a good ol' boy like me doing in a business like this?'

'Something like that,' he said.

'I'm a nosy son of a bitch,' I said.

'Me too,' he said, and grinned again. 'Maybe we'll get along.'

'I'm supposed to keep an eye on you, Mr. Trahearne, not be your faithful Indian companion,' I said.

'Horseshit.'

'And gunsmoke?'

'You'll do,' he said.

'How's your ass?'

'Getting better,' he said. 'I've survived worse. Of course, I was a younger man at the time. But the Marine Corps didn't have vodka deliveries.'

'Glad to be of service,' I said.

'It's the boredom that's hard,' he said. 'I need a couple of favors.'

'I'm yours to command.'

'I'd rather it be a favor.'

'Whatever,' I said.

'Get me some reading material,' he said. 'Paperback novels and popular magazines by the pound – I go through them like a kid through potato chips – whatever you pick up off the shelf will be fine. Also, it would be wonderful if you could arrange to have my dinners delivered. I don't care if it comes from McDonald's, just so it isn't hospital food.'

'Okay,' I said. 'What about the dancing girls and a marching band?'

'I like a man who knows how to entertain,' he said. 'If I'm stuck here too long, maybe you can arrange for a working girl interested in oral gratification. But no bands. Maybe a string quartet.'

'I'll look into it,' I said, 'but I can't promise anything. I'm out of my territory.'

'If you can't work that foot-shuffling, hayseed, ma'am routine,' he said, 'I've got several interesting telephone numbers in San Francisco.'

'Okay,' I said. 'I've got a favor to ask of you.' He stopped grinning. 'It won't interfere with your errands.'

'What sort of favor?' he asked quietly.

'Seems that Rosie has this runaway daughter,' I said, 'and I told her I'd look into it while you were in the hospital, if it was all right with you.'

After a moment, he said, 'It's all right with me. I like to see a young man trying to get ahead in the world.'

'I don't know if I qualify as a young man anymore,' I said, 'and I don't give a shit about getting ahead. I like the old lady and I said I'd do her the favor. If you don't mind.'

'I don't mind,' he answered.

'Probably a waste of money and time,' I said.

'How much money?'

'Eighty-seven dollars,' I answered, and he grinned again.

'Hell, how much time can you waste for eighty-seven dollars?'

291

'Whatever time I spend will be wasted,' I said.

'Why?'

'The daughter ran away ten years ago, and that's too – '

'By God, I seem to have some drunken recollection of Rosie telling me that,' Trahearne said quickly, then shook his head. 'I'm afraid this is my fault.'

'How's that?' I asked.

'I'm afraid that I told her that a private eye would come sniffing down my cold, cold trail,' he said, then hit the bottle, 'and suggested that she hire him. Thought that it might divert whomever Catherine sent for a few more days.' He laughed. 'So how can I mind?' He added. 'How do you go about this missing person business?'

'Depends on who's missing and how long,' I said, 'but mostly I just poke around.'

'Doesn't sound like much of a method.'

'If you want method, you hire one of the big security outfits,' I said. 'They're great at method. Straight people don't know how to disappear, and crooks can't because they have to hang out with other crooks.'

'And where do you fit in?'

'I'm cheaper,' I said, 'and my clients usually still believe in the small, independent operator. They're usually romantics.'

'You must be working all the time,' Trahearne said with a chuckle.

'And every year I have to tend bar more often,' I said.

'By God, boy, I knew right away that there was something I liked about you,' he said.

'Everybody likes bartenders,' I said. 'By the way, your ex-wife asked me to tell you that Melinda was home, throwing fits or something.'

'Pots.'

'What?'

'My wife,' he explained. 'She's a potter and a ceramic sculptor.'

'Oh.'

'I can see by your face, boy, that you aren't aware of my situation,' he said grimly. Since I wasn't, I didn't say anything. 'We all live together – or nearly together – my mother, my ex-wife, my present wife, and me, on a little ranch outside Cauldron Springs.' Trahearne stared at the institutional beige wall as if it were a window overlooking the mountains, as if he could see himself standing in a crowded postcard scenic view. 'One little happy family,' he said quietly.

I knew I would have to listen to the story of his life eventually, but I preferred later to sooner, so I excused myself. As I turned to leave, his large hand wrapped around the small bottle as if it were his only hope of salvation.

There's no fool like a fool who thinks he's charming. On the way out, I stopped by the nurses' station to say hello to the tall nurse again. I asked her about having Trahearne's meals delivered, and although she didn't seem pleased about it, she promised to check with the doctor.

'And what are you doing about dinner tonight?' I asked.

'Fixing it,' she said as she held up a banded finger.

'I'm not,' a perky voice said behind me.

Before I picked up the line, I turned around to see who had dropped it. She was shorter than the other one but rounder, with a pert, snub-nosed face framed by curly blond hair and a solid, muscular body. She had bowlegs, but what the hell, so did I.

'Is that a date?' I asked her.

'Only if you want it to be,' she answered quickly, her blue eyes brightly smiling.

'Eight o'clock,' I said, 'in the bar at the Sonoma Lodge?' I'm not a monster but I've got a beer gut and a broken nose, and strange women never pick me out of a crowd for blind dates, but gift horses and all that. Also, she had a small mobile mouth, and the straightforward approach of a bedroom lady.

'Wonderful,' she said, then extended a square, no-nonsense hand. 'Bea Rolands,' she added. 'Are you a writer too? Like Mr. Trahearne?'

'Not exactly like Trahearne,' I admitted, holding on to the hand as things became clearer. The only writer around was out of action, and I had read enough books on bored afternoons in Army gymnasiums to fake it, maybe even pick up Trahearne's slack. 'I do research for him, sometimes, and take care of his affairs,' I said with a leer.

'Isn't he a wonderful writer?' she gushed. 'I just love his books. I have them all, you know. Hardbacks. Even his poetry. And I've seen all the movies, three or four times, and I just love them, too. Do you think he'd mind if I asked him to autograph them for me?'

293

'Well, I don't know,' I said. 'He's really shy, you know, and that sort of thing embarrasses him, but why don't you bring them along tonight, and I'll ask him tomorrow.'

'Oh thank you,' she bubbled, bouncing on her heels. Her small firm breasts bounded about quite nicely in the thin bra she wore beneath her uniform.

'See you at eight,' I said, finally releasing her hand. 'And thanks for saving me from a solitary dinner.'

'Oh, the pleasure's all mine,' she answered, giggling.

Walking out of the hospital, I decided that Trahearne was all right. At least he wasn't boring. Things happened around him: blood, gunfire, a night in jail, and now a devoted fan with sexily bowed legs. I found myself hoping he would run away again. Soon. And often. Once every five or six months. Maybe he could just stop by and pick me up on the way, then we wouldn't have to waste all that party time while I busted my ass hunting for him.

4

At the supermarket, I asked the check-out lady for a receipt for the fifteen pounds of magazines and paperbacks, then flashed a deputy sheriff's badge – obtained under extremely suspicious circumstances – from Boulder County, Colorado. I told her I was investigating the material for hidden pornographic meanings. She didn't turn a single artfully tousled hair. Which was one of the things I had always liked about California: Everybody's so crazy, you have to be really weird to get anybody's attention.

When I delivered my load to Trahearne's room, he was sleeping like a grizzly gone under for the winter, curled on his unwounded hip, spitting out snores that seemed to curse his sleep, great phlegm-strangled, whiskey-soaked, cigar-smoked, window-rattling roars. I wondered how he slept in all that racket, how his wives, past and present, ever got any sleep. I hid his afternoon ration of vodka between something called *The Towers of Gallisfried* and a thin Western, *Stalkahole*, then tiptoed out quietly, trying not to awaken the monster.

At the nearest pay telephone, I found the high school drama teacher's number listed. When I called Mr. Gleeson and told him why I wanted to talk to him, he sounded vaguely amused rather than surprised. He didn't have to thumb through his memory to recognize the name, though, which was a good sign. He agreed to talk to me as soon as I could drive out to his house, but only for a short time, since he had a student appointment later that afternoon. Then he proceeded to give me a set of directions so confusing that it took me thirty minutes to drive the ten miles out to his house at the base of the Oakville Grade. By the time I found it, I had stopped myself

295

twice from driving on over the Grade into the Napa Valley and a wine tour.

Charles Gleeson lived in a cottage in a live oak glade, a small place that looked as if it had been a summer retreat once, with a shake roof and unpainted walls that had tastefully weathered to a silver gray. Some sort of massive vine screened his front porch and clambered like crazy over the roof, as if it feared it might drown among the large flowering shrubs that cluttered the yard. He came to the screen door before I could knock, a small man with a painfully erect posture, a huge head, and a voice so theatrically deep and resonant that he sounded like a bad imitation of Richard Burton on a drunken Shakespearean lark. Unfortunately, his noble head was as bald as a baby's butt, except for a stylishly long fringe of fine, graying hair that cuffed the back of his head from ear to ear. He must have splashed a buck's worth of aftershave lotion across his face, and he was wearing white ducks, a knit polo shirt, and about five pounds of silver and turquoise.

'You must be the gentleman who telephoned about Betty Sue Flowers,' he emoted as he opened the door. A cruising fly, hovering like a tiny hawk, banked in front of me and sped for the kitchen. Gleeson swatted at it with a pale, ineffectual hand and muttered a mild curse.

'I'm sorry I'm late,' I said.

'The directions, right? I must apologize, but my conception of spatial relationships is severely limited. Except on the stage, of course. My God, I can block out a monster like *Mourning Becomes Electra* in my head but I can't seem to tell anyone how to find my little cottage in the woods,' he prattled as he twisted the heavy bracelet on his wrist. Then we shook hands, and he patted my forearm affectionately and drew me into his Danish modern, Neo-Navajo living room. 'It's lovely out,' he suggested, touching the squash-blossom necklace, 'so why don't we sit on the sun deck? I fear the house is a disaster area – I'm a bachelor, you see, and housekeeping seems to elude me.' He waved his hand aimlessly at some invisible mess. We could have lunched off the waxed oak floorboards or performed an appendectomy on the driftwood coffee table. I didn't mind going outside though. His sort of house always made me check my boots for cowshit. Unfortunately, this time they were innocently clean.

The sun deck, built out of the same silvered planks as the house and threatened by the same heavy vine, was done in wrought iron and gay orange canvas. At least it was outside. With a deep, throbbing sigh, Gleeson collapsed into a director's chair and genteelly offered me the one facing him.

'It's a bit early for me, but would you care for a *cerveza?*' he said, idly swirling the ice cubes in the blown Mexican glass he had picked up from the neat little table that matched his little chair. 'A beer?' he added, just in case I hadn't understood.

'Right,' I growled, 'it's never too early for me.' Then I chuckled like Aldo Ray. If I had to endure his *l'homme du monde* act, he had to suffer my jaded, alcoholic private eye.

'Of course,' he murmured, then reached into a small refrigerator on the other side of his chair and came out with a can of Tecate, a perfect pinch of rock salt, and a wedge of lime already gracing the top of the can. He had prepared, the devil. 'Do you like Mexican beer?'

'I like beer,' I said, 'just like Tom T. Hall.'

'I see,' he said, trying to hide a superior smile with a supercilious eyebrow. 'Mexican beer is quite superb. Perhaps the best in the world. I'm quite fond of it myself. I summer in Mexico, you see, San Miguel de Allende, every year. Takes me away from the mundane world of high school,' he said as he handed me the beer.

'Must be fun,' I said, guessing that he spent his summers wearing a three-hundred-dollar toupee which looked like a dead possum and boring hell out of everybody for forty miles in every direction.

'A lovely country,' he sighed, meaning to sound wistful and longingly resigned to a life unworthy of his talents. Then he glanced up and said, 'A touch of salt on the tongue, then sip the beer, and bite the lime.'

'Right,' I said, then gobbled the salt, chug-a-lugged the whole beer, ate the lime wedge, rind and all, and tossed the empty can onto the lawn. Gleeson looked ready to weep, and when I belched, he flinched. 'Got 'nother wunna them Mexican beers?' I said cheerfully. 'That weren't half bad.'

'Of course,' he said, the perfect host, then doled me another can as if it were rationed. Before I had to destroy that one too, I was saved by the bell. Or the chirp. His telephone chirped like a baby bird. 'Oh damn,' he said. 'Please excuse me.'

After he went back inside, I stood up to let the heavy beer lie down. Out of an old nosy habit, I checked Gleeson's glass. Cranberry juice and a ton of vodka. He was either a secret tippler, a pathological liar, or more nervous about my visit than he cared for me to know. I sidled up to the kitchen window but I couldn't hear anything except the distant throb of his voice and the insane buzz of a frustrated fly. I opened the back door to let the poor starving devil out, then sat down to watch a humming bird suck sugar water from Gleeson's feeder. I couldn't believe the little bastard had come all the way from South America for that. Or that I had come all this way to talk about a girl who had run away ten years before.

Gleeson came back muttering gracefully about the foibles of his simply, simply lovely students. 'Now,' he said as he leaned back in his chair and clasped his hands around his knee with a soft clink of silver rings. 'What can I do for you?'

'Betty Sue Flowers.'

'Quite.' A brief frown wrinkled his forehead up toward the fragrant, glistening expanse of his scalp. 'Betty Sue Flowers,' he sighed, then shook his head and smiled ruefully. 'I haven't thought about her in years.'

'What comes to mind?'

'Such a gauche name for such a lovely, talented child,' he said. 'When it became apparent that she was more than just a good amateur actress, I advised her to change her name immediately, discard it like so much childhood rubbish.'

'I sort of like the name,' I said. I didn't like women who changed their names. Or men who wore jewelry before sundown.

'Quite,' he said. 'What exactly was it you wanted to know? I haven't seen or heard of her since the Friday before she ran away. What was that? Six, seven years ago?'

'Ten.'

'How time does fly,' he whispered with a dreamy lilt, mouthing the cliché like a man who knew what it meant.

'Quite,' I said.

He glanced up, narrowed his eyes as if he was seeing me for the first time. 'It isn't polite to mock me,' he suggested politely. He sounded half pleased, though, that I had taken the trouble.

'Sorry,' I said. 'A bad habit I have. What did she talk about that day?'

'I'm afraid I don't have the slightest notion,' he said, then held up

298

a finger. 'Wait, I seem to remember that she stopped by my office to tell me that she had tickets at the ACT for the next night.' He started to explain the initials, then stopped. 'I'm afraid I don't remember what they were doing. It has been quite some time, you understand.'

'Too long,' I admitted for the tenth time.

'Do you mind if I inquire into your motives in this matter?'

'Her mother asked me to look for her,' I said.

'Do you do this for a living? Or are you a member of the family?'

'Both,' I said. 'I'm a cousin on her mother's side and a licensed private investigator.'

'Would you be insulted if I asked for some identification?'

'Nope,' I said, and took out my photostat.

'I would have thought, from your accent,' he said as he handed it back, 'that you were from the Texas or Oklahoma branch of the family.'

'Texas,' I said. 'But they let us live just about anywhere we want to nowadays.'

'I see,' he said. 'Has there been some new information about Betty Sue that prompted her mother to hire you?'

'Nope,' I said. 'I was just handy. Down here on another case. And both Mrs. Flowers' sons are dead now, and she just thought she'd like to see her baby girl again.'

'I don't imagine she's a baby anymore,' he said, smiling at his own joke. 'But if I were you I would get in touch with her father. For reasons I don't quite understand – perhaps because he withheld his affection from her – Betty Sue had an unhealthy fixation on him. I would think she would have been in touch with him. Yes, I would look for the father,' he said, then leaned back in his chair, sipped his drink, and sighed heavily, like a detective who had just broken a big, sadly corrupt case in an existential movie.

My temper and my mouth had always gotten me in trouble. And occasionally prevented me from picking up the information I needed. I wanted to tell Gleeson to stuff his stupid advice. I also wanted to tell him to stuff his *Time* magazine analysis, and to explain what *fixation* meant, but instead of carping, I kept my mouth shut, my temper in hand.

'I never had a chance to meet Betty Sue when she was growing up,' I said, changing directions. 'What sort of girl was she?'

299

'One in a million,' he answered, quickly but softly, then paused abruptly as if he had confessed to something. I knew I had him now. 'Why?'

'Why?' he whispered. 'When I first saw her, she was playing in a grade school production of *Cinderella*, which I had to attend for reasons I don't even want to think about now. A simply dreadful production, even for grade school, and Betty Sue had been wasted in the fairy godmother role, but let me tell you, my friend, when that little girl, that mere child, was onstage, all the other children seemed like creatures of a lesser race. She had the best natural stage presence I had ever seen. Offstage, she wasn't anything special, a pleasant-looking child, no more, but onstage she was in charge. Such presence. Such a natural sense of character, too.' He paused to chuckle. 'Her fairy godmother was a queen, her gifts bestowed grandly on her inferiors. And even then, she had a frighteningly sexual presence. You could almost hear the middle-aged libidos in the audience whimpering to be unleashed.

'After the production, I went backstage to talk to her,' he continued, 'and found her staring with such awful longing eyes at the little girl who had played Cinderella that I gave her a lecture then and there about how good she had been. I'm afraid I quite lost control for a bit. When I finished, she looked up at me and said, "It's just a prettier dress than mine, that's all. I wouldn't be Cinderella, anyway. I wouldn't stand for it." She was nine, my friend, nine years old.

'After that, of course, I took her in hand, and whenever possible I arranged my high school and Little Theatre productions with a role for her in mind. I also tried to get that horrid mother of hers to allow me to enroll her in an acting class in the city – even offered to pay all the expenses out of my own pocket. Of course, she refused. "Buncha damn foolishness," I believe were her exact words.' He paused again and clasped his hands together. 'Her damned mother foxed me at every turn. I suppose she had been considered good-looking in her youth – though the idea escapes me now – and she resented Betty Sue. And who wouldn't, stuck in that horrid trailer house behind that sordid beer joint. Once, when Betty Sue was fifteen, I had a friend – a professional photographer – take a portfolio of photographs of her. They were lovely. Later, when I asked Betty

Sue what she had done with it, she told me that it had been lost, but I remain convinced that her mother destroyed it.

'So sad,' he said, sipped his drink, and hurried on. 'At fifteen, she played Antigone in Anouilh's version, and at sixteen, Mother Courage. I wouldn't have believed it possible.'

'Pretty heavy stuff for high school,' I said.

'Little Theatre productions,' he said. 'We had a great company then. Even the San Francisco papers reviewed our productions favorably. She was so wonderful.' He sounded like a man remembering heroics in an ancient war. 'With a bit of luck, she might have made it on Broadway or in Hollywood. With a bit of luck,' he repeated like a man who had had none. 'The luck is nearly as essential as the talent, you know.' Then he gazed into his empty glass.

I broke into his reverie. 'How old was she when you seduced her?'

Gleeson laughed lightly without hesitation, his capped teeth gleaming in the sunlight. The hummingbird buzzed the sun deck like a gentle blue blur, pausing to check Gleeson's fragrance. But he wasn't a flower, so the bird flicked away. Gleeson rattled his ice cubes and stood up.

'I think I'll have that drink now,' he said pleasantly. 'Would you care for another Tecate?'

'I'd rather have an answer to my question,' I said.

'My good fellow,' he said as he fixed a drink, 'you've been the victim of sordid rumors and vicious gossip.'

'I got your name from Mrs. Flowers,' I said, 'and that's all. Except that I understand now why she gritted her teeth when she said it. Otherwise, I don't know a thing about you that you didn't tell me.'

'Or that you surmised?'

'Guessed.'

'You do the country bumpkin very well, my friend,' he said as he handed me another beer. 'But you slipped up when you didn't ask me to explain what ACT stood for, and you didn't learn about Brecht and Anouilh in the police academy or in a correspondence course for private investigators.'

'I'm supposed to be the detective.'

'I imagine you play that role quite well, too,' he said, 'and I suspect that it isn't in my best interest to continue this conversation.'

'I don't live here,' I said. 'I couldn't care less how many adolescent hymens you have hanging in your trophy room. Better you here with candlelight and good wine than some pimpled punk in the back seat of a car with a six-pack of Coors.'

'I'm not that easily flattered,' he said, but I could see smutty little fires glowing in the depths of his eyes. 'However, I do occasionally indulge myself,' he added, smiling wetly. 'Most of the simple folk in town think I'm a faggot, and I let them. A very nice protective coloration, don't you think?' I nodded. 'But Betty Sue and I never had that sort of relationship. Not that I wasn't sorely tempted, mind you – she had a fierce sexuality about her – and not that she might not have been willing. Certainly, if I had known . . . known how things were going to work out, known that she wouldn't pursue a career in the theatre, I would have snatched her up in a moment. But I was afraid that a sexual relationship might interfere with our professional relationship.'

'Professional?'

'That's right,' he said. 'I may be only a high school drama teacher now, but I have worked off-Broadway and in television, even taught in college, and I know the business. Betty Sue might have made it. And I confess that I intended to use her if she did.' He sighed again. 'Athletic coaches often rise on the legs of their star players, and I saw no reason why I shouldn't have the same chance. So I abstained. Betty Sue, as young girls so often do, might have grown bored with the older man in her life, and confused the sexual relationship with the professional one. So, my friend, I kept my hands off her,' he said with just the right touch of remorse mixed with pride.

'I'm sorry,' I said, trying to see his face behind the wistful mask. 'You must still have friends in the theatre,' I said, 'and I assume that you have asked them about Betty Sue over the years.'

'So often that I've become an object of some derision,' he said ruefully. 'But no one has ever seen or heard of her. That's a dead end, I'm afraid.'

'Could she have been pregnant?'

'She could have, yes,' he said. 'I assumed that she wasn't a virgin much past her fourteenth birthday. But, of course, I had no way of knowing.'

'You know,' I said, still bothered about the earlier lie about his drink, 'sometimes people confess a little thing – like your selfish intentions about her career – to cover up something larger.'

'What could I possibly have to hide?' he said blandly.

'I don't know,' I said, then leaned forward until our hands nearly touched. 'I've got a little education,' I said, 'but I'm not particularly sophisticated – '

'Still a country boy at heart?' he interrupted.

'Right. And, like you said, you're a professional – you know all about acting and lying, wearing masks,' I said, 'and if I find out that you've been lying to me, old buddy, I'll damn sure be back to discuss it with you.' I crushed my empty beer can in my fist. An old-fashioned steel can.

Gleeson laughed nervously. 'You're a terrible fraud,' he said as cheerfully as he could. 'You couldn't fool a child with that act.'

'Unlike yours, old buddy,' I said, 'mine ain't an act.' Then I grabbed his wrist and squeezed the heavy silver bracelet into his soft flesh. 'Intellectual discourse is great, man, but in my business, violence and pain is where it's at.'

'My God,' he squeaked, squirming, 'you're breaking my arm.'

'That's just the beginning, man,' I said. 'Keep in mind the fact that I like this, that I don't like you worth a damn.'

'Please,' he whimpered, sweat beading across his scalp.

'Let's have the rest of it,' I whispered.

'There's nothing, I swear . . . Please . . . you're breaking . . .'

'Listen, old buddy,' I said pleasantly, 'the U.S. Army trained me at great expense in interrogation, filled my head with all sorts of psychological crap, but when I got to Nam, we didn't do no psychology, we hooked the little suckers up to a telephone crank – alligator clips on the foreskin and nipples – and the little bastards were a hundred times tougher than you, but when we rang that telephone, the little bastards answered.'

'All right,' he groaned, 'all right.' I released his wrist. 'Can't you get this off,' he grunted as he struggled with the bent bracelet.

'Sure,' I said, then straightened the silver. His face wrinkled and his eyelids fluttered. He rubbed his wrist as I fixed him a drink. 'You had something to tell me.'

'Yes, right. Once, some time ago,' he babbled, 'I thought I saw her in a porno flick over in the city. The girl was fat and awful, a pig, but it might have been her, it looked like her, the print was bad, all grainy, and the lighting even worse, but it looked like her, except for this scar, this ugly scar in the middle of her belly.' When he stopped talking, his ruined mouth kept moving like a small animal in its death throes.

'Why lie about that?' I asked, honestly amazed.

'I was . . . I am ashamed of my interest in that . . . that sort of thing,' he said, then rushed into his drink. 'And it was so sordid, that awful fat girl and all those old men . . .'

'You remember the name of it?'

'*Animal* . . . something or other. *Lust* or *Passion*, something like that. I can't remember, it was so horrid,' he moaned, then began to weep.

'And so exciting,' I said, and he nodded. 'That's all you had to tell me?' I asked, and he nodded again.

It didn't sound right, but I didn't know what sounded wrong. I did know that I couldn't push him anymore. I didn't have the stomach for it. The only interrogation I had seen in Vietnam had made me sick, but I didn't remember if I had vomited because of the tiny Viet Cong's pain, the Vietnamese Ranger captain's pleasure, or my own fatigue. I had been in the bush for twenty-three days, and I could sleep standing up with my eyes open, which was good, because I couldn't sleep lying down with them shut. A few days later, I made the mistake that got me out of Nam and two years later out of the Army. Those times seemed far away, usually, but listening to Gleeson sob into the clear sunlight, they seemed too close.

'Hey,' I said, 'I didn't mean to hurt you.'

'Oh, I understand,' he blubbered, 'that horrid war twisted so many of you boys.'

'I left Nam nine years ago,' I said, 'and I'm no boy, so don't make excuses for me.'

'Of course,' he said as sincerely as he could, 'of course.' Then he took his hands away from his face and wiped at the tears. 'Will you do me one small favor?'

'What's that?'

'If you find her, will you call me? Please. I'll pay anything you ask. Please.'

'You might have thought of that ten years ago.'

'Ha,' he said, rubbing his eyes. 'Ten years ago I was still in my thirties, instead of nearly fifty, and I had no idea that I was going to be here ten more years, no idea that the peak of my career was going to be some little high school actress. No idea at all. I didn't know what she meant to me then. I do now. I'd just like to see her, talk to her again. Please.'

'I won't find her,' I said.

'But if you do . . .'

'I'll let you know for free,' I said. 'Sorry about your wrist, and thanks for the beers.'

'My pleasure,' he answered, a slight smile curling his lip, then his head dropped into his hands again.

I left him there on the sun deck, his huge head cradled in his arms like that of a grotesque baby. As I stepped out the front door, a young girl wearing a halter and cut-offs took that as her cue to push her ten-speed bike up the walk. I wanted to tell her that Gleeson wasn't home, but her greeting and smile were shy and polite with wonder, her slim, tanned thighs downy with sweat.

'Hello,' she said. 'Isn't it a lovely day?'

'Stay me with flagons,' I said, 'comfort me with apples, for I am sick of love.'

'What's that?' she asked, sweetly bewildered.

'Poetry, I think.'

Instead of taking her in my arms to protect her, instead of sending her home with a lecture, I walked past her toward my El Camino. Youth endures all things, kings and poetry and love. Everything but time.

5

Since it was getting on into Saturday afternoon, and since I didn't feel like Christian charity on the hoof, I hoped Albert Griffith wouldn't answer his telephone. No such luck. After I explained what I wanted, he agreed to meet me in his office at five. He even sounded anxious to talk to me. I drove to Petaluma and found an anonymous motel bar and a dirge of a Giants game on the television with which to slay foul time until five.

After a couple of deadly dull innings and slow, carefully paced beers, the bartender drifted by and I asked him for a drink.

'Stay me with CC ditches, my friend, for I am bored shitless by all this.'

'Hey, fella, take it easy, huh,' he said, then walked away.

'That's Canadian Club and water, you turd,' I shouted at his back. 'But I'll have it someplace else.'

'That's fine with me, buddy,' he said.

For a tip, I left him the remains of a stale beer. When even the bartenders lose their romantic notions, it's time for a better world. Or at least a different bar. I found the local newspaper and the nearest bar.

Albert Griffith, though, had enough romantic notions to gag Doris Day. He kept an office in a restored Victorian house on a quiet side street just outside the downtown area, sharing the house with another lawyer and two shrinks. And he had dressed for the occasion. A dark blue, expensively tailored, vested, pin-striped suit and a silk tie. As he ushered me into his office, he offered me a wing-backed gold brocade chair and a taste of unblended Scotch. I accepted them both. In my business, you have to buy everybody's act. For a few

306

minutes. Usually lawyers are too devious to suit me. They seem to have the idea that justice is an elaborate game, that courtrooms are tiny stages, and clients simply an excuse for the legal act. They also have a disturbing habit of getting elected to political offices, or appointed to government commissions, then writing laws you have to hire a lawyer to understand. But Albert Griffith acted as if he were my best friend. For a moment.

As soon as I was settled, he leaned against the front of his massive desk, his arms crossed as he towered over me, smiling in a friendly way beneath sardonic eyes. After I had a taste of his great Scotch, he leaped into his act.

'All right, Mr. Sughrue,' he said, 'let's get something straight from the very beginning. I don't know how you persuaded Mrs. Flowers to hire you for this wild goose chase, and I don't know how much money you have managed to weasel out of that poor woman, but she's a personal friend of my mother's, and I intend to put an end to this nasty little gambit of yours.'

'You want me to cut you in, huh?' I said. 'Okay. There's enough for everybody.'

'What?'

While he worked on his confusion, I stood up and walked around behind his desk, took a cigar out of a burled walnut box, lit it, sat down in his leather swivel chair, and propped my boots on his desk.

'What the hell are you doing?' he asked.

'Making myself comfortable, partner,' I said, then blew smoke in his face.

'Get up from there,' he sputtered. He couldn't have been any angrier if I had sat down on his wife's face.

'Listen, Buster Brown,' I said, taking a fistful of his cigars for my pocket, 'you've got a fancy setting here, but you're just another second-class creep. Your daddy, when he can stand up, holds a sign for the highway department, and your momma put you through law school with a beauty operator's tips. Your daddy-in-law is springing for this antique whorehouse decor, this whole lawyer scam, and you, Mr. Griffith, aren't only a failure, you're a courthouse joke, so get out of my face with this big-shot attorney crap.'

'If you don't get out of my office this instant, I'm calling the police,' he said in a voice on the verge of sobs.

'After you apologize,' I said, 'maybe we can start this whole thing over again.'

At the moment, though, he didn't have anything to say. I watched his face change hues about four times and examined the shoddy dental work on his back lower molars. At the newspaper bar, I had found an AP stringer who, for the price of a 7 & 7, had given me Albert Griffith's life history.

'If it will improve your attitude,' I said, 'give Rosie a call. She's got eighty-seven bucks, two beers, and a smile into this, and I might take another beer or two, and I might only lose a hundred bucks on this, but she's paid all she's going to pay. So call her while I have another taste of this overpriced whiskey.'

While I stiffened my drink, he called Rosie and spoke softly to her for a minute. Then he hung up, loosened his tie, and made himself a really stiff drink. I didn't have much of a picture of Betty Sue Flowers yet, but just the mention of her name seemed to drive grown men to drink.

'Let's sit on the couch,' Albert said, and we sat at opposite ends of a long leather expanse. 'Please accept my apology,' he said. 'I'm sure you've been in the business long enough to understand that most independent operatives are scumbags. Even the corporate security people are frighteningly ugly beneath that slick exterior they maintain.'

'Thanks.'

'For what?'

'For not thinking I have a slick exterior.'

'You're welcome,' he said, glancing at my faded Levi's and worn work-shirt and laughing. A bit too long to suit me. 'Rosie explained everything, Mr. Sughrue, and I am sorry for acting so hastily.'

'That's okay,' I said. 'I'm used to it.'

'Well, I am sorry,' he repeated. I wished he would stop. 'Rosie even said that you told her it was probably a waste of time and money,' he said, then smiled sadly. 'Let me tell you that it is definitely a lost cause.'

'Why's that?'

'I was a student at Berkeley when Betty Sue ran away,' he said, 'and I spent all my spare time for two years searching for her in the city. Let me tell you, my transcript showed it too. I nearly didn't get into law school,' he said dramatically. I wasn't impressed yet. 'I never turned up a single lead. Not one. It was as if she walked away from my car that afternoon and off the edge of the world, off the face of the earth. I even had a friend from law school – he's in Washington – check her Social Security payment records, and there hasn't been a payment since she worked a part-time job the summer before she disappeared.' He sucked on his whiskey glass, his hand trembling so badly that the lip of the glass rattled against his teeth. 'I can only assume that either she doesn't want to be found or that she's dead. Though if she is, she didn't die in San Francisco or any place in the Bay Area. At least not in the first five years after she ran away.'

'How do you know that?'

'I checked Jane Does in county morgues for that long,' he said softly, as if the memory made him very tired.

'You went to a lot of trouble.'

'I was very much in love with her,' he said, 'and Betty Sue was a very special lady.'

'So I've heard,' I said, then regretted it.

'From whom?' he asked in a voice that tried to be casual.

'Everybody.'

'Which everybody, specifically?'

'Her drama teacher, for one,' I said.

'Gleeson,' he snorted. 'That faggot son of a bitch. He didn't know anything about Betty Sue, didn't care anything about her. He encouraged her acting so she would think he was a big man, that's all. She was good at it but she didn't even like it. She used to tell me, "They just look at me, Albert, they don't see me." '

'I thought Marilyn Monroe said that.'

'Huh? Oh, perhaps she did,' he said. 'I'm sure it's a common psychological profile among actresses. Betty Sue was very sensitive about her looks. Sometimes when we would be having a . . . spat, she would cry and tell me, "If I were ugly or crippled, you wouldn't love me." '

'Was she right?' I asked without meaning to.

'Damn it, man,' he answered sharply, 'I haven't seen her in ten years and I'm . . . I'm still half in love with her.'

'How does your wife feel about that?'

'We don't talk about it,' he said with a sigh.

'Could Betty Sue have been serious enough about the acting to have run off to Hollywood or New York, something like that?'

'Do girls still do that?' he asked, glancing up at me.

'People still do everything they used to do,' I said. 'What about her?'

'Oh, I don't think so,' he said, then asked if he could freshen my drink. When I shook my head, he got up and made himself a new one. 'I don't think so at all,' he said from the bar. 'She enjoyed the work-rehearsals and all that – but for her, the play wasn't the thing.' He sat back down. 'She suffered from passing enthusiasms, you know,' he said, as if it were a disease from which he had been spared. 'One month it would be the theatre, the acting just a preparation for writing and directing, and the next month she would be planning to go to medical school and become a missionary doctor. Then she would want to be a painter or some sort of artist. And the worst part of it was that she could do damn near anything she set her mind to. For instance, I wasn't a great tennis player – though I nearly made the team at Cal – and when I could get her on the courts, she gave me a hell of a time, let me tell you.' He paused to look at his drink, then decided to drink about half of it in a gulp. 'And, you know, in spite of all the things she could do, she was the loneliest person I ever knew. That was the heartbreaking part of it, that loneliness. I couldn't help her at all. Sometimes it seemed my attempts just made it worse. I couldn't stop her from being lonely at all.'

'Not even in bed?'

'You're a nosy bastard, aren't you?' he said quietly.

'Professional habit.'

'Well, the truth is that I never laid a hand on her,' he said with proper sadness. 'Maybe if I had, I wouldn't still be carrying her around on my back.'

'Did anybody else lay a hand on her?'

'I always suspected that she wasn't a virgin,' he said with a slight smile. 'But she wouldn't talk about it.'

'Did you two fight about it?'

'I fought, but she wouldn't fight back,' he said. 'She'd just sit there, drawn into some sort of shell, and weep. Or else she'd make me take her home.'

'Did you have a fight the day she walked away?'

'No,' he murmured, shaking his head. 'It was just a normal day. We drove over to San Francisco for dinner and a movie, and on the way she decided that she wanted to drive through the Haight to see the hippies. We got stuck in a line of traffic, and she just opened the car door, stepped out, and walked away. Without looking back. Without saying a word,' he said slowly, as if he had repeated the lines to himself too many times.

'You didn't chase her?'

'How could I?' he cried. 'I didn't know she was running away, and I couldn't just leave my car sitting in the street, man.'

'I thought you had tickets for a play,' I said.

'Hell, I don't know,' he said. 'It was ten years ago, ten goddamned years ago.'

'Right.'

'Need another drink,' he either said or asked. When he stood up, I handed him my glass, but he paced around the office with it in his hand.

'Can you tell me anything else about her?' I asked.

He stopped and stared at me as if I were mad, then started pacing again, taking the controlled steps of a drunk man. But his hands and mouth moved with a will of their own; he waved his arms and nearly shouted, 'Tell you about her? My God, man, I could tell you about her all day and you still wouldn't see her. Tell you what? That I had loved her since she was a child, that I couldn't just stop because she ran away? I tried to stop, believe me I tried to stop loving her.' Then he paused. 'It all sounds so silly now, doesn't it?'

'What?'

'That the disappearance of a damned high school chick that I'd never touched was the most traumatic experience of my life,' he said. 'And let me tell you, I know something about trauma, growing up with a drunken father. What do you want to know anyway?'

'Everything. Anything.'

'That I married a safely dull woman and fathered two safely dull children that I can't bear to face and can't bear to leave and can't bear to love because they might all run away too,' he said.

'Hey, man,' I said, 'take that crap upstairs to the shrinks. Don't tell me about it. I asked about her, not you.' He stopped to stare at his feet. 'You've already been upstairs, right?'

'I've been going for two years now,' he said with that mixture of pride and shame people in analysis so often have. 'And, in spite of the jokes, it's working. I meant to go to medical school, you know, but all those visits to the morgue, all those anonymous faces beneath

311

the rubber sheets, were too much for me.' He went to the bar to splash whiskey aimlessly into our glasses, then kept mine in his hand. 'As you so aptly said, as a lawyer I'm not even a good joke. But I'm enrolled in next fall's medical school class out at Davis. Thanks to Betty Sue, it's taken me ten extra years to get started, but now I'm finally going to make it.'

'Good luck,' I said.

'Thank you,' he muttered, not noticing my irony. 'Anything else?'

'One more question,' I said, 'which I hate to ask, but I really would appreciate an answer.'

'What's that?' he asked, then saw the two glasses in his hands. He still didn't give me mine. 'And why do you hate to ask it?'

'I heard a rumor that Betty Sue had made some fuck films in San Francisco.'

'That's so absurd I won't even bother to answer,' he said, and finally gave me my drink.

'You don't know anything about that, huh?' I asked as I stood up and put some ice in the warm whiskey.

'Don't be ridiculous,' he said, facing me across an expanse of Persian carpet.

'Okay,' I said. 'Do you remember a girl named Peggy Bain?'

'Of course. She was Betty Sue's best friend. Only friend, I guess.'

'You wouldn't know where she's living?'

'Actually, I might,' he said. 'I handled a divorce for her some years ago, and she sends me a Christmas card once in a while.' He stepped over to the desk and thumbed through his Rolodex, then wrote an address and telephone number on a card with his little gold pen. The simple chore had restored some of his façade, but his knuckles were white around his glass when he picked it up. 'Two years ago she was living at this address in Palo Alto. If you see her, please give her my regards.'

'Thanks,' I said, 'I will.'

'Say,' he said too loudly, 'let's sit down and have a drink. Pleasure instead of business.'

'No thanks,' I said, setting my unfinished Scotch on the coffee table. 'I've got a date.'

'Me too,' he said sourly as he checked his watch. 'With my wife.' We shook hands as he led me toward the door, then he held my hand and asked, 'Would you do me a favor?'

'What's that?'

'If you should, through some insane circumstance, find Betty Sue, would you let me know?'

'Not for love or money,' I said, and took back my fingers.

'Why's that?' he asked, confused, and nearly crying.

'Let me tell you a story,' I said, which didn't help his confusion. 'When I was twelve, my daddy was working on a ranch down in Wyoming, west of a hole in the road called Chugwater, and I spent the summer up there with him – my momma and daddy didn't live together, you see – and my daddy was crazy, had this notion, which he made up out of whole cloth, that he was part Indian. Hell, he took to wearing braids and living in a teepee and claiming he was a Kwahadi Comanche, and since I was his only son, I was too. And that summer I was twelve, he sent me on a vision quest. Three days and nights sitting under the empty sky, not moving, not eating or sleeping. And you know something? It worked.'

'I'm not sure I understand what you're telling me,' he said seriously.

'Well, it's like this,' I said. 'I had a vision. And I've been having them ever since.'

'So?'

'You know, when you were telling me about those Jane Does and those rubber sheets, I had another one,' I said.

'Of what?'

'I saw your face all scrunched up in disappointment every time you didn't find her under that rubber sheet,' I said, and he understood immediately. After two years on the couch, he had begun to have visions of his own. 'I know you're a nice person and all that and that you didn't mean to feel that way, but you did, and if I find her, you'll never hear about it from me.'

'Why are you doing this to me?' he screamed, but I shut the door in his face. I didn't have a vision for that yet.

As I opened the outside door, I held it for a thin, lovely woman with fragile features and a brittle smile. She thanked me with a voice so near to hysteria that I nearly ran to my El Camino. No visions, no poetry for her. Just a road beer for me. I sat for a bit, holding the beer from the small cooler sitting in the passenger seat like an alien pet, thinking about my mad daddy and those days and nights sitting cross-legged on a chalk bluff above Sybille Creek, sitting still

313

like some dumb beast or a rock cairn marking a nameless grave. Of course I had visions. At first they were of starving to death, or being so bored I died for the simple variety of the act, then it was maybe freezing to death under the stars or finding myself permanently crippled, locked into my cross-legged stance like a freak on a creeper. Later, though, the visions came: a stone that flew, a star that spoke like an Oxford don, Virginia Mayo at my feet. I guess I wasn't a very good Comanche; I had seen too many movies, and besides, my crazy daddy had made the whole thing up. But, by God, I had visions. And none of the drugs, or combinations thereof, I had ingested as an adult had ever matched those first ones. But I had never gone back up Sybille Creek to that chalk bluff either. And never would.

6

As I drove back to Sonoma, I wondered what Gleeson and poor Albert had done to draw the meanness out of me. I had bullied Gleeson unmercifully and picked Albert open like a scabbed sore, left them both alone talking to empty drinks. Maybe I just had a natural-born mean streak. That's what the last woman I loved had told me when she refused to marry me. She said that she had two children to raise and that she didn't want them to learn about being mean from me. That, and other things. If it hadn't made me feel so mean, I would have tried to feel guilty about Gleeson and poor Albert. Maybe even the lady who wouldn't marry me. But I had washed her out of my system with the binge that had ended in Elko's ashtrays and toilets. Then I went home and cleaned up my act so well that I leaped at the chance to follow Trahearne on his reckless binge.

If not forgiveness, at least I had found work again. I had even found Trahearne, though I knew I didn't have a chance of finding Betty Sue Flowers. Not in a million years. So I drank my beer and pushed my El Camino down the road. That's my act. And has been for years.

Trahearne's act, however, was turning up like a bad penny or an insistent insurance salesman. When I walked into my motel room, his hulk was beached on the other double bed. A half-gallon of vodka, tonic, and ice sat on the nightstand between the beds, and a scrawled note sat on my pillow. *Stop me before I kill again.* In the corner of the room, a motley heap of unopened magazines and paperbacks sat in a silent pile.

I shook his shoulder and asked him what the hell he was doing in

315

my room, but he just smiled like an obscene cherub between snores. I cleaned up, changed into my good Levi's, and left him sleeping there without a comic note. My day hadn't lent itself to comic notes at all.

Bea had been raised in Sacramento, had never heard of Betty Sue Flowers, and didn't find out I was a fraud until much too late in the evening to make any difference. We did the town, such as it was, entertained the nightlife with laughter, lies, some of her home-grown grass, and some of my whiskey. Then we went stumbling back to the motel for the grandest lie of all. We also carried a stack of Trahearne's books up to the room, but the great man couldn't autograph them in his sleep.

'We could wait until tomorrow morning,' I suggested, leaning toward my bed.

'Oh, I couldn't do that,' Bea giggled. 'I've got to drive to Sacramento before one tomorrow afternoon, and besides, I couldn't do it with him sleeping right in the next bed.'

'Want me to wake him up?'

'No, silly,' she said. 'That's what I'm afraid of.'

'Don't worry about that, love,' I whispered into a suddenly accessible ear. 'The old boy sleeps like a stone. And there's one other thing . . .'

'What?'

'Well, I don't know if I should tell you.'

'Do.'

'Well, the old man can't get it up anymore,' I said seriously. 'Whiskey and war wounds, you understand. But he really likes to sleep right next to it while it's happening.'

'You're kidding.'

'Not a bit,' I said. 'He claims that the force of the sexual emanations gives him absolutely wonderful dreams. He says that's just about the only pleasure left for him in life.'

'No,' she said, shaking her head but still leaning into me.

'Yes,' I said into the soft little ear. 'You never know, he might have a great dream tonight and write a poem about it tomorrow. I'll make him dedicate it to you.' Then I had to fake a coughing fit to cover Trahearne's badly stifled giggles.

'You think he might do that?' she asked shyly.

316

'I think I can arrange it.'

She stepped back and smiled. 'Do you do this sort of chore for him very often?'

'Not nearly often enough.'

'Okay,' she murmured, then stepped into my arms again, 'but you have to turn out the lights.'

'I won't be able to see your freckles,' I said.

'You can taste them, silly.'

The next morning as the three of us breakfasted in our beds — hothouse strawberries and real cream, turkey crêpes, and three bottles of Californian champagne — Trahearne sighed deeply and finished signing the last of Bea's books, then said to her, 'My dear, I'm certain that my faithful Indian companion there was terribly indiscreet last night, that he spoke to you of matters most private, matters too private to discuss in the light of day, matters I would consider it a personal favor if you mentioned to no living soul. If word got around, it might be embarrassing, you understand.'

'Oh I'd die before I'd say a word, Mr. Trahearne,' Bea cooed, then popped a berry into her wonderful mouth.

'Please call me Abraham,' Trahearne said formally. 'I consider myself in your debt.'

'Call me Isaac,' I muttered around a mouthful of turkey.

'And what shall we call me?' Bea asked prettily.

'The Rose of Sharon, the lily of the valley, not black but nonetheless comely,' Trahearne said gravely.

'How about the whore of Babylon?' I suggested.

'Don't be mean,' Bea said sweetly, then set a sharp elbow loose against my ribs as she glanced at her watch. 'Whoever I am,' she said, 'if I'm not at my mother's house in Sacramento by one o'clock, my name will be mud.' Then, as if it were the most natural gesture in the world, she slipped from beneath the covers, buck-naked, gathered up her neatly folded clothes, and strolled slowly and unselfconsciously into the bathroom, the morning sunlight glimmering off her untanned breasts as they bobbed, off her switching hips.

'Absolutely beautiful,' Trahearne muttered as she closed the door. 'And that routine of yours, Sughrue. I thought I'd heard them all — but sexual emanations and erotic dreams for the poor impotent old man! Where did you come up with that?'

317

JAMES CRUMLEY

'Drugs,' I said. 'You don't think she bought that crap, do you?'

'Women love that sort of lie,' he said, 'they love the role of helpmate. That's where they get their power over us, my boy, their victory in defeat, their ascendancy in submission.'

'Should I write that down?'

'You never stop playing the jaded detective, do you?' he said. 'How do you like my sadly wise old man act?'

'If a pig's ass is pork, old man, how come they call it ham?'

'Envy, my young friend, is such a mean, small emotion,' he said. 'Did you hear me envy your lady friend's inspired thrashing last night?'

'I heard you breathing hard,' I said. 'Does that count?'

Trahearne laughed and I poured the champagne. When Bea stepped out of the bathroom, Trahearne said, 'Let me thank you, my dear, for that beautiful display. It warmed, as they say, the cockles of my heart –'

'Is that anything like warming over your cliché?' I interrupted.

' – and restored my faith in human nature. You're simply too kind to an old, sick man.'

'You're more than welcome, Mr. Trahearne,' she answered, then leaned over to kiss his plump cheek. His great hand slipped up her thigh to fondly stroke her rump. 'Also, you're a terrible old fraud,' she added, and her firm nurse's hand shot under the covers and gave his unit a ferocious honk. 'Gotcha,' she giggled. Trahearne actually blushed, then sputtered around trying to regain his dignity. She came over to my bed and presented me with a kiss that was supposed to make me long for home and hearth, to give up my wandering ways – for a few days at least – then she said, 'And you, C.W., you're the most terrible liar in the whole world – sexual emanations, my ass – but you're sweet, too. Give me a call anytime.' Then she swept out of the room, her books under her arm, scattering bright laughter like coins, leaving a faint trace of woman scent lush in the air.

'By God, that's an exceptional young lady,' Trahearne harrumped.

'You old guys are too easily impressed.'

'Ah ha! Do I hear the strains of true love hidden behind the bite of tired cynicism?'

'True love, my ass,' I mocked. 'It's the sexual revolution, the open marriage, the growing-together-apart relationship. She's meeting her boyfriend, the doctor, at her mother's house. He spent last night pranging his second ex-wife, her sister, her sister's boyfriend, and a bisexual Airedale.'

'If that's true, that's sad.'

'It's fairly accurate,' I said.

'That's sad, then,' he said. 'I remember true love.'

'You mean the old days when you had to get engaged before you could show your girl's ass to your buddies?'

'Cynicism doesn't become you,' he said blithely.

'I'm sorry; it's the champagne, I guess.'

'That's odd,' he said. 'It always fills me with romance.'

'No shit.'

'Where in the world did Catherine find you, boy?' he asked. 'Surely not in the Yellow Pages or something as mundane as that.'

'I'm listed,' I said, 'but she found out about me in a bar.'

'Of course,' he said, raising an eyebrow built like a woolly worm. 'Where?'

'The Sportsman in Cauldron Springs,' I said. 'The guy who owns it is an old Army buddy of mine.'

'Bob Dawson?'

'Right. She went in to see if anybody had seen you, and he told her he had a friend who found lost things, like ex-husbands, and one thing led to another.'

'I'll just bet it did,' he said, oddly bitter, then I understood.

'She's your *ex*-wife, isn't she?' I said. 'So what the hell do you care?'

'For myself, I don't,' he said. 'It's just that it embarrasses my mother.'

'Your mother?'

'Catherine lives with my mother. In her house,' he said, 'and it upsets her when Catherine whores her way across the state.'

'You live with your mother?'

'My house is within a stone's throw of hers.'

'You don't sound very happy about it,' I said.

'Sometimes I'm not.'

'Move.'

'It isn't that simple,' he said. 'She's an old woman now, crippled with arthritis, and I promised her I'd live on the ranch until she died.

319

I certainly owe her that, you understand, at least that. And besides, every place is the same,' he said.

'The people are different,' I said, but he ignored me as he took a long drink from the champagne bottle, drank until he choked, then he smiled at me with wet eyes.

'If I had known how much fun we were going to have, Sughrue,' he said, 'I would have let you catch up with me sooner.'

'Pretty expensive fun,' I said.

'Worth every penny,' he said as he tossed the empty bottle on the carpet. 'I would have spent it all just to see that lady walk across the room.' He eased himself upright, propped on his good buttock. 'Wonderful naked ladies, by God, I love them,' he said. 'I've seen a horde of them in my time, boy, but I just can't get used to it.' He shook his head and grinned. 'Pop the cork on that other bottle,' he said, 'and let's drink to naked ladies.'

When I did, the cork bounced off the ceiling and skittered across the carpet like a small rabid animal. Then I filled our glasses, and Trahearne held his up into a soft beam of sunlight that had filtered through the eucalyptus trees, watching the bubbles rise like floating jewels.

'That's funny,' he said.

'What?'

Then he told me about naked women and sunlight. And that he was a bastard.

His mother had been an unmarried schoolteacher in Cauldron Springs when she was impregnated by a local rancher, who was married, and the school board had run her out of town. She had moved to Seattle to have the baby and stayed there after he was born, working at menial jobs to provide for them. By the time he started school, his mother had begun to publish stories in the Western pulps and free-lance articles in newspaper supplements and magazines, so they moved uptown into a tenement neighborhood on the edge of Capitol Hill. After school Trahearne walked home through the alleys to talk to the people his mother wrote about, the unemployed seamen and loggers, the old men who knew about violent times and romantic faraway places.

Sometimes, though, on these aimless walks, he saw a woman standing naked in front of her second-story back window. Only when it rained, though, as if the gray rain streaked on her dark window made her invisible. But the child could see her, dim but clearly visible beyond the reflections of the windows and stairways across the alley. In the rain, at the window, sometimes lightly touching her dark nipples, sometimes holding the full weight of her large, pale breasts in her white hands, always staring into the cold rain. Never in sunlight, always in rain. Sometimes she tilted her face slowly downward, then she smiled, her gray eyes locked on his through the pane, and hefted her breasts as if they were stones she meant to hurl at him. And sometimes she laughed, and he felt the rain like cold tears on his hot face. At nights he dreamed of sunlight in the alley, and woke to the insistent quiet rush of the gentle rain.

Even after high school, through the first years of college at the University of Washington, when he still lived at home, he saw the woman. And even later, after he had moved closer to the campus, he came back to the neighborhood on rainy days to once again stride the bricks of that littered alley, red bricks glistening in the rain. Only when he graduated and could find no work in Seattle, after he moved to Idaho to work in the woods setting chokers, only then did he stop haunting the alley behind her house, watching, waiting.

There were girls, of course, during those days, but it was never the same in cheap tourist cabins or upon starlit blankets beneath the pines. There was one, almost, once. A plump Indian girl who went skinny-dipping with him at dawn in a lake, which had flooded an old marshy forest and filled with tiny dark particles of wood fiber held in pellucid suspension, the naked girl near but distant too, like a skater twirling in a paperweight snowstorm. One, once, almost.

Then the war came. Trahearne enlisted in January of 1942, in the Marines, and after officer's training, his gold bars brightly gleaming, he took his leave in San Francisco instead of going back to Seattle to see his mother before he shipped out to the Pacific war. In the center of the Golden Gate Bridge, he met a young widow, still in her teens, whose husband had been an ensign on the *Arizona* at Pearl Harbor. At first, seeing her black dress and pale young face ruined with tears, he thought she might be preparing to jump, but when he spoke to her he found out she wasn't. She had only come there to throw her wedding ring into the bay. One thing, as he said ruefully, led to many others, and they fell in love, the young lieutenant anxious to be away to the war, to glory, the teenaged widow who had already

321

lost one man to the war with a sudden violence that was as shocking as that first blot of blood that had marked the end of her girlhood only a few years before. Their love, he said, was sweet with the stink of death from the beginning, and each time they coupled, it was as if it were the last time for both of them.

On his final day of leave, they went back out on the bridge, and there on a blustery spring afternoon, the wind full of sunlight, booming through the girders like the echoes of distant artillery, cold off the green sea, fragrant as a jungle, there he told his new love about the naked woman and the rain. Before he could finish, though, she began to unbutton her blouse, and oblivious to the people around them, she bared her small breasts to the afternoon sunlight, then nestled his face between them, sending him off to die.

'Of course,' he said to me, 'it was the most exciting thing that had ever happened to me. And maybe still is. I don't know.' Then he paused, and in his rumbling voice, added, 'I'd never been so touched. Such a lovely gesture.'

'What happened to her?'

'Always with the questions, huh,' he said, and gave me a long, hard stare. 'What happened to everybody then? The war happened, that's what. But I don't suppose you remember much about that.'

'I remember my daddy went away, then he came back, and went away for good,' I said.

'Killed?'

'No,' I said. 'After seeing North Africa, Italy, and southern France, he said south Texas didn't look like much. He came out West, and my mother and I stayed home. She said the war just gave him an excuse to be as worthless and shiftless as he always wanted to be.'

'Women are like that, boy,' he philosophized. 'They don't understand moving on. Give them a warm cave and a steady supply of antelope tripe, and they're home for good.'

'Maybe so, maybe not,' I said. 'But what happened to the woman?'

'What woman?' he asked, seeming confused and angry.

'The one with the tits.'

'For a man with at least a touch of imagination, my young friend, you have a callous soul and a smart mouth.'

'I told you I was a nosy son of a bitch.'

'I'll buy that,' he said. 'What's the C.W. stand for?'

'Nothing,' I lied. 'What happened to the woman?'

'Hell, boy, I don't know,' he grumbled. 'She married a 4-F or a dollar-a-year man or another officer with a longer leave than mine. What difference does it make? It's the story that counts.'

'Not until I know how it ends,' I said.

'Stories are like snapshots, son, pictures snatched out of time,' he said, 'with clean, hard edges. But this was life, and life always begins and ends in a bloody muddle, womb to tomb, just one big mess, a can of worms left to rot in the sun.'

'Right.'

'And speaking of messes,' he said, smiling, 'what are you going to do now?'

'Take you home, I guess.'

'What about Rosie's missing daughter?'

'It's a waste of time,' I said. 'If I had a year with nothing else to do, I might be able to find her, or find out what happened to her. But not in a couple of days. I'll just tell Rosie that you got out of the hospital sooner than I expected.' But that wasn't what I wanted to say.

'Listen, boy, I don't have a damned thing to do at home,' he said as I poured the last of the champagne into our glasses, 'and I feel that I've earned a few days of entertainment – what the hell, I've been shot again and survived – so why don't you give it a couple more days.'

'Well, sure, if you don't mind . . .'

'Mind, boy? Hell, I insist,' he said grandly.

'Great.'

'But I've got one little favor to ask,' he said as he sat up gingerly on the side of the bed.

'What?'

'Take me along,' he said shyly, mumbling and scuffing his feet on the carpet.

'What?'

'Let me go with you,' he said. I laughed, and he jerked his head up. 'I won't get in your way. I promise.'

'Promise to stay relatively sober,' I said, 'and you're welcome to come along for the ride.'

'How sober?'

'At least as sober as me.'

323

'That's no problem,' he crowed. 'You sure you don't mind?'

'It's your ass, old man,' I said.

'Please don't remind me,' he muttered, grinning as he stood up stiffly. 'It's a lovely day, boy. Let's stop by and pick up my barge, let the top down, and have some fresh air and sunshine, let the four winds blow the hospital stench and the, ah, ineffable odor of lust out of our noses. By God, I'll even buy the gas and the whiskey.'

'What will I do for expenses?' I asked as he hobbled toward the bathroom, but he waved his hand at me as if to say: *The devil take the expenses.*

While I replaced the rotor and moved our gear into his convertible, Trahearne tried to lure Fireball, dour with a hangover, out of the back seat, but the bulldog obviously intended to defend his position to the death. Or at least until Trahearne poured a cold beer into a rusty Hudson hubcap. Muzzle-deep in his morning beer, Fireball ignored us as we climbed in and lowered the top, but when we drove away, he glanced at the locked doors of Rosie's, then followed us down the road with a damned and determined trotting waddle, as if he knew we had the only cold Sunday-morning hangover beers in Northern California, as if he intended to fetch the Caddy by a rear tire and shake them loose. I slowed down to keep an eye on him.

'Dumb bastard's bound to quit,' Trahearne said after we had driven nearly half a mile.

Maybe that's the definition of dumb bastards: they never quit. After another two hundred yards, I stopped the car to wait for the dog. He showed up petulant and thirsty. Trahearne opened his door, let him in, and gave him a beer. Fireball turned up his nose at it and scrambled into the back seat, where he sat with a great deal of dignity, waiting like a stuffy millionaire for the help to drive on. I did. His jowls quivered in the slipstream, and he seemed to enjoy the sunlight and the Sunday drive.

'All he needs is a cigar,' Trahearne grumbled. I handed him the ones I had lifted from poor Albert, but he kept them for himself. 'What a lark!' he shouted as he fired up a fog and settled back to enjoy the ride. 'What a fucking lark!'

Outside of San Rafael, I had to brake hard to avoid a gaudy van as it cut across three lanes of traffic toward an exit. Trahearne flinched,

then propped his haunch higher on the pillow we had stolen from
the motel.

'By God,' he said, 'if I were a younger man – or hell if I were just
whole – we'd run those punks down and see if they couldn't learn
some manners.'

'You sure this is what you want to do, old man?' I asked.

'Son, this is all I've ever wanted to do,' he said, still grinning
through his pain. 'Hit the road, right? Move it on. And here I am
wandering around America with an alcoholic bulldog, a seedy private
dick, and a working quart of Wild Turkey.' He reached into the
glove box, took a nip, and passed the quart on to me. 'But don't call
me *old man*. That's all I ask.'

'Don't call me a seedy dick.'

'It's too lovely a day to be crude,' he said. 'And if you'll pass the
painkiller instead of holding it, I'll see about easing the pain.' He hit
the bottle hard when I handed it to him.

'No thanks,' I said when he offered it to me again. 'Do you mind
if I ask you a personal question?'

'We're in this together, aren't we?'

'What were you doing on the road?' I asked. 'Looking for your
runaway wife?'

'She hadn't run away,' he said. 'Like most artists, Melinda needs
a change of scene occasionally – fresh vistas and all that – a chance
to be alone, to be anonymous, to see the world with an eye unclut-
tered by companionship. My God, I understand. If I can't understand
that, who can? I need the same things myself. Luckily, in this marriage there's plenty of room for that sort of freedom, in this marriage,
unlike my first, my wife and I aren't completely dependent upon
each other.' Then he paused. 'Goddamned Catherine. I divorced
her, but I can't seem to get her off my back. I think she had some
insane idea that Melinda *had* run away, which I'm sure delighted her
no end, and that I was searching for her with murder on my mind.
Or something equally melodramatic. She thought she could save me
by sending you to find me. Or something like that. I don't know.
Damn it, I was married to the woman – saddled by the woman – for
more than twenty years, and I still don't have any idea what goes on
in her mind. I wouldn't be surprised to discover that she had hired
you to have me shot in the ass.'

'Pretty slick, the way I handled it, right?'

'Don't make jokes about Catherine,' he said, grinning, 'she's great at arranging things. She arranged my life for years.' He was telling me something more than I had asked, but I had no idea what. 'You're not married, are you?'

'Never have been.'

'I thought not,' he said. 'You're not complex enough to survive it.'

'That's what I always said.'

After a long pause as he watched the frail monuments of apartment complexes soar past the moving freeway, he asked, 'Do you mind if I ask you a question?'

'Nope.'

'Where the hell are we going?' he asked, then laughed wildly.

When he stopped, I told him what I had found out about Betty Sue Flowers, what I planned to do, and where I meant to look, shouting above the road noise until we kicked off into the windy, blue space of the Golden Gate. As I talked, Trahearne drank, and as we crossed the bridge, he stopped listening, thinking, I suppose, of the young widow. He stared at the bottle, clutched in his hand like a grenade, then frowned, the feathers on his lark already sadly ruffled.

In the back seat, the bulldog hunkered like a heathen idol, some magical toad with a ruby as large as a clenched fist in his head, glowing through his stoic eyes, an inscrutable snicker mystic upon his face.

7

They say the gods watch over fools and drunks – surely Trahearne and I qualified – and whoever *they* are, they're right too often for comfort.

Once we were downtown, we stopped at a quiet bar, and I called every dope dealer, police officer, and old girl friend I knew. They gave me some names and numbers, all of them absolutely useless. How was I supposed to know that every porno kingpin and czar in the city spent Sunday afternoons in religious retreats, consciousness raising sessions, or *est* seminars? Out of boredom and hoping to stay sober, I hit the bars and theatres around Broadway and found a bored college student taking tickets. He knew a sociology professor who knew more about pornographic movies than either the Legion of Decency or the Mafia.

The professor was home on Sunday afternoon like any good citizen, watching an old silent porno flick about a young fellow who is fooled by two young girls at the beach into fucking a goat through a knothole in a fence. Several months later, the girls con him out of his walking-around money when one of them slips a pillow under her old-fashioned bathing suit and accuses him of having fathered it.

'I'll be damned,' Trahearne whispered as he wriggled on the hard metal folding chair. 'That's almost funny.'

'Almost?' Professor Richter said, glancing down his sharp nose. 'Almost?' he repeated with the proprietary air of someone who had written, directed, and starred in the movie. He did resemble the young protagonist. 'It's hilarious!' he screeched. 'And that is the major problem of modern pornography: it's too serious. With minor exceptions, of course. Usually, when it attempts humor the modern pornographic film tries for the lowest level, and when it succeeds, however slightly, as in the case of *Deep Throat*, they have a national hit on their hands,' he said gravely. 'It's the same in all the arts: as technology advances, humor declines. The limits and definitions of art disappear, then the art is forced to satirize itself too earnestly, and the visual arts become literary, and that, my friends, is the very first sign of cultural degeneracy.' Then he slapped his slender, dusty hands together lightly, lifted the corners of his mouth, and added, 'Don't you agree?'

He had the glittering eyes and pained smile of a fanatic, the long face unmarked by emotion, so Trahearne and I nodded quickly. His face wasn't unpleasant, just blandly, hysterically objective. Maybe a steady diet of porno flicks had softened his features, but I couldn't begin to guess what had happened to his clothes. Perhaps he had slept in his shiny black suit. Several times. Badly. Certainly he had dined in it. Or off it. A blossom of tomato sauce with a dried mushroom bud served as a boutonnière, and his thin black tie, tugged into a knot the size of an English pea, as a napkin.

'What can I do for you gentlemen?' he asked as it became apparent that we hadn't come to discuss the state of the art.

I showed him my license and explained my business. Before I could finish, he scampered to a 5×8 file, rifled it, and came up with both hands full of cards, waving them at the walls of his small apartment, which were banked with file cabinets and shelves and stacks of film cans.

'*Animal Passion*,' he said, holding out his right hand. '*Animal Lust*,' he added with his left. 'Take your choice, gentlemen. Not a particularly imaginative title, either of them, but damned popular.' He simpered at his own joke.

'Low, low budget,' I said, 'with a group grope for a finale.'

'Aren't they all,' he said with his frail laugh. 'Could you give me an approximate date?'

'Late sixties maybe.'

'Major actress blonde or brunette?'

'Blonde.'

'Right,' he said, then replaced the cards into their file, shuffled them again. 'Perhaps this is it,' he said as he read a card, his narrow bloodless lips mouthing a long number. He dashed over to a stack of film cans and jerked one out of the middle so quickly that the ones above it fell down with a neat solid thunk. 'If I remember this one correctly, it's simply trash,' he said, 'without a single redeeming feature. Would you like to see it?'

'You mind?' I asked Trahearne.

'Why should I mind?' he said, looking very confused.

'Your romantic illusions,' I said, then laughed.

'Oh,' he said, 'oh yeah. Those.' His confusion seemed to clear itself up. For him, though, not for me. 'Roll it,' he said crisply, and Richter threaded the film.

It was basic, all right, perhaps even pitiful. It was Betty Sue Flowers, too. No matter how often I looked away, when I looked back she was there. She had gained enough weight to make her figure more than Reubenesque, and if she hadn't been able to move it with some grace, she would have seemed grotesque and comic as a chubby young housewife clad only in a frilly apron, her thick blond hair gathered into two unbraided pigtails that framed her fat face.

At least the plot was thin. First, a little minor-league action with a pair of bewildered toy poodles, then some major-league work with the neighborhood help: a postman, a milkman, two meter readers, and a grocery boy with pancake over his wrinkles. Among the five men, they had enough beer guts, knobby knees, blurred tattoos, dirty feet, and crooked dicks to outfit a freak show. In the finale, as they gathered in a carefully arranged pile about the kitchen table, they looked even more distraught than the poodles had, and their faces contorted with pain as they all tried to come at once as Betty Sue worked at all of them together. Everybody was stoned blind, and the crew kept stumbling on camera or into the lights or jerking the camera in and out of focus. You could almost hear the sigh of relief when they ran out of film. The whole thing seemed about as exciting as jerking off into an old dirty sock.

But Betty Sue, in spite of the fat and her eyes, which were as blank as two wet stones, had something that had nothing to do with the way she looked. She seemed to step into the degradation freely, without joy but with a stolid determination to do a good job. In spite of myself, I was excited by her, which made the whiskey curdle in my stomach. I worked on righteous anger but only came up with quiet sadness and a sick sexual excitement. I saw why Gleeson hadn't wanted to talk about the film; I didn't either. No more than I wanted

329

to look at a large, ugly scar that split the center of her pudgy abdomen.

'That wasn't funny at all,' Trahearne growled as the film unthreaded itself and flapped like a broken shade.

'Don't blame me,' Richter said as he began to rewind it.

'Think I'll hobble outside for a breath of fresh air and about a gallon of whiskey,' Trahearne said as he heaved his bulk out of the chair.

After he left, I asked Richter if he knew any of the actors' names.

'Surely you jest,' he said. 'In this business, only the *crème de la crème* have names, and usually they are assumed. However, I did recognize the chap who played the milkman – in another context, of course.'

'What context.'

'He once ran a pornographic bookstore downtown,' he said, 'and I think his name was Randall something . . . Randall Jackson.'

'Is he still in town?'

'No, he left after this film,' he said, 'which was his single effort. I seem to remember someone telling me that he was some sort of paperback distribution agent. In Denver, I think.'

I asked if he knew anybody else or anything else about the film, but he had never seen the girl again, which meant that she had dropped out of the business. I thanked him, then stood up to leave.

'Do you mind if I ask you a question?' I said.

'Of course not,' he answered pleasantly.

'What are you doing with all these films?'

'Catalogue, classification, and cross-indexing. Preparing for a scholarly study of the decline of the American pornographic film.'

'Isn't all this expensive?'

'I have a grant,' Richter said blithely. I didn't ask from whom. I didn't want to know. As I left, he was humming as he reloaded his projector.

Outside, Trahearne and Fireball were sitting back, drinking and watching the Sunday traffic on Folsom Street – two cabs, a babbling speed freak, and an Oriental wino. I climbed into the car, wishing I had a greater variety of drugs with me. Or less blind luck.

'Was that the girl you were looking for?' Trahearne asked.

'No,' I lied. 'It looked something like her but it's some chick named Wilhelmina Fairchild.'

'Could be a stage name,' Trahearne suggested.

'No,' I said. 'Richter knows the lady personally. She's working in a massage parlor over in Richmond. So unless she's developed a German accent since she left home, it wasn't Rosie's daughter.' I wasn't sure why I lied to Trahearne. Maybe because I was embarrassed for Rosie. Or for myself. Whatever, I didn't want him to know that it had been Betty Sue on the screen, flickering among so many hands.

'For Rosie's sake, I'm glad,' Trahearne said. 'I stopped in her place by accident and drank there a couple of days because I liked the place and her bulldog. I didn't talk to her much, but I liked the way she poured the beer and handled the bar, so I'm glad her daughter didn't end up like that. Or worse.'

'Me too,' I said.

'What now?'

'Palo Alto.'

'Why?'

'To talk to Betty Sue's best girl friend from high school,' I said.

'Maybe she's out,' he said. 'Maybe you should call first. Maybe we should hang around the city tonight. Have a few drinks, you know, relax and rest a bit.'

'No rest for the wicked,' I said, then tucked the Caddy between a taxi cab and a semi-truck, ripping off two dollars' worth of Trahearne's tires. 'It's a nice day and a pretty drive,' I added as soon as the truck driver stopped blowing his horn.

'If we survive it,' he said.

'You want to drive this fucking barge?' I asked angrily, mad about my lie and the movie.

'You just drive it however you want to, son,' Trahearne said, holding up his hands. 'But don't get mad at me. I'm not in charge of the world.'

'Sometimes I can't tell if I'm crazy or the world's a cesspool,' I said.

'Both things are true,' he said, 'but your major problem is that you're a moralist. Don't worry, though.'

'Why?'

331

'It'll pass with age,' he said. 'But talking about crazy – what was that fellow doing with all those films?'

'You wouldn't believe me if I told you.'

I was partially right. It was a nice drive. Except for a scuffle Fireball had with a large gray poodle who wanted to sniff his ass at a rest area, and except for the rich lady in the Mercedes who belonged to the poodle who slapped Trahearne when he suggested she do something impossible and obscene with her lousy damned play-pretty mutt, it was a lovely drive. But Trahearne was right about calling Peggy Bain first.

The girl who lived in the apartment address Albert had given me didn't know where Peggy Bain lived, but she did know somebody who might. We spent the afternoon kicking around from apartments to bars and back again, talking to a long series of people who knew where she might be. Finally, as we tried the last possible place, a backyard barbecue all the way up in La Honda, the sun headed behind the coastal hills and Trahearne began to whine like a drunken child. He had forgotten his promise to stay at least as sober as me. Trahearne and Fireball were as drunk as dancing pigs. At least the bulldog had the decency to pass out in the back seat. As we parked in the string of cars beside Skyline Drive, Trahearne sniffed the air, muttered *party*, and stopped whining.

'Maybe you should stay in the car,' I suggested.

'Nonsense,' he said as he tugged a fresh quart of Turkey from under his seat. 'If my famous writer act doesn't work, lad, I'll show them my invitation,' he added, waving the whiskey. 'I'm always welcome at parties,' he said as he lurched out of the car.

Of course the old bastard was right. The bearded young man who answered the doorbell had met Trahearne some years before at a poetry reading in Seattle, though Trahearne didn't remember him, and he welcomed us into his house, introducing Trahearne to his guests as if he had been the guest of honor all along. Within minutes, he had arranged glasses and ice and Peggy Bain sitting across a picnic table. Trahearne shooed the host and his fans away, sat down beside Peggy Bain, and flopped a heavy arm over her shoulder as he called her *honey*. She was a genial lady with a face as round as a full moon looming above her thick wool poncho. When Trahearne explained what we wanted, she glanced at him, then me, then broke

332

out in a fit of stoned laughter so fierce that she had to remove her rimless glasses and set them among the dirty plates on the table.

'You've got to be kidding,' she said over and over again, only stopping to giggle. Then she lowered the pitch of her glee, rubbed the tears out of her eyes, and said, 'Man, I haven't seen her since high school.' She paused long enough to shake a hash pipe out of her sleeve and light it, then offered it to Trahearne. He took a greedy hit, then held his breath and muttered *dynamite dope!* like some kid. When she offered it to me, I shook my head, trying to stay straight for a few minutes longer. 'I ran into her father down in Bakersfield a few years ago, and he said Betty Sue had been living in a commune up in Oregon, but she had left.'

'Remember the name of it?' I said.

'Man, who can remember those names,' she said. 'Sunflower or Sunshine Starbright Dreaming or Sun-fun or Sun-kinda-pretentious-hippie-shit.' After she stopped chuckling at her own joke, she added, 'Whatever its name was, it was somewhere outside of Grants Pass, I think.'

'When did you talk to her father?' I asked, and Trahearne muttered *yeah* as he fondled her square shoulder through the rough wool.

Peggy's face stiffened and she slipped her glasses back on, sighed and lifted her hands. I thought I was about to get a long question about who the hell I was to ask about Betty Sue, but she turned to Trahearne, saying, 'Hey, man, I ain't into star-fucking, okay? See that lady over by the back door? The one with the scarf around her head and all that heavy metal hanging off her neck? That's where your action is, man, okay?' Then she lifted his large hand off her shoulder by the fingers, dangling it as if it were a dead crab, and dropped it in his lap.

'Excuse me,' he muttered without a trace of sincerity, looking at his lap and peeking toward the back door at the same time.

'Don't be bummed out, man,' Peggy said.

'No sweat,' he said, then slid off the bench and limped toward the house.

'What's wrong with him?' she asked.

'Artistic temperament,' I said. 'He thinks famous writers are supposed to get fucked a lot.'

'Not that, dummy,' she said. 'What's wrong with his leg?'

'Old war wound,' I said.

333

'Which one?'

'Pick one,' I said, 'they're all the same.' I had been trained in the right radical responses by a crew-cut first lieutenant with a text on radical responses.

'Right on, man,' she answered on cue.

'But back to Betty Sue,' I said. 'How long ago did you talk to her father?'

'At least six years ago,' she said. 'I know because I was still married to that redneck asshole from Santa Rosa. We were down in Bakersfield on some kind of United Farmworkers blast, and I saw Betty Sue's daddy's name in the paper. He was playing at a place called the Kicker, which I assumed was short for Shitkicker, so a bunch of us got high and went out to test the rednecks. Of course, we took two of the biggest hippies in the world, two logger kids from up around Weed. We wanted to look back to see how the other half lives.'

'How were they doing?'

'Just like you'd expect, man, living high, wide, and handsome in Bakersfield,' she answered, grinning. 'But old man Flowers, he was one cool dude.'

'How's that?'

'Singing in the band, running the bar, and dealing nose candy like a bandit,' she said.

'Cocaine?'

'Nothing else makes you feel so good,' she said. 'At first we thought he was bragging to impress the hippies – you know how straight people do – talking about selling coke to all the big names playing around Bakersfield, but after the second set, he took us back to his office, and we did a ton and bought five grams. Good stuff and fairly cheap.'

'And you talked about Betty Sue,' I said, trying to bring her back from her cocaine memories. And mine too.

'Right. I asked if he'd heard from her, and he said she'd called once, a year, maybe two years before, asking for money to split from the commune scene. Probably one of your typical fascist hippie scenes, you know, man.'

'But you don't remember the name?'

'Like I said, man, Sun-something,' she said, then paused to glance up at me. 'You looking for her because she's in trouble?'

334

'No, not that,' I said, then realized that after the film I didn't know why I was looking for Betty Sue anymore. 'I stumbled into her mother, and she hired me to look around for a few days,' I said.

'Sorry, but I can't help.'

'That's okay,' I said, 'she's been gone too long anyway.'

'Just barely long enough,' Peggy whispered, looking down, all the stoned laughter gone now.

Behind her, the clouds surrendered their last crimson streaks to a soft, foggy gray. A single tall evergreen tilted against the falling sky. Behind me, the party began to rumble like thunder. Peggy relit the hash pipe, and this time I accepted it from her. We shared the smoke as the evening winds rose off the cold sea, rose up the wooded ridges, and herded the party inside, people muttering thin complaints like little children called from play to the fuzzy dreams of their early beds. The plate-glass windows along the back of the house reflected the last vestiges of the sunset, and beyond, like a double exposure, the party trundled silently onward, mouths opening, wounds without sound, gestures without meaning. Beside a doorway against the opposite wall, Trahearne stared sadly at the sunset.

'What else can I tell you, man?' Peggy asked when the pipe had gone out.

'I don't know,' I said, then moved around the table to sit beside her, close but not too close, my fingers locked behind my head as I leaned against the littered table. 'I just don't know,' I said as I tried to see the ocean swells and the evening fog below the wide and empty sky being overcome by a nascent darkness. 'Maybe you could just tell me about her,' I said. 'All about her.'

'That's too much,' she said.

'Just barely enough.'

'Like what?'

'Oh, I don't know,' I said. 'Tell me what she looked like in the sixth grade with pigtails and elbows and knees, or tell me–'

'I'll be damned,' she interrupted. 'I'll just be damned.'

'Why?'

'You've never met her, right?'

'Right. Why?'

'I can tell by the way you're talking,' she said, 'that you're stuck on her.'

'It's a professional hazard,' I said, trying to wriggle out of it. 'I get

335

stuck on everybody I hunt for. They stop being pictures and words and become people, that's all.' I nipped at my drink to ease the dry bite of the hashish. 'Sometimes the people I think I'm hunting for don't turn out to be the people I find,' I babbled. 'Or something like that.'

'Cut the bullshit, man,' she said. 'You're stuck on her. I never met a man who wasn't. Goddammit, she could do a lot of things well, but nothing better than that.'

'What?'

'Getting men stuck on her – she did that best of all. They used to come for miles around just to sit at the queen's feet, just to touch her hem – oh, hell, that's not fair.'

'What?'

'She just never found anybody as good as she was,' Peggy said, then picked up a wine glass in her stubby fingers. 'She was the most beautiful woman in the world and she was only a girl – just like me, man, just a little high school kid from Sonoma, but she was so beautiful, a beautiful, lonely lady, lonely because nobody was good enough for her.'

'Stuck up?'

'Not a bit of it, man,' she said, 'or why would she like me? Listen, man, I spent my school years watching pretty girls try to be my friends so they'd look good standing next to me, but Betty Sue, she didn't care about that, she was my friend, and better-looking than the whole bunch of them, and smarter and nicer – the whole bit.'

'You've thought about her some?'

'Not a day goes by, man, that I don't.'

'I see.'

'You don't see shit, man,' she said quietly. 'I loved her, you see, loved her. I didn't know what it was all about until I had survived two nightmare marriages, but since then I've found out, and I loved her. When she ran away, I cried my eyes out, man, cried myself blind. Before that, I thought that was a cliché, but when she left, I wept until I couldn't see.'

'I'm sorry,' I said.

'I hated her too,' she confessed, 'but that was my fault. I lined up with the smitten swains but didn't know what I was doing for years. And hell, if she was here tonight, you and I could stand around with

336

our tongues out.' Then she tried to laugh as she socked me on the arm. 'Lined up to meet the lady.'

'I never stand in line for anything,' I said lightly.

'This is a lady you'd kill for a chance just to stand in line,' she said with a sad smile. 'Or something like that. That didn't make sense, did it?'

'I know what you meant,' I said. 'Thanks for your trouble.'

'No trouble, man,' she said. 'I'm like this all the time now. And when I finish law school, I'm gonna make the world pay for it.'

Since it was the first happy thing I had heard her say, I wished her well and thanked her again. Then I wandered toward the far side of the yard to find a bush to water.

Betty Sue Flowers. I had talked to three people but hadn't found out anything worth knowing, except that everybody who knew her was stuck on her still. Maybe I was too. Maybe I didn't have any choice in the matter any more. But I had to make up my mind. Her daddy lived down in Bakersfield, Randall Jackson might still be in Denver, and the remains of the commune were in southern Oregon – long trips in three different directions, and none of them on the way to Montana. Rosie's eighty-seven dollars was getting a workout, and I was getting nowhere, but that's always where I knew this one was heading anyway. So I shook it off and headed back to the party.

When I walked through the kitchen, Trahearne was leaning against the wall beside the lady with the chains, offering her the slug they had removed from his hip, saying, 'You charming little devil, you, I'd like you to have this as a good-luck piece.' He tickled her under the chin.

'Why don't you lick her on the arm,' I said, but they both ignored me. She giggled and accepted the good-luck gift, and Trahearne lifted her hand to his lips. As I tried to walk past, he grabbed my neck with a meaty hand and hugged me toward him, his huge face rubbery and flushed with the whiskey, hanging over mine like something butchered in a nightmare.

'And what did the little dyke have to say?' he asked.

'Nothing I didn't already know,' I said. 'Let's get the hell out of here.'

'The party's just getting interesting.' He leered at the chained lady, sloshed whiskey into my glass, and patted my shoulder. 'Hang

337

around,' he said, gathering the lady with silken clinks beneath his arm and leading her into the twinkling night.

'Have a good time,' I said. 'Have a hell of a good time.'

'You've got to learn to relax,' he advised over his shoulder, 'learn to have a good time.'

Ah, yes, the good times. The parties that last forever, the whiskey bottle that never runs dry, the recreational drugs. Strange ladies draped in denim and satin, in silver and hammered gold. Ah, yes, the easy life, unencumbered by families or steady jobs or the knave responsibility. Freedom's just another word for nothin' else to lose, right, and the nightlife is the right life for me, just keep on keepin' on. Having fun is the fifth drink in a new town or washing away a hangover with a hot shower and a cold, cold beer in a motel room or the salty road-tired taste of a hitch-hiking hippie-chick's breast in the downy funk of her sleeping bag. Right on. The good times are hard times but they're the only times I know.

The next morning, I woke up with a faceful of sunshine in the back seat of Trahearne's convertible, sodden with dew, dogspit, and recriminations of high degree. When I sat up to look around, it looked like California, then a passing paperboy told me it was Cupertino, but that didn't tell me anything at all. Two houses up the street, a curly-headed guy was standing in his driveway, sucking on the remains of a half-pint as he tried to dodge a barrage of kitchen utensils that flew from an unseen hand inside the house and glittering out into the morning light. He ducked a large spoon and a heavy ladle, chortling and dancing, but a potato masher caught him on the lower lip with a sudden burst of bright blood. As he started weeping, a blond woman in a housecoat rushed outside and led him back inside.

I shook my head, shared the last cold beer with Fireball, then let him out to water somebody's lawn. As soon as he was finished, I leaned on Trahearne's horn until he stumbled out of the house across the street, his shirt in one hand, his shoes in the other, his tail tucked between his legs.

'Damned crazy woman,' he complained as I drove away. 'How was I supposed to know she wanted to wear all that goddamned junk jewelry to bed. Jesus Christ, it was like fucking in a car wreck.'

'Beats sleeping in the car,' I muttered.

'Wasn't my fault,' he grunted as he tied his shoe. 'You refused to come in the house.'

'At least you could have put the top up.'

'I did,' he said. 'Twice. But you insisted on having it down, and you gave the world a forty-minute speech about sleeping under the stars to clean out your system, so I left you alone.'

'Good idea,' I said.

'You're a surly drunk, Sughrue.'

'Surly sober, too.'

'What happened to the woman?' he asked.

'What woman?'

'The one with you.'

'Whatever happened,' I said, 'I'm sure I enjoyed it. What did she look like?'

'Soft and furry,' he said. 'She's not dead in the trunk or something awful, is she?'

'I don't have any idea,' I said, 'and I'm not about to look before I have a drink.'

'Let's not even act like we're going to have breakfast,' he said, grinning. 'Let's just find the nearest bar.'

'Then it's off to Bakersfield,' I said.

'Oh my God,' Trahearne groaned.

8

Between drunks and hangovers, it took Trahearne and me two days to drive to Bakersfield, but as we drove from the motel to Betty Sue's father's place, we were both sober and not in any great pain, which was good because his place looked like the sort of dance hall and bar where a man wanted his wits about him when he went inside. The marquee promised dancing nightly to the strains of Jimmy Joe Flowers and the Pickers, and the bar, a cinder-block square building in the middle of a parking lot, promised all the trouble you could handle. Since it was early, though, we went inside with the lunch rush – two welders and a traveling salesman who wanted beers and Slim Jims. The daytime bartender told me that Mr. Flowers usually came in about one-thirty, and sure enough at two o'clock sharp, his ostrich-skin boots thumped through the doorway. Ostrich skin makes a lovely boot leather – if you like leather that looks as if the animal had died of terminal acne – and it went well with Flowers' wine Western-cut double-knit leisure suit, just as his suit matched the woman who followed him.

Flowers was all happy handshakes and smiles until I showed him my license and told him what I wanted. Then he frowned and led his secretary into the closet he called his office. When I didn't follow on his heels, he stepped back out and waved me hastily inside. He said he had something he wanted to say to me. At some length.

'Ungrateful little bitch,' he said, then slapped his flimsy desk. 'I never thought a child of mine would turn out to be a hippie, you know, never thought it for a minute. I mean, what the hell, I like to see kids have a good time, but they got to work for it, and you know, I lost a boy over there in Vietnam, and might have lost the other one, but he had a bum knee, and here I turn around and find this damned hippie for a daughter. I mean, you know, first I hear she's run off without finishing school – and you know how important an education is nowadays – and here I am her own loving father, you know, and I don't hear a single solitary word from her for four, maybe five years, then one night she calls, collect, mind you, and wakes me out of a dead sleep.' He paused to look up at his secretary. 'You remember that, don't you, honey?' he said to her, and she reached down to pat his freshly shaven and powdered cheek as if the effort of waking up had been just more than he could bear.

'And you know what she wants?' he asked me suddenly. He didn't give me time to answer. 'Money, by God, she wants money so she can leave that damned dirty commune where she's been shacked up like some animal.' He paused to shake his head. 'And you know what I told her?' I didn't make a move. 'I told her that I hadn't sent her a single thin dime to get herself into trouble, and I wasn't going to send a damned cent to get her out. Not by a damned sight I wasn't, you know what I mean.'

Even if he knew anything else, Betty Sue's father wasn't going to tell me, so I didn't have to be nice for effect. 'You mean those dirty hippies were probably stuffing drugs up their noses, too,' I said.

'You got a smart mouth, fella,' he said, his eyes as flat as yesterday's beer. Then he smiled with just his mouth. 'But that's okay, because you must have a smart head on your shoulders to come into town and tell me that.'

'Peggy Bain told me,' I said, not wanting him to think I was too smart.

Flowers sighed heavily, as if the conversation had been the hardest work he had done in years. His secretary patted his shoulder again. 'Remember your heart, honey,' she murmured. She had dressed for the occasion too, but her idea of a sex kitten looked like something the cat had dragged in.

'Most drugs make you stupid,' he lectured me, 'but cocaine is a smart man's high. You have to be smart to enjoy it and rich to afford it.'

'A man in my business needs his wits,' I said, 'so I don't know anything about drugs.'

'I can see that,' he said scornfully. 'How much is Rosie paying you for this wild goose chase?'

'Not nearly enough,' I said, meaning to insult him.

341

'She was always tight with a dollar bill,' he said, ignoring my tone. 'Goddamned old woman.'

'Well, her place isn't doing as well as yours,' I said. 'You must have done well in the aluminum cookware business.'

'How would you like that smart mouth on the other side of your head, fella?' he said quietly. 'Or maybe one of your legs busted at the kneecap.'

'You'd need help,' I said stupidly.

'All I have to do is snap my fingers,' he said as he held up his hand. 'You know what I mean?'

'You have the right connections, right?'

'You could say that.'

'What's a good ol' boy like you doing with connections like that?' I asked pleasantly.

'Making a living,' he said.

'Okay,' I said, 'I'm sorry.'

'Don't let the door hit you in the butt on the way out,' he said.

'Give my best to the family,' I said, then left. He could have been bluffing, but I didn't want to find out. I made a quick exit, which made Trahearne happy.

'This place gives me the creeps,' he said as we left.

'Me too,' I said, and on the way to the car I told him why.

Since I needed some time to think about Betty Sue Flowers, and since Trahearne demanded a few days of luxurious recuperation, we drove straight through to San Francisco, and he checked us into a suite at the St. Francis.

Some time for reflection and recuperation. Cigarettes and whiskey and wild, wild women. One commercial type spent the whole time babbling in my ear about her shrink, so I faked an orgasm for her and hid in the shower until she went about her business. Then there was a lady poet, an old friend of Trahearne's, who was so mean that she scared me into hurrying. Hiding in the shower didn't help a bit. She came in and gave me an endless lecture on my responsibility to women in general and herself in particular. Somewhere in the drunken blur, Trahearne walked off the balcony bar in the lobby and fell headfirst into a rubber tree, much to the consternation of the management. Somehow, I drove his convertible into the rear of a cable car. Nobody was hurt, but I had to endure a monsoon of abuse

342

about trying to destroy a national monument. The conductor and his passengers acted as if I had run over a nun. The worst thing that happened, though, was that Fireball took to wearing a rhinestone collar and drinking Japanese beer.

One afternoon, it finally came to an end. Fireball was drinking water out of the toilet bowl, a naked blond woman wearing red boots slept on the couch in an extremely revealing position, and the suite smelled like a Tenderloin flophouse.

'This is no way for a grown man to live,' Trahearne announced as he woke me up. 'Let's go home,' he said.

'Home's where you hang your hangover,' I said.

'Let's have more movement, Jack, and less pissant redneck homilies,' he grumbled, holding his head very carefully.

When he decided he wanted to go home, Trahearne wasn't about to wait for anything. Not even to wake up the blond lady. He griped about the length of time it took me to pack, then he whined all the way to Sonoma as I detoured by Rosie's to drop off her dog and pick up a tow bar and my El Camino. But there was a strange woman behind the bar. She told me Rosie was asleep in her trailer house, and not to bother her, but I had to.

Rosie came to the door after Fireball and I had spent several minutes standing on the steps. She was hastily wrapped in a faded purple chenille bathrobe, her hair tangled with sleep and sweat. Fireball elbowed past me and trotted toward the rear of the trailer, where the sounds of masculine snoring rumbled.

'What the hell's that thing around his neck?' she asked, not sounding all that happy to see me. 'You shoulda called, gimme a chance to clean up,' she added.

'Sorry,' I said, 'but I didn't know we were coming until a few minutes ago.'

'Been on a toot, huh?'

'Had about as much fun as a man can stand,' I said.

'You find my baby girl?' she asked.

I shook my head and looked down. Rosie tried to hide her long, crooked yellow toenails, first with one foot, then the other. I looked back up.

'You come up with any leads?' she asked.

'One rumor,' I said, 'that she was living up in Oregon six or seven years ago.'

'Where'd you hear that?' Rosie looked puzzled.

'From her daddy.'

'You talk to that worthless bastard?' she asked.

'Just about as long as I could,' I said.

'How's he doing?'

'Got his own band,' I said, 'and a place to play it in.'

'Somebody must be running it for him,' she said.

'He's got himself a secretary,' I said.

'Naw, it wouldn't be that,' Rosie said. 'Jimmy Joe's scared sideways by a smart woman. He might've loved Betty Sue if she hadn't been so smart.'

'Maybe so,' I said. 'Listen, since I didn't come up with anything definite, why don't you take your money back?' I tried to hand her a sheaf of folded bills.

'Get away with that,' she said.

'Take it.'

'You earned it.'

'Okay,' I said, 'I'll stop in Oregon on the way through and ask around some more.' Which was exactly what I didn't want to do. I didn't want to look anymore, didn't want to find any more scraps of Betty Sue Flowers. 'If I find anything, I'll give you a call.'

'I'd appreciate that,' she said, 'but you've already done more work than I paid for.' Down the hallway behind the living room, the squeak of springs and a series of muffled curses filled the close air. Fireball had joined the gentleman in bed, and the gentleman hadn't enjoyed it. Rosie looked embarrassed and turned to quiet the man. When she did, she exposed a life-sized poster of Johnny Cash on the wall behind her. Then she glanced back at me. 'You did more work than I paid for, didn't you?'

'I told you it was wasted money,' I said.

'It's mine to waste,' she said, 'and I thank you for trying. Give me a call, collect, you hear, whatever you find in Oregon, and if you're ever down this way, you got a place to drink where your money's no good.'

'Sounds like heaven,' I said, and Rosie smiled.

'You taking the big fella's car home?' She nodded over my shoulder. I had already hooked Trahearne's Caddy to the tow bar and my El Camino.

'The big fella too,' I said.

344

'What's the matter? Can't he drive?'

'He can't even walk yet,' I said.

'Must be nice,' Rosie murmured.

'What's that?'

'To have enough money to hire somebody to tow you around,' she said.

'I don't know,' I admitted, then as Rosie and I exchanged good-byes, a bald, hairy man, his beer belly drooping over his sagging boxer shorts, wandered into the picture, demanding cold beer, scrambled eggs, and true love. Rosie asked me in for lunch, her eyes pleading for me to leave, so I did. I had to drive Trahearne home anyway.

Trahearne had made his literary reputation with six highly praised volumes of poetry, two of which had been nominated for national prizes, but he had made his fortune with three novels, the first published in 1950, the second in 1959, and the third in 1971. I had read all three, and although they were set in different places with different characters, I couldn't keep them separate in my mind. The first one, *The Last Patrol*, had been set on a nameless island in the Pacific during the final week of World War II. A Marine squad had been sent on a mission behind Japanese lines to blow up a crucial bridge. Before they can make the march, though, they receive a radio signal telling them that the war is over, but the young lieutenant who is leading the patrol keeps the information to himself. At the bridge, the Japanese soldiers, sick and hungry, rush out to surrender, and the Marines slaughter them. During the one-sided fire-fight, the young lieutenant takes a round through the chest, and as he is dying, he tells his men the truth, and he laughs, happy that he is dying before the fighting ends. The war is over, he says, and the peace is going to be hell.

In the second novel, *Seadrift*, the survivors of a yachting accident, cast adrift on a small raft, work hard to elude their rescuers. One of the survivors, a Hollywood screenwriter, convinces the others that surviving on their own is more important than living. By the end of the novel, I expected them to be eaten by a whale, but only the screenwriter dies, leaping into the jaws of a shark, his sole regret that he doesn't have time for a dying speech.

In the third one, *Up the River*, an alcoholic playwright and his

345

pacifist son team up to wreak a terrible vengeance on a party of elk hunters who have accidentally killed the wife and mother. Even as the last of the hunters dies in a bear trap, the father and son still don't know which hunter actually did the shooting, and they don't even care, trapped as they are by their love of this wild justice. The son joins the Army to go to Vietnam and the father sobers up to write a great play about love.

All three novels were best sellers, all made into successful movies, and perhaps because of his reputation as a poet, well reviewed. But as far as I could tell, the books were fair hack work cluttered with literary allusions and symbols. Fancy dreck, one unimpressed reviewer called them. The male characters, even the villains and cowards, cling to a macho code so blatant that even an illiterate punk in an east L.A. *pachuco* gang could understand it immediately. The female characters serve as stage props, scenery, and victims. And the stories were always incredible. But Trahearne had found his niche and mined it as if it were the mother lode instead of a side vein, and he made a great deal of money, back in the days when money was still real.

But maybe that was the only choice he had. When he came back from the war, he found that his mother had become a rich and successful writer with two novels about the tender, touching, and comic adventures of a young widow with an infant son as she makes her way in the world as a teacher in a one-room school-house in western Montana. As Trahearne said, she made a million dollars, then never wrote another word, and she made it up out of whole cloth, since she only taught one year in Cauldron Springs before she became pregnant and lost her job. And he told me also that she didn't bother to write the best novel of all, she lived it. When the money came flooding in, she left Seattle and moved back to Cauldron Springs, where she bought the hot springs and the hotel and most of the town, and she kept the town running through the lean years when hot baths were no longer in vogue, when the cattle market fluctuations ruined the ranchers. She never said an unkind word to a soul, never mentioned the fact that the small town had run her off, she just lived in her house on the hill and looked down, smiling kindly, watching the town look up.

With his first money, Trahearne had built a house across the creek from hers, and except for occasional trips to Europe and a few visiting-writer jobs at colleges, he had never lived anyplace else, but had never written a poem set within fifty miles of Cauldron Springs. He wrote about the things he saw on his binges, about the road, about small towns whose future had become hostage to freeways, about truck-stop waitresses whose best hope is moving to Omaha or Cheyenne, about pasts that hung around like unwelcome ghosts, about bars where the odd survivors of some misunderstood disaster gathered to stare at dusty brown photographs of themselves, to stare at their drinks sepia in their glasses. But he never wrote about home. As I drove him there, I had too much time to think about all the runaways.

My El Camino was a bastard rig – half sedan, half pickup, a half-crazy idea out of Detroit for lazy drugstore cowboys who want to drive a pickup without driving a pickup – and I loved it. The Indian kid up in Ronan who had ordered it out had it set up so he could hit the rodeo circuit as a calf-roper, which means plenty of high-speed travel towing a heavy load. The kid got tired of the circuit and bored with making payments, and when I repossessed it, I bought it from the dealer cheap. It was a beauty, fire-engine red with a black vinyl roof and a fancy topper for the pickup bed, all chrome and conception, but it had a heavy-duty racing suspension, a four-speed box, and a tricked up 454-cubic-inch engine stuffed under the hood. It was a real beast, it could dust a Corvette on the straight, outcorner a Porsche Carrera, and I carried an honest ticket from a South Dakota radar trap for 137 mph. Of course it got six miles to the gallon, if I was lucky, and not even Lloyd's of London would sell me insurance, but with a CB radio, a radar detector, and a stack of 15-grain Desoxyn speed tabs, even a child could make time towing Trahearne's barge, and I burned up the highway.

We were in Lovelock, Nevada, before Trahearne woke up from his nap, and when I stopped for gas there, he moved up to ride with me. He was quiet, except for the occasional gurgle of Wild Turkey, until we reached Elko.

'I'm tired,' he said, 'and my ass hurts, so let's stop and sleep.'

'Why don't you go back to your car and sleep there?' I said. 'I've got so much speed in my system that I couldn't sleep if you knocked me out.'

'That's not my fault,' he said. 'Let's stop.'

'I thought you were in a hurry to get home.'

'Listen, son, I'm paying the ticket here, and when I say stop, we stop, you understand,' he said.

'Right,' I said. 'One minute I'm your best drinking buddy and the next I'm your nigger for the day.' I pulled into a darkened service station and got out.

'What are you doing?' he asked. Then he followed me to the rear of my rig to repeat the question.

'I'm taking this son of a bitch off,' I grunted as I heaved on the tow-bar nuts. 'You can drive yourself home, old man – you can go when you're ready, stop when you want to. I quit.'

It took him a bit, but he finally said it. 'Hey, I'm sorry. And hell, I'm not even sleepy anymore.'

'You sure?'

'Yeah.'

'You ain't going to change your mind?'

'No,' he said. 'And I am sorry. Money makes a man stupid sometimes, you know.'

'I don't know yet,' I said, 'but when your ex-wife pays me, I'll have a better idea.'

Trahearne laughed and got me a beer out of the cooler. 'You have to learn to relax,' he said, 'to take it easy.'

'I didn't want to stop,' I reminded him, and he laughed again as we drove on.

South of Arco as I watched the headlights flash across the sagebrush and desert scrub, Trahearne woke up again and wanted to know what Betty Sue's father had had to say.

'I tried to tell you on the way back to San Francisco,' I said, 'but you wanted to talk about this lady poet I was going to love.'

'She's mean, son, but she's full of life,' he said, then he laughed. 'She gave you a hard time, huh?'

'You could say that.'

'You don't like them mean, huh?' he said.

'Do you?'

'Sometimes,' he murmured, 'sometimes it helps.'

'Helps what?'

'Helps me forget that I'm performing a mindless act that I've performed too many times already,' he said quietly, 'with too many different women in too many shabby places.'

'That's a different tune,' I said.

'Right,' he said without further explanation. 'Did her father know where she had been in Oregon?'

'No. And if he had, he wouldn't have told me anyway.'

'I sort of thought you might drive back that way,' he said.

'I thought about it,' I admitted. 'Then I decided to take you home first. I'll drive down next week.'

'You're going to a lot of trouble over that girl,' he said.

'Storing up my treasures in heaven,' I said. 'Rosie promised me free beer for a month the next time I'm down in Sonoma.'

'Don't kid me,' he said. 'You're obsessed with the girl.'

'Maybe,' I said. Then we passed a sign telling us how far it was to the Craters of the Moon National Monument. 'Hey,' I said, changing the subject. 'We banged the same whore at the Cottontail, you know.'

'Why did you do that?' he asked.

'Thought it might give me a clue.'

'Jesus Christ,' he said, 'no wonder you're such a cynic, you're a goddamned mystic in disguise.' Then he paused. 'Did she tell you anything?' he asked nervously.

'She expressed some doubts about man having conquered the moon,' I said, 'but that's all she said.'

'That's the way women are, son – either too easy to fool or too hard,' he said, then sighed. I didn't ask him what that meant. I just drove on toward the dark heaps of the mountains beyond the desert, trying to push Betty Sue Flowers to the back of my mind with the gentle shove of Trahearne's whiskey.

In spite of a minor drunk, I got Trahearne home around midnight the next evening. His house was a long, low expanse of log and stone set over a daylight basement that jutted into the side of a shallow hill. As we parked in front, I saw a woman leaning in the open doorway, silhouetted against the light, her arms and ankles crossed patiently as if she had been waiting for us, had stood for days like a woman on a widow's walk staring into a dark and stormy sea.

'Home again,' Trahearne said. 'Every time I get home, I'm surprised that I made it back alive. I keep thinking I'm bound to die on the road. But I guess I'm doomed to die in my own bed.'

'I know what you mean,' I said.

'You'll stay the night, of course,' he said.

'If there's going to be a big domestic strife scene,' I said, 'I'd just as soon drive back to Meriwether.'

Trahearne laughed loudly, breaking the quiet in the cab, and said, 'Don't worry. Melinda's a saint. She forgives me even before I transgress. So come in and let's have a homecoming drink.' Then he slapped me on the shoulder and climbed out, shouting, 'Whiskey, woman!' His great voice echoed across the shallow valley. Across the creek, a light appeared in an upstairs window of his mother's house, and the dark blot of a woman's head came to the window.

'In which order?' the woman in the doorway asked, her soft, unaccented voice unhoned by even a hint of rancor.

'Order be damned,' Trahearne shouted back. 'Celebrate, love, the sailor, home from the sea, the hunter home from the hill.'

'On his cliché or bearing it?' she answered happily.

As the big man limped up the redwood steps to the deck, I followed with his suitcases and my duffle like some faithful native bearer.

'Who's that behind you?' his wife asked. 'Gunga Din?'

'Come, Gunga Din, you swine, sahib needs water for the whiskey,' he said as he came back to help me with the bags.

'Thanks,' I said, then paused on the steps to ease the amphetamine trembles in my legs. Trahearne and his wife embraced in the doorway as she fondly murmured *you maniac*, and she chuckled as she led him through the doorway. In the silence, the creek whispered in its rocky bed, and the face at the far window seemed to be staring at me. I crept up the stairs in silent guilt, away from the face.

By the time I reached the doorway, which opened directly into a living room as big as a house, Trahearne had fallen into a huge leather lounge chair and propped up his feet. His wife was behind a small bar, rattling ice cubes. Across the room, in a fireplace large enough to roast a Volkswagen, three four-foot logs crackled merrily against the mountain chill. From where I stood, it looked like a cozy little fire.

'A drink, Mr. Sughrue?' Trahearne's wife asked.

'A beer, please,' I said, and she opened a bottle and poured it into an earthenware mug, then brought the drinks around, Trahearne's first, then mine.

As she handed the mug to me, she said, 'I'm afraid Trahearne has the social grace of a stone. I'm Melinda Trahearne.' She held out a rough hand, which I shook as I introduced myself. 'Make yourself at home,' she said, then smiled. 'Walk around until your butt wakes up, then have a chair.'

'Thanks,' I said as she walked back to Trahearne.

So I stood around like a knot on a log while she sat on the arm of his chair and fiddled with his sparse hair. She was so obviously pleased to see him home that I did my best not to watch them, not to overhear her whispered greetings.

I had been so wound up with Betty Sue Flowers that I hadn't thought about what Trahearne's second wife might look like, and even as I tried not to look at her, she seemed a rather plain woman of about thirty, not at all what I would have expected if I had thought about it.

She wasn't ugly, just plain, and she looked as if she had just come in from a hard day's work in the fields. Her hair was a dull shade of brown, neither dark nor light, and she wore it in a closely cropped tangle that made her nose seem too long, her mouth too wide, and her eyes set too far apart. Except for a streak of pinkish-gray clay across her forehead, her face was unpainted, and even in the soft light, her tan seemed sallow, the skin color of a convict or a barmaid. She wore a pair of baggy jeans and a loose velour sweatshirt, so I couldn't tell about her body; she didn't seem fat or skinny but she moved with the sort of controlled grace rich girls seem to learn as soon as they take their first steps. Her bare feet, too, were slender and elegant, well-manicured, although her hands were as rough and hard as a brick mason's, and her eyes were an odd shade of blue-green, which might have made them striking, but they didn't seem to match her hair or coloring.

She glanced at me, caught me watching her, and her smile was generous, her teeth as straight and even as money could buy. If her voice hadn't been so completely without accent, I might have thought that she was one of those rich East Coast girls who majored in English Lit and field hockey at one of the seven sisters. As I watched, she slipped off the arm of the chair to stand behind Trahearne, her

351

strong hands kneading the thick muscles of his shoulders. It looked like it felt good, but he groaned.

'Enough, woman,' he said, 'the cure surpasseth the disease.' Then he patted her hands to hold them still.

'Sissy,' she said, laughing as she walked over to pick up his bags. When she lifted them, heavy as they were, her shoulders didn't dip, and she carried them toward a dark hallway as if they were empty. I knew they weren't. As she walked away from me, the firm outlines of her hips swayed with a force of their own beneath the baggy jeans. As I turned back, I caught Trahearne watching me watch his wife.

'How long have you two been married?' I asked, then applied my mouth to a worthier project, my beer.

'Nearly three years,' Trahearne answered without interest.

'Seems like a nice lady,' I said.

'Yeah,' he answered. 'A nice lady.' His voice seemed to drift away with fatigue.

'Maybe I should unhook the cars and hit the road,' I said.

'Nonsense,' Melinda said from the hallway. 'You've been on the road too long, and I insist that you at least stay the night.'

'Thank you, ma'am,' I said, 'but I don't want to impose.'

'No imposition at all,' she said graciously. 'The basement is filled with guest rooms – it's private, quiet, and you can come and go without bothering us at all. There's a wet bar, an icebox full of beer, a small kitchen, and two color televisions. You must stay.'

'Well . . .' I said.

'Oh to hell with him,' Trahearne growled. 'He's some kind of ultimate redneck country boy, and he can't sleep except under the stars. Besides, he's never been married and he's scared shitless of domestic strife.'

'Don't be silly,' Melinda said, then laughed. 'The only strife in this household is the sound of Trahearne's snores.' She walked over and picked up my duffle bag. 'Come on, I'll show you your room.'

'And I'll show myself to bed,' Trahearne said as he stood up. 'Good night, C. W., and all that social grace crap,' he added, then lumbered toward the hallway like a wounded bear.

'In the morning,' I said, then followed his wife through the large, open kitchen to the stairway.

Downstairs, a large room with full-length glass walls on the daylight side filled most of the basement, and the bedrooms lay down a hallway that followed the track of the upstairs hall. Melinda carried my bag to a small bedroom beside the bathroom, then led me back to the game room to show me the bar and the small kitchen.

'Please make yourself at home here,' she said. 'You'll find everything you need for breakfast in the icebox. For lunch too. I'm sorry, but because Trahearne and I work at different hours, we only eat one formal meal at dinner. Usually around seven. Until then, I'm afraid you'll have to fend for yourself.'

'I'll be fine,' I said.

'I'm sure you will, Mr. Sughrue,' she said. 'Bachelors always make the best houseguests. They're more capable of fending for themselves than most married men, it seems.' She smiled slightly. 'You never married?'

'No, ma'am.'

'Do you mind if I ask why not?'

'I don't mind,' I said, 'but the truth is that I don't rightly know why not. I've never jumped out of an airplane on purpose. Even in jump school they had to kick me out. I guess nobody ever kicked me into marriage.'

'I've done some skydiving,' she said softly, 'and found marriage to be just as exciting.'

'You seem to be happy,' I said.

'Yes, I am,' she said. 'And as I'm sure you noticed, I'm very fond of my husband.'

'Yes, ma'am.'

'And he seems fond of you,' she said. 'I'm pleased about that. I don't begrudge my husband's friends. I only hope we can be friends too.' Then she held out her hand again.

'Of course, if you call me "ma'am" again, I'll have to knock the shit out of you,' she said calmly, then burst out in a fit of giggles.

'I guess I could break down and call you Miz Melinda,' I said, and we both smiled.

'That's an improvement,' she said, then wished me pleasant dreams.

As she left me, her voice echoed in my head, words and phrases that seemed to have no meaning – 'my husband' and 'icebox' – but I didn't pay any attention to myself.

The drive and the Desoxyn had left me too rattled to sleep, so I sat down in front of the television to drink beer and catch the late movies by cable from Spokane. Although they were quiet for twenty or thirty minutes, after that the Trahearnes made a great deal of commotion for a couple not engaged in domestic strife. Since I began in the business, I always did the whole number, so I had done more divorce work than I should have, more than my share back in the days when I still had a partner. I didn't want to hear it unless I got paid for it, so I turned up the volume on the television, but I could still hear the heavy rumble of Trahearne's voice through the thick floors. Whatever he was angry about, he told her about it all the way through the second half of *Johnny Guitar* and through the first half of *The Beast with a Thousand Eyes*. I switched to whiskey, found a pack of cigarettes behind the bar, then stepped outside through the sliding glass doors. Even there, the sound of his complaints, of her lilting compliance still echoed. I went back to the movie and turned up the sound again.

Finally, it was over, and the noises changed to the groan of bedslats, the slap of flesh. That made me even sadder than the fight. I left the basement again and walked all the way out to the cars and leaned against the dew-damp fender of the El Camino. In the pasture, cattle shifted their hooves and breathed in soft, snuffling grunts, and their flat teeth ground gently against the grass. Across the creek, the other house was dark now, but I still felt the watching face, hidden behind the frail glimmer of a nightlight that glowed like a spectre beyond the black windows.

Once more, I took Betty Sue Flowers' picture out of my pocket. I had been carrying it for over a week and hadn't shown it to anybody but myself. In the sudden flare of a match, she looked somehow familiar, as if she were a girl I had grown up with, but as the flame died, the flickering image of the film filled my blindness. I didn't even know why I cared about it, didn't know what to think. I was like the rest of them now, I suspected, I wanted her to fit my image of her, wanted her back like she might have been, but I feared the truth of it was that she wanted to stay hidden, to live her own life beyond all those clutching desires. Unless she was dead, and if she was, she had already lived the life she made, as best she could. I stared at the picture in my hand, the one I couldn't see, and saw the pictures I couldn't look at without flinching, the pale, doughy flesh that moved with an undeniable grace, both fragile and determined, endlessly vulnerable but unharmed. Ashamed that I had been aroused, ashamed that I was ashamed, and aroused again thinking about it, I went back to the now-silent house, back to my empty bed.

Not to sleep, though, or even unpleasant dreams. I drank and smoked and watched the ceiling. When the ashtray beside the bed was filled, I took it to the bathroom to empty it, and out of habit I wiped it clean. It was a lump of glazed clay, as formless as any rock, with a smooth, shallow depression in the center. As I wiped away the caked ashes, a woman's profile came into view, a high, proud face moulded into the clay, a tangle of long hair streaming away from the face, as if the woman stood in a cosmic wind. When I looked more closely, I saw what seemed to be a ring of watchers, lightly impressed eyes around the rim of the depression, staring at the woman's face with a lust akin to hatred. Then I noticed a slim ceramic vase on the bathroom counter, which held a small bundle of straw flowers, and on the vase a series of women's faces, their hands over their eyes, their long, tangled hair bleeding over their shoulders. The pieces must be Melinda's, I thought, a plain woman understanding the curse of beauty, and I was impressed. The ashtray was as heavy as a stone, the vase as light as if it had been molded from air, and the women's faces too fragile for words.

Usually, on those sleepless nighttime trips to the bathroom, I had to take a long look at my own battered, whiskey-worn face, searching it for a glimpse of the face it might have been but for the wasted years, the bars, the long nights. But this night, I rubbed my thumb over the faces locked beneath the brown translucent glaze, all the weeping women, and I had no pity left for myself.

I had made my own bed and went to it to sleep, then to rise and do what I knew I had to do, to pay what I owed the women.

9

An old drinking buddy of mine had come home from a two-week binge with a rose tattooed on his arm. Around the blossom was written *Fuck 'em all/and sleep till noon*. His wife made him have it surgically removed, but she hated the scar even more. Every time he touched it, he grinned. Some years later she tried to remove the grin with a wine bottle, but she only knocked out a couple of teeth, which made the grin even more like a sneer. The part that I don't understand, though, is that they are still married. He is still grinning and she is still hating it.

I didn't have any tattoos or any marriages, but the morning after I brought Trahearne home I slept till noon anyway. When I woke, I knew that I had to roll out of the sack and shuffle into my sweat suit and jogging shoes. I had been on the road too long, and I could hear various invaluable parts of my body whine for exercise. Maybe it would clear my mind. Maybe I would break my leg and have to forget about driving to Oregon.

Eventually, I did just that, dressed in tired athletic gear and strolled outside into the noon sunlight. I sat down in a deck chair to survey the landscape.

Trahearne's mother owned a half section of land northwest of the small town of Cauldron Springs. Her land lay in a shallow valley between two low ridges. At their highest elevations, the ridges were timbered, but on the lower slopes they were covered with sagebrush scrub. Between the houses and the highway, she kept a few head of cattle in a small pasture. Cold Spring Creek ambled between the ridges to the pasture, where it broke into a series of long smooth willow-choked bends, then it flowed alongside the highway until it joined the warm mineral waters of Cauldron Springs Creek east of the small town. Trahearne's house sat on the east side of the creek, his mother's on the west. Her house looked like something off the Great Plains, a square and sturdy farmhouse, its only decoration a porch across the front, and it seemed to stare down upon the small town with the austere gaze of a wheat farmer driven mad by the whims of the weather.

The town had grown up around a hot spring that bubbled up in a limestone cup the size and shape of a washtub. An old man who had made his fortune in silver and tin mines had built the hotel and the bathhouse, claiming great curative properties for the spring waters. He had sunk his fortune into the project, built a huge wedding cake of a spa around the spring, then settled back to enjoy his declining years, but he had built his spa too far from the people, and the flow from the spring didn't have enough volume to keep his pools and baths hot enough to please those few who came. When he died, he was the only guest in his hotel, the only bather.

Trahearne's mother had reopened the bathhouse and one floor of the hotel, but only as a courtesy to the town, like the tennis courts she built behind the bathhouse, a reminder of her money. She wouldn't have the buildings repainted, though. She let them fade and weather from white to an ashen gray as dull as raw silver.

As I jogged slowly down the gravel road toward the highway, Melinda ran past me like a deer. Six seasons of Army football and four at various junior colleges had left me with legs that only remembered running swiftly, and I envied Melinda's easy, quick pace. She ran as nicely as she walked but she still kept her body bundled, hidden now beneath a loose sweat suit. She reached the highway and turned west up the long rise toward the end of the pavement. When I got to the highway, I followed her briefly, then slowed to a walk as she topped the rise and turned back. I waited where I stood, and when she came back, I swung alongside her, and we jogged back to the gravel road.

'You'll never get in shape that way,' she said, breathing slow and easy.

'This is penance,' I puffed, 'not physical therapy.'

She laughed, then ran away from me, dust spurting from beneath her tennis shoes with each powerful stroke of her legs, her short hair bouncing ragged in the sunlight.

When I finally reached the house, she was standing up on the deck watching me, her fists on her hips, her legs spread in a wide, strong stance. I limped up the steps and fell into a redwood lounger.

'I wish I could get Trahearne to exercise,' she said.

'I wish you could get me to stop,' I huffed.

'Don't you just love to run?' she asked.

'It's not as bad as getting poked in the eye with a sharp stick,' I said, 'but at least that's a quick pain.'

'Exactly,' Trahearne boomed as he stepped out the front door. 'How about a Bloody Mary?' he asked as he rattled a pitcher at me as if it were a magic charm.

'Only because it's before breakfast,' I said as he poured me a drink.

'Around here, this is breakfast most days,' Melinda said.

I turned around to study her face for some evidence of wifely irony, but she was smiling, almost prettily, and patting Trahearne on his plump cheek. Whatever the shouting had been about during the night, they both seemed to have forgotten it, or had chosen to act as if they had. Melinda kissed him lightly on the corner of his mouth, then stepped inside. Trahearne settled into a lounge chair beside me.

'That's an exceptional woman,' I said, 'for a wife.'

'You don't know the half of it,' he said, then blushed. I grinned at his blush, but he didn't smile back. He just filled up my glass again, saying, 'Drink this, my boy, and then I'll show you what real people do with their hangovers.'

'So this is what taking the waters is all about?' I said as Trahearne and I lowered ourselves into the warm waters of the hotel's main pool. He just grunted and sank to his shoulders. His white T-shirt, which he had insisted upon wearing, billowed briefly with trapped air, then burped under his neck. After we had finished the Bloody Marys, Trahearne had forced me to drive him to town to take the waters. He had a key to the back door and to a private dressing room, where we changed, and we had the pool to ourselves except for an old couple from Oklahoma. They had left as we climbed in, on their way to a hot mud bath for their feet, behind a door appropriately labeled The Corn Hole.

'How do you like it?' Trahearne sighed.

'It's okay,' I said, lying to be polite. The water, which stank faintly of sulphur and other minerals my nose refused to identify, was tepid rather than hot and it seemed slimy like a fever sweat.

'It beats the hell out of running around,' he said, 'and I guess it works. My mother swears by it – she's down here every morning at six – and Melinda comes down late at night to swim laps after she's been working.'

'And what do you do?' I asked.

'I come down for hangovers,' he said, 'and sit around until I break a sweat.' Then he ducked his head under the water and stood up. 'Am I sweating?' he asked, then smiled. 'I feel like I'm sweating.'

'You're certainly all wet,' I said, trying not to look at the maze of purple scars glowing across his chest through the wet T-shirt. He lowered himself into the water again.

'Anytime you're ready to go, let me know,' he said.

'This wasn't my idea,' I said.

'Let's get out of here,' he said, 'this place always stinks like a hospital.' Then he stood up and lumbered toward the steps. He had even more scars on his back. They looked like the deep painful gouges of shrapnel wounds, reminders etched into his flesh of a long-forgotten war. I followed him out of the waters to the dressing room.

As we changed clothes, he said, 'Okay, so I'm bashful about my scars.'

'They're not that bad,' I said.

'Bad enough,' he answered. 'Hurry up,' he added, 'I think I may be sober enough to try to write this afternoon.'

'I know I'm sober enough to drive back to Meriwether,' I said.

'Tomorrow,' Trahearne commanded. 'Melinda's got a steak thawing for you.'

'Yes, sir,' I said, then walked with him out to the car, which was parked between the back of the pool house and the tennis courts. An elderly man was bouncing balls off a backboard, and two teenaged girls were engaged in a furiously contested point.

'Don't watch,' Trahearne said as he climbed into the passenger seat. 'All that nubile flesh will drive you mad.'

'It already has,' I said as I drove us away.

Later that afternoon, after a short nap in the sun, a shower, and a light lunch, I called Trahearne's mother's house to let Catherine

Trahearne know that I hadn't forgotten who had hired me. She said that she was on her way to town to play tennis, but she told me to come over for a drink before dinner, and I accepted. Trahearne was ensconced in a large study off the living room, rattling papers and ice cubes and cursing loudly, and Melinda had gone up the hill to her studio, so I fixed a drink and wandered along the graveled footpath toward the creek and a narrow wooden bridge across it. The creek was small and choked with rocks and brush, but it picked its way energetically through the clutter, pausing occasionally in a shallow pool. Creek-watching is a patient art, and I leaned on the bridge rail and practiced, sniffing the cool riffles of breeze over the creek, watching the pan-sized trout shimmer in the crystal water, their gills fanning like vestigial wings as they waited for dusk and whatever fly hatch the day demanded.

'You must be the detective,' a gruff woman's voice said from the shadowy willows beside the pool, and I nearly jumped into the creek. 'Sorry,' she said. 'I didn't mean to startle you but I was having an unplanned nap when you got here.'

'That's all right,' I said as she stepped out of the shade.

She was a tall, angular woman with short gray hair, wearing a worn red flannel shirt, Malone pants, and a pair of battered Bean's hunting boots. She carried a knotty cane and leaned on it heavily as she limped along the creek side to the path.

'I'm Edna Trahearne,' she said as she offered me a gnarled hand to shake. She had to be in her late seventies, but her eyes were clear, her handshake firm in spite of the twisted fingers. Deep wrinkles had eroded the strong features of her face, and her heavy but withered breasts hung loose beneath the flannel shirt like useless flaps of flesh. 'And you're that Sughrue fella.'

'Yes, ma'am.'

'How's my son?' she asked.

'A little tired,' I said, 'but he's got the constitution of an ox.'

'He comes by it naturally,' she said, 'but someday he's going to tie one on and there won't be anybody around to untie the knot. I told Catherine not to send anybody after him this time – a waste of money and effort – but of course she refused to listen to me. I don't know what that slut he lives with does to him – I haven't spoken to him since she arrived – but his binges come on the heels of each other now, and he hasn't written in over two years. If he doesn't rid himself of her, he'll be in his grave before me.' Then she paused to stare at me with a look that almost seemed coy. 'You don't agree?'

'I don't know,' I said. 'She seems to love him,' I added lamely.

'He doesn't need love, young man, it confuses him,' she said. 'He needs tending like a child. From what I can tell, my son's young wife makes the mistake of thinking he's a man. He's an artist, and all artists are children.'

It's true, I thought, some men do need tending, but it's degrading to talk about it to strangers. I decided to see if the old woman was as tough as she acted. 'I understand that you once wrote,' I said.

'It was the only way for a woman alone to work at anything besides serving men, and as soon as I had the money to afford this place, I stopped.'

'You weren't dedicated to the art?' I said.

'If you've read my two novels, then you know what sort of fairy tales they are,' she said, 'and if you've talked to my son, you know the truth of my life here. I took money from fools, boy, and I earned it, but don't give me any bullshit about art.'

'All right,' I said. She was as tough as she seemed to be, so I went back to watching the little creek.

'Are you a fisherman?' she asked suddenly. 'Or just another dude with a fancy fly rod?'

'I'm not much of a fisherman, no, but I have caught a few trout.'

'If I were to loan you my fly rod, do you think you could catch half a dozen of those little trout?' she said. 'I can't see well enough to tie a leader anymore,' she added, 'even if I had the hands for it, and I would dearly love a mess of pan-fried trout tonight.'

'I've got my fly rod in the pickup,' I said, then sat my drink down and trotted toward it as obedient as a son.

The creek hadn't been fished in some time, and the trout rose to whatever fly I offered them, but I caught more willow branches and wind-tangles than trout, and it took me an hour to get a stringer of small cutthroat trout. The old woman watched me like a fish hawk, but she didn't offer any snide suggestions or sage advice about my back-casting. I cleaned the fish in the creek, then followed her to the back door of her house and into the kitchen. While I washed my hands, she got me a beer and asked me to join her on the front porch.

We walked through the living room slowly, as if through a museum. A war museum. The walls and tables were covered with mementos of Trahearne's war: framed pictures of young, freshly commissioned Marine officers, a thinner Trahearne standing tall among his contemporaries; the same faces during the jungle campaigns, hollow-eyed and worn among the gray rain-forest debris after the fire storm of battle; Japanese battle flags, a .25 Nambu automatic pistol, and an officer's Samurai sword hanging crossed with Trahearne's Marine officer's dress sword; and embroidered pillows and shell necklaces and bone earrings – all the random junk they brought back from the islands. One of the photographs was a wedding picture, Trahearne in dress blues beneath wind-twisted Monterey pine with white beaches and a phony blue ocean tinted into the background, but the attractive woman holding the white bouquet beside him was dressed in black. It was odd, as if he had been killed in the war. Nothing of his life after the war was in the living room, and I half expected to see a faded gold star hanging in the front window. When I looked, though, the old woman was waiting at the front door, looking irritated. I shook off the chill the room filled me with and followed her outside, where I took a deep breath, the air in the living room too old and bloody to breathe.

'Were you in the war?' she asked politely.

'Not that one,' I said. She shook her head and smiled as if I had given the wrong answer. I stepped around her, careful not to touch her, to introduce myself to the handsome woman sitting in a rocker on the front porch.

She was dressed in white today instead of black, a short tennis dress, with a racket and ball bag set beside her chair. Beads of sweat sparkled across her forehead and up into the hairline of her tied-back copper hair. The years hadn't hurt her at all. If anything, she was even more lovely now, her complexion smooth and tanned, her flesh firm and elastic.

'I'm Catherine Trahearne,' she said unnecessarily as she stood up. 'I've been playing tennis in town, and I haven't had a chance to clean up, so you will have to excuse me.'

'That's okay,' I said. 'I've been fishing.'

'Any luck?' she asked.

'Enough for our dinner,' the old woman said, 'but just barely.' It sounded like both a rebuke and a command, but for what and to do what escaped me.

'Every one I catch is luck,' I said.

'You found Trahearne,' Catherine said, 'so I choose to believe that you fish with skill rather than luck.'

'Ha,' the old woman snorted. 'A complete waste.' I didn't know if she meant my fishing or my hunting.

'Whatever, thanks for bringing him home in one piece,' Catherine said. 'I'm certain that it was no easy task.'

'It wasn't all that hard,' I said.

'Ha,' the old lady added.

'Mother Trahearne, may I get your glass of wine?' Catherine asked.

'I think I'll wait until I go to bed,' the old woman said. 'Maybe I'll sleep tonight if I wait.'

'Of course,' Catherine said, then to me she added, 'I would ask you to stay for dinner but I'm sure that you have other plans. You must excuse me now, though. I must shower before dinner.' I had the uneasy impression that she had told me she was going to shower not out of politeness but rather so I would think of her tanned and naked body standing under the rush of hot sudsy water. 'If you will send me your bill, Mr. Sughrue, I'll see that it is taken care of immediately. And let me thank you once again. It has been a pleasure meeting you.' She shook my hand and went inside the house, the flat, smooth muscles of her thighs rippling in the afternoon sunlight.

'How my son could give up a woman like that, I'll never understand,' Edna Trahearne said.

'I wouldn't know about that,' I mumbled.

'Don't be such a twit,' the old woman chided me. 'I appreciate the trout, son, but not enough to allow you to be a twit on my front porch.'

'I'm sorry,' I said.

'Don't apologize, either,' she said.

I picked up my rod and said goodbye. As I walked back to Trahearne's house, I was convinced that I had been manipulated in ways I didn't even begin to understand, for reasons way beyond me. Maybe I was just a convenient target. Or maybe I had wandered into a loony bin. They all had to be slightly crazy to live so close to one another, but I didn't know what was going on. My job was over anyway. All

I had to know was that Melinda had promised steaks for dinner. I wanted red meat, two drinks of good whiskey, a sober night's sleep, and then I wanted to get the hell away from all of them.

Dinner was ready when I got back to the house, but Trahearne was too hammered to eat. He sat in his study, looking at his desk, which was covered with scraps of yellow paper off a legal pad, idly twirling an old .45 service automatic while Melinda tried to hold the steaks at medium rare.

'Now you know,' he mumbled as I stepped into the study with drinks for the two of us.

'I know dinner's ready,' I said.

'You've met the crone and the dragonlady and seen the hall of lost dreams,' he said, 'so what else is there to know?'

'Let's eat,' I suggested.

'Eat, eat,' he said, then broke into his poetic brogue. 'Matched with an aged wife, I mete and dole unequal laws unto a savage race who eat and sleep and breed and know not me – '

'It little profits that an idle king,' I added, moving back a line, 'fucks up the dinner.'

'How the hell do you know that line?' he asked, drunken puzzlement twisting his face.

'When I was a domestic spy at the University of Colorado for the United States Army,' I said, 'I took an M.A. in English Literature.'

'You're shittin' me,' he said, rearing back in his chair.

'Not at all.'

'By God, boy, let's have a drink,' he said, 'an' you can tell all 'bout your life as a spy.'

'Over dinner,' I suggested.

'All right, goddammit,' he grunted as he heaved his hulk out of the chair. 'All right, you bastards and your goddamned dinner,' he complained, but he followed me to the table.

If I had known how he was going to act, I would have left him in his study quoting bad Tennyson. His steak was overdone, his baked potato cold, his salad too vinegary – or so he claimed in a loud, drunken voice. He ate a few bites, moved his food about his plate as if he were playing some sort of victual chess, then he slumped in his captain's chair at the head of the table, sleeping, thankfully, with only a few light snores. Melinda smiled at me and shook her head. But not in reproach.

'Poor dear,' she whispered. 'His work never goes well when he first gets home. If you don't mind, we'll just let him sleep there while we eat.'

'I don't mind,' I said. 'I'm so hungry I could even eat with him awake.'

'Don't be mean,' she said lightly, then smiled again and brushed her hand through her short hair, the clay dust in it fluffing out in a soft cloud. She went back to her steak, eating like a farm hand at the end of the harvest season. When she finished it, she sliced off a portion of Trahearne's, then ate that too with equal relish. When she finished that, she suggested coffee on the deck, and we left the big man sleeping in his chair.

It was past eight o'clock but the northern sun still settled slowly toward the low mountains in the west. The grass of the pasture grew darkly lush in the limpid air, and the forested hills shifted from green to a darkness as black as dead coals. Over the flats, nighthawks flitted with throbbing cries through the willows, and small trout leapt into the floating haze above the creek. In the near distance, the lights of Cauldron Springs flickered like signal fires.

'It's a shame,' Melinda said softly, 'that he can't write . . . about this place. My work has never gone better, his never worse, and yet he says it isn't my fault. Sometimes I wonder, though . . .' She paused to sip her coffee and stare at me over the cup.

I had had all the confidences I could stand for one day, so I turned to idle conversation.

'Were you raised around here?'

'What?' she said. The fading light was kind to her features, and I thought that if she worked at it – maybe fixed her face and let her hair grow and wore something besides baggy clothes – she might be an attractive woman. As I studied her, she blushed, and I wondered what she felt when she saw the polished beauty of Catherine, wondered what her fingers felt as she molded the lovely profiles on her clay.

'Were you raised in Montana?' I asked.

'Oh no,' she answered quickly, almost as if she felt guilty because she hadn't been. 'Marin County,' she said, 'across the bay from San Francisco, and Sun Valley, and the south of France.' It sounded like a line she had said so many times it had begun to bore her. She noticed it too. 'I'm sorry,' she added, 'I love this part of the country, and I'm afraid that I sounded a bit supercilious. Poor little rich girl, you know, and all that. I wish I had been raised on a little ranch just like this, but my parents were both well off – not wealthy, mind you, but well off – incomes from estates and trusts – and they dabbled at things, you see, the cello and violin, abstract painting, scuba diving, and skiing. The worst sort of dilettantes, I'm afraid,' she said with a gentle laugh, 'but very good and kind people.'

'Are they still traveling about?' I said, still making conversation with the poor little well-off girl to whom Trahearne, for all his faults, must have seemed as real and exciting as a storm in the North Atlantic.

'My parents?'

'Yes.'

'No, I'm afraid they're dead.'

'I'm sorry,' I said.

'My mother died in a skiing accident in the Alps,' she said, 'and my father died of grief. Or so I told myself. He ran his Alfa off a curve on the Costa Brava.'

'I'm sorry,' I repeated.

'Thank you, but there's no need,' she said. 'It seems so long ago now, so far away.' Then she sat up and brightened. 'I'm certainly glad that you two weren't hurt in the accident.'

'Just a fender bender,' I said, wondering what Trahearne had told her.

'Oh, it must have been more than that,' she said, 'for Trahearne to be in the hospital for three days.'

'Observation,' I said, glad that I had my wits about me. If Trahearne didn't want his young wife to know that he had been shot, then I certainly wasn't going to tell her.

'He must have taken quite a spill when he was thrown out,' she said. 'Those scars on his ham look as if it might have been serious.'

'Minor stuff,' I said.

'How did it happen?' she asked, but I didn't have the impression that she was pumping me.

'Frankly, I was too drunk to know exactly what happened,' I said.

'Well, thank you for taking care of him,' she said.

'We had a pretty good time,' I said, 'and I'm not sure who was taking care of whom.'

'It sounds like . . . sounds like a wild trip.' She paused. 'You know, we got to know each other on just the same sort of trip. I was teaching in a summer workshop in Sun Valley and having a drink with some of my students in the lodge, and Trahearne came in off the terrace, this huge, beautiful, alive man, and he sat down at the bar beside me, bought me a drink, then another, and somehow we ran away with each other. I didn't realize who he was until we had driven all the way to Mexico – we wouldn't tell each other our names, it was like that, you know – and then I heard him spell his name for the Mexican border people, for that form – visitor's card, you know – and I just couldn't believe it. Here he was, the most *alive* man I had ever met, and he turned out to be Abraham Trahearne. Life is so strange. Who would have thought all this could come of a simple thing like buying me a drink.'

'Speaking of the great man,' I said, trying not to be ironic, 'would you like me to help you get him to bed?'

'Not at all,' she said. 'He'll wake up in a couple of hours shouting for whiskey and wild, wild women.' The grin on her face suggested that she could handle the wild woman part perfectly well. For an instant I believed her, then she turned her face, and I thought that if she was wild, she kept it well hidden behind plain. 'I've bored you, haven't I, with my little love story?'

'It's not that,' I said. 'I thought I'd hook it up and leave while I'm still sober.'

'Trahearne will be so disappointed,' she said as if she meant it.

'Yeah, but I've got this other case I'm working on,' I said, 'and I need to be in Oregon yesterday.'

'Tomorrow's never soon enough, is it?'

'No.'

'And that's such an exciting phrase.'

'What's that?'

' "Working on a case," ' she said. 'It suggests dark intrigue, tangled mysteries, the sort of romance denied to mere mortals.'

'I'm afraid the reality is usually repossessing cars and combing bars for runaway husbands,' I said.

'Or runaway children.'

'Sometimes.'

367

'That should be exciting,' she said. 'A prince stolen by gypsies or something like that.'

'I don't know any gypsies or princes,' I confessed.

'That's no reason to quit looking,' she said, a plaintive note creeping into her voice, soft like the cry of a lost and dying animal. 'I do wish you wouldn't leave.'

'I have to go,' I said.

'I understand,' she said. 'I'm sure that Trahearne would want me to tell you that you're always welcome in our house. I feel the same way. Please come back whenever the mood suits you.'

'Sure,' I said, 'thanks.' But I couldn't think of any moods that would bring me back to this crazy place. We said our good-byes, and as I drove away, in contrast, my search for Betty Sue Flowers seemed almost sane.

Driving hard, I made it to Grants Pass in one straight shot, nineteen calm hours behind the wheel, then checked into a motel and slept like a child until ten the next morning.

At the Josephine County Sheriff's Department, when I stopped by to let them know I was in the county and I wasn't planning to break any laws, they seemed bored by the prospect but they told me where to go. They didn't tell me what to look for, though, and a couple of hours later I was driving up into the Siskiyous, following a washboard gravel road along a small creek that ran into the Applegate River. About ten miles up the road, the land opened up into a nice little valley, and I understood the smile on the deputy's face.

A prefab A-frame cabin sat beside the road surrounded by multi-colored plastic flags flying from loose guy wires. A large sign in front announced SUNDOWN SUMMER ESTATES. When I parked, a tall young man bounded out of the cabin, his hiking boots rattling the cheap pine porch.

'Yes, sir,' he said brightly, 'what can we do for you today?'

'I think I'm looking for a place to retire,' I said, and it sounded suddenly true. A quiet place where I could settle back and think about all the wild goose chases of my life.

'I've got just the place for you,' he said quickly, 'a ten-acre plot with creek frontage, a spring, and a great building site. Unimproved, of course, but cheap.'

'Actually, I was looking for a hippie commune,' I said.

'You're in the wrong place,' he said, his spiel over, his voice hard now.

'This place belong to you?'

'That's right,' he said.

'No hippies, huh?'

'Not now.'

'Where did they go?' I asked.

'Wherever hippies go when they find out that living on the land in the old way is hard work.'

'How did you get the place?' I asked.

'If it's any of your business, I inherited it from my grandmother,' he said, then looked away and shuffled his feet. 'You're some kind of law, right?'

'Private,' I said, then showed him my license.

'Wouldn't you know,' he grumbled. 'I've had three prospective buyers today – a Fresno chicken farmer, two kids driving a brand-new Continental, and a rent-a-cop.'

'Didn't mean to raise your hopes,' I said.

'That's what they're for, aren't they?' he said sadly.

'It was your commune, right?'

'Everybody makes mistakes.' He grinned. 'What the hell, man, I turned twenty-one in Nam and came into this place and a little bread, and when I came back, all I could think of was peace and dope and hairy-legged hippie chicks. Sounded like heaven on earth.'

'What happened?'

'Times changed,' he said simply, 'and my money ran out. I thought we could make a living up here, but nobody wanted to be on the duty roster. The lazy bastards wouldn't work, so I got a little freaked on acid and conducted a search and destroy mission of my own, burned their hooches and relocated the fuckers. Man, you should've seen them run.'

'So now you're selling out?'

'Everything but the back quarter section,' he said. 'It's either that or another six months up on the pipeline, and Alaska is great, man, if you don't have to work out in the cold – but it's always cold.'

'How long ago did everybody leave?'

'Four or five years ago,' he said. 'Who're you looking for?'

'Betty Sue Flowers,' I said, then showed him the picture.

'You've got to be kidding,' he said as he looked at it.

369

'No, I'm really looking for her.'

'Not that, man, I mean you got to be kidding that this is her,' he said. 'When she was here, man, she was a cow. A sweet fuck but as big as a barn.'

'You remember her, huh?'

'Nobody ever forgets a fuck like that,' he said, then sighed darkly, as if he remembered too many other things, too. 'Say, you wouldn't have another one of those beers, would you?' I nodded and got two fresh ones out of the cooler. We strolled over to sit on the steps of the A-frame porch. 'She was wild, man, too much. How come you're looking for her, anyway?'

'She hasn't been in touch with her family for a long time, and they'd like to find her, see her again.'

'Probably not.'

'Why?'

'Man, I've known some crazy ladies – in Nam and up on the pipeline – and I've done some numbers I don't like to remember during the daylight hours, but this one, she was something else.'

'Was she your lady?'

'Everybody was everybody's,' he said. 'You know, trying to destroy the concept of private property and personal ownership. What the hell, man, you do enough drugs, it sounds okay.'

'At least you hung on to the land.'

'Just barely,' he said. 'They were pushing me to put the title in all our names, you know, telling me that I was on some sort of power trip because I owned the land, and that's when I finally freaked.'

'Was that when she left?'

'No, she was gone by then,' he said. 'She didn't stay around too long before she split with this older dude. She may have even come with him, you know, but I just can't remember.'

'Remember his name?'

'Jack. Something like that. We weren't too heavy on last names, you know, shedding another vestige of the middle-class fascist life or some such crap.'

'Randall Jackson.'

'Sounds good to me, man, but I don't remember.'

'Potbellied, bandylegged, balding?'

'That's the creep,' he said.

'Creep?'

'He wanted me to finance a skin flick dressed up as a sociological study of sexual freedom in the communes. He said he had all sorts of distribution connections and claimed we'd make a bundle. You know him?'

'We haven't exactly met,' I said, 'but I know him.'

'Whatever happened to him?'

'I heard a rumor that he was in Denver dealing dirty books,' I said.

'Figures,' he said, then we sat for a bit listening to the flutter of the plastic flags. 'Looks like a fucking used car lot, doesn't it?' I nodded. 'I guess when I decided to sell out, I wanted it to look as sleazy as possible,' he said. 'Hey, if you've got another beer, maybe I'll trade you a lot for it.'

'You can have a beer,' I said, 'but I've already got five acres up in Montana on the North Fork of the Flathead. Sorry.'

'Don't be sorry,' he said as he came back with two fresh beers.

'How are the plots selling?'

'Like cold hot cakes,' he said. 'Two five-acre plots in the last month, and I had to carry the paper on those. Money's too tight. But I've got a standing offer from a land syndicate – you know, one of those outfits that sell acre lots on television and in the Sunday supplements. Only thing is, they want the whole place, you know, they say that if I keep my quarter-section, it ruins the development potential or some such shit, but if I don't sell some more plots soon, I'll have to take their offer.'

'Better than nothing, I guess.'

'Just like nothing,' he said, 'just money, and damn it my great-grandfather was born on the Oregon Trail in Applegate's second train, and my grandmother was born in a log cabin that is still standing five miles up the creek, so here I am sitting under a raft of plastic flags.'

'Like you said, times change.'

'Yeah,' he murmured, 'but you know what I hate most of all?'

'What's that?'

'One of these nights, man, I'm gonna be sitting down in Santa Cruz stoned out of my mind watching the late movie, and some washed-up TV cowboy is gonna come on the tube offering my land in pissant lots, and man that's gonna be a bummer.'

'Maybe you could run a few cattle or something.'

371

'Hell, have you seen the market quotations lately?' he said. 'You've got to have a wad of capital just to get into the cattle-raising business and lose your ass,' he said. 'Besides, I've been lazy too long to quit now,' he said, then paused. 'Say, man, you look like you might have been high once or twice, and I've got this dynamite number in my pocket. If you've got a couple more beers, we can sit here and get high and wait for the customers who ain't about to come here anyway.'

We smoked his dope and drank my beer, watched the sun ride the wide open spaces of high blue sky, talked about wagon trains and trails, about what it might have been like, talked about the motorcycle shop he might open down in Santa Cruz, but we didn't talk about Betty Sue Flowers and we didn't get very high.

10

Two afternoons later, I knocked on Randall Jackson's office door. He worked out of a cubicle in the corner of a large warehouse filled with cartons of books and magazines. He hadn't been hard to find. The clerk in the first porno bookstore I had hit on Colfax told me where to look. But I guess I arrived at a bad time. After my knock, the voices inside the office stopped suddenly. The cheap door opened quickly, nearly jerked off its hinges, and a very large, very ugly man with a dark face and a three-hundred-dollar suit stepped outside and asked me what I wanted. I should have known, I suppose. Where there's money, there's dirt, and when you work my side of the street, you have to expect to deal with those people. They're everywhere. Not as well organized as they would like you to think, but organized well enough.

'Can I help you?' he asked politely, a soft trace of a Mexican accent in his voice. His twenty-dollar haircut looked as if it belonged on somebody else's face.

'I'd like to talk to Mr. Jackson,' I said, even more polite than he had been.

'I'm sorry but he's busy right now,' the big man said.

'Who is it, Torres?' a voice from inside asked.

'Nobody,' he answered, not meaning to insult me.

'Tell him to wait,' the voice inside said.

'It's a nice day,' Torres said. 'Why don't you wait outside?'

'I'll be on the loading dock,' I said.

He nodded, and we went our separate ways. I was just as glad. The hairy pie of pornography is a big business with a small capital investment and a great cash flow, and freedom of the press is a fine theory, but none of it is any of my business. I waited outside, watching

373

two black dudes hand-truck cartons into the rear of an unmarked blue van. It wasn't a nice day at all, but I didn't complain. Denver had a dose of smog as thick as L.A.'s, but I stared through the gray, dirty haze toward the Rocky Mountains as if I could see the peaks, standing like ruined cathedrals against a crystalline cobalt sky.

Randall Jackson wasn't the man with the voice inside the office. He had a wheedling whine, as unctuous as old bacon grease as he ushered the man with the voice into the back seat of a black Continental with blank silvered windows. The large dark gentleman drove it away. Then Jackson turned to me, his whine gone.

'You wanted to see me, bud?' he said. Time hadn't been kind to him. His gut had grown rounder, his hair thinner, and his legs more bowed. His wardrobe didn't help, either – a maroon blazer with electric blue slacks that sported a bright chrome stitch in the weave. His fancy loafers had a new shine and dandy tassles, but they were run-over at the heels. His name might be on the business license, but he didn't even flush the toilet without permission. 'Well, what was it?' he demanded.

'I'm looking for Betty Sue Flowers,' I said. I didn't think he was going to tell me anything anyway, and I knew I didn't want him to know my name, so I didn't explain anything or show him my license.

'Never heard of her,' he said quickly.

'Maybe she was using another name,' I said. 'I've got information that you were with this girl in Oregon several years ago.'

'You got shit for information, bud, I ain't never been to Oregon,' he said, his tiny black eyes glittering like zircons.

'Must be the wrong Randall Jackson,' I said. 'Sorry to have bothered you, Mr. Jackson.' Then I climbed back into the El Camino and drove away.

That was that. For now. I couldn't muscle him with a warehouseful of help watching. But he had lied to me, probably out of habit, and I intended to find out why. It had to be the hard way, though. His telephone would be unlisted, his home address in the city directory faked, and he had seen my El Camino, so I couldn't tail him in it. I had to have another car.

One of the reasons that I spend so much time driving back and forth across the country, aside from the fact that airplanes scare me spitless, is that I can't rent a car when I arrive in a strange city. I can't rent a car because I don't have any credit cards. I don't have any credit cards because I can't get one without stealing one. It's easier to steal cars. I have more experience in that line of work.

Nobody likes to talk about it because it's such a shoddy business, but private detectives spend a lot of time repossessing cars. That's how I got in the business, in fact. After my third hitch in the Army, a friend of mine got me a job on the sports desk of the Wichita *Eagle-Beacon*, which is what I did in the Army when I wasn't playing football, and since I was short of money and bored, I started moonlighting for a finance company skip-tracing and repossessing cars and stereos and furniture and televisions. When I got fired from the paper for being a lousy reporter, I headed out to San Francisco, where I hustled runaways for a year, then up to Montana, where my father had died, and took up skip-tracing and repo's as full-time job. I had stolen lots of cars legally with court orders in my pocket, and without, and I thought I could at least borrow one in Denver without too much trouble.

I drove out to Stapleton Airport and parked in the lot farthest from the terminal, then waited for the right car, something inconspicuous in a company car preferably, driven by a tired salesman with his flight luggage in his hand. I didn't have to wait very long for the right one, and as soon as the salesman was out of sight, I lifted a brown LTD that belonged to the Hardy Industrial Towel Company. With the right tools, it only takes a minute. I was out of the lot before the salesman hiked to the terminal.

I had a supply of blank titles and a set of Alabama plates in my toolbox, plus a batch of blank repossession papers, but I didn't have time to fill any of them out, so when Jackson pulled his plum-colored Cougar into the afternoon rush-hour traffic on Santa Fe, I had to stay close but drive carefully. He made it easy, and I stayed behind him all the way back downtown to a topless place on East Colfax. Two hours later, when he stepped out of the bar into the dusk, his face inflamed with whiskey and visions of naked, dancing flesh, I stuck a revolver in his ribs, and he drove us to a cheap motel out in Aurora. We didn't even have to get out of the car.

'Okay,' he admitted, 'I knew her, all right. We came down here together, and I was flat busted, so I put her on the street, and she took a soliciting fall the first night. I couldn't make the fine, so she did thirty days down on the county farm.'

375

'And then?' I said.

Jackson lit a cigarette and glanced up at the motel rooms. 'After that she wouldn't have anything to do with me.'

'Can't blame her, can you?'

'Guess not,' he said.

'Where'd she go after that?'

'Up around Fort Collins, I heard,' he said. 'There's some rich lady who lives up in Poudre Canyon, and she does rehab work, you know, pulls girls out of the slam and takes them home. A real do-gooder, you know, and I heard that Betty Sue had stayed there for a while. Then I didn't hear any more.'

'Nothing?'

'Nothing at all,' he said.

'How come you lied to me?' I asked.

'I thought you might be some of her family,' he said, 'the accent and all, you know, come to get even or something.'

'Even for what?' I asked.

'You know,' he said, 'she was just a kid.' As if that explained everything.

'You shouldn't have lied,' I said.

'I see that now,' he said as he glanced at the .38 in my hand. 'What did you have in mind up in that motel room, man?'

'Taking you apart,' I said.

'That's what I figured,' he said. 'Hell, I thought you were going to blow me away on the street, man. You should've seen the look in your eyes. You were crazy, man.'

'I'm tired,' I said.

'What the hell are you looking for Betty Sue for?'

'I don't even remember,' I said, then Jackson drove us back to his car. 'No hard feelings,' I said as he got out.

'None at all,' he said, then hitched his pants and walked away.

As I drove back to the airport, it crossed my mind that it had been too easy, and I thought about going back, but I had enough trouble as it was. I parked the salesman's company car near the spot where I had taken it, then picked up my own and headed north toward Fort Collins up I–25. Halfway there, my hands began to shake so badly that I had to pull into the nearest exit and off the road. I didn't think it was nerves, though. Mostly anger working its way to the surface. Jackson had been right. When I shoved the piece in his back on the

street in front of the topless place, I had wanted to pull the trigger
as badly as I had ever wanted anything, pull it and pull it until I had
blown him all over the sidewalk. I thought about what Peggy Bain
had said about me being willing to kill just to stand in line for Betty
Sue. I thought about it, but the line just seemed too damned long.
I crawled under the topper and locked my .38 in the toolbox, then
drove on north, the mountains to the west, the vast empty stretch of
the Great Plains to the east.

One summer when I was a child, after my parents separated, I
had lived with my father out on the plains east of Fort Collins, north
and east of a little town called Ault, during that summer, stayed with
him and a short widow woman and her three little kids. He was
trying to dry-farm her wheat land, and we all lived in a basement
out on the plains, a basement with no house over it, where we lived
in the ground like moles, looking up through the skylight, waiting
for the rain that never came.

When I turned off the freeway at the Fort Collins exit, I thought
about driving east to try to find the basement. I had found it once
in the daylight when I was living in Boulder but I knew I would
never find it in the dark. So I checked into another motel, went into
another bar, had another goddamned drink.

The next day I had some luck. First, a little good luck that turned
bad, then a little bad luck that turned worse.

The second probation officer I called told me where to find the
right rich lady. The first one I talked to could have told me but she
just didn't want to.

Selma Hinds lived in a large octagonal cabin of log and glass set
on the spine of a ridge south of the Cache la Poudre River. As I
drove up the canyon, I could see it sitting up there like a medieval
fortress. I parked by her mailbox at the base of the ridge and changed
into hiking boots, throwing longing glances at the old mine cable
hoist at the side of the road, but it was for groceries and firewood.
I had to trudge up the steep, winding trail for three quarters of a
mile, wondering if Selma Hinds had many casual visitors or door-
to-door salesmen. She didn't have a telephone, so I also wondered
if she was home. If she wasn't at home, I would just have to wait,
unless I wanted to walk the trail twice in one day.

Finally, sweating and sucking for air, I broke out of the scrub pine into a large clearing on the saddle of the ridge just as half a dozen dogs discovered my presence. They greeted me happily, though, especially a large three-legged black Lab who stabbed me in the groin with her single front leg. The others, mostly medium-sized mutts, were content with a gale of barking.

The octagonal cabin sat on the highest point of the saddle with a large garden in the swale between it and five smaller cabins and a bank of wire cages set in the edge of the trees on the other side of the clearing. Two young girls and a boy were working in the garden among the spring planting, which was protected by sawdust and plastic sheeting, and the dry, rocky soil of the ridge had been mixed with compost until it was as black as river-bottom land. In the wire cages, small animals and birds seemed to gaze at me with the dazed eyes of hospital patients. The young people looked up from the garden but then went about their work.

A tall, smooth-faced, motherly woman with brown hair streaked with gray stood in the doorway of the large cabin holding a big yellow cat in her arms. Her hair was tucked neatly into a bun, and she wore a long, plain dress. Even from twenty yards away, her gray eyes stared at me with a calm kindness, the sort you might expect to see in the face of a pioneer woman standing outside a soddy on the plains, a woman who had seen all the cruelty the world had to offer, had seen it and found forgiveness beyond reason or measure.

She was nothing like my mother, who was a short, pert Southern woman, bouncy and mildly desperate, somewhat giddy, slightly sad because rogue circumstance in the guise of my father had left her working below herself as an Avon lady in Moody County, Texas, but as I walked toward Selma Hinds, I felt lightheaded and joyous, as if I were coming home after a long and arduous war. She smiled, and I broke into a childish grin, nearly ran to throw my arms around her, but as I stopped in front of her, something in her gaze, perhaps a slight lack of focus in her eyes, lessened the impression.

We exchanged introductions, and she invited me into her home. Inside, among the plain wooden furniture in the open cabin, a number of cats lay sleeping or walking about, switching their tails as they kept a weather eye on the dogs standing with drooping tongues and wistful faces just outside the door. As soon as Selma Hinds sat down on the couch and waved me to the opposite chair, the dogs sat too, their dark eyes watching us calmly, their frantic barking stilled.

'You have the look of a man searching for something,' she said quietly, 'or someone.'

'A girl,' I said. 'Betty Sue Flowers.'

'I see,' she said, 'and as you can see, I take in strays – the halt, the lame, the sore of foot.' She paused to smooth the fur of the calico that had replaced the large yellow cat in her lap. 'And the spiritually damaged too, I take them in, do what I can to restore them – rebuild the body, replenish the spirit. Those who have homes they want to return to, I provide for their trip, and those who don't I help to find a place to go, and sometimes, those who aren't able to leave, I keep by my side.'

'Yes, ma'am,' I said, thinking that she must be mad or way too good for this world.

'Mostly it works out that the human animals go on, and the others stay . . .' She paused again, just long enough for me to think that Betty Sue might still be here. 'These are trying times for the young, and I provide a place away from the world, the violence and the drugs, a haven with a sexual king's-ex,' she said.

'And Betty Sue came here?'

'Yes, for a time.'

'Then she left?' I asked, confused now.

'She left her spirit among us, it walks among us, it walks among us even now,' she said, 'and her ashes are mixed with the garden soil.'

'I beg your pardon?'

'She's dead, Mr. Sughrue,' she said. When I didn't say anything, she added, 'You seem shocked. We all must die many times.'

'I don't know if I can explain that to her mother,' I said.

'Tell her then that while Betty Sue was among us, she regained her innocence, restored her youth,' she said. 'She was happy here, she grew young again.'

'I've heard it's possible,' I said, still stunned, 'but I've never seen it happen.'

'That's a pity, sir, since it is one of life's delights to watch the young grow young again.'

'What happened?' I asked, wanting to know how she died.

'She blossomed like a flower here,' Selma said, misunderstanding, 'she came to value herself again. If you have been searching for her for some time surely you know something about her life after she ran away from home. She came here from jail, beaten and whipped by life, fat and ugly, but once she fasted and cleansed her system of animal mucus, the compulsive eating stopped, and she grew lovely again, whole. She stayed longer than any of my charges, before or since, even though her stay was more difficult than most.'

'Do you mind if I ask why?' I said.

'This isn't just a job to you, is it?'

'No, ma'am.'

'You're not a member of the family, are you?'

'No, ma'am.'

'I sensed both those things immediately,' she said, 'which made it possible to talk to you. You understand that I do not judge or criticize my charges or their life before, but when they come here, they must follow my rules or leave. No meat, no drugs, no sex. What they do when they leave is their business, and if they come back up the mountain in emotional rags, I take them in gladly, but while they are here, they must obey the rules or leave.'

'And Betty Sue had trouble?'

'The boys followed her like a bitch in heat,' she answered flatly, 'as well they should. Betty Sue had a great capacity for love. She fended the boys off, but it was so hard for her. She seemed to need that sort of male affection – I suppose her father never gave her the sort of love she needed – but she fought it to a standstill.' Then Selma paused to laugh. 'She also admitted to an intense longing for red meat, but she never gave in to that desire either.' The bit of light laughter seemed to bring back memories, and her gray eyes turned cloudy. 'Then one afternoon in late summer,' she continued, whispering so softly that I had to lean forward to hear her, 'just after she had decided to leave in the fall to return to school, she drove my pickup down into town for supplies, and as she drove back, a stray dog ran in front of the truck, and she swerved to miss it, off the pavement and into the river . . .' She rose and walked to the window, the cat limp over her arm, and pointed down toward the sparkling flow. 'It happened on that corner right down there.'

I followed the finger's direction down the ridge to a narrow bend, a sharp curve ending in a swift green pool.

'She survived the crash but drowned,' Selma said. 'I am so very sorry.'

'You had no way to notify her mother?' I said.

'Her mother? No. I did what I could, placed advertisements in the San Francisco papers, but Betty Sue never talked about her childhood,' she said. 'Never. Not a word the whole time she was here. In that, too, she was different from others who have stayed with me for a time.'

'I understand,' I said.

'Why do you think she wouldn't talk about her childhood?' Selma asked, her eyes damp and serious.

'I don't know,' I said. 'Maybe she felt like a princess stolen by peasants. I don't know.'

'Children feel that way too often,' she said, 'it's so sad.'

'I guess the trick is to take what you get for parents and try to live with it,' I said lightly.

'That's very easy to say,' she said, 'and often very difficult to do.' I understood that I had been rebuked for a lack of gravity. 'Parents must make their children feel loved and wanted. If they do nothing else, they must do that, they owe at least that to their children,' she said with such a brittle tone to her voice that I thought she must have been either an unwanted child or a failure as a parent. But I didn't ask.

'You had the body cremated?' I said.

'Graves are too sad, don't you think?' she said.

'Yeah,' I said, 'it's just that her mother might not like the idea – country people are sometimes funny about cremation.'

'It's done,' she said sharply, 'and there's little to like or dislike about it now.'

'Of course,' I said. 'You wouldn't have a snapshot of Betty Sue?' I asked, nodding toward a corkboard covered with photos. 'Her mother might like a picture.'

'Those are photographs of those who have found other lives after leaving,' she said. 'They send them back. We take no photographs here, no reminders of how they looked here to remind them of how they came to be here.'

'I guess I can understand that,' I said. 'Do you mind if I ask why you do all this?'

381

'I would mind very much,' she answered. 'My motives are my own.'

'Then I won't ask,' I said, and she smiled at me. 'I'm sure Mrs. Flowers would want me to thank you for your kindness and love, and I want to thank you for talking to me.'

'I'm sorry to be the bearer of sad tidings,' she said, then shook my offered hand. 'Once, years ago, I believed that after death we moved on into some universal consciousness, some far better life than this flawed world upon which we must somehow survive, but now I know, I understand that terrible knowledge that the dead do not rise again to walk the earth, and I take no false joy in the knowledge, I simply endure it, so I am immensely sad to tell you of Betty Sue's death.'

'I guess we should be glad she had some happy times here,' I said, 'since she was so unhappy everywhere else. You have a lovely place here.'

'Thank you.'

'Thank you,' I said. 'I'm a little old to give up strong drink, red meat, and women all at once, but some morning you might find me curled up on your front steps,' I added. 'If I can make the hill.'

'I'll take that as a compliment,' she said as she patted my hand. 'My door is always open.'

'Thanks,' I said. 'I guess I should know the date of her death, too. Her mother will want to know.'

She told me without hesitation, and I left.

Down the switchbacks of the dusty path, I walked without looking to either side, and as I drove down the sweeping curves of the canyon highway, I didn't watch the sunlight dancing on the riffles, didn't see the towers and battlements of pink rock rising above the river. I didn't stop or think or look until I reached the Larimer County Courthouse and checked the death certificates. It was there. I cursed myself for a suspicious bastard, cursed the emptiness of my success, the long drive to California before the long drive home. Then I thought about getting drunk, a black ceremonial wake, a sodden purge.

Thus did the good luck turn bad.

The bad luck turning worse came later when I stumbled back to my motel room more tired than drunk, tired of trying to get drunk without success. As I reached with my key for the lock, somebody sapped me just hard enough to drop me to my knees, to bring bright flashes of darkness, stunned me long enough to hustle me soundlessly into the room, pat me down, and shove me into a corner. When I could see, I saw the man who had been inside Jackson's office sitting relaxed in the motel chair, his large ugly associate, and another hired hand with his back against the wall as he covered me with a small silenced automatic.

'No trouble,' I muttered.

'You're in no position to cause any trouble at all,' the man in the chair said mildly.

'That's what I meant,' I said.

'Mr. Sughrue, you have to understand that I can't allow you to treat my friends badly,' he said.

'Hired help,' I said.

'What?'

'Jackson's hired help,' I said, 'not your friend.'

'Whatever, I can't have you shoving a gun down his throat and making empty threats,' he said.

'Okay, I'll give it up for Lent.'

'I'm afraid that won't do,' he said.

'Listen,' I said, 'if you wanted me dead, you wouldn't be here – '

'Don't be so sure,' he interrupted.

' – wouldn't be within thirty miles of here, but if you've got some misguided sense of vengeance for whatever it was I was supposed to have done to Jackson, I'm willing to take my medicine,' I said as I eased up the wall, 'and I'll be as quiet as I can.'

'How nice,' the man in the chair said.

'Nothing personal,' Torres said softly as he eased a glove on his right hand.

'Nothing personal,' I agreed, then took it as best I could.

They didn't seem to have their hearts in it, and I didn't resist a bit, didn't give them the slightest reason for any emotional involvement. Maybe it worked or maybe they didn't plan to hurt me too badly from the beginning. Whatever, they didn't do any permanent damage. No broken bones, no missing teeth, no ruptured spleen. I had forgotten, though, how much a professional beating hurts, and I was very glad when they stripped me, strapped me with tape and sat me in the bathtub. I didn't know why they did it, I was just glad the hard part was over. Maybe they knew what I had planned for Jackson in the motel room in Aurora.

Before they gagged me and turned on the cold shower, the one in charge said, 'Hey, buddy, you've got discipline, and I like a man with discipline. You ought to come to work for me.'

'Leave your name with the desk clerk,' I muttered.

'Your only problem is that you think you're both tough and smart,' he said as he patted me on the cheek, 'and the truth is that you're only tough because you're dumb.'

'What the hell,' I grunted. 'I don't take orders worth a damn, either.'

'Maybe you should take up another line of work,' he crooned, as he held up the photostat of my license.

'Is that an order?'

'You never quit, do you?' he said, laughing. 'I hope this was worth it, you know, hope you found the chick you were hassling Jackson about.'

'She's dead,' I said. 'She's been dead for nearly five years. It was a waste of time.'

'Too bad,' he said, then laughed again. 'Just be thankful that you didn't hurt my friend and be thankful that I'm in a good mood.'

'I am,' I said.

Then his associates gagged me with a sock. I was thankful that it was clean, thankful that after they left I was able to shove the water control off with my foot, and thankful too that when the maid came in the next morning, she jerked the sock out of my mouth instead of screaming. I had no idea how I might begin to explain my condition to the police. I tipped the maid and told her to tell the desk that I would be staying over another day. I needed the rest.

11

'It's just not true,' Rosie said for the fifth time.

'I'm sorry,' I repeated, 'but I saw the death certificate and talked to the woman she was living with who saw the body. I'm sorry, but that's the way it is.'

'No,' she said, and struck herself between the breasts, a hard, hollow blow that brought tears to her eyes. 'Don't you think I'd know in here if my baby girl had been dead all these years?'

It was an early afternoon again in Rosie's, soft, dusty shadows cool inside, and outside a balmy spring day of gentle winds and sunshine. Even the distant buzz of the traffic seemed pleasant, like the hum of bees working a field of newly blossomed clover. After a quick visit to the emergency room for an X-ray and some painkiller, I had left Fort Collins and driven straight through on a diet of speed, codeine, beer, and Big Macs, and had arrived at Rosie's dirty, unshaved, and drunk. My nerves felt as if their sheaths had been lined with grit and my guts with broken glass. Even bearing good news, I wouldn't have looked like a messenger from the gods, and with bad tidings, I was clearly an aged delivery boy from Hell's Western Union. I looked so bad that Oney hadn't even asked me to sign the cast on his foot, and Lester expressed real concern. He even offered to buy me a beer. Fireball woke up long enough to slobber all over my pants, but when I didn't give him my beer, he slunk over behind the door. Rosie wouldn't look at me, though, not when I came in, not even when I told her the news.

'I'm sorry,' I said again, 'but she's dead.'

'Don't say that anymore,' she said, not pausing as she furiously wiped off the bar one more time.

'She is,' I said, 'and you'll have to accept it.'

Finally, she stopped cleaning and looked at me. 'Get out. Just get out.'

'What?'

'Out of here,' she said softly. 'Get out.'

'Aw now, Rosie . . .' Lester began, but she turned on him.

'You just shut your damned mouth, you worthless bastard. And get out. All of you get out. Especially you.' She pointed an angry finger at my face.

'I'll get out, all right,' I said, then threw her eighty-seven dollars on the bar, 'but you take your damned money back.'

'You keep it,' she said, her voice as flat and hard as a stove lid. 'You earned it, you keep it.'

'You damned right I earned it,' I said as I picked it back up. 'I've been lied to, run around, and beat up, by God, and I've driven four thousand goddamned miles and I'm still twelve hundred from home, and you're damned right I earned it.'

'Nobody asked nothin' extra of you, so don't come whinin' to me,' she said. She couldn't look at me, though. Her eyes faded to a brittle, metallic gray, like chips of slate. 'Just get the hell away from me.'

'I'm going,' I said.

'And take that damned worthless dog with you too,' she added. 'He ain't been worth killin' since you brought him back.'

I snapped my fingers and Fireball woke up and followed me out the door. Lester and Oney had beat us outside, and they were walking in aimless circles like children during a school fire drill.

'Woman's got a temper on her,' Lester said, shaking his head

'She's got some grieving to do,' I said as I walked toward my pickup.

'Where're you headed?' he asked.

'Home,' I answered, as if I knew where that was.

Home? Home is Moody County down in South Texas, where the blackland plain washes up against the caliche hills and the lightning cuts of the arroyos in the Brasada, the brush country. But I never go there anymore. Home is my apartment on the east side of Hell-Roaring Creek, three rooms where I have to open the closets and drawers to be sure I'm in the right place. Home? Try a motel bar at eleven o'clock on a Sunday night, my silence shared by a pretty barmaid who thinks I'm a creep and some asshole in a plastic jacket who thinks I'm his buddy. Like I told Trahearne, home is where you hang your hangover. For folks like me, anyway. Sometimes. Other times home is my five acres up beyond Polebridge on the North Fork, thirty-nine dirt-road miles north of Columbia Falls and the nearest bar, ten miles south of the Canadian border. There's an unfinished cabin there, a foundation and subflooring and a rock fireplace, and wherever home might be, I had been up on the North Fork for a week or so when Trahearne found me.

I was working. On my tan and my late afternoon buzz. It had been a dry spring, and I saw the plume of dust rising like a column of smoke ten minutes before I saw the VW Beetle convertible that had caused it as it charged through the chug-holes like a midget tank. It skidded into my road and braked to a stop about six inches from a stack of stripped logs. Through the beige fog of dust, Trahearne looked like a man wearing a bathtub that was too small for his butt.

'What the hell is that?' I asked as he pried himself from behind the wheel.

'Melinda's idea of transportation,' he grumbled. 'My car's in the body shop.'

'Well, listen, old man, the next time you come up the road raising a cloud of dust like that,' I said, 'one of the natives is liable to shoot holes in the poor beast until it's dead.'

'Spare me your country witticisms, Sughrue,' he said as he pounded dust from his khakis like a cowhand after a long drive. 'Where the hell have you been?' he demanded.

'Here and there,' I said.

'You're the devil to find,' he said.

'I wasn't hiding,' I said. 'You just don't know how to look.'

'Cut that crap,' he said. He hadn't shaved or changed clothes in several days, and he still limped, but he seemed reasonably sober.

'What's happening?'

'Not a thing,' he growled as he sat down on my steps and struck a kitchen match on the subflooring, 'not a damned thing, and since you do nothing as well as anybody I know, I thought we could do it together. It's not as dangerous or boring as when I do it alone.'

'Is that a compliment or an insult?'

'Just give me a beer and shut up,' he said, and I pitched him a can from the cooler I had been using as a footstool. 'So what are you doing?' he asked out of a billow of beer foam and cigar smoke.

'Working on my retirement home.'

'Nice place you've got here,' he said, looking around.

'Thanks,' I said. 'I like it better than cheap irony.'

Actually, I liked it far better than that – enough so that finishing it seemed redundant. I had built the foundation and subflooring three summers before, and had helped with the fireplace and the chimney base the summer after that. Instead of walls and a roof, though, I had erected a wooden-framed surplus officer's tent that faced the fireplace. Beyond the missing front wall, a small pine grove caught some of the road dust, and beyond the North Fork road, a range of soft, low mountains partially blocked the western sky. To the north, Red Meadows Creek scattered across a grassy flat, then gathered itself to plunge through a large culvert and on into the spring-thaw swollen waters of the North Fork. Across the river to the east, the towering spires of the peaks in Glacier Park rose into a sky as pristinely blue as an angel's eye. To the south, however, the view, mundane on the best of days, was sullied by the dirty haze that still roiled and billowed in the road thermals.

'I guess it's all right,' Trahearne allowed, 'but there's no place to hang the Mondrian.' Then he chuckled and finished his beer.

'Abstract painting gives me – '

'Goddamn it,' he interrupted, 'can I hole up here for a few days?'

'Be my guest,' I said.

'That's what I had in mind,' he said. 'Thanks.' He sat, waiting for me to ask him why, but when I didn't he told me anyway. Trahearne was dependable that way. 'Nothing was happening at home. I couldn't work. Not a lick. Goddamn it, sometimes I wonder if I haven't topped the last good woman, had the last good drink out of the bottle, and written the last good line, you know, and I can't seem to remember when it happened, can't remember at all.' He glanced up at me, tears brimming his bleary eyes. 'I can't remember when it happened, where it went.'

'Try to relax,' I said.

'Don't give me my own lines.'

'You shouldn't have given it to me in the first place,' I said, as I pitched him another beer.

'You can be a real bastard, can't you?' he muttered, his trembling fingers struggling with the pull tab.

'Want me to open that for you, old man?'

'I guess that's why I came,' he said, smiling suddenly and brushing at his tears with fingers as thick as sausages, 'for the quality of the sympathy. It's got a sharp edge on it here, Sughrue, and I can deal with that.' He sounded like a man who got more sympathy than he wanted at home, but I wasn't about to say that. He did it for me anyway. 'I just can't stand all that damned solicitude. It's as if she was an intensive-care nurse and I was about to croak.' Then he paused. 'I always go back to work eventually,' he said. 'I just haven't found the right moment yet.'

Since I didn't have anything to say, he finally shut up, and we sat around enjoying the silence. A light wind rustled the lodgepole pines, clearing the road dust, and behind us the river roared mightily in its stony course. The afternoon drifted slowly toward dusk, lingering like wisps of feather ash in the air, and Fireball returned from his afternoon explorations, trotting down the road like a man returning from a serious mission. He nosed Trahearne's ankle, and the big man leapt up.

'What the hell's he doing here?'

'Rosie said we had ruined him for polite company,' I answered.

'You've been back to California?'

'There and other places,' I said. 'I've been on the road so much I think I've worn out my ass.'

'Looks like you've done considerable damage to some other parts, too,' he said, nodding toward the yellowed bruises on my abdomen. I hadn't been working on my tan hard enough to hide them.

'I took second-best in a political discussion in Pinedale, Wyoming,' I lied. I still didn't know what to think about the beating, and even if I had known, I didn't want to talk about it.

'Did you find Rosie's daughter?' he asked as he rummaged through the ice for another beer.

'Found out that she died some years ago,' I said.

'How?'

'Drowned after a car wreck.'

'That's too bad,' he said. 'How'd Rosie take it?'

'She ran me off her place,' I said.

'Why?'

389

'She didn't believe me,' I said.

'Why not?'

'Said she knew in her heart that her daughter was still alive,' I said. 'But I checked the death certificate and talked to a woman who identified the body.'

'That's too bad,' he said again.

'Runaways get killed all the time,' I said. 'For every three or four I find, one will be toes-up on a slab. Running away is not a good life. At least Rosie's daughter had six good months before she died.' I stood up and struck a match and dropped it into the logs laid in the fireplace. The kerosene-soaked sawdust caught swiftly, and the logs began to crackle. Instead of a cheery fire, though, it seemed too much like a funeral pyre. 'Six good months,' I repeated.

'Sometimes I think I'd give up the rest of my life for six good months,' he said softly.

'It doesn't work that way.'

The flames rose without smoke, sparks flaring up the stubby chimney and into the velvet night waiting to the east.

Trahearne stayed sober that night, easing by on slow beers, and the next day he stayed dry. The third morning he limped the five miles down and back to the Polebridge store to buy a box of pencils and a Big Chief school tablet. The fourth morning he went to work at the picnic table beside the tent. After that, for more than a week, our days and nights became as orderly and measured as the rising and falling of the sun, the gentle waxing and waning of the fickle moon.

In the mornings, I jogged up the North Fork road, heading for the border and dodging logging trucks. I never made it, of course, but the walk back was always nice. Until I stopped at the creek for a heart-stopping plunge into the shallow pool below the culvert. When I got back to the cabin, Trahearne would close his tablet, boil another pot of cowboy coffee and fix breakfast on a Coleman stove while I sat on the steps with a cup of coffee and my first cigarette of the day, coughing and spitting up phlegm and what felt like scraps of lung tissue.

One morning as he stroked a fluffy pile of scrambled eggs in the skillet, he asked, 'What's all that running about?'

'It makes me feel so good.' I choked, then coughed and spit again.

'Boy, I guess I'm the lucky one,' he said grinning.

'Why's that?'

'I can feel like shit without doing all that work,' he said, then laughed like a man full of himself and empty of cares.

In the afternoons and evenings, we talked about things – our wars, our runaway fathers, the nature of things – then we crawled into sleeping bags to wait for the next day, wait for it to begin all over again.

Then one morning I came back to find a note nailed to the steps. *Sorry*, it read. *Back in a few days.* I thought about the bars myself but went fishing instead.

Two nights later, about three A.M., he roared back, crunched the right front fender of the VW on the pile of logs, then stumbled into bed, muttering about his life and hard times. I acted like a dead man until he finally went to sleep. He stayed in bed the next day, rising only to piss, guzzle water, and gobble aspirins and Rolaids. The next day he wasted bitching about the weather: it was too nice to suit him. Then he went back to work.

This time he only lasted four days. On the fifth morning, when I showed up dripping cold water, he had the whiskey bottle sitting on the tablet like a child's dare. In the fireplace wads of crumpled paper huddled like the scat of some odd nocturnal beast.

'How long do you think you can stand this goddamned solitude?' he asked peevishly as he splashed Wild Turkey into his cup.

'What solitude is that?'

'Goddamn it, Sughrue, has anybody ever talked to you about your hospitality?'

'Never twice,' I said.

As I dried on a dirty sweat shirt, he grunted to his feet and huffed over to the VW convertible, then raced away on a cloud of dust. Perhaps the same one he had ridden in upon.

That evening, as I used the scraps of poetic paper to start a fire, I found one that seemed longer than the others, and I smoothed it out on the table.

It read:

Once you flew sleeping in sunshine, amber limbs
locked in flight. Now you lie there rocky
still beyond the black chop, your chains

blue light. Dark water holds you
down. Whales sound deep into the glacier's
trace, tender flukes tease your hair,
your eyes dream silver scales.
                              Lie still,
wait. This long summer must break before
endless winter returns with tombstone glaciers
singing ice.
                    I will not mourn.
When next the world rises warm, men will chip
arrowheads from your heart . . .

His large, childish scrawl raced across the page, breaking at times
into an almost indecipherable frenzy. I didn't know what he meant
by the poem, but the handwriting was that of an insane child. For a
moment, I felt sorry for him. I folded the poem and slipped it into
my wallet. It seemed mannered and stilted to me, but for reasons I
wouldn't think about, I wanted to keep it.

Later that evening, I took a tin cup full of his whiskey down by
the river. A new moon burnished the rough waters. The river was
rotten with the stink of old snow, cold and brackish green, roaring
like a runaway freight, an avalanche of molten snow.

Once, when I summered with my father in that basement on the
Colorado plains, he had come home drunk and awakened me to take
me to see my first snow. He lashed me behind him on his motorcycle,
an old surplus Harley with a suicide shift, and drove across the
midnight plains toward the mountains, flying as if he were being
pursued by fiends, the rear wheel spitting gravel on the twisting
curves. He found snow, finally, on the northern face of a cut bank,
and he stopped and we took off our clothes under a slice of moon
to bathe in the snow. He meant something mystic, I think, but like
me, he was a flatlander who had grown up without knowing snow,
and within minutes the two of us were engaged in a furious snowball
fight, laughing and screaming at the stars, wrestling in the shallow
skim of frozen snow. On the way home, tied once more to his back
with baling twine, I slept, my cold skin like fire, and dreamed of
blizzards and frozen lakes, a landscape sheathed in ice, but I was
warm somehow, wrapped in the furs of bears and beaver and lynx,
dreaming of ice as the motorcycle split the night.

As I thought of that and sipped the smoky whiskey, I heard Trahearne return, more slowly than he had departed. He parked by the cabin and left the engine running, grinding like teeth in the darkness, as he gathered his gear, stumbling about like a drunken bear. I waited by the river until I heard his car door slam, then I walked back to the cabin. He drove away slowly, jammed into the tiny car, slow and almost stately, like a funeral barge loosed on a black, deep-flowing, silent river. The embers of his taillights grew pale in the dust.

It wasn't until the next morning that I missed the bulldog.

12

I drove back down to Meriwether the next day, and for lack of anything better to do, I went back to work. One midnight repossession up on the reservation, some lackadaisical collection work, and a divorce case so sordid that I checked my bank account and found it still fat with Catherine Trahearne's money. I shut down the operation, closed my office, and told the answering service that I was unavailable, out of town on a big case, then I spent a few easy days and nights playing two-dollar poker and staring at the remains of my face in barroom mirrors. In the right light, I could pass for forty, though I was a couple of years younger than that. I stayed fairly sober and faintly sane, and although the highway called to me several times, I stayed in town. Then a bartender out at the Red Baron had to take off for his mother's funeral over in Billings, so I filled in for him.

When I first moved to Meriwether, and for years before, the Red Baron had been a fine working and drinking man's bar called the Elbow Room, the sort of place where the bartender comes out into the parking lot at seven A.M. to wake up the drunks sleeping in their cars, then helps them inside, and buys the first drink. The Elbow Room didn't have a jukebox or a pool table or a pinball machine. Just a television set for the games and an honest shot of whiskey for the watchers. Then one summer old man Unbehagen died in his sleep a few weeks after I had come into the possession of a bundle of very hot cash, so hot nobody would claim it. So I went in with the Schaffer twins as a silent partner and we bought the license and premises. Unfortunately, the Schaffer boys were as loud and ambitious as I was silent and outvoted. They took my favorite bar and turned it into a business, a topless-dancer, pool, and pinball

394

success. Since I was tied to the hot money, I couldn't even raise my voice in silent protest. I took my cut and kept my mouth shut.

On Monday nights the Baron was the scene of amateur topless dancing, feckless young ladies exposing their mediocre bodies with enthusiasm in place of talent to a horde of young men driven quite mad by the mere idea of amateurism. The middle of the week was devoted to straight semi-pro tits and ass, and the maniacs usually settled into a dull roar, broken by the occasional drunken fistfight. Friday and Saturday nights were given over to heavy metal rock or bluegrass and free-form boogie, but Sundays were, thankfully, a day of rest from the reckless abandon of entertainment. On Sunday night, the drinkers had to have their own fun, and the place was usually as quiet as a graveyard.

Catherine Trahearne could have come in on a Sunday night, but she didn't. It had to be Monday. When she came in the vinyl-padded door that night, she looked as out of place as a chicken in church, but she walked directly to the bar and stood behind a group of flushed shame-faced young men until they cleared a space for her. Dressed in wool and leather – soft beige slacks, a dark cashmere pullover, and a deerskin vest – she looked even better than she had in a tennis dress. The dark umber tones of her clear skin hinted at sultry, mysterious nights, and her slim, athletic body promised to fulfill the hints. Whatever women were supposed to lose in their early fifties, she hadn't lost it yet. Not a bit of it. A hunk of polished but uncut turquoise as large and roughly the same shape as a shark's tooth dangled from a heavy silver chain between her breasts.

When she sat down at the bar, she took out a cigarette, and I leaped to light it for her. She stared over my shoulder toward the stage, where Boom-Boom, our resident amateur heavyweight, lifted her shift to reveal breasts as large and round as a bald man's head with a screaming giggle that should have shattered glassware. As always, the crowd exploded into hoots and cheers, table-thumping fists and whistles. In her real life, Boom-Boom was an improbably demure barmaid, but on Monday nights she came out and killed them. Catherine smiled at the furor, seemingly with honest amusement. I ignored the shrill pleas of the topless dancers doubling as cocktail waitresses, ignored the bar customers, and asked her if she wanted a drink.

'What an odd way to make a living,' she said, then blew out the match before it burnt my fingers.

'She's an amateur,' I said.

'But joyously enthusiastic, don't you think?' she said, staring into my eyes with a steady gaze that reminded me of how I had felt when she told me she had to take a shower the first time I met her. To get away from the gaze, I glanced over my shoulder. Boom-Boom was having a hell of a time, and I felt like a cretin for not having noticed before. 'Actually, though, I was talking about your new line of endeavor, Mr. Sughrue.'

'Just filling in for a sick friend, Mrs. Trahearne.'

'Catherine,' she commanded softly.

'C.W.,' I said.

'What do the initials stand for?' she asked, smiling.

'Chauncey Wayne,' I confessed.

'C.W. will do fine,' she said, then laughed.

'Would you like a drink?'

'Actually, I'm here on business,' she said. 'But it could be conducted over a drink. Later, perhaps? Some place more conducive to conversation?'

'Where are you staying?'

'The Thunderbird.'

'They've got a quiet piano bar,' I said, 'and I could meet you around midnight. If that isn't too late?'

'Not at all,' she said, 'it's a date.' Then she extended her slim hand. Her nails were painted a dark, dusky red that matched her lips and picked up the tones of her skin and hair. When I shook it, she held my hand and focused her bright green eyes on mine until I nearly blushed. 'Trahearne is quite fond of you,' she said, 'and I hope we can be friends.' I had heard that before; all Trahearne's women wanted to be friends of mine. Catherine gave me an expensive smile and left. As she walked out, even the dumbest, drunkest of the kids turned away from Boom-Boom's mighty breasts to watch Catherine's delicately switching hips.

In the rosy, diffuse light of the piano bar, she looked even better. She could have passed for thirty. A great thirty. And she damn well knew it. After we had settled into a plush booth with our drinks, she went to work on me with the wise eyes, the slightly amused smile, and more random body contact than the law allows in public places.

'Thank you for coming,' she whispered.

'You said something about business,' I said nervously as I finished my drink before the cocktail waitress walked back to the bar. As much as I had enjoyed the first trip, I didn't feel up to chasing Trahearne around Western America just yet, and I certainly didn't want to mess around with his ex-wife.

'Yes, I have a small complaint about how you handled the recovery of my ex-husband,' she said with mock seriousness.

'What's that?'

'When you called from the hospital,' she said, 'you told me a little white lie about Trahearne's accident which we won't even bother to discuss, but now I want a full report into all the lurid details of his latest odyssey.'

'Right,' I said. It seemed odd that Trahearne's ex-wife seemed to know more about what had happened than his present wife did. I assumed that he didn't care if I told Catherine. 'What do you want to know?'

'Everything,' she answered sweetly. 'Where he went, how you found him, how he came to be wounded in the butt. All the sordid details.' She sipped her vermouth. 'I've always wanted to know exactly what transpired on one of his trips,' she continued, 'but his versions were already literature by the time he returned, and none of the other gentlemen I hired were able to either find him or provide me with the details. They seemed to lack both intelligence and imagination. Are most of the members of your profession as pedestrian as those I've done business with in the past?'

'This may sound strange,' I said, 'but the only other private investigator I know is my ex-partner here in town, and he's an even worse drunk than I am. I know PI's have conventions, but I've never been to one. They're all about electronics and industrial security and crap like that. I just repossess cars and chase runaways and follow cheating husbands, stuff like that.'

'You don't sound very ambitious,' she said.

'I'm not,' I said, 'not about anything. I spent nine years in the Army in three separate hitches, mostly playing football or sitting in a gym or writing sports stories for post newspapers, and I spent four years playing football for three different junior colleges under two different names, and I got in this business strictly by accident, so I'm not Johnny Quest or the moral arbiter of the Western world. More like a second-rate hired gun or a first-rate saddle tramp.'

'A classic underachiever?' she said.

'Classic bindle-stiff, apple-knocker, pea-pickin' bum,' I said.

'But still you found Trahearne,' she said, 'and you must tell me about it.'

As I told her what I thought she wanted to hear, she moved closer, occasionally smiled and touched my hand with her fingers, then our hips and thighs were nudging each other, and her nails drifting across my wrist. When I finished, she told me to tell the rest of it now, and she laughed and held my hand as I filled in the gaps. When I finished the second time, she hugged my arm against her breast.

'How simply delightful,' she said.

'Hey,' I said, trying to make a joke of it, 'you're going to have to turn it down a few notches.'

She didn't play coy at all, just laughed openly, the tones ringing crystal through the cozy bar like vesper bells chiming in a pastoral dusk.

'Don't be so serious,' she said. 'I won't attack you.'

'Damn it,' somebody using my voice complained. I knew better than to fool around with the ex-wives of friends, and for all our troubles, Trahearne had become a friend. But I said it again anyway, 'Damn it.' And Catherine lifted my hand to touch a flattened knuckle with her lips. Damned if I wasn't as spooky as a sixteen-year-old kid as I followed her out of the lounge.

Afterward, as we lay on her motel bed, my hand resting on the taut muscles of her thigh, I asked her, 'Is this what you drove down for?'

'Flew,' she said, and laughed. 'I flew down by way of Seattle. I'm supposed to be visiting friends there. This is what I came for, yes, and I would have walked.'

'Why?'

'Please don't be shocked when I tell you this,' she said, pausing to light two cigarettes, 'and please remember that I might have chosen you anyway. I work like the very devil keeping this aged body intact, and I endure yearly humiliations at the hands of expensive plastic surgeons so I can enjoy my declining years. You see, I sleep with whomever pleases me' – she paused again and her voice grew hard – 'especially Trahearne's friends. Do you mind?'

'Well, it makes me feel a little like I've been rutting in the old man's track,' I said, thinking about the skinny whore in the desert, 'but it's a damn fine track. So I guess I don't mind.'

'Thank you,' she said. 'I've only a few more years before I become withered and old – don't interrupt me – and I have a great many lonely years to recover.'

She stopped to look at me. I watched the cigarette smoke drift across the shadowed ceiling in mare's tails.

'You're not curious about my motives?' she asked, her fingernails lightly plucking at the hair on my chest.

'Nope.'

'I thought detectives were endlessly curious,' she said.

'Only in the movies.'

After another long silence, she said, 'It's odd, you know.'

'What?'

'I almost never explain my actions to anyone,' she murmured, 'but since you didn't ask, I feel somehow obligated to tell you.'

'Old Chinese interrogation tactic,' I said, and she chuckled and slapped me on the belly.

'Be serious,' she said, still chuckling. 'I'm about to tell you the story of my life.'

'Okay.'

'We met during the war, you see,' she said as she leaned over to stub her cigarette out. 'I was still a child, only eighteen, but already widowed. My first husband was one of those smart young men from Carmel who stabled his polo ponies and dashed off to join the RCAF, visions of the Lafayette Escadrille dancing in his head. In the excitement of his departure, he took my virginity, then with a burst of daylight remorse he drove us up to Reno, where he made an honest woman of me. Six months later, his Spitfire went down into the Channel during Dunkirk. It was like something out of a novel at the time, and I suppose it still seems that way to me.

'Then I met Trahearne, and it seemed like the next scene,' she continued. 'To the horror of everyone concerned, I married him still wearing widow's weeds, then sent him too off to the war.'

'You're the woman on the bridge,' I whispered.

399

'Oh, he told you that absurd story too,' she said. 'I didn't know what it all meant to him, but something inside me knew what to do.'

'I wonder who the woman in the window was,' I said absently.

'His mother, of course,' Catherine answered softly.

'Jesus Christ,' I said, then sat up and fumbled for another cigarette. 'That's why I'm not curious,' I said. 'I find out too many things I don't want to know as it is. Jesus Christ.'

'I don't suppose it was that terrible,' she chided me. 'And it was such a long time ago. Trahearne only acts as if it was so important because he's never been able to write about it.'

'Let's get back to the war,' I said, 'something I can understand.'

'Four long years of wretched fidelity,' she said, 'then another fifteen years while he worked out his guilt because I could be faithful and he simply couldn't. I don't think I minded his whoring, you know, not nearly so much as I minded his guilty rages of which I was the object of hatred. It wasn't an easy life at all.' She took my cigarette from me. 'One day two years ago he called from Sun Valley to tell me that he was divorcing me. I wasn't surprised; he had done that sort of thing before. This time, though, he went through with it, and let me tell you, he paid dearly for it. I stripped him, as he said, like a grizzly strips a salmon, left him wearing fish eyes and bones. That might have been enough to bring him back, but he had already remarried before he realized just how badly I had taken him. Now he has a wife who is as recklessly unfaithful as he is, so he doesn't have to feel guilty anymore, and he hasn't written a word worth keeping in two years. It's driving him quite mad, I suspect.'

'And you're living with his mother,' I said in amazement.

'Edna was quite kind to me during all those years,' Catherine said, 'and it was the least I could do. She was more like a mother than my own had been, and living with her, I can keep an eye on Trahearne. I have my freedom now, more money than I can possibly spend before I die, and I also have my revenge.' She paused and rolled over to hold me, saying, 'Don't let them tell you that revenge isn't sweet, either.'

'You still love the old fart,' I said.

'Of course,' she said as she straddled my hips, 'but I love this, too. You don't mind, do you?'

The complications and confusion worried me a bit, but Catherine was a sweet and loving woman, her passion fired by the years when she had kept it banked, and during the night I didn't seem to mind at all. The next morning, though, when she checked out of her motel and moved her bags into my apartment, I had a few doubts. We laid those to rest, though, for the next three days. She cooked a better breakfast than Trahearne and she was easier to get along with, but I had to admit that I was relieved when she announced that she had to fly back to Seattle, then home. It wasn't until we were standing in the airport terminal that I realized how much I was going to miss her.

'Somehow, this stopped being a weekend fling,' I said as we watched the passengers disembark from her flight.

'I know, I know,' she said, squeezing my hand angrily. 'It sounds so terribly trite, but I wish I had met you twenty years ago. It's not only trite, it's a lie. Thirty years ago would be closer to the mark, and you didn't have your first pair of long pants yet.'

'I was born an old man,' I said, but she ignored me.

'You or somebody like you might have saved me from this damned emotional martyrdom I seem to have chosen,' she said bitterly. Then it was time to go, and she presented me with a tilted cheek for a matronly goodbye kiss. 'We'll pretend you were some anonymous lover I picked up in a cocktail lounge,' she said.

'Whatever you say.'

'This is goodbye,' she said, then tilted her cheek toward me again.

'To hell with that,' I said as I grabbed her shoulders and kissed her on the mouth so hard that it blurred the careful lines of her lips, mussed her hair, and made her drop her carry-on bag.

'You bastard,' she muttered when she caught her breath and picked up her bag. A blush rose up her slender neck like a flame, touching her cheeks with umber sweetly burnt. She reached up to wipe my mouth, repeating, 'You bastard. That was the last one.' Then she walked through the security check and boarded the airplane without glancing back.

As she climbed the steps, I swallowed some dumb pain and walked away too.

Nobody lives forever, nobody stays young long enough. My past seemed like so much excess baggage, my future a series of long goodbyes, my present an empty flask, the last good drink already bitter on my tongue. She still loved Trahearne, still maintained her secret fidelity as if it were a miniature Japanese pine, as tiny and

401

perfect as a porcelain cup, lost in the dark and tangled corner of a once-formal garden gone finally to seed.

After she left, I wandered around in a dull haze for days, telling myself what an idiot I was, trying to swallow with measured amounts of whiskey the stone in my chest. It was June in Montana, high enough up the steps of the northern latitudes to pass for cruel April. Blue skies ruled stupidly, green mountains shimmered like mirages, and the sun rose each morning to stare into my face with the blank but touching gaze of a lovely retarded child. I drove down to Elko to try to find a landscape to suit my mood, but the desert had bloomed with a spring rain and the nights were cool and ringing with stars. I put Rosie's eighty-seven dollars in a dollar slot machine and hit a five-hundred-dollar jackpot. Then I fled to the most depressing place in the West, the Salt Lake City bus terminal, where 1 drank Four Roses from a pint bottle wrapped in a paper bag. I couldn't even get arrested, so I headed up to Pocatello to guzzle Coors like a pig at a trough with a gang of jack Mormons, thinking I could pick a fight, but I didn't have the heart for it. Eventually, none the worse for wear, I drifted north toward Meriwether like a saddle tramp looking for a spring roundup.

13

One of the advantages of my business was that it didn't leave me much inclined to mourn lost loves too long. Back in town, I worked a couple of divorces and repossessed a few televisions from households where domestic strife was the commodity of exchange. It worked like a charm. My cynicism restored itself, and my bank account remained flush. Then Trahearne called one afternoon.

'Hey, I'm sorry I left the cabin in such a snit,' he said.

'Looked more like a funky blue huff,' I said.

'Always with the jokes, Sughrue,' he complained. 'When are you coming up to get your damned dog?'

'My dog?' I said. 'You stole him, old man, you bring him back.'

'Not a chance. I'm at home for as long as I can manage it,' he said.

'How's Fireball?'

'Last I saw him, he was the bull of the woods around here.'

'The last time?'

'Yeah, he took to Melinda like a long lost brother,' he said, 'and they're off on a little trip. You know how Fireball likes to travel.'

'In style,' I said. 'If she's down this way, maybe she could drop him off.'

'Be too far out of her way,' he said too quickly.

'You don't know where she is, do you?'

'Not exactly, no,' he said, 'but it's okay.'

'Want me to go looking for her?'

'She's not lost.'

'Neither were you,' I said, 'but I found you anyway.'

'Yeah, thanks,' he said. Over the telephone, his sneer sounded

403

like the snort of a wounded cape buffalo. 'What's the matter? Are you getting bored down there?'

'I was born bored.'

'Well, hell, drive up and help me stay dry,' he said. He almost sounded serious.

'Isn't that like the halt leading the lame or something like that?'

'I'm doing pretty good on my own,' he said. 'I'm just about ready to go back to work.'

'Your public's waiting with bated breath,' I said. 'Hey, you're a literary type – what the hell's that mean?'

'How should I know? Maybe it just sounds good.'

'Great,' I said. 'Give me a call when she comes back with my dog, and I'll drive up for a weekend.'

'All right,' he said cheerfully.

Then we chatted aimlessly about the weather and the fishing we intended to do – all the assorted foolishness that keeps Ma Bell whistling a happy tune. It wasn't until we had hung up that I thought of Catherine, which I assumed meant that I was cured. As they say, I heaved a sigh of relief. When I tell folks that I've never been married, I neglect to mention the fact that I've been engaged about forty times.

Once I decided that I had stopped moping about, though, my foot started itching so badly that I had to take my boot off. I scratched it furiously, but the itch went deeper than I could reach with anything but five hundred road miles. I got back on the horn and called every bailbondsman I knew, but nobody had any jumpers to chase. Then I tried all the usual things – walking around my tiny office, three steps one way, four the other. I got a glass and tried to listen to the marriage counselor next door, but the aluminum walls didn't do much for vocal reproduction. My office is in a double-wide trailer house that I share with the marriage counselor, who gives me a lot of business, and two shady real-estate salesmen. None of my neighbors were known for their conversational versatility, so I moved the plastic drapes to look at my view. How long can you stare across an alley at a battered Dempster Dumpster behind a discount store, though. I thought about going out to talk to the current inept secretary I shared with my neighbors, but she buzzed me before I could leave.

'You have a call,' she said.

'Who is it?'

'Long distance,' she crooned.

'Ol' long calls a lot,' I said.

'Sir?'

'Nothing,' I said. 'If it's not collect, put them on.'

'Oops,' she muttered. 'I'm sorry, sir, but we seem to have been disconnected.' Which meant she had forgotten how to use the hold button again. 'Maybe the party will call back.'

'Hope so.'

The party did. It was Rosie. Before I could say hello, she said, 'I tol' you she wasn't dead.'

'You told me,' I answered. The itch raced up my leg and burrowed under the skin between my shoulder blades. 'What happened?'

'Jimmy Joe called me and said he got a picture postcard from her this morning,' she said, 'mailed from Denver.'

'Was he sure it was her handwriting?'

'It had to be,' Rosie said. 'Who'd be playing a mean trick like that?'

'I don't know,' I said.

'He read it to me and it sounded like Betty Sue,' she added.

'You haven't heard from her in ten years,' I said. 'How would you know what she sounds like?'

'I just know,' she said.

'I'll be damned.'

'Don't be down on yourself, C.W., anybody can make a mistake,' she said. 'How much would you charge to go down to talk to that lady who said my baby girl was dead and in her grave?'

'Not a cent,' I said.

'Now, don't be that way,' she said.

'Okay, I'll send you a bill. If I find anything,' I said. 'You can do me a favor, though.'

'What's that?'

'Call your ex-husband back and ask him to send me the postcard general delivery in Fort Collins, Colorado, okay?'

'Good as done.'

'I'll call you in a couple of days,' I said.

'If you should just happen to find her, just tell her she don't have to come home or nothing,' Rosie pleaded. 'Just ask her to call me collect. That's all. Just hearing her voice would be more than enough.'

'Okay.'

'Say,' she said, 'how's that worthless bulldog doing?'

'He's doing fine,' I said, 'but he's homesick. I thought I might tote him back down that way sometime. If you'd like me to.'

'I guess I would at that,' she said. 'And, say, I'm terribly sorry for the way I talked to you before . . . when . . .'

'Don't worry about it,' I said. 'Take care.'

'You too, son.'

Within the hour, I had the El Camino packed and headed out for Colorado.

During the fourteen-hour trip, I had plenty of time to think about things, this all-too-convenient postcard and the beating I had suffered on my last trip to Colorado, but nothing made any sense. Even if I had had fourteen years instead of fourteen hours, I probably wouldn't have worked it out. That's not how I work. My ex-partner once found me in a bar puzzling over a contorted divorce case that had me completely baffled – I couldn't find out who was doing what to whom – and he advised me to forget about thinking and to get my ass out on the street and put my hands on somebody. He was drunk, of course, but drunk or sober, he was a hell of a divorce detective.

But I was on the road, instead of the street, and didn't have any idea who to put my hands on. Either Selma Hinds had lied, for reasons that made no sense, or somebody had lied to her, which made even less sense. If she had lied and wanted to keep on lying, my hands were tied. Unlike Jackson, Selma Hinds was a proper citizen, and if I laid a finger on her, she would scream for the law, and I would probably end up in the slammer down in Canon City doing twenty to life. I didn't know what was going on, didn't understand a bit of it, didn't like any of it. Maybe that's why the first thing I packed was my guns. If your brain won't work, wave a gun around. Sometimes that helps.

As it turned out, though, all the worry and thought was wasted. When I pulled off the Poudre Canyon highway at Selma Hinds' trailhead, I parked behind a red Volkswagen convertible with Montana plates and a crunched right front fender. At first, I wondered what the hell Melinda Trahearne was doing up at Selma's, then I wondered why I had been so blind and dumb. That crazy, goddamned Trahearne had been leading me around by the nose from the moment I had found him in Rosie's. Maybe even before that, which would explain that long insane jaunt through the bars, explain why he had been so easy to follow and so hard to find, why he waited at Rosie's. He wanted me to look for Betty Sue Flowers, wanted me to nose around in her past, like a hungry dog turning up the buried bones and ripe flesh of her life so he could have an excuse for the bitter taste in his own mouth, the stink of corruption in his nose. If I hadn't been looking so hard for Betty Sue, I would have seen her face in Melinda's the first time. Goddamned Trahearne. I had been bounced around like a foolish little rubber ball on an elastic string, and seeing it now made me so tired that I didn't even care who held the paddle – I just wanted off the string.

Selma and Melinda were on their knees weeding the garden, their soft voices and laughter echoing across the ridge like windchimes. At the edge of the garden, curled in a shallow depression, Fireball slept among dry pine needles. The rest of the dogs were sleeping too, in a wire kennel beyond the small cages.

'Excuse me,' I said when I stopped at the edge of the garden.

The two women paused, then stood and turned toward me. Selma's face wore the same forgiving look, but now it seemed like a gaze painted on a stone, passive and permanent. When she recognized me, though, her face broke into a thousand fragments, wild and frightened like that of a deer poised to run. Melinda sighed and relaxed with the patience of an eternal victim flooding her eyes.

'I guess I knew that you'd come,' she said. 'I guess I've been waiting. How did Trahearne find out?'

'Find out what?' I said. 'Your mother sent me.'

'But I'm her mother,' Selma whimpered.

'Didn't you tell her I was dead?' Melinda said.

'She wouldn't believe me,' I said. 'And then you sent your daddy a postcard.'

'A postcard?' she said, looking amazed.

'I'm her mother,' Selma repeated, trying to draw herself back together.

'If you didn't, somebody did,' I said. 'Trahearne, maybe, or some of your friends in Denver. Somebody sent a postcard so Rosie would know you're alive, so I'd come here. I just don't understand why.'

'I don't either,' she said. 'Nobody's looking for me anymore but my mother.'

'I'm your mother,' Selma wailed, then sank to her knees in the soft dark soil, weeping.

'It's all right,' Melinda said, holding Selma's head against her thigh.

'Tell him I'll pay . . . pay anything for his silence,' Selma sobbed. 'Pay anything.'

'Listen,' I said, 'as far as I'm concerned Betty Sue Flowers is dead. I only walked up that damned hill to be sure. If you want your mother to think you're dead, that's on your conscience, and if you want to act like Trahearne doesn't know who you are, that's between the two of you. I'm out of it. I'm going home.'

'I'll pay anything,' Selma moaned.

'Hush,' Melinda said kindly. 'It had to happen sometime. It'll work out.' Then she looked at me. 'Wait for me, please,' she said. 'At the bottom of the trail. I've got to take Selma inside and calm her down. But please wait. I have to talk to you.'

'You'll just tell me things I don't want to know,' I said.

'I'll pay!' Selma screamed. The dogs in the kennel woke and began to yap, which in turn woke Fireball out of his sun-dazed stupor. He yawned, sniffed the air, then trotted over to greet me. As I scratched his head, Melinda helped Selma to her feet and led her toward the cabin. When they were inside, I headed down the hill.

'Please wait for me,' Melinda said from the doorway. 'Please.'

'All right,' I said from the edge of the clearing.

Fireball followed me down the trail, plodding steadily through sunlight and shade, his nose lifted in the morning air as if he could smell a beer.

'No drugs on the mountain,' I said to him, and he quickened his step.

At the bottom of the trail, I crossed the highway to wash my face in the river, to lave the miles away with cold water. Fireball gave me a dirty look, then lapped up a quick drink, shaking his head as if the water horrified him. I took him back across the road and gave him a beer. We had both earned one.

I woke up with the can warm in my hand in the middle of the

afternoon. Melinda was sitting in the passenger seat, dressed now in hiking boots, shorts, and a tank top. It was as if she had shed her baggy clothes to show me what it was all about – long, shapely legs rippling with muscle, high, firm breasts, the sort of body men dream about.

'You were sleeping so hard, it seemed a shame to wake you up,' she said. 'Selma doesn't have any coffee, but I made you some herb tea,' she added, holding up a thermos.

'I'll have a beer,' I said. 'I don't want to get too healthy.'

As I rustled up a beer, she said, 'Trahearne must know, then?'

'He led me right to your mother's place, and then after Rosie hired me to find you, he encouraged me. He must have had it in mind.'

'I should have told him the truth about my . . . my life,' she said as she poured herself a cup of the weak tea.

'You should have told him,' I agreed. 'In the course of my search, he had the wonderful chance to see your acting debut.'

She sighed. 'Oh, that poor, poor man. Now he'll never believe me.'

'About what?'

'I have to travel a lot, have to be alone, too,' she said, 'and he's convinced that I . . . I sleep with other men when I'm away from him.' When I didn't say anything, she added, 'And it isn't true. He just wants it to be true. I know he does, and it doesn't matter to me, but I don't fool around.'

'Okay.'

'You don't sound convinced,' she said.

'I don't care,' I said, 'and it's none of my business anyway what either of you do or don't do, okay?'

'You don't even care why Betty Sue had to die, do you?'

'Nope.'

'They came looking for me,' she said, 'and I had to die to make them leave me alone.'

'Randall Jackson and the Denver hoods,' I said.

'You know them?' she asked, amazed all over again.

'Intimately.'

'I was in jail,' she said defiantly, 'and I . . .'

'I know,' I said. 'You got busted for soliciting.'

'. . . I lost thirty pounds in jail, a pound a day,' she continued as

409

if she hadn't heard me. 'Selma came to the jail when I was in, and I wanted to come up here, but I had to go by Jack's place to get some things, some books and things, and he saw me, you know, with all the fat gone, and he made me go to work for those awful people. It wasn't like San Francisco at all – that time we were just high and having fun and making money for bread and dope – this was a business, and they made me go to the hospital to have this scar I have ... made me have plastic surgery on this scar, and they spent a lot of money and they wouldn't let me leave. You understand, don't you?'

'Right.'

'So I stole a little money from Jack's billfold and ran up here to hide, but they came looking for me in a week or two, and I had to hide in the woods and Selma had to lie – she hates to lie, she hated lying to you before. Then later that summer her daughter drowned in the wreck, and she told the sheriff it was me, you see, and I could start over again, could act like none of it ever happened, don't you see?' She sat the plastic thermos cup very carefully on the dash, then began to weep. 'But you don't care, do you?' She sobbed between her hands.

I had had a bellyful of weeping women. 'Jesus fucking Christ!' I shouted as I threw my unfinished beer can out the open door and across the road. 'Your mother paid me eighty-seven dollars to find you,' I said, 'and I chased you all over the fucking country, and I don't know if I did it for Rosie or for myself or for some idea I had of you, but I know fucking-a well that I didn't do it for eighty-seven fucking dollars, so don't tell me I don't fucking care!'

'I'm sorry.' She giggled, then moved her hands and began to wipe away the tears. 'I was so involved in my own problems that I forgot how hard you had worked trying to find me.'

'You didn't know,' I said huffily.

'I understood without knowing,' she said with a smile.

'Bullshit.'

'You're cute when you're mad, C.W.,' she said.

I got out of the pickup and kicked a few rocks around, raising a cloud of dust that nearly choked me.

'So what now?' I said as I climbed back into my seat.

'I truly don't know,' she said. 'I'll have to think about it for a few days. That was always the trouble before – I did so many things without thinking about them first.'

'In spite of what I said up there, I've got to tell your mother something.'

'Will you wait for a few days?' she asked. 'Just until I've straightened this out with Trahearne?'

'I've got to call your mother tomorrow,' I said.

'All right, I'll call Trahearne tonight,' she said. 'I'd rather not do it by telephone, but if he already knows about me, I can tell what he thinks about it. Come back tomorrow. I'll meet you down here about ten. I think it might be best if you didn't come up the hill . . . you know, for Selma's sake. She's taken this whole thing so hard. She buried her daughter with my name, and of all the things I owe her, I owe her most for that. She gave me my life back, you see, and that's the most one person can do for another. That's how I feel about Trahearne sometimes – that I can give him his life back, take it back from those two awful women who have held him captive so long. You've seen them – you understand.'

'Maybe I do,' I said, 'and maybe I don't. It doesn't matter. I would like to know one thing, though.'

'I thought you didn't want to know anything,' she said with a gentle smile. I was amazed that I hadn't noticed how beautiful her smile was before. 'I thought you had no curiosity at all.'

'Don't be a smart-ass,' I said. 'Just tell me why you ran away in the first place.'

'Well, you don't know everything, do you?'

'Nope.'

'I was pregnant,' she said, 'and my boy friend took me to San Francisco for an abortion. On the way out of the hotel where they did it, I started hemorrhaging – it's an old story, you know, so old it's almost trite until it happens to you – and he ran off and left me bleeding to death on the emergency room steps of the Franklin Hospital. He dumped me there and ran away – '

'Albert Griffith?' I interrupted.

'You know some things, don't you?' she said. 'They stopped the bleeding all right, but I came down with a raging case of septicemia, and they had to do a hysterectomy to stop the infection. Pretty, isn't it? I had left my purse in Albert's car and lied about my name and my age, so nobody knew. I was afraid for anybody to know, ashamed, too, I guess. Anyway, by the time I was released from the hospital, I had been gone too long to go home, or so I thought, so I lived on the streets in the Haight until Jack took me in, and then so many other things happened that I just couldn't face going home at all. Not even when I heard about Bubba getting killed in Vietnam.'

'Is that your brother Lonnie?'

'Yes.'

'Your little brother's dead too,' I said.

'I know,' she whispered. 'I sneak back every now and again to hang around Sonoma, and I heard about it. I nearly went home then, too.'

'You should have gone home in the first place,' I said. 'A lot of grief could have been spared a lot of folks, including you.'

'I know,' she said, 'God, I know, but my daddy was gone and he didn't care, I called him once and he didn't care, and my momma was a slut – '

'Hey,' I said.

She looked at me. 'Guess I've no right to judge, huh?'

'Not even if you had lived the life of a vestal virgin,' I said.

'You're right,' she sighed. 'It seemed so important back then. Momma tried to act like it didn't mean anything when she divorced Daddy, but I could tell it did. She got to drinking a lot and bringing men into the trailer house, and I'd lie back there in the back bedroom and listen to them laughing and banging around and tell myself that if she'd stop that, my daddy would come home, which was silly, since he never paid any attention to me when he was there. About the nine hundredth time he looked at me like a stranger when I was a little girl, I decided I had been adopted. I guess every little kid does that, huh?'

'It's an easy way out,' I said.

'And it was all so long ago,' she whispered.

'Now it's all come back.'

'I think I'm glad, you know,' she said as she patted me on the thigh. 'I really think I'm glad it's all over.'

'Me too.'

'You drove straight through from Montana, didn't you?'

'Right.'

'You must be exhausted,' she said, then moved her hand from my thigh to the back of my neck. 'Go check into a motel and sleep,' she said, 'then come back tomorrow about ten. I'll meet you down here. Is that all right?'

I yawned. 'It's fine.'

'You've been so kind to me,' she said, 'kind to everybody – Trahearne and Selma and my momma. It's always like that, you know, for me. Every time things look bad somebody shows up in my life, and they're so much kinder than I deserve – like you and Selma and Trahearne, even poor old Jack in his own twisted way.'

'Maybe you deserve it,' I said.

'Nobody deserves it,' she said, 'it just happens. I'll see you tomorrow.' Then she leaned over to kiss me lightly on the corner of my mouth, a sisterly kiss, but her breath smelled of herbs and dried flowers and spring water, fresh and cool. 'About ten,' she whispered, and I kissed her on the mouth. Her lips parted slightly, our tongues touched for a brief electric moment, and her eyes widened, darkened to a stormy blue. 'I'm sorry,' she said, apologizing for something she hadn't done, something she wouldn't do, then she climbed out of the pickup, snapped her fingers at Fireball, who lumbered out from under the VW, and they pranced up the trail.

In that sudden sleepy moment, it became clear to me that, like it or not, I was standing in the lady's line and I didn't care about my position. She left me breathing like a hard-run horse. As I eased back down the sweeping curves of the canyon highway, I told myself that if I didn't watch out, Trahearne's women were either going to break my heart or change my life or be the death of me. I also told myself to drive north toward home as fast as the El Camino would go, but I didn't. I had a few drinks instead of lunch, but the taste of her mouth remained in mine like a sweet communion cracker unbroken before the bitter wine. In the middle of the afternoon, I checked into a Holiday Inn, checked out into a dreamless sleep, a wake-up call waiting like a death sentence.

413

14

The next morning, the condemned man, who had slept like a child and showered like a teenager preparing for a date, ate as hearty a breakfast as the Holiday Inn could provide, then stepped outside to contemplate the delicate air and the clear blue sunshine of the high plains. Interstate 25 was two hundred feet to the east, though, and the diesel stench took the edge off my enjoyment. Sixty-five miles south, the gray cloud of Denver's smog humped over the horizon like a whale's back. But the morning was finally ruined when I saw Trahearne sitting in his Cadillac barge, an obscene grin on his round face. He looked like a fat, mean child.

'What's happening?' I said, trying to stay calm.

'Hell, boy, I checked every motel in town before this one,' he said. 'I thought you had more taste than to stay at a Holiday Inn.'

'Some of my best friends are Holiday Inns,' I said. 'What are you doing here?'

'Looking for you, what else?' he said. 'After we talked, I decided to drive down to Meriwether, and when I got there, your secretary told me that you had driven down here, so I picked up a couple of hitchhikers, and they helped with the driving, and we drove all night and here I am . . .' His voice ran slowly down, like one of those talking dolls whose string had been pulled too many times.

'Let's not have any more lying, okay?' I said as I opened the door of the Caddy and got in. 'No more lying.'

'I couldn't find her without you, son,' he sighed. 'I didn't know where to look.'

'You were already here when you called me, weren't you?' I asked, and he nodded. 'And you sent her daddy a postcard, didn't you?' His head rose and sank once, then lay heavily on his chest. 'Why?'

'I've got to know who she's seeing,' he muttered.

'Okay,' I said, 'I'll show you.'

'Would you drive?' he asked.

There seemed no need to hurry, so I eased the convertible through town. Trahearne didn't say anything until we were four or five miles on the other side of town on the Laramie highway. As we topped the first hill and dropped into a little valley beyond a hogback ridge, he said something, but the wind through the convertible covered his words.

'What?' I asked.

'I'm sorry,' he said.

'Not sorry enough to suit me, old man,' I said, and he started to weep. 'Stop your goddamned whimpering,' I said. 'Just stop it. You know what she said when I told her that you'd seen that movie?' He shook his head. 'She said, "That poor, poor man." She's too good for you, you know that?'

'God do I ever know it,' he said.

As we turned off 287 onto the Poudre Canyon road, I asked him, 'Why? What the hell did you have in mind? How did you know where to go?'

'I didn't have anything in mind,' he said, 'except finding her. I was out there, driving around in circles and drinking, you know, hoping to find her but not looking for her, you know, and when I stopped at the Cottontail, I couldn't . . . Well, the little whore must have told you.'

'Told me what?'

'I couldn't get it up,' he said blankly.

'She didn't even remember you,' I said.

'That's even worse.'

'If you want them to remember you, old man, stay out of whore-houses,' I said. 'How did you know to go to Sonoma?'

'Once she was gone, off on a trip, and I went through her things and found a clipping from the San Francisco paper, a review of a Little Theatre group production of Anouilh's *Antigone*. When I read the description of the girl who played the lead, I knew it had to be her.' Then he paused. 'I've always known she wasn't who she said she was,' he admitted, 'knew right from the beginning. She had never been to the south of France, never been to Sun Valley before that summer. At first it seemed exciting, you know, not knowing who she really was. But it was like the promise she made me give her before she would marry me – the novelty wore off quickly and began to drive me mad.'

'What promise?' I said as I parked the Caddy behind Melinda's VW. A battered gray GMC pickup was parked in front. It looked like it had been wrecked once, then towed out of the river. 'What promise?' I repeated.

'That she could come and go as she pleased,' Trahearne muttered. 'That I wouldn't ask any questions.'

'She promised you the same thing, didn't she?'

He nodded, and glanced around. 'Does he live here?' he asked. 'He?'

'You know, the man . . . the man she sees.'

'She's supposed to meet me down here around ten,' I said. 'I'll let her tell you about it.'

'It's you now, isn't it,' he said sadly, a statement, not a question. 'It's you.'

'Just shut the fuck up, all right?' I said, then got out and walked across the road to watch the river.

What a case. Private detectives are supposed to find missing persons and solve crimes. So far in this one I had committed all the crimes – everything from grand theft auto to criminal stupidity – and everybody but poor old Rosie and I had known where Betty Sue Flowers was from the beginning. I had the odd feeling that if I didn't go home soon, instead of ending up with a bank account fat with Catherine Trahearne's money I would end up with holes in my boots and moths in my pocket. The more I thought about it, the angrier I became. I stood up and charged back across the highway, shouting at Trahearne.

'I'm sending you a bill, old man, and I don't care if it breaks your ass, you better come up with the scratch!'

'All right,' he answered meekly.

'Oh, stop being such a damned dope,' I said. 'She's up on that mountain staying with a woman who saved her life once and she's not doing a number with me – she's never done a number with anybody since she made the colossal mistake of falling in love with your sorry ass.'

'All right,' he said, not believing a word of it.

As I thought about it, I wasn't too sure that I believed it either. Like too many men, Trahearne and I didn't know how to deal with a woman like Melinda, caught as we were between our own random lusts and a desire for faithful women so primitive and fierce that it must have been innate, atavistic, as uncontrollable as a bodily function. That was when I stopped being angry at the old man.

'What time is it?' I asked him.

'Ten-thirty,' he said.

'She should be here soon,' I said. 'Let's have a midmorning nip.'

He looked startled, then reached under the seat for the bottle. As we shared the whiskey, I wondered how long men had been forgiving each other over strong drink for being fools.

At eleven, when Melinda still hadn't shown up, I hiked up the trail toward Selma's place, Trahearne following at his own pace, ten steps and a halt for some heavy breathing.

'I'll go ahead,' I told him, 'and warn them of your arrival so it won't be so much of a surprise.'

'It'll be a hell of a surprise if I get there,' he joked as I went on ahead. Two switchbacks up the hill, I could still hear his tortured breaths.

By the time I reached the clearing, my lungs were working overtime too. As I paused to rest a bit, I noticed a black splotch in the dust of the trail and splatters of dried blood on the rocks beside it, then I wondered where the dogs were. Across the clearing, the kennel gate stood open, as did the bank of small animal cages.

I ran to the large cabin, but it was empty, so I ran outside and around it. A young boy was digging a large hole with a pick and a young girl knelt beside a pile of dead dogs and birds and small furry animals. Selma sat on the far side of the clearing, her back against a pine, a shotgun cradled on her knees.

'What the hell happened?' I said to the boy.

He started, then climbed out of the hole quickly, the pick raised like a club. An ugly mouse closed his left eye, and he spit blood between broken teeth.

'You'll have to kill me this time, you son of a bitch,' he said as he came at me with the pick.

'Hey,' I said, holding up my arms and backing away. He didn't

417

stop. The girl beside the grave moaned and covered her face with her hands. 'Hey, wait a minute,' I said, but he kept coming. 'Calm down, son,' I said, still walking backward, 'I didn't do anything.'

'You led them here!' Selma screamed as she stood up and pointed the double-barreled shotgun in my general direction.

The boy with the pick glanced over my shoulder, and I heard the scuffle of feet on the rocky dirt. I didn't wait to find out what the sudden inhalation of breath behind me meant; I ducked and rolled away, catching a glimpse of the other young girl as she swung the ax she carried. When it hit the ground where I had been standing, the blade glanced off a rock and the ax bounced out of her hands. She didn't take her eyes off me, though, she just locked her fiercely calm gaze on my face as she picked up the ax again. There's nothing like a woman with an ax to get you moving. I chunked a handful of dirt and stones at the boy with the pick, scrambled to my feet, and ran back to the trail, stepping high and moving out. The ax looped and whistled over my head, and I picked up the pace. Just as I hit the tree line, Selma touched off the first barrel, and shot dusted a small pine to my left. I dodged, and she got a piece of me with the second barrel. The edge of the pattern stung me high on the right side but it didn't knock me down. It helped my progress, though. I abandoned the trail to leap straight downhill through the small trees.

Combat at close range is the sort of thing you have to train for until you operate by reflex. Once the ball is rolling, there usually isn't much time to think and just barely enough time to react. It had been nine years since I led a squad with the 1st Air Cav in the central highlands of Vietnam, and Trahearne's Pacific war was twenty years beyond that. When I found him on the trail midway down the hill, we were two civilians scared out of our wits, as effective a combat unit as a couple of headless chickens.

'Jesus Christ, what happened?' he asked me in a breathless whisper.

'I don't know,' I said, trying to think. 'Go back down the hill,' I told him. 'Take your car a mile up the highway and if I'm not back in an hour, go get the sheriff.'

'I've got a shotgun in my trunk,' he said.

'There's already too many shotguns up here,' I said. 'Just do what I say.'

'What are you going to do?' he asked with a hurt look. When he remembered his war, he remembered being in command.

'Going back up the hill,' I said, 'and you get your ass down it.'

'Lemme go with you,' he whined.

'Move,' I said, then hit him on the shoulders with the heels of my hands.

The big man went ass over teakettle, and I dodged into the trees, circling right over the lower end of the ridge and into the next drainage, then I dropped down the far side of the ridge about a hundred yards, and worked my way back up toward the clearing. If I had been in better shape, I would have gone the other way, uphill, and dropped down on the clearing. If I had had any sense, I would have gone home.

Fifteen minutes later, I bellied up to the clearing behind the large cabin. Three of them were on the far side, peering into the trees behind the trail – Selma with the shotgun, the boy with his pick, and the crazy girl with her ax – but the other young girl sat on the edge of the unfinished grave, still weeping into her hands.

Sweat poured off me so furiously that I couldn't tell if my back was still bleeding, and I was too tired to crawl on my belly anymore. I stood and walked up behind the girl as quietly as I could, with all the cunning and grace and animal stealth of an old milk cow, but she didn't hear me until I sat down beside her.

'Don't be afraid,' I said to her. 'I won't hurt you.'

She fainted right into my arms. I lifted her in front of me like a shield, then shouted at the others. They turned and walked back toward me.

'One more step and I break her neck!' I shouted melodramatically. She was so limp her neck might as well have been broken. The three of them stopped, then took a hesitant step. 'Throw all that crap away!' The boy flung his pick to the ground in disgust and Selma sat the shotgun at her feet but the girl with the ax kept it on her shoulder. 'You gotta throw it away, honey,' I said.

'Don't *honey* me, motherfucker,' she answered calmly, clutching the ax handle tightly.

'Please, young lady,' Trahearne growled from the trail as he lumbered into view, 'please put it down.' His face was fiery red and his shirt completely soaked with sweat, but he walked straight up, carrying the ugliest shotgun I had ever seen – a riot gun, a 12-gauge

Remington pump with an 8-shot magazine, a 20-inch barrel, a pistol grip, and a metal stock that folded over the receiver and barrel. I knew what it was because I had one just like it. 'Please,' he said again.

She let the ax head fall to the ground beside her tennis shoe but she kept her hand on the handle. I was willing to settle for that. Without their weapons, Selma and the boy lost their angry spirit, and their shoulders sagged like empty sacks, but the girl stood defiant and erect. She even managed to spit on the ground toward me. I couldn't have spit if my life depended on it. I lifted the unconscious girl and walked toward the cabin.

'Where the hell did you come from?' I asked Trahearne.

'I don't know,' he said, 'but wherever it was, it was a hell of a walk.' A grin brightened his tired face.

'Let's go in the house and sit down,' I told everybody as I carried the girl toward the doorway. They all followed like ducks in a row.

'They came just at dusk,' Selma said as she lifted her hand to touch her swollen cheek, 'came up the hill with silenced revolvers and began shooting the dogs. They shot the dogs and some of the animals and birds in the cages, then they took Melinda away.' She moved her hand from her cheek, down to caress the forehead of the girl sleeping in her lap. Her voice sounded so distant and hollow that the interior of the cabin seemed to darken as she spoke. 'Benjamin tried to stop them but they beat him senseless, then one of them hit me when I tried to help him.'

'I should've been here,' the other girl said bitterly, then banged the head of her ax against the floor.

'You'd have just been hurt too,' Selma said quietly. 'I'm glad you were gone.' Then she stared at me. 'Melinda kept screaming that she would go with them, go with them gladly, but they kept laughing and kicking poor Benjamin and shooting at the dogs.'

'They shot the bulldog?' I asked, already knowing the answer.

'Gut-shot him,' the girl with the ax answered, 'but he and the three-legged bitch were still alive this morning when I left the vet hospital down at CSU.'

'They're gonna be damned sorry for that,' I said.

'What about kidnapping my wife, for God's sake,' Trahearne said.

'That, too,' I said. 'For all of it.' Then I straightened up. 'How many of them were there?'

'Four,' Selma answered.

'Was one of them a big dude, a Mexican with a pug's face?' I asked.

'They all seemed like giants,' Selma said blankly, 'and they wore ski masks.'

'You didn't call the sheriff, did you?' I asked.

'They said they would kill Melinda if we did,' she answered, 'then come back and kill all of us. I believed them. You should have seen them shooting the dogs, the crows and hawks and the bobcat in their cages. I believed them, so I didn't call the sheriff.' She raised her hand to touch her face, palpating the bruise as if the wound went deep within her. 'What could we do?' she pleaded. 'What can we do?'

'I can damn sure do something,' Trahearne threatened, lifting the shotgun as if it were a holy ikon, the rallying banner for his private jihad.

'Try to relax,' I told him. He gave me a foul look, then stood up and walked about the cabin, glaring down his puffy nose at the sleeping ranks of cats. Then I asked Selma, 'Why did you jump me?'

'We thought you must have brought them,' she said.

'Why?'

'You're the only one who knew who she was – where she was,' she answered. 'Why did you come back?'

'She wanted to talk to me,' I said, 'to tell me what to tell her . . . her natural mother.'

'And what are you going to tell her?' Selma asked.

'I don't know,' I said. 'Maybe I'll tell her that I have climbed the mountain and seen the prophet, but all I know is that I'm getting too old for this sort of foolishness.' I tried a wry grin, and it seemed perfectly at home on my face.

'You're hurt too,' Selma said with a brief smile. 'I suppose I did that.'

'It's nothing,' I scoffed like John Wayne.

'Stacy,' Selma said to the girl with the ax, 'why don't you see to Mr. Sughrue's wound.' She leaned her ax against the low couch where she sat, then walked across the room with a sheepish grin. 'Stacy has attended a year of vet school,' Selma said.

'I guess that's good enough for me,' I said. 'I was delivered by a vet.'

Trahearne laughed. 'Goddammit, Sughrue, if you were any more country, your feet wouldn't fit shoes,' he said, then laughed again.

Stacy peeled the dried bloody shirt off my back with hydrogen peroxide and professional fingers, then she cleaned off the wounds. The pattern of shot was larger than I had suspected, circling from the back of my neck to the middle of my upper arm.

'I'm glad you weren't any closer,' I said to Selma.

'You haven't spit up any blood, have you?' Stacy asked.

'Not lately,' I answered.

'Don't try so hard to be funny,' she said. It sounded like medical advice.

'How many pellets?' I asked.

'Eleven,' she answered as soon as she finished counting them.

'What size shot?' I asked.

'Seven and a half,' Benjamin answered.

'Steel or lead?'

He had to go over and open a drawer to check the shell box to answer that. 'Steel,' he said.

'If you've got some sort of antibiotic salve,' I said to Stacy, 'we can leave them in for a few days.'

'I've got probes and some local anesthetic that I use on the animals,' she said. 'I could freeze 'em and pop 'em right out, then suture up the wounds.'

I looked over my shoulder at her. She had high cheekbones, dusky skin, and dark brown eyes. If I hadn't seen her in action with the ax, I would have thought her a delicate type.

'What the hell,' I said, and she went after her bag.

As she worked on me, Trahearne persuaded Benjamin to go down the hill for the bottle of whiskey. For himself, though, not for me. When the boy brought it back, I had a drink anyway. As soon as Trahearne took a second hit off it, I made him give me the bottle. I held it until Stacy finished working on my back. She put the last circle of tape over the sutures so they wouldn't catch in the weave of my shirt, then she patted me on the shoulder lightly.

'What now?' she asked.

'We go get the lady back,' I said.

'You know where she is?' Trahearne asked anxiously.

'I know how to find out,' I said.

'You need some help?' Benjamin asked.

'Right,' Stacy said.

'We'll all go,' Selma said, and the girl sleeping in her lap stirred.

It was a great romantic notion, a band of righteous misfits rescuing the princess, and I even thought about it for a second, but we already had enough troubles.

'You been in the service?' I asked Benjamin.

'No, sir,' he answered, then hung his head.

'You stay with Selma, then,' I said. 'Help her take care of things here.'

'I've never been in the service either,' Stacy said with heavy irony, 'but I'm meaner than any Marine in the world, by God, pound for pound.'

'I can use you for bait,' I said, 'but you'll have to be nice to a creep.'

'That should be easy,' she said, smiling, 'I've spent my life doing that.'

'Are you afraid?' I asked.

'Damn right,' she said, 'but I'm too mad to give a shit about being afraid.'

'It won't be very pretty,' I said.

'I can tell you things about ugly that would make your ears curl up in self-defense, mister,' she said.

'Okay,' I said, 'you're on.'

'Take care of her,' Selma said in a quiet voice.

'I'll be fine,' Stacy said firmly, letting me know that she damn well meant to take care of herself.

'You all take care,' Selma said.

'This is what I'm supposed to do for a living,' I said, which made me laugh. I don't think I sounded full of joy with the laughter. When I glanced around the room, nobody would meet my eyes. Except Trahearne, and he looked infinitely sad.

As Stacy, Trahearne, and I walked down the trail, he paused to rest, leaning against a stone outcropping.

'What are we going to do?' he asked, and slapped me on the shoulder.

423

'First of all, we're going to stop slapping me on the shoulder,' I said, meaning it as a joke, but he took it seriously.

'I'm sorry,' he said. 'Goddamn it, I haven't done anything right since the war.'

'You came back up the hill with that shotgun,' I said.

'It was all over by the time I got there,' he said, looking up at me. 'You're going to need me, aren't you?' he asked.

'Of course,' I said. 'Particularly your plastic money.'

'And what am I supposed to provide?' Stacy asked.

'Your nubile body,' I said.

'Well, you ain't gettin' no cherry,' she said jauntily, then led off down the trail.

After a wildly hectic afternoon down in Denver – renting two cars, buying Stacy a new dress and me a wig and fake mustache, and finding a ground-floor motel room with a private entrance near the airport – we put it all together in time for a freshly scrubbed Stacy, looking sixteen in spite of the twenty-four on her driver's license, to be sitting in Tricky Dickie's topless bar on Colfax when Jackson came in after a day at the office. He was all polyester and smiles as he arrived for his vodka martini and his visual fix of female flesh. Just as I feared, though, he had a hired tough with him.

Stacy had been great – street-wise and tough. The bartender didn't want to believe her ID at first, and when she bullied him into giving her a drink, he wasn't sure he wanted a strange hooker in his place. She set him straight, then fended off the stag line until he believed her. When Jackson made his play, she held him off a bit.

'Listen, man, I'm looking for work,' she told him, 'not a party. No citizens, no johns, and no traveling salesmen, okay?'

'What sort of work were you looking for, honey?' Jackson asked.

'The same sort of work I was doing back East,' she answered, 'until the weather got to me.'

'The weather?'

'The heat, man,' she said.

'Oh, yeah,' he said as if he had understood all the time, 'right, the heat. What a . . . what sort of work was that?'

'I'm in the fucking movies, man,' she said. 'What did you think? Hanging paper, maybe? Boosting groceries? Get off my case and outa my face, okay?'

'Listen, babe,' he said as he sidled closer while pretending to wave his empty glass at the bartender, 'I've got some friends, some business associates actually, who sometimes make movies. Just for fun, you know.'

Stacy sneered. 'Fun and profit.'

'You got it, kid.'

'And I guess you'd like to check my moves before you put me in touch with these friends of yours, right?'

'Why not?'

'Right.' She snorted. 'Hit the road, man. You want a free sample, call the Avon lady.'

'I, ah, don't mind paying,' Jackson said cautiously.

'A hundred for a half and half,' Stacy said quickly. 'You look like the kind of john who'll need it.'

'A hundred!' he said so loudly that the bartender and most of the patrons looked around.

'If you can't afford the merchandise, man, get out of the store,' she said, then became very interested in her drink. I don't know how Stacy knew to play him tough instead of giving him the hooker's usual honey and promises, but it worked like a charm.

'Sure,' Jackson said. 'Sure, that's fine. Let's do it.'

'Let's see the bread,' Stacy said without looking at him.

The poor bastard had to cash a check and endure the bartender's sly grin when he brought the bills. He handed the money to Stacy and chugged his third martini.

'You hold it,' she told him. 'I just wanted to see it.'

'My car's right out front,' he said, falling over himself trying to be casual.

'My motel room's at the airport,' Stacy said. 'Let's hit it.'

'Right,' Jackson said, then turned to his hired friend. 'Hey, man, let's go.'

'Who the fuck's that?' Stacy asked, holding back against Jackson's hand.

'My driver,' he answered loftily.

'Is he going to hold your dick, man?' she said.

'I'll be back,' Jackson said, and his friend sat back down quickly and ordered another drink.

I brushed the curly-haired wig out of my eyes and followed them

425

outside. This was the only part where I had told Stacy what to say. I didn't want her in Jackson's car.

'Hey, man,' she said, 'I got a rented car right there. Why don't you follow me?'

'I'll bring you back,' he offered grandly.

'What if I don't want to come back here?' she asked.

'When I get through with you, honey, you'll follow me anywhere,' Jackson insisted, ushering her into his Cougar.

I stood on the curb and watched them drive away, wondering where the hell Trahearne was with the other rented Ford. I kicked myself for trusting the old man to wait outside, for not having another ignition key for Stacy's rental unit. Five minutes later, Trahearne finally showed up, his big face flushed, a sorry smile twisting his lips.

'They took off, huh?' he murmured as I opened the door and shoved him from behind the wheel.

'Where the hell have you been?' I asked as I gunned the car down the street and made the corner in a four-wheel drift.

'Listen, son, we left the whiskey in the other car,' he said, waving a pint of vodka at me, 'and I knew we'd need a drink. We're too old to do this kind of crap without a drink. So I went around the block to buy a bottle. What the hell difference does it make?'

'He wouldn't follow her,' I said as I slipped through a yellow light ahead of a bus. 'She's in his car, and if they're not at the motel when we get there, if he took her home or someplace else, I'm gonna have your ass, old man, and have it good.'

'Goddammit, C.W., I didn't know,' he whined, then he changed his approach with the sort of clumsy grace drunks think of as quick-witted. 'What the hell, boy, that little lady can take care of herself. You can be damn certain of that.' Then he slapped me on the shoulder again, hard enough to start the bleeding from torn stitches. I jerked the wig off and threw it on the floor at his feet. He picked it up and laughed, holding it out like a prize beaver pelt. 'You looked like shit in this, you know,' he said, then sat it on his head like a hat. 'Of course, I look like a million dollars,' he said, then laughed again. He reached over and ripped the phony mustache off and stuck it crookedly on his upper lip. 'How's that?' he asked, grinning. When I didn't answer, he said, 'Aw hell, come on, don't be so damned serious. Have a little drink and try to relax.' He nudged me with the pint, and there didn't seem to be anything else to do. 'They got my

Melinda, boy, and I don't know what to do,' he said as I handed the bottle back. 'I don't know what to do.'

'Try doing just exactly what I tell you to do,' I said. 'For a change.'

'You're in charge,' he said, 'but it better come out right.'

'Wonderful,' I said, as I turned off Colorado onto 32nd through a service station.

When we got to the motel, the plum Cougar was parked in front of Stacy's room. I left Trahearne in the car, told him to wait, then went in through the other room and the connecting door. Jackson was already in the saddle. Stacy's eyes were pleading over his fat, pimpled shoulder. Before I could get his attention by sticking a silenced .22 in his ear he grunted and moaned, trembling, and Stacy's eyes filled with tears. I clubbed him on the back of the neck with the automatic's butt, then jerked him off her onto the floor and kicked him in the stomach hard enough to twist my ankle. I started to kick him again, but Stacy jumped out of bed and grabbed my arm.

'It's all right,' she said, 'it's all right. It doesn't matter.' Then she shook my arm hard. 'It doesn't matter. Really.'

'I'm sorry we were late,' I said.

'It doesn't matter,' she said again.

'It does to me,' I said.

'My fault entirely,' Trahearne apologized grandly as he came through the connecting door, 'all my fault, honey, but it couldn't be helped.'

Stacy took one glance at Trahearne, then one step, and she slapped him so hard she nearly knocked him down. 'You drunken pissant,' she whispered, then slapped him again.

'What did I say?' he wondered as she raced past him into the other room. Then he saw Jackson naked on the floor. 'Lemme get my hands on that son of a bitch,' he roared as he moved toward Jackson. I hit him on the point of the shoulder with the butt and he sat down on the bed. 'Jesus Christ,' he muttered.

'Just sit there and shut up,' I said.

'Goddamn it, it's my wife they took, you son of a bitch, it's my wife,' he said.

'If you don't shut up,' I told him, 'it's going to be your widow. I thought I told you to stay in the car.'

427

'It's my wife,' was all he answered, then he made himself comfortable on the bed, sighing, 'I always fuck it up.'

I took a roll of strapping tape and bound Jackson at the ankles, knees, wrists, and elbows, then I stuffed his dirty sock in his mouth and locked it there with a loop of tape around his neck. As I worked, I heard the sound of Stacy brushing her teeth and showering in the other room's bath. The noise of her toilet went on long enough to get Trahearne's attention.

'I never do anything right,' he whined.

'I told you to shut up,' I said. 'Get off your ass and give a hand with this piece of shit.'

'Yes, sir,' he said, then giggled, covering his mouth with a finger. It was like trying to deal with a two-hundred-fifty-pound fifty-seven-year-old baby. I couldn't understand how Catherine or Melinda found the patience or energy. Hell, I couldn't even understand how Trahearne found the energy to be such a bastard. At least he got off the bed, grabbed Jackson under the arms, and before I could help, carried him into the bathroom and deposited him in the tub. 'Was that okay, sir?' he said with a Gary Cooper smile somehow fitted on his moon face. Schizophrenia – that was the word I had left out. Trahearne sober and during certain stages of drunkenness was a sad old man with a hell of a load of character, but during other stages of his drunks, he was a two-hundred-fifty-pound fifty-seven-year-old schizophrenic child.

'Just get the hell out of here, okay?' I said.

'I'm all right now,' he said. 'I know I've been a fool and an idiot but I'm all right now. We've got business to tend to, I know, and I'll slow the drinking down, drink myself sober. I've done it before. So have you. You know what I'm talking about.'

'Just stay out of the way, then,' I said.

'Of course,' he said, sounding as sober as Oliver Wendell Holmes. 'This is your show.'

'What now?' Stacy said as she walked into the bathroom, dressed in jeans and a black sweat shirt.

'Go back in the bedroom,' I said.

'I signed on for the duration, man,' she said, suddenly resolute, 'and after fucking that creep, if you blow his brains out, I deserve to watch. I earned it. Shit, if you did it, that would be a ray of sunshine in my life.'

428

'You are the sunshine of my life,' Trahearne crooned, then sipped from the vodka.

'Let's have some of that,' Stacy said as she jerked the pint from his hand.

I guess I grinned without meaning to and shook my head without thinking about it. When I saw Jackson's face, he looked like a man in the clutches of the Manson Family, and I didn't blame him.

'Are you going to tell me where she is?' I asked him, and he made the mistake of shrugging. 'Get me the telephone book,' I said to Trahearne.

'The phone book?' Stacy went into the bedroom and brought it back.

I lifted Jackson's feet and sat them on the thick book. His genitals had balled up in his crotch and they looked like some vital organ that had slipped from his body. I stood up and took the .22 out of my belt.

'You don't know where she is?' I asked. He shrugged again, and I said, 'Okay.' I let the automatic dangle from my hand as I waited for the sound of a jet making its final approach over the motel. 'Last chance,' I said before the noise got too loud for him to hear. He shrugged again. 'You know I'm not going to kill you, don't you?' I said. He shook his head, but his eyes smiled. He might be a piece of shit but Jackson had some balls on him. Either that or he was more frightened of his business associates than he was of me. That was a real mistake on his part. When the landing jet swept over the motel, I leaned down and pumped two rounds into his right foot. Blood splashed over the telephone book and the bathtub, as red as Jackson's face was white.

'Jesus Christ,' Trahearne muttered as he sank onto the toilet. As he slumped, Stacy leaned over the sink and vomited with a single quick motion.

'I'm all right,' she said, then she rinsed out her mouth. 'Shoot the fucker again.'

'You didn't have to shoot him twice,' Trahearne said.

'Once to get his attention,' I said, 'and once to let him know I was serious.' Then I looked down at Jackson. 'I am serious, you know.' Without waiting to see if he believed me, I jerked him up and shoved the telephone book under his butt. 'You understand?' He nodded quickly.

'I don't like this,' Trahearne said.

'Then get out of the room,' I said without turning around. He didn't leave. Then I tapped Jackson under the chin with the silencer. 'Now, the first thing you have to get straight in your mind is that you're through in this town. This part of your life is over. Either you leave this room dead or you leave it having told me where Betty Sue is, which won't make your friends happy, so give up this part of your life right now. Get your mind straight on that. We'll even buy a ticket, but get this part out of your mind right now. Okay?' He didn't nod, he jerked his head up and down in a blur. 'Now I'm going to take the gag out, and you're not going to make any noise at all, right?' As soon as his head quit bobbing, I took out my pocket knife and sliced the tape over the sock and tugged it out. He moaned with amazing restraint. I took the vodka from Trahearne and gave Jackson a quick hit off it. 'Now can you tell us where she is?'

'Yes, sir,' he whispered.

'Where?'

'This guy I work for, Mr. Hyland – I think maybe you met him up in Fort Collins once – he has a house between Evergreen and Conifer, a big red brick colonial on the west side of the road on a three-acre lot. You can't miss it. Up there it sticks out like a sore thumb, and he's got his name on the mailbox.'

'She's there?'

'Yes, sir.'

'What kind of security has he got?' I asked.

'Security?' Jackson said, looking very confused. I gave him another sip of vodka.

'How many men does he have guarding the place?'

'Guarding the place?' he asked. 'Oh, yeah, well, when they're shooting – '

'Shooting?' I interrupted.

'Yeah, you know, making a flick,' Jackson explained to me. 'When they're shooting, Mr. Hyland has a guy on the gate and another dude walking the grounds. To keep the neighborhood kids away, you know – kids don't have any respect for private property anymore, so Mr. Hyland has Peter and Mike sort of watch things when they're shooting.'

'What about the big Mexican?'

'Torres? He's Mr. Hyland's personal man and he's always next to him,' Jackson said.

'Don't they know we might try to take her back?' I asked.

'I don't think they know who you are,' Jackson said, trying to be as polite as possible. 'I know I don't.'

It didn't seem necessary to explain who we were, and as I glanced around the crowded bathroom, I wasn't all that sure myself.

'How did they know where to find Betty Sue?' I asked.

'Her daddy, you know, out in Bakersfield,' Jackson said. 'He knows some people we know and he got this postcard – we thought she was dead – I mean that's what we heard a long time ago, and that's what you said after they roughed you up – so anyway, when her daddy's friends called about the postcard, Mike flew up to Montana and followed you down.'

'Great,' I said. I didn't even bother to turn around to give Trahearne a dirty look. He cursed under his breath and walked back into the bedroom. 'Do they have Betty Sue locked up?'

'I don't think so,' Jackson said. 'They're shooting tonight.'

'Tonight?'

'Yeah, they rent the equipment to use in the daytime at Hyland's ad agency, so they have to shoot at night.'

'Cheap bastards,' Stacy muttered.

'Has he got a fence around the place?' I asked.

'Yeah, a chain-link fence,' he answered.

'Any dogs?'

'Dogs?'

'You know, guard dogs,' I said.

'No, nothing like that,' he said. 'Hyland hates dogs.'

That reminded me. 'Did you go with them after Betty Sue?'

'I drove the car, that's all,' he said. 'I didn't go up the hill. I wouldn't shit you, man, not about that.'

'It doesn't matter,' I said. 'Listen, I'm going to cut your hands loose, and I want you to draw me a layout of the grounds and a floor plan of the house, okay?'

'Could I have another hit of that vodka first?' he asked.

'Sure,' I said, then cut the tape, and let him hold the bottle himself. When he finished his drink, he held the pad on his knees and drew for me. 'Do your best,' I said.

431

'I'll try,' he muttered, then wet the pencil lead with his furry tongue.

'Act like your life depended on it,' I reminded him, and he applied himself to his task with renewed vigor. When it was done, he handed it to me. It wasn't bad. 'Only three doors?' I asked. 'Front, back, and garage? No patio doors or sliding doors or French windows?'

'Right,' he said.

'Where do they film?' I asked.

'In this downstairs bedroom here,' he said, pointing it out with the eraser.

'Okay,' I said, 'you've done great so far. Now I'm going to leave you here in the company of this young lady . . .'

'I'm not staying here for a minute,' Stacy said.

'Like I said, I'm going to lock you in the trunk of our car, and if everything goes well, we'll put you on a plane in the morning.'

'Couldn't you just take me to the hospital?' he said. 'I wouldn't call anybody.'

'You jerked me around once,' I said, 'and you're sleeping in the trunk until tomorrow morning.'

'I guess I can understand that,' he said.

'Good,' I said, then I cleaned up his foot. Both wounds were through and through, and the bleeding had nearly stopped when I went to work on his foot.

'You reckon it's fucked up pretty bad?' he asked as I wrapped gauze around it.

'You're going to limp for lying the rest of your life,' I said. He nodded as if that were a system of justice he understood. 'Will you get me his clothes?' I asked Stacy. She snorted but she went to get them, then tossed them on the floor and went back into the bedroom.

As I helped Jackson dress, I asked him, 'Why did they go to all this trouble? Not over a five-year-old doctor's bill.'

'That was part of it,' he said as he limped into his pants, 'yeah, but the forty thousand, that was what pissed them off.'

'The forty thousand?'

'You don't know about that, huh?' Jackson said with a superior smile.

'Tell me,' I said.

'When Betty Sue split, she hit the till for forty K, man, and Mr. Hyland, he had to make it up out of his own pocket. He's gonna work Betty Sue until he figures he's made his bread back, then he's gonna dump her down a mine shaft.'

'Nice people,' I said.

'Just good business,' Jackson said.

Instead of knocking a wad of his teeth out, I gave him two codeine tablets left over from my last visit to Colorado.

'What's that?'

'For the pain,' I said.

'You know, it's amazing, but my foot don't hurt all that bad,' he said as he gingerly pressed the ball of it against the bathroom floor.

'Take the fucking pills,' I said, and he did.

By the time Trahearne and I carried him to the car and stuck him in the trunk with a blanket and pillow, Jackson was nodding away and calling us 'Mummy.'

'What's going to happen to him?' Trahearne asked as I slammed the trunk lid.

'If we're alive tomorrow morning, we'll give him a head start on his friends,' I said. 'But if we're dead or in jail or in the hospital, he'll probably die locked in that trunk. Hell, even if everything goes like it's supposed to, he's probably a dead man already.'

'That doesn't bother you?'

'Not a bit,' I said. 'He's a piece of shit, man, and he lied to me. I gave him every chance I could, and he still lied to me, so fuck him.'

'I lied to you too,' Trahearne said, looking away toward the shifting lights of the airport.

'Yeah,' I said, 'but that's the difference between you and him.'

'What's that?'

'He's worth killing and you're not,' I said, then I went back into the motel room and left him standing outside.

433

15

Like everybody in the world, I had seen too many movies. I expected Hyland's place to be a large estate, a fortress with high walls and a massive gate guarded by a brace of men with automatic weapons, but it was just a good-sized brick house on a suburban lot with a four-foot-high chain-link fence. A man stood beside the gate, but it was wide open, and he was obviously bored stupid as he slumped against a gatepost. In the flash of our passing headlights, I recognized him as a man I had seen drinking coffee in a truck stop in Sheridan, Wyoming. Even standing guard, he looked like a trucker with bleary eyes, swollen feet, and itchy hemorrhoids. I, on the other hand, had come dressed for the party, decked out like a mercenary in jungle boots and a tiger-striped fatigue uniform, even done up in blackface like a night-fighter, and armed to the teeth, a K-bar combat knife strapped to my calf, a .38 S&W Airweight in a shoulder holster, and the silenced .22 Colt Woodsman under my belt.

As we drove past Hyland's gate, Trahearne laughed and asked, 'You loaded for bear, boy?'

'Be prepared,' I said. 'That's my motto.'

He sneered.'That's for Boy Scouts.'

Before I could answer, Stacy said, 'He's just jealous because he doesn't have a uniform.' Which shut Trahearne up.

She dropped me around the first curve north of Hyland's gate, and I crept back up the ditch toward the fence corner. Once there, I vaulted it, then bellied slowly toward the back of the house, watching for the other guard. I found him peeking through a slit in the blackout curtains at a back bedroom window. Some guys just can't get enough of that sort of thing. Even though the mountain air was chilly, the air-conditioning unit was going full blast. I used the noise for cover and walked up behind him. It seemed a shame to spoil his fun, but I slapped him silly, then trussed him like a pig for slaughter. When I finished with him, I took his place at the window.

Banks of movie lights filled the large bedroom with white heat that seemed intensified by the huge mirror over the king-sized bed. A naked black woman sat on a stool, fanning herself with one hand and smoking a joint with the other. On the bed, a blond, tanned guy was being worked over by a chesty girl in shorts and a halter, her head bobbing at his crotch with an angry exasperation. Two guys stood beside the camera chatting and smoking dope, and a short, fat fellow paced around the room talking to himself. In the shadows beyond the light, Hyland and Torres sat on a couch, flanking a woman with a ton of blond hair who wore a flimsy robe, a very blank expression, and too much make-up. Hyland had a tall, cool drink in one hand. The other was draped casually over the blonde's shoulders, where it kneaded her large firm breast regularly, as if he were exercising it. Only when I glanced at the woman's face again did I recognize Melinda, then I looked away as quickly as I could.

At the gate I was supposed to wait for Stacy to stop the car on the highway and ask the guard for directions, but when I went around the house to wait for her, he was off in some other world. I walked up behind him and put him to sleep too. When Stacy stopped the car, I stepped out of the shadows and waved her into the driveway. She cut the lights and pulled in.

'Just a second,' I told her, 'I've got to finish gift-wrapping this one.'

She stomped on the emergency brake and followed me behind the shrubbery. As I leaned over to finish taping the guy's ankles, Stacy jerked the sap out of my back pocket, and before I could stop her, she had flattened his nose, crunched some teeth, and given him a lump as big as a walnut between the eyes.

'Jesus Christ,' I muttered as I wrestled the sap from her.

'That'll teach the motherfucker to shoot dogs,' she said calmly.

She went back to the car, and I had to rummage around behind his gag for fragments of teeth so he wouldn't choke to death, but it was a hopeless task. I cut the gag off him. His mouth was going to hurt so bad that he probably wouldn't make much noise. If he woke up at all. The knot between his eyes looked nasty, maybe fatal, and I knew that Stacy didn't need his death on her conscience.

435

It had been a long day, so I rode up the driveway on the car fender, then hopped off and removed the valve stem from the tires of the three-quarter-ton Dodge van and the black Continental. Sitting on four flats, the vehicles looked comic, but I was too tired to smile. As Stacy turned the car around to face down the driveway, I used the keys I had taken from the guards to try the garage door that opened into the kitchen, but it wasn't locked. I dropped the keys on the steps and went back to organize Trahearne and his shotgun.

'You stay outside,' I told him as I checked again to be sure that he didn't have a shell in the chamber. 'Don't come inside unless you hear gunfire, and if you do come inside, don't shoot anybody until you're sure who they are. Right?'

'Teach your grandma to suck eggs,' he said.

'That's my line,' I said.

He glared at me. 'I had a platoon on the 'Canal when you were still in diapers.'

'Just stay outside,' I said, 'and try not to think about it.'

He grunted and that sounded like the closest I could get to an agreement. I changed clips in the .22 so I would have three rounds of rat shot above six rounds of hollow-point hot loads, then I got a Browning 9mm automatic out of the car for Stacy, jacked a round into the chamber, and left the hammer back.

'If it happens,' I said, 'hold it like I showed you and aim for their kneecaps and keep pulling the trigger until it's empty.' She nodded, breathing shallowly, her eyes wide. 'You sure you want to do this?'

'Let's do it before I change my mind,' she said, and followed me into the house.

As we eased through the darkened rooms, she covered me while I cut telephone wires, which I had forgotten to do outside. Every time I glanced over my shoulder, she was standing in a crouch, the heavy automatic clutched in her right hand, her left hand holding the right wrist, the pistol covering the rooms in long, smooth arcs. She had seen too many movies too. I just hoped that she would pull the trigger if I needed her. After we had checked both floors and found all the rooms empty, we paused at the bottom of the stairs to catch our breath, then went down the hallway toward the bedroom where they were filming.

I listened for a moment at the door. Somebody was complaining about the working conditions, the late hours, and the dubious physical accomplishments of *some* so-called actors. 'Have you ever had an erection?' the voice inquired as I opened the door, stepped in, and shot the top of Hyland's glass with the hollow point in the chamber. Just for the effect.

'Everybody be calm,' I said as Stacy backed into the corner beside the door. 'Be real calm.'

It almost worked. Everybody froze for a second. Except for Torres. With one smooth motion, he stood and reached under his left arm. At seven feet, a round of .22 long rifle shot will pulverize a rattle-snake's head, and when I shot Torres in his right hand, it seemed to explode, but he didn't make any more noise than the silenced round.

'You'll have to hire somebody to wipe your ass and pick your nose,' I said. He chuckled and let his hand fall to his side.

As if that were some sort of signal, the film crew broke out in a fit of small movements and aimless chatter, but as soon as Stacy swept the automatic across them, they all stilled and shut up. All but the chubby director.

'All right,' he demanded, 'what's going down here?'

'If he opens his mouth again,' I said to Stacy over my shoulder, 'blow the back of his head off.'

He opened his mouth, then shut it quickly as he looked down the barrel of the automatic. He took another look, sighed, and fainted into a puddle.

'All you film folk,' I said, 'I want you lying flat on the bed, face down, with your fingers laced behind your necks. Right now.' Melinda stared at me, confused, but when I jerked my head, she dashed for the bed and joined the scramble for a place.

'Now, you two gentlemen assume that old familiar position against the wall behind the couch,' I said to Hyland and Torres. They were too tough to hurry but they got there anyway. 'If they lift a finger,' I said to Stacy, 'start pulling that trigger and don't stop until it's empty.' She nodded and moved to my left to cover the two men while I patted them down. Hyland was clean, but Torres had been reaching for a .357 magnum Colt Python with a six-inch barrel. 'It'd take you a month to get this sucker out,' I said as I unloaded it, but he didn't answer. He just leaned against the wall, watching the blood from his hand creep down the plaster. 'Now, you boys just stay right

there,' I said as I stepped away and tossed the Colt under the couch.
'We're going to have a little conversation.'

'What do you want?' Hyland asked calmly.

'The girl,' I said, 'and a little satisfaction.'

'Take her,' he shrugged, 'enjoy her to your heart's content, buddy,
because you're a dead man.'

Just to see if he was as tough as he acted, I skimmed him across
the buttocks with another round of rat shot.

'Jesus Christ,' he wailed, and broke into a slick sweat.

Torres glanced at Hyland with contempt, then at the .22 with
interest. I fired the last round of shot into the row of bottles standing
on a dry bar against the far wall.

'That's the last round of rat shot,' I said, 'and I don't know how
far you'd get with a hollow point between your eyes, but you can try
if you want to.'

He relaxed and leaned harder against the wall, but before I could
start the conversation, Trahearne lurched into the room, shouting,
'Where is she!' as he jacked a round into the chamber of the riot
gun, then let it off into the ceiling. The large mirror exploded like
shrapnel, a bank of lights flared, then went black. Hyland rolled over
the arm of the couch to hide behind it, and Torres shoved off the
wall, heading like a mad bull toward Stacy and the automatic. He
didn't even glance at me and didn't hesitate. He didn't think the
little girl would have the nerve to pull the trigger, and it was very
nearly the last mistake he ever made.

Stacy fired five rounds as quickly as she could pull the trigger,
holding low. But the automatic jerked a little higher with each shot.
The first splintered the floor between his feet, the next two went
between his legs, and Torres could see what was coming. He hit the
floor in a headfirst slide. When he finally halted his skid, Stacy had
stopped firing, and he glanced up. She held the pistol steadily pointed
at his head. How she had missed him at that range with five rounds,
I'll never understand. Torres couldn't either.

'Enough,' he whispered, then crawled back to the couch. 'You
mind if I lie down for a minute?' he asked.

'Be my guest,' I said.

He climbed up on the couch and rested his head on the arm that
Stacy had blown to stuffing and splinters.

'How the fuck did I miss?' she asked herself.

'Where's my wife?' Trahearne asked. The gunfire had brought him to a dead halt too.

'I thought I told you to stay outside,' I said, but he didn't even look at me. 'She's over there.' I pointed to the pile of people who had hidden behind the bed. Trahearne handed me the shotgun and went to get Melinda. 'Get her out of here,' I said as he helped her up, clucking like a mother hen.

As they walked past me, Melinda slipped the wig off and dropped it on the floor. Trahearne tried to kick it but he missed and would have fallen down if Melinda hadn't grabbed him. Even with her cropped hair and smeared make-up, she still looked worth a man's blood, maybe even his life. A line of red from a small cut ran down her smooth cheek, and as she glanced at me, I could see she was crying as they made their way across the littered room.

The film crew had moved off the floor back onto the bed, and they were examining their wounds from the flying glass. From where I stood, nothing looked too serious, just small cuts. The male star had the worst one, a shard of mirror about four inches long sticking through the loose muscle below his left shoulder blade. When he started whining about it, though, the black girl jerked it out and told him to shut up.

'Mr. Hyland,' I said as I walked over to the end of the couch, 'you can come out now.' He didn't, though. When I looked over the arm, he was crouched in a puddle of blood. One of Stacy's rounds had blown the side of his head all over the wall. It was an incredible effort, the hardest of the whole lousy night, but I turned to Stacy and said, 'Mr. Tough Guy's over here in a dead faint. Why don't you herd those other folks down the hall to the bathroom so they can clean up.'

She nodded, then jerked the automatic at the people on the bed. The black girl had to slap the male star to get him going, and the head girl and one of the cameramen had to carry the director, but they got it together, finally, and trooped out the doorway.

'Is he dead?' Torres asked as soon as the room cleared.

'He's all over the wall, man,' I said as I walked over to the dry bar and picked up a bottle of Scotch out of the broken glass. 'Let's go to the kitchen and have a drink.'

'That's the first good idea you've had tonight,' he said, then rolled

439

off the couch and stood up. 'Maybe the first good one in your whole life.'

I stuck the .22 under my belt and propped the shotgun across my arm. Torres shut up. As we left the room, I cut off the light and closed the door.

'Doesn't taste like Chivas, does it?' Torres asked as we lifted our glasses.

'Right now it tastes like shit but it tastes great,' I said. On the way to the kitchen, I had locked the crew in the bathroom and sent Stacy outside to cover the front of the house. Just in case the gunfire had attracted anybody's attention, I told her.

'Hyland,' Torres went on. 'He buys four-ninety-eight Scotch and pours it into a Chivas bottle, then the dumb son of a bitch expects nobody to notice it.'

'Nice eulogy,' I said.

'More than he deserves,' Torres suggested. 'What happens now?'

'Depends on how you want to play it.'

He took a long swallow of his drink, then stared at me. 'Okay, let me lay it out for you,' he said, then held up his hand wrapped in a bloody dishtowel. 'I think my working days are over, man, and I'm used to living good . . .'

'All your days were nearly over,' I interrupted.

'No shit,' he sighed. 'I still don't know how that chick missed me.'

'I wish she had missed Hyland,' I said.

'If you don't tell her, man, she won't know,' Torres said, 'and in a way she did both of us a favor.'

'How's that?'

'He's the sort of dumb bastard who would have taken this personally,' Torres said. 'He didn't know when to cut his losses.'

'And you do?'

'Right,' he answered. 'Look at it like this, man, Hyland was an idiot – I mean how dumb can you get, making flicks in your own place – and the uncle who got him into the business is no longer in business, if you know what I mean, so there are a few people who won't cry when they find out Hyland is out of it, you see.'

'And you're one of them?'

'I know more about his business than he did,' Torres said, 'and with him out of the way, I can step in and run it right.'

'So I just walk away with the girl? Clean?'

'Absolutely,' he said. 'Except for one thing.'

'The forty thousand.'

'You got it,' he said.

'That was a long time ago.'

'Right. But everybody concerned knows about it,' he said.

'I think you're jerking me around,' I said, 'trying to make a little profit on the side.'

'Can you blame me, man?' he said, then grinned. 'And I ain't kidding you, if I had that forty K, there would be a lot less heat.'

'That's your ticket to the movies, isn't it?' I said.

'You got it.'

'Not in my pocket,' I said, 'but if you'll give me sixty days, I'll do what I can.'

'Quicker would help,' he said.

'Listen, don't press me,' I said, 'not when I'm holding this shotgun.'

'Aw hell,' he said, then waved his bloody hand at me. 'If you were going to kill me, man, you'd've done it right out of the bag instead of screwing around that dumb shit rat-shot bit. It's too messy, man – dead, I'm just more trouble than it's worth, but alive, I can clean up this end.'

'Sixty days,' I said, 'and no promises.'

'Okay, what the hell, it's worth it,' he said. 'Deal?'

'I've got to have an edge,' I said.

'Like what?'

'Your prints on the piece that killed Hyland,' I said, 'and the account books out of his safe.'

'Or what?'

'Or I'm talking to a dead man,' I said. 'I'll leave you in the room with Hyland, the Browning in your hand, the .22 in his, and take my chances.'

'The pieces aren't registered to you, huh?'

'Out of Arkansas,' I said, 'as clean as whistles.'

'You ain't exactly a model citizen.'

'I'm no kind of citizen at all,' I said.

'You get the piece, I'll get the books,' Torres said calmly.

'You get the books, I'll watch.'

'Right,' he said, then knelt in front of the sink cabinet, opened it up and removed what looked like ten years of accumulated kitchen cleaning materials. He lifted the floor of the cabinet to expose a round safe sunk into the concrete foundation. He worked the dial, and paused before opening the door. 'The first thing out, man, is a piece, but it'll come out slow,' he said, then opened it up and lifted out a nickel-plated .32 automatic and handed it to me.

'A beautiful piece,' I said as I unloaded it.

'Yeah,' Torres said, 'he must've paid at least twenty dollars for it.' He laughed, then stood up and handed me a stack of narrow ledgers. 'Can I ask one more favor?'

'What?'

'If you send me copies of these,' he said, 'it'll make the changeover all that much smoother.'

'Okay.'

'I almost believe you,' he said.

'You mail me a receipt for a thousand-dollar contribution to the Humane Society,' I said, 'and I'll mail you copies.'

'You got it, man,' he said. 'I'm sorry about the dogs. Hyland, he hated dogs and when this bulldog bit him on the ankle, he went crazy. I tried to stop him, really, but he – '

'Just shut up,' I said as I leveled the shotgun at his nose. 'You got it?' He nodded. 'Now let's go get the Browning.' I herded him outside, took the automatic from Stacy, then prodded him back into the kitchen. 'Unload it,' I told him, 'and wipe it clean, then reload it.' He did it quickly and professionally. I didn't even have to tell him to take each round out of the clip. When he finished, he found a large plastic bag and dropped the piece in it. 'Now let's go down the hall and pick up those five pieces of brass,' I said.

'You're a careful son of a bitch,' he said as he handed me the plastic bag.

'That's what I'm doing here,' I said, 'practicing my careful act, scumbag.'

'You don't have to insult me,' he said as I followed him down the hall.

'I wouldn't know where to begin,' I said, then stepped back as he opened the door and switched on the light. The five shell casings were clustered behind the door, and he picked them up and gave them to me. 'Now get me the magnum out from under the couch,' I said.

'Come on, man, that's my favorite piece,' he complained. 'Besides, it's registered to me.'

'That's even better,' I said, and he knelt down to reach under the couch. 'Nothing personal,' I said as he pulled the revolver to the edge of the couch and I clubbed him with the shotgun butt behind the ear. His face slammed into the floor, his back arched, and his feet tattooed across the rug. 'Nothing personal at all.' I picked up the .357 and stuck it in my belt, then drew my boot back to kick Torres in the face, but I knew it wouldn't help. I put my foot down. I had gotten Melinda out, but it hadn't provided any satisfaction at all.

When I got to the car I motioned Stacy behind the wheel, then climbed into the passenger seat and dumped my load of arms on the floorboard along with the ledgers.

'What took you so goddamned long?' Trahearne asked as Stacy drove us away. 'We must have been sitting in the car for a goddamned hour.'

'Honey,' Melinda chided him in a whisper, 'honey, hush. He got me out.'

'Yeah, well, I'm paying him good money for it,' he said.

Stacy slammed on the brakes, skidding across the gravel of the driveway, and turned round and shouted at Trehearne, 'You old fat bastard, you shut up! No – you say thank you and then you shut up! You haven't done a thing tonight but piss and moan and fuck up, and if it wasn't for him, Melinda would be doing it under the lights with that good-looking blond dude, so you say thank you and then you shut the fuck up!'

'It's okay,' I said.

'Stop making excuses for him!' she shouted at me.

'I don't have to thank the hired help,' Trehearne huffed. That made Stacy so mad that she flounced back under the wheel and stuffed the accelerator to the floorboard. The car shot down the drive and fishtailed onto the highway.

Nobody said anything for a long time as we headed back toward Denver, the silence only broken by the whisper of tires, the gurgle and plop of Trahearne's bottle, and Melinda's sobs.

I had a long drink of water out of a canteen, then wet a towel to

443

scrub away the camouflage paint on my face. When I finished and leaned back in the seat, Stacy reached over to pat my thigh.

'Thank you,' Melinda said softly, 'thank you so very much.'

'Yeah,' Trahearne grunted as nicely as he was able. 'You want a drink?' He reached the pint of vodka over the seat back.

'Is that your answer to everything!' Stacy shouted, wheeling in the seat and nearly running the car off the freeway.

'Don't make him mad,' I said as I grabbed the steering wheel, 'or he won't give me one.'

'Oh,' she muttered, then settled back to driving. When I offered her a hit off Trahearne's pint, she cursed, but took a long swallow. 'I don't know why you drink that terrible stuff,' she said, spitting and coughing.

'It's the only way to get drunk,' I said, and everybody laughed as if I had said something funny.

'I'm sorry,' Trahearne said, and that sent up gales of laughter.

'You should be,' Stacy said, giggling. 'I can't believe I missed that son of a bitch,' she added, then giggled louder.

'You couldn't've stopped that big bastard any quicker if you had blown his head off,' Trahearne said, and they chuckled.

'Meaner'n a Marine,' Stacy squealed.

'That's not saying much,' Trahearne said. 'My mother's meaner than any Marine that ever lived.'

'No kidding,' Melinda offered in a soft, shy voice. 'She wouldn't have missed,' she added, and they all laughed again, so happy to be alive that they would have laughed at a stop sign.

Back at the motel, we moved all the gear out of the car into the room, then I left them there while I unloaded Jackson from the trunk to the front seat. Stacy's driving had left him some the worse for wear. He wasn't bleeding too badly, but he looked like a man who had just survived a terrible auto accident. I drove him to the emergency-room entrance at Denver General and left him on the curb, a shoe in one pocket, a half-empty pint of bourbon in the other, assuming that he would work it out after I explained that Hyland was dead and nobody was looking for him. He nodded briskly, then hobbled toward the hospital, hopping quickly off his right heel.

'I'm sorry!' I shouted out the car window, but he waved his hand without turning around, as if to say it was all in a day's work.

When I got back to the motel again, it wasn't even midnight yet,

and I found the troops sitting down to delivered pizza and room-
service beer, and we ate and drank furiously until a flurry of fatigue
swept over us like a tropical rainstorm, dropping us like sodden flies.
Trahearne fell asleep with a piece of pizza in his hand moving toward
his mouth, and as she helped him to the bed, Melinda tumbled down
beside him with a quick, sudden snort like a woman clubbed in the
back of the head. Within seconds Trahearne, flopped on his back,
began to snore as only he could.

'Jesus Christ,' Stacy whispered, 'how can she sleep through that?'

I yawned. 'She must love him.'

'She must.'

'I guess I have to sleep in your room,' I said.

'Of course,' she answered sweetly, then took me by the hand and
led me through the connecting doors. Stacy was asleep on her feet,
and as I collapsed toward the bed with her, I went under too.

But it was, as I knew it would be, a quick, uneasy sleep, dreamless,
but broken by fits and starts of waking out of darkness into the
unfamiliar room – like the first few nights back from the bush in the
base camp at An Khe – a treacherous sleep. And the second time I
woke up, around three A.M., I didn't want to go back into it. I
untangled myself from Stacy's arms as gently as I could, but she
woke up too.

'Every time I close my eyes, I see that room with the mirror
exploding like knives,' she murmured dreamily, 'and I don't understand why I don't feel bad.'

'The good guys won,' I said, loosening her grip on my neck.

'Where're you going?'

'The john,' I said.

'Come back,' she whispered. 'I don't feel bad but come back,
okay? I don't understand why I don't feel bad.'

'I'll be back,' I said, climbed up and closed the connecting doors,
then went to the john. When I came back, she had taken off her
clothes and lay naked above the covers, her hands holding her small
breasts as if they were as painful as wounds.

'It's not like hers,' she said quietly – she didn't have to explain
who *her* was – 'but it's all I'm ever going to have.'

'You're lovely,' I said.

'I know you want hers,' she said, trying to smile and cry all
together, 'but make love to me.'

445

I lay down and held her as the sobs rippled like convulsions through her slim body, held her until she cried herself to sleep. I covered her up and went to the bathroom to make a drink, meaning to drink until I could sleep again, but I heard a tapping at the connecting doors. When I opened them, I wasn't surprised to see Melinda waiting there.

'I guess we should talk,' she whispered, then held her index finger up to her pale lips. Sometime during the night, she had scrubbed the make-up from her face, but even wrapped in a sheet and wearing a wan face, the beauty I hadn't been able to see at first was as clear as the troubled look darkening her eyes.

'I guess we should talk,' I echoed her, then led her into the bathroom and closed the door. She sat on the floor, cross-legged, her elegant feet rosy in the harsh light. I sat down on the toilet seat in my classic thinker's pose. 'I seem to be having a lot of conversations in johns tonight.'

'I'm sorry,' she said, as if she could reach back and change it all now. 'I'm sorry.'

'Me too,' I said, 'but it's too late to do anything about it. Way too late.'

'How do you know when it's too late to change things?' she asked with a sad smile. But she didn't want an answer. Not to that question. 'What did take you so long after Trahearne and I left the house?'

'I had to clean up the mess,' I said, 'talk to Torres and Hyland about the details.' It didn't seem necessary for her to know that Stacy had killed Hyland. I didn't want anybody else to know.

'What details?' she asked casually.

'Like what to do with your body if you don't come up with the forty thousand,' I said, and she dropped her face into her hands. 'You can't steal from those people,' I added. 'Didn't you know that?'

'I didn't have any choice.' She raised her head to stare at me. For the first time since I had known her, I could see Rosie's influence on her features. She had the same patient eyes, the same cocky defiance in the tilt of her chin. 'I just couldn't make another movie,' she said. 'I couldn't . . . couldn't do it . . . Hell, I can't even say it anymore . . . I couldn't fuck any more strangers. When I first started it seemed like a lark. I mean, it seemed like fun, you know, I was stoned all the time and fucking everybody anyway, so getting paid for it seemed like a great bonus. What I did with my body didn't matter. Only the mind and the spirit mattered, I thought. But I was wrong. Everything you do matters. Every action causes complications, repercussions. I learned that in jail.'

'What happened?' I asked.

'Nothing all that dramatic,' she said. 'I went in thinking that I was Betty Sue Flowers – a little fucked up, right, and thirty pounds overweight, but still smarter and prettier than any of that trash in jail. I was wrong. I met a woman who was brighter and better looking than I could ever hope to be, more talented, more promising in school. She was also the meanest, toughest person I had ever met. She beat me senseless the first night, and humiliated me every day and night after that, but the worst thing she did was tell me that in ten years I would be just like her. She was dead right, of course, so when I got out, I knew I had to change my life. The money gave me a chance, and I had no other choice, so I took it.'

'What did you do with it?'

'When I left Selma's, I went to stay with a friend of hers in St. Louis, and she got me admitted to Washington University as a special student – '

'The great American dream,' I interrupted, 'finance and education with mob money.'

'It seemed like a good idea at the time,' she said quietly. 'So I went to college until I discovered ceramic sculpture. Once my pieces started to sell, I came back out West. Everything was fine until . . . until all this happened.'

'I don't know if all this was Trahearne's fault or mine,' I said, 'but I'll apologize anyway.'

'That's not necessary,' she said. 'If it's anybody's fault, it's mine.' She sighed. 'What's going to happen now?'

'You have any of the money left?' I asked.

'I have about thirty-five hundred in the bank,' she said, 'and I can raise some more – maybe another three or four thousand – if I sell all my finished pieces. That isn't forty thousand, is it?' She chuckled. 'Maybe they'll let me pay them back on the installment plan.'

'Us,' I said.

'Us?'

'I'm on the hook now too,' I said. 'I've bought a little time, but I don't have a big enough edge to keep them off our backs forever.

447

They're really touchy about their money. They'll spend a hundred grand just to get the forty back, and then they'll cut off our hands.'

'What can we do?' she asked tiredly.

'Borrow it from Trahearne,' I suggested.

'He's so broke, I have to buy groceries on his BankAmericard,' she said.

'How about Selma?'

'She's done too much already,' she said.

'Ask Trahearne to borrow it from his mother,' I said.

'I'd let them cut off my hands first,' she said, then held them out in offering. The long, darkly red fake nails had been clumsily pasted over her own. As she looked at her trembling fingers, tears of anger gushed from her eyes, and she started tearing at the fake nails, scraping and biting, ripping nail and cuticle and flesh until the ends of her fingers were covered in blood, then she jammed her hands into the folds of sheet bunched at her lap. She stared at the stains and whispered, 'I've made such a mess of things, and people I don't even know have to come to my rescue again and again . . . Maybe I should call Hyland and tell him I'll come back to work.'

'I don't think that would work,' I said.

'Why not?'

'He told me he never wanted to see you again,' I lied.

'And I've probably made a mess of your life now, too,' she said.

'It's always been a mess,' I said lightly.

'You've done so much,' she said, 'and I don't even know why.'

I didn't either but I reached for my wallet and took out her high school picture and handed it to her.

'I killed that girl a long time ago,' she said quietly, 'you've been looking for a ghost.' She touched her face in the picture, smearing it with blood. She didn't sob, but tears coursed unbidden down her cheeks. 'That cameo was my grandmother's, you know, the only thing she had left when they got to California – that cameo and seven kids and a husband with a cancer behind his eye,' she said. 'She raised them all, made them all finish high school. She ruined her feet and legs slinging hash in a truck stop in Fresno, and when she got too old to work she went to the county home. She wouldn't live with her kids, wouldn't trouble them that way. When I was a little-bitty girl, my mother would take me to visit her, you know, and I hated that dry stink of the old folks. They were so crazy with

448

loneliness, they always came out of their rooms to touch me and fuss over me, and I hated it, just hated it.

'While she talked to Granny, my momma would kneel down in front of her chair and rest her legs on her shoulders and rub the varicose veins in Granny's legs, rub them until her hands began to cramp. Then she'd ask me to rub Granny's legs for a minute while she rested, and I wouldn't do it, wouldn't touch those veins like big ugly worms under her stockings. I couldn't make myself touch them, those legs she had ruined so her children would finish high school.

'Jesus God, why didn't I understand?' she moaned. 'I didn't go to her funeral because I was playing at being tragic in *Antigone* . . . Playacting, my God, what a foolish child I was . . . a foolish child I have been.' Then she stopped and stared at me, tears and blood smudged on her cheeks, like some ancient mask of grief. 'Why?' she asked simply.

'I don't know,' I said, and she tucked her legs under her, let her head fall into my lap.

'I haven't dreamed in ten years,' she said, her voice muffled against my thigh, her breath hot against my skin even through the fatigue pants. 'They say I dream and don't remember but I know I don't dream at all. My hands dream for me,' she said as she rocked back on her knees and held her hands out again, offering them to some angry god. I reached for the hands, but she grabbed my face between them, clutched my cheeks and pulled me toward her, kissing me through the tears, whispering against my mouth, 'Lie down with me, make me forget, please, please . . .'

With the last strength of my hands, I took her wrists and pushed her away. As she rocked back on her knees, the sheet unwound from her shoulders like a shroud, and her naked breasts stood between us.

'You don't want me,' she said, 'and I can't blame you, not after all you know.'

'It's Trahearne,' I said.

'He doesn't want me anymore,' she said. 'He wants me gone, out of his life. I've known that for a long time but I chose to ignore it.'

'He went to a lot of trouble for a man who doesn't want you,' I said.

'He thinks I'm a slut,' she whispered, 'and he just wanted to make sure. That's all. That's not the same thing as wanting me. A woman

449

knows. You want me, I can tell. I don't know why you won't lie down with me.'

'I'm afraid,' I said.

'Of me?' she asked, then twisted easily out of my grip.

'Of myself,' I said, and she stared at me again, long and hard. 'You love Trahearne,' I added as I put my hands on her bare shoulders. She waited, as still as an animal resigned to a trap, waited for me to pull her toward me or push her away.

'You're right,' she said, tilting her head so her cheek rested on the back of my left hand. 'I'm sorry.' She rose and wound the sheet around her body. 'You think you're in love with me, don't you?' she said with her hand on the doorknob. I nodded slowly. 'You don't even know me,' she said, and I had to nod again. 'It's very kind of you to care, but you don't even know me at all.' Then she left, walking out of the sterile light of the bathroom and into the darkness. To my blurred eyes, the white sheet seemed to leave a drifting afterimage that glowed like swamp-fire.

When the connecting door clicked shut, Stacy got out of bed and walked over to the door. 'You missed your chance,' she said quietly. I stood up and mixed another drink. 'Men are such romantic old farts,' she said, smiling. 'Come on to bed.'

We woke at ten the next morning, but Melinda and Trahearne had already gone, leaving me like some hired retainer to clean up.

16

I tried to get Stacy to go back to Selma's place while I tidied up the rest of the mess, but she wouldn't hear of it.

'I've got my first new dress in five years,' she said, 'and you're taking me out to dinner tonight, dummy.'

'Right,' I said, glad of the chance.

She waited at the motel while I ran errands. I returned the two rental cars, had the account books copied, sent the copies to Torres and stuck the originals in a safe-deposit box along with a note explaining what they were about. I made dinner reservations at a Chinese place and bought two bottles of French champagne, which we drank as we dressed for dinner.

'I've never had real French champagne.' Stacy sighed as she slipped her dress over her head. 'But I intend to have it again.' Then she fell back across the bed, laughing softly until she fell asleep.

I ordered dinner over the telephone and sent a cab driver after it. When he brought the cartons back, I paid him, then lay down beside her. Sometime during the middle of the night, we woke up making love in our clothes. After, we undressed and sat down to our cold dinner, which we ate silently like two starving peasants, then crawled back into bed.

'You know,' Stacy said dreamily, 'I must be well again.'

'Why's that?'

'Here I am drunk on champagne, shacked up with a strange older man, the reek of gunpowder still fresh in my innocent young nose, and I feel absolutely great,' she said. 'How about you?'

'I've got these holes in my shoulder,' I said, 'a swollen ankle, Chinese indigestion, and nothing to look forward to but a champagne hangover and a long drive home.'

'Isn't it wonderful,' she whispered. 'I'm gonna be a great horse doctor, you know, goddamned great horse doctor. When I grow up. Whadda you gonna be when you grow up?'

'Older,' I said, but she was already asleep again.

The next morning, as I parked at the head of Selma's trail, I had to line up behind her pickup, a fence company truck, and Melinda's Volkswagen.

'You think she's still here?' Stacy asked.

'I think I'm back in the goddamned towing business,' I said as I climbed out to look at the note under the VW windshield wiper. A key was folded up in the paper, which had one word written on it: *Please.* I shook my head, and Stacy and I picked up our tired feet and headed them up the trail.

Selma was sitting in the living room watching four young men struggle as they tried to dig post holes in the rocky hillside.

'I never thought it would come to this,' she said as we joined her.

'You think it's enough?' I asked.

'I've ordered two guard dogs from a place in Broomfield,' she confessed. ' "The world is too much with us, late and soon," ' she recited. 'No one will ever trespass here again,' she added, then touched her bruised cheek. 'Ever again.'

'I hope not,' I said. 'I bought us some insurance, but put up the fence and get the dogs anyway. Just in case.'

'You sound like a man about to make his goodbyes,' she said. 'You should stay a few days, should rest.'

'Do,' Stacy said, grabbing my arm.

'I'm too tired to stay,' I admitted. 'Why don't you all pack and head up into the mountains for a few days? Find a little lake and some air that nobody's breathed. I'm going to town to pick up a tow bar and my dog, then I'm going home while I still can.'

'Perhaps you're right,' Selma said. She glanced at Stacy, who nodded slowly and released my arm. 'You're always welcome here, you know.'

'Thanks.'

'And if you need doctoring,' Stacy said lightly, 'give me a call. Any time at all.' She gave me a quick hug and walked out of the cabin toward her own, her narrow back firm and erect.

'She's a lovely woman,' Selma said, 'and I think as terrible as all this has been, it has been good for her.'

'She's a tiger,' I said, 'she'll be fine.'

'Melinda told me,' Selma said. 'I always think I know my charges, and they always find some way to surprise me. You didn't surprise me, though.'

'Why?'

'I knew that you would get Melinda back,' she said, 'and I want to thank you for it. You saved her life.'

'If I hadn't been so stupid, they would never have found her,' I said.

'One can't be blamed for believing lies,' she said softly.

'I get paid for knowing the difference,' I said, 'but this time – '

'This time was different,' she interrupted.

'Yes, ma'am.'

'Will you do me one last favor?' she asked.

'Of course.'

'Keep an eye on Melinda,' she said, 'check on her from time to time. I have this feeling that she's going to need a friend soon.'

'I'll do my best,' I said, 'but I can't promise anything.'

'Thank you,' she said, 'and please don't blame yourself for this last spate of her troubles. They began many years ago, and none of this was your fault.'

'I'm not sure about that,' I said, then left her there with her cats and her chicks and her shiny new fence.

But the really bad ones never end. They drag on like an endless litigation or a chronic jungle fever. I thought this one was over, though, except for the forty thousand dollars, which was mostly Melinda's worry. I had plenty of time to think about it, too, as I headed north one more time with Melinda's VW in tow and Fireball lying in a drugged stupor on the seat beside me. The bulldog was heavily bandaged to hold the drains in place. When I picked him up, the vets released him to me as if he didn't have much chance to survive. They had removed a portion of his stomach and resectioned his small intestine, so I babied him toward home as gently as I could. By the time we reached Meriwether, he looked so bad that I put him in the vet's while I towed the VW up to Cauldron Springs.

I had had a bellyful of the Trahearne family circus, so I left

453

Melinda's car parked behind the hotel pool house, then went home to keep an eye on Fireball and tie up the loose ends. I sat in my office holding the telephone until it was slick with sweat, then I hung it up and dug up some postcards. It seemed a fitting form of communication. I sent one to Rosie with Trahearne's telephone number on it. Another to Melinda, telling her to call her mother. A third to Trahearne, which said simply: *You owe me, old man.*

As I left the office, I stopped by the secretary's desk and interrupted her as she buffed a higher gloss on her blue fingernails.

'If anybody calls,' I told her, 'tell them that I'm out of town indefinitely.'

'How long is that?' she asked without looking up.

'Almost forever,' I said, and she wrote it down.

I picked up Fireball, who was still hanging on, and drove him up to the cabin on the North Fork. His wounds healed slowly, but they healed. A fresh froth of white hairs grizzled his muzzle, he walked carefully as if trying to control his natural waddle, and he couldn't lift his leg to pee, but he survived. Finally I drove him down to Columbia Falls to have the drains and stitches removed. When we got back to the cabin, Trahearne's Caddy was parked in front and he was sitting at the table with a half-gallon of vodka and a jug of tonic. He didn't say anything as I picked up Fireball and carried him up the steps. When I sat him down, the bulldog walked toward Trahearne to sniff him, but halfway there he changed his mind and lay down to lick his scars.

'I suppose you blame me for that, too,' Trahearne said casually.

'I guess I don't blame anybody for anything,' I said.

'Must be tough being a saint,' he suggested. He sounded sober but his eyes were red and drunk. A white crust of antacid flaked at the corners of his mouth.

'What are you doing here?' I asked.

'I couldn't work,' he said, and hung his head.

'Maybe you're standing too far from your desk,' I said.

'What the hell do you know about it?' he asked, his anger changing to sadness in the middle of the question.

'Nothing.'

'Then don't try to tell me how to do it,' he said as he tried to pour vodka into his glass. It was too much trouble, though. He lifted the half-gallon and drank from the bottle, using the tonic water as a chaser.

'I don't think that's how you make vodka tonic,' I said.

'Fuck you.' He belched painfully and had another drink.

'Let's start this conversation over,' I said.

'Whatever you say,' he mumbled. He stood up and staggered over to the edge of the cabin. He fell to his knees as if he were about to pray, gagged once or twice, then projectile-vomited a huge gout of blood off the side.

'Jesus Christ,' I said. He did it again, and collapsed over the side, three feet down to the ground on his face. I went over and helped him to his feet and wiped his face, then hooked an arm over my shoulder and walked him toward his car.

'What are you doing?' he asked.

'Taking you to the hospital,' I said.

'Lemme die,' he muttered, 'lemme die.'

'You'd draw flies,' I said as I stuffed him into the Caddy. As I went back to get Fireball, Trahearne laughed and gagged again. It took me a few minutes to throw some clothes into a knapsack, and when I stepped out of the tent, Trahearne had gotten out of the car and was stumbling toward the river. 'Hey!' I shouted as I ran after him.

'Get away,' he said as I caught him by the arm. When I didn't, he jerked his arm so hard that he threw me into a tree. Then he set off for the river again.

My first impulse was to leap up and knock the hell out of him, but I didn't want to break my hand on his giant jaw. This time when I caught him, I wrapped a forearm around his neck to choke him down. He thrashed and raged and bucked like a wounded bull, but I stayed on his back until he fell to his knees, then I turned him loose. He shook his great head, struggling for breath and oxygen for his brain, then rose without a word and took off for the river again. This time it was easier. The third time easier still.

'I can keep this up all day,' I told him as he stood up the last time.

'You're going to have to,' he whispered, still strangling on his words.

'To hell with it,' I said as I turned away from him, then I swung around and hit him on the point of the jaw. It was like hitting a tree, and it felt as if I had broken all the bones in my right hand and wrist. 'God damn,' I said as I held it gently with my left hand. Trahearne stood upright for a moment, then took a step toward me and fell into my chest. We both went down, the big man on top, and I felt a couple of ribs tear loose. At least he was finally out, though. I crawled from under him and grabbed his collar to drag him to the car before the pain got too bad. But I couldn't budge him. I had to drive down to the Polebridge store to get help loading him into the back seat of the Caddy. By the time I drove to the hospital in Kalispell, Trahearne was snoring peacefully, and my right hand looked like a rubber glove full of water.

Two days later I went back down to visit him. When I walked into his hospital room, he smiled painfully.

'You're going to be the death of me,' he said.

'I broke six bones in my hand, old man, and dislocated three ribs – trying to keep you alive.'

I held up my cast.

'I guess I owe you again, huh?'

'Damned right,' I said.

'Well, thanks.'

'What the hell did you have in mind?' I asked as I sat down in the nearest chair.

'Who knows,' he murmured. 'Who the hell knows?' Then he paused for a long moment. 'Melinda told me about the forty thousand,' he said, 'and I made the mistake of going to my mother to borrow the money.'

'Mistake?'

'The crazy old bitch laughed at me,' he said, blushing with shame. 'I knew better than to ask,' he added, 'knew I had to work it out on my own.'

'What did you do? Mortgage your house?'

'I would if I could,' he said, 'but the bank already has two overdue notes on it now. The only reason they don't kick me out is because my mother went down and guaranteed the notes. Goddamned crazy old woman. I've never understood anything about her, you know, nothing. Maybe she wants me around, but only on her terms. I don't know . . .'

'So she laughed and you hit the bottle, huh?'

'Not then,' he said, 'not just yet. I called my publisher and got
him to give me a forty thousand advance against this new book – '

'What new book?' I interrupted.

'Whatever new book I write,' he answered. 'But I have to finish
at least a hundred pages of it before he'll give me the money. That's
why I came to see you.'

'You want me to write it?' I asked. 'Or just hold your hand while
you do it?'

He nodded slowly. 'If you could come up and keep me dry for a
month, I could do it.'

'You're kidding.'

'Not at all,' he said. 'I know how much I owe you, C. W., but if
you could just do this last thing, I'd . . . I'd do anything for you, pay
you anything. I've just got to get back to work, you see, just have
to . . .'

'For the forty thousand?' I asked. 'For Melinda?'

'Yeah, right,' he muttered.

'You son of a bitch,' I said. 'I'll do it, but not for you or your
damned stupid book . . .'

'For her,' he said quietly. 'I'll take that. I guess that's more than
I deserve.'

'What's she think about it?' I asked.

'She doesn't know yet,' he said. 'She rented a truck and loaded
up her pieces and took them down to San Francisco.'

'Great,' I said. 'Why didn't you give her a hand?'

'She wouldn't let me,' he confessed. 'She said it was her trouble
and that she'd handle it. But when I get the money, you can give it
to them, and she'll be off the hook.'

'Me too,' I said, but he wasn't listening.

'It must be tough,' he said softly.

'What's that?'

'To finish the grand quest and find the fair maiden sullied,' he
said, almost whispering.

'Only by you,' I said, 'only by you.'

'That's what I meant, of course,' he said, 'to find the fair lady in
love with the dragon, married to the shaggy, foul-breathed beast . . .'
He stopped and stared at me. 'You should have let me make it to
the river.'

'I thought about it.'

'Why didn't you do it?'

'Because she loves you, I guess,' I said, 'though I don't understand why.'

'Neither do I.'

'What about you?' I asked. 'Do you love her?'

He paused for a long time before he answered, then he said, 'I'm not sure what that means anymore, but I know I can't live without her.'

'You don't seem to live with her too well.'

He paused again, even longer this time, then he said, 'You know, I used to look forward to the day when I got too old to give a damn about women. I used to think that when that day came, all that wasted energy I spent chasing them would go into my work. I thought I'd grow old and wise, sexless as an oracle, but it didn't work that way, son, not at all. It came on me sooner than I expected, it drove me crazy – or crazier. And when Melinda rekindled the fires, I was so grateful that I married her. Now I'm afraid to lose her.'

'You don't need a detective, old man, you need a shrink.'

'Maybe so, son,' he said, 'but you're all I've got. I'd rather give you the thirty dollars an hour anyway. At least you buy me a drink every now and again.'

'But no more,' I said. 'The first drink you take is the last one I buy.'

'I'll be as meek as a lamb,' he said, and grinned. 'You'll see.'

As soon as the doctors could run a series of tests, they found out that Trahearne didn't have a perforated ulcer at all. Just an attack of acute alcoholic gastritis. They let him check out of the hospital the next morning.

'Put the top up,' he said peevishly as he settled into the passenger seat of his Caddy. His face was so white that it seemed to have been painted with clown make-up.

'Shut up and enjoy the sunshine,' I said as I wheeled away.

'Where are you going?' He sighed. 'You're going the wrong way.'

'I've got to get my pickup.' I popped the top on a beer.

'I can't drive,' Trahearne said, staring at the beer.

'I know,' I said, 'I've got a tow bar in the trunk. You just bought me one. I got tired of renting the damn things. Almost as tired as I am of towing your damned cars back and forth.'

'You're going to make me ride up that forty miles of gravel road?' he said. 'All the way up and back?'

'And you get to watch me drink beer all the way, too,' I said. 'What the hell, if Fireball can make it, you can,' I added, nodding toward the back seat where the bulldog slept.

'Sughrue, you're a mean son of a bitch,' Trahearne said as he swiped at his sweaty face.

'You want two-bit sympathy, old man, or hundred-dollar-a-day efficaciousness?'

'How about six-bit words?' he asked, almost smiling.

'Uncle Sam bought me a pocketful,' I said, 'but I never have any place to use them.'

Trahearne grinned until I made him open me another beer, then we drove north into the mountains. I drank and he watched all the way to the cabin, where I hooked our cars together again. On the way back down, I hit a couple of bars in Columbia Falls and Kalispell, then every one after that on the way to Cauldron Springs. The big man never complained. He just sat in the car sipping 7-Up and scratching Fireball's head. By the time I parked in front of his house, it was late afternoon, and I was drunk as a coot. When I opened the door of the El Camino, Catherine Trahearne nearly took it off with her Porsche. She locked all four brakes and slid to a stop in front of us, then leaped out and raced to help Trahearne out of the pickup.

'How are you feeling?' she crooned. 'You should have let me come to the hospital, you know.'

'I'm fine.' Trahearne sighed heavily as she fussed over him. 'Just fine. A little tired, though. Maybe I'll take a little nap.'

'Is that *nap?* Or *nip?*' I asked as I climbed out. Trahearne gave me a sad, tired smile as he shook his head, but Catherine looked at me with such intense anger that it nearly sobered me. Nothing like a little naked hatred to get a drunk's attention. 'Sleep tight,' I added stupidly as she eased Trahearne up the stairs.

When they disappeared through the front door, I went around to help Fireball out. He nosed across the lawn slowly, looking for a bush. Not to pee on, though – to hide behind. Having to squat like a mere puppy embarrassed him no end. Finally, he found a bit of ragged evergreen shrubbery and he lowered himself behind it.

'What the hell are we doing here, dog?' I asked. But he didn't know either. He finished his business, then came back to curl up in

459

the shade beside my feet. I leaned against my fender and went on with my beer.

Catherine came out of the house and walked down toward me, the short pleated skirt of her tennis dress fluffing as she bounced hurriedly down the stairs.

'You're looking particularly lovely today,' I offered.

She was, too. The summer weeks of tennis had darkened her tan without drying her skin, and deep red highlights glowed in her cheeks. She smelled of perfume and lady-sweat, of coconut oil and sunshine.

'Damn fine,' I added, hefting my beer can in toast as a warm flicker of old desire kindled inside my belly.

She stopped in front of me and slapped the beer can out of my hand. It clattered against the gravel driveway and spewed a froth of foam across the road.

'What the hell do you think you're trying to do?' she asked, breathless with anger.

'He's had all the tender loving care he can stand,' I said as I tried to swallow my own anger.

'What the hell do you know about it?' she demanded.

'Almost everything there is to know about it,' I said. 'He hired me to keep him dry, and I just wanted to see if he's got the guts.'

'Alcoholism is a disease!' she screamed at me. 'It has nothing to do with guts.'

'Well, he hired me, not you,' I said.

'You're not even doing it for him,' she said, 'you're doing it for her.' I didn't bother to deny it. 'Oh, the goddamned bitch,' she hissed. Rage flattened her lips and stretched the skin tightly across the bones of her face until they seemed to glow like a mummy's skull through parchment. Fine white lines glimmered hotly at the corners of her eyes, her temples, and along her jawline. She hissed a silent curse, stomped her foot, then ran over to her Porsche and roared away in a cloud of gravel and dust.

I went around and got another beer and watched her leave. She made the turn onto the highway with a very nicely executed four-wheel drift. Halfway back to town, her brake lights flared as she locked the wheel and skidded to a stop in the middle of the highway, where she sat for several minutes. Then, slowly and deliberately, she turned around and drove back toward the house.

'Please accept my apology,' she said as she stopped the car beside me. 'I'm truly sorry.'

'Don't apologize,' I said as she stepped out, 'it's a sign of weakness.'

Her anger came back in a single swift rush, but she gulped it down, and sweetly asked, 'What?'

'That's what John Wayne says,' I said. 'I can't remember which movie but I know he said it.'

'He's your hero, is he?' she said.

'Only fools have heroes,' I said.

'I see,' she said, smiling slowly. 'I always make the mistake of underestimating you, don't I?'

'That's better than overestimating me, isn't it?'

'I'm not certain of that,' she said, 'but I'm certainly sorry.'

'Forget it,' I said. 'It's a fool's errand, and I'm probably doing it foolishly. It's the only way I know. Pride and guts – that's the only thing that will work for Trahearne.'

'When the going gets tough, the tough get going?' she asked slyly.

'Make fun if you want to, but that's what character is all about.'

'I'm sorry.' She laughed and touched my arm. 'I just couldn't resist teasing you. You were *so* serious, you know.'

'Drunks are always serious at the wrong times,' I said.

'Do you think you can keep Trahearne dry for a while?'

'If he really means it, I can help, I guess,' I said. 'It's worth a try.'

'Perhaps I should come over later to prepare dinner for the two of you.'

'Thanks,' I said, 'but we'll manage.'

'I'm being, as they say, invited out?'

'Something like that,' I admitted.

'Perhaps you're right,' she said. 'Come over for a drink after dinner.'

'I'll see,' I said.

'Of course.' She reached up to kiss the corner of my mouth. 'Take care of him for me.'

'I'll do my best,' I said, and she nodded as if she knew I would. She went back to her car and drove slowly around to Trahearne's mother's house. Once again I loaded up with our baggage and toted it up the stairs to the house.

Instead of napping, though, Trahearne was sitting in his shorts

461

and T-shirt at his desk, idly working the slide of the .45 Colt automatic. A freshly poured glass of neat whiskey sat at his elbow.

'Don't worry,' he said as I set the bags down in the living room, 'I'm not about to blow my brains out. I prefer the slow suicide of drink.' Then he lifted the glass of whiskey. 'And don't worry about this, either,' he said as he put it back down. 'Its presence comforts me somehow.' He picked up the .45 again and spun his chair to face me. The large automatic was almost dwarfed by his huge hand. He let it dangle from his fingers as if it were a broken wing. 'You took that house down in Colorado like a good soldier,' he said. 'Were you?'

'It seemed like the only choice at the time,' I said, 'the best way to stay alive.'

'That's the big difference,' he said quietly, 'between your war and mine. You kids knew that if you survived the tour of duty, you'd survive the war. We all knew we were going to be killed. That's the only way we could go on – we accepted our deaths in advance just so we could go on. But that's not the point, is it?'

'What's the point?' I asked as I sat down.

'What's the worst thing you did in the war?' he asked suddenly.

It wasn't a casual question, and I didn't have a casual answer.

'We were fighting through a village south of An Khe, a hole in the road called Plei Bao Three,' I said, 'and I grenaded a hooch and killed three generations of a Vietnamese family. Both grandparents, their daughter, and her three children.'

'Were you a good soldier before that?' Trahearne asked.

'I guess so.'

'And afterwards?'

'There wasn't any afterwards,' I said. 'I was in the stockade afterwards. A Canadian television news team was covering the attack, and I made the evening news the next day, so they had to lock me up.'

'That's politics,' Trahearne said, waving his empty hand at me, 'not combat.' After dismissing the central trauma of my adult life with a flip of his hand, Trahearne went on. 'I'm going to tell you something I've never told anybody.'

'Great,' I said, but he didn't notice.

'When we landed at Guadalcanal, I wasn't much of a Marine,' he said. 'I mean, I walked and talked and fought like a Marine but it was all an act. I guess I thought I was supposed to survive the damned war or something – I don't know – but I was just going through the motions, trying to look good. Then we were dug in up on the Tenaru River, and the Japs pulled a night banzai charge. We held, we held and kicked the shit out of them, and I got some idea of what I was doing wrong. After it was over, though, I worked it all out in my mind.

'We were checking the bodies, the Jap bodies, and I found this Jap enlisted man floating face up in the shallows. There was just enough starlight to see that he was alive, enough for him to see me. I leaned over and shot him between the eyes with this .45.

'I guess I don't have to tell you what it looks like up close, I guess you know, but I made myself watch, made myself not flinch, and then I knew what the war was about. It wasn't about politics or survival or any of that shit, it was about killing without flinching, about living without flinching.' Then he paused and tossed the pistol onto a pile of loose papers. 'That's how I've lived ever since that night, and that's what's wrong. If you can't flinch, you might as well be dead.'

'That was a long time ago,' I said. 'Maybe it's time to stop blaming yourself.'

'Have you stopped blaming yourself for all those dead civilians?' he asked quickly.

'Some.'

'You're lucky, then,' he said sadly. 'I can't stop. So I'm going to give in to it. Listen, I know what sort of sentimental nonsense my poetry is, and I know what sort of macho dreck my fiction is – I'm as phony as my goddamned crazy mother – but I've learned something out of these past few insane months, and I'm through with all that other crap. And it's all your fault.'

'It's always my fault,' I said lightly.

'In the beginning, I wanted you to find out about Melinda so I would know – if Rosie hadn't hired you, I would have found some way to do it – but I watched you go after her for a smile and eighty-seven dollars, and you never judged her, not once, you forgave her without asking anything in return. When I was in the hospital, I thought about it all the time, and I finally understood it. All this time, all these years since the war, I worried about how tough you had to be to live, how I had to live without flinching, but when it came down to it, when it had to do with living instead of dying, I

463

didn't have the guts to forgive the woman I loved. I couldn't cut it, son, not a bit.' He paused long enough to pick up the .45 and shove the stack of pages off his desk. 'So now I'm through with all that. I'm going to write a novel about love and forgiveness. Even if it kills me. And that's why I'm not about to blow my brains out with this.' He tossed the pistol back on his desk. 'It's nothing but a paperweight now.'

'Good.'

'I've pulled my last trigger, boy,' he said, grinning. 'Hell, I didn't even pull the trigger on the shotgun that night – I just jacked a round into the chamber and I was so drunk that I had the trigger back when I did it, and the son of a bitch went off. Nobody there was more surprised than me.'

'Some of us were pretty surprised,' I said, grinning back at him.

'Nobody more than me,' he said, then he chuckled and handed me the glass of whiskey. 'Now get out of here, boy, I've got work to do.'

'Right,' I said. As I stood up and watched him gather his sharpened pencils and a fresh legal pad, I discovered an odd knot in my throat and a burning in my eyes, but I went off to do my chores before the old man noticed.

Trahearne worked until dinner, then he ate scrambled eggs and sausage at his desk, waving me away when I offered him more. Since he seemed locked in, I decided to wander outside to check on the bulldog. Fireball had eaten most of the baby food in his dish and had fallen asleep with his nose still touching the bowl. I left him alone and drifted over toward the creek. Catherine met me at the bridge. She was wearing a long knit gown that rippled across her body in the twilight.

'Were you coming for a drink?' she asked as she locked her arms around my neck and socketed her groin against mine.

'Something like that,' I said as I slipped my arms around her firm waist.

As she kissed me, she murmured against my mouth, 'We've no place to go, lover.' It didn't seem to matter, though. She moved her hands down and quickly unfastened my Levi's, then lifted the long folds of her skirt and gathered them about her hips so I could hold her naked buttocks in my good hand as I bent my knees.

When we were finished, I glanced over her shoulder toward Trahearne's mother's house. A curtain at an upstairs window wavered as if someone had just stepped away from it.

'I think the old woman was watching us,' I said.

'To hell with her,' Catherine said as she smoothed her skirt down over her finely muscled legs.

'Did it ever occur to you that we shouldn't be doing this?' I asked.

'It never occurs to me until afterward,' she answered, then laughed prettily. 'Tomorrow evening,' she added, 'same time, same place.' Then she walked away from me into the fading dusk, walked away before I could say no.

But the next evening when I showed up at the bridge after dinner, Edna Trahearne was waiting for me. She was dressed, as usual, in her retired fishing clothes, to which she had added a knit Irish hat against the evening chill. As I walked out on the bridge, she snorted as if I were late for a fly-casting lesson.

'Try to contain your disappointment,' she growled at me. 'Catherine is still clearing the dinner table. She'll be along shortly.'

'It's nice to see you again, Miz Trahearne,' I said as I leaned against the rail beside her. 'Fish bitin'?'

'Aren't you the polite one?' she sneered. 'How did you get mixed up with all these mortal folk?'

'How did you?'

'A moment of foolish passion, boy,' she answered, then broke out in a cackle, a rash, fevered laugh that split the evening like a loon's call. 'What's your excuse?'

'I guess I don't have one, ma'am.'

'You'd best find one, boy,' she advised cheerfully. 'You've stepped into a nest of vipers, and if you're here without a good reason, you got no business being here.'

'A day's work for a day's pay,' I said, and she laughed again. 'You're in a good mood tonight,' I added.

'Every time that little slut is gone it improves my mood considerably,' she said, then smiled as she waited for me to rise to the bait. When she was convinced that I wasn't going to bite, she snorted again, then asked, 'What happened to your hand, boy?'

'I hit your baby boy in the chops,' I admitted.

'A fella in your line of work ought to know better than to hit a man that size with your fist.'

'I knew better,' I said, 'but I did it anyway. Just for the pure pleasure of it.'

'You're polite, boy,' she said with a smile as twisted as her fingers, 'but you're not nice. Not a bit.'

'Yes, ma'am,' I answered, and the old woman turned away to hobble toward her house, pausing for a moment to speak to Catherine, who was walking toward the bridge. I couldn't hear what Edna was saying, but Catherine glanced over her shoulder to smile at me, the sort of smile my mother used to call a snake's grin. When they finished talking, the old woman went on toward the house, and Catherine strolled toward me slowly. She wore the same long soft green gown and carried a tall glass in her hand.

'I understand that you aren't always respectful toward your elders,' she said as she stepped onto the bridge, the smile still sly on her face.

'I'm always nice to you,' I said.

'You find it amusing to remind me of my age?' she asked, the smile suddenly wiped from her face.

'Just a little joke,' I said by way of apology.

'I am not amused,' she said as she swirled her drink furiously.

'I'm sorry.'

'Why don't you go back and play nursemaid?'

'You got it, lady,' I said, then walked away from her.

'C. W.,' she said softly, but I kept on walking.

17

For nearly two weeks everything worked smoothly, and Trahearne and I lived together as pleasantly as two old impotent bachelors, much as we had during his long visit up on the North Fork. It was like a vacation for me. In the mornings I ran, then sat in the sun and read my way through a large portion of his library. After lunch, I moved my chair into the shade and picked up whatever book I had just put down. Trahearne worked all day, though, writing in his furious scrawl and muttering to himself. About five every afternoon, he would stroll out of the house, stretch and growl, 'Scribble, scribble, scribble, eh, Mr. Gibbon?' then chuckle as he walked down the stairs for his daily exercise, whistling for Fireball.

The big man and the bulldog walked toward town every afternoon while I followed in the Caddy like a trainer watching my fighters do their roadwork. When Trahearne tired, I would pick them up and drive on to the hotel pool, where Trahearne lolled about like an old walrus until his head began to nod. Then I drove the two invalids home and fed them. After dinner they both went to sleep, and I went downstairs to drink beer and watch television until I, too, found refuge in sleep.

Every morning, while I was away from the house running, Catherine brought Trahearne a sheaf of typed manuscript and picked up his pages from the day before to transcribe them. Once, though, she was late, and I was sitting on the porch, back from my run and breathing hard as she came up the steps. She nodded at me, then went on into the house. When she came out, though, she stopped.

'I suppose you find this odd?' she said, rattling the long yellow sheets at me.

'Nobody else in the whole world can read his handwriting,' I said.

467

'I'm pleased to do what I can,' she said huffily, then went away.

'Aren't we all?' I whispered to her departure.

Trahearne stayed dry, seemingly without effort, except for a sip of my beer the afternoon we toasted Fireball the first time he managed to raise his leg to take a leak.

'God, that's good,' Trahearne sighed after he had swallowed the beer, 'so goddamned good.'

'The first one always is,' I reminded him as I took my beer can back.

'Right,' he said, then trundled off on his walk.

Fireball followed dutifully, marking every bush and rock in sight. When they reached the highway, Fireball waddled across the road to the creek to fill up again, and on the way toward town, Trahearne fussed at the bulldog constantly, telling him to put his damned leg down and come on.

That night, as he lowered himself into the pool, Trahearne asked me why I didn't come in with him anymore.

'It's like swimming in somebody's snot,' I said.

'Sughrue,' he said softly, 'Sughrue, you're the most disgusting human being I've ever had the displeasure to meet.'

'At least I don't swim in – '

'My God, don't say it again,' he cried, then buried his head under the water. As he bobbed back up, he faked a great sneeze and splashed water all over me. His laughter rattled around the large tiled room, filling it with the sound of breaking glass. Then he drenched me again, shouting, 'Never again! Don't ever say that again!'

I reached out with a damp boot and shoved his head back under the water. He grabbed my ankle with his huge hand and jerked me off the side of the pool. We both came up laughing like kids.

Later that same evening, as I was watching television and letting my clothes dry, I heard a knock on the large picture window of the daylight basement. When I glanced up, Catherine was standing there, grinning at me. My pants were nearly dry, so I slipped into them before I went to open the door.

'Aren't you the bashful one?' she said, still grinning.

'My mother was an Avon lady,' I said, 'and she taught me never to answer the door unless I was dressed.'

'That makes perfect sense,' she answered, then she sighed and her grin didn't come back. 'Listen, I'm coming down with cabin fever. When I finished typing this evening, I decided that I needed to get out of the house. Why don't we call a truce, and you can take me to town and buy me a drink.'

'Good idea,' I said.

When the Sportsman Bar closed at two, I bought half a dozen drinks in go-cups and carried them out to Catherine's Porsche. As I balanced them and climbed into the passenger seat, she reached over to touch my cheek.

'Let's take a midnight dip,' she suggested.

'Good idea.'

She eased the sports car through the darkened town and parked it behind the hotel, then got out and unlocked the back door of the pool house. Inside, I lined the paper cups up along the edge of the pool as Catherine rustled out of her clothes. Then she came over to help me with mine.

'Shall we swim before or afterward?' she whispered when I was as naked as she was.

'During,' I said as I grabbed her and we tumbled into the warm, slick embrace of the water.

Sometime later, we sat on the edge of the pool with our feet dangling into the water. Wisps of steam hovered across the rumpled surface of the water, and like a distant echo of thunder, the spring rumbled gently at the far end of the room. The last quarter of the moon ticked slowly past a skylight window.

'It's so odd here at night,' Catherine whispered. 'It's like the entrance to some underground world where it's always warm and silent. That's why I whisper. When it's closed up like this, they couldn't hear you over in the hotel even if you screamed.'

'Don't scream,' I whispered as I held my hand over her mouth. She giggled against my fingers. When I moved my hand, she screamed, a quick high note that shattered the silence and echoed around the walls.

'I'm sorry,' she said quietly, then giggled against her hand.

'You're drunk, lady,' I said as I fumbled for another drink. The ice had melted, but I gunned it anyway.

469

'Isn't it wonderful,' she sighed, leaning against me. 'I'll tell you a secret,' she said.

'Then it won't be a secret.'

'You won't tell anybody,' she said.

'I'm too drunk to remember.'

'In the wintertime, when I come down at night, I climb out of the pool and dash outside and roll in the snow, then dash back into the pool.'

'Everybody in town knows that,' I said.

'Oh you,' she hissed, then slapped me gently on the chest. 'You should try it sometime. It's like being reborn.'

'Rolling around naked in the snow is not my idea of a religious experience,' I said.

'Sissy.'

'That's what they called the brass monkey after he rolled around in the snow,' I said.

'What brass monkey?'

'The one that froze his balls off.'

'You're terrible,' she said. 'Except when you're being wonderful.'

'That's what I always say.'

'I'll tell you another secret, you terrible man.'

'I already forgot the other one,' I said.

'You're the first man I've ever come here with,' she said, watching her feet as they stirred the water. 'The very first.'

'I'm touched.'

'Don't be cynical,' she said. 'This place is very special to me.' She sat up straight again. In the darkness, the strips of untanned skin glistened, and as she turned to face me, her white breasts were as luminous as small moons. She must have seen me looking because she covered them with her darkly tanned hands. 'The plastic surgeon who does my work says it's nip and tuck from now on,' she said lightly. 'He also reminds me how lucky I am that I didn't have children. Trahearne wouldn't have them, you know.' When I didn't respond, she added, 'Considering how things worked out, perhaps he was right.'

'Trahearne's all the children anybody needs,' I said.

'Trahearne is a great artist,' she said quickly, 'and if I've made sacrifices, they were offered to that greatness.'

'Okay,' I said, sounding, I thought, properly chastised.

470

'You don't sound convinced,' she said.

'Look, I'm fond of the old fart,' I said, 'but I'll let the folks in charge of greatness and all that crap decide that for me.'

'C. W., sometimes you exhibit an unbecoming smallness of mind,' she said.

'Provincial, huh?'

'A goddamned redneck,' she said, then laughed. 'You damned phony,' she added, 'I know all about you. Trahearne has told me everything.' I didn't have anything to say about that, either. If Trahearne wanted to talk to his ex-wife, she was *his* ex-wife. 'I don't tell him everything,' she said, 'if that's worrying you.'

'I never worry.'

'I worry about Trahearne,' she said seriously.

'Maybe it's time you quit,' I suggested.

'No, he needs me more now than ever,' she said. 'You can understand that.'

'Sure.'

'You're not jealous, are you?'

'I don't think so,' I said. 'My needs are small, and if you want to baby Trahearne, that's between the two of you.'

'Not exactly,' she said softly.

'What?'

'Melinda,' she whispered.

'Right.'

'You know, I think I would hate her even if she didn't have my husband,' Catherine said calmly.

'Jealous?' I asked.

'Only of her backhand.'

'What?'

'Oh, when she first moved up here, back when I was still trying to be gracious about all this, I asked her to play tennis one afternoon,' Catherine said.

'What happened?'

'She humiliated me, on the court and in the dressing room later when we came in for a swim,' Catherine said. 'I understand that you've seen that body she keeps hidden under all those baggy awful clothes and you can imagine how it made me feel when I saw it.' Then she paused. 'Not that she showed it to me. She did her best

471

to hide it – I have to admit that – but I peeked into the shower. That was the hardest moment of many hard moments.'

'You're a lovely woman too,' I said.

'It's kind of you to think so,' she said. 'I suppose she's better in bed than I am, too.'

'I wouldn't know,' I said.

'Really,' she said, sounding genuinely surprised. 'I thought she was fairly free with her favors.'

'You're not the only one who thinks that,' I said.

'You're a little bit in love with her, aren't you?'

'Maybe.'

'Trahearne thinks you are,' she said.

'Maybe I am, maybe not,' I admitted. 'I don't know anymore.'

'Damn it.'

'What?'

'Are you sober enough for me to ask you something very important?'

'Sure.'

'Do you think she would leave him? Under the right circumstances?'

'I don't know about that,' I said. 'She loves him but she thinks that he doesn't love her anymore. She might leave, but I wouldn't know what the right circumstances might be.'

'Think about this for a moment,' she said. 'In my purse I have three cashier's checks. One for forty thousand made out to the bearer. Another for twenty thousand made out to a Miss Betty Sue Flowers. And a third in your name for ten thousand.'

'No,' I said. I stood up and walked toward my clothes.

'Listen to me,' she said as she followed, 'hear me out. Trahearne is working now, he isn't drinking and he has a chance to live and work for the rest of his life. If she comes back to live here, he will die within the year. You must know that.'

'No,' I said, 'I don't want any part of this.'

'When she flies back from San Francisco, Trahearne will ask you to pick her up at the airport in Meriwether,' Catherine said as she rummaged in her purse, 'and all you have to do is convince her to get back on that airplane – or another airplane – and fly out of our lives.'

'No.'

'Please,' she said as she handed me a long white envelope.

'Trahearne would just send me after her again,' I said as I hefted the slim bit of paper. Seventy thousand dollars seemed as light as a feather, yet so heavy that my hand could barely hold it up. I tapped it against my cast, which was crumbling after being dunked twice that day. 'He'd just send me after her again.'

'But if you took a long time to find her, long enough for him to finish this new book,' she said, 'it wouldn't matter by then.' When I didn't answer, she added, 'I wish you could read the beginning of this new book. It's beautiful, and you would understand why this is so important.'

'I can't do it,' I said as I tried to hand the envelope back to her.

'Just think about it, then,' she said. 'Keep the money and think about it. You owe me that much.'

'I guess I do,' I said as I set the envelope down and worked into my clothes. 'Whose money is it?' I asked as we finished dressing.

'Does it matter?'

'Maybe.'

'Edna and I put up equal amounts.'

'I'll think about it, but I know I won't do it,' I said.

'If you don't convince her,' Catherine whispered as she stepped into my arms, 'Trahearne's a dead man.'

'I can't,' I said, then buried my face in her damp hair. Beneath the sharp mineralized odor of the spring water, the light flowery touch of her perfume lingered.

'Everything would be so simple if you could,' she whispered against my neck, 'and it will be so awful if you don't.'

'It's already awful,' I said.

We rode in silence back to Trahearne's house, and when she dropped me there, we didn't even say good night. I watched her drive over to the other house and park her car in the garage on the far side, watched the progression of lights turned on, then off as she moved through the house. The light in the living room stayed on for several minutes, as if Catherine had spent time looking at Trahearne's war trophies again. Then the downstairs went dark and a soft glow lightened the upstairs windows as if a hallway light had been turned on. As I turned away, both upstairs windows on this side of the house flared, and I could see the two women's shadows moving behind their separate curtains. The old woman had been sitting downstairs in the darkness among the remains of that old war. A shudder swept across my back, and I went over to my El Camino, unlocked the topper, then crawled inside to lock the envelope in the gun case in the bottom of my tool chest. I went on to bed before I could think about any of it.

Catherine was right about one thing, though: two days later Trahearne asked me to drive down to pick up Melinda so he wouldn't miss a day's work.

When she came down the ramp, I almost didn't recognize her. She wore a tailored, vested suit in a dark shade of peach, her hair was blond again, short still but smoothly cut instead of hacked into a rumpled mess, and she even wore light touches of make-up. When she walked briskly across the asphalt and through the terminal doors, everything came to a halt at the airport while everybody watched her. She wore a new pair of leather boots, too, with stacked heels, and she didn't have to reach up to give me the light hug and kiss with which she greeted me.

'How do you like the new me?' she asked, her smile so warm and dazzling that it nearly blinded me.

'Jesus Christ,' I murmured.

'Thank you,' she said, accepting the compliment as if she felt she deserved it. 'How are you?'

'Overcome with desire,' I confessed.

'Thank you again,' she said calmly, then swung her shoulder bag around and headed for the baggage claim. Two matching leather suitcases came down the conveyor. She nodded toward them, and I picked them up.

'What the hell's in here?' I grunted.

'A new life,' she said, still smiling.

I followed her out to the El Camino, hurrying to keep up with this new, confident stride. Even from the rear, she looked happy. When she swung open the passenger door, Fireball tumbled out to greet her. If he had been any more excited, he would have rolled over on his back and pissed on himself like a puppy. As it was, he bounced around and barked and slobbered until he ran out of breath.

'Old Fireball MacRoberts seems to have recovered,' she said as she knelt to rub his stubby ears.

'Roberts,' I said as I tossed her bags under the topper.

'What?' she asked.

'Fireball Roberts,' I said, 'not MacRoberts.'

'Oh, who cares?' she said joyously, and I had to agree.

'I'm almost afraid to ask what happened,' I said as we drove away.

'Buy me a beer and I'll tell you all about it,' she said as she opened the cooler between the seats and cracked two beers. She handed me one, then drank half the other in one long rippling swallow, the smooth muscles of her throat working fluidly. 'How's your hand?'

'Still broken,' I said as I pounded the ratty cast on the steering wheel.

'What happened?' she asked.

I had made the mistake of assuming that she knew, but it seemed that Trahearne hadn't told her. If he hadn't, I certainly wasn't going to.

'One of those things,' I said.

'Well, if you want to be mysterious,' she said, then laughed and attacked the beer again. When she finished it, she crumpled the can like tissue paper, tossed it behind the seat, and went after another. 'You ready?'

'Not just yet,' I said, hefting the nearly full beer. 'What did you do down there?'

'I don't know where to begin,' she said, 'so many wonderful things happened. I found a gallery in Ghirardelli Square, and they liked my work well enough to arrange a show – which sold out in three days; can you believe that? – and I shipped the rest of my pieces to a place in L.A., so that's settled.

'Then I went to see all the old ghosts. Rosie and I got roaring drunk, had a terrible fight, then fell weeping and laughing into each other's arms.' She paused long enough to laugh giddily. 'I went up to see Mr. Gleeson, and he was a pathetic old fool. Then I dropped in unannounced on poor Albert, and it took him two Valium and a giant Scotch before he stopped stuttering. I forgave the bastard for being a bastard, and you know what he did?'

'No, but I can guess.'

'He came on like Mister Smooth-action,' she said, 'and when I wouldn't have any of it – I laughed in the creep's face – he burst into tears and dashed upstairs to see his shrink. I loved it.' She laughed again, then dug into her purse. When she jerked out a long white envelope, I occupied myself with the beer can, but she slapped me across the chest with the envelope. 'Five thousand dollars cash money,' she said. 'Will you see that Hyland gets it for me?'

'All right,' I stammered, then stuffed the money in my shirt pocket.

'A down payment on a new life.'

'Melinda – ' I started to say.

'Betty Sue,' she interrupted quietly, 'Betty Sue Flowers. It's a decent name.'

'I've always thought so,' I said.

'How's Trahearne?' she asked. 'He didn't have much to say over the telephone.'

'Nose to the grindstone, dry as a bone,' I clichéd.

'He did mention that you were a great nursemaid,' she said. 'You'll stay, won't you? As long as he needs you?'

'I guess so,' I said. 'Unless you want to run away with me.'

'Don't be silly,' she chortled as she slapped me heavily on the thigh. 'I've just come home again.'

18

As soon as we got back to the house, Betty Sue tumbled out of the pickup and raced up the stairs toward the front door. Fireball and I followed slowly – I was trying to be polite and he was practicing his aim – but she met us at the doorway, her finger lifted to her soft lips.

'He's working,' she whispered.

'Listen,' I said as I set her bags down, 'I think I'll go fishing this afternoon. You know, so you can be alone with the great man.'

'Don't be mean,' she said shyly. 'And it isn't necessary for you to go away.'

'I'm going anyway,' I said, then told Fireball, 'let's go kill a trout.' But he was sitting stolidly beside Betty Sue's heel. 'Will you keep an eye on the dog?' I asked her.

'He'll keep an eye on me,' she said. 'You have a good time.'

'You too,' I answered, trying to mean it.

As I walked to the pickup, beneath the heat of the late summer sun, a hint of cool, crisp air tickled my nose. Autumn soon, I thought, and another Montana winter waiting in the wings. Every fall I considered drifting south to San Francisco and renewing my California license, but I never went. Maybe this would be the year. But for now, I knew where there was a little roadside lake up in the mountains behind Cauldron Springs. Moondog Lake, where the trout had an affinity for worms, a place to waste an afternoon watching my bobber dance across the windy chop.

I drove down to the highway and turned right, away from town, but Catherine's Porsche caught up with me before I crested the first rise. I pulled to the edge of the road, parked, and got out.

'What did she say?' Catherine asked as she walked over to stand beside me. 'Well?'

'We didn't talk about it.'

'Why not?' she demanded flatly.

'This whole idea is . . . is terrible,' I said. 'You can't expect to pay people to do this sort of thing.'

'Why not?'

'There's more than money involved,' I said.

'That's why Edna and I are willing to spend so much money.'

'Well, you're going to have to get somebody else to do it,' I said. 'Or do it yourself.'

'You're the only one who could do it,' she said, 'and if you don't, whatever happens is on your head.'

'Sometimes I get the awful suspicion that this whole thing has been out of my hands from the very beginning,' I said, 'so it can't be my fault. But even it if is, I'm not going to try to bribe her to leave the man she loves.'

'If she loved him, Sughrue, she would leave him for free.'

'Betty Sue doesn't – '

'So it's Betty Sue now,' Catherine interrupted. 'That's very interesting.'

'That's her name.'

'Fitting,' Catherine sneered.

'Look,' I said as I stepped behind the pickup to unlock the topper, 'I'm going to give you those damned checks back and then wash my hands of this whole fucking mess.'

'It's on your head now,' she said, then ran back to her car and drove away before I could climb into the pickup bed.

'My ass.' I coughed into her dust as I locked up.

I didn't leave Moondog Lake until full dark, so it was nearly midnight before I drove down the highway toward Trahearne's house. The lights were still on, so I went on into town for a drink, then drove back out to check again. This time the lights were out. I eased up the driveway, parked, and let myself in through the basement door. As I mixed a drink the household above was silent. I switched on the television to catch the late movie from Spokane by cable, hoping for something rich with romance and scenery. *The Hanging Tree*, maybe, or *Ride the High Country*. Instead I caught *The Rise and Fall of the Roman Empire*, which put me to sleep. Occasionally I woke for a barbarian attack, a Christopher Plummer screeching speech, or Sophia Loren's breasts nudging the small screen, then fell back into a confused sleep.

I woke to the sound of gunfire and the instant memory of a preceding scream. I glanced at the television, where an aggressive young man urged me to buy a new pickup from the thousands on his lot. Then another shot boomed through the house. Down the hallway, I heard glassware break in the basement bathroom. I dashed to my bedroom for the .38, then raced back and up the stairs to the main floor, listening to the grunts and thuds of a struggle. As I slipped through the darkened kitchen, another shot banged. I dove across the living room rug and rolled into a left-handed firing position behind Trahearne's lounge chair.

The desk lamp in the study was on, but it had been knocked askew and it shined out the doorway directly into my eyes. Beyond it, though, I could see two shadowy figures struggling, wrestling for possession of the .45 automatic, which went off again. A shelf of books scattered into smoldering pulp. I fired a round through the ceiling and shouted *Freeze!* but nobody paid any attention to me. As I charged the door, I heard a fist strike soft flesh, and Betty Sue staggered toward me. I shoved her aside and crouched just outside the door. When Trahearne bulled his way through it, I slammed him on the side of the neck with the butt of the .38, then again as he was going down. As he fell, he swung the .45 toward me, but I clubbed it out of his hand with my cast. He hit the floor unconscious and belched a small puddle of vomit, which smelled like straight whiskey. I picked up the .45, unloaded it, and tossed it on his lounge chair.

'Is he all right?' Betty Sue panted behind me.

'He's alive,' I said as I knelt to check his pulse, which beat along as strong as a bear's, 'but he's dead drunk. Are you all right?'

'Just had the breath knocked out of me.' She huffed and puffed. 'That's all.' She moved over to kneel beside me. 'Help me get him to bed.'

'Right,' I said, stuffing the .38 into my belt. 'Glad I didn't have to shoot anybody,' I added. 'I'm terrible with my left hand.'

'Help me,' she answered, and the two of us levered the big man upright and walked him toward the bedroom. As we dropped him on the bed, he woke up long enough to tell us that he didn't need our damned help, but he went to sleep before we could debate the point. 'Thank you,' Betty Sue said, still breathing hard and deep.

'What the hell happened?' I asked.

'I need a drink,' she answered, then walked out of the bedroom.

'Me too,' I said as I followed.

But she wouldn't talk to me in the living room, either. I poured whiskey into two glasses and handed her one.

'Can I have a cigarette?' she said. I lit two, and she grabbed one out of my hand and sucked a cough out of it.

'Maybe you better sit down,' I suggested.

'Outside,' she said, and I followed her again.

As I leaned against the door frame, she paced back and forth across the desk, hitting the cigarette and the whiskey until she finished them both. When I went back inside, I noticed that the lights were on in Trahearne's mother's house. I hoped that they hadn't heard the shots. Outside again, I handed Betty Sue a fresh drink.

'What happened?' I asked.

'I'm not sure,' she said in a small voice. 'When he finished working this afternoon, we went into town for dinner, and he started drinking – he said it was all right, a celebration, you know, because he'd just finished a section and I had come home. And it was all right. He was in great form, full of good spirits and jokes . . .'

'Until?' I said into her pause.

'Until we went to bed,' she murmured. She blushed and hugged herself against the chill night air, wrapping the new yellow nightgown tightly around her body. 'He went to sleep – finally – and I guess I dozed off too,' she said. 'When I woke up he was gone. I went down to see if he was in his study working – he does that sometimes when he can't sleep at night. He was there. He was . . . he was holding the gun to his head . . . He was holding the gun and staring me right in the eye . . . It was almost as if he was daring me to make him pull the trigger. I don't know . . . I remember screaming, then after that we were fighting for the gun. That's all I – '

'You better pull yourself together,' I interrupted as I saw the blue lights of a sheriff's car racing out of Cauldron Springs toward the turnoff to Trahearne's house.

'Why?' She was close to crying.

'Because the law is here,' I said.

'What should I say?'

'Don't say a word,' I said. 'Just sit down on that lounge chair and whenever somebody asks you a question, you break into tears. All right?'

As if taking me at my word, she fell on the chair and began sobbing loudly. I stepped back inside the house and flipped on the porch lights, then stood empty-handed in their glare as the sheriff's unit skidded to a stop at the bottom of the stairs. The officer stepped out and leaned across the hood, covering me with his revolver.

'Shoot him!' came a wail from the direction of the creek. 'He's killed my baby boy! Kill him!' The old woman floundered out of the shadows, dragging Catherine as she tried to hold her back. 'Kill him!' she wailed again.

'Mr. Trahearne is perfectly all right,' I said to the deputy behind the car. 'No one's been hurt.'

'On your knees, buddy,' he growled, 'and lace the fingers behind your neck.' I didn't even bother to hesitate. As I assumed the position, he moved from behind the car and eased up the steps with his piece aimed steadily at my thorax region. 'Tighter,' he said as he stepped behind me. 'I want to see white knuckles.'

'The right hand and wrist were broken recently, officer,' I said as he grabbed my fingers and a handful of hair. He patted me down, sighing in my ear as he jerked the .38 out of my belt.

'Stand up,' he ordered as he cuffed my left wrist. As I stood up, he pulled it down behind me and grabbed the right and cuffed it above the cast.

'Easy,' I said as quietly as I could. 'I told you that nothing has happened. There's no reason to rebreak the wrist.'

'Kill him!' the old woman screamed again as she scrambled up the stairs like a wounded crab. Catherine didn't even try to hold her back.

'Tell the old bitch to shut up,' I said to nobody in particular.

'You shut up, buddy,' the deputy said as he jerked the cuffs. 'The sheriff will be here shortly,' he added, then jerked the cuffs again as if the alignment of my shoulder sockets didn't suit him.

'Your baby boy is safe and sound, sleeping off a drunk,' I said to the old woman as she hobbled up and bared her gums at me.

'I told you to shut up,' the deputy said, then did his act with my arms again.

481

'Don't do that again,' I said mildly.

He laughed and did. Some people never learn. Particularly country cops. They never get enough action to stay in shape. I grabbed the deputy's heavy leather belt with my left hand and tugged him closer, then stomped the instep of his right foot and cracked him on the nose with the back of my head and butted him with my ass. As he staggered backward, reaching for his holstered revolver, I turned around and kicked him in the crotch so hard that his feet came off the deck. He hit the floor in a fetal position, but I untangled his arms with my feet and knelt on them and sat on his chest.

'You didn't listen to me,' I said to him. He rolled his head sideways and spit blood. I heard grunting and scrambling feet behind me. Catherine kept a good hold on the old woman, though. From the smile on her face, I assumed that Catherine had decided that after what I had done to the deputy, I was going to be out of action for a while. Betty Sue sat on the chair, her mouth open as if she had stopped in the middle of a sob. 'Hey,' I said to her, 'get this dummy's keys and unlock the cuffs.'

She didn't say anything, she just did it.

'He really is all right,' I said to Trahearne's mother when Betty Sue got the cuffs off me. 'He just got drunk and decided to redecorate his study with a .45. That's all.'

'Really?' Catherine asked with a cocked eyebrow.

'Take his mother down to the bedroom so she can see for herself,' I said as I lifted the deputy's revolver and unloaded it. The two women glanced at each other, then went into the house. 'Hey,' I said to Betty Sue, 'could you get me a towel and a bowl of ice?' After she had stepped into the house, too, I stood up and released the deputy. 'Did you hear all that?' I asked. He nodded and crawled toward the vacant lounge chair. 'What kind of fool do you want to look like when the sheriff gets here?'

'You're the fool, son of a bitch,' he muttered. 'Just wait till I get you in a cell.'

'You think you'll have a job ten seconds after the sheriff finds out a cuffed prisoner took your piece off you?'

The deputy sneered. 'He's my uncle.'

'But Roy Berglund's no fool,' I said. 'Nephew or not, he'll shuck you like a hot tamale. He doesn't get elected by hiring kinfolk who look like fools.'

He thought about that for a minute or two, long enough for his pride and his family jewels to stop aching quite so badly, then he glanced up at me, asking, 'What did you have in mind?'

'Watering the grass,' I said, but he just stared at me. 'It always gets those damned stairs wet and slick as owl shit.'

'Goddamned stairs,' he muttered, then grinned and wiped at the blood on his face.

Betty Sue brought a bowl of ice and two dishtowels. I handed them to the deputy, then went to arrange the lawn sprinklers. Afterward, we sat down to wait for the sheriff. Everybody except for Edna Trahearne. She went home mad.

Roy Berglund looked like a sheriff. He was tall, blond, with crystal-blue eyes and a craggy face. As far as I knew, he wasn't dumb or corrupt. But he was an elected official, more interested in how he looked than how he did his job. And he looked great in a uniform. He had taken time to dress in a fresh one before he picked up two extra deputies and a medical examiner. As he strode like a giant through the sprinklers and up the stairs, they followed like the mere mortals they were. Roy looked great until he stepped, with a leather boot heel, on the wet redwood landing. As he skated across it, his huge arms windmilled furiously as he fought for balance, and he felled a deputy with a backhand right. Betty Sue had to break into sobs to cover her giggles and the deputy on the chaise lounge snorted with laughter until his nose started bleeding again.

'Turn off that goddamned water,' he shouted at the deputy lying on the ground. Sheriff Roy was angry. The most important citizen, the son of the richest woman in the county, had been foully murdered, and Sheriff Roy's dignity had been damaged. 'Now, what's going on here?' he demanded.

'I'm afraid it has all been a terrible mistake,' Catherine said as she stepped out of the shadows, taking charge with smooth assurance. 'We – Edna Trahearne and I – heard gunshots and assumed the worst. We leapt to a hasty conclusion.' Sheriff Roy looked both confused and disappointed. 'My husband – my ex-husband, that is,' Catherine said with a slight smile, 'was cleaning his pistol when it accidentally discharged. No harm done, I'm pleased to say.'

'Oh,' the sheriff said, tugging on his thick lower lip. 'Okay.' Then he turned to his nephew. 'What happened to you?'

'I was going down to call you on the radio,' he mumbled, 'and I slipped on them damned stairs.'

'Oh,' the sheriff said again. 'Well, Miz Trahearne, I'm sure glad nobody was hurt, but I've got to make out a report. If you could drop over to the county seat sometime during the next few days, I'd surely appreciate it.'

'Of course,' Catherine answered before Betty Sue could.

'Let's wrap it up,' he said to his courtiers, then, as if it was an afterthought, he added, 'Why don't you walk down to the car with me, Mr. Sughrue?'

'Sure,' I said.

The sheriff waited until everybody else had a head start, then he wrapped a heavy arm around my shoulder and led me down the stairs.

'Watch your step there, C.W.,' he said pleasantly. Up close I could see that he had taken time to shave too. 'Now,' he said softly when we were at the bottom of the steps, 'what happened? The old boy try to punch his own ticket, huh?'

'I was asleep,' I said.

'It's all right,' he murmured, drawing me still closer. 'It's just between us.'

'Just between us, huh?'

'Absolutely.'

'Just between us, Roy, I was asleep,' I whispered.

'Don't jerk me around on this, boy,' he answered, 'or I'll have your ass in a sling you can't begin to carry.'

'It's your sling, sheriff.'

'How about three to five in Deer Lodge for assault on a police officer?' he said.

'I think it's two to ten,' I said, but I didn't know either.

'Whatever it is, you won't like it,' he said, but when I didn't answer, he tried another tack. 'How come you didn't stop by my office to let me know you were working in my county?'

'I'm not working,' I said. 'I'm just visiting.'

'Hope not for long, boy,' the sheriff said, then slapped me on the shoulder and laughed as if he had just made a joke. 'Don't you even throw a beer can in the ditch, boy,' he added.

'You think knowing that Trahearne tried to blow his brains out will buy you anything?' I asked.

'A man who has everything don't need no presents,' the sheriff said over his shoulder. 'I know what happened and I don't care. I just hate to have a man lie to me.'

'Me too,' I said.

He laughed as he walked away. 'See you around, Sughrue,' he said, then climbed into his unit and had a young deputy drive him home.

Back up on the deck, Catherine stood at the head of the stairs and Betty Sue sat on the lounge chair. They were both watching me as I climbed tiredly toward them.

'Betty Sue, would you excuse us, please?' Catherine said without looking at her.

'Of course,' Betty Sue answered, and went into the house.

'Let's talk about it tomorrow,' I said as I lifted my foot up the last step. 'Okay?'

'Tomorrow will be too late,' Catherine said. 'Talk to her now.'

'I'm going to bed.'

'I'll just bet you are,' she said to my back.

Inside, I went to the bar for a fresh drink. I was in the middle of my second one when Betty Sue came back from the bedroom. She had changed out of her nightgown and into her old baggy clothes.

'I liked you better the other way,' I said.

She didn't bother to answer as she stopped to lean against the frame of the study door. The glare of the tilted desk lamp fell harshly across her pale, worn face.

'Let him clean up his own goddamned messes,' I said.

'I can't,' she said. 'What if you had felt that way about my mess?'

'That's different,' I answered lamely, but she had already stepped into the study.

The angle of the light lowered, the line of shadow sweeping across the carpet toward the doorway, and the desk chair squeaked as if she were sitting down. I poured myself another splash of whiskey and went outside, switching off the deck lights as I stepped through the door. My .38 Airweight still huddled on the pad of the chaise lounge where the deputy had tossed it. I unloaded it and stuck it in my back pocket. A slice of moon like a hairline fracture opened the night sky, the dark bulk of the remainder clearly visible. As I stared at it, I heard Fireball whimper down on the lawn. I called him and heard his slow scuffle up the stairs. Up on the deck, he waddled over and climbed painfully up into my lap as I sat down on the lounge chair. His haunches were trembling furiously.

'That's okay,' I said as I patted his head. 'Everybody is gunshy the first time.' The bulldog whined as I rubbed his neck until he stopped shaking. Then I sat him down and went back into the house. He followed, his nose brushing my heels.

Betty Sue still sat at the desk, her head in her hands as she leaned over the pile of tangled yellow pages. Her eyes were dry, though, when she glanced at me. Fireball walked over to her, and she lifted him into her lap. I went over too and leaned against the desk.

'Are you all right?' I asked.

'What did I do wrong?'

'Nothing.'

'Then why did he try to kill himself?'

'He can't handle it, I guess.'

'Handle what?' she asked as she wiped at her nose with the back of her hand.

'Love and forgiveness,' I said.

'I think I'm leaving him,' she said softly.

'That's probably the best thing.'

'For whom?'

'Both of you.'

'You're probably right,' she said. 'It might be the best for everybody.'

'Where are you going?'

She stared at me for a long time, then answered slowly, 'I'm ten years late but I'm going home.'

'At least I'll know where to find you,' I said.

'Don't,' she whispered, 'please don't.'

'Whatever you say.'

'And don't worry about Hyland and the rest of the money,' she said. 'I'll take care of it somehow.'

'Are you really leaving?' I asked.

'Yes.'

'Wait a minute,' I said, then went out to the El Camino to pick up the checks and her five thousand cash.

'What's this?' she asked, as I gave her the envelope.

'Look at it,' I said.

'My God.' She sighed as she pulled the checks out. 'Catherine?'

'And his mother.'

'If they want him back this badly, I guess I have to let them have him,' she said, then handed me the checks and the cash. 'Give the checks back to Catherine and the cash to Hyland,' she said. 'I pay my own way.'

I folded up the checks and stuck them back into my pocket along with the five thousand in cash. 'In the morning,' I said. 'I'm going to the bank to cash this one for forty thousand, then I'm driving down to Denver and put it in their hands. Catherine can have your five thousand and these other two checks back.'

'Please don't,' she pleaded.

'Listen,' I said, 'you're not the only one involved – my ass is on the line too.'

'I'm sorry,' she answered. 'Thank Catherine for me – tell her I'll pay her back.'

'You tell her.'

'I'll be gone before daylight,' she said. 'I've got a few things to pack up in the studio and a few clothes, then I'm gone.'

'I'll be gone before that,' I said.

'Come here,' she said, and I leaned toward her. She slipped a hand behind my neck and pulled my face toward hers. Our lips brushed lightly. 'Thank you,' she whispered. 'Thank you for everything.'

'Do me one favor,' I said as I stood up.

'What?'

'When you go home, take that goddamned worthless bulldog with you.'

'Thank you,' she said again, a touch of laughter rising through a mist of newly born tears.

I touched her cheek with the fingers of my broken hand, then left her that way.

19

While I was packing, I went into the bathroom to pick up my toilet articles and found the large mirror broken by the round Trahearne had fired through the floor. A large piece had fallen off it and crushed the slim vase with its burden of straw flowers and lonely women's faces. I reached into the tangle of glass and pottery to pick out a large piece with a woman's face upon it. I stared at it for a long time, then tossed it back on the counter and finished packing.

After I loaded the El Camino, though, I didn't have anyplace to go. I drove down the gravel track to the highway, anyway, then turned right toward the mountains again. When I reached the crest of the first rise, I stopped and got out, lit a cigarette and opened a beer. The Trahearnes' houses were dark, but a flood light spilled out of the studio up the hill from his house, and behind the windows, Betty Sue's shadow walked back and forth briskly. In the darkness of the valley, the studio seemed like a crystal island in a sea of black water. I finished the cigarette and the beer, then drove on up to Moondog Lake to wait out the rest of the night.

At dawn an early loon filled the far end of the small lake with his maniac gibber. I kicked out my poorly tended campfire and headed back toward Cauldron Springs.

When I reached the edge of town, I stopped at an outdoor telephone booth to call Torres to tell him that I had his money, then I eased through the waking town, searching for a cup of coffee. Everything was still closed, though. I toured the town aimlessly, the only person awake except for an arthritic old man shuffling from a cheap motel toward the hulk of the hotel and its hot spring waters. I stopped to offer him a ride, but he refused, cackling as he told me that he needed the exercise. I drove slowly on past the hotel and as I turned,

488

I saw Betty Sue's VW parked in the alley behind the pool house and the tennis courts. Staring at it, I went past, then turned around and eased down the alley to park behind her car, which was stuffed with her gear.

The back door was unlocked, but when I went inside the pool house, the waters lay flat and empty, filled with a luminous viscosity from the underwater lights, a light as ashen as that seeping through the skylights. I walked over to the pool and shouted her name, but her naked body floated face down in the pellucid waters, her right arm draped over the small body of the bulldog, as if she had tried to protect him from the bullets. Three black holes clustered in the middle of Betty Sue's back, and another glowed like a coal behind Fireball's ear. Below them, the .45 nestled like a poisonous sea plant against the bottom of the pool, and a cloud of blood, undissipated in the still water, surrounded the bodies like a hazy halo around a dark moon.

It wasn't what I wanted to do, but what I had to do. I went back outside to open the hood of the El Camino and remove the air cleaner. I hid the checks and the cash inside the paper element of it, then went back inside and over to the hotel. The old man who had refused a lift and an even more crippled and older desk clerk were discussing their ailments. I let the conversation die a natural death before I told the desk clerk to call the sheriff's office.

The first thing Sheriff Roy did, of course, was arrest me. I spent two weeks and three days in the Logan County jail without saying a word to anybody except my public defender lawyer, and I only told him that I didn't have anything to say. If the Trahearnes didn't push, the county attorney had no case, so I kept my mouth shut, and they didn't push. They came once, though, Catherine and Trahearne, to visit me in jail. We sat at the end of a long table, my attorney at the other end. Trahearne looked downcast, but Catherine smiled as she told me that I wasn't going to be charged.

'Thanks,' I said.

'We told them about those people in Denver,' Catherine said, 'but of course they all have iron-clad alibis.'

'Those sort of people always do,' I said.

'What happened to the money?' she asked casually.

'It's in a safe place,' I said. 'Do you want it back?'

'You've earned it,' Catherine said, smiling.

'Right,' I said.

Trahearne started to say something, but Catherine reached over to press her fingers to his mouth. I assumed that she was living in his house again, comforting him, protecting him.

'I hope it was worth it,' I said, then stood up and went back out into the hallway to pick up my jailer.

That afternoon as I drove out of town, Sheriff Roy followed on the tail of my El Camino. He flashed his headlights at me, then when I wouldn't stop, switched on his spinning blue lights. I didn't even slow down, not even when he opened up his siren, and ten miles out of town, he cut it all off and left me alone. When he stopped to turn around, I stopped too and backed up. We both climbed out and met midway between our cars.

'You got a lot of guts, boy,' he said.

'And you've got a lot of gall,' I answered.

'I just didn't want you making the mistake of coming back up here to straighten things out,' he said.

'What things?'

'Person or persons unknown,' he said. 'Leave it at that.'

'They paid me more than you,' I said, then headed back toward my pickup.

'They didn't pay me nothing,' he claimed behind me, and I believed him.

In jail, I had missed the funerals, but when I got to California, I saw the graves. Betty Sue had been buried between her brothers in one of those modern, tasteful cemeteries, nothing but lawn and flat stones. It keeps the upkeep down. They can mow right over the headstones. Right over the rotting meat. Oney and Lester had dug right through the concrete and buried Fireball in front of the doorway of Rosie's place, then poured a new concrete plug upon which his name and dates were scrawled in a drunken scribble.

The afternoon I got to Sonoma, Rosie and I were sitting on the front steps, looking at his grave, Lester and Oney flanking us with the beers I had bought them.

'You boys go on inside,' she said, and they did. 'I thank you for all your trouble,' she said.

490

'I'm sorry,' I said.

'At least I saw her that once,' she said, 'and that's better than nothing.' Then she paused to hit on her beer bottle. 'She told me about . . . about everything,' she said softly, 'but I just don't understand why they had to kill her. She would've paid the money back, you know that, or if they could've waited, her husband would've paid it – he told me that when he came down with the body – they didn't have to kill her.'

'No,' I said.

Then she turned to me, saying, 'I don't reckon I could hire you again to . . . to take care of those people out in Denver . . . would you?'

'No,' I said, 'you couldn't hire me, and it wouldn't do any good anyway.'

'The man who killed her, he probably didn't even know . . . didn't even know her . . . didn't even know why . . .' she stammered, then dropped her head into her arms.

'That's right,' I said, letting her think it had been that way.

'I won't cry yet,' she said as she lifted her head quickly.

'Will you do me a favor?' I asked.

'What's that?'

'I've got some of Betty Sue's money,' I said, 'and I know she'd want you to have it.' I dug the five thousand out of my hip pocket and handed it to her. I had already sent Torres his money. If he was afraid to cash the check, that was his problem. 'Why don't you get on an airplane and go to Hawaii or some goddamned place? I could run the place for you.'

'That's too much to ask,' she said as she slapped the sheaf of bills against her thigh.

'Do it,' I said, sounding angrier than I meant to.

'You sure?' she asked.

'Dead sure.'

'I'd rather fly back to Oklahoma to see some of my kin,' she said quietly.

'Stay as long as you like,' I said, and finally Rosie turned loose the tears. When she stopped, she went back to the trailer to pack, and Lester and Oney used my pickup to take her over to San Francisco and the airport.

While she was gone, I tended the bar, ran the place, and spent my days waiting for him to show up.

It took him a week, but finally, on a Thursday afternoon, Trahearne showed up, rolling through the front door like a drunken bear. He paused long enough to exchange boozy condolences with Lester and Oney, then he ambled back to the far end of the bar, where I waited. As he shuffled onto a stool, I walked back down the bar, cracked two beers for the boys and a third for the old man.

'How you doing, boy?' he said as I sat it in front of him.

'Better than you, old man,' I said.

'How's that?'

'My conscience is clear.'

'Yeah, I know,' he mumbled. 'If I hadn't been so broke, none of this would've happened. That Hyland son of a bitch!'

'Who?'

'Hyland,' he answered. 'That son of a bitch down in Denver.'

'He was dead when we left the house,' I said.

Trahearne didn't say anything for a moment, then he said, 'You don't know that. He might have talked his way out of it or something. You don't know that.'

'I saw the body, old man.'

'Then it must have been that big ugly son of bitch,' he said.

'It was a big ugly son of a bitch,' I said, 'but he didn't have the guts to pull the trigger.'

'What's that?'

'He got his ex-wife to pull the trigger,' I said.

'I don't understand,' he said.

'She pulled the trigger,' I said, 'but you put the gun in her hand. And all for nothing, old man. Betty Sue was gone, already gone.'

'Oh, come on, boy, you've got to be kidding,' Trahearne said, then laughed hollowly. 'Let me buy you a beer, boy, before I take off? I've got to get home, you know, get back to the old desk. Like you said, I've been standing too far from it. So get yourself a beer, boy.'

'Go home,' I said as I jerked his bottle out his hand. 'Get your ass home, old man.'

'Come on, boy, gimme my beer,' he whined.

I threw it on the duckboards beside me.

'Okay, if you feel that way, boy, I'll take off,' he said.

492

'When you get home,' I said, 'I want you to do me a favor.'

'What's that?' he asked as he stood up, drawing himself up like a wounded man.

'Wait for me.'

'I don't know what you mean,' he said, confused, rolling his head.

'Go home and wait for me,' I said. 'I've got a brand new elk rifle, a 7mm magnum, old man, and some afternoon, some afternoon, you're going to step out on your front deck after a day of scribble, scribble, scribble, and I'm going to put a 175-grain hunk of lead right through your gut.'

'Always with the jokes, Sughrue,' he said as he stumbled back from the bar.

'Go home, old man,' I said, 'go home and wait for me and try to work, old man.'

'Come on,' the big man pleaded as he banged into the pool table.

'You're dead,' I said. 'Go home before you start to stink.'

I guess he did. The last I saw of him, he was hurrying out of Rosie's place, stumbling over Fireball's grave.

DANCING BEAR

*for the Dump Family Singers
Orris, Nelson, Young Eugene, Ma,
and Little Shorty*

. . . and remember, my little grandchildren, in the old days there were more bears than Indian people, black bears and brown bears, cinnamon bears and the great grizzly, and we had no honey, no sweetness in the teepees, and Brother Bee was always angry, going around stinging the Indian people. The bears always found the bee trees before the Indian people, ripped them apart, ate the honey-comb, and stole the honey with their sharp claws and rough tongues. And the bees were always angry, because the bears, poor souls, did not know about the sacred smoke to make the bees feel friendly, and the bears did not know about the songs of thanksgiving so the bees would forgive them, but worst of all, the bears suffered from greed and they always took all the honey, left none for the bees. The bears knew about honey but not about bees, so the Indian people had no sweetness in the teepees.

Then one day, little grandchildren, a young man of peace, Chil-a-ma-cho, He Who Dreams Awake, came upon a ruined bee tree. Even though there was no honey left for him to take and even though the bees were very angry, he smoked his pipe with the bees and sang the songs of thanksgiving for all the good things of the earth. And when the bees smelled the sacred smoke and heard the songs, they settled down and went about their business. In return, the Grandmother Bee gave Chil-a-ma-cho a vision.

When he woke from the dream, he blessed the Grandmother Bee for her wisdom, then followed the tracks of Brother Bear across the mountains to the edge of a chokecherry thicket by the meadows where once we dug the camas root, singing the songs of thanksgiving and the songs of sadness as he went along. In the thicket he found Brother Bear sleeping, his breath still sweet with honeycomb, and Chil-a-ma-cho prayed to the spirit of Brother Bear for forgiveness, then plunged his lance into the bear's throat. Once again, as we always should, little grandchildren, Chil-a-ma-cho prayed for forgiveness for killing one of Mother Earth's precious beasts. Then he skinned the hide from Brother Bear, ate the liver and the heart dipped in gall, scraped the fat from the hide, saved it, then worked the skin for three days and three nights with the brains until it was as soft as a deerskin shirt. For another three days and three nights, he purified himself with fire and fasting and bathing away his man smell. Then he rubbed his skin with the fat of Brother Bear and put the hide on his shoulders.

When the moon rose high over the meadows, little grandchildren, Chil-a-ma-cho walked on all fours into the open, grunting and snuffling, speaking the bear language the Grandmother Bee had given him. When the other bears around came to greet their new brother, Chil-a-ma-cho began to dance the steps the Grandmother Bee had given him. The first night the other bears thought their new brother must have come from someplace beyond the mountains where the bears were crazy, so they went back into the lodge-pole pine to watch. The second night a few danced with him to be polite, as we must be to our brothers from beyond the mountains, and on the third night they all joined in, danced and danced in the sacred circle, danced until all the bears dropped.

The next day as the bears slept, Chil-a-ma-cho led the Benniwah as they followed the bees, the bees whose legs were hairy with pollen, led them to the bee trees and the honey. The People were happy, in a hurry for honey, but Chil-a-ma-cho made them make the friendly smoke, made them leave half the honey for the bees, made them sing the songs of forgiveness. The bees forgave the Benniwah, and stopped going around stinging everybody.

After that we had sweetness in our lodges – except for Chil-a-ma-cho, who gave himself to the dancing and the bears and never ate honey, and it is for his memory that the Benniwah forsake honey during the days of the Bear Dance before we harvest the honey with the sacred smoke and sing the songs of forgiveness for sweetness in the lodges.

Of course, as you well know, little grandchildren, sometime later the white man showed up, and now there are not too many Indian people and even fewer bears, and even Brother Bee, bless his spirit, lives in a little square house and works for the white man. There has not been much sweetness in this world, or the next, since then, not much dancing either. Even He Who Dreams Awake, Chil-a-ma-cho, sleeps.

– A BENNIWAH TALE

1

We had been blessed with a long, easy fall for western Montana. The two light snowfalls had melted before noon, and in November we had three weeks of Indian Summer so warm and seductive that even we natives seemed to forget about winter. But in the canyon of Hell Roaring Creek, where I live, when the morning breezes stirred off the stone-cold water and into the golden, dying rustle of the cottonwoods and creek willows, you could smell the sear, frozen heart of winter, February, or, as the Indians sometimes called it, the Moon of the Children Weeping in the Lodges, Crying in Hunger.

I worked the night shift for Haliburton Security, though, and didn't see or smell much of the mornings that fall, since I spent them wrapped in a down comforter with the creek-side window open wide to the cold morning breeze, only my nose, stuffy with cigarette smoke and the sweet stench of peppermint schnapps, exposed to the wind.

On this particular November morning, though, when a rumbling clatter crossed the loose boards of my front porch and a sharp rattle at my screen door jerked me halfway out of a hangover sleep, the cold breeze in my nose told me it was nowhere near noontime, far too early in the morning for civilized behavior. In the first confused moments of waking, I thought it might be a bear rummaging in my trash cans. Then I remembered it was fall, and the bears usually came down out of the Diablo Range in the spring after a hard winter sleeping. Besides, the city of Meriwether had grown up the canyon over the years, a flood of houses and people that stretched for miles beyond my small log house nestled at the head of Milodragovitch Park, so the bears did not come down to my house anymore. Even if they chanced a journey through all the pastel plywood houses, they wouldn't find an easy meal waiting in a tin trash can, but all my garbage securely bound in a fifty-five-gallon drum with a locking lid. A meal only a grizzly could eat; and nobody had seen a silvertip on this side of the Diablos in forty or fifty years. The only danger to my garbage can came from the huge new automated trucks that picked them up; sometimes the front lift held the cans too tightly, ruptured them like rotten fruit, or banged the sides flat as the lift dumped the trash into the bed of the tasteful blue garbage trucks. Progress, they called it: garbage untouched by human hands, safe from hungry bears.

Then the pounding on my front door brought me back to the present as it clearly became the rap of knuckles falling directly on the large plastic sign that politely asked that I not be disturbed before noon. During the two years and four months I had been working for Haliburton Security, I hadn't been sleeping very well. The boredom of the work – rattling doorknobs, guarding twenty-four convenience markets, and holding the hands of lost children in shopping malls – had caused a sudden, and unseemly in a man of my years, affection for cocaine. I slept through the mornings, true, but badly, lightly. I had taken the bell out of my telephone and put the sign on the front door, but it seemed nothing helped.

The pounding went on, a dull echo bound within the thick log walls, booming inside my head. I hadn't been asleep long enough to have a hangover; I was still half drunk. I feared I knew whose fist tolled for me. Sometimes my next-door neighbor came over in the mornings after her husband had left for work. Usually she wanted a toot or two, then some sordid business in my bedroom. She was young and athletic and not bad-looking for a mean, skinny girl, and I might have enjoyed her visits a bit more if I hadn't known that her husband worked two jobs just to keep her outfitted in a rainbow's hue of ski clothes and lift tickets and to keep up the payments on her new white Corvette. Ignorance might not be bliss, but too often knowledge took the fun out of some parts of life.

As I rolled out of bed and struggled into my jeans I tried to think of some way to put her off, but I had run out of exotic venereal diseases and disabling prostate disorders. Resigned to my fate, I stumbled to the door. But when I opened it, a postman in a summer uniform holding a clipboard stood on my porch, his hairy fist raised for another resounding knock. He looked as bad as I felt and as if he didn't care if he hit me or the door.

'Can't you read?' I groaned, jerking a thumb at my sign.

'Of course,' he grunted, 'but she said it would be all right.' Then he nodded to where my next-door neighbor was standing in her driveway, dressed in a heavy sweater and a down vest while she serenely washed the dew and pulp mill smog off her beloved automobile. She smirked wisely, an eyetooth glistening in the curl of her thin upper lip.

'Special Delivery Certified Mail,' the postman announced with chattering teeth. 'Sign here,' he said, then prodded me with the cold metal ring atop his clipboard.

'Ouch,' I said, then looked at him.

He stared at me out of two painfully bloodshot eyes sunk into a swarthy, unshaven face. His short-sleeved shirt and short pants fit him like a dirty sack. Even his shoes looked too large, and when he danced as the cold breeze licked his legs, his shoes didn't move.

'Sign here,' he said again.

'Who's it from?' I asked. Back in the old days when I worked as a private investigator out of my own office and when I made enough money to afford the string of ex-wives I had somehow accumulated, I learned the hard way not to sign for mail I didn't want. 'Well, who's it from?'

'What the hell difference does it make?' he answered, then held the clipboard to his chest. 'Just sign the son of a bitch before I freeze to death.'

'No way,' I said, then briefly wondered if it was against the law to impersonate a mailman to deliver a subpoena. 'I'll just pick it up at the post office,' I said; 'maybe your supervisor will be kind enough to tell me who it's from.'

'Stuff my supervisor,' he said as he got me in the belly with the clipboard again. 'Either sign here, man, or I'll shit-can it, and you can whistle Dixie, asshole.'

'I'm a taxpayer, jerk,' I said, which was partially true, 'and you've got a dirty mouth for a government employee. What's your name?'

'No more shit,' he muttered, dancing in a small circle, the clipboard raised, 'no more fucking shit.' Then he broke the clipboard over my head.

For a moment both of us were too stunned to move, then we went

to the ground growling like a pair of rabid dogs, snarling and snapping, biting and scratching as we tumbled off the porch and onto
the dew-damp grass, our hands at each other's throats, our teeth
bared, too mad to consider technique, and if my next-door neighbor
hadn't turned her hose on us, we might have hurt ourselves, but
once we were wet, we were just too cold to fight.

Things took a bit to straighten out, but ten minutes later we were
warm again, sitting at my breakfast bar wrapped in blankets and
huddled over cups of coffee and shots of schnapps while my next-
door neighbor ran the postman's uniform through her dryer. We
compared wounds and laughed at ourselves, discussed the long-term
tensions of marital discord. He had spent the night before drinking
and fighting with his second wife, and when he passed out on the
kitchen floor in his boxer shorts, his wife, in some demented vision
of revenge for unnamed sins, gathered up every stitch of his clothing
and threw them off the Dottle Street Bridge into the Meriwether
River below. Unfortunately, the only uniform he could borrow that
morning was dirty, summertime, and three sizes too large. She had
done things like that before, he added sadly. Once she had cut off
the left legs on all his pants, and another time she had snipped the
toes out of all his socks. I had been there before, far too often. Ah,
women, I thought, God love 'em. And especially my five ex-wives.
But, Lord knows, don't piss them off. They can be fiendish in search
of revenge. I kept my thoughts to myself, though, and when my next-
door neighbor brought his uniform back, we shook hands and parted,
if not friends, at least veterans of the same wars.

All's well that ends well, I thought contritely as I poured myself
another shot of schnapps. The postman had a dry uniform, slightly
cleaner if no better fit, his pride, and my signature; I had my mail,
slightly damp; and my next-door neighbor had her morning's amusement.

I had only glanced at the envelope while we talked, just long
enough to see that I didn't know who had gone to such a fuss to
write to me. I picked it up again, the heavy butternut bond of
envelope rich against my fingers, and stared at the return address
embossed in gold script. Mrs. T. Harrison Weddington, of 14 Park
Lane, Meriwether, Montana, had something to say to me. The
message on the deckled-edged stationery had been written in brown

ink with a spidery but firm, old-fashioned hand trained in the Palmer method.

> My dear Mr. Milodragovitch, since I have been unable to reach you by telephone, either at your office or at your home, I have taken the liberty of writing you. If you find this to be an intrusion upon your personal privacy, please accept my deepest apologies in advance. However, it is imperative that we meet at your earliest convenience. I may have a case for you.

The note was signed 'With kindest regards, Sarah Weddington,' and included a postscript in another, more modern and casual hand with the telephone number. When I looked at the letter again, it didn't seem to make much sense. The text was clear but the words seemed strung together oddly, as if they had been written by somebody who had learned English in another country. And the name, Sarah Weddington, seemed familiar, but I didn't know why. And the phrase 'a case' . . . My God, even when I worked for myself, I never got cases. Whiskey came in cases; the sort of work I did came in crocks.

I hadn't had my own office in nearly five years, not since the day the trustees of my father's estate evicted me from my own building because of a small matter of six months' back rent. Actually, it wouldn't be my building until I turned fifty-two and finally came into my father's estate.

A case, I thought, then dug out my city directory, which told me nothing more than I already knew. Park Lane was a short twisting street in an old residential neighborhood, the McCravey development, just west of the campus of Mountain States College, and the houses along Park Lane were all old Victorian dowagers set on two- and three-acre lots. Just the taxes and utility bills on one of them would keep me in steaks and cocaine for a year. Even if this 'case' turned out to be a crazy old woman who had lost her favorite cat, I suspected I would be well paid for my time, so I called the number.

A young woman's voice answered the telephone, said she was not Mrs. Weddington, said my call had been expected and I could see Mrs. Weddington at either eleven that morning or four that afternoon. I thought about dumping a shift at Haliburton's so I could have a nap and go at four, but I settled for eleven. No sense in losing a day's pay for a wild-goose, or -cat, chase.

'You wouldn't know what this is in regard to, would you?' I asked the young woman.

'Nope,' she answered, then hung up.

Even though I had just over two hours to make the appointment, I found myself hurrying to my closet to see if I had any appropriate attire in which to call upon rich folks. But I had torn the knee out of my blue pin-stripe three-piece courtroom suit and lost one of my black boots in a scuffle on the courthouse steps a few years back after I had testified in a rather messy divorce hearing, and my last wife's cat had thrown up the remains of a garter snake on my only sport coat. Not a thing to wear, I thought, then saw myself in the dresser mirror. It wasn't going to make a bit of difference what I wore. A scrape on my forehead still bubbled watery blood and my left eye was already turning black.

After I cleaned up as best I could, showered and shaved, I went down into my basement to my mad-money cache. It had gotten thin, but I took it anyway. On the way back I patted the haunch of the cow elk I had poached with my trusty crossbow the weekend before. Meat for the winter, skinned and aging in the cool cellar light. Steaks and roasts, sausage and chilli, and the memory of the elk's wide dark eye glistening in the spotlight as she leaned over the salt block. I patted her flank again, thankfully, then headed upstairs and out to my beat-up old Ford 4×4 red pickup.

Carlisle Drive skirted the eastern edge of Milodragovitch Park, sixteen wildly overgrown bushy acres that had been my backyard when I was growing up rich, then plunged out of the dark, shaded canyon into the full daylight filling the valley of the Meriwether. The air was clear, but a high hot haze made the sunshine diffuse and painful, almost like snow glare, and I fumbled in the glove box for my sunglasses, as blindly as a junkie coming out of a shooting gallery into unexpected daytime, but I couldn't find them. So I stopped to buy gas at the corner of Main, slipped into the john for two quick snorts of coke off the end of my pocketknife blade, then drove on out to the shopping mall on the south side of town, where I dropped nearly five hundred bucks on a new pair of Dan Post lizard boots and a Western-cut leather jacket. Only by the grace of God did I manage to avoid a string tie with a hunk of turquoise the size of an elk turd on it. Western clothes are all the rage these days, even back East, I understand, but when I climbed back into my pickup in the mall parking lot, I may have looked like a fashion plate, but I smelled like an old leather couch and creaked like a new saddle. Maybe these rich folk would look at my clothes and not notice my worn-out, battered face.

Meriwether was one of those old Western towns where every one of the early developers of residential neighborhoods had expressed his God-given and constitutionally guaranteed individuality by laying out his streets at cross-purposes to those of the surrounding neighborhoods. And the McCravey development was the most cantankerous of all, an absolute maze of wandering lanes, nooks and crannies, irregularly shaped lots, dead-end streets, circles, and tiny parks in the most unexpected places.

Even though I knew the neighborhood, I still missed the angled turn off Tennessee into Park Lane and had to go around to Virginia and come back to Park Lane. A few of the grand old mansions on Park had been cut up into student apartments or converted into fraternity or sorority houses, but most were owned by ancient professors at the college or survivors of the original families.

Number fourteen was the largest and most impressive of all, a grand old Victorian, sparkling with a new coat of paint in the fall sunshine, a great dame spreading her majestic wings, adrift on a small sea of mature, well-tended greenery, an eccentric old lady given over to whim and fancy: an off-center porch, a tower here, a cupola there, bay windows of rounded glass trying to balance French doors on the other side; and on the south side of the second story a huge solarium with a balcony on three sides looked as if it had been lifted bodily out of another, more modern house.

It was the old McCravey mansion, and I kicked myself for not remembering. The house had changed hands several times since the McCraveys had taken their mining and timber fortunes on to rape and pillage larger and more distant economic horizons. Whoever owned it now had restored it beautifully, expensively. I could almost feel my wallet expand, and began to consider a vacation somewhere south for the winter months.

Two towering blue spruces flanked the entrance to the brick driveway, but I didn't want to park my pickup like a soiled dove beside the dowager queen, so I pulled up to the curb and tried to hide it behind a lilac bush. I walked back slowly along the spiked wrought-iron fence to the gate, trying to keep the leather noise down, trying to keep my new boots from eating my feet, but the silences of my pauses just made the animal squeal of the dead hides that much louder, and my little toes were already as sore as boils.

The lower story of the house seemed dark, draped behind heavy velvet, so I rested my dogs on the porch steps. Above the oak double doors, a stained-glass fanlight glowed faintly in a dull, unfinished wink. Before I could turn the brass handle of the bell, though, the front doors jerked open wide.

'So,' came a voice from the gloom, 'you're late. She said you'd probably be late. And now I'm late. For my graduate organic lab. Thanks a bunch.' The voice paused while I wondered what sort of madness I had blundered into. 'Well, don't just stand there like a knot on a log. Come on in.'

Before I could step inside, a young woman stepped out on the porch to glance at the high haze. 'Weather,' she said calmly, meaning, as they always do in Montana, bad weather coming. She wore a pair of white painter's overalls, a cashmere turtleneck, and a chamois shirt-jacket. A small knapsack full of books dangled off her left shoulder. She stared at me through a pair of oval gold-rimmed glasses.

'I beg your pardon,' I said.

'Weather,' she repeated, 'goddammit. And you're late. And I've missed my chem lab. But what the hell, Sarah could have used the elevator. I can make it up tonight, so come on in . . .'

As she rattled on, I followed her inside, and she shut the heavy doors with a crash that should have pulverized the stained glass of the fanlight. For a man with sore feet, I thought I managed to step aside quite deftly. She swung her daypack off into a walnut deacon's bench, then headed down the broad hallway toward the wide stairs. The cleats of her hiking boots clattered on the polished parquet floor, and I expected to be showered with wooden tiles as I followed in her noisy wake. She rushed up the stairs, and I wondered where the elevator might be, then I wondered why she had swaddled such a nicely pert butt beneath the baggy overalls. Halfway up to the landing she realized she was talking to herself, so she stopped, turned, flipped back the tails of the chamois shirt, sighed as she hooked her thumbs into the side loops of the pants, and her young breasts rose sweetly under the thick layers of fabric. When she shook her head, her short blond hair ruffled shortly.

'Are you coming or not?' she asked sharply, then added as I hobbled up the first few steps, 'New boots, huh? You guys drive me crazy, you guys in those silly goddamned boots. You might as well bind your feet like a Chinese whore – '

'Chinese princess,' I interrupted.

'Huh?'

'Nothing.'

'Well, as far as I'm concerned, that's the major problem with this whole goddamned state . . .'

'What's that?' I asked.

'Cowboy boots and bulldozers, that's what,' she said, 'goddamned romantic affectations. And I'll lay odds that you haven't been horseback ten minutes in your whole life . . .'

Although she waited on the landing for me, her mouth didn't slow down a bit. My feet hurt and I was trying to stop the cocaine sniffles, so I didn't hear much of what she said. Something about animal skins and latent homosexuality, about poor harmless iguanas slaughtered to satisfy the vanity of dudes. When I finally caught up with her at the top of the stairs, I grabbed her elbow.

'Fuck a bunch of horseback,' I said. 'You want to see my saddle sores?'

'Nice talk,' she said, but she smiled.

The solarium was even larger than it looked from the street, filling the whole south third of the second floor. The sunlight flooded the huge room through three walls of French doors and two huge skylights; so much light so suddenly that I seemed not only blinded but somehow deafened too. White wicker furniture with gaily flowered cushions rested peacefully among a forest of large potted plants, mostly ornamental citrus trees and fan-leafed ferns. An array of Oriental throw rugs broke up some of the light as it reflected off the pale oak flooring, but most of the sunlight glanced off the floor and plunged like tiny knives into my already bleary eyes. I had done either too much coke or too little, a constant problem in my life.

Between spasmodic blinks, I watched the young woman thump across the room and out to the balcony, where an old woman leaned

509

lightly against the rail, her face lifted into the fall sunlight. I heard their voices but not the words, and they seemed far away, as if we all stood in the brilliant salt-air haze of some Mexican Pacific beach, paralyzed by the sun and the softly pounding surf, reduced into an infinite languor, language lost in the muffled, sun-struck crash of the waves in the throbbing air. I felt like falling on the nearest couch for a long winter's siesta. The old woman raised a finger to her smiling lips, and the young woman stopped jabbering, lifted *her* hand to her mouth, but a stream of giggles slipped quicksilver through her fingers.

The old lady turned toward me, the sunlight catching her fine white hair, the polished burl of the cane in her left hand, and the stainless-steel brace on her left leg, then she came toward me out of the sun, slowly, limping, but with the grace of long-practiced motion, and when she paused just inside the French doors to set a pair of binoculars on a small table, her hand seemed to float in the air.

'No problem, Sarah,' the young woman said, her hand placed lightly under the old woman's elbow, 'I'll just hit the night lab, and – ' Then she banged her forehead with the heel of her other hand. 'Oops. Forgot the coffee. Be right back,' she added, patting the old woman's elbow.

'You do drink coffee?' she asked as she stopped in front of me. When I nodded, she looked at my face. 'Jesus,' she said, 'some shiner.' Then she darted past.

The old woman started to walk across the room. My hand rose to finger my swollen eye and the scrape on my forehead, and I had to wipe the blood off my fingers before I could take her extended hand.

'Sarah Weddington,' she said in a gently hoarse voice. 'Thank you for coming, Mr. Milodragovitch, on such short notice,' she added with a smile, 'and please forgive me for being so mysterious in my note.'

'Yes, ma'am,' I admitted, 'I'm sorry...' Then I looked at her again.

She wore a white linen suit and a raw-silk blouse that set off the sun-tanned flush of her finely boned face. Even her sensible, low-heeled shoes looked expensive and handmade. Her years, as they too often are to women, had done their cruel work to her face, but she hadn't tried to recapture her lost beauty with cosmetics but had let her face grow old with character and repose, with a serenity only highlighted by the hard touch of time. Although her blue eyes had paled, when she smiled, as she did now still holding my hand, they became clear, the limpid blue of the dawn sky rising over a mountain ridge.

'Oh, Bud,' she said, grinning now, 'and you had such a reckless crush on me back then.'

My given name is Milton Chester Milodragovitch III, a name chosen by my great-grandfather, Anglo-Saxon names chosen to leaven the Slavic curse of our surname. My grandfather was called Milt, my father Chet, and my mother tried and failed to call me Milton. My friends called me Milo. Only my father had called me Bud, and when he blew his head off with a shotgun when I was twelve, the name died with him.

'Seven Mile Creek,' she said softly, and it all came back.

'I'll be goddamned,' I whispered, and she lifted her cane, took a small step into my arms, and we hugged each other tightly, our arms wrapped around all the dead years.

My father grew up rich and useless, the scion of an old Meriwether family, interested only in fly-fishing, expensive whiskey, hunting, and any woman who wasn't my mother, which was the main reason my mother made him write his will to keep the family fortune out of my hands until I turned the ripe, and hopefully mature, age of fifty-two. She planned some useful life for me, working for a living at a job, making some small contribution to society. A life she had probably planned for my father when she met him in Boston the fall before he was asked to leave Harvard for drinking, gambling, and shooting squirrels in the Harvard Yard with a Colt .44 Dragoon pistol.

All her plans failed. My father never had a job in his life. When she said 'social contribution' to him, he wrote a check and told her that was his job. Even her body betrayed her. After seven wild and painful years in Meriwether she left him, only to become morning-sick with me on the long train ride back East. I failed her too, even after her death. Except for a tour of duty in the Army during the Korean War, ten years as a Meriwether County deputy sheriff and this last terrible stint at Haliburton Security, I never held a steady job in my life.

Although I gave up fly-fishing years ago and only hunt for meat,

I certainly inherited my father's taste for aimless sloth, whiskey and philandering, even without his money. And I still admired his taste in women, since Sarah Weddington was the only one of them I had ever met. Forty years ago she was the most beautiful woman I had ever seen, and the first time I saw her I fell asshole over teakettle in love.

We had been fishing up Seven Mile, my father and I, at the end of a long summer's afternoon, hard into the evening hatch and catching pan-sized cutthroat trout with each cast, when a random gust of wind or an artless back-cast lodged a 04 Royal Coachman all the way through my right ear. My old man couldn't find his wire cutters to clip off the barb, so we trudged through the lengthening shadows of the Hardrock Peaks across a newly mown hayfield toward the nearest house, a small farm house with a collapsing barn and a concrete-block toolshed behind it. I remember Sarah coming to the front door, a grown woman as shy as a girl, apologizing because her husband was away on a long trip and hadn't left her the keys to the toolshed, then apologizing still more because she didn't even have any coffee to offer us. My father, usually as glib as an auctioneer, must have been taken by this vision, this dream woman standing before us, because he too stood as silent as a stone. Her rich blond hair fell straight to her waist, the late afternoon sunlight glowed brightly across the smooth angles and planes of her lovely face, and her lush body seemed on the point of bursting through the thin housedress she wore. She asked if she might look at the fly in my ear, and I cocked my head like a daffy pup. Her long white fingers were cool on my blushing face. Finally my father found his voice: when he mentioned that he had a thermos of coffee down by the creek, she smiled and nodded slowly, almost sadly, as if she already knew what was about to take place.

We all hurried back across the hayfield to the creek, the Royal Coachman resplendent in my ear. They had coffee, then whiskey, and the next thing I knew, my old man and this strange, lovely woman were heading back hand in hand upstream through the willows.

'Keep working that hole, Bud,' my father shouted over his shoulder, laughing, 'and if the worst comes to worst, stick your head in the water and see if you can catch some of those little bastards on your ear.'

At the time – I must have been seven or eight – I didn't think that was very funny. I sulked on a cool gravel bar, kicking rocks into the shallows, occasionally pausing to wiggle the fly riding on my ear, tugging it forward until I could just catch a glimpse of the hackles at the edge of my vision. It didn't hurt, but it tickled, and I grew enamored with the idea of wearing this gaudy decoration like a totem for the rest of my life. Or at least around the neighborhood for a few days. Until, perhaps, I felt the woman's cool fingers on my skin once more.

When Sarah and my father came back in the long mountain twilight, their arms around each other's waists, flushed and smiling, a deep, hollow ache filled me, followed by a flood of anger. I fled the creek side, leaving my fly rod and tackle box and the gunnysack of trout, plunged through the brush, snagging the fly on leaves and branches until I felt the string of warm blood eddy down my neck and across my chest, and ran breathless to where my father's Cadillac was parked beside Seven Mile Road.

'He'll be all right,' I heard my father say. 'He's my little buddy.'

As always, on the way back, we hit a couple of bars, my father drinking, silent and darkly grave, me silent, spinning on my bar stool, refusing the money he offered for the pinball machine. Finally he reached over, ruffled my hair, smiled, and said, 'You look like a pirate, Bud, or one of those goddamned Hottentots.' I thought he had said 'hot-to-trot' and I found that pretty funny, until I got home and showed my mother the fly in my ear and mentioned proudly that I hadn't shed a single tear. I also asked her if she didn't think I looked like one of those hot-to-trots, and she slapped the living hell out of me, Royal Coachman, bloody ear, and all. Hours later, when I finally fell asleep upstairs, I could still hear their angry voices rumbling in the huge old house.

After that, we fished Seven Mile two or three times a week during the season. Sometimes while my father worked a hole, standing thigh-deep in the cold water, his fly line stacked like a gossamer string over his head, Sarah and I sat on the bank, our feet cooling in the water, and she told me tales of men at arms and jousts, mountain glens rich with the smell of crushed heather. But never a word about her life.

Then, suddenly one summer, we no longer fished Seven Mile. In fact, my father packed his fly rod in its case and never took it out again. That fall, with an accident so carefully arranged that it took me thirty years to understand what had happened, he committed suicide late one night. I heard him tell my mother that he smelled a skunk and that he was going to get his shotgun; then as he lifted the Browning over and under out of the gun cabinet, he caught the trigger on the bolt of his elk rifle, and blew his head all over the living room.

2

'I'm sorry, Mrs Weddington,' I said as we sat down on one of the wicker couches facing the sun, 'it was so long ago, and this house . . . I'm sorry.'

'Please call me Sarah,' she murmured, then cradled her hands on the crook of her cane. 'And please don't apologize, Bud. I meant it to be a pleasant surprise, not a shock.'

'That's all right,' I said. 'It just took a moment to sort out all the memories.'

'Pleasant ones, I trust.'

'Oh, yes,' I lied, 'fond memories.'

'I saw your advertisement in the Yellow Pages when I came back from Europe – what was it? – ten or twelve years ago. I – I can't recall exactly,' she said, lifting her fingers to gently stroke her temple. 'I didn't know how you would react to hearing from – from the other woman in your father's life.' She smiled sadly, then forced cheer into her face. 'But I suppose your father had many other women in his life.'

'You're the only one I knew about.'

'Thank you for that kind lie,' she said. 'I meant to telephone many times, Bud, but I got involved with the restoration of this old white elephant, and then I – I had this damned stroke' – she clanked her cane against her leg brace – 'goddamned stroke . . . I'm sorry now that I didn't call. You look so much like your father, you know, nothing at all like that little boy with that fly dangling from his ear. Nothing at all, except for the black eye and the scrape on your forehead. You were always the most beat-up little boy I ever saw.'

'I was always biting off more than I could chew and sticking my nose in somebody's business,' I said. 'Some people never grow up.'

'But we all grow old,' she said, then continued, 'I never felt guilty

515

about the affair – you understand that it was a godsend for both of us – but I always felt slightly guilty for leaving you alone that first day, bleeding and so hurt.'

'Don't,' I said. 'I might have been a squirt but I wasn't a total dope. You guys looked great when you came back. I was pissed but I got over it.'

'I could tell,' she said. 'I was charmed . . . by you, such a brave little boy, and your father, such a bear of a man but so sweet and even more unhappy than I was, and the coffee . . . Perhaps that was the first time in the long history of the seduction of married women – outside of the Mormon Church, that is – that a wife was ruined by a cup of tepid coffee. Goddamned Harry, every time he went off on one of his dental peregrinations, he locked up the coffee in the toolshed so I wouldn't have neighbor ladies over for coffee, as if we had any neighbors out there – '

'Dental peregrinations?' I interrupted.

'Oh,' she said, 'you didn't know about any of that, did you?'

'No, ma'am.'

'Harry was a traveling dentist. He started out with a chair, a pedal-driven drill, and an old Reo truck. He hit all the small towns and ranches and homesteads in Montana. Did quite well for himself, the old bastard . . .' She seemed to drift away, into her own past, unshared.

'What happened?' I asked.

'Oh,' she said, coming back, misunderstanding, 'the old tightwad son of a bitch was changing a tire in a rainstorm over by Roundup and a cattle truck ran over him. Served him right. The old lecher always thought he'd die in the saddle. Or be gunned down by an angry husband . . . But you were asking about something else, weren't you? Forgive me, but since the – the stroke, I have a tendency to lose track of the conversation. Your father and I . . . well, your mother put a detective on him, don't you know, and she made Chet choose between you and me. She meant to take you back East . . .'

'I didn't know.'

'Ironic,' she said, 'that you would take up this sort of work.'

'Ironic,' I said, then stood up and walked toward the balcony, cursing all the divorce work I had done over the years.

'I'm sorry,' she said.

'No problem,' I said. 'It was a long time ago.'

But she was still back there. '. . . then your father had that – that horrible accident. I couldn't – couldn't do anything, come to the funeral, cry, I was already cried out, send flowers, throw myself in the grave with him, nothing . . . Then Harry was killed, and suddenly I was a very wealthy young woman . . . or perhaps not so young. All those years, being locked in that tiny, cheap little house out at Seven Mile had made an old woman out of me, long before my time.

'At first I spent as much of Harry's tightly hoarded money as I could – sailed around the world, twice, wore furs and jewels, drank champagne by the gallon, I lived like a queen, or a famous courtesan – the south of France, Scotland, Spain – lived out my revenge, praying that Harry was spinning in his grave like a pin-wheel.

'Then my looks began to fail, the wild nights grew so much like the night before that I couldn't tell one from another, so I came back home to Montana, came back – and please forgive an old woman's romantic affectations – came back to be near the memory of the only man I ever loved . . .

'I'm sorry, Bud, to go on, to stir up foul memories.'

'That's all right, Mrs Weddington,' I said. 'It's always seemed as if it happened yesterday to me.'

'How true that is, Bud,' she whispered. 'I remember that first day, the smell of the sun on the hayfield, the coffee' – she wiped her watery eyes with a brusque motion of her wrinkled hand, then she laughed – 'and the smell of the fish on your father's hands.' Pausing, she touched her lips with a stiff, knotty finger. 'Oh, I remember what I meant to say.'

'Yes, ma'am.'

'Please call me Sarah, Bud.'

'Yes, ma'am.'

'I suppose no one calls you Bud anymore.'

'No, ma'am.'

'I'm sorry,' she said. She seemed to falter, her hand rising again, touching her temple, her lips, then back up again, as if she could form the words with her finger. 'I know – I know I should know your given name, but I – I just can't find it in there. So many things are gone, just not there anymore . . . names, places, the faces of old friends . . . I'm truly sorry.'

'Most people just call me Milo,' I said.

'Milo,' she said quietly, resting her head on her hands holding the

517

cane; in a minute or two the young girl came barging into the room with a coffee pot and china cups on a silver serving tray, which she placed on the low table in front of us.

'Shall I pour, mum?' she asked in the worst parody of an English accent I had ever heard.

'Thank you very much, Gail,' Mrs Weddington said, raising her head, 'but I'm sure Mr. Milodragovitch will do the honors.'

'As you wish, mum,' she said, then curtsied, holding out the tails of her shirt. In the doorway she stopped, saying. 'If you need anything, Sarah, I'll be in the kitchen making zucchini bread, so just ring.' Then she was off again, waffle-stompers pounding down the stairs.

'Such a sweet child,' Mrs Weddington said as I poured the dark, rich coffee from the silver pot into delicate china cups.

Neither a child nor all that sweet, I thought as I raised the fragile cup in my trembling hands. I couldn't tell if the sharp quivering in my blood came from a lack of sleep, drug abuse, or the flood of memories.

'Who is she?' I asked, trying to settle in the present, but Mrs Weddington was involved with her coffee. She inhaled the warm fragrance for a long time, took a tiny sip, then set the cup back on its saucer and pushed it deliberately to the far side of the table.

'Oh, I do miss my coffee,' she sighed. 'I'm sorry, Bud, you were saying something . . .'

'I just wondered who that girl is.'

'Gail? Oh, she's my grandniece. I cannot abide nurses or house-keepers, so Gail has lived with me since she was a freshman at college. She has been delightful company these past years, and I will miss her dearly when she finishes her master's.'

'She takes care of the whole house and goes to graduate school at the same time?' I asked, impressed or amazed.

'Oh, goodness no,' she said, chuckling. 'One afternoon a week the two of us go out for a long leisurely lunch while a sanitation crew – "sanitation"? That can't be right, can it? Doesn't that mean "garb-age" these days?' She touched her forehead with the back of her wrist. 'Housecleaning,' she said, 'a housecleaning crew comes in, and when we come back – slightly tipsy, I must confess, very much against my doctor's advice – the house is sparkling again. As if by magic . . . Sometimes money seems almost magical, doesn't it?'

'I'm afraid I wouldn't know,' I said without thinking.

'But you must be quite well off! Your father's – '

'It's all tied up.' I said, 'But you were telling me about Gail.'

'Gail? Oh, yes,' she said, laughing. 'Gail and housecleaning. the poor child might be able to clean up the world when she finishes her degree in environmental engineering, or whatever it is, but I'm afraid she'll never be a housekeeper. Never.

'Oh, but I will miss her when she goes,' Mrs. Weddington added. 'Most of my friends are either dead or *old*, and Gail has filled that gap. She keeps me young.' Then she laughed again. 'However, I fear that the little devil has become rather an evil influence in my life.'

'Ma'am?' I said, afraid that I was in no shape to follow her meandering conversation.

'My politics have become embarrassingly radical,' she said. 'You should see some of the groups she makes me support. I know they are the sort of people the FBI watches constantly. And, much to my chagrin, I fear she has – You're not connected with the police, are you, Bud?'

'Anything but, ma'am.'

'I've become something of a "pothead," ' she said with a sweet smile.

'There are worse vices,' I said, trying not to giggle.

'Quite,' she admitted. 'Greed, penury, the lust for power and money that makes men rape this lovely country – quite a number of far more evil vices, I am sure, but still I find myself quite embarrassed about this little bit of pot smoking that I indulge in, quite.' Then she quickly put her fingers to her lips. 'Oh,' she whispered, 'Bud, you must forgive me. I promised myself that I would not become over-excited by your visit, but it seems I have – seems I have said "quite" nine times in the past ten seconds. Would you kindly excuse an old lady for a few moments.'

'Of course,' I said, standing up, not knowing what to expect. But Mrs. Weddington simply leaned her cane against the arm of the couch, folded her hands in her lap and let the heavily creased lids of her eyes fall softly shut. Within seconds her breathing grew deep and regular, and I assumed she had gone to sleep.

For a minute I stood around dumfounded, confused, like a mourner who has wandered into the wrong funeral parlor, then I picked up my cup and saucer and tiptoed in my squeaking boots outside to the balcony, set my coffee on the rail and lit a cigarette.

The balcony commanded a grand view of the old neighborhood and sat high enough so that I could see over the yellowing trees and up the valley of the Hardrock River as it flowed north into the Meriwether. On the eastern flank of the broad valley, the gently rounded humps of the Agate Range rolled south, and on the western side the mighty broken peaks of the Hardrocks, tough, hungry mountains, loomed stark over the fields and pastures of the wide, pleasant valley.

A case, I thought. I didn't mind if the old woman had only invited me for coffee and memories, didn't even mind the chunk of mad money gone to clean up my act. Already my new boots had begun to mould themselves comfortably to the knotty contours of my feet, and the leather jacket smelled sharp and clean like the interior of a new, expensive car. A fair trade, and the view a bonus. Twelve miles up the Hardrock, Seven Mile Creek still babbled merrily in my mind, brimful of pan-sized cutthroats, and the graceful loops of my father's fly line still hung in the air. Quarts of Lorelei beer still cooled in the arching curves under cut banks, and the print skirt of a lovely young woman still folded around her legs with the wind ... Though in truth I knew that an invasion of pastel tract houses cluttered the sides of Seven Mile, that the only trout there were shit-fed stockers, and that the young woman had grown old and crippled and was taking a nap in the solarium behind me. And the kid with the Royal Coachman in his ear, Hottentot that he meant to be ... well, God knows what became of the little fart –

'*Quite* the view,' Mrs. Weddington said behind me, and when I turned she smiled to let me know she meant this 'quite.' She looked refreshed, not rumpled and puffy as if after an uneasy sleep, but truly rested, the angles and wrinkles of her face somehow smoothed, softened, filled with peace. 'A beautiful view,' she added, 'but too often I find myself closing my eyes in hope of seeing the land as it once was back when we knew it.'

'I think I still have a crush on you, Mrs. Weddington,' I said.

'Sarah, please,' she ordered. 'And thank you for that charming lie. I take it that you are your father's son about women.'

'Worse, maybe. I've got enough ex-wives to start a basketball team.'

'Something in the blood,' she said softly. 'I hope there were no children.'

'Just one,' I said. 'He looks like his mother. He doesn't even have the name. When my wife remarried, her new husband adopted the boy, gave him his name.'

'Does he live here?'

'No, ma'am, he's a junior at Washington State,' I said and added conversationally, 'Did you have a nice nap?' Enough of my sordid past, I thought, enough.

'Not a nap,' she said, 'but a few moments of meditation – Gail taught me – and at my age much more relaxing than sleep. I have grown to hate sleep of late, which means, I suppose, that I fear death, which is unseemly in a woman of my years. I let Harry take so much of my life, though, that sometimes it seems as if my life has just begun and now that it is almost over.' She leaned against the rail, easing the weight off her braced leg.

'Would you like to sit down?'

'Not for a bit, thank you. The sun feels so good.' Then she said, 'I realize we haven't discussed our business yet, but if you would indulge the ramblings of an old woman with only half a brain left, I feel that you have a right to know why your father was so important to me.'

'Of course,' I said. 'I'll listen as long as you want to talk.'

'Thank you, Bud,' she said. 'I hope you are not just being polite.' She paused, and I could see her face visibly clench with effort. 'My father had a small ranch,' she began, 'down along the Missouri on the edge of the Breaks, one of those hard-luck little outfits where the man spends every waking hour trying to stay ahead of the bank notes falling due like some curse each year, and the children grow up as wild and skittish as jack rabbits, and the woman . . . ah, the woman looks as if she has spent her entire life in a coal mine, or in a root cellar gnawing on seed potatoes and withered apples.

'The only time I ever saw my mother smile was when she was reading Sir Walter Scott aloud to my sisters and me. Every winter she seemed to grow smaller and smaller through the cold months, then she would regain her stature in the spring. One spring, though, she kept getting smaller and smaller until she finally disappeared . . . into a spring blizzard without a coat.

'The summer I turned sixteen I ran away with the first man who

521

promised to take me as far away from that damn endless horizon as I could get. Or at least the first one who did not arrive on horseback. I had had a bellyful of men on horseback – gawky cowboys, all elbows and Adam's apples, shy when sober, mean when drunk, and they only talked to cattle, horses and each other, never to their women. So when old Harry Weddington rolled up in that Reo with his torture chair in the back . . . well, as they say, the rest is history.

'Everybody in eastern Montana assumed that Harry had seduced me – he had that sort of reputation, had been in that sort of trouble before, shot at by irate husbands and angry fathers, even had a piece of his heel shot off by a rancher over by Sidney – but the truth of the matter is that I did all the seduction that morning.

'Harry talked to me,' she said, somehow still amazed after all the years, 'he talked to me, and his hands were soft and gentle, his voice low and sweet, crooning . . . I remember the day perfectly, even remember the dress I was wearing, but have not the slightest notion what he said. Probably just his usual spiel to a frightened young girl in his chair. Whatever he said, though, it reached me. When he tried to take his fingers out of my mouth, I bit down, hard, and held on for dear life. Poor old Harry, he thought he was dead for sure, but then he realized what I wanted and thought all his lecherous dreams had come true.

'Of course,' she said with a bitter grin, 'once he had me, he didn't want me anymore, not as much, but we were already married – at my insistence – but he wanted to make sure that no other man had me, so he kept me locked away like some medieval princess out at Seven Mile . . .

'And if you hadn't caught that fly in your ear' – she paused, then patted my hand once softly – 'well, I hope you got over it,' she finished, then sighed as if *she* hadn't. 'Thank you for your indulgence,' she added. 'I hope I haven't presumed too heavily on a rather ancient and tenuous connection.'

'Don't be silly,' I said, sniffling, hoping it was the coke.

'Old women have little purpose in this world,' she said, 'so they usually become either mean or silly. I prefer silly.' She giggled, oddly, and the strength and composure seemed to melt off her face in the warm sunshine. Her hands began to skitter about, moving from the rail to her cane to her face as if she had lost something. 'And I fear you will think me even sillier when I-I tell you why I wanted to engage your-your services. It will-will take a moment to explain, you see, a moment . . . every neighborhood needs – every neighborhood has one – needs-needs one, every neighborhood has a busy-busy-busy . . .' Then her right hand flew toward her trembling lips, catching the edge of my saucer, flipped it and the cup over, the bone china glistening as it fell, tumbling in slow motion to the brick wall below, where they shattered in a glittering splash of sharp fragments.

'. . . Body,' she muttered to herself, 'body, goddammit, *body*, busy-body, busybody.' Her aching fingers pried at her temple, pleading with the throbbing veins as soundless tears poured down her cheeks.

'Sarah,' I said, taking her arm, 'would you like to sit down?'

'Please,' she murmured, 'thank you.'

As I led her back to the couch her arm quivered beneath my hand, a frail and pitiful anger trickling through her body. This time she slept. I found an Afghan and folded it around her legs, watched her until she fell into the regular sputtering breath of a sleep near death, then I took her cold cup of coffee out on the balcony, where I smoked and stared blindly back up the Hardrock Valley. I would have given anything for a good stiff drink.

In July of 1952 my outfit was making its third assault up the ruined slopes of Old Baldy, the one west of Ch'orwon, when a two-hundred-and-forty pound Hawaiian staff sergeant from G Company of the 23rd jumped into the shell hole where I had taken cover. He broke three of my ribs and my collarbone, and my left wrist so badly that it had to be pinned. He probably saved my life. In the nine days of fighting over Old Baldy, my outfit took eighty percent casualties.

Six weeks later, when I was at the Oakland Depot waiting for my medical leave to begin, the chaplain came by my bunk to tell me my mother had just died. It wasn't much of a surprise, since she had been in and out of hospitals for years, at first with imagined complaints but later with liver and stomach complications as a result of her secret drinking. Then the chaplain switched to his Dr. Kildare voice and gave me the kicker: she had hanged herself with her silk stocking at a fat farm in Arizona.

I spent my leave at the Mark Hopkins, smoking cigarettes and staring through the foggy afternoons at the Bay as if I could see the great ocean rolling beyond. Somewhere out there, the war, where I would not go again. Somewhere behind me, back East, my mother's grave, which I never saw. After my discharge I went to Mexico for

523

the first time, lost myself in a sea of mescal until I felt like an agave grub floating in the clear, fiery liquid.

Standing on Sarah's balcony, I wanted to fall back into the bottle one last time, bottom-out in some open sewer, but when I went to work for Colonel Haliburton, I had promised him that I would quit trying to kill myself with a whiskey bottle. So I drank schnapps, which I hated, and stayed fairly sober, but right then I longed for an ocean of whiskey, one last chance with self-destruction.

Twenty minutes later Sarah woke and excused herself shyly, then limped slowly toward the upstairs hallway. When she came back, she had combed her hair and freshened her light make-up, but the cosmetic changes weren't even skin-deep. She looked tired, afraid, sick unto death, but she forced a game smile, a sly wink, even a small lilt into the dark huskiness of her voice.

'I know you noticed the binoculars when you came in,' she said, 'and I assume you didn't think I was engaged in bird-watching.'

'No, ma'am.'

'Because of my view of the neighborhood, because of my loneliness, perhaps because of my addled mind – whatever, I have taken to watching my neighbors. It is an ugly habit, true, but I keep what I learn to myself.' She paused. 'And I am willing to pay your usual daily rate plus liberal expenses and a substantial bonus ...'

'To do what?' I asked, wondering if I had missed something.

'To satisfy an old woman's curiosity,' she answered, 'nothing more than that. Nothing illegal, I assure you, nothing complex or dangerous.'

'How?' I said, surprised that I felt a small pang of loss at the promise of nothing illegal, complex, or dangerous.

'Come with me,' she said as she raised herself slowly from the couch. I took her arm and followed her outside to the balcony. 'See that small park?' She pointed south-southeast to a wedge of green between Park and Virginia. 'Every Thursday afternoon for the past six weeks, two cars park there, a man in one, a young woman in the other – he looks to be in his forties and rather scruffy, and I would guess she is in her late twenties, an attractive young woman – and they sit in her car for an hour or so, talking, it seems.' Then Sarah turned to me. 'I would very much like to know who they are, what they talk about, why they meet like this. Could you do that for me?'

When I didn't answer immediately, she added, 'Or more to the point: Will you?'

'Well . . . ah, I don't know, I've – '

'What these people do is probably none of my business,' she said as she led me back into the solarium, 'but I can afford to indulge my curiosity.' She opened the drawer of the small table where the binoculars sat, took out a long white envelope, and set it on the table. 'This envelope contains five thousand dollars in cash, an assortment of my credit cards, which have been cleared for your use, and the license-plate number of the man's car – a Washington plate – the young woman arrives in a different automobile each time, rented, I assume. Are you interested?'

'I don't know what to say, ma'am. This is a little weird, you know.'

'I'm sorry, my dear boy,' she said, smiling, 'but rich old women are eccentric, not weird.'

'Of course.'

'Take a few days to think about it, if you like,' she said, putting the envelope back in the drawer and closing it slowly. 'If you would just let me know by Thursday morning what you decide. If you decide against it, perhaps you can recommend one of your colleagues.'

'I'll let you know.'

'And one last favor?'

'Yes, ma'am.'

'See that huge globe in the far corner?'

'Yes, ma'am.'

'It is, in fact, a liquor cabinet,' she said, smiling again, 'and inside you will find a large brandy snifter and a bottle of cognac. Would you please bring me three fingers and the joint sitting beside the snifter.'

Although it wasn't much past noon, I felt like joining the old woman, but the day had been so crazy already, I knew I wouldn't stop.

After I settled her in a lounge chair with her drink and the lit joint, she thanked me, and added, 'Please think about it seriously, Bud, but whatever you decide, please visit again, whenever you like.'

I promised both things, then kissed her soft old cheek and said goodbye.

Downstairs, I wandered toward the rear of the house until I found the large kitchen, where Gail was leaning against the counter, a textbook in one hand, a batter-coated beater in the other. I watched the tip of her pink tongue slide slowly up one of the blades.

'Lose your way, cowboy?' she asked without looking up.

'I need a broom and a dustpan,' I said. 'There seems to be a broken cup and saucer on the sidewalk.'

'Clumsy jerk,' she muttered.

'What time do you get out of lab tonight?' I asked.

'About ten. Why?'

'Want to meet someplace for a drink about eleven?'

'You married?' she asked.

'Not now.'

'You as old as you look?'

'Not nearly.'

'You going to wear normal clothes?'

'What's normal?'

'Okay, why the hell not,' she said, then smiled. 'I'll be at the Deuce about eleven. You know where that is?' Her smile grew wicked. The Deuce of Spades was a mountain-hippie, biker, dead-beat hangout, complete with watered drinks, bluegrass stomping, and aging freaks. Also my cocaine dealer, Raoul, spent most of his free time there.

'Sure,' I said, 'it's a date.'

'It's a drink,' she said. 'I'll let you know when it's a date.'

'Okay.'

'And that's the broom closet,' she said with a motion of her thumb.

When I came back inside to empty the dustpan, Gail asked me how Sarah was feeling.

'Tired,' I said. 'Those hikes down memory lane ain't always easy. But when I left, she had drink and smoke and sunshine.'

'She is one beautiful old lady,' Gail said.

'You should have seen her back when.'

'I've seen pictures,' she said. 'Do you look anything like your father?'

'Some.'

'Are you anything like him?'

'A lot poorer.'

'That's probably to your advantage,' she conceded. 'Is that your cowboy Cadillac hidden out front behind the lilacs?'

'You got it.'

'How many miles do you get to the gallon?'

'No idea, love,' I said. 'When it gets empty, I give some Arab a twenty-dollar bill and he gives me half a tank of gas.'

Gail gave me a sharp frown that should have cut me to the quick, or at least shamed me into a Volkswagen diesel Rabbit.

Outside, when I paused to unlock the door of my pickup, I glanced northwest and saw the high, telltale horsetail haze drifting swiftly south. Gail had been right: weather. The first serious wave of winter forming for an assault on the Meriwether Valley. Even in the sunshine I shivered and thought of Mexico. This winter, for damned certain sure, I would go. Even if I had to finally sell the last and only thing I owned in my name, my grandfather's three thousand acres of timber up in the Diablos, land he had stolen from the Benniwah Indians – a legal theft, but an outright theft nonetheless. I had had three recent offers: one from a rich kid from Oregan who wanted to horse-log the timber; one from an automobile-parts company in Detroit that wanted to turn it into a corporate hunting lodge; and one from the government, which wanted to include the land in the proposed Dancing Bear Wilderness Area.

The kid struck me as a smart-ass and he tried to impress me with a suitcase full of cash, the people from Detroit seemed bored by the whole deal, and the government . . . well, to hell with them. Wilderness areas were good ideas, but I still like chain saws and snowmobiles and four-wheel-drive vehicles too much to have to have them outlawed on my own ground in my own lifetime. As it was now, they had blocked my access to the land, so that I had to drive seventy miles out of my way – up to the Benniwah Reservation in the foothills of the Cathedrals, then across the old C, C&K Railroad sections, up past the abandoned mine to Camas Meadows – seventy miles, just to poach an elk on my own land.

Maybe Gail was right, and bulldozer and cowboy boot mentality had ruined Montana. Or maybe the Indians were right, and the land belonged to itself. Whatever, this particular piece of rough, sidehill timber and open meadow belonged to me. Maybe, I thought as I climbed in my pickup, trying to ignore the cold front coming, maybe I would do Sarah Weddington's crazy job, grab her money and take the sort of Mexican vacation my father would have loved.

3

The swiftly moving Arctic front hit Meriwether in midafternoon with thundering gusts of wind that swept the street clean of all those people still dressed in light clothes who believed in Indian summers that lasted forever. Then a stiff, cold rain began to fall, sliding down the wind. By the time I headed across town to pick up a car at the Haliburton offices, the temperature had dropped into the thirties and the raindrops hit my windshield in slushy pellets.

As I swung left off Railroad onto Dottle, I noticed one of Haliburton's armored trucks parked at an odd angle in the lot in front of Hamburger Heaven. The driver, leaning out of his door, his revolver dangling from his hand, shouted at the passing traffic, occasionally lifting the pistol and aiming it at cars. During the few moments it took me to drive down the short block of Dottle, I saw four cars and a beer truck bolt like frightened cattle right through the red light.

The driver's eyes glowed in the ashen light, drunk or drugged or simply crazed. The man, whose name I couldn't remember, was one of Colonel Haliburton's basket cases, a Vietnam vet with a good war record and a terrible employment history. The colonel was a do-gooder, one of those unusual career military men who also think of themselves as soldiers in God's compassionate army. He had given this guy a chance at a steady job, but things didn't seem to be working out too well.

After I parked my pickup on the other side of the armored truck, I tore my uniform coat open, loosened my collar and tie and mussed my hair, thinking that if I looked as disheveled as the driver did, he might not waste me out of hand. I had never been a master of disguise, though, and when I stepped around the back of the truck and said hello, the driver dropped out of the door into a combat stance and laid a bead right on the old trembling thorax area.

'What the fuck are you doing here, man?' he asked, his voice shaking and his knuckles white on the butt of the .38.

'Oh, shit,' I said, 'I don't exactly know.' And I meant it.

'Just like over there, right, dad? Nobody fucking knew.' I didn't have to ask where *there* might be. 'Nobody knew, and you don't know shit from wild honey about it, dad, what it was like.'

'I spent time on the line in Korea,' I offered lamely.

'Korea?' he sneered. 'The line? Well, kiss my rosy red ass.' Then he lifted the revolver straight up into the gray, windy rain, pulled the trigger six times, six flat ugly splats as the hammer fell on empty chambers. He laughed wildly as he tossed his piece onto the front seat of the armored truck. 'Tell the colonel to stuff his charity, right, and his goddamned empty guns. I ain't much into limited warfare, man. If I'd gone to Canada, dad, I'd have both my kidneys and all my marbles, right? Ain't it the shits.' He sighed, shook his head, then stumbled off toward the nearest bar, the Deuce down on Railroad, his lank hair poking wetly from under his uniform cap.

I stood there a long time, it seemed, the cold rain seeping down my collar, then decided I wasn't going to wet my pants or collapse into a frightened puddle, so I locked up the truck, took the keys and the empty .38, then drove very carefully across town, trying not to look at the bars. Some security outfits, I had read, equipped their rent-a-cops with rubber guns for their own safety. Symbolic fire power, I thought, an idea whose time has come. The .38 that I carried at work, wrapped in its holster belt on the front seat of the pickup, was, like the driver's, empty. By choice. A few years back, when I still worked for myself, I had killed two men at close range, and although I couldn't bear to throw away all that lovely, lethal machinery I had collected over the years, I did throw all my live rounds into the Meriwether River.

Haliburton's had me working relief that shift, filling in for piss-calls and dinner breaks for the first four hours, easing around the now freezing streets in my yellow Pinto with the little blue light on the roof – barbecue pits on the hoof, we called them – my door unlocked and my seat belt off. As happened every winter, most of the drivers in Meriwether seemed to have forgotten all about ice during the summer months and they drove as if the streets were bare and dry, which made my job more dangerous than philosophical discussions about war as an arm of diplomacy with armed crazy people. Dangerous, but so goddamned boring. And I felt like a clown dressed in my brown-on-brown uniform with its old-fashioned Sam Browne belt like a mule's harness across my chest.

At least the last four hours of my shift would be warm and safe, off the streets, sitting behind a sheet of one-way mirrored glass in the back room of an EZ-IN/EZ-OUT twenty-four-hour convenience market and filling station out on South Dawson. Warm because I had a small electric heater for my feet, and safe because we had video tapes of the guy we were trying to catch who had been knocking over convenience markets all over town, a tall, skinny kid in a ski mask who we knew owned a police-band radio because he only hit stores when the police were busy with fires or drunken wrecks out on the interstate, and who held the clerks at bay with what looked like a starter's pistol. In Montana, where we have more guns than people and cattle, maybe even trees, this dude had been knocking them down with a goddamn blank pistol.

After I checked in with the Haliburton dispatcher on the company band, I settled into the little room, turned on the police scanner and the CB radio, checked the television cameras and the tape monitor, then made a fresh pot of coffee. Sipping that first good cup out of the pot, I thought about Sarah, the way she savored the smell, enjoyed her tiny sip. Most of the time, instead of considering old age and preparing myself for some wise gentle assaults on those last years, I thought about fifty-two and my father's money. My final days might not take too long when they came around, but I intended to enjoy them.

The CB crackled in the background. Out on the interstate where it sliced through the northern edge of the city limits, long-haul truckers were complaining about the slick roads, their piles, and Smokey the Bear. On the police scanner, all the units were too busy with a rash of fender benders and resultant fistfights to complain. Ah, winter wonderland, I thought as I leaned back in the swivel chair and stared through the one-way glass, down the aisle, and out the glass front of the store. Across the street, the blue blinking light of the Doghouse Lounge made it look like a more romantic and mysterious place than it really was. It was a workingman's place, and the parking lot was full of pickups with rifles racked in rear windows. At least they served whiskey there, and I could think about a drink as I watched the customers string through the store, grumbling about the thirty percent extra they paid for *convenience*.

Two teenaged girls on their way to the movie down the street used the mirror side of the glass to make certain that their eyelashes were as thick and furry as tarantula legs, giggling about some poor unsuspecting lad named Shawn they planned to surprise at the theater, then they gaggled away in a cloud of youthful laughter. A bit later a lanky kid came in, swiped a can of Coke and a package of red licorice rope, stuffing them into the game pocket of his 60/40 parka, then spent a few minutes working on his zits in the mirror before he left, paying for a package of gum. I started to hit the shoplifter switch, but the clerk behind the counter had his nose in a motorcycle magazine, and I decided this shoplifter was Shawn of the giggles and already in more trouble than he could handle, so I let him walk. In the days before juveniles had legal rights, a shop-lifting bust could be worked out between the parents and the store manager. But legal rights meant paperwork, which in turn meant records, and no governmental body of any size, shape or function had ever found a way to dispose of records. After the kid had gone, I went out front, paid for the candy and Coke, and made sure the clerk rang up the sale instead of skimming it.

About nine-thirty, with an hour left on my shift, a seven-car pile-up blocked the Dawson Street bridge, and an 'every available unit' call went out on the police band. Fifteen minutes later out on the interstate, a semi-load of frozen turkeys locked its trailer brakes, skidded on the iced pavement, and jackknifed into the median, spreading toms and hens like small boulders all over the landscape.

Meriwether lived off lumber, and with interest rates up and hous-ing starts down, two mills had closed their saws forever the previous summer, and the pulp mill had been on half shifts for three months. So Meriwether was chock-full of surly unemployed folks facing a Thanksgiving with little to be thankful for and a Christmas even more grim. When news of the turkey wreck swept through town by CB radio and telephone, a lot of unhappy people piled into their four-wheel-drive rigs and headed for the highway, muttering 'Thanksgiving' under their collective breaths, 'Christmas.' I cheered them on. They might as well have the turkeys because the USDA

531

would show up the next day, condemn the meat, and consign it to the dump.

As riots go, it didn't sound like a big one, but large enough to involve three sheriff's deputies and two highway police patrolmen. No fatalities, either, just two broken legs when a drunk on a snowmobile ran down a housewife in the median, and a minor concussion when her husband knocked the drunk off the snowmobile with a well-aimed twelve-pound hen.

Unfortunately, I wasn't paying attention to business. When I stopped laughing long enough to glance up, a tall skinny kid in a ski mask held a small pistol behind a loaf of white bread while the frightened clerk shoveled bills and change into a paper bag between frightened looks cast my way. I wasn't ready; the rusty snap on my holster took forever to open and I couldn't have loaded my piece if I had wanted to. I hit the silent alarm, even though the police units were all busy, slipped out the door, hid behind the upright Coke cooler. When the bandit turned away from the cashier, I leapt out into the aisle to do my bit for law and order and the American way of life.

'Police!' I shouted. 'Freeze!'

Well, it works on television. But this guy jumped three feet in the air and got off two rounds at me before his bandit shoes hit the tile floor. Starter's pistol, my ass; the video tapes had lied. I dove back behind the cooler, then bellied over to peek under the potato-chip rack just as the kid hit the front door. He didn't make it out, though. Two fiery muzzle flashes flamed out of the Doghouse parking lot, followed by the roar of high-velocity hunting rifles. The kid spun wildly, scattering folding money and change as he fell into a rack of motor oil and antifreeze beside the door. A whole shelf of onion-and-sour-cream-flavored potato chips exploded over my head, and a rack of Coke cans crashed through the glass doors and fell on my back, hissing like angry snakes.

Two more muzzle flashes came out of the parking lot. The rounds popped through the plate glass, spraying fragments like grenade shrapnel, ripped out whole shelves of dry and canned goods, snipped through the glass doors of the beer cooler behind me, releasing a sea of foam.

'Had enough in there?' somebody shouted from across the street.

I, for one, certainly had, but I was curled too tightly into a damp ball to answer. The bandit, though, grunted 'Fuck you, white-eyes,' then let off a useless round into the ceiling. The rifles answered with a four-round volley, and the whole interior of the store seemed to explode. Even a row of fluorescent lights on the twelve-foot ceiling disintegrated, the shards of tubes drifting like snow through the dust.

'Enough now?' the voice shouted again, laughing.

'Enough!' I screamed, then started to throw my piece out into the aisle until I remembered I was supposed to be one of the good guys. I stood up, praying the bastards could see my uniform under the soggy coat of chips. Behind me I could hear rivers of cold beer rushing and a punctured aerosol can wheezing in a slow circle. Out front, two men darted across the street like some dream of combat infantryman under attack. When they didn't shoot, I stuffed my empty revolver back into the wet holster, then went up front to separate the dead from the dying.

Somehow the clerk hadn't been hit. When he saw me, he leapt from his hiding place beneath the counter, vaulted over it, and ran out the door into the freezing rain without a jacket. I knew the kid in the ski mask had been hit, knew it was going to be bad, with the way hunting rounds mushroomed and fragmented on impact and killed with hydrostatic shock. He looked dead, too, where he lay in a pool of antifreeze, oil, and blood. But when I tried to pry the cheap .22 revolver out of his hand, he had live resistance in his fingers.

Two guys wearing down vests over flannel shirts, their scoped elk rifles at port arms, charged through the front door. I asked for their help as I tried to ease the kid out of the muck, but they were too busy admiring their handiwork. When I asked a second time, louder, the nearest one said 'Fuck him' and nudged the bandit's arm with a heavy hunting boot.

'Hey, that's right,' I said, standing up, 'we're the good guys and we don't have to mess with shit like this.' When I tried for a good-old-boy grin, it felt as if my face cracked. 'Damn good shooting,' I said. 'What the hell you guys using?' I reached for the nearest one's rifle. He let me have it rather absent-mindedly as he stared wide-eyed around the ruined store. When I hit his buddy in the forehead with the rifle butt, he still didn't seem too concerned. He had enough sense left to shake his head at me once, but maybe he didn't shake it hard enough. I took him out, too, then dragged them outside and cuffed one's wrist to the other's through the front-door handle. Up close, there seemed to be some family resemblance between them, except that one's forehead hung over his eyes and the other's nose was three inches wide and flapjack-thick. Then I quickly unloaded their rifles and made junk out of them against the curb.

When I got the bandit out of the slippery mess to a fairly clean part of the floor, I slid off the ski mask, and a long stream of bubbly froth looped out of his mouth. He was just a kid, maybe twenty, with the dark coppery skin and flat round face of a Benniwah. When I cut off his shirt and jacket, I saw that he had the small delicate chest of a malnourished child. The round had taken him just below the right collarbone. Because the bullet must have been wobbling after passing through the plate glass, it caused an unusually large entrance wound, and the exit wound through his shoulder blade was as large as the bottom of a beer can. The round must have clipped the top of his lung, too, because both wounds were sucking air. Finally I found enough gauze pads on the shelf to pack them, and I bound them tightly with tape.

By then the inevitable crowd had begun to gather from the bar and the theater and the vehicles parked along the street to see the real blood, the real dying. While I was working on the kid they had stayed back, staring through the ruined windows, and they shied from my glances as if they had seen a caged animal they were afraid to recognize. As usually happens, too, some had come to help. One man held the crowd at bay, another took a flashlight and waved passing cars past the store, and a stout young woman wearing glasses and a full-length leather coat pushed through the crowd. She slipped out of her coat, under which she wore a long pink wool dress. 'I'm a nurse,' she said calmly as she came through the door and draped her coat over the kid. 'Are you okay?' she asked as she patted my cheek.

'A little shaky,' I said, 'but the kid's hurt bad.'

We knelt beside him and noticed that his breath turned sour and shallow, rattling, bloody spittle snaking out of his mouth. She took his pulse, and it seemed I could feel his blood flow dwindle to a thread under her fingers.

'We're losing him,' she said quietly, staring at me over the narrow, bottomless gulf.

She got on his chest, and I propped his chin back, checked to see if he had swallowed his tongue, then pinched his pug nose and started the mouth-to-mouth. Sometimes we can breathe for each other, muscle the heart. Somehow we kept him going ten, maybe fifteen minutes until the EMS technicians arrived with the ambulance. He seemed to be breathing on his own when they strapped him onto the stretcher. The nurse tossed her coat to a man she seemed to know – a husband or a date – and the two of us leaned against the counter breathing hard for ourselves, then we fell into each other's arms so hard that it knocked off her glasses, held each other like old lovers. Over her shoulder I could see her date or husband or whatever holding her bloody coat as if it were something he had found in the street.

After most of the police had come and gone, after I had stood ankle-deep in the back cooler for half an hour, breaking my schnapps vow and drinking beer after beer, then promptly throwing them up, I went out front to stand in the freezing rain with Colonel Haliburton and the chief of police, Jamison, my old buddy, asshole buddy from childhood, Korea, adopted father of my son. The three of us stood outside, even beyond the roof of the overhang, as if somebody had died inside the store, and watched three Haliburton uniformed guards set up sawhorse and rope barricades around the lot. The young couple who managed the store, dressed in matching maroon bathrobes and white flannel pajamas covered with tiny red and green reindeer, huddled in the dim, smoky light just inside the front door. Occasionally one or the other would break into a tiptoe trot through the mess to pick up a can of dog food or a box of breakfast cereal off the floor, place it carefully on the shelf, then gently straighten the row.

'They might as well have used hand grenades,' the colonel said softly, shaking his head.

'Fucking assholes,' I muttered.

The colonel lifted his flat cap off his balding head and frowned into the darkness, away from me. In spite of all his years in the Army, profanity still embarrassed him as much as it must have when he was a good little Lutheran farm boy growing up outside Grand Forks, North Dakota. He cleared his throat in disapproval, then stared even harder into the distance, as if he were watching the fresh snow on the Hardrocks. 'I don't know how you do it, Milo,' Jamison said sadly. 'I don't know how you get into so much trouble.'

535

'Just lucky, I guess.'

He looked at me hard and for a long, silent time. We hadn't been friends since I was bounced off the sheriff's department for looking the other way from some illegal punchboards. Then he married my first ex-wife and adopted my son, which hadn't improved our affairs.

'I would like to see you in my office tomorrow morning,' Jamison said bluntly, 'eight A.M. sharp, Milo, not one minute later.' He paused and ran his hand through his rain-wet hair. 'Why did you have to break up their rifles?' he added. 'Why?'

'The heat of passion,' I said.

'Just be there,' he said, 'because I think you've bought the farm this time.' Since Evelyn – my ex-wife, his wife – had recently left him to take up residence with a twenty-eight-year-old vegetarian French professor at Reed College in Portland, Jamison had trouble focusing his anger on me. 'Just be there,' he repeated.

'Ah-hem,' the colonel said, 'my lawyer will be there also.' Then he walked over to comfort the young couple. I started to follow him.

'Just a minute, Milo,' Jamison said. 'I've been meaning to call you. Evelyn has this idea that we have to be civilized about all this shit.'

'Civilized,' I said. 'What shit?'

'You and me and her and the boy,' he sighed, 'and whatever it is she lives with. She says we should all be adults about this, and she's got tickets to the Washington State-Stanford game, and she wants us all to gather on neutral ground to watch the boy play.'

'How's he doing?' I asked. Eric played defensive end for the WSU Cougars.

'Great,' Jamison said, nearly smiling. 'He's started the last three games. Kicking ass. Or so I read in the papers. I haven't been able to get away for a game this year.'

'I'll think about it,' I said, 'even though I don't want to.'

'Call me,' he said, 'and I'll see you in the morning.' Then he stalked away in the rain, some of which had turned to sleet. The tiny white pellets gathered on the stooped shoulders of his tweed overcoat.

When I turned around, the colonel had his hands on the young couple's arms, reassuring them all over again that his men would hang plywood sheets over the broken windows and would watch the store for the rest of the night. Then he gave them a gentle shove toward their Toyota pickup. The wife burst into tears and her husband looked as if he wanted to do the same, but he just clutched a milk carton to his chest so tightly that it leaked down the front of his robe as they walked away.

The colonel strode over to me, saying, 'I want you to know that the entire legal resources of the corporation are at your disposal, Milo.'

'Even if I quit?' I said.

'Even if you quit,' he said, 'but don't quit.' The colonel had some romantic notion that because I had once worked a one-man office he had to keep me employed just in case he ever needed my old-fashioned, peculiar talents. 'Don't quit.'

'Sir, I can't stand any more of this monkey-suit business.'

'Boredom and the bottle,' the colonel said, looking at his ox-blood cordovans. His wife, it was rumored, drank. 'Oh, Lord,' he whispered, 'there's just no call these days ... but I did get a query from an outfit on the Coast today. They needed someone to tail a woman for a couple of days until they can get their own security people on it. I don't know the outfit, but I'll accept the job, and you can do it, then take a week or so off, with pay of course, to think about it.'

'Jesus,' I said, suddenly so tired that my head seemed to spin. 'Sir, I just don't know – '

'Two weeks,' he said, 'as a favor to me.'

'Only because you ask.'

'Thank you,' he said. 'I want you to know that you handled that incident with Simmons this afternoon perfectly. I do appreciate that, Milo.'

'Simmons?'

'The driver of the armored truck.'

'Never can remember that kid's name,' I admitted. 'I just happened to be passing by, sir, and I didn't really do anything.'

'Which was perfect,' he said, then added to nobody in particular, 'I've got to get that boy some help, somehow.' Then he turned back to me, extended a hand. 'I do thank you, though.'

'Anytime,' I said, shook his hand, then loaned him my handkerchief so he could wipe the sticky Coke slime off his hand.

'I'll leave the woman's name and address with the dispatcher,' he said, 'and you can pick it up after your, ah, chat with Jamison ... You don't mind if I ask about the trouble between the two of you?'

'A long story,' I said. 'History.'

'I see,' he said, then waved aimlessly as he marched off toward his gray Mercedes, a staunch, stocky, erect figure of a man, a good soldier to the end. The colonel had retired to Meriwether and started a small security service so he could afford his fishing trips, but he was too good at the business. It kept expanding. First into alarm systems, then into armored transport, then into branch offices all over the Mountain West. I knew for a fact that he hadn't wet a fishing line in over two years.

When he started the engine of his Mercedes, the diesel clattered loudly. I wondered what sort of man tried to keep aging detectives out of the bars, to provide jobs for half-crazed Vietnam vets, and drove a thirty-five-thousand-dollar automobile that sounded like a truck, wondered, as always, what to think about the colonel. Usually, professional military men and successful businessmen gave me a pain in the ass, but I liked the colonel. I didn't even mind that he had stolen my handkerchief.

When I walked around to the rear of the store to pick up the Pinto, the cold beer in my shoes felt like frozen slush, and most of the glass had been blown out of the little tin car by errant rounds. Only a railroad embankment behind the store had saved the two vigilantes from spreading misery and mayhem throughout the neighborhood. I wiped the shards of safety glass off the front seat, as best I could in the darkness, then drove across town to pick up my truck, the sleet funneling into my face through the broken windshield.

By the time I had showered the soda syrup and chips out of my hair and off my back, changed clothes, and indulged myself in a short toot, I felt as old as I was ever going to get. Even though I was already an hour late for my meeting with Gail, I heaved myself off the couch, eased the pickup over the icy streets down to the Deuce, where a bluegrass band fretted through its last set. She was nowhere to be found in the crowded bar or among the dancers stomping on the floor. Even Raoul, my dealer, had gone home. I saw a biker gang I knew, but we didn't exchange greetings, and the armored-truck driver, whose name I had forgotten again, still in his Haliburton uniform, sleeping at a table in the shadows beside the back door. I gave up and walked across the street to Arnie's, a bar for serious drinkers, where nobody either cared or noticed if your hands trembled so badly that it took both of them to get a shot of schnapps to your mouth.

I saw my postman there, though, also still in the baggy sack of his borrowed uniform, but he had a fat lip I hadn't given him, so I had one shot, then went home to my little log house in the canyon.

Since the colonel's lawyer – a sharp young dude dressed in Western clothes and wearing, fastened to his string tie, what looked to be the piece of turquoise the size of an elk turd that I hadn't bought – and I were both on time the next morning, the police took my statement politely and with a minimum amount of fuss and bother. Jamison didn't even show up.

When I got to the Haliburton offices, the colonel hadn't come in either, so I picked up the name and address from the dispatcher. A wildly impressive name, Cassandra Bogardus, but a rather shabby address over on the north side beyond the tracks, 1414 Gold. None of the women I knew on the north side could afford the sort of trouble that called for a two-hundred-a-day tail. I didn't really care, though, because I was so glad to be out of uniform. Two days of this, I thought, then I can do Sarah Weddington's crazy number and head south.

I signed for a white Chevy van without checking the fake magnetic signs on the doors, transferred my surveillance gear to the van from my pickup, and headed for the north side of town. By ten o'clock that morning I was on station half a block down Gold from the Bogardus house.

The freezing rain and sleet had, as the weatherman had predicted, changed to snow, and the temperature had stabilized in the low twenties. Weather, as Gail had said. But it didn't bother me; I had all the comforts of home. A snowmobile suit and down booties kept me snug and warm as I lounged in the plastic web of a lawn chair in the back of the van. If I leaned forward a bit, my eye nestled easily against the 25X spotting scope that hid behind the smoked glass of the rear window. On my right I had a huge thermos of coffee, egg salad on rye with a slice of Walla Walla white onion as thick as my finger – and if nature called, I was ready. In the corner of the van sat a Port-a-Potty like a faithful robot companion prepared for duty. I might not know why I was doing what I was doing, but I had done enough in the old days to know how to do it in comfort.

539

The Bogardus house sat on a large corner lot. An untrimmed hedge and clumps of shrubbery drooped under the load of heavy wet snow. Two vehicles were parked in the driveway – a beautifully restored 1964 Mustang convertible with New Hampshire plates, and a brand-new three-quarter-ton 4×4 GMC pickup with a load of firewood in the bed and Maryland plates. Firewood, neatly split and stacked, also covered most of the side porch. In the backyard, a huge compost pile stood next to a large garden already winter-bedded and covered with straw. The small window in the front door showed no light in the gray, snowy day, and the other windows were dark behind half shutters and tie-dyed drapes. A wisp of woodsmoke trickled out of the chimney, though, curling among the large drifting flakes.

I settled in for the waiting, oddly excited to be working again. During the next two hours, while nothing happened, I decided that Sarah's job might be fun – picking up two unknown people, filling in their history, finding out what sordid little secrets drew them to their weekly rendezvous. An old Chicago cop had taught me how to tail by choosing a perfect stranger off the street and making me dog the man or woman for days on end, put them to bed at night, wake them in the morning. I was surprised to find out how few strangers, when I watched their lives for a few days, turned out to be perfectly boring. Almost everybody, it seemed, led at least one secret life. Except me. I was the watcher, the uninvolved observer. Sometimes a boring job, but usually safe.

Or so I thought until I was halfway into my first sandwich and somebody started pounding on the side of the van. With the blackout curtain hanging behind the front seats and the smoked glass in the rear windows, I knew nobody could see inside, so I sat very still until a face peered blindly through one of the back windows. I peeked out of the other one. It was a wiry old man in house slippers, shiny black slacks, and an old-fashioned undershirt. He wore a huge mustache, yellowed with age but neatly trimmed and combed, long enough to nearly reach his defiant little chin. The hands of a much larger man dangled off his corded arms. He raised one of them and slapped the smoked glass hard enough to shake the van.

'I know you're in there, you lazy son of a bitch!' he shouted, then slapped the glass again while I ducked away.

When he grabbed the rear bumper and began rocking the van, I gave up. 'I'm coming,' I shouted, 'I'm coming.' Then, swaddled in the snowmobile suit and as clumsy as a drunken bear, I wrestled through the blackout curtain and out the passenger door.

'I called you sons a bitches yesterday afternoon,' the old man said when he saw me, 'yesterday goddamned afternoon. And you promised you'd be here before noon. So what the hell do you do? Show up and take a snooze right in front of my yard.' Then he shook a fist the size of a steer's kneebone under my nose, and tiny drifts of snow fell off his bare shoulders. As he looked at me, his eyes didn't seem to focus correctly, and I saw the pinched creases on the bridge of his nose where his glasses usually rested.

'Why me?' I muttered as I stepped backward to see what sort of sign hung on the van's door. Not Floral Delivery or Washing Machine Repairs, not Knife Sharpening or Housecleaning Services – nothing safe for me – but TV REPAIR in large black letters.

'Well?' the old man said, raising his fist again.

'I don't know what you're talking about,' I said. 'You must have talked to the girl in the office.'

'Didn't talk to no girl,' he growled, 'talked directly to you.' Snowflakes gathered in his eyebrows and on his thin hair began to melt, but the old man ignored the icy water trickling down his wrinkled face.

'Not to me,' I said, 'you didn't talk to me.' Then I chanced a glance at the sign. 'Not to me – Clyde "Shorty" Griffith,' I read.

The old man looked at me as if I was crazy. He raised one woolly eyebrow as if to say, 'What sort of damn fool has to read his name off a sign to remember it?' Then he squinted at the sign again, shifted his shoulders, and grumbled. I thought I had him until he said, 'Did so.' Even caught in confusion and blindness the old man wasn't about to retreat. 'Damn sure did.'

'Couldn't have,' I said, retreating myself. 'I . . . ah, I was out with the flu.' Then added with a whine, 'And I wasn't taking a nap, I was having lunch.'

'Whiskey flu,' he said, 'and a two goddamned hour whiskey lunch.'

'No way,' I said, but the old man had me backing up so fast that I didn't even believe myself anymore. 'Not true.'

'Well,' he said, licking the snow water off his mustache, 'you damn sure promised, Mr. Whatever-your-name-is, to have my TV fixed before one o'clock' – he tugged a large Hamilton railroad watch out of his pants, consulted it about six inches from his face – 'and I've got a lady friend coming over in forty-seven minutes to watch *General Hospital*, and if my set ain't fixed by then, I'm gonna call the Better Business Bureau, maybe even the county attorney ... you people think you can treat old folks like shit ... well, I'm here to tell you that don't go with Abner Haynes – '

'Okay,' I said, thinking I had run into enough crazy people in the past two days to last me a lifetime. If my cover hadn't already been blown, it certainly would be if I spent any more time in the street debating the issue with the old man. I needed to move the van now, anyway, so maybe if I took a few moments to run his set downtown to a repair shop, leave it, and rent a loaner, then I could race back, drop it off, and find another location quickly. I glanced at the Bogardus house. Nothing had moved. Maybe it would work, unprofessional as it was. Maybe I had been a security guard too long. 'Listen, pops,' I said to the old man, 'I don't know nothing about this call, okay, but I'll take a quick look at your set – I can't promise to fix it here, may have to run it to the shop and pick up a loaner – '

'Don't you "pops" me, you ugly bastard,' he grunted when he found his voice under the anger. He was giving away sixty pounds and twenty-some-odd years, but he didn't care. Either I apologized, and quickly, or he was going to take a poke at me.

'Listen,' I said, 'I'm sorry.'

'My name is Abner Haynes,' he said, his fists still clenched. 'Mr. Haynes to you, by God.'

'Yes, sir, Mr. Haynes,' I said. 'Now if I could take a look at your set?'

Abner shrugged and sighed, then led me toward his little frame house. The sidewalk in front of his yard, his walk and his porch steps had been shoveled often enough since the snow started so that they were bordered by substantial drifts, and the old man had carefully scattered rock salt on the concrete. The rose bushes by the porch had been pruned and wrapped in burlap, and even under six inches of snow I could tell that Abner's lawn lay as smooth and level as a golf green.

When I stepped out of the cold and into Abner's living room, I broke into an immediate, showering sweat. I wiped my forehead and Abner chuckled.

'That old sawdust furnace works like a charm,' he said proudly. 'Smells good and don't smoke at all, and,' he added, 'those goddamned environmentalists with their smoky wood stoves . . . Ha! Fools. Almost every house in the neighborhood had wood or sawdust furnaces when they were first built. Then all those fools who thought they was progressive, they switched to natural gas – ain't nothing natural about burning something you can't see or smell, something that's as likely to turn a man's house into kindling wood as keep it warm . . .'

Abner carried on about the state of the world and the nature of progress while I looked at the wall covered with framed pictures above the television set: Abner in his gandy dancer days, young and cocky, as lean and tough as the hickory handle of his pick, as sturdy as the stack of ties he leaned against in some mountain pass, his mustache as black as India ink and as big as the switch on a cow's tail; Abner's wedding picture with him standing a head shorter than his large blond wife; Abner as brakeman, fireman, conductor . . . Abner's life captured in fading yellow prints.

'. . . so what's with my TV?' he asked and tried to poke me in the ribs through the bulk of the snowmobile suit.

I didn't have any idea – it looked as if the bottom half of the picture had folded itself halfway back up the tube – but I knew how to make it work long enough for me to move the van and take off those goddamned signs.

'Well, what you've got there, Mr. Haynes,' I said, 'is an ABS forty-two-slash-eleven tube going bad on you, and I can tell you right now, sir, that I ain't got one on the truck, maybe not even one in the shop – don't get much call on that model these days – but I can make it work for a couple of hours, and I'll put that tube on order just as soon as I get back to the shop.' Then I began to disconnect the set, wrapped the cord around it, and picked up the huge old-fashioned, misnamed 'portable' color set.

'Where the hell you going with my TV?' he asked.

'Well, sir,' I grunted, 'I'm gonna set it out on the porch here and let that ABS tube cool off – you see, when it gets too hot, the resistance builds up and it pulls off the aim of the gun –'

'The gun?' he interrupted.

'Trust me,' I said. 'I'll leave it outside while I finish my lunch, then at five to one I'll carry it back inside and hook it up for you.' Abner looked extremely doubtful. 'Believe me, sir, it'll work,' I said.

543

'One time I watched the whole second half of a Raiders-Jets game sitting in a snowstorm with a garbage bag over the top of my set – '

'A garbage bag?'

'God's truth,' I said, and it was.

'Well,' Abner said, tugging on the corner of his mustache, 'I guess we can give it a try, but if it don't work, I know Yvonne'll sneak over to that damn Tyrone's, even though he's only got a black-and-white, to watch her soap . . .'

Abner opened the front door, still worrying, and I put the set down on the porch and headed for the van before he could find a new argument, promising to keep an eye on his TV while I finished my lunch.

Nothing had changed at the Bogardus house, and nothing happened while I waited. The whole neighborhood seemed frozen, except for two children, who looked like bear cubs in their snowsuits, and a malamute pup playing in a yard down the street. At five to one I lugged the set back into Abner's house and connected the antenna wires, and it worked like a charm. Once again I promised to order him a new tube, and Abner reached into his pocket and asked how much he owed me.

'On the house,' I said.

'Don't need nobody's charity,' he grumbled but left his hand in his pocket. 'Thanks,' he added, and we shook hands.

'That's some 'stache,' I said on the way out, and good old Abner grinned somewhere behind it.

I was halfway back in the van when a tiny old woman with a painted face that looked as if it had been left too long in the weather minced down the sidewalk toward Abner's walk. She tried out a smile on me, an expression so coy and phony that not even a child would have fallen for it. Lord knows what a stand-up dude like Abner saw in a piece of fluff like that. Then I wondered if perhaps Abner and Sarah might want to double-date with Gail and me some night. I drove away, laughing.

My new location on the cross street didn't give me quite as good a view. I couldn't see the front door, but both vehicles were still parked in the driveway. Still more nothing with snow. If I decided to take Sarah's job, I hoped the weather would clear by Thursday. The money would be great, but it seemed a little crazy to me. And when I worked for myself, I had done some insane shit – divorces and child custody cases so obscene and degrading that only a month of whiskey could get the taste out of my mouth; repossessions of everything from combines to tropical fish; and once I had flown to Hawaii to steal back a dual champion Labrador retriever at Honolulu airport from a Japanese businessman who had stolen it from a Texan in southern Alberta. However strange the jobs had been, though, they had a purpose, and somehow the satisfaction of an old lady's curiosity seemed a bit too eccentric for me.

It would be an easy job, sure, tagging two people who weren't thinking about somebody tailing them – if they were worried about tails, they wouldn't have met at the same place so many times – maybe too easy for a man of my talents . . .

But as I was complimenting myself, a police car pulled in behind the van, good old Abner glowering in the passenger seat. Nothing is ever simple or easy in my work. This took an hour to straighten out, an hour at the police station.

The colonel finally got Abner to stop shouting about lazy, crazy bastards who gave him a line of crap a mile long then set his TV out on the goddamned porch in the snow and called it fixed. He stopped because the colonel promised that Haliburton Security would buy him a new television set, which Mr. Milodragovitch would personally deliver the next morning. Then the colonel and Jamison both shook their heads and gave me the sort of look you give a puppy who brings back a dog turd instead of the stick. I even had to give Abner a ride back to his house. All the way, Abner kept his nose curled as if I was the dog turd.

4

This time I parked two blocks west of Abner's house down Gold, nearly three blocks away from the Bogardus house, and I had to keep my eye on the spotting scope constantly. At three-forty, I got to log my first entry of the surveillance. A slender brunette in slacks and a blue down parka emerged from the side door of the house and began to scrape the windshield of the Mustang. As she leaned over the hood, her tight gray slacks stretched rather nicely over good strong legs and a great ass. I didn't put that in my report but I did make a note of it.

Then she climbed into the convertible, backed out of the driveway and took off like a shot east on Gold. By the time I had lumbered into the driver's seat, started the cold engine, and performed a full-bore three-hundred-and-sixty-degree spin instead of a U-turn on the icy street, the Mustang was nearly out of sight. If she hadn't caught a red light at Dawson, I might have lost her. When she bounced across the old rail bed on Main, the bump knocked the snow off the bottom of her license plate. 'Live Free or Die,' it said.

The Mustang led me east on Main and into the parking lot of the Riverfront Lodge, where the woman parked and locked her car and headed for the bar entrance, her buttocks jingling with muscle each time her boot heels hit the pavement. She was a pleasure to tail. I gave her a minute while I struggled out of the snowmobile suit and booties – winter exercise, changing clothes to match the temperature – and back into my new boots and a Japanese tractor 'gimme cap.'

Inside the plush bar, all mirrors and wood and décor abounding, I saw the woman up on a bar stool, chatting with the daytime bartender, my old friend Vonda Kay. I slid into a dark circular booth and tried to hide, but Vonda Kay spotted me. She charged over to

546

pull me out of the booth, cursed me for not saying hello, then dragged me over to the bar to meet a new friend of hers. When she led me up to the woman, I tried to look anonymous, but when she started to introduce us, I gave up.

'Hey,' she said as she tapped the lady on the arm, 'I want you to meet an old friend of mine.' The lady turned and smiled. 'Carolyn Fitzgerald, shake hands with Milo Milodragovitch. Carolyn's new in town – with the Forest Service or some crap – and Milo's a rent-a-cop.'

Carolyn Fitzgerald, whoever she might be, shook my hand warmly and asked, 'And just how much does it cost to rent a cop these days?'

'One shot of schnapps,' I said, then excused myself to go to the john and call the colonel.

He apologized for not giving me a description of Cassandra Bogardus, then told me to let it go for the day, to pick up the tail in the morning.

'Like flies on shit, sir, I promise.'

The colonel coughed politely into the telephone, told me where to pick up Mr. Haynes's new television, then wished me luck.

Well, sometimes you get lucky. Carolyn Fitzgerald's broad, flat face was too blunt to be pretty, but she had grand, unfettered breasts bobbing and weaving beneath her soft gray sweater, and something even better, something women who own their own lives often find in their thirties, an intelligent, happy mind, a generous smile, and an honest laugh. We smoked and drank and exchanged those inevitable details of our histories. She had grown up in Burlington, Vermont, where her father and mother both taught government and economics in the local high schools, and she had a master's from Cornell in recreational management, whatever that might be, and had just finished a law degree at Georgetown, and had been hired as a legal consultant by the Friends of the Dancing Bear Wilderness Area to keep an eye on the Forest Service land swaps and purchases.

'And I've been trying to get hold of you for weeks,' she said as she crushed a cigarette butt in the ashtray. 'You don't seem to answer your telephone,' she said, 'or my letters.'

'I took the bell out of my telephone,' I admitted, 'and I don't even open that kind of mail.'

'Philistine,' she said.

'With a vengeance.'

'Oh, that's true, honey,' Vonda Kay said from the back bar, where she was making something tasteless in the blender. 'Don't believe a word he says.'

'He has an honest face,' Carolyn said, then touched my crooked nose with the tip of her finger.

Vonda Kay just laughed and put another strawberry into the machine. The two of us went way back, all the way to high school, and had served each other well over the years, safe harbors in our stormy domestic lives. Once we even took off at four in the morning to drive to Jackpot, Nevada, to get married, but somewhere among the cliffs of the Salmon River in Idaho we both realized that neither of our divorces was final. We hadn't seen much of each other lately, but I knew Vonda Kay wasn't mad at me. She had introduced me to Carolyn out of friendship.

When I finished blushing, I told Carolyn that I was no more honest than the next man.

'Which also means no less,' she said. 'Except for the old C, C&K Railroad sections and your three thousand acres, Mr. Milodragovitch, I think I've got the Dancing Bear settled from the waterworks dam up the Hell-Roaring drainage and over the Diablos' divide to the Stone River Reservation. We're having a little trouble finding out who really owns the C, C&K sections, but when we do, I've worked out a swap of their sidehill trash timber and that old mine for a nice stand of second-growth pine down on Forest Service land in Idaho. What's holding you up, sir?'

'You can call me Milo,' I said, 'and I'm more than a little reluctant to give up my grandfather's timber land for money, marbles, or match sticks, or even virgin ponderosa, but I wouldn't mind discussing it with you up at my place.'

'What did you have in mind?' she asked, then sipped her martini, her eyes twinkling above the glass.

'Elk steaks cut off a dry cow killed this weekend,' I said, 'a bit of blow, if you're so inclined, and whatever.'

'You don't look the type,' she said.

'For whatever?'

'For cocaine,' she answered. 'You look like a cop.'

'And you, lady, look like a hell of a lot of fun,' I said, feeling a lot better already.

We settled our tab, got our change and Vonda Kay's blessing, and Carolyn followed me up the canyon to my house.

She *was* fun, too. She walked around the cellar, drinking gin on ice and occasionally hitting the lines I had chopped on the top of the freezer, pouring me the odd shot of schnapps and talking about this and that while I butchered the right hindquarter of the cow elk. She didn't act like I was insane when I pan-fried the steaks and made home fries and gravy, and she ate dinner with a good appetite, in spite of the coke.

'You're pretty classy,' I told her as we took our coffee into the living room, 'for a tourist broad.'

'You're not too bad either,' she said as she poked at the crackling apple-wood fire, 'if you'd just stop playing Gary Cooper.' Then she dug a fat bomber joint out of her purse, lit it, and said as she passed it to me, 'Just in case.'

'In case of what?' I asked, and she gave me a wicked smile.

And wicked she was, that long, firm body gleaming in the firelight, sweet shadowed hollows, smooth skin, muscle tone worthy of an Olympic swimmer. She waited for a long time as we played to speak.

'I've got one rule,' she said, her voice in the darkness above me, 'one rule you should know about.'

'No business in bed,' I suggested with a muffled voice.

'No all-nighters and damn few repeaters,' she said, moaning and moving under my tongue. 'That's how-how I keep my life simple. No-no baggage.'

She meant it, too. Sometime after midnight she gathered her clothes and hiked toward the bathroom. When she came back, freshly showered and dressed, she knelt beside me where I lay on the carpet like a gut-shot bear, bleeding where she had raked my back and thighs and ears, bleeding even from the scrape on my forehead. I meant to roll over to hold her, but the weight of her cool hand held me to the floor.

'What do you want for your timberland?' she asked.

'My grandfather's timber,' I groaned, correcting her, 'my grandfather's.'

'He's been dead for forty-three years,' she said, pressing on my chest, 'and your name is on the deed.'

'What's in a name?'

'Be serious.'

'Maybe I am.'

'How about more money?'

'Sure,' I said, 'and a plaque in the middle of Camas Meadows with my grandfather's name on it.'

'That's easy.'

'And a suspension of the rules, too.'

'The rules?'

'Sure,' I said. 'When you get the C, C&K sections, if you get them, give me a call . . .'

'On a telephone that doesn't ring?'

'Come by the house,' I said. 'I want to be one of those lucky damn few repeaters. A weekend in Seattle maybe?'

'All right,' she said, but somehow it sounded more like a threat than a promise.

'And one time on my grandfather's grave.'

'His grave?'

'His ashes are scattered in Camas Meadows.'

'You son of a bitch,' she said, laughing. 'Thanks for the evening – all of it, old man – and the next time we discuss this matter, I expect you to be serious.'

'Three times is about as serious as I get these days, love . . .'

She slapped me on the chest, kissed me, and left, her laughter and smell still warm in the living room, mixed with the fragrance of the apple wood, as I let the snowy darkness flow around my log house and over my eyes . . .

I woke around four, though, with a mild case of the cocaine jangles and a terminal case of the post-coital blues. The good ones always seem to get away, I thought, and second best is no way to love. Shit. As the child of two suicides, depression always hovered about me like a cloud while self-pity waited in the wings. I made myself get up and stumbled to the bathroom to take an old Serax left over from my hard-drinking days. In theory, it would ease the shakes. I went out into my backyard, anyway, to roll naked in the snow, to have a reason for the quivering inside. The front had passed, the sky cleared, and the temperature dropped into the teens. A sliver of moon tried, unsuccessfully, to compete with the stars.

After a long hot shower I wiped the bathroom mirror clear of mist and tried to talk to myself. 'No all-nighters,' I said, 'and no damn repeaters at all. Travel light. You're forty-seven years old and you're carrying more baggage than you need . . .' Then I had to laugh. Sometimes when you try to talk to yourself there's nobody home. I knew all the signs, far too well, knew I was on the verge of something. Another marriage maybe, another failure at love with the first woman who would have me. Another life, another place, any place, any love.

Later that morning I was glad I woke up early and stayed awake. I was parked down the street from 1414 Gold before six o'clock, and at six-thirty a tall blond woman in a red velour robe stepped out of the front door, stretched backward so hard that her large, heavy breasts seemed to lift like wings, then bent gracefully from the waist like a dancer to pick up the Meriwether *Avalanche-Express*. She moved as smoothly as light wind across water, Cassandra in the morning, and when she bent, her long, straight blond hair rippled like gold off her shoulders. The spotting scope gathered the dawn light, and I could see her face, the high cheekbones of a model, the wide, firm mouth and dark eyes of a lover, the broad, unruffled forehead of a woman at peace with herself. I had tailed Carolyn Fitzgerald by mistake, and we had ended up in bed. I couldn't help hoping that tailing this woman on purpose might lead to that same bedroom. Cassandra Bogardus stretched again, then walked barefoot through the snow to the pickup, empty of firewood now, started it and left it idling, then went back into the house without even brushing the snow off her feet. Tough, too. I liked that.

Half an hour later she came back out dressed like a model for an Aspen ski advertisement, carrying a shoulder bag and a large purse, then jumped into the pickup and roared away west on Gold toward the interstate. By the time she passed the remains of the turkey-wreck debris, she was doing seventy. It looked like we were headed out of town, so I checked the glove box to be sure the company credit cards and the trip ticket were there, then I settled in two hundred yards behind her. What the hell, I could stand a bit of road time; but before I could get comfortable, she took the airport exit. Ten minutes later we were standing in the check-in line for the 7:48 flight to Salt Lake City. I heard the ticket agent check Ms. Bogardus through to Los Angeles, so I ducked out of line and called the colonel at home. He told me to stay with her and promised that backup help would meet me at LAX.

Since I didn't want her to see my face too many times, I stayed in the downstairs coffee shop until the arriving passengers from Missoula disembarked. I waited five minutes after the final call for the Salt Lake flight, then dashed upstairs to claim my seat. Once aboard the airplane, I hurried to the rear with my head down, fell into an empty seat in front of the aft bulkhead, shut my eyes, then did a fair imitation of a man sleeping.

I didn't wake up until we were halfway to Salt Lake. I went to the john and washed my face, then wandered forward to thumb through the tattered magazines in the rack. On my way back I checked out the passengers. Cassandra Bogardus wasn't aboard. Maybe she's in the john, I told myself, or maybe you've been had. Then I remembered that when I was sitting in the coffee shop watching the disembarking Missoula passengers – as you do in airports, looking for a familiar face – I had seen a tall, erect gray-haired woman in a tweed suit who had looked oddly familiar. Now I suspected I knew why. There had been enough commotion around the white van in her neighborhood the day before – Abner, the police, my aborted U-turn – that it would have been a wonder if she hadn't made my van. And she certainly had ditched me very neatly.

The colonel met my flight back from Salt Lake. He seemed tired but not too upset as I told him how the Bogardus woman had dumped my tail.

'Pretty goddamned smooth,' I told him again. 'I'm sorry.'

'A one-man tail is tough,' he said as we walked out to the parking lot. 'We just didn't have enough information. That's why I didn't want to take the job in the first place, but I thought you would enjoy the work.'

'I'll find the bitch,' I said, 'and she'll – '

'They have their own security people on it now,' he interrupted. 'Ms. Bogardus is no longer our concern.' He coughed politely into an expensive deerskin glove. 'I took the liberty of driving your pickup,' he said, 'and I'll take the van back to the office. Your paycheck, with the extra two weeks' pay, is in the glove box.' We traded key rings. 'And Mr. Haynes's new television set is in the cab. If you wouldn't mind . . .'

'Not at all.'

'Go someplace warm,' he said, 'and enjoy yourself. We'll talk about your job when you get back.'

'Thank you, sir,' I said. 'You ought to take off yourself, if you don't mind me saying so. How long's it been since you wet a line, sir?'

'Far too long,' he said, smiling sadly, 'far too long. I meant to get down to the Florida Keys for some bone fishing this year, but I don't seem to be able to find the time.'

'It's a long time to next year's trout season, sir.'

'A long time, yes. Did you hear what happened up at Downey Creek?'

'No, sir,' I said. Downey Creek was the nearest blue-ribbon trout stream to Meriwether.

'That gold mine on the west fork,' he said, 'they're using some sort of acid process on the old tailings and one of their ponds broke . . . forty percent fish kill . . . Sometimes, Milo, I wonder what's happening to this country.'

'Me too,' I said, and the colonel patted me on the arm and said good-bye.

'By the way,' he said, reaching into his pocket, 'I believe this is yours.' He handed me my handkerchief, washed, ironed and neatly folded.

'Thank you,' I said. 'Would you do me a favor, sir?'

'What's that?'

'If you find out what this Bogardus deal is about, will you tell me?'

'If I find out, Milo,' he said, then walked across the lot to the van.

As I drove back to town on the old highway, I wasn't very proud of myself. Perhaps Sara's little job was just about my speed. Next day was Thursday. I decided to do Sarah's job, to take her money, easy as it was, put it in a pile with mine and head south for the winter. Maybe for good. Even though I had been born and raised in Meriwether, it didn't feel much like home anymore. Across town, the south hills had been gobbled up by developers, the softly rounded slopes layered with rows of ticky-tacky houses. Even with the pulp mill on half shifts and with the millions of dollars' worth of scrubbers the mill had installed, the air smelled like cat piss and rotten eggs whenever the wind came out of the west, and the current rage for wood stoves was already filling the valley with a yellowish-brown haze, clotted thickly in the air like something you might cough up, and after a week of winter inversion, you would. All my favorite downtown bars were either closed or filled with children. Mahoney's had become a place to buy expensive coffee, sweet European baked goods, and overpriced glassware. The Slumgullion was still on the corner of Dottle and Zinc, but under new management, and they didn't serve brains and eggs or fried mush and fresh side pork anymore. Even all my old wino friends seemed to have disappeared.

Right, I thought, south for the winter, for all the winters. I knew a dope dealer in Tucson who always needed a new bodyguard, and an ex-con in Albuquerque who owned a used-car lot and always needed a salesman also licensed to do repossessions. *Right!*

Old Abner was like a kid at Christmas when I took his new television set out of the box. It was a Sony, and when I turned it on, he stared, entranced by the bright, sharp colors, then he broke into a jig, clapping his hands and dancing around the room in his flopping slippers. I had a vision of Abner and Yvonne transfixed for days in front of the endless soaps as a surly Tyrone lurked outside the windows.

On my way out, Abner caught me on the porch, grabbed my arm, thanked me again, and asked, 'Are you really one of those private eyes?'

'I used to be,' I said, trying for a mysterious air, then I split.

Back at my house I tried to call Sarah, but the line was busy. I thought about a drink but decided to get ready to leave instead, half afraid that if I didn't pack now, I would never get out of town when the time came. I stripped all my guns, cleaned and oiled them, put them all, along with my poacher's crossbow, behind the false panel in the basement. Then I finished quartering the elk, wrapped the front quarters, put them in the freezer, and took the remaining hindquarter over to my next-door neighbor. She wasn't home, so I left it on the front porch. I went back to try Sarah's number again. Still busy. I had a shot of schnapps, then packed. Before I knew it, I was through. All my worldly goods, everything I would need for an extended visit, fit into two B–4 bags, a duffle bag, and one cardboard whiskey box. Now I was ready. When I finished Sarah's job, I could throw my crap into the back of the pickup in five minutes, and five minutes later I would see Meriwether in my rear-view mirror.

No all-nighters, damn few repeaters, no baggage, traveling light.

When Gail finally answered the phone, she didn't sound very happy to hear my voice. I apologized for missing our drink.

'Fuck it,' she said. 'What do you want?'

'To see Sarah.'

'You going to work for her?'

'Guess so.'

'She's resting now. Why don't you come by about four.'

I agreed, and she hung up without saying good-bye.

This time I wore my old boots and a down vest and parked my truck right in front of the old McCravey mansion. Gail stood in the driveway, her daypack full of books on top of a Honda Civic. She looked as if she had been standing there for a long time, and her face looked red and chapped, her eyes watery with the cold.

'I'm sorry I was so abrupt on the telephone' she said, 'but I had just spent an hour talking long distance to my mother and she took forty-five minutes of small talk to tell me that my father's in the hospital.'

'Nothing serious, I hope.'

'Lung cancer, they think.'

'I'm sorry,' I said. 'I keep meaning to quit smoking myself.'

'He didn't smoke,' she said, 'he worked in a shipyard on the West Coast during World War II. Goddamned asbestos. The fibers curl up in your lungs like heartworms. Goddamned government.'

'That's too bad,' I said lamely.

'Well, I am sorry about being so short on the phone.'

'Don't worry about it.'

'Maybe we can have that drink after you talk to Sarah,' she said. 'I read about the excitement the other night, in the paper.'

'I don't read the newspaper,' I admitted.

'Don't you care about what's happening in the world?'

'What's the world?'

'A fucking insane asylum,' she said, then laughed bitterly and rubbed her eyes. 'Let's go see Sarah.'

When we got there, the gray afternoon light seemed to fill the solarium like a light fog. Sarah looked tired, and when I leaned over to kiss her cheek, her hand trembled on my arm.

'It's so nice to see you, Bud,' she said. 'Would you like some coffee? Or a drink?'

'No thanks.'

'Gail tells me that you are going to-to do this bit of eccentric nonsense for me.'

'Yes, ma'am.'

'That's very kind of you,' she said, then reached into the pocket of her dark-blue dressing gown and withdrew the envelope and handed it to me. 'I've changed my mind slightly, though . . .'

'Yes, ma'am?'

'The five thousand is your fee,' she said, 'and we will settle the expenses later.'

'That's too much, way too much.'

'Hush,' she said. 'Don't argue with me, young man. I never let my employees disagree with me.' Then she chanced a weak smile. Over by the French doors, Gail laughed her way into a coughing fit. 'Except for Gail, and I fear she is a hopeless case.'

'It's too much . . .'

'Hush,' she said again. 'And I expect you to be profligate with expenses and my credit cards.' I sighed, and she took it as a sign of my agreement. 'If you do not mind my asking, Bud, how do you plan to do it?'

'Well, I was going to pick up one of the cars after tomorrow's meeting,' I said, 'but with this much money I can afford to hire some help to tail the other one, too.'

'I-I would rather you handled it alone,' Sarah said quickly. 'You-you can appreciate my feelings.'

'Yes, ma'am, you're the boss,' I said. 'So tomorrow I'll – ah, there's an outdoor telephone booth on the corner of Virginia and Dottle. I'll call to give you the number.'

'I don't . . . I can't . . . talk – I don't like to use the telephone,' Sarah stammered.

'Will you be here, Gail?'

'Sure,' she said, shrugging. 'I wouldn't miss this cloak-and-dagger action for the world. But why so far away?'

'So they won't see my pickup on Virginia,' I explained. 'Anyway, I'll give you the number of the telephone in the booth, and you can call me to tell me which car is coming my way.'

'Right,' Gail said.

'And-and after that?' Sarah asked.

'I'll tail whichever one comes my way, stick on them until I find out who they are,' I said, thinking about my bad luck that morning. 'Then I'll figure out some way to pick up the other one later.'

'Sounds real precise,' Gail said under her breath.

'Trust me,' I said, 'it's what I do for a living.' Or used to, anyway.

After a silence that seemed to last for minutes, Sarah finally said, 'Thank you again, Bud.'

'For this kind of money you could have them killed,' I said, trying for a joke, but I didn't get any laughs.

'Now,' Sarah said, standing slowly and leaning heavily on her cane, 'I'm afraid you will have to excuse me. This hasn't been one of my better days. I'm afraid I must retire.' Then she limped toward the door.

'I'll be back in a minute,' Gail said and helped Sarah to her bedroom.

While I waited I thought about my plan, which I had made up the moment Sarah asked me what I intended to do. If I wanted to get really fancy and modern, I could rent a directional mike and a couple of contact bugs, maybe even a movie camera. But, hell, old-fashioned and cheap would work on a cream puff of a job like this . . .

'Thank you for doing this for Sarah,' Gail said as she came back. 'I know it sounds crazy, but this is the sort of thing that keeps her alive and kicking. How about that drink now?'

'You have any schnapps?'

'Schnapps? God, I don't think so.' Gail walked over to the large globe and checked it out. 'Nope. Bourbon, Scotch, gin, brandy – beer in the refrigerator downstairs.'

I hadn't had many beers in the past two years, and suddenly all the work I had put into staying sober seemed a waste of time. 'Damn right,' I said. We went down to the kitchen, where we had a beer, then another, and one of the bomber-sized joints I had lit for Sarah the other time.

'I know I'm trying to evade my problems,' Gail said after she threw the roach into the garbage disposal, 'and I know I'll start thinking about my father when I'm coming down in a couple of hours, and then I'll get so goddamned mad I can't see straight, and then I'll cry . . .'

But she didn't wait for the process to work itself out. She turned and hammered her fists on the edges of the sink as she sobbed. When I touched her shoulder she spun around quickly and huddled against my chest, still crying. One thing led to another, and a few minutes later we were on the kitchen floor, tangled in our clothes, involved in a frenzied coupling that had nothing to do with love or sex or even comfort, but two frightened, befuddled animals seeking a warm place to weep.

Afterward, as she hopped around trying to fit her overalls over her hiking boots, she said, 'Goddamn, it's nice to know I'm handling this like an adult. Shit.'

'What's an adult?' I said, turning my back politely to look for my shirt, to keep from seeing her naked anger and grief.

'Jesus Christ,' she said, 'you must lead an exciting life.'

'What?'

'Those scratches on your back,' she said. 'An exciting life.'

'Or sordid,' I said.

'Shit, now I've made you sad,' she said. 'Sorry.'

'No problem.'

'Want another beer?'

'No thanks,' I said. 'I think maybe I should go.'

'Maybe you're right,' she said. 'How old are you?'

'Forty-seven,' I said. 'Why?'

'Sometimes old guys get sad afterward,' she said.

'I'll be goddamned,' I said.

'Why?'

'Six, maybe seven years ago, a little hippie chick said the same thing to me.'

'Maybe it's true,' she said as she opened another beer.

'Maybe,' I said.

'Whatever,' she said, 'thanks for being kind to Sarah ... and to me.'

'You're welcome,' I said, but I didn't feel like I had been kind, not even once in my life. 'I hope your father's all right,' I said, kissed her cheek, then carried myself and my life home.

5

The next afternoon I called Gail from the phone booth at the corner of Dottle and Virginia to make sure that she and Sarah were set. They were, Gail on the telephone, Sarah on the balcony with her binoculars. I had mine, too, around my neck and hidden under my down vest, even though I couldn't see the meeting place from my angle. I told Gail to stay on the line to keep it open, which she did, but she wasn't interested in any chitchat. Maybe the night before had embarrassed her, maybe she wanted to forget it.

I kept the booth occupied by opening the paper to the Houses for Rent section and pretending to make calls. I wondered what sort of response I would get from landlords if I were an unemployed sawyer with three children under six, two tomcats, an unspayed female German Shepherd, and a wife who worked as a barmaid. I probably couldn't rent a house with a gun.

But while I was waiting I got a good look at the driver of the little yellow Toyota Corolla as he waited to make a left turn off Dottle onto Virginia. Lank blond hair, acne scars across a tired, bony face – a sad face rather than troublesome. As he disappeared down Virginia, I remembered Sarah telling me that they always parked on opposite sides of the street, which probably meant the woman would be coming my way. But Gail came on the line and told me the guy had made a U-turn and parked facing in my direction.

Although I couldn't see down Virginia very far, I could make out a group of young girls trying to build a snowman on the front lawn of a sorority house while a gang of young boys pelted them with snowballs. As I watched, one of the new blue automated garbage trucks with EQCS, INC. painted on its bed turned into Virginia and worked its way slowly out of sight, the arms of the loader doing its job

559

on the fifty-five-gallon drums. It looked like some sort of prehistoric monster dreamed up by a cartoonist who had taken one too many acid trips.

Sometimes I didn't know what to think of a world where garbage had become big business, where dumps had become something called landfills, a world where some of our garbage was so terrible we had to consider burying it in salt domes or launching it into outer space –

'The woman's here,' Gail said, interrupting my thoughts.

'Ask Sarah what kind of car.'

'A little blue one,' she answered after a moment.

'Great,' I said. 'License number?' In the silence I felt the old juices begin to flow. But when Gail gave me the number, she didn't sound too sure about it.

'The guy's walking over to her car,' Gail said. 'Now he's running back to his car, he's coming your way.'

'I got him,' I said, then hung up quickly and ran to the corner with my binoculars in hope for a glance at the woman's car. I had time for a glimpse of a little blue Subaru with Montana plates, Silver Bow County, Butte, and the back of the woman's head in a blue-and-white striped ski hat, then I raced back to my pickup and waited for the man in the yellow Toyota Corolla.

When he turned right on Dottle, heading north, I was waiting for him, and I tucked the pickup into the traffic five cars behind him. After he crossed the bridge, he made several left and right turns in the downtown area, and I nearly lost him, but he didn't seem to know the one-way-street grid in Meriwether, and he ended up behind me heading west on Main. I watched his blinkers, wondering how I would catch him if he turned, but we went straight out Main to the interstate entrance. He signaled for the westbound ramp, so I went east in front of him, went a quarter of a mile, then whipped an illegal U-turn across the median, spraying snowy mud and grass behind me, praying that no cops were around. Then I punched the old pickup westbound. The four-barrel carburetor on the 302 engine screamed like a tornado as it sucked down gasoline at about six miles to the gallon, and we caught the Toyota five miles west of town.

The old Corolla was covered with rusty dents and almost all the glass was cracked but the little car went fine, and I had to keep the foot-feed almost to the firewall to keep him in sight. Both saddle tanks were full, but if the guy was on his way to Washington, I would need gas before we got there. On the interstate west of Meriwether there weren't many exits, and I knew where they were, down to the mile marker, so I could stay way behind him between exits, then catch up to watch for a turn. Twice he got off the interstate, then went across the intersection and back up the westbound ramp. He still thought he might have a tail but didn't have the slightest idea how to shake one. Mostly, I just kept heading west, ignoring his fakes, wondering what the hell was going on, wondering what the woman had said to him to make him think he was being tailed. *Flee! All is lost! My husband knows everything!* Maybe. Or *Run for your life! The killers are on the loose.* Maybe not. Who knew? Certainly not me. I just knew that if something didn't happen soon, I was going to lose him.

East of Missoula, I switched tanks. West of Missoula, he signaled for a turn onto Highway 93, then headed north toward Flathead Lake, Kalispell – the Canadian border, maybe – Sandpoint, Idaho, or the back road into Spokane, Washington. I didn't know but I had to go with him, tailed him up the black ice on Evero Hill, but when he slowed down and eased into the lot of the Evero Bar across the road, I went past like a man with Canada on my mind.

As soon as I could I turned left onto somebody's private road, dashed into a stand of pine trees with my binoculars. Although the sun had dropped behind the farthest edges of the mountains, enough light remained glowing in the clear sky so that I could see the man as he came out of the Evero Bar with a six-pack of Oly dangling from each hand. He stood in the parking lot, drinking a beer and watching the traffic. Then he climbed back into his car and headed back south toward the interstate, crossed it and pulled into a truck stop. I parked in front of Fred's Lounge, watched him until he walked into the café, sat down at the counter, and picked up a menu, then I drove like a madman toward the Missoula airport to rent another vehicle.

I wanted something that would go but ended up with one of those new General Motors front-wheel-drive cars the Arabs shamed Detroit into manufacturing, a car with all the guts of a moped.

When I got back to the truck stop, a waitress was pouring the blond guy another cup of coffee, so I drove over to Fred's, went in to buy a bottle of schnapps, a handful of jerky, and a roll of Tums. While I waited in the rental car, I had a small toot off my knife blade, a shot of schnapps, and a piece of tough dried jerky. Now I was ready. A real Western private eye again, completely outfitted.

We went back to Missoula on the old highway, then south on the 93 bypass. He drove slower now, picking his teeth and drinking a beer as we skirted Missoula in the fading light. He seemed convinced that he had lost any sort of tail, and his overconfidence gave me the break I needed to maintain a one-man tail at night. We went south on 93 to Lolo, then west up Highway 12 along Lolo Creek toward Lolo Pass and the Idaho border along the old Lewis and Clark Trail, along the Nez Percé escape route. Before we reached Lolo Hot Springs, I passed him, then pulled off on a Forest Service road, disconnected a headlight, then picked him up and followed him one-eyed over the pass into Idaho along the Lochsa River to Clearwater Crossing where the Lochsa and the Selway merge to become the Clearwater. When he stopped at Syringa to take a leak I went past him again, reconnected the headlight, and got behind him as we wound down Highway 12 toward the Snake River and the Washington border.

At Kooskia, though, he changed direction and turned left on Idaho 13, going south, and a few miles later he turned left again on Idaho 14 up the crooked course of the South Fork of the Clearwater, which we followed sedately almost all the way to Elk City, where he pulled off into the parking lot of a small motel with a NO VACANCY sign clearly displayed. I had no choice but to go on by, turn around beyond the next curve, then go back with my lights out.

Although it was only a bit after eleven, the motel and café were dark, the little Toyota nowhere in sight. I didn't know what all these people were doing in Elk City this time of year. It wasn't on the way to anyplace. On the west side of town the paved road ended, and a dirt road led over the Bitterroot Mountains to Connor, Montana, but the first snowfall of the season had closed the road. Maybe it was elk season in Elk City, I thought, laughing as I crept around the shadowed parking lot.

Finally I hid the rental car behind a camper, then took off on foot looking for the yellow car, which I found about fifty yards up a dirt road beyond the motel, parked in front of a small cabin. I saw his shadow moving aimlessly across the window curtains. I slipped out of my boots and eased across the pine needles, the sharp rocks, and the patches of snow around to the back of the cabin, where I peeked inside through the flimsy curtains.

A can of Dinty Moore beef stew with the top cut sat on the stove bubbling. The guy dumped the bottom third of a Tabasco bottle and two eggs into the boiling stew. Whatever sort of trouble he might be involved in, he couldn't be all bad – he cooked a lot like me. Kept house much the same way, too. Newspapers, magazines, paperback books, and dirty clothes lay in heaps all over the one-room cabin; the bed looked as if it had been slept in by a man with bad dreams; and the garbage had overflowed its can onto the dusty floor.

While he waited for the eggs to cook, he kicked his dirty clothes into one pile, then stuffed them into a plastic garbage bag. He emptied the small dresser and put his clean clothes on top of the dirty ones, glanced around the room to see what he had missed, then shuffled the rest of the trash into a corner. The smell of the beef stew slipped through the walls of the clapboard cabin, and my stomach grumbled so loudly that I had to get away from the window.

After I picked up my boots I went back to the motel and sat in the car waiting for him to leave, making my supper out of schnapps, jerky, and Tums. After half an hour, though, the Toyota still hadn't come down the track, so I went back up. The little car was still parked in front of the dark cabin, and when I leaned against the outside wall I could hear the snuffles and snores of a beery sleep, which left me looking at a long night.

I thought about it a bit, then hiked on up the dirt road to where it ended against a bulldozed hump beyond the next switchback. I walked quietly back down to my car, picked up the small traveling bag I had remembered to move from my pickup to the rental unit – winter emergency road gear, a space blanket, a bag of hard candy, matches, a toothbrush, a pint of schnapps – then crossed the highway to the river to clean up in the cold, rushing water.

An hour later I moved the car up to the dead end, where he couldn't spot it, turned it around, then took the space blanket and the pint of schnapps back down the hill until I found a hollow beneath a dead-fall ponderosa where I curled up, planning to balance the occasional shot of schnapps with the odd toot of coke, hoping to sleep a little but lightly enough so I would hear the guy when he started his car in the morning.

It had snowed up the South Fork, too, but not as much as it had

over in Montana. High clouds swept overhead, flirting with the
snickering slice of moon, and in the shadows of the lowing pines,
the patches of snow glowed and faded and glimmered like dying
phosphorescent creatures jerked from the bottom of the sea. All
around me the pines creaked and sighed in the wind like mourners.
I couldn't tell if I trembled from the cold or from the excitement of
working again. When I smoked, I cupped the match and hid the
cigarette the way I used to that long winter on the line in Korea,
and although I don't remember sleeping, I remember dreaming of
the war. All through the night, it seemed, shadowy figures rose from
the snow and moved silently past my position, and when I woke just
before dawn as the guy slammed shut the front door of the cabin, I
rolled over reaching for my M–1 and was amazed in my sleepy
confusion to find it wasn't there.

Sleeping in the cold on the ground was not something I did well
at my age, and when I tried to stand up, my joints groaned like truck
axles packed with frozen grease. Even before I got to my knees I
heard his car door bang shut, the starter grinding angrily against the
resistance of the cold engine, the pump of the accelerator hard
against the floorboard. On my knees, I heard the muffled bang, then
threw the space blanket aside and stumbled downhill through the
brush.

The explosion had blown all the glass out of the small car, popped
open both doors and the trunk lid, and when I got to the man, his
face was covered with freckles of blood, his shirt and jacket tattered
on his chest. There were smoldering bits of seat-cover fabric and
clots of cotton stuffing on his naked shoulders. When I reached for
him, I saw a gaping hole in the floor. His left leg was gone below
the knee, his right above, and blood gushed from the nerve on his
cheek, and most of his fingers were stubs, the pink, pork-chop flesh
not bleeding yet. When I reached around his chest to pull him out
and away from the biting stink of gasoline, he grabbed my left arm
with what was left of his right hand. He could not stand to be moved.
After a few seconds, while he held me so tightly with the maimed
hand that I couldn't run either, he died, and his hand fell quivering
from my elbow.

I wanted to run, God, I wanted to run away from the blood and
the smell of raw gasoline, but I made myself roll him over so I could
empty his pockets into mine, then I grabbed the garbage bag out of

the back seat, holding his goods tightly with my arms around the
shredded plastic. I took a moment to glance in the open trunk, where
I found a green duffle bag. I slipped the strap over my shoulder, and
ran.

Okay, I panicked. I had stepped in shit and I was scared. If you
don't see that sort of thing regularly, you lose your touch for dealing
with it, the cynical layer that lets you see a shattered body, shake your
head once, then go about your business. I tampered with evidence,
obstructed justice, and ran away, leaving the dead body propped like
a side of beef in the front seat. And ran.

When I started the long uphill flight to my rental car, I couldn't
get enough air in my lungs, and when I got to the dead end beyond
the switchback, I fell on the ground beside the driver's door, sobbing,
sucking empty air, thinking, trying to remember how to survive a
world at war. Think. It hadn't been a bomb connected to the ignition,
or the car would have gone up when he first turned the key. Whatever
it was had been under the front seat. Whoever put it there must have
known I was around, must have tailed me tailing him. Think. I
crawled around to the passenger door, opened it slowly, carefully,
searching with bleary eyes for a wire. Nothing. Nothing under the
seat on that side. Under the driver's seat, though, a simple booby
trap, something I had seen explained in *Time* magazine during the
Vietnam war. A grenade with the pin pulled and stuffed into a tin
can to hold the handle down – a Del Monte crushed-pineapple can,
a killer with a sense of humor – and a length of soft soldering wire
run underneath the floor mat and tied to the clutch pedal.

My hands were shaking so badly that I thought I would never get
the grenade out from under the seat without dropping the can, but
I did, eventually, then I held it tightly as I crawled out the driver's
door and looked for a place to put it, a safe place, but what if a kid
came along, or a hunter or a bear turning over rocks looking for
grubs, no safe place. I set it on the roof of the car, threw the dead
man's goods in the back seat, took the grenade and the can and
myself and put us behind the wheel, the grenade lodged snugly in
my crotch.

I wanted to weep, and did. My balls wanted to climb back up into
my body, and they tried, sweating with the effort. I started the car
and tried to ease down the trail, but my foot hammered the accelerator against the floor, and the cold engine flooded and died. 'Oh,

Jesus God,' I heard myself say, then I started the engine again, let the car coast in neutral down the hill, idling to warm it up. Even before I reached the ruined Toyota, though, I hit it again, fleeing, crazy, trying to brake, to go slow through the motel parking lot, but when I hit the highway the little car was going so fast that it lifted two wheels off the ground, which made the grenade rattle in the can, but still I jammed the throttle down, ran the gutless little bastard as hard as it would. A few seconds down the road, the gas tank of the Toyota went off behind me like a bomb, the fireball rolling through the rear-view mirror.

When I finally stopped running up and down Forest Service roads, I had no idea where I might be, but I knew I had to stop. The panic only stops when you stop running. I longed for the warm weight of my Browning 9mm automatic hanging heavy under my arm. At least I have a live grenade, I thought, laughing hysterically, riding between my legs. I shot off the road onto a logging skid trail and bounced the goddamned little car as far as it would go up it. When I got out, though, with nobody in sight as far as I could see, it still didn't help. I could feel gunsights crawling like ants across my back whichever way I turned. I reached in the back seat, hefted the duffle bag; it was heavy, it rattled, that was enough, maybe a pistol, maybe a big knife, anything . . . But I couldn't make myself wait to look there, standing by the car, so I threw it over my shoulder and ran, the can in my other hand.

When I was about seventy-five yards uphill and across fifty yards of granite scree from the car, I fell into the shadow of an outcrop, lay flat behind the lip of the shattered rocks, and decided I had run as far as I was going to. I laid my head on the duffle bag, propped the can and the grenade securely between two rocks, and waited to catch my breath. Then I unsnapped the duffle bag, dug into it, and felt better almost immediately.

Right on top were three fragmentation grenades still in their cardboard tubes. Below them, two flat packages wrapped in heavy plastic. I opened the first one and nearly shouted with joy. Not that guns kept you from running – I saw men in Korea shot in their foxholes, wrapped around their unfired weapons – but if you're done with running, a gun feels better than a woman, more comforting than your mother's breast. Although I had only seen them in movies and in magazines, I recognized the small submachine gun at once. An

Ingram M–11. Not much larger than a .45 automatic pistol. Eight hundred and fifty rounds a minute. So simple a child can operate it. I dug deeper, looking for clips and ammo.

I found what I was looking for, and more. Ten loaded clips of .380 rounds, a bat-shaped suppressor. A kilo of marijuana. A bag of white powder, heroin or cocaine, I assumed. Two more grenades. The guy in the yellow Toyota might be a bad guy, but he was Santa Claus to me.

Everything except the grenades had been wrapped in the heavy black plastic, and all the packages were covered with a light pinkish-gray, dusty powder. I brushed it off my hands and the two M–11s, then turned the duffle bag inside out to see if something inside had burst, but the bag was empty. I loaded the kilo of smoking dope, its plastic wrapper still intact except for the tear I had made to look at it, and one of the M–11s back into the bag, then got ready.

I fitted the suppressor to the other Ingram, loaded it, and fired a short burst at ponderosa about thirty yards downhill and to my right. Then two more to get the feel of the kick. On the fourth burst, which emptied the clip, I chipped enough bark off the big yellow pine to convince me that I could hit a man, and the little submachine gun didn't make enough noise to frighten away the chipmunks that had come out on the scree to watch me. Then I changed clips, moved back deeper into the outcrop's shadow, stacked the grenades beside me, checked my field of fire, and waited.

After a while, I opened the baggie of white powder, tasted it. Cocaine. Maybe four or five ounces, more than I had ever seen in my life. I snorted a bit off my knife blade, and it nearly took the top of my head off. The coke must have just come off the boat, not even stepped on hard yet, maybe seventy, eighty percent pure. My admiration for the dead guy rose another few notches. He didn't look like much, he lived like a tramp, and his car was a seven-year-old wreck, but he carried good stuff in his trunk. I had another tiny snort. What the hell, I thought, if the bad guys are behind, they may have a little trouble doing in a drug-crazed, scared-shitless, middle-aged old fart like me. Especially since I had a good position, half a dozen grenades, an automatic weapon, and two hundred and seventy rounds of ammo.

But nobody was behind me – good, bad or indifferent – and by

567

midmorning, most of the fear washed with occasional nips of coke, I had become bored enough to be half sane again.

What in God's name had Sarah gotten me into? What *had* the woman in the blue Subaru said to the man to make him run? They hadn't been dealing weapons or drugs, not if they had met so often at the same time and same place. Never. The man was dead, the woman gone, and I had no idea who either of them might be. At least I had the license-plate number off the woman's car, and even if it was rented, I could catch up with her. And the plate number off the man's car, too, written on a slip of paper somewhere . . .

I now remembered rolling over his dead body to rifle his pockets. I checked the thinly timbered hillside and what I could see of the road, then emptied my pockets.

The leather of his wallet was wrinkled and stretched, as if it had been emptied of everything nonessential – those slips of paper with telephone numbers and names you don't remember, out-of-date insurance cards, expired credit cards, pictures that have lost their meaning. In it I found only three twenties, two tens, a five, four ones, and a two-dollar bill folded in a square with 'Shit' written across it in red ink, and a Washington State commercial operator's license in the name of John P. Rideout at an address in Wilbur, Washington. Stuck to the back of the license, not with glue but from wear, was a small snapshot of a plain chubby woman with three small and indistinct children huddled at her baggy knees. The group stood in front of a small frame house on the edge of a meadow, around which loomed a dark evergreen jungle. Certainly not Wilbur, which sits on the lava-broken high desert plains of eastern Washington, but perhaps somewhere west of the Cascades.

In my other pocket I had found half a pack of Salems, and stuffed behind the cellophane, a matchbook from a bar called Nobby's in West Seattle. I used the last match out of the book to light one of my own cigarettes.

Okay, I had a place to begin, with Rideout, and a plate number for the woman. But no notions. Why had somebody blown the poor devil to bits? To rip him off? No, they left the goodies in the trunk. Maybe he ripped somebody off. And why me? And did they know who I was? Probably. All they had to do was open the glove box and read the rental agreement. But why me?

And the trembling began all over again. My cigarette slipped out of my fingers and fell inside my down vest. As I slapped at the sparks flying across my chest, I found the small bloody streaks left by his fingers. They knew me, all right. And I had to either find the bad guys to tell them I had a poorly developed sense of law and order and didn't talk even in my sleep. Or go to the law. I didn't know what kind of fall it was in Idaho to tamper with evidence and obstruct justice. I didn't even know where the Idaho State Prison was. Even turning state's evidence, probation was the best I could hope for. And what evidence? No law, not until I knew what the hell was going on. I couldn't even hang around the house and wait for the bad guys to come by for a chat, a few last words. I had to go to ground, hide as I tried to find out why Rideout had been killed, why they tried to kill me.

I wondered how many people they had working the tail – at least four, I guessed, and damn professional work at that. I thought about taking Sarah's money and the colonel's paycheck and simply running, my sense of justice superseded by my sense of survival, wondered where the bastards had picked up our trail . . .

Then I had a terrible vision of somebody watching the meeting through binoculars, like me, casing the neighborhood to be safe, seeing the old woman with her gleaming silver hair, seeing the sun low in the southern sky flash off her binoculars. Shit, I had to find a telephone, had to get that beautiful old woman out of her house for a while, someplace safe until I could find out what was going on. And I had to get rid of the goddamn live grenade too.

Although I didn't know exactly where I had ended up, I did know that I was north of the South Fork and that if I kept heading north on the Forest Service roads, eventually I would come out on the Clearwater and back on Highway 12, which we had come over the night before. Highway 12 was the only place I could hope to find a telephone without going back to Elk City and whatever law-enforcement attention the explosion of Rideout's car had drawn. From the paved roads, national forests looked like vast impenetrable barriers, but that was strictly for show, for the tourists. In fact, all those acres of forest land were threaded by an endless maze of roads built by the Forest Service with taxpayers' money for the logging industry, access for the heavy machinery necessary to clear-cut great swaths of timber. I couldn't complain too much, though, since roads gave me a chance to get away from Elk City, from the minions of the law and the outlawed gathered there by the charred remains of John P. Rideout.

The mountain air was fresh and cold, but the road was mushy with snow melt along the sunny stretches. At least the rental car was good for something – the front-wheel drive pulled it right through the boggy places. When I finally came down off the side of the mountain to cross a creek, I stopped the car and tossed the grenade into the middle of the culvert in about two feet of running water. It seemed a safe place to dispose of the bomb. Even through the thick metal sides of the culvert and the three feet of roadbed, the explosion shook me. I stumbled about for a moment, slapping at myself, checking for wounds with an old combat habit. When I leaned over the edge of the creek to see if I had damaged the culvert, peering through the smoky mist, a great lunker of a cutthroat came floating out, belly up. I went down the bank and out into the knee-deep water, which was so cold I felt the ache all the way up to my hips, to pick up the trout. Such a fucking waste, I thought, holding the slippery length of the fish, and I felt like weeping again. 'My fucking nerves are shot!' I screamed. 'Shot to fucking hell!' Then I threw the fish back into the water, threw him as hard as I could. The small burst of adrenaline carried me out of the water, back to the car, down the road. But my hands were shaking on the wheel within minutes, my balls still trying to crawl away from the grenade.

Finally, in the middle of the afternoon, I reached Highway 12 and drove west to the Syringa Café, where I had a huge order of ham and eggs while I waited for a truck driver to get off the telephone. When I called Sarah's number, though, no one answered. I called the colonel, asked him to put a man on Sarah's house around the clock. He didn't ask me why or where to send the bill or what kind of trouble I was in now. He just said, 'Certainly.' A good soldier all the way. I headed west toward Lewiston on the Washington border, where I traded my piece of rented Detroit crap for a Datsun station wagon. The girl behind the counter started to ask me why but when she looked at my face again, she just shook her head and filled out the forms. I borrowed the key to the rest room to take a look at myself. I had only been on the job twenty-four hours and already I looked like hell, like death warmed over, like a man on the run from himself.

On the way north I tried to drive close to the speed limit, as one must when carrying the sort of load I had in the back seat, but it was a battle all the way. When I went through Pullman, where my son went to college, I had a terrible urge to give him a call, to drop by his dorm just to give him a bear hug, but it would just have confused him, so I pressed on to Spokane, then west on Highway 2 to Wilbur.

When I drove by the address on Rideout's license, the house didn't just look empty, it looked abandoned forever. I had to sleep, I thought, so I checked into a motel and called Sarah's number one last time, and Gail answered.

'Don't you people ever pick up the phone?' I asked a bit more curtly than I meant to.

'Sarah doesn't,' she said, 'and I've been out.'

'I'm sorry,' I said. 'How's your father?'

'They flew him back to the Mayo Clinic this morning,' she said, 'for tests, more fucking tests. I wanted to be a doctor once, you know, until I found out that they don't know shit.'

'Nobody does,' I said. 'Listen, I want you to do me a favor.'

'What? I hope it doesn't take too long, Milo, because I've got two quizzes tomorrow, and I haven't cracked a book for either of them.'

'Just listen a minute,' I said, 'please. I am in a world of trouble – '

'I told Sarah not to give you that much money,' she interrupted.

'Just listen – '

'What sort of trouble?'

'Will you please just shut up for a minute!'

'Don't you be telling me to shut up, asshole,' she said.

'Ah, Christ,' I sighed, 'whatever happened to that moment of tenderness between us?'

'You dudes in your needle-nosed boots always think you're so fucking tough,' she said, 'but underneath you're all just a bunch of sissy cream puffs. It went where it was supposed to, old man, the way of all flesh, ashes to ashes, dust to dust, down the toilet of life . . .' She sounded as if she was crying.

'I don't believe this conversation,' I said.

'I don't either,' she said and hung up.

When I called back, the line sounded permanently busy. I took a shower, tried again without luck, then lay back on the bed hoping I didn't have bad dreams . . .

. . . and I didn't. I didn't sleep enough, but spent most of the night wrapped around the submachine gun, my hands still heavy with the empty weight of the dead fish, the dead man as I rolled him over to rummage through the pockets of his life.

6

Even though I suspected it would be wasted time, I spent the next morning working Wilbur without finding a soul who had either seen or heard of John P. Rideout, and even though I knew nobody was behind me, the back of my neck kept twitching. Everything was wrong, nothing fit, and nobody answered the telephone at Sarah's house. I called a lawyer in Butte to get him to check out the plate number on the woman's car, but his secretary told me that he was in California on vacation. I thought about the matchbook from Nobby's in Seattle. Maybe it really was a clue, and Seattle was a lot closer than Butte. I could drive over in a couple of hours, check out the bar, and with a little luck, drop the rented Datsun at the airport, and catch a night flight back to Missoula to get my pickup.

Right. So I cut across the back roads south to the interstate, across the fields of wheat stubble and sagebrush hills sliced by lava dykes. After eighteen months, the volcanic ash from Mount St. Helens still lay along the roadsides. We had even had enough ash fallout in Meriwether to close the bars for four days, which was as near to a natural disaster as I ever wanted to get.

When I picked up the interstate at Moses Lake, I tried Sarah again. Still no answer. So I called the colonel. He told me that none of his men had reported any activity, unusual or otherwise, at the Weddington house. Then he asked where I was.

'Moses Lake,' I said, 'heading for Seattle. But don't tell anybody if they ask.'

'Why would anybody ask, Milo? Are you in some sort of trouble?'

'No, sir,' I said. 'Just doing a little free-lance work.' My crimes were all mine, and I didn't want to make the colonel an accessory after the fact.

'Enjoying yourself?' the colonel asked pleasantly, and I had a little trouble answering him. 'Still drinking schnapps?'

'My goddamned tongue tastes like fucking peppermint stick,' I said, and decided to do something about it immediately. He told me to be careful and have fun, then we rang off. I went straight to the nearest market, where I bought a Styrofoam cooler, a bag of ice, and two six-packs of Rainier, then to a secondhand store to buy a trunk that locked and loaded the guns, grenades, and coke in it. Even if the Washington state patrol popped me for drinking and driving, they couldn't open the locked trunk without a warrant.

I felt pleased with myself, fairly or unfairly, as I headed west, on I–90, but I still kept an eye out for the law, checking all directions before I took a drink of beer on the highway, watching my ass. And that's how I saw them watching me.

There were four of them and they were good. A four-wheel-drive Chevy pickup decked out for show, big tires, and chrome roll-bar with quartz lamps on it. A green Ford sedan, company car stripped, with suits and shirts hanging in the back seat. A Volkswagen van. And a dude in a red Porsche 924 who thought he was the cutest one of all. These people had some money to spend, too. A four-car tail, a tap on the colonel's telephone line. Cute. I didn't seem to mind, though, it got the juices flowing. I sort of wished that I hadn't locked up the two M–11s and the grenades, but I didn't think they would try to take me out on the highway. At least not after I found a state patrol car and dogged him at fifty-seven miles an hour all the way into Seattle.

I took the boys downtown to get in line for the Bremerton ferry. I got the silenced Ingram out of the trunk, emptied my knapsack, and put the gun in it. Then I went back down the line of waiting cars, collecting a few ignition keys. They knew what was in the sack, so they went along nicely. Except for the big dude in the Porsche. First he tried to play dumb, then he acted like he wanted to get Western right in public, but I slapped him in the throat with the suppressor and he didn't have anything else to say. I even took his billfold, but it contained even less information than Rideout's had. Ninety-seven dollars in bills but nothing else.

After the ferry docked and the lanes in front of me cleared, I turned around and left the ferry traffic blocked for half a mile, headed south down the freeway to the Sea-Tac airport, where I swapped cars one more goddamn time. I wanted a Corvette, but nobody had one, so I settled for a black T-bird. I made it back to Nobby's just in time for the five o'clock rush, really pleased with myself now, pleased enough to order a Chevas on the rocks.

The bartender was too busy to talk, so I waited for business to die down, waited too long, and found myself ambushed by a two-for-one happy hour, and suddenly, miraculously, sweet gift of whiskey and fatigue, it was nearly nine o'clock, and I was drunk as a pig. I didn't care who those guys had been. In fact, I thought about looking for them, but I finally stopped the bartender and showed him Rideout's fake license. Like any good citizen, he wanted to know why. I flashed my old Meriwether county deputy sheriff's badge, but he wasn't buying any of that. So I stacked up the change from a fifty.

'Maybe I've seen him a few times with the ferryboat crowd,' he said sadly, fingering the sheaf of bills. 'But not in a long time.'

'Which ferryboat?'

'Usually the last one. Sometimes he came in after work and stayed until the last boat. But like I say, it's been a while.'

'Vashon Island or Port Orchard?'

'Who knows?'

'Ever say what he did for a living?'

'I think he was a long-haul trucker,' he said, 'coast-to-coast number.'

'But you're not sure?' I prompted, nudging the bills closer to him with my finger.

'Not at all,' he said, then leaned back and shoved the bills toward me. 'Listen, buddy, you mind if I say something?' I shook my head. 'You keep your money there, and use it to get a room or something, because, my friend, you look like a dead man, and you are somewhat drunk.'

'You mind if I say something?' I asked, and he shook his sad pale face, the face of a reformed drunk. 'I been listening to bullshit advice all my life,' I said. He didn't look angry, just sadder. I dropped a ten-dollar tip on the bar and staggered out. Pretty picture. My first lungful of cold air off Puget Sound sobered me up a little bit, and I started to go back to apologize, but I had learned the hard way that drunken apologies to strangers usually just confuse them.

I got lost among the side streets of West Seattle looking for some of the Colonel's chicken, then lost again, gnawing on a drumstick,

575

as I tried to find the ferry dock. I think I meant to show Rideout's picture to some of the boat crew, but before I had a chance, I got hassled for smoking on the car deck, then for drinking beer on the passenger deck, then severely chided when I held up disembarking traffic on Vashon because I couldn't remember which one of the six sets of keys belonged to the T-bird.

I had been on Vashon Island once before in daylight and knew there was a tavern on the short main street of the small town in the middle of the island, but in the dark, salt-misty night, I couldn't find my ass with either hand. I spent what seemed hours wandering around before I found the main street and the tavern, and I was wildly surprised to discover it was still open.

As soon as I walked in, though, I knew I had made a mistake. It was a real hometown bar. Everybody knew everybody else, and nobody wanted to talk to a weird drunken stranger who looked as if he had just escaped from the federal lockup on McNeil Island. Nobody. Especially a swarthy fellow at the end of the bar who looked like an ex-con and who reminded me of the hapless postman. As I wandered down the bar, trying to start drunken conversations, he watched me carefully out of the corner of his eye, and when I pulled up on a stool near him, he chugged his beer and scooted out the back door. Even though the Supreme Court doesn't buy it, cops can smell the bad actors. I went out right behind him.

'Hey, asshole,' I said when I caught up to him in the alley, 'why don't you just hold it right there.'

'Shit,' he groaned, 'why don't you fucking guys get off my ass.' And they can smell the cop stink, too. 'Just leave me the hell alone,' he added, but when he turned around to face me his shoulders slumped, as tired as his voice. He had been in the joint a long time, had his ass kicked by pros. 'Alone,' he whined.

'How long you been out?'

'Three and a half years,' he said, 'and I can promise you, man, I ain't doing nothing, ever, to go back.'

'Relax,' I said, slapping him on the arm lightly. He flinched anyway. 'Take it easy,' I said, 'I ain't the man no more.'

'Right,' he said, 'sure. Let's just get it over with.' He pulled up the sleeves of his flannel shirt so hard that he popped the cuff buttons, and presented me with the insides of his elbows. Somebody had been rousting the poor guy.

'That don't mean shit,' I said, trying to sound like somebody in authority. 'Just take a look at this picture.' Even in the dim light I could see his eyes cloud and the old practiced lies forming on his mouth. 'Don't jerk me around, asshole.'

'Okay,' he sighed, 'what the hell. He told me his parole was up a long time ago.'

'Can you put the right name to the face?'

'John. That's all I ever knew,' he said, 'but I ain't seen him in six or eight months. Not since him and his old lady split.'

'She live here on the Island?'

'Maybe.'

'Here?' I asked, showing him the small snapshot. He nodded. 'Where is it?'

'Somewhere on the south end, toward Tahlequah,' he said. 'I was only there one time, and it was dark and raining, and we were – '

' – Fucked up?'

'Right,' he said sadly.

'I'll find it.'

'Not on a night like this,' he said with bitter humor as he lifted his hands into the foggy mist.

'Don't sweat it,' I said, trying to sound tough and competent. 'Just tell me how to find a motel.'

'A what? Oh, sure,' he said, smiling around broken teeth. 'Hey, you really ain't the heat, are you?'

'Maybe something worse,' I said.

'It shows, man,' he said, his smile growing larger, then he gave me a set of rather complicated directions to the only motel on the island. I gave him a ten and told him to buy himself a beer, and he whistled down the alley into the murky night.

It took me a number of beers and a length of time that should have been counted in years instead of hours as I roamed the black wet roads for me to realize what the ex-con's smile had been about. No motels on the Island, no ferryboats back to the mainland, no way I could take a chance, not with all the crap in the trunk of the T-bird, on sleeping in the car beside the road or on the ferry dock, and no way I could drive around all night. Although it had been only two nights with little sleep, my body said sleep.

When in doubt, go right to the source. I remembered passing a King County police substation on my meanders, so I back-tracked until I found it, then parked in the lot, put a note on my windshield explaining I was a tourist, lost and drunk and ignorant of ferry schedules, then climbed into the back seat, where I slept far better than I had any right to.

At five-thirty a patrolman rapped on the side window until he woke me up. I climbed out to stretch and thank him. The mist had turned to a light rain that couldn't wash the fog out of the air. When I yawned, the cold damp filled my lungs, like trying to inhale wet wool. The policeman was surprisingly pleasant for that time of day, even complimented me on my good sense. I shook his hand and thanked him again.

'No problem,' he said, yawning too. 'Happens all the time, all the goddamned time.' Then, as he walked back to his unit, he added over his shoulder, 'Goddamned islands.'

On the ferry back to West Seattle I stood on the bow in the cold wet wind and tossed the four sets of car keys into the dark pulsing waters of the Sound. On a bright sunny day I could have seen Mount Rainier looming like a misshapen moon on the horizon, and even through the fog and rain I thought I could feel its rocky weight. I drove back out to Sea-Tac to the large anonymous motels nearby, parked the T-bird in the lot of one, checked into another, paying cash and signing a false name. Unlike that person of the evening before, bloated with expensive Scotch and fake self-confidence, this guy wanted a few hours of untroubled sleep and no truck with the bad guys.

When the wake-up call came at noon, I was still scared, tired, hung over, and suffering that terrible morning-after, horny itch. I thought of how cool Gail's body might feel next to mine, how warm the comfort of Carolyn's heavy breasts, and the icy fire of Cassandra Bogardus' face. Nothing but hangover fantasy, though. No repeaters, Carolyn had said. The way of all flesh, down the toilet of life, said Gail. And I was still half angry at the Bogardus woman for dumping me so easily at the airport. I took a cold shower and stopped torturing myself. I had things to do.

First, I needed a new image. The bad guys were going to be looking for me with a vengeance. Professionals did not like to have their ass kicked by anybody, much less an alcoholic security guard. It took a ton of Sarah's money, but I bought a new image. A four-hundred-dollar blue pin-striped three-piece suit. Black loafers with tassels for a hundred and thirty bucks. A forty-dollar blow-dry haircut. A zircon pinky ring out of a pawnshop on 1st Avenue. Fifteen bucks.

While I waited for the alterations on the suit, I sent the colonel a hand-delivered-only telegram, telling him to have his telephones, office, and house swept for bugs. I sent Gail a telegram telling her to get Sarah out of town. Then I went over to pick up the suit. As I looked at myself in the triptych of mirrors, I thought about what the athletic young man with the wedding band had said when he finished cutting my hair. Even looking at my dirty, wrinkled Levi's, my bloodstained Woolrich shirt with pine needles still clinging to the back, he turned me around in the chair, patted the helmet of hair on my head, and said, 'It's you, sir.' I turned to the salesman, watching me look at myself in the mirrors, and said, 'It's me.' He didn't even raise an eyebrow. I went crazy and treated myself to one of those wonderful London Fog trench coats with a zip-out lining and a gray Tyrolean hat with a bright feather in the brim. 'Mother-fucker, it is *me*,' I said to the salesman, but he just thanked me sincerely. Then I drove this new, well-dressed me out of Seattle for safety's sake down the interstate to Renton, where I checked into a fancy motel under another cash-paying name. The new me and the old me, we did a couple of lines of that wonderful cocaine, then drove back up to West Seattle and the Vashon Island ferry to look for the former Mrs. Rideout.

Although there were no Rideouts listed on Vashon, it only took me half an hour to find the little frame house by the meadow. Even in the daylight, the low gray clouds and the drizzle made it feel like night. The three children had grown since the picture and they were dressed in matching yellow slickers that glowed in the ashen light. When I pulled into the muddy driveway, the smallest one looked at my car with the frightened eyes of a startled animal, then darted around the side of the house toward the dull, clumping sound of a splitting maul, but the largest, a pale blond boy who looked as if he lived in the rain, put his arm around his little sister and waited, his thin shoulders pulled tall and erect under the loose slicker. When I climbed out of the T-bird and walked toward him, he saluted smartly. Without thinking, I returned it, and he smiled.

'My daddy was in the army for a long time,' he said proudly.

'So was I,' I said, thinking, The rockpile army.

579

'He was a captain,' he added.

'Then I should have saluted you,' I said, 'because I was only a PFC.'

'That's right,' he said very seriously, and we exchanged salutes again, in the proper order this time.

'And what's your name sir?'

'John Paul Rausche, Junior,' he said, 'and this is my sister, Sally.' I shook the boy's hand, but when I offered mine to the little girl, she turned away shyly to hide her face against her big brother's shoulder. 'Sally's got a cancer behind her eye,' the boy explained, 'and she don't like people looking at her.'

'Is your mother home?' I asked. The name wasn't Rideout, but this was his father's son.

Before he could answer, though, she came around the corner of the house, the splitting maul held like a club in her raw, chapped hands. The smallest child clung to her left leg, but she walked steadily, as if she had become so accustomed to his weight that she might limp without it. Sweat drenched her red, plain face, and rain had beaded like a damp cloak across the shoulders of her buffalo plaid wool shirt.

'You kids go inside,' she said, her voice as flat and hard as the slap of a piece of kindling wood against starched jeans. 'Now.' John Jr. and I exchanged salutes again, but quickly, and the children disappeared into the house like sparks dropped into wet grass. 'If you be looking for John, mister, he ain't here. He ain't been here in a long time, and if I got anything to say about it, he won't ever be here again.'

The body hadn't been identified yet, and I wasn't about to be the one to tell her what had become of her ex-husband.

'You wouldn't know where I might find him?' I said. 'I am – '

'Like I told that fella last week,' she interrupted, 'I ain't seen hide nor hair nor support checks for eight months and two weeks . . . three weeks now.'

'I don't know where he is either,' I said, making it up as I went along, 'but I owed him some money and I'm on my way to California, moving out of this damned rain, and I wanted to pay him before I left.'

'Ain't nobody ever owed John money,' she said suspiciously. 'It's always him does the owing.'

580

'He did some work for me,' I said, 'but he took off before I had a chance to pay him.'

'That's my Johnny,' she said, some sort of perverse pride in her tone. 'Elk season must've opened.'

'Maybe I could give it to you,' I suggested, 'and you could hold it for him.'

'Maybe,' she said quietly as I dug out my billfold, fat with Sarah's money, and started pulling out one-hundred-dollar bills, meaning, I think, only to take a couple, maybe three, but I had to make myself stop when I got to ten. God hates a piker, I said to myself, Jesus loves the little children of the land. Then I counted ten more. When I handed her the money, her face dropped, then grew bright, not with greed, but with sheer joy. 'What in the name of the Lord did John do for this much money?' she asked, stammering as she counted. 'Kill somebody?'

'He hauled a couple of loads for me,' I said.

'Loads?' she said.

'This is his bonus,' I said. 'He did a good, quick job.'

'I didn't even know he was hauling again,' she said, still counting.

'Who was he hauling for before?' I asked, but she wasn't listening. She brushed a damp strand of hair out of her eyes, wet her thumb, kept counting.

'Holy Jesus, Joseph, and Mary,' she said when she finished.

'This other guy who was looking for John,' I said, trying to get her attention, 'what did he look like?'

'Like you,' she answered without looking up, 'except he drove a Lincoln.'

'What did he want?' I asked, hopelessly, great cross-examiner that I am.

'Huh? Oh, he said John owed him money,' she said, 'but I just laughed in his face.' Then she sprang at me, gave me a fierce hug and a wet kiss on the cheek. 'Lord, thank you, mister,' she said. 'You know he'll never see penny one of this, don't you?'

'I like to pay my debts,' I said, 'and I consider this one paid in full.' But she was back at the money, and I could have been talking to the wind or the soft rain or the stately, silent firs.

Driving away, I hoped Sarah would forgive me as I felt the plain woman's kiss burning on my damp face.

581

While I waited, parked on the ferry dock, for a ride back to the mainland, the effects of my grand gesture wore off quickly. What the hell did I have in mind? Here I was passing Sarah's money around like Christmas candy, and all the things I knew about the driver of the yellow Toyota filled me with sadness instead of knowledge, and I couldn't tell Sarah about his death without making her an accessory to my crimes. I climbed out of the T-bird and leaned against the dock rail. And what was I doing in these goddamned rich man's clothes? Maybe I thought they would make me bulletproof? Shit. I felt like ripping them off and throwing them into the cold green scummy water slapping under the dock. I settled for sailing the stupid gray hat over the gentle waves. Several gulls checked it out in the air, decided it wasn't worth eating, even though gulls will eat garbage that would gag a buzzard. While it still floated on the water, one of the gulls landed on it and seemed terribly surprised when the hat promptly sank. Jonathan Livingston Seagull Shit.

During the boat ride I sulked in the car, decided I would go back to the motel and clear my sinuses before I made any more major decisions – such as what I was going to do with all that dope. I had kept it so long after Rausche's death that not even my best friends would believe that I had kept it out of any other impulse than greed. It was great cocaine. I could keep on keeping it, maybe, but considering the sort of addictive fool I had proved to be throughout my life, that much good coke in my hands would probably be the death of me. Maybe I could sell it to make up for some of Sarah's money. But I was six hundred miles from home. When I got back to the motel down in Renton I played my only card; called my dealer in Meriwether, Raoul.

Raoul tried to act like a street-wise Puerto Rican from New York, and he affected leather slouch hats, brightly colored leather jackets, and red-tinted glasses day and night, but in fact, he was the son of a Jewish fuel-oil dealer in Pittsburgh. He had even gone to Harvard for a couple of years before he split to become a cook on the Alaskan pipeline, where he had discovered the joys of dealing and of freedom in the Wild West. He knew better, knew he was on a one-way ticket to the slammer, but he had been popped once in Phoenix, lost his stash and his cash, and now he was in debt so badly to the wholesalers and the lawyers that he had to keep dealing just to stay out of jail and alive.

When I finally got him on the telephone, he wasn't very happy about it, but I promised him a sixty-forty split, and he said he would see what he could do. Twenty minutes later he called me back, told me I wouldn't believe these people, wouldn't believe how flaky they were, told me to carry a piece and to hire some armed backup if I could. Just as I had with the bartender's advice the night before, I dismissed it without thought.

As a result, two hours later in a country house on the Olympic Peninsula across the Sound from Seattle, I found myself lying flat in a dusty hallway while a skinny girl with pimples subjected me to a very thorough and not very pleasant search, and another, even more emaciated woman, who looked like a high-fashion model, held a sawed-off 12-gauge shotgun against the back of my neck. At the end of the hall a fat girl in a baggy gray sweatshirt covered with the names of famous women held two huge and slobberingly angry Rottweilers on a short leash. Lying there, convinced I had dug my grave this time, I vowed to start listening to more advice. If they didn't blow my head out from between my ears, that is.

'He's clean,' Pimples said, 'nothing but car keys and this.' And she tossed *this*, a small packet of cocaine, down to the fat girl. She caught it and growled at the Rottweilers, who sat down at her feet, stopped drooling and started wagging their tails like dumb puppies. I stayed put, the shotgun barrels and Pimples' knee holding me on the floor. Hysterical, hushed giggles came from the mouths of unseen people and skittered like day-blind bats down the hallway.

'Shut up,' the fat girl said, and the laughter stopped at once. She walked away, came back a few minutes later, and said, 'Okay, bring the jerk in here.'

'Does she mean me?' I asked as the bony knee and the black steel holes lifted.

'Oh, does she ever,' the model answered in one of those cultured drawls that always makes me think of Vassar or Smith. 'Jerk.'

As I hobbled stiffly down the hallway, easing around the dogs, who were bored with me now, my knees shook so badly that I nearly collapsed. One scare too many. Once during Korea, Jamison and I had spent thirty-six hours under a Chinese artillery bombardment. We had started screaming 'no more' before the first five minutes had passed. That's how I felt now.

'Well, I do believe the big boy's just about to wet his pants, momma,' the cultured voice murmured behind me.

'You bet your sweet ass,' I whispered over my shoulder. She sneered like a brain-damaged collie, dug the shotgun into my kidney, then shoved me toward a Victorian chair, where I collapsed on the brocade in a sweat-damp puddle. She stood behind me, tapping the barrels lightly on the wood trim, and the fat girl sat down on a couch on the other side of the room.

'This is pretty good shit,' she said. 'Where'd you get it?'

'Does it matter?'

'If it's hot, it might matter one hell of a lot.'

'It's not exactly hot,' I said.

'What the hell's that mean?' she asked, smiling. Oddly enough, the smile made her plump face sweetly pretty. If she washed her hair and lost thirty pounds, she could turn heads.

'It came into my hands by accident,' I said, 'as part of another business deal. And nobody knows I have it.'

'We do,' the model said, stroking my ear with the shotgun.

'Usually I like a little more history,' the fat girl said, 'before I do business . . . but Raoul vouches for you, and if anything goes wrong, I'll send Lovely there to see you . . .'

'And I'll blow your fucking head off, jerk, cut off your nuts and stuff them down your throat,' the model crooned.

'Lovely,' I said, and the fat girl laughed.

'Where's the rest?' she asked.

'In a briefcase in the trunk of the car,' I said. Not all of it, though. I had taken the liberty of buying two briefcases and had mailed one to myself with about a quarter of an ounce hidden in the handle.

The fat girl picked up the car keys off the coffee table and tossed them to Pimples where she stood at the edge of the hall. But her aim was slightly low, and one of the Rottweilers snapped them out of the air as if he were catching flies. 'Orlando,' the fat girl said quietly, 'give.' And the dog dropped the keys on the floor, curled up, and started licking his anus.

'Orlando?' I said.

'He's from Disney World,' the model drawled. 'Aren't you?'

The fat girl's eyes crinkled with amusement, and the strange giggles came again, creeping out of a side room, followed by a string of coughs and a cloud of marijuana smoke.

'Carry the briefcase flat and with both hands,' I said to Pimples, 'because there's a live grenade inside with the pin pulled.'

The fat girl burst into honest laughter, but the model slapped me on the head with the shotgun. 'Aren't you Mr. Smartypants,' she said. 'Let's kill the asshole, momma, and drop him in the Sound.'

'He's too much fun,' the fat girl said, and I tried to look charming in my sodden three-piece suit.

When Pimples brought the briefcase to me, she handled it as if it were her very own baby. I sat it on the Oriental rug, disarmed the booby trap, held the grenade in one hand and the pin in the other, then scooted the briefcase across the rug to the fat girl.

'Now we can negotiate,' I said, 'on semi-even terms.'

Out of the corner of my eye, I saw a teenaged boy with long hair, wearing tattered overalls but no shirt, stick his head around the edge of the doorframe. 'He ain't shittin',' he whispered to somebody behind him.

'You cretins sit down and shut up,' the fat girl said without looking up as she hefted the loosely wrapped black plastic bundle.

'I'll go with your weight,' I said into her silence, thinking that was why she kept holding the package. But she wiped some of the pinkish gray powder on her sweat shirt and looked up at me.

'Jesus Kee-rist,' she muttered, 'that fucking pimp Raoul don't know shit from wild honey. He told me you were some jerk off the street, man, but you must have balls the size of a gorilla. I am truly impressed.' I didn't have any idea what she was talking about, but I tried to sneer confidently and look casual at the same time. The fat girl shook her head, gathered the dusty black plastic into a wad, and tossed it to Pimples. 'In the woodstove, baby,' she said, 'and now.'

'Good idea,' I said. Even if I was a jerk, Raoul, whose real name was Myron, was going to regret his mouth when next I saw him.

As she took her scales out of an inlaid Japanese box on the coffee table and weighed the cocaine, the fat girl kept glancing at me, a coy, little-girl's smile flickering about her mouth. 'I make it a hair more than five and a half ounces,' she said, finishing her work. 'Let's all do a couple of lines,' she added, taking a screen, a razor blade, and a small mirror out of the inlaid box, 'and call it five and a half. Okay?'

585

'I never touch the stuff,' I said primly. 'Five and a half is fine with me.'

'The way you make your living, man, I don't blame you,' she said as she chopped lines.

I nodded like a man who knew what was going on, shifted my damp shorts out of the crack of my ass, and took a tighter grip on the slippery grenade.

The fat girl snorted two short lines, as did Pimples, but the model declined, saying she would wait until I had gone, downer that I was, then she tapped me lightly again with the shotgun.

'Can't you get her to stop that?' I said. 'What sort of business are you running here, anyway?'

'We're sort of a family,' the fat girl said, even happier than she was before. 'Usually we conduct ourselves in a more professional manner, but this is a different deal. That's why we're doing it – for fun. You've got a fucking grenade, Lovely's crazy about using her shotgun – what the hell, let's enjoy.'

'Let's finish our business,' I said as Pimples carried the mirror into the side room, where the teenaged voices burbled and the 'Oh, wow's' and 'Good shit's' twanged.

'Right,' the fat girl said. 'You want to dicker or you want to get down.'

'Down.'

'Okay, fine,' she said. 'It's worth eleven, but it ain't got no history, you understand. I was going to offer you six, but I figure you've got your ass covered pretty good, and I've loved meeting you, so I'll go seven, tops . . . No, seven and a half, fuck it.'

'Done,' I said. During this last part of the business, the model had grown bored, wandered toward the gray, rain-streaked window, the shotgun propped against the exquisite flare of her collar bone. 'There's another item under the back seat,' I said.

'Get it, Lovely,' the fat girl said, and the model slinked out, looking even more bored. 'You sure you don't want a taste?' she asked me.

'If it goes to shit,' I said, 'it might as well go to shit with happy noses.' She laughed, shouted at Baby in the other room. When she brought the mirror back, the fat girl brought it to me, held the mirror and the glass straw for me, and when I had finished, she kissed me on the forehead. 'Thanks,' I said.

'Any time,' she said. 'No chance you'd put the pin back in the grenade, huh?'

'No chance.'

She laughed as the model came back inside with the kilo of marijuana. She threw it to the fat girl, snarled something I didn't hear, then went back behind my chair.

'I like your style, man,' the fat girl said as she sliced the black plastic wrapping off the smoke with a silver dagger, 'but we don't handle pot.'

'It's a gift,' I said, 'a bonus.'

'Ah, do I ever like your style,' she said, wadding up the plastic and giving it to Pimples to dispose of. 'Listen, man, anytime you want to do business – buy or sell or just get purely fucked up – you call me at this number' – which she repeated several times – 'and ask for, ah . . . Joan, and tell her that you're, ah . . . Leroy, and that you've got a bushel basket of fresh Dungeness crab. Leave a number, and I'll get back to you. And listen, man, now you really can put the pin back in the grenade, man, because I wouldn't jerk you around for love or money.' Then she paused to laugh. 'Well, maybe love. I've always got enough money, but nobody ever has enough love.' Then she stood up, headed for the back of the house, still laughing.

'She eats pussy, you understand, don't you?' the model whispered in my ear. I nearly jumped out of the chair. She had moved back behind me as quietly as a snake. 'But you wouldn't know about that, would you, tough guy,' she said, then smacked me along the jaw line with the shotgun.

Enough is enough. She might be mean, but she didn't know not to touch the person you're covering with a gun. I dropped the pin out of my left hand, grabbed the shotgun, and shoved it toward her, pointing the barrels toward the ceiling. Shit, she had the safety on, so I jerked the gun out of her hands, and popped her lightly in the gut with my right hand heavy with the grenade. I dropped her like a bad habit, and she fell to her knees like a nun seeking sudden forgiveness. I had forgotten about the dogs, but they just ambled over to lick the model's face. Pimples grinned at me, then walked into the side room where the teenaged boys were whispering.

'What happened?' the fat girl said when she came back in the living room with a sheaf of bills in her hand.

'Philosophical disagreement,' I said.

587

'Lovely *can* be a bitch, can't she?' she said, then slapped the bills against her wrinkled jeans. 'You want to count it?'

'It doesn't seem necessary now, does it?'

'Way beside the point,' she agreed.

'Then put it in the briefcase,' I said, 'and carry it to the car for me, okay?'

'Of course,' she said. 'You wait right there, Lovely.' But Lovely didn't answer, she just lay on her side, her eyes clenched tightly shut as the two Rottweilers mouthed her gently. As she opened the five locks on the steel-core front door, the fat girl said, 'Aren't you forgetting something?'

'What's that?'

'The pin.'

'Fuck it,' I said, 'it's somewhere in the living room.'

She laughed wildly all the way down the driveway, laughed as I unloaded the sawed-off, laughed even as I handed her the gun and the grenade. She tossed the shotgun into a rain puddle, and as she took the grenade from me, our hands seemed to fire in the damp air.

'Now give me a kiss,' she said, brandishing the grenade. I tried, but we were laughing too hard. 'And give me a call, you crazy son of a bitch.'

'Maybe I'll just do that.'

As I drove down the muddy road, I watched her in my rear-view mirror, watched her pitch the grenade underhanded across the road and into a deep, thickly overgrown barrow ditch. The shrapnel must have blown a tiny clear-cut in the evergreen brush. In my last glimpse of the fat girl in the rear-view mirror, she was standing over the ditch in the smoke rising in the misty rain, surveying the damage and still laughing.

I couldn't remember who said it – Freud? Margaret Mead? Phyllis Schlafly? – that no civilization could afford to send women to war because they would be too fierce.

If I had been the right sort of person, I would have had some sort of remorse while I waited for the Bainbridge-Seattle ferry, would have suffered at least a modicum of moral regret, but, what the hell, if I started worrying about the horrors of cocaine, who knew where I would stop worrying. Fluorocarbons out of our armpits and into the ozone? The next Ice Age? The dinky little star that made life possible going into nova? No, no, too much on my mind, too many troubles of my own. Sarah's and Gail's safety, and my own . . .

The pale, thin-faced man who had tried to look like a traveling salesman as he had tagged me from Ellensburg to Seattle leaned over the passenger deck rail watching the cars as they rumbled down the ramp onto the ferry. I turned up the collar of my trench coat, tried to look bored, and drove underneath him. I wanted a drink, and bad, but the shot of peppermint schnapps didn't cut the fear out of my mouth.

I took my time going to the motel, circling back on my trail several times, until I was sure my tail was clean, but in the motel room I shoved the two heavy easy chairs in front of the door, checked the M–11 with trembling fingers, and thought about drying out. This was no time, though, for the shakes, so I had another shot of schnapps and looked at myself in the mirror. My four-hundred-dollar suit looked as if I had worn it on a cross-country hike – dusty and damp from cuffs to collar – and my forty-dollar hairdo had a case of the terminal frizzies. Even naked after a shower, I still looked like a failure – saggy, bloated, and gray, like a stiff just fished out of Elliot Bay. I took the money out of the briefcase and spread it across the bed, but that didn't make me feel any better either. 'Balls like a gorilla,' the fat girl had said, meaning what I didn't know. But I had to laugh. If only she could see them now.

I fell on the bed and picked up the telephone to call the colonel, but fell immediately asleep with the dial tone buzzing in my hand. And woke four hours later, long past sundown, drenched in sweat, hundred-dollar bills pasted like leeches all over my body.

The colonel answered his home telephone before the first ring finished. I said, 'Milo,' and he gave me the number of a pay telephone, adding, 'Ten minutes.' When I called him back, he didn't even say hello, he just wanted to know who had tapped his lines. He sounded angry enough to curse, but he didn't.

'I don't know, sir,' I said, 'I'm sorry. And sorry, too, for involving you in my mess.'

'What sort of mess?'

'I can't say.'

'Why not?'

589

'I don't want to get you in trouble.'

'Okay,' he said. 'Are you going to find out who tapped my lines?'

'Yes, sir,' I said with more confidence than I felt.

'Then you're back on payroll as of yesterday.'

'Save your money, sir.'

'If you're not working for me, Milo, I've got to call the FBI about this.'

'I'm working for you, sir.'

'Good,' he said. 'And I've got some bad news for you . . .'

'Yes, sir,' I said.

'After twenty-four hours with no activity at the Weddington house, Milo,' he said, 'I took the liberty of entering the house – we handle the alarm system – and nobody was there.'

'Maybe they left town,' I said, hopelessly.

'Not as far as I could tell,' he said. 'Both vehicles were in the garage, no signs of packing, no signs of a struggle, nothing, and when I checked with airport security, nobody remembered them taking a flight.' When I finished cursing, the colonel coughed, then added, 'Remember, Milo, that I have a rather large organization, if you need any help.'

'Thank you, sir,' I said, 'but this one has to be mine.'

'Good luck,' he said.

'I'll check in tomorrow night, sir, same time,' I said, and we rang off. Then I called the airport, made reservations on a morning flight to Butte, hoping to pick up the trail of the woman in the blue Subaru. Waiting for morning made for a long night.

7

They sell picture postcards all over Montana bearing the legend 'The Most Beautiful Sight in Montana.' It is a picture of Butte in the rear-view mirror of an automobile. Butte isn't a pretty sight, coming or going. The great maw of the Berkeley Pit is eating the old town right off its mountainside, digging for copper they ship to Japan to be smelted. In many ways it is a sad city, a crumbling monument to both the successes and the failures of unbridled capitalism, seduced and abandoned first by the copper kings, then by the international conglomerates, but even as it dies, the old city still lives, filled with perhaps the best bars in a state of great bars, and rich with an ethnic mixture of Irish and Finns, of Poles and Mexicans. No true son of Montana can deny a deep fondness in his heart for the grand old whore, and a lot of people, myself included, don't think you can qualify as a native son unless you have spent at least one St. Paddy's Day in Butte.

But it is no place to be confused and depressed on a bleak and cold November afternoon. The north sides of the reddish, gray boulders up the mountainside shadow scraps of snow as dingy as a wino's sheets, the cold winds cut with a metallic edge, and the sky is the color of snot.

Only one place in Butte rented Subarus, and I didn't even have to bribe the woman behind the counter to get a look at the rental agreement for the dates in question. I suppose I shouldn't have been surprised by the name, but I was: Cassandra Bogardus.

Blind horse on a merry-go-round, back to my hometown, where not even my rich man's suit would hide me. I turned in my T-bird and rented the blue Subaru – cheap irony at the daily rate – then went out to the mall on the Flats, looking for a new image to carry me home. A blond frizzy wig with matching mustache, a double-knit lime-green leisure suit, Hush Puppies, an order pad, and a seventy-five-dollar twenty-pound Bible.

I made it back to Meriwether just before dusk, prime time for door-to-door salesmen, checked into the Riverfront, then drove over to the north side. Unless my hunch was completely wrong, the bad guys knew about the meetings between Cassandra Bogardus and Rausche, knew where she lived, and more than likely had somebody watching her house, and mine too, so I thought I would try to sell the Good Book, check out the neighborhood, and hope that I could find the watchers to watch them myself. I parked a block down from the Bogardus house on Gold, tucked the huge Bible under my arm, and began to ring doorbells. I chatted with a lonely old woman, survived the outrage of a drunk, got asked for my city business license by a young housewife, and took an order for a Bible from a puffy-faced middle-aged man who looked as if he had just been released from one of the rubber rooms over at Warm Springs.

As darkness fell, bringing with it a light snowfall, I came to the Bogardus house. Since no lights showed behind the windows, I could pass it by without drawing attention to myself. I tried to look confused and Christian, dejected as I sighed and crossed over to the other side to call on Abner's house to hire some surveillance of my own.

Abner was not happy, to say the least, when he opened the door to a Bible salesman. He cursed and tried to slam it in my face, but I shoved my way into the living room.

'Don't swing, Mr. Haynes,' I said, once I had shut the door, 'it's me, Milodragovitch.'

'Jesus Christ,' he said, 'you look like one of those homos on TV.'

'You got a glass of water,' I said. Even on the cold day in the light suit, sweat poured from under the wig. I tossed it and the giant book on the couch, took off the window-glass horn-rims, and sat down, trying to wipe the sweat out of my hair.

'Are you undercover?' he asked seriously, tugging furiously at the drooping end of my mustache.

'I'm under something,' I said. 'How do you sleep, Mr. Haynes?'

'What?'

'How do you sleep?'

'How the hell does anybody sleep when they're sixty-seven,' he grumbled, then narrowed his eyes as if he suspected I might try to sell him a dose of sweet rest.

'Working men never sleep worth a damn after they stop working,' I said, 'that's why retirement is such a damned hard job.'

'You can say that again,' he said, pulling at the straps of his undershirt in the warm room.

'How would you like to work for me?'

'Doing what?' he asked, lifting his large hands and flexing the fingers.

'See that house over there,' I said, leaning over to open the drapes slightly, but the angle of the porch cut off the view, so I led him into his neat bedroom, where the side window had a clear shot. 'That one there.'

'Where the big blonde lives?'

'That's the one,' I said. 'How long has she lived there?'

'Since the Johnsons went to Alaska this summer.'

'The Johnsons? Who are they?'

'He teaches wildlife biology out at the college,' he said, 'and she grows organic vegetables. What about it?'

'Can you see it good?' I asked, remembering his mistake with the sign on the van.

'I'm just old,' he growled, 'not blind.' I looked at him for a moment. He shrugged, went into the living room, and came back wearing gold-rimmed spectacles. 'All right,' he sighed, 'I can see it good.'

I explained that I wanted him to keep an eye on the house for me, not on any particular schedule, just watch it and call me at the motel day or night if he saw the blond woman come in, or anybody else around the house.

'Just watch it, that's all?' he asked.

'Don't watch it all the time,' I said, 'just take an occasional glance at it when you're awake, maybe every fifteen or twenty minutes. That's all I ask.' He looked disappointed that I hadn't asked more of him, so I added, 'And I'll pay you the same thing I would pay a professional operative.'

'How much would that be?' he asked, shuffling his slipper against the worn rug.

'One hundred dollars a day,' I said, 'a three-day minimum in advance.' I couldn't tell if it was the money I counted out or the phrase 'professional operative,' but the old man leapt at it.

'You mind if Yvonne helps?' he asked slyly, sneaking a glance at the old oak bed.

'As long as she keeps her mouth dead-tight shut,' I replied as seriously as if I were the reincarnation of J. Edgar himself, but laughing on the inside. Old Abner still had some healthy vices left in his worn, wiry frame.

'You've got my word on it,' he said, reaching out his hand.

As I shook it the thought of Sarah and Gail missing hit me again, and the laughter inside died. 'I mean it about Yvonne not talking,' I said.

'You've got my word,' he repeated.

'Day or night,' I reminded him as I went back into the living room to don my shoddy disguise, 'and if I'm not there, leave a message for Mr. Sloan – '

'Phony name, too,' he interrupted. 'Damnation, I thought this only happened on TV.'

Me too, I thought. I slapped the old man's shoulder, picked up the Bible and my wig, then left. When I hit the steps – splay-footed on the foam soles, with a smile so smarmy it would have made a dog puke – I paused long enough to curse a world that teaches a man to work until he can't live without it, works him nearly to death, then shoves him out to die.

Although with the five grenades and the two submachine guns I had enough firepower to start a coup in some small Central American country, I wanted my own guns and some backup, and since I couldn't pick up my mail without getting tagged by the bad guys, some cocaine. Purely for my nerves. All three, for my failing nerve. I went back to the motel to change into something warmer and less gaudy to wear while I broke into my own house, but the telephone was ringing when I went into the room. Old Abner on the job. He said he could see what he thought to be a flashlight moving around inside the Bogardus house. I went to check it out.

I nearly missed them when they came out the back door of the Bogardus house and slipped through the snow-dark shadows of the side yard and out a gap in the hedge. Two guys in jogging suits, their hoods up and snugly tied to hide their faces. I tagged them at a distance as they circled the block once for show, then went into a small frame house east on Gold and across the street, on the same side as Abner's. I started to go up to the front door and try to get them to order a Bible, but even if I hadn't left my red-letter edition in the car, I just didn't have the nerve. Not without some help, whiskey, or cocaine. Just following them had filled me with trembling fear. I knew where they had set up the surveillance and could deal with them later, so I went after some nerve.

My next-door neighbor's driveway was empty – his rattletrap pickup had taken him to his night-bartending job, and her Corvette had carried her out on the town to boogie – so I parked there, vaulted the back fence and went into my house through the cellar door. Very quietly. I meant to take all my guns out of the house, but by the time I removed the false panel my hands were shaking so badly that I only took three handguns – the Browning 9mm, a .357 Colt Python and an S&W five-shot, hammerless Airweight .38 – the shoulder holsters for them, and a box of shells for each. I strapped myself into the Browning in the cold basement air, but it looked like a thick steak under my arm beneath the thin leisure-suit coat, so I changed to the .38, trembling, then crept up the cellar stairs, opened the door to the kitchen and slammed it hard, then went back out through the cellar door.

Outside, I dashed across the street, dove into a clump of snow-heavy creek brush and waited. The bastards had my house bugged, just as I thought. Within two minutes a light-blue van arrived and parked right in my driveway just as if it belonged there. Two men who moved like professionals went into my house, one through the front, one through the back, so quickly I knew they had already had keys cut. I wondered if they were supposed to kill me there, or take me for a ride and kill me later.

After they had checked out the empty house they came outside, stood around as casual as tourists, discussing the vagaries of electronic surveillance. In the streetlight I could see their faces—the small dark dude in the pickup and the large guy who wanted to get Western in the Porsche when I messed up their pretty four-man tail in Seattle. Huddled in the snowbank, I wished I knew what to think. Too much cocaine, though, too much fear. I didn't want to think; I wanted to run, never think again.

When they turned around and left, I ran across to the Subaru and tailed them around the park to the apartment complex at the south end. I watched them go back to their apartment, made a note of the number, then dug into my wallet for the Snowseal packet of coke. There wasn't much left by now, so I just did the last of it right off the paper. It didn't help. And stopping wouldn't help either. Maintaining the buzz, that was my only choice. Otherwise, as scared as a street punk on his first mugging, I was going to kill somebody. And soon. And probably the wrong person. I headed for the Deuce and Raoul, the dealer, the little car fishtailing across the snow-covered streets.

Raoul was amused by my disguise, when he finally recognized me, and further dismayed when I dragged him out into the alley behind the Deuce by the lapels of his leather coat. When I had him in the shadows, I jerked him back and forth so hard that his leather hat fell into a pile of frozen dog shit. He protested, and I lost it for a second, slapped off his red sunglasses, and ground the lenses into the bricks with my Hush Puppies.

'Jesus shit, Milo,' he whimpered, 'take it easy.'

'What the fuck are you afraid of, Myron,' I hissed, 'some jerk off the street?'

'Okay, man, okay,' he said, wiping my spittle off his face. 'I made a small error in my judgement, okay, man, I thought those crazy bitches would be easy on you if they thought you weren't anybody, that's all, just some guy off the street, okay. What did you want me to say – that you used to be the man, that you're an alcoholic who has occasional lapses into cocaine psychosis?'

'Right,' I sighed, trying to get a handle on myself. 'I'm sorry. Too much shit going down, okay. I'm sorry.'

Myron took a deep breath, let it out easy, closed his eyes like a man chanting his mantra silently. 'Jesus,' he said, 'when you did my glasses, I thought I was next . . . Are you okay?'

'Shit.'

'I think you gave me whiplash,' he said, but he smiled. 'What can I do for you, man?'

'I brought your cut,' I said as I stuffed the roll of bills into his pocket.

'Keep it,' he said. 'I'm out of this. All the way. I talked to the fat lady, and I'm out. I don't know what you did, don't know what's going down, but I'm out.' He handed me the three thousand back.

'Keep it.'

'Absolutely not.'

'Okay, fuck it,' I said, counting off five bills. 'I need a quarter-ounce, okay?'

'You be hurting, huh?' he said softly. 'Sure. But this is too much bread.'

'For the glasses,' I said. 'The price of stupidity, okay?'

'Only for you,' he said, reaching down to pick up his hat. 'Thank God for cold weather and frozen dog shit. I'll catch you inside in half an hour or so.' Then he paused, and added, 'Maybe you ought to wait someplace else, Milo.'

'Why?'

'You ain't exactly dressed for the Deuce, man.'

'Fuck it.'

'It's your party, man,' he said, then hustled down the alley.

Inside, I tried to ease through the crowd politely, but when I went past the head hog of the local motorcycle gang, I stumbled over my Hush Puppies and jostled his beer. He was leaning against the end of the bar, daring somebody to bump into him, copping feels off passing ladies, hoping to start a fight so he and his tawdry minions could take some poor drunk dude back into the alley and put the boots to him. He looked at me as if I were some sort of subhuman species.

'What the hell, buddy,' I said under the bluegrass stomp, 'you never seen a Bible salesman before?' The .38 felt warm under my armpit as the blood rose. Goddammit, I thought, I knew I was going to kill the wrong person. Back off. But before I could apologize, he did. In his own way.

'Hey, dad,' he said, hitching his balls, 'you best take it cool and easy.' Then he sauntered off toward the pisser.

Sitting at the bar, trying to nurse my shot of schnapps, which must be something like nursing hemlock, I saw the armored-truck driver, whose name I couldn't remember, at a table near the back door with three other aging mountain hippies. He had been under fire, wounded in Vietnam, and I knew he was at loose ends. Maybe he wanted to work backup for me. If I could just remember his name.

Raoul came back during my third shot of schnapps, eased up to the bar beside me and bummed a cigarette, and when he handed the pack back, I knew the quarter-ounce was inside.

597

'Thanks, man,' he said, letting the smoke drift slowly out of his mouth. Under his breath he added, 'Try to remember, Milo, that sometimes you eat the bear, but sometimes the bear eats you.' It is something they say in Montana; I think it means that life has consequences. Raoul adjusted a new pair of red shades, shook his head, and went about his business.

I gunned the shot in front of me, walked toward the back door, and stopped at the table where the unemployed armored-truck driver sat. 'Hey, dude,' I said and tapped him on the shoulder, 'remember pulling down on me in front of Hamburger Haven the other day?' He stared at me for a long time, then nodded and smiled as if he was sorry he hadn't blown me away. 'Let's talk some business,' I said, 'outside.' Then I moved toward the door.

'In a minute,' I heard him say.

But as I waited in the alley, watching the tiny crystalline flakes float in the blue light from the street lamps, the tall, slouching bulk of the biker strolled out the back door and headed toward me, walking slowly, like a man with a mission.

'Hey, man,' he said as politely as anyone in his position could, 'you ought not to brace me like that, man, not a man like you.' When I didn't say anything, he scratched his chest beneath his jacket. 'I may not look it now, man, but I was brought up Pentecostal, and I've still got respect for believers, but a man like you ought not to be in a place like this. I'm lost, man, but you got a chance. Don't backslide, not like me, man; go back to the one true – '

'I'm Federal heat, son,' I interrupted, holding the double-knit jacket open to show him the .38, 'and you best be about your own business. Now.'

No matter how tough you are, you don't rise to the leadership of even a crappy small-town biker gang without a certain amount of ability to be articulate, even if only in the argot of bikers, and this guy looked as if he had never been at a loss for words in his life.

'You-you-you fucking – you pigs,' he stammered, 'you dudes will do anything for a bust, any-anything – '

'Forgive your enemies,' I said, hoping I was quoting something, 'as I forgive you, my son.'

But he just muttered a string of curses as he hurried back into the bar, pushing the armored-truck driver out of the way as he tried to get into the door.

'What the hell's wrong with *him?*' he asked as he stepped over to me.

'Salvation just turned to shit in his hands one more time,' I said.

'Say what?' he asked, but I didn't answer.

In fact, I didn't say anything for a long time. Or so it seemed. The small insane encounter with the biker had shaken me more than I could admit. I was tired of being half drunk, or half sober, tired of measuring out those shots of candied alcohol. The world was simply too crazy for me to handle sober. Maybe not the whole world, but at least the world where I lived – the bars and back streets, the shadows from which I watched, that world was too crazy for me to handle sober. Maybe the whole world was too crazy. Religious wars, political wars, economic wars . . . Did that world out there reflect us? Or we, that world?

I didn't much know, didn't much care. I knew I had to find out who wanted my ass, and negotiate, accommodate as much as I could and still live with myself. I had to find Sarah, if they had her, and Gail, and when I found the old woman, I had my own peace to make. That old lady and I would get happily stoned and talk about my father. And if I didn't find her, or if I found her dead, I intended to wreak havoc across the land until the guilty were punished under my hand. Even if it cost my life.

Then I realized what a coward I had been. It had been coming on me for years, the closer I got to fifty-two and my father's money. That was over now, here in this dog-shit alley, it ended, all the running, hiding, and I found myself grinning, not like a rabid animal, but like a child.

'Hey, man,' the armored-truck driver asked, 'are you all right?'

'I'm fine,' I said, 'absolutely fine. If a guy can't stand the occasional mid-life crisis, then fuck him, right?'

'Damn straight,' he said. 'But listen, man, I'm really sorry about the other day. I was behind a handful of downers and a pint of vodka, and my liver just won't handle it anymore, so I tend to get a little crazy – '

'What did you do in Vietnam?' I interrupted.

'What'd I do?' he said. 'Well, shit, man, I did what every grunt worth his C rations did, man – I killed people. What difference does it make to you?'

'Can you still handle yourself?'

599

'If I need to, Jack. Why?'

'I need somebody to cover my back,' I said. 'You want the job?'

He brushed his hair out of his face, wiped the melted snow off his forehead, then held his hands out toward me, palms down, so I could see the fingers tremble. 'I can just barely wipe my ass,' he said sadly.

Perhaps because we had shared that frozen moment in the gray, gusting rain or perhaps because I had finally lost my mind – whatever, I dumped a patch of cocaine on my fist and said, 'Will you at least do what I say?'

He hesitated for a moment, brushed his sleeve across his wet nose and snorted off my hand. 'Why?'

'Money, fun, fire power, and enough of this to keep us fairly sane,' I said.

'When?'

'Now,' I said, laughing, having a touch of nose myself, 'right now.'

'I can't remember your name, man – I know it's one of those long Polack numbers . . .'

'Russian,' I said.

'But you just hired a hand.'

'I can't remember your name either,' I said, and we both laughed wildly in the dark alley.

'Simmons,' he said, still laughing. 'Bob Simmons.'

'Milodragovitch,' I said, and we went to work.

I left Simmons in the car, clutching the .357, while I slipped across the yard to have a look through the windows of the surveillance house on Gold. Just as I thought, it was the other two guys from Washington, the salesman and the VW van driver, sitting on folding chairs in a bare living room. A small black-and-white television screen flickered on top of a stack of radio receivers. The two guys were sitting so closely together in the chairs that it almost looked as if they were holding hands. I went back to the car and we drove down to Abner's house.

When I introduced Simmons to him, Abner wrinkled his nose as if he smelled a dead rat.

'Don't pay any attention to how he's dressed,' I told him. 'Simmons is undercover, too.'

'Looks like he's been hid under a pile of garbage,' the old man muttered.

I borrowed Abner's flashlight, his hammer, and a towel – it would be a sloppy job breaking into the Bogardus house, but since my lock picks were in the tool box of my pickup, I didn't have much choice – and told Simmons to watch the other house.

'If they come out running,' I said, 'you come out behind them, find some cover, and shout "Freeze!" as loud as you can.' He stuffed the .357 in his belt and wiped his hands on his dirty jeans. 'Don't worry,' I added, 'they're probably not going to start a fire fight in the street.'

'Right,' he said, 'right.'

Abner shuffled over to a closet, drew out a Long Tom 10-gauge single-barrel shotgun. 'This'll blow their shit to kingdom come,' he said.

'Put that away,' I said. 'I didn't hire you for gunfire, Mr. Haynes.'

'Make that Corporal Haynes of the AEF,' he said. 'And you can have your money back, son.'

'Okay, but for God's sake, be careful!' I said. 'That goddamned cannon will blow somebody's house down.' Crazy old bastard. 'Please be careful,' I said again, but he just sneered. I gave up and left.

The house was a cracker box, though, so I slipped the side-door lock with Sarah's Gold American Express card and left the hammer and the towel on the stack of firewood. At least the Hush Puppies were good for something – they were quiet. I went through the house as quickly as I could and found out a great deal about the Johnsons – bounced checks and past-due credit duns, a collection of S-M magazines, some Polaroid nude studies of a dumpy dark-haired woman who was rather proud of her labia – but almost no evidence that Cassandra Bogardus had ever lived there. Just the tweed suit and the gray wig she had used to fox me at the airport. So I gave that up too.

When I got back to Abner's house, the old man asked me if I had had any luck.

'I got out alive,' I said.

'Yeah, but you're a pro,' the old man said proudly, 'and that's not luck.'

'You watch too much television, old man,' I said thoughtlessly, and Abner pouted and grumbled as he put away his shotgun. He sulked for another fifteen minutes while I waited to call the colonel at the telephone booth, waited in a dead silence because Abner refused to turn on his new Sony.

When I called the colonel, he picked up the telephone on the first ring, and I asked him to meet me at the office. I wanted to see who had hired Haliburton to tag Cassandra Bogardus.

On our way across town Simmons asked, as politely as a very nervous man could, what was going on.

'You just cover my back,' I told him, 'and don't worry about anything else.'

He got a little sullen too, so I left him in the car while I went into the colonel's office.

'Milo?' he said from behind his desk. 'You look terrible.'

'I assume you had the building swept,' I said.

'This morning,' he said. 'It's clean. They just bugged the telephone lines.'

'Bastards,' I said, and for once the colonel didn't look away when I cursed.

'I would certainly feel better if I knew what was going on,' he said.

'Me too, sir.'

'I don't like working in the dark.'

'Me either, sir,' I said.

'Well, what did you get me down here for, Milo?' he said tartly. This was my night for pissing people off.

'I need to borrow a couple of those down vests with the bulletproof lining.'

'Sure,' he said, tossing me his keys. 'They're in the weapons locker.'

'Sir, Simmons is out in the car,' I said. 'He's giving me some backup on this. Maybe you can talk him into coming back to work when we're done.'

'Simmons?' he said. 'Good man. A little confused from the war still, but a good man all the same. And a good idea, Milo. Thanks. I'll give it a shot.' Then he put on his flat cap and went out.

When I heard the front door close, I used the colonel's keys to unlock his file cabinet. The Cassandra Bogardus surveillance had been instigated by a Seattle firm, Multitechtronics, Inc. I jotted down the address and telephone number, locked the files, and hurried

602

down the hallway to pick up the vests. When I carried them out to the car, the colonel was talking very softly while Simmons stared out the windshield.

'Thank you, sir,' I said as I climbed into the Subaru. 'I'll be in touch.' I stepped on the gas, leaving the short man standing in the snow-covered parking lot.

'What the hell was that all about?' Simmons asked.

'The colonel wants to give you another chance,' I said.

'I'll be damned,' he said.

'He's a good old man,' I said. 'A little stuffy, but he'll go to the wall with you.'

'Ain't bad for an officer,' Simmons said, then laughed bitterly.

'Where do you live?'

'I've got a dump over the Deuce.'

'Living close to home, huh?' I said. 'You want to pick up some clothes and whatnot.'

'Why?'

'We've got a suite at the Riverfront,' I said.

'Guess I should.'

'Got a match?'

'Sure,' he said.

'Then dip it into here,' I said, handing him the vial of coke, 'and let's fix our noses.'

'You're the boss,' he answered.

Although the late-evening traffic on the Franklin Street strip was light enough so that any cop cars would easily be visible, I took two or three close, searching looks to be damn sure before we did any coke. And luck was with me again. I spotted the light-blue van that had carried the two bad guys to my house earlier. They had settled in about forty yards behind us.

'Shit,' I said and blew the coke off the match stick. 'We shouldn't have used the same telephone booth twice.'

'What?' Simmons asked.

'Do me quick,' I said, 'then climb over and jerk the back seat out and see if you can reach that orange knapsack in the trunk.'

'What?'

'Do it!'

Simmons seemed to have some experience breaking into auto

trunks through the back seat because he did it quietly and smoothly, without much effort.

'This what you want?' he asked, handing me the knapsack.

'Right,' I said and slipped the silenced M–11 out of the sack.

'Jesus,' he sighed. 'What the hell is that?'

'An interesting toy.'

'You are into some serious shit, huh?'

'You want out?' I asked as he climbed back into the front seat.

'No way, man. No way.'

'Okay. Now the vests,' I said, and we struggled into them. Although I had never personally tested the Kelvar mesh vests, I had seen them stop a .357 magnum round on a dummy. 'Let's go for a ride,' I said.

I took them out to the interstate, not running, but not poking along either, driving like a man on business. The van stayed with me as I headed west to the Blue Creek Road exit, where I turned south up the creek. The snow seemed to be falling harder on the dark, empty stretch of road, and the wind kicked small ground-blizzard swirls through my headlights. The van had cut its headlights, but I could still catch an occasional glimmer of its parking lights in the rear-view mirror. I punched the Subaru a bit, and it pulled away smoothly across the snow-packed ruts.

When I got to the long wooden bridge across Blue Creek, which led to Moccasin Flats Road, then back to town on the old highway, I raced across the slippery planks, then another twenty yards just around the belly of a curve, where I stopped the car and told Simmons to get behind the wheel. I ran to the bridgehead and dove behind the biggest rock in the ditch. The van came on faster now, its tires crunching through the frozen snow crust as it followed our tracks onto the bridge. It seemed I could hear the men chuckling while they checked their guns.

Thinking I didn't want to just drop them in cold blood, thinking maybe I could work something out, I let the van get to the middle of the bridge before I tried to put a short burst into the left front tire. I had held too low, though, so it took a second burst to hit the rubber. The van veered sharply into the railing, bounced and slithered, but it kept coming on the flat. The guy in the passenger seat leaned out the window; a spurt of flame exploded from the end of his arm, followed by the sharp, ugly splat of a silenced revolver. I rolled to the other side of the rock, put a burst into the grill. Steam and sparks and the hiss of a ruptured gas line filled the darkness. The fan belt began to scream like a hysterical woman, and the van came to an abrupt halt.

'Listen, you guys!' I shouted. 'It doesn't have to be this way!' When they didn't answer, I added, 'Let me have the old lady and the girl back, I'll keep my mouth shut about Elk City and we can call it even!'

Then they answered. Three rounds ricocheted off my small boulder, rock chips and dust mixing with the snowflakes. To hell with it. I sprayed the bridge and the van to get their heads down, saw the first flickers of flame off the engine and then crawled down the ditch around the curve, jumped into the car, and told Simmons to hit it. He did, and it was the most dangerous thing we did all night. Fifty yards down the road he nearly put us into the creek.

'Jesus!' I said. 'Let me drive.'

'Right,' he said, his voice trembling.

As we changed seats we heard a muffled roar and watched a fireball rise through the snowy night.

'Hope those boys were wearing their winter coats,' I said, 'because it's a long walk home.'

'Shit, was that the van? On the bridge?'

'People up here have been trying to get the county to build a new one for years,' I said.

8

After we picked up Simmons' gear, we packed all the guns into the small truck, then called a cab, leaving the little blue Subaru abandoned in the alley behind the Deuce with the keys in the ignition. I would report it stolen, eventually. Back at the Riverfront, the bar was closed, so Simmons and I had to make do with the remains of my schnapps.

'I'm sorry I can't tell you what's happening,' I said over the last shots. 'Some people are trying to kill me, and I'm trying to work a deal with them without killing any of them. Anything else I tell you would make you an accessory after the fact.'

'Whatever,' he said. He had been strangely silent since the bridge. 'You're the boss.'

'Look, if anything happens,' I said, 'you're looking at a piece of a Federal firearms rap and a cocaine bust – '

'Listen,' he interrupted, 'I gotta tell you something . . .'

'What's that?'

'You ever kill anybody up close?' he asked. 'I mean face to face?' I nodded, but I didn't want to talk about it, even if he was going to. 'Well, shit, man, I spent my sixteen weeks of the war riding an armored personnel carrier and firing fifty-caliber rounds into the fucking bush. Man, I never even saw Charlie. I was a fuck-up before the war – got into the Army because a judge in Denver gave a choice of the slammer or Uncle Sam on a little pot bust – and I got my Purple Heart when a gook rocket hit the half-track parked in front while I was sitting on the side of the APC reading a Spiderman comic, took a piece of shrapnel no bigger than a pencil eraser . . .' He paused, tugged his shirt out of his jeans, and pulled it up. 'Look at this shit.' The doctors had opened him up from pelvis to sternum,

606

gutted him like a game animal, but he was pointing to a tiny blue dimple just to the right of his belly button. 'So I ain't no kind of hero, man, and both times tonight, I was scared shitless, so if you want to look for some real backup, man, I'll understand . . .'

'Just shave clean in the morning,' I said, 'and we'll get you a haircut and a new suit. I can't have my bodyguard looking like a tramp.'

He grinned and tossed off the last of the schnapps. 'How do you drink this shit?'

'I'm with you there, son,' I said, 'and you'll do to ride the river with.'

'What the hell does that mean?'

'I don't know,' I admitted, 'but I heard it in a Western movie one time. And another line – "Let's hit the hay." '

I heard him laughing all the way into the other bedroom of the suite, heard him, like me, switch on the television set for the all-night company in our sleep, hoping to dream Western movies instead of our lives.

And woke the next morning to a full-blown blizzard, six inches of fresh and six more coming, hard icy winds off the Pole, and single-digit temperatures. My kind of weather, born and bred to it, and those web-footed sissies from Seattle were in trouble. I needed some clothes and winter gear out of my house, wanted a chat with Carolyn Fitzgerald about her connection with Cassandra Bogardus, but first I needed more wheels.

After I dressed in my rich man's clothes, I folded the leisure suit neatly, set it in the trash can with the snow-stained Hush Puppies on top of it, hoping the maid had a husband with no taste, then Simmons and I took a cab down to the car-rental agency, where I picked up two four-wheel-drive rigs, a Blazer for me, an American Eagle for him. I wondered if I was about to set some sort of record for rent cars, wondered if I would ever see my trusty pickup again, wondered, as we drove out to the mall, what Simmons would look like in a suit and a haircut.

As it turned out, he looked very nervous in the vested tweed, so I brought him a full-length leather overcoat, something a pimp or an actor might wear, and he felt okay again. So we went to work, Simmons tagging me around town while I looked for Carolyn Fitzgerald.

She didn't have a listed telephone number, nor, I found out for twenty dollars, an unlisted one either. When I tried calling her at the Friends of the Dancing Bear, they said she didn't come in too often, but took my message to call Mr. Sloan at the Riverfront. Thinking perhaps Vonda Kay might know where she lived, I went back to the motel bar when it opened at ten; the lady bartender told me she had called in sick.

'So she's at home?'

The bartender looked at me for a long time. Although she was dressed in ruffles and lace and made up like an actress, she had those hard bartender eyes. If it had happened, she had seen it.

'Maybe,' she said.

'I'll give her a call.'

'I can't give you her number,' she said.

'I've got it, babe,' I said, 'and if I miss her at home, tell her Milo stopped by.'

'Oh, you're Milo,' she said, glancing about the empty room, then leaning across the bar. 'Listen, she's on a tear. She called me at ten last night, drunk out of her mind, and asked me to cover her shift for a couple of days, so I don't know where she is. Your guess is as good as mine.'

'Thanks,' I said, then went up to the room to call Vonda Kay's favorite bars.

I caught her day-drinking at the Doghouse, and when she came to the phone, she was mumbling drunk. 'Winter, winter,' she kept blubbering, 'I can't stand another goddamned winter alone, Ralph.' Ralph was an ex-husband twice removed. When she finally understood who I was and what I wanted, she lurched out of tears and into cursing. 'Why don't you want to know where *I* live, bastard, why?' Then she hung up. By the time I drove out to the Doghouse, she had left. I called some more bars without luck. Lady bartenders live a tougher life than anybody knows.

As Simmons and I went back out to our cars, I stared across the lot at the EZ-IN/EZ-OUT, but it looked permanently closed, the plywood panels, gleaming like raw meat in the gray light, looking as blank as dead faces. I thought about the two kids in their reindeer pajamas, about the Benniwah kid locked in the maximum-security cell in the hospital, about the two hunters who probably had their lawyers after my ass at this very moment.

'You okay?' Simmons asked through his open window.

'Sure.'

'Where now?'

'The cop shop,' I said, and he frowned. I climbed in, locked the 9mm automatic and the .38 Airweight in the glove box, stuffed the M–11 to the bottom of the knapsack beneath a dirty sweat shirt, then went to see Jamison.

'Goddamn, Milo,' he said as I walked into his office, 'you are looking prosperous. Come into the money?'

'Don't be a jerk,' I said.

'I'm glad you stopped by,' he said, smiling. Although he hadn't treated me with active disgust as often as he used to, it was odd, after all the years of enmity, to see him smile at me as if he were actually glad to see me. It made me uncomfortable, made me feel the cell doors clank shut.

'Why?'

'I wanted you to be the first to know.'

'Know what?'

'I asked the colonel to let me be the one to tell you,' he said.

'What?'

'He's opening a new office in Portland,' he said, 'and I'm going to run it . . .'

'And?'

'And Evelyn and I are getting back together.'

'She dumped Captain Organic, huh?' I asked, and he nodded. 'What happened?'

'I'm not quite sure,' he said thoughtfully. 'Hell, I was never sure why she split in the first place, but, anyway, she said she hit him in the face with a two-pound T-bone and he ran away.'

'She always did have a way with words,' I said. 'Congratulations. I guess.'

'Thanks,' he said, 'and I've got some good news for you.'

'I could use some.'

'But don't tell anybody it went down this way, okay?'

'What?'

'The Blevins brothers, those upright citizens with the vigilante turn of mind who blew up the EZ-IN/EZ-OUT the other night . . .' he began, almost happy. 'Well, they're not pressing charges against

609

you, and they're not filing civil suits against you or Haliburton Security, and they're not going to Deer Lodge Prison.'

'Wonderful,' I said. 'What about the Indian kid?'

'I suspect he will,' Jamison said sadly.

'Too bad.'

'You're right,' he said.

'That doesn't sound like you,' I said, 'and I can't believe you're resigning, either.'

'You know, Milo,' he said, leaning back in his swivel chair and lacing his fingers behind his neck, 'I can't quite believe it either. You told me years ago, you remember, that I was carrying too large a burden of morality to be a good cop, and, you know, you were right.'

'Did I say that?'

'That,' he said, 'and I think you also asked me out into the hills for a round of fisticuffs. Several times. Maybe I would have been a better cop if I had gone with you.' I didn't say anything, more than uneasy with this new Jamison. He had tried like crazy to be my friend all the years when we were growing up, while we were playing ball together at Mountain States, while we were in Korea in the same outfit. We had even gone into law enforcement – his term – together; he had joined the police department the same month I went to work for the sheriff. It had taken a long time for him to understand that I didn't much give a damn about enforcing some laws, and even longer for him to forgive me for my attitude. 'So what was it you wanted?' he said after the long silence.

'A favor. Or two.'

'If I can.'

'I need you to run a couple of names through your computer hookup.'

'Not a chance,' he said nicely. 'You know that.'

'What do you have on that van they pulled out of Blue Creek this morning?' It hadn't made the paper yet, but the radio news was full of wild reports about bullet-ridden vans, burned bridges, and drug wars.

'It will be in tomorrow's paper,' he said, fingering a sheet of computer print-out, 'and on tonight's news.'

'What?'

'No vehicle identification number,' he said, 'no engine block number until we get somebody over from Helena to do an acid test, stolen plates – you know the scenario. Why do you ask?'

'Just curious,' I said.

'Goddammit, Milo,' he groaned, 'you draw trouble like honey draws flies.'

'Or shit.'

'Right,' he said. 'You coming to the ball game?'

'If I can.'

'Try,' he said. 'Here's your ticket.'

'Thanks.' I put the ticket carefully in my wallet. 'I will try.'

'Buddy will be glad to see you.'

'I said I'd try.'

'And if you figure out a favor I can actually do,' he said, 'let me know.'

'I will,' I said, and we left it at that.

After we dropped Simmons' rental unit at the motel, and since there didn't seem to be anything else to do, we spent the rest of the day drifting with the storm around Meriwether, up and down the snow-covered streets, looking for Carolyn Fitzgerald's Mustang, looking for Vonda Kay, occasionally checking the motel for messages, without luck, rolling past the dark Bogardus house, the even darker Weddington mansion, doing cocaine and schnapps and worrying until I was half-crazy, maybe full-bore bull-goose loony.

Anyway, just after dark I parked the Blazer in my next-door neighbor's driveway, with something really insane in mind. I saw her come to the window to see who had pulled in, so I went to the front door and knocked.

'Milo,' she said when she opened it, 'you look beautiful. Come on in. Where have you been?'

'Maybe in a bit,' I said. 'Can I leave my rig in your driveway for a few minutes?'

'Of course,' she said, giving me one of her wild, thin-lipped kisses, all teeth, tongue, and suction, which nearly pulled me into her house. 'Oh, do come back,' she said as I turned to leave, patting the Airweight under my arm. 'You know how much I love it when you've got your gun on.'

'Sure,' I said, wishing that I didn't know how she felt about it, wishing I had lived a somewhat saner life. 'Sure.'

611

I went back to my house. Simmons and I got in through the cellar door and gathered up down parkas and sleeping bags, clothes, my .30–06 elk rifle, a Ruger .44 magnum autoloading carbine, a 12-gauge riot shotgun, my grandfather's .41-caliber derringer, two pairs of snow pacs with flannel liners. Simmons, as crazy as I was, kept stifling giggles, and when I would mouth 'Bugs' at him, he had a bigger giggle to choke. It took two trips, and on the second I picked up my chain saw case, and Simmons kept his fist stuffed in his throat until he got control of himself, then he whispered, 'We've got enough arms to start a goddamned war, man, but if we're getting into Texas Chain Saw Massacre, I'm getting out.' Then he had to hold his jaws shut to keep the laughter inside.

Back in the Blazer, though, it broke out, and neither of us could stop until long after the tears had come. My next-door neighbor came out of the house to see what we were doing, but I gave her a toot off my fist and sent her back inside with empty promises.

'Where you going now, dad?' Simmons asked as I climbed out of the rig one more time.

'One last thing,' I said, a short burst of laughter barking into the sideways snow.

Thinking about the grenade under my seat in Idaho, I went back inside, muttering, 'Booby-trap me, bastards,' all the way. I carried the crossbow upstairs to the kitchen, cocked it and ran a string off the back-door handle through a cabinet-door handle, then to the trigger, and set the bow on a kitchen chair aimed at the back door. Then I unscrewed the hunting point off the bolt, cut a hole in an old handball, and stuck it on the end. That would make the bastards think twice about messing with me again, and maybe they would want to talk when they finally realized what a sneaky bastard I was. I opened the front door, slammed it, turned on the television, rattled my old couch, then slipped quietly out through the basement.

Back in the motel parking lot I decided I had had enough time looking like somebody else, and Simmons kept tugging at his tie as if it were attached to a hangman's knot, so we went up to the suite and put on normal clothes. It felt great, especially after another toot, so we rushed down to the bar to catch the tag end of the Happy Hour.

Sometimes when hard work fails, luck succeeds. Carolyn Fitzgerald sat at the bar holding a beautiful martini. Lord, how I wanted a martini, but one would be too many and ten thousand wouldn't be enough. I perched on the stool beside her, motioned Simmons to the other side, and ordered a cup of coffee. Working-time again, and me in no condition for it.

After we exchanged trite pleasantries, and I realized that she wasn't at all pleased to see me, I said, 'I need to talk to you. Privately. I've got a room upstairs. You can carry your drink up there.'

'What about?' she said.

'Business.'

'The last time I saw you, Milo, you were more interested in jokes than business,' she said, 'and from the size of your pupils, I assume you're going to be even funnier now.'

'Damn right,' I said and picked up her hand as if I were admiring her bevy of rings, then guided it to the place under my arm where the Airweight nestled like a snake in a skull. 'Serious business.'

'My God,' she whispered.

'Laugh,' I said, 'smile, and bring your drink. My friend behind you is carrying an even bigger gun.'

Her hollow laughter followed a bitter smile, but she came, and I could tell she hated every step of the way. The strap of her purse kept slipping off her trembling shoulder, and even though she held her drink with both hands, by the time we reached the door of the suite, all the gin had splashed out to run like crystalline tears over the turquoise and silver, the sapphire and ceramic of her rings.

'I'm sorry,' I said, once we were locked in the room. 'I'm terribly sorry, but this is damned serious.'

She didn't answer but tossed her empty glass on the bed, flopped into an easy chair, and buried her face into her bejeweled hands, her long red fingernails digging into her forehead. I told Simmons to go into the other room. He looked like I felt, like a man coming down off stone-crazy giggles into the black maw of reality. Finally Carolyn raised her head, smiled like a woman resigned to a fate worse than death, and clawed some cigarettes out of her purse.

'I didn't mean to lose it like that,' she said through a streamer of smoke, 'but guns scare the hell out of me. Three years ago I was raped in my apartment in D.C., at gunpoint, so I'm still a little touchy.'

'I understand,' I said. 'I'm sorry . . . Shit, I guess no man ever

613

understands that sort of violation. Unless he's been gang-raped in prison . . .'

'That happened to you?'

'No, no – I didn't mean that. I'm just trying to say I'm sorry, but you didn't seem inclined to talk to me, and – '

'And you're drug-crazed.'

'Truth be known.'

'I hope you have a good reason for this,' she said, a good, tough lady gathering herself.

'Cassandra Bogardus.'

'Cassie?'

'I need to see her.'

'You don't need to jerk me out of the bar at gunpoint,' she said, 'just to see Cassie. From what I understand of her life, men get to see her just about whenever they want – never as long as they want, but just about whenever.'

'Not like that,' I said. 'I just need to talk to her.'

'Don't you all.'

'Shit,' I said, unfit for human conversation, thinking that perhaps Carolyn didn't know anything worth knowing.

'I've got her telephone number,' she said, stubbing out the cigarette and lighting another, 'and her address.'

'So do I. But she's never home.'

'That's not my problem.'

'What is?'

'You, Milo, your gun, your friend with the crazy eyes, and wondering how you know I know Cassie.'

'I was watching her house the day I met you here,' I said. 'I followed you here thinking you were her.'

'And just why the hell were you supposed to be following her? If you don't mind my asking?'

'You know, maybe it was a real coincidence,' I said, 'but so many strange things have happened lately, cause and effect have gotten all confused in my mind. Truth is, lady, I don't have any idea what's going on.'

'That makes two of us, buster,' she said and clicked her long fingernails against the surface of the small table beside her. I felt the scars on my back itch, the flesh tremble with the old gunsight fear.

'I need to see her,' I said. 'People are trying to kill me, and I think she knows why.' I walked over to her chair, leaned over her and took out the Airweight, set it on the table next to her hand, and backed away. 'I can't hard-ass answers out of you, babe – maybe it was just one night, but it was a night – and if you know where she is, I'm asking you, please call her, tell her I need to talk to her.'

'Maybe she's hiding from you,' she said softly through a billow of smoke as she moved the revolver away with the backs of her fingers. 'Ever think about that?'

'Maybe she's hiding from me,' I said, sitting down on the bed. 'Sometimes it doesn't help to know who you're hiding from. Whatever, you've got the gun, you set the meeting, I'll come alone, unarmed – you can strip-search me if you want,' I added, and the idea made laughter bubble in my throat.

'Can I use your phone?'

'Sure.'

'You go in the bathroom, shut the door, and turn on the shower,' she said casually, and I obeyed, leaving the .38 on the table, even though I felt unbalanced without its comforting weight. It seemed that I spent an hour in the bathroom, sitting in the steamy air as the shower flowed, but it couldn't have been more than ten minutes before Carolyn knocked on the door.

'You can come out for a bit, lover boy,' she said without a trace of a smile to soften her coarse features.

'Any luck?'

'She's supposed to call back in fifteen minutes.'

'You want a drink while we wait?'

'A Beefeater martini on the rocks.'

I went into Simmons' bedroom and asked him to go down for drinks. Back in my room, I sat down across the table from Carolyn.

'I would appreciate it if you would put that away,' she said, staring at the ugly little .38. I tucked it back under my arm. 'You've killed people, haven't you?'

'In Korea,' I said, 'when I had to. I didn't go out of my way looking for it, though. Spent ten years as a deputy sheriff without firing a serious shot. Seven years ago I shot two men who were trying to kill me.'

'How does it feel?'

'Now or then?'

'Both.'

'At first it makes you numb to keep you from being sick,' I said, 'then it makes you sick and sad, then you get over it.'

'How?'

'The same way you get over anything, I guess. Time passes, you become a different person. You're thinking about the rape, aren't you?' She nodded, lit a new cigarette on the butt of the old one. 'Would you have killed him?'

'No,' she said flatly. 'I don't want to kill anybody. Ever.'

'I feel the same way.' I was thinking about how careful I had been not to shoot at the guys in the van even when they were shooting at me.

'Why?'

'Enough people die in this world without my help, and I don't think I can stand it anymore.'

'Interesting,' she said.

'Tell me about Cassandra Bogardus.'

'She's the toughest woman I've ever met,' she began softly. 'I think she would have killed my rapist, or died trying . . . but I don't really know her that well.'

'Why not?'

'We met in D.C. some years ago,' she said, 'then ran across each other out here a few months ago.'

'What's she do for a living?'

'Clips coupons. Also works as a free-lance news photographer and magazine journalist, covers the occasional war.'

'War?' I said. 'She looks like a model or something.'

'Don't let it fool you. She's been to at least two Middle Eastern wars and one Central American revolution.'

At this point Simmons came back with a tray of drinks – two martinis for Carolyn, two *Dos X's* for himself, two shots of goddamned schnapps for me – but after he went back to his room Carolyn didn't want to talk anymore, so we smoked and drank until the ringing of the telephone broke the silence.

'Yes,' she said into the receiver, then listened for several moments. 'Unarmed, alone, and damn sure you aren't tailed,' she repeated, glancing at me. 'Can you handle that, lover boy?'

'Right,' I said, which she echoed into the phone before she hung up.

616

'I'll meet you in the bar at ten o'clock,' she said as she stood up. 'And wear something warm.'

'Want to finish your drinks?'

'You need them worse than I do,' she said, heading for the door.

'Can you give me some small idea about what's happening?'

'Yeah,' she said, her hand on the doorknob. 'I'm sick and tired of this goddamned cowboy-and-Indian crap.' Then she left, slamming the door behind her with a sudden and furious finality.

'Cowboy-and-Indian crap,' I said to myself as Simmons came in the room.

'What happened?'

'I don't know,' I said. 'Maybe we should eat and try to come down a little bit.'

'Eat?' he said. 'Shit, man, I can just barely chew this Mexican beer.'

'I know what you mean,' I said. I put one finger in Carolyn's full martini, stirred the ice, sucked the gin off my knuckle. 'Let's take a walk up to my place. Maybe we'll have an appetite when we get back.'

'Walk?' he said. 'Goddammit, Milo, there's a blizzard out there!'

'And an unsightly snowstorm in my head,' I said. 'Let's do it.'

We laced ourselves into the Soral pacs and tucked ourselves into down parkas and shearling mittens, headed into the storm. All that talk about killing had made me want to disassemble my little joke of a booby trap.

But we were too late. Even though the snow had drifted into the tracks, we could see where they had already gone into the house, front and back doors again. At the kitchen steps the crossbow bolt stuck out of a snowbank, the handball intact on the point, and beside it, a deep wallow where someone had fallen, and gouged trenches where someone else had dragged him away through the snow. A two-foot drift like the beginning of a great sand dune had billowed against the kitchen cabinets through the open door. I shut the door quietly, and we left, trekking back through Milodragovitch Park toward the warm motel room, pausing just long enough at the apartment complex on the south end of the park to look for a light in the windows of the apartment where I had seen the two thugs go in, but the panes were as black as the wintery night.

9

Carolyn was on time, dressed as warmly as I was, and she didn't want one for the road. Out in the parking lot I asked which car we should take, and she said to take mine. Once inside the Blazer, she checked every nook and cranny in the rig, then she searched me very carefully. True to my word, I had moved the rifles, the shotgun, and the Ingrams to the trunk of the AMC Eagle. True to my word as best I could be as scared as I was – my grandfather's .41-caliber derringer nestled inside my right mitten, tossed carelessly on the dashboard. She missed it, as I knew she would, and I felt slightly guilty that it was so easy, but I preferred guilt to death.

'Okay,' she said, 'now tell me how you're going to be sure that we're not followed.'

'Just trust me, and watch. If there's a tail, I'll drop it. But there isn't any.'

'Do it anyway, whatever it is you do,' she said, 'but what about those electronic things they put on cars to track them?'

'Beepers?'

'If you say so.'

I drove across town to the Haliburton offices, bullied the dispatcher into giving me the key to the electronics locker, then went over the Blazer carefully. 'See that dial,' I explained to Carolyn. 'If there's a transmitter aboard, it'll go crazy.' But it didn't move. 'Now the visual tail,' I said when I came back from returning the equipment.

We drove up the dark corridor of Slayton Canyon to the end of the pavement, then I switched the Blazer into four-wheel drive, and headed down the dirt road to Long Mile Creek, bulling through the drifts while Carolyn tried to chew the knuckle out of her wool gloves, down the mountain road until I found the right sort of tree, an eighteen-inch-thick pine that leaned over the road toward the sidehill. I stopped just past it, got out my chain saw, checked the gas and the oil levels, and prayed it would start.

'What are you doing?' she asked, leaning out of her window.

'Roadblock,' I said, tugging on the reluctant starter rope.

'This is a national forest,' she said. 'You can't do that.'

'Just shut up, will you,' I said, pulling on the rope again.

The engine coughed and died in a burst of smoke, but the next time I choked it, the Poulan fired again, sputtered, then broke into smooth running. I let it warm up, then cut it off, and stepped off the side of the road into the hip-deep snow, cleared the brush around the trunk, then started it up again. It wasn't a beautiful cut, or quick, and for a second I thought I was going to drop the sucker on the Blazer, but it fell just where I wanted it blocking the road, and when the pine tree bounced, it didn't take my head off.

After I had loaded the chainsaw into the back of the Blazer, I got back behind the wheel, huffing like a gut-shot bear, and turned the heater all the way up.

'Sometimes, you know,' Carolyn said, then hit her cigarette, 'sometimes you people out here don't seem to know what you've got in this beautiful country, because you treat it like shit.'

'When I want some goddamned East Coast tourist to tell me how to live in the place where I was born and raised,' I said, 'I'll let you know. All right? But for now, just shut the fuck up. When you see places like Butte and the coal strip mines in eastern Montana and the goddamned clear-cuts, try to remember that we may be whores, but it's those pimps playing squash in the Yale Club in New York fucking City who are living fat on their cuts. So shut the fuck up.'

'I'm sorry,' she said, almost as if she meant it.

I didn't have anything left to say, nothing to do but drive, covered in frozen sweat, trembling as the last of the alcohol and cocaine washed like acid rain out of my system, feeling all the old frost-bitten parts – the tip of my nose, both cheeks, both ear lobes, my left little finger, the outside of my left foot – begin to sting and burn as if somebody held cigarettes to the spots. And I was so tired, I almost didn't care if I ever saw Cassandra Bogardus.

When we finally got down Long Mile Road to the interstate, Carolyn directed me back to town, where we changed to her Mustang, which had been parked on a side street on the south side of town. She made me climb into the back seat and cover myself with a blanket.

When she let me out, we were parked beside the end door of the new wing of the Riverfront. I was not happy.

'Too goddamned cute,' I said as she unlocked the side door with a room key and led me upstairs. 'Just too goddamned cute for words.'

'I am sorry. Truly,' she said. 'But Cassie's afraid, and if she's afraid, I'm scared to death.'

She paused in front of a room door and gave it two taps, three taps, one, and I curled my fingers around the derringer.

'Coded knocks no less,' I grumbled.

'Wait until I'm gone,' she said stiffly, 'then knock twice.' She touched my cheek with her fingers. 'I'll be in touch.'

'You ain't going noplace, lover lady,' I whispered into her ear, tucking the derringer against her throat. 'It was a great night, but only one night, and I don't trust you worth a shit anymore.'

Her eyelids fluttered as the breath rushed out of her in a warm stream against my burning face. I thought she was going to faint, but she took a deep breath, sighed, then knocked on the door twice. When it opened, I held the small pistol to my lips to shush Cassandra Bogardus' greeting, then shoved Carolyn inside, slammed the door with my back, and motioned the two women to the floor. Then I checked out the room.

Nobody hiding anywhere, not under the bed, not even on the balcony that overlooked the black rush of the river. Wherever Cassandra Bogardus had been staying, it wasn't in this room. The dresser drawers were empty, the bathroom pristine, and a pair of stylish, dripping snow boots and a ski parka were the only objects in the closet, her large, expensive leather purse the only blot on the smooth, unruffled bedspread.

I nudged the bottoms of their feet, and the two women rose, Carolyn frightened and angry, her shallow breath coming like blasts from a blacksmith's bellows across a white-hot bed of coke, but the Bogardus woman only arched one perfect eyebrow in amusement, the corner of her perfect mouth slightly curled.

'Outside,' I mouthed silently as I handed her the coat and boots and her purse. Once the three of us were in the hallway, I steered them down toward my room. Halfway there, Carolyn stopped and turned on me. 'You son of a bitch,' she hissed, 'whose side are you on?'

'I don't even know what we're playing,' I whispered.

'I'll scream my head off,' she said, 'then what are you going to do? Shoot me?'

'Knock you out and hope I don't break your jaw, hope your tongue isn't between your teeth, because you'll bite it off, maybe scream myself . . .'

'Tough guy,' she sneered.

'Take it easy, Carolyn,' the Bogardus woman said softly, her hand reaching for Carolyn's. 'Can't you tell that he's as frightened as we are. Let's just do what he says. It'll be all right.'

Carolyn took a long moment to decide, and I took the time to look at Cassandra Bogardus. If she had looked beautiful in the spotting scope that morning, up close and in person, she was stunning, the loveliest woman I had ever seen in real life: flawless skin made up so carefully that I couldn't see it even in the bright hallway, but make-up she could have worn under the harshest camera lights, the whitest and straightest teeth I had ever seen, jade-green eyes with flashing flicks of amber, and glowing blond hair that fell full and soft across her shoulders to curl in ardent dismay at her heavy breasts. She wore an open-weave sweater, which nearly matched her eyes, over a dull-gold turtleneck, designer jeans so tight they made me uncomfortable, and golden high-heeled sandals, which made her taller than me, with straps as delicate as spider webs.

'If you're through, lover boy,' Carolyn said, 'let's get on with it.'

'Huh? Right, right,' I said. 'When we get to my room, ladies, not a sound – '

'He's afraid of electronic surveillance, darling,' Cassandra said to Carolyn, 'and I don't blame him a bit.'

'Huh? That's right. Let's go.'

Inside my room, while the two women sat at the table, I went through their purses looking for bugs and information. As far as I could tell, they were who they said they were, and not bugged, but I went through their coats and snow boots, anyway. The Bogardus woman stood up and slipped the open-weave sweater over her head, draped it over the back of the chair, then her earrings and rings clattered to the table. She slid neatly out of her shoes, tugged the turtleneck out of her jeans, and started to take it off, but she stopped just below her breasts.

I guess my mouth was open because she said, 'Don't you want me to strip? And go into the bathroom with you where we can turn on the water and talk?' Before I could say it wasn't necessary, she was naked, strolling toward the bathroom, saying over her shoulder to Carolyn, whose jaw had dropped even farther open than mine, 'Wait for me, darling. We'll be a bit.' Then she paused by the bed, picked up a large manila envelope, went into the bathroom, and turned on the water. I took off the parka and the vest, stuffed the derringer into my hip pocket, and followed. Behind me, I heard Carolyn sigh long and hard.

For a motel, it was a large bathroom, but when I walked in, it seemed terribly crowded. She stretched her leg, arched her lovely foot, and shut the door, then she reached for my hand, ran my index finger around the inside of her mouth. 'See, nothing there,' she whispered, then drew it into her crotch, 'and nothing there,' then farther back, 'or there.' I swallowed something in my throat that lodged like a stake in my chest. 'See, darling, I'm clean. We can talk here, safe from directional mikes, spike mikes, or those funny lasers that pick up sound vibrations off window-panes.' She reached over to turn on the hot-water faucet, too, bouncing her breast solidly off my arm. 'Quite safe,' she said.

'You seem to know a lot about electronic surveillance,' I said lamely, seemingly unable to point out that any wireman worth his fee could filter out the sound of rushing water his first pass on the tape. 'Maybe too much.'

'Only what I read in books,' she said. She reached for my hand again, squeezing my limp fingers until I answered her touch, saying, 'I'm so glad to finally meet you, Mr. Milodragovitch, and so sorry to have played that awful trick on you at the airport the other day. But I thought you were one of them.'

'Them?'

'The people who have been watching my house and trying to follow me. Mr. Rideout warned me, but I made the mistake of thinking he was just being melodramatic. Poor chap's dead now, isn't he?'

'That's right,' I said, sweating now.

'A crispy critter, poor fellow,' she said sweetly, 'as the boys in

Nam used to say. A disgusting term, but all too accurate, I suppose.'

'How did you know I knew about him?' I asked dumbly. Since I had gone to a lot of trouble to talk to her, it seemed only right to stop looking at her breasts and ask a question, any question.

'Oh, I was watching you watching him that afternoon,' she said. 'I recognized you from the airport, and when I told Rideout that I thought I had been followed, he left like a shot, running back to wherever he had been hiding. I simply assumed that you were able to follow him, even though he knew you were there. He wasn't exactly the brightest sort of man, you understand. Almost repellent, too, but he didn't deserve to die that way, not burned to death.' She bit her lower lip, then added, 'And I hope you'll forgive me for thinking you might have something to do with his death.'

'Would you put something on, please?'

'Of course,' she murmured. 'Forgive me.' She twisted her hair into a bun and wrapped a towel round it. Almost as an afterthought, it seemed, she wound a towel about her body, then leaned against the counter, her arms crossed under her breasts. She, too, sweated now in the steam coming off the hot water running in the sink. I reached around her, careful not to brush her, and turned off the hot water. 'Don't be so prissy, Mr. Milodragovitch,' she said, then leaned over into the shower stall. 'Oh, you've got one of those steamers,' she said, turning it on. 'It will feel wonderful, don't you agree, as cold as it is outside.'

'Sure,' I said as she moved close to unbotton my chamois shirt and gently tugged the tails out of my jeans.

'You're quite well built for an older man,' she said, her long fingernails lightly scratching through the thick gray fur on my chest. Then she patted my belly and stepped back. 'I like a bit of gut on men,' she said, 'it gives them presence.' Beads of sweat began to glisten on her body, and the perfumed smell of her seemed to fill the cloudy room.

Only a fool wouldn't have known he was being played for a fool, but knowing it didn't help. I swallowed something larger, more painful, and asked finally, 'What was your connection to Rideout?'

By way of answer, she picked up the limp manila envelope and slid an eight-by-ten photograph out of it. The picture had been taken at a great distance with maximum magnification of the telephoto lens, then the negative had been cropped and enlarged, so the photograph

623

looked ghostly gray, indistinct in the steam-clouded room. I stepped over to the counter, switched on the lights around the mirror, and tried to ignore the soft tug of her fingers on the hairs on my forearm. Blurred as it was, I could make out the faces of the two men huddled over a huge supine silvertip boar grizzly with its throat gaping open like another, larger, more awesome mouth. A 10-gauge sawed-off shotgun, a guide's weapon of last resort when leading someone after grizzlies, and a tranquilizer rifle leaned against a log behind them. The men were laughing, clearly, in the shot, John P. Rideout/ Rausche and a large Indian with a braid hanging over his shoulder, a curved skinning knife held in his raised hand.

'What the hell is this?' I asked, moving away from her hand.

'Poachers,' she said calmly.

'Poachers? All this shit is about poachers? That doesn't make any sense.'

'Not just any poachers,' she said, 'but an organized gang of poachers. Do you have any idea what that hide and head are worth back East? Ten thousand dollars is my guess. Taken legally, that's a Boone and Crockett head. Can't you just see some fat-cat bastard in Chicago or Cleveland or Pittsburgh showing off that grizzly mounted in his den? Can't you? I understand that full-curl Rocky Mountain sheep ram heads go for five grand, so think what that bear must be worth.'

'This can't be about poachers,' I said, thinking about the goods I had lifted out of the trunk of the yellow Toyota, about the dead man's stubs clutching my arm. 'No.'

'Think about it. This is big business,' she said, 'and when you threaten their profits, they are always ready to kill.'

'I've tampered with evidence, obstructed justice, over a bunch of dumb-ass poachers,' I whispered.

'What?'

'Nothing,' I said quickly. 'Where'd you get this?'

'A little background,' she said, holding up one long slim finger. 'The last time I came back from Beirut, I promised myself to give up all that foolishness, gunfire and all that, dead bodies stacked like cordwood, so I came out to take pictures of peaceful things – snow-fields in the winter sun, glaciers in slow drift, elk calves at play – and I just stumbled onto this.

'I was up in Glacier Park, on the south side of Upper Quartz

Lake, back in September, climbing toward the rim to take some sunset shots, when I stopped, looking back at the lake through my telephoto lens, when I saw this. I took a half-dozen shots, but this was the best after I developed and enlarged. But I knew I was on to something. Really, I mean, these two guys weren't park rangers disposing of a rogue boar or anything.

'So while they were skinning it, I hurried back down to the head of the lake, watched them load the hide and head on a raft, bring it back to the campground, then pack it on a mule they had tethered there. I tried to follow them out, but by the time I got to the trail head at Lower Quartz, the Indian and the hide were long gone, and I only caught Rideout because he was changing a flat. I followed him across the Flathead to Polebridge, then down the North Fork Road, and when he stopped for beer in Columbia Falls, I went into the bar behind him. The rest, as they say, is history.'

'How did you get him to talk?' I asked, and a warm, lovely flush rose across her chest and flamed up her neck.

'How do you think?' she said, touching herself between her breasts as if it were somebody else's body.

'I'm sorry,' I said. 'Listen, will you wait here a bit. I need to think and I can't – '

' – look at me,' she said sadly, twisting her mouth and cocking her head, her neck bowed, it seemed, by the lovely burden of her face. 'Of course.'

When I went out of the warm, damp bathroom, I was surprised to see Carolyn still sitting at the table. I had, shamefully, forgotten she was there. She stubbed out a cigarette into the overflowing ashtray, then sipped at the watery remains of one of the old martinis. I couldn't say anything, I just nodded as I walked past her, opened the sliding door, and stepped out onto the balcony. 'Too hot for you in there, lover boy?' I heard her say as I closed the door.

Outside, the sweat froze quickly on my face, and I knew the frostbite would be with me a long time that night. The storm still raged, cloaking the black waters on the Meriwether with frozen froth. With the first lungful of cold air, a thousand questions formed and dissolved in my mind, but the image of the woman remained clear. Like a moonstruck teenager, I sniffed my index finger but only smelled the cold, clear bite of the snow. I felt as if I wouldn't be

625

able to think clearly anywhere for a long time, so I went back. Carolyn ignored me this time.

'Why Thursdays?' I asked as I barged into the bathroom. 'Why that business at the airport? What's your stake in this?'

'Easy,' she crooned as she finished wiping her body down with the towel, then wrapped herself back inside it. When she faced me, she said, 'Shut the door. You're letting the steam out.'

'How much does Carolyn know about this?' I asked, closing the door.

'Nothing,' she said, mounting the counter around the sink with a single graceful motion, 'nothing at all. Just that I'm in trouble, that she's a friend trying to help. Now, what were those other questions?'

I repeated them. 'Thursdays, because that was his day off – '

'From what?'

'He never said. And as for the airport . . . after all his warnings, I began to be careful, a little, and I saw your white van parked three different places in the neighborhood the day before, saw the police take you away, saw you follow Carolyn, called her early the next morning, heard what a wonderful man she had met, a rent-a-cop with a Russian name, so when I saw your van again the next morning I took precautions . . . the wig and the tweed suit belonged to Don Johnson, a very kinky fellow – '

'I know,' I said, 'I went through the house.'

' – and the idea came out of a novel, and my stake in this is exactly nothing. Not after what happened to poor Mr. Rideout, darling. I'm not about to die to protect the wildlife habitat of the northern Rockies. What's your stake, Mr. Milodragovitch?'

'My life,' I said. 'The bastards have tried twice, they've been on my ass like warts on a toad, and' – I thought about Sarah and Gail, missing – 'and there are some other considerations, but mostly I want to talk to somebody in charge, to let them know that as far as I'm concerned, I don't know shit . . .'

'Add my vote to that,' she said, wiping sweat off the wings of her cheeks. 'I've burned my notes, burned my tapes, and lost my memory. If you find them, tell them that, and that I've gone as far away as I can get from all this.' Then she dropped both towels in the puddle at her feet. 'This has given me too much pleasure to see it turned into charcoal – don't you agree?' She moved into my arms, her fingers busy at my belt buckle and the buttons of my jeans. 'Just a touch, darling,' she whispered as she pushed down my pants, pulled me to the counter, and into her sweet warm body. 'Just a touch, because I don't have my diaphragm with me, darling.' A touch like dying inside her, then she shoved me gently backward, and knelt before me.

Afterward, as she shut off the steam and turned on the shower, I tried to say something, but all my words were jammed in my throat.

'You'd like to see me again?' she said calmly. 'Of course. But not here. Not until this – this mess is cleared up. And someplace warm, darling. I find I've lost my taste for winter.'

'Me too,' I croaked, 'someplace warm. And this rabbit hole is cold but too hot. When you're someplace warm, and safe, call Goodpasture's Used Cars in Albuquerque, tell him – tell him that the fat lady called, and leave a number where I can reach you.'

'The fat lady?' she asked, smiling sedately around the shower door.

'Like they say, the opera ain't over till the fat lady sings.'

'How quaint,' she remarked and closed the door.

Locked in a daze as Carolyn and I watched her dress, put on her clothes as if she had been born for nothing else, and dazed through the goodbyes – one bitter, one sweet – I lay back on the bed, holding the photograph of the hunters and the grizzly, but staring at the ceiling. I stayed, unbuttoned, dismayed, for a long time, nearly sleeping, thinking I dreamed, until Simmons knocked lightly on the connecting door and came in when I was unable to raise an answer.

'Boss, I think you better see this,' he said as he walked over to my television, snapped it on, and found a local channel on the cable. Meriwether sometimes thought of itself as a city on the make, and the local stations had joined in the community spirit, had gotten themselves a mobile news van and a remote camera for live news events. And dead ones. In the hazy colors of the motel set, they showed live coverage of a burning house, firemen and hoses, innocent bystanders, the lot – my fucking house. Even at that, I had to have a snort of coke to bring my limp body to life, to button up, grab my parka and race Simmons down to the car. But by the time we got to my house, it was real life, not television, my house.

The police had blocked off the only road to my house, and I had sense enough not to argue with them. Simmons turned around, drove back to the apartment complex, where we parked, then plunged into the thickets of the park, heading for the dull red glow in the north, rising and falling on the wind like the northern lights.

By the time we got as close as we could, another fire truck had arrived, but they had already lost. The cedar shake roof had already fallen in on the west side, and the old logs of the walls burned like rubber tires, the thick coats of shellac funneling black smoke into the storm-tossed sky. The two large cottonwoods beside the creek had caught, then toppled under the weight of the water from the fire hoses. A blue spruce in the backyard exploded into flame and burned like a giant torch.

'It's gone, boss,' Simmons said.

'It's been gone for a long time,' I said.

The same year my mother donated the land to the city for a park, she had also sold the big house to the country club – they had cut it into four sections and moved it out to the golf course – and donated all the family pictures and artifacts to the county historical society, but she had missed an old safe from my grandfather's bank and a portrait of my great-grandfather dressed in a Cossack uniform, carrying a knout and wearing his Meriwether County sheriff's badge. When the trustees evicted me from my office, I donated those two bits of memorabilia to the historical society.

'Are you okay?' Simmons asked.

'Not too bad,' I said. 'Why?'

'You seem awfully calm for a man whose house is burning down.'

'I say: Don't get mad, get even.'

Back at the Eagle, I picked up the M–11 and tucked it under my parka, and Simmons followed me upstairs to the dark apartment. It took two tries to kick the door off its hinges, and even less time to check out the empty apartment. Before anybody bothered to see what the noise had been, we were on our way back to the motel. As we packed, Simmons asked, 'Where now?'

'Mr. Haynes' for a minute,' I said, 'then I'll let you know.'

Abner wasn't all that glad to see us, until I explained that somebody had just burned down my house, and then he was so angry that I felt guilty for being calm. But it made sense. Abner's house was his home. What he hadn't built himself he had worked to pay for. But my little log house had come to me because of my name, not because

I had worked for it. Our investments were much different, and I understood the old man's anger and my calm, even if he didn't.

'Take it easy, Mr. Haynes,' I said, but the old man kicked his living-room rug so hard that his house shoe flew across the room and crashed into the venetian blinds. 'You two wait right here,' I said, 'until I get back.'

'Where are you going?' Simmons asked.

'Reconnaissance,' I said, checking the submachine gun one more time before I went out.

Every light in the surveillance house down the street was on, blazing into the storm as if a late-night party still raged. I crept around the house and a silence that seemed louder than drunken conversations and rock'n'-roll music roared into the night. When I peeked through the living-room shades, the stack of radio equipment still sat in a pile, the black-and-white television on top, Johnny Carson looking wry as the picture rolled. One of the men seemed to be sleeping on the floor beside the equipment. The other sat at the kitchen table, facing the back door, his service revolver on the table in front of him. Occasionally, he spun it idly, as if trying to start some engine inside himself. He didn't look much like an imitation traveling salesman anymore. He had the gray, crumbled look of death in his face.

I stood on the back porch watching him and I found myself filled with a confusion so intense that it washed the need for revenge right out of me. I was almost willing to think that my house had burned down by accident. The time for gunfire had passed. It was time for talking. I waited until the man at the table had his face in his hands, not touching the revolver, then I covered him through the glass with the Ingram, and tapped the silencer on the window.

'It's open,' he muttered without looking up, as if he had been waiting for me.

I reached for the doorknob and he went for the .38. I meant to give him every chance, meant to keep my trigger finger still until the last possible moment, but when he lifted the revolver, he put it in his mouth instead of pointing it at me, and blew the back of his head all over the kitchen.

If you have been unlucky enough to see something like that, you don't want to hear about it, and if you haven't, I promise you, you don't want to know what it looks like.

I did what I had to do, numb for now, slipped out of my pacs at the back door, walked in my socks, careful not to disturb the gore. The guy in the living room wasn't asleep but dead, a dark ugly bruise over his crushed trachea. He must have ducked as he went into my back door, and caught the handball bolt right in the throat. Holding on to numbness as if my life depended on it, careful about fingerprints, I went through his wallet, writing down the information, then did the same with the dead man on the kitchen floor.

They were both retired Seattle cops, both held current Washington State driver's and PI licences and Multitechtronics employee cards, and both had the same home address on Mercer Island east of Seattle, a neighborhood usually too expensive for retired cops.

Finished, still numb, I let myself out into the blizzard, the soft drumming of the snow that had muffled the sound of the shot. Thinking of any number of things I should do – let the cops know, let Abner and Simmons know, call the FBI and let them hunt for Sarah and Gail – I went back to the Blazer and drove to the nearest bar.

After my second whiskey with a beer chaser, I called Jamison at home. He was sorry about my house, which he had seen on the newsbreak, and he asked if he could help.

'Remember that favor?' I asked.

'Sure. Anything, Milo.'

'Tell the reporters that you have it on good information that Milton Chester Milodragovitch III was in the house at the time it burned down.'

'What?' he said, suddenly excited. 'You think somebody torched it?'

'A favor,' I said, then hung up.

I think I meant to go back to Abner's, but I stayed in the bar until last call. And for last call I ordered two fifths of Seagram's and a case of Rainier beer. When I checked the glove box to be sure the cocaine was still there, it was, and when I slammed the glove box shut, it sounded hollow, like cheap tin, so I drove out toward the interstate, turned west for Missoula and my pickup. But things got in the way – snowstorms, shitstorms, the dull muffled roar of a .38 or a 12-gauge or a silken noose . . .

Whatever, at ten o'clock the next morning I was parked in front of the Eastgate Liquor Store and Lounge in Missoula when Janey,

the best damned daytime bartender in America, opened the bar, and
I went inside like a man on his way to his own funeral.

10

On the third morning when I sat backward on the toilet lid in the Eastgate chopping up the last of the cocaine, I heard the bathroom door open, so I stopped the click of the razor blade on the porcelain. But somebody kicked the stall door and the latch popped and whistled over my head, then the same somebody grabbed my collar and jerked me off the stool, stood me against the wall, and started slapping me. Jamison.

'Aren't you a little bit out of your jurisdiction, sir?' I said, slumped with the giggles.

Holding me up with one hand, Jamison brushed all the coke to the tile floor, and I whimpered, and then he opened the toilet lid and pulled my face toward the bowl as if it were a mirror where I might see myself, a pool where I might drown in my own image. 'Look at that,' he said, shoving my face closer to the bloody froth. 'Janey says you been puking blood for two days.'

'Damned old tattletale,' I said, giggling again.

Jamison shouldered me into the wall, grabbed me by the vest, and began to bounce me off it until I heard the plaster crack behind my head. When he stopped, his fingers were working at the Kevlar mesh inside the vest. 'What the hell are you doing wearing this?' he growled, but I didn't have an answer. 'Why?' he asked, and bounced me again.

'I forgot.'

'Forgot what?'

'I don't know, man,' I said, 'that's what "forgot" means in our language.' I must have thought that was funny because I started laughing again.

'What kind of trouble are you in?' he asked, and slapped me again when I didn't answer.

'I'm dead,' I said, 'don't you read the papers?' Then I had one of those flashes of memory that sometimes come in the worst parts of dog-shit bottom-out, a memory of reading about my death in the *Missoulian*, and telling Janey not to tell anyone I was alive. 'But I'm not dead, am I?'

'It was your idea, son of a bitch,' he said, tears in his eyes, 'and if I wasn't an officer of the law, I think I'd kill you myself, or at least let you kill yourself.'

'You ain't got it anymore,' I whimpered, 'and I ain't got it anymore – dead people suck.'

'What are you doing here, anyway?'

'Having a taste of whiskey,' I said, 'and a touch of nose – or least I was until you came in – and then I was going out to the airport to get my trusty old pickup – '

'Your pickup?' he interrupted. 'Shithead, your pickup is parked out front.'

'Huh,' I said, giggling again, 'spaced that out. Wonder what I did with the Blazer . . . burning down poor Sarah's credit cards . . .'

'Who's Sarah?'

'Nobody you know, a better class of people than you'll ever know, you pissant, small-town hick copper . . .'

'Milo, Milo,' he said softly.

'Sorry 'bout that, chief,' I said with more giggles, 'lemme buy you a drink, chief.'

'Sure,' he said, but when he led me out of the john we went right past the bar. When I tried to resist, he put me in an arm lock as easily as he might twist a soft pretzel. 'Thanks, Janey,' he said, 'for calling.'

'Yeah, thanks, you old tattletale,' I said. 'Fu – oops, sorry, Jane. Onion off, okay?' Janey didn't much like the f-word, always made me say 'onion' instead. That's how you can tell if you like a bartender – you appreciate their foibles no matter how twisted you are. 'Onion off, and thanks but no thanks, okay?'

'I'm sorry, Milo,' she said, her eyes as soft and kind as a mother's. 'I don't mind your having a good time, but if you're going to kill yourself, you can't do it in my bar, okay?'

'Prig,' I said as Jamison hustled me out the door. 'Where the hell you taking me, ossifer?'

'Home,' he said, waving away the patrol car, which must have brought him in from the airport, 'home.'

'I ain't got no home,' I said, 'you dumb straight-arrow son of a bitch, I ain't got no home.'

'My house,' he said as I wept into his shoulder, 'my house.' Then he stuffed me into the pickup.

Surely in this vale of tears we call life, the ill, the halt, and the lame find it curious that some people with constitutions like bull calves sometimes consider their good health and strength a curse rather than a blessing. It *can* be, though. In fistfights, even beaten senseless, we don't fall down nearly soon enough; the joys of drug abuse don't seem to take their proper toll; and, sometimes, when we try to drink ourselves to death, we fail miserably. Miserably.

My mother's father, whom I only met once when he drove from Boston to Meriwether in his seventies, started drinking a quart of Jamaican rum and smoking at least ten cigars a day during the great Spanish influenza epidemic of 1917, a habit that he maintained saved his life while thousands of others died, a habit that he maintained until he died at eighty-two. My father's father drank a fifth of whiskey and smoked Prince Albert cigarettes every day from his twenties to his seventies, then he quit and lived another twenty years. God might know what it means; doctors don't. Have a good constitution and don't be miserable? I don't know either.

But after twenty-four hours on Jamison's couch and a bait of steak and eggs at a truck stop west of town where I hoped I wouldn't run into anybody I knew who would ask me why I wasn't dead, I should have been happy, but strolling out to my pickup, I realized I had to face the troubles, had to stop running, start working.

Driving through Meriwether on my way to look at the remains of my house in the daylight, I let my mind drop into idle for the slow drive. In my absence, the blizzard had blown itself out but left its heartbroken tracks behind. A gray, heavy overcast loomed dark over the afternoon as Meriwether dug itself out of the snow to face another long winter. The clotted wood-smoke smog drifted like a noxious, killer fog over the city, the mountains ranging like shaggy ghosts somewhere beyond it. The faces of the people on the streets seemed pale and empty, small animals huddled beneath fur caps and woolen scarfs or tucked into hoods. Although I knew it wasn't true – most of these people lived there because they wanted to live there, and wintertime was a cheap price to pay – it seemed that laughter had gone into hibernation for the season. Maybe just my drunken laughter, my cocaine giggles.

When I got to my house it seemed to me that the random lumps bellied up under the snow could have been anything, a battlefield, a pile of frozen corpses, the debris of a melting glacier, anything. While I was parking in front, my next-door neighbor came rushing out of her house, waving her arms and weeping.

'Milo, Milo,' she shouted into my window, 'you're alive!' I had forgotten I was supposed to be dead. 'Come in,' she said, 'come in – for coffee or something – I've got some mail they delivered, and come on in. For coffee.'

'Sure,' I said. I didn't see how I could refuse.

Sitting at her kitchen table, sipping instant coffee, I opened my mail. Mostly bills, but a few reminded me what sort of world we live in. Three people, who evidently did not read the newspapers very carefully, wanted to build me a new home as soon as I got the insurance settlement. The city wanted to know what sort of arrangements I had made to clean up the debris, which constituted a public health hazard. Also, they had delivered the briefcase I had mailed from Seattle.

'Listen,' I said to my next-door neighbor, 'I've got a large favor to ask you.'

'Anything,' she said, 'almost anything.'

'You know, you introduced yourself the first day you moved into this house, and we've known each other for a year or so . . .' She smiled when I paused, and I realized that I had never really looked at her, never really even thought about her except as something that came by occasionally and did the dirty number. Behind that facile sneer of a smile dwelt a real live woman, probably massively unhappy, certainly confused, if she took up with somebody like me for casual carnal carnage. 'I'm sorry,' I said, 'I don't have any idea what your name is.'

'I know that,' she said. 'I realized that a long time ago and decided I sort of like it that way. Oh, and I had a wonderful cry, Milo, thinking about you dead and not even knowing my name . . . Ann-Marie.'

'Thanks,' I said. 'Ann-Marie, I have a huge favor to ask you.'

'What's that?'

'Don't tell anybody I'm not dead for a while,' I said as I unwrapped the briefcase and stuffed my wonderful mail inside.

'Why?'

'That's the favor,' I said, 'you don't ask why.'

'Whatever you say.'

'Thanks.'

I split the stitches on the briefcase handle, pulled out the rolled packet of cocaine, and gave her a half-gram-or-so present. She couldn't thank me enough, but I didn't have time for that.

The AMC Eagle was still parked in front of Abner's house, so buried in plowed snow that I was sure it hadn't been moved during my absence. Simmons had waited, like a good lad, but when I opened the front door and found him sitting on the couch next to Abner and Yvonne sipping tea, with his little finger cocked in the air like a dog's leg, nibbling gingersnaps, and laughing at Richard Dawson's wisecracks between the families feuding, I wondered if I should have left him there.

He even stood up, blushing, when I came into the room. 'Jesus H. Christ,' he said, and then, 'Oh, excuse me, Mrs. O'Leary – I didn't know what to do, boss, when you didn't come back, so I just waited . . .'

'You did fine,' I said. I could tell that Abner, hopping from foot to foot, wanted to introduce me to the simpering Yvonne, but I told Simmons to get packed. 'Excuse me a second,' I added, 'I'll be right back – I promise.' Then went back outside and down to the surveillance house.

Through the windows I could see that somebody had cleaned up, the rooms were empty, sparkling, the kitchen walls repainted, the floor tiles replaced, even the appliances changed. Neat, professional work. I wondered what they had done with the garbage, how they had disposed of the bodies. I pulled out the pocket notebook to look at the men's names for the first time since that night. Willis Strawn. Ernest Ramsey. I had to assume that Strawn had torched my house out of some terrible grief over the death of his partner at the hands of my dumb joke of a booby trap, and then had waited for me to take his perverse revenge. Rather than kill me, he had left me with an image of death I would carry to the grave. There was so much I didn't understand. How did he know I would find him? Maybe he had seen my tracks in the snow the night I had peeked in his window. I just didn't know. Like so many things in life, an artful guess was the best I could come up with.

Heading back to Abner's, I felt so tired that the snow seemed to suck at my pacs, to hold me frozen in a block of cold, icy ignorance. Maybe I could find some answers in Seattle amid the past lives of Strawn and Ramsey, behind the doors of something called Multitech-tronics, Inc. Maybe Simmons and I could catch the afternoon flight. But as I glanced at the sky, the overcast seemed to settle lower over the valley, leaving only the bases of the mountains visible. Even if planes were taking off from the Meriwether airport today, I didn't want to fly through that rough, freezing tumble of clouds, which meant driving twelve hours or more, long hours on black ice and snowpack to Seattle.

Back at Abner's, the old man refused to take any more money, and I was too worn out to argue. Simmons and I thanked him, said our good-byes, and headed west.

The interstate was clear traveling until we were west of Missoula, but a fresh storm began its assault outside of Alberton, horizontal snowfall skidding across the icy road. We stayed sober, clean-nosed, creeping through the blizzard, but even at that, we lost it just before midnight, spun out on the east side of Lookout Pass and into the barrow pit in about four feet of snow. It only took an hour or so of serious labor to dig out the pickup and get the chains on all four wheels, serious labor in a wind chill of forty below. Once, while we were warming up in the pickup cab, Simmons turned to me and asked through his chattering teeth, 'You reckon them old folks are getting it on?'

'Abner and Yvonne?'

'Yeah.'

'That's what the old goat has in mind,' I said, trying to grin with a frozen face.

'You know, when you're young,' he said, 'you're just so damned dumb. I never thought about old folks doing it, you know, and I

637

wondered how, ah, they go about it, you know.' I couldn't tell if he was blushing or finally getting some blood back in his face.

'Are you implying that I'm old enough to know, bud?'

'No, nothing like that, boss,' he said. 'I just thought old men lost it, and old women . . .'

'With courage,' I said, 'all things are possible.' And we laughed. 'Now let's get that last chain on, and get out of this mess.'

But even the chains didn't help. We had to get the sixteen-pound sledge and a steel stake out of the toolbox to give us an anchor for the winch. As we were pounding the stake into the frozen roadbed, Simmons stopped hammering to catch his breath.

'I hope he's banging the holy hell out of her at this very moment,' he said, smiling into the wind. 'I really liked that old son of a bitch, you know. I ain't never been around old folks much before – just the daytime winos in the Deuce – and them two old people are cool.'

'And I'm freezing to death, son,' I said. 'Get on that hammer.'

Before long, winter driving began to seem like an Arctic expedition – chains off on the other side of Lookout Pass, back on for Fourth of July Summit in Idaho, then off, then on again for Snoqualmie Pass, then off – and for all the good it did, we might as well have stayed in Meriwether, where I would have been warm, wrapped in dreams of Cassandra Bogardus.

When we got to the Mercer Island address I had for Strawn and Ramsey, we found a burned-out hulk beside the calm gray waters of Lake Washington dimpled with light rain.

'What are we supposed to be looking for, boss man? Burned houses?' Simmons asked, then laughed, brittle with fatigue.

'Some serious bad guys,' I said, 'serious.' And Simmons' hand crept under his vest to touch the butt of the .357, shivering perhaps with fear or with the memory of the freezing wind and snow.

'Easy,' I warned when I noticed a woman coming out of the house next door bundled in a bright-blue rain parka and heading toward us.

'Hi,' she said quietly as she walked up to us. She had one of those intelligent, perky, expensive faces you expect to find on Mercer Island, the second, younger wife of a doctor or a lawyer or a rich Indian chief. 'Can I help you?' she asked politely.

'We were looking for Mr. Strawn or Mr. Ramsey,' I said, 'but I can see they're not home.'

'Then you didn't know,' she said softly. 'I hope you weren't friends of theirs . . .'

'Associates,' I said, and she nodded as if she knew what I meant.

'A terrible accident,' she offered, 'the furnace exploded, and they never had a chance . . .'

So that's how they cleaned up the garbage, brought the bodies to Seattle and blew up a house, which also meant the bad guys had enough clout to buy an arson investigator, an autopsy, and a police report. Poachers, my ass. Cassandra Bogardus was crazy.

'I was never very fond of policemen,' she continued. 'The sixties,' she added, as if that explained everything. 'But Willie and Ernie were different than you would expect . . . Excuse me, I hope you gentlemen aren't policemen.'

'No, ma'am,' I said, and Simmons muffled his laugh with a cough.

'They were so nice, you know, quiet and neighborly, both of them wonderful French cooks, and they had the most fantastic collection of big-band records and a stereo system that covered an entire wall, and now it's all . . . ashes.' The sad little smile looked painted onto her pert, liberal face. 'I'll miss them so much,' she added. 'My husband always claimed they were, you know, odd – ah, homosexuals. But I always maintained that they wouldn't, you know, let homo-sexuals be policemen – would they?'

'No, ma'am, I wouldn't think so,' I said.

'Well, I wouldn't care if they were,' she whispered in a rush as two large tears bloomed in her eyes.

'Yes, ma'am,' I said as Simmons and I retreated toward the pickup. Driving away, we watched her standing in the driveway, her figure bent with grief as she gazed across the ashen water like a woman whose man went to sea years and years ago. A small bit of life, light, and laughter had dimmed forever in her snug suburban nest.

'You're still not going to tell me what this is all about, are you, boss?' Simmons said.

'Even if I knew, son, you're better off not knowing,' I said, 'but it's bad enough that if I were you, I'd get out now.'

'Not a chance, boss man,' he said. 'They can't put you in the slammer because you're dead, or me, because I'm crazy.' He sounded almost happy about it.

'Jail is the least of our worries, the least,' I said, but the kid kept smiling.

639

Multitechtronics turned out to be an empty office over a porno shop on 1st Avenue just south of Pike Place Market, a mail drop, an answering service, defunct. I tried the painless dentist next door, but he was feeling so little pain that the only thing he could tell me was what he had drunk for lunch, and I had already smelled the bourbon and ether fumes in the hallway. I had a number of choices, checking with the owner of the building, digging out the incorporation documents, but I thought I had better have another, less personal conversation with Ms. Bogardus, so I found a hungry, lanky young lawyer named McMahon, gave him a retainer, and set him on what I assumed would be a paper maze to track down the owners of Multitechtronics, Inc.

Then we went down to Ivar's for lunch, where I had three dozen raw oysters, which disgusted Simmons so much that he couldn't even eat his chicken-salad sandwich.

On the way home that night we crashed in Ellensburg, and I dreamed not of Cassandra Bogardus, but of the fat lady cocaine dealer. Oddly enough, it wasn't a bad dream, as my dreams go, and for that I was grateful.

Back in Meriwether the next afternoon, we checked into a truck-stop motel east of town, showered the tire-chain mud and slush and cold off ourselves, and then I called Jamison at the station. His greeting seemed distant, uncomfortable.

'I guess I owe you a vote of thanks,' I said.

'Milo, I don't know how you do it.'

'Get twisted?'

'Survive,' he said.

'It's my hardy-pioneer genes,' I said, and Jamison coughed disgustedly. When my great-grandfather was sheriff of Meriwether County, he founded the family fortune on a string of opium dens, gambling hells, and cotes for soiled doves.

'I don't think I can keep you dead much longer, Milo,' he said.

'A few more days,' I said, 'whatever you can manage.'

'I'll try,' he said, 'but the arson investigator is pressing me. He also mentioned that although he can't find anything, he smells something hinkty about the fire.'

'Well, I can promise you I didn't torch my house for the goddamned insurance money.'

'I know. I've already checked that out.'

'I need one more favor, Jamison.'

'Lock you up for your own protection?'

'Not just yet,' I said. 'I need permission to visit the Benniwah kid in the hospital lockup. The one from the EZ-IN/EZ-OUT.' The only people I knew up on the reservation I knew from my days as deputy sheriff, and not a single one would talk openly to me, not even the police. Maybe the kid felt as if he owed me something, maybe he would give me a hand trying to find the Indian in the photograph with Rausche and the grizzly bear. 'Okay?'

'That's easy,' he said. 'Our Good Colonel Bleeding Heart has arranged for his lawyer to handle the defense, so you're his investigator, right.'

'Right. A Mr. – ah, Grimes from Seattle. Thanks.'

'And, Milo . . .'

'Yeah?'

'The game is Saturday after next.'

'Right,' I said and hung up. 'Rich man's clothes,' I told Simmons, and he sighed as if that were the worst chore of all.

On the way out to the hospital I stopped long enough to buy another Tyrolean hat and a pair of expensive sunglasses. Rich dudes can afford to wear sunglasses even in the worst snowstorms.

The Benniwah tribe was notoriously suspicious of strange white men. And with good reason. The first white trader to discover the small peaceful tribe, an Alsatian by the name of Benommen, gave them a corrupted version of his name (*they* called themselves the Chil-a-ma-cho-chio, the people of Chil-a-ma-cho) and swapped them blankets from smallpox victims of the Mandan tribe for prime beaver pelts. The survivors fled into the high valleys of the Cathedral Mountains, where most of them slowly starved to death. The remainder, although they never shed a drop of white blood, watched as their ancestral lands were slowly stripped and stolen by various government officials, including my great-grandfather of the hardy-pioneer spirit, who had paid a quarter an acre for the three thousand acres of timberland. Finally the tribe managed to secure a small reservation on the north and middle forks of the Dancing Bear River between the Cathedrals and the Diablos. What little they had left, they meant to keep. Unlike many tribes, they never sold or leased land to white men, not even to those few who married into the tribe, and when you drove across the reservation, even the children stared darkly at your pale face as if they still smoldered with racial regret for rivers of white-eye blood unshed.

For somebody who had taken a .30–06 round in the recent past, Billy Buffaloshoe looked remarkably hale and hearty sitting propped up against the pillows, staring at the green placid walls of his unhospitable cell. When the jailer on duty at the door unlocked it, Billy turned slightly, just enough to bump the elbow of his cast against the metal bed rail. His face became instantly gray, and I waited politely, staring through the heavily meshed one-way glass until he regained his naturally high, burnished color. Then I told Simmons to wait for me in the lobby, and went in.

'And who the hell are you, man?' he said when I was inside. 'Another rich lawyer bearing the white man's burden? Another cop? Maybe a social worker?' I took off my glasses and hat. 'Nope. You don't look social enough, man.'

'Just a guy looking for a favor,' I said, paused at the end of the bed, and we could hear the jailer drop the dead bolt with a clunk that seemed to shake the snow off the barred windows.

'A favor?' he said. 'Wow, man, I am honored, but I ain't exactly on the uphill side of success right now. You can dig it, right, man.'

'I just want you to look at a picture for me,' I said, taking out the eight-by-ten of the poachers.

'And what are you going to do for *me*, man?'

'I've already done it,' I said, 'the night you got shot.'

'The rent-a-cop,' he sneered. 'Jesus, man, you look good for a rent-a-cop. So you saved my life, man. Big fucking deal.'

'I'll make a good witness at your trial,' I said, 'and at least you can beat the assault with a deadly weapon – '

'What trial, man?' he said. 'I'm copping a second degree on the armed robbery, so I'm looking at Deer Lodge whatever happens.'

'You don't care what I say at the pre-sentencing hearing?'

'Who listens to jerks like you, man,' he said, 'so you ain't got shit to trade.'

'Money?'

'How much?'

'You tell me, tough guy.'

'Five hundred and a television in this stinking goddamned room,' he said, 'and that's my first and last price.'

'I can't do nothing about the entertainment, son,' I said, 'but the five is okay.'

'You got it on you?'

'Sure,' I said, 'but they'll just take it away from you.'

'Hey, man, *I* ain't no jerk,' he said, as if I was. 'I been there before. Ain't nobody gonna take it off me.'

Screening the door window with my back, I counted out five bills, and handed them to him with the photograph. As he leaned over to slip the money into his crotch, he started coughing. When he worked up a bloody froth, I leaned over for the stainless-steel bowl, let him spit and catch his breath.

'You okay?' I asked. 'Need a nurse or anything?'

'Fucking service in this hospital is for shit, man,' he gasped, then glanced at the picture. 'Don't know the white dude, man, or Brother Bear, man . . .' He laughed and brought up another coughing fit, more blood. 'And I don't know the other dude's name – he's not one of us, he's a breed, Assiniboin, Cree, I don't know, don't even live on the res, man, just hangs out at the bars in Stone City – ask Tante Marie.'

'Tante Marie?'

'The grandmother lady, man,' he said, then sighed and told me how to find her, stirred in the bed in the telling and pulled out the end of his lung drain from the bedside bottle.

'You sure you don't want me to call the nurse?'

'Not only do they have piss-poor service here, man,' he gasped between shallow breaths, 'but this hospital is renowned for its shitty drugs.'

'Thanks for the help,' I said and held out my hand.

He stared at me for a long time before he took it and gave it a brief pump, but our eyes held – his, growing dark and deep like that narrow passage to the other side, where the eternal spring-time sang, where the maidens' breath always smelled sweetly of honeycomb, where the ghostly deer leaped lightly into the humming flight of the arrow. He had nearly made it this time, and his knowledge made the back of my throat taste bloody and raw. Next time, his eyes said, he would go.

643

The clouds had lifted and the snow stopped, but as we eased across the black ice up Wilmot Hill toward the reservation, the pickup rose into the lowering overcast, and a corn-snow squall swept out of the gray fog and lashed at the windshield. Even though I had the heater cranked all the way up, Simmons and I had been cold too long and tired, and the cold air seemed to rush into the cab on clattering hooves.

'How long's it been since you had a drink?' I asked Simmons.

'Not since you left that night,' he said, tugging at his tie, 'and it's really weird, you know, I don't seem to want one.'

Lord, did I want one. Whiskey for warmth in the gut, for fire to burn the ugly taste of violent death out of my throat, whiskey for laughter. I thought about stopping at the Wilmot Bar for a quick one, at least one, but my old friend Jonas no longer stood behind the bar, surveying his domain like a crazed dwarf king. Like too many of the old ones, the crazy ones, he was dead. Fat Freddie, the Chicago cop; and silent Pierre, who had drunk the English language right out of his brain; Leo from Mahoney's, the recorder of our faces; and good Simon the Roamer. Dead. Me, too, according to recent reports. But maybe it was really true, I was really dead. What a wonderful joke. After death, the crossing over, we find neither heaven nor hell, not even happy hunting, but just more of the same sad, silly life we thought we left behind. Confusion and muddle, disorder and despair.

But just as I worked myself into an alcoholic's glorious and sober self-pity, as we rolled past the shadowy outline of the Wilmot Bar, we popped out of the clouds and into the blinding winter sunlight firing back off the snowfields. I locked all four wheels of the pickup, scrambling in my pockets for the new sunglasses. When I had them on, I saw before me the snow-capped towers of the Cathedrals glistening against a sky as blue as the backside of heaven, the sort of vision that makes you forget tire chains and frostbite, makes you remember why you live in Montana until you die.

Tante Marie, Billy had told me, was the most honored woman among the Benniwah, the keeper of the tales, the teller of the sacred stories, and in a tribe where all the grandmothers, once having put away the bloody stain of womanhood, were honored for their patience, wisdom, and kindness, and entrusted with the most treasured objects of a tribe that had nearly disappeared, the children and the old stories. Tante Marie was the grandmother of grandmothers, more obeyed than a war chief, more trusted than a peace chief, and more powerful than the lawyers who advised the tribal council.

Even with all that tradition resting on her shoulders, Tante Marie didn't live in a teepee or an earthen lodge, but in a small yellow frame house up the Middle Fork of the Dancing Bear, just beyond where the South Fork Road turned south up the north side of the Diablos, a road that led into the mountains past the old C, C&K sections, the abandoned mine and over the divide to Camas Meadows and my grandfather's timberland. Fifty yards down the Middle Fork Road beyond her house sat the locked gate that protected the last bit of sacred Benniwah land from the roaming gangs of white-eye hunters, fishermen, and beer drinkers.

Because it was on a school-bus route, the Middle Fork Road had been plowed that morning, and it looked as if the South Fork Road had been too, which seemed odd, but maybe the Forest Service was keeping it open for loggers. A small school bus was parked in front of her house, and past it I could see a new gate across the Middle Fork Road. When I was a kid, the old gate was an easy one, and we could either shoot the lock off or ride around it on dirt bikes, but over the years, every time I saw that gate it had become a more formidable barrier. Now it was constructed of steel pipe, fastened with a Master padlock as large as a sandwich, set in concrete and flanked by rocky berms higher than a man's head. A long-dried and frozen coyote skin had been draped over the top rail.

After I parked behind the school bus, I asked Simmons to wait in the pickup, then trudged toward the shoveled walk where the drifts were piled four feet high on either side, my rich man's shoes useless in the snow. They had had even more snow than we had down in the Meriwether, and some of the drifts reached nearly to the roof eaves.

When I paused on the front steps to try to kick the snow out of my shoes, a deep voice, happy in its seriousness, rumbled inside the small house.

'. . . and that, little grandchildren,' it said, 'is why poor Brother Raven is cursed with his black, black feathers and his ugly caw. He traded his pollen-yellow feathers, his sky blue and his cloud white, traded even his once sweet song that filled the air with the sacred rainbow, traded his honor for one chew of the white man's tobacco, and even to this day, little grandchildren, he caws and caws but cannot spit that bitter, dishonorable taste away . . .'

Then the voice grew soft and low, the words indistinct, replaced by the shuffle and hum of children, broken now and again by respectful laughter.

When Tante Marie opened the door, she saw me but ignored me so furiously that I naturally stepped aside to watch as she gently ruffled black-haired heads before she tucked them into snow hoods and patted tiny rumps to speed them on their merry way. Although they still had wonderfully solemn looks gracing their faces, the line of small children filing out the door toward the bus carried happy smiles, bronze cheeks glazed with apple, and dark, singing eyes. The driver, an old snaggled-toothed man named Johnny Buckbrush, who knew me from my deputy sheriff days, glanced at me once, then lowered his eyes. I had known him in his days of shame.

'You're looking great, Johnny,' I said, 'a new man.'

'Thank you, Milo,' he answered, his face turned away from me as he followed the troop of happy children.

Tante Marie watched them until the bus was loaded and on its way, watched until it passed a granite outcrop beyond the South Fork turn, then she looked at me, and said, as if it were a command, 'Yes.'

From the way Billy had talked about her, I expected some sort of Hollywood version of a female shaman, an ancient English actress in wrinkles and copper face, draped in buckskin and beads, but Tante Marie was a large, strong woman, wearing high heels that matched her beige sheath. Her long, heavy face, framed by a pair of horn-rimmed glasses, could have belonged to a Mexican, or an Italian, or a rich white woman with a deep-water tan.

'Yes,' she said again.

'Excuse me,' I said, 'but I couldn't help overhearing the end of your story, ma'am – and please correct me if I'm wrong – but wasn't it the Indian people who introduced the white man to tobacco? When Columbus discovered – ah, the Indies.'

'True enough,' she said as if this were a question she had waited all her life to answer. 'Indian people smoked – tobacco, kinnikinnick, red-cedar bark – but we smoked for ceremony, not for pleasure, for what you white people might call prayer, thanksgiving for the sun and moon, the wind and rain, the coming, and going, of life. Smoking for pleasure, for the tobacco lobby and the government subsidy, for sophistication, *is* hazardous to your health.' Then she flicked a finger against my breast pocket, and the cellophane of the cigarette pack rattled like a snake.

'Yes, ma'am,' I said, 'you win,' trying to be friendly, but the face she offered me had been carved out of something harder than stone. 'Billy Buffaloshoe sent me,' I explained, 'for a favor.'

'A favor?'

'Yes, ma'am,' I said again, tugging the rolled photograph out of my overcoat pocket. 'Did you know Billy was in jail?' I added, but her face didn't even bother to answer. She knew everything. 'Maybe I can help keep him out of prison.'

'Ha,' she snorted, 'he was born for Deer Lodge.'

'Maybe I can help postpone his fate,' I said. 'Do you know this man?' I asked, holding up the picture.

She took it and looked at it for a long time, nodded, then stepped back inside the house out of the snow glare and removed her glasses. I started to follow, but she raised that stony gaze and I moved away, nearly falling on the icy porch. While she stared at the photo and I tried to regain my balance, one of the bright-blue EQCS garbage trucks rumbled around the outcrop and turned up the South Fork Road.

'What the hell – ' I started to ask.

'They have the reservation contract,' she explained, and left it at that. 'Which man?'

'The Indian.'

'Is it about the bear?'

'Sort of,' I said. Tante Marie wasn't the kind of woman I wanted to lie to. 'The bear and other things.'

'He's the sort,' she said, nodding, 'to do something like this. A jailhouse Indian, a mixed breed without honor. His real name is Charlie Two Moons, but he calls himself Charlie Miller. At this time of day you can find him – ' She paused and looked at me. 'Take off those glasses and that silly hat.' After I complied, she said, 'You're a Milodragovitch, aren't you?'

'Should I confess, ma'am, or admit it proudly?'

'It's your name,' she said, 'you decide.'

'I am the last of the Milodragovitches,' I said.

'Good,' she said. 'How badly do you want to find this man?'

'I'll find him,' I said, 'with or without your help, ma'am.'

'Not if I make a telephone call,' she said. 'I'll trade you my help for Camas Meadows. We'll even buy it at a fair price.'

'Okay.'

'I love a joke, coyote tongue,' she said, not laughing. 'You'll do everything you can to have Billy placed on probation in my care?'

'Yes, ma'am.'

'All right. At this time of day you can find Charlie Two Moons leaning on a bar down in Stone City.' I must have raised a frozen eyebrow because she answered a question I didn't ask. 'Before I came home to the land,' she said, 'you might have found me there, too.'

'Thank you.'

'You've got frostbite on your face,' she said, then reached up to peel a tiny sliver of black skin off the side of my cheek. 'Take care of it.'

'Yes, ma'am,' I said, 'and I do appreciate your help.'

'Don't mention it, coyote tongue,' she said, then shut the door so firmly in my face that I felt as if I had been locked out of someplace very important.

Stone City sat just west of the Benniwah reservation, the sort of small ugly town you find embedded like a tick along the borders of dry reservations or military encampments, a town forged of homesickness and grief, greed, a town of bars and pawnshops where nobody ever grew up. I found Charlie Two Moons in the fifth joint we tried, huddled over a shot of bar bourbon and a short draw of beer. He had looked large in the photograph, but in real life he was one big son of a bitch, at least six-six and grown up toward two-seventy, and there was no way even two of us was going to waltz this half-drunk and completely unhappy giant out of the bar.

'What's happening, boss man?' Simmons asked while the bartender ignored us.

'I think maybe we better have a drink,' I said. 'See that big dude behind me? Well, we need to have a serious conversation with him about a felony.'

'How did you ever get into this business, man?'

'It was back in my hard-drinking days, bud, and I don't exactly

648

remember,' I admitted as I rapped my knuckles on the bar to get the bartender's attention.

The silence in the small bar was suddenly very intense. A group of day-drinkers at a back booth stopped laughing, the three other customers at the bar besides Charlie Two Moons halted their drinks in midair, and the bartender gave us a murderous scowl. But he came down the bar anyway, slowly.

'Can I help you gentlemen?' he said as if we were going to need more help than he could provide.

'Yes, sir,' I said as if I hadn't heard the silence. 'My friend and I would like shots of Black Jack and beer backs,' I ordered, lifting a fifty from my wallet, 'and get yourself one too, sir – hell, get everybody in the bar one . . . I just hit the poker game at the Slumgullion down in Meriwether, so let's all have a drink for luck.'

'For luck,' the bartender said, seeming to imply that we were going to need that too.

But after I bought a second round for the house, the silence eased, Simmons and I took a deep breath and sipped slowly at our drinks.

'You hear the one about the great North Dakota artist?' Simmons whispered in a low voice. In Montana, what the rest of the country calls 'Polack jokes' we set in North Dakota.

'No,' I said.

'The North Dakota Historical Society hired the most famous painter in the state,' he whispered even more quietly, 'to paint a giant mural depicting the Battle of Little Bighorn, and when he finished, they had this big party for the unveiling, all these fat-cat preachers and society matrons gathered to see the finest work of North Dakota's greatest painter. But when they pulled back the curtain, there was this picture of a huge goddamn fish with a halo over its head surrounded by thousands of Indian couples balling.

'Of course, all the fat-cat preachers swallowed their snuff and all the society matrons peed in their girdles and everybody went charging out of the room in a great North Dakota huff. So the president of the historical society goes over to the artist, who has been too busy admiring his work to notice the fuss, and he says to the painter, "What in the world do you call this?" And the painter smiles and says, " 'Custer's Last Words.' " " 'Custer's Last Words'?" the president says. "Right," the artist says, " 'Holy mackerel, I've never seen so many fucking Indians.' " '

When Simmons finally stopped giggling into his hand, he added, 'You can understand what made me think of that, boss – "Custer's Last Words." ' Then he laughed again. Some people will laugh at anything.

'I love a joke, coyote tongue,' I said, quoting Tante Marie, 'but how are we going to get this big son of a bitch outside?'

'No problem,' Simmons said. 'He's on his way out now.'

I picked up my change, and we followed his wavering gait out into the cold, windy street. As I came up behind him I slipped my Buck folding knife out of my pocket and opened it.

'Charlie Two Moons,' I said, grabbing his right shoulder with my left hand, and jabbing the blade into his right armpit through the wool coat and shirt until I felt flesh. 'If you jump, man, you'll never lift that arm again.' When he hesitated, I gave him a bit more of the knife point, and the sharp, unexpected pain took the fight out of him. He puked without jerking forward, then spit on the sidewalk.

'Whatever you say, dude, you got the blade.'

'You got a rig?' I asked. 'I don't want blood and vomit all over mine.'

He bobbed his head sourly, spit again, then led me down the street to a battered pickup, a 1965 Dodge Power Wagon, the best back-country rig ever to come out of Detroit City. Maybe I was too busy admiring it, but as we eased into the cab he got away from me. We engaged in a very silent, very tense struggle that ended with my blade under his ear and with the .38 snubnose he had hidden in the crack of the seat partially blocked by my left hand, but still nuzzling coldly into my left thigh. He didn't seem sick or drunk now; he seemed to fill up the whole cab.

'What we've got here, dude, is a Mexican stand-off,' he finally said, his lips barely moving.

'My buddy's behind you with a .357,' I pointed out. Simmons had his piece out, the barrel resting on the window ledge and shielded by his leather overcoat.

'A .357, dad, will make mush out of both of us at that range,' he said.

'A Mexican stand-off,' I said, the sweat freezing on my face. 'I'll be crippled, Charlie, but you'll be dead.'

'I don't much give a shit, man.'

'Neither do I,' I said, and was surprised to discover that I meant

650

it. 'If you're going to pop that cap, sucker, do it now because this conversation is over.'

'Whoa, man, hold it,' he said quickly as he let the revolver fall to the cluttered floorboard. I let him slide, trembling, to the far side of the seat, where he buried his face in his shaking hands, moaning, 'It ain't even loaded, man, ain't even loaded.' I picked it up and checked it. Empty. When I looked at him, Charlie Two Moons looked like a much smaller man.

'Afraid of doing yourself?' I guessed, and he nodded with shame.

'What do you want with me, man?' he whimpered. 'I ain't done nothing to nobody. Not in a long time.' I put the photograph in his lap. He took one glance and handed it back. 'Bad medicine,' he said quietly. 'We should've never killed that grizzly. It's all gone to shit since then. I lost my job a week later, my old lady split, then I got drunk over in Butte, got the shit kicked out of me by two miners in the alley behind the M&M Bar, and they cut my braid, man, they cut my braid. Bad medicine.' He sat silently for a bit, staring at his huge hands as if he couldn't believe they had failed him. 'So what's going down, dad?' he said. 'It's clear you're not Fish and Game or Park Service, not with that cute blade-in-the-armpit number. So what is it? The goddamned Sierra Club hiring hoods now, putting out contracts on poachers? Ducks Unlimited, maybe?' Then he laughed, the taut, bowstring squeal of a man on the edge. 'Goddamned liberal phony white folks . . .'

'Who's the other guy?'

'Johnny Rausche,' he said, 'calls himself Rideout now. He's a brother.'

'A brother?'

'Yeah, dad, we used to share the same accommodations over at Walla Walla.'

'Who did you guys work for?'

'Well, I used to run a fork lift at that wholesale grocery warehouse down in Meriwether,' he said, 'and Johnny, he was a long-haul trucker – '

'No, not that,' I interrupted. 'The gang?'

'The gang?' he said, seemingly honestly amazed.

'Poachers, you know, don't jerk me . . .'

'Poachers?' he said, then loosed a fairly healthy bray of laughter. 'Who the hell do you work for, man?'

651

'That's a damn good question,' I admitted. I turned to look out the side window, fogged now with our breath, and cleared a small circle, a peephole, but all I could see was the snow rustling down the gray street, a few cars and pickups parked in front of the line of bars, some idling in the cold, banners of exhaust wind-whipped out of their tailpipes, others abandoned to the frozen drifts.

'Where's the grizzly hide?' I asked, even though I already believed him. There was no gang of poachers. Or if there was, Charlie Two Moons certainly didn't belong to it. I wondered if Rideout/Rausche had been stringing Cassandra Bogardus along just to keep her around, or if she had been blowing angel dust in my ears to, to . . . to what? To keep me around. Hell, all she had to do was blow in my ear, and I'd follow her anywhere. To keep me away? From what? Shit. 'Where's the hide?'

'In the hock shop across the street,' he said. He took out his billfold and found the pawn ticket. 'Two hundred bucks,' he said.

'Let's go take a look at it.' I knew in my bones that he wasn't lying, but I wanted to see the grizzly hide, anyway, wanted to touch it, as if the coarse, thick hair held the answer to questions I hadn't even been smart enough to ask yet.

The chubby old man behind the counter smiled when the three of us came in, kept smiling even after Charlie told him he wanted to redeem his pledge, but his smile didn't blunt his hard, greedy eyes, and I could tell the old man had just been waiting for ninety days to pass so he could claim the hide for himself. But he had to live in the same town with Charlie. He didn't mutter as I counted out two hundred, didn't grumble as he led us to the fur storage vault in the back. The hide and head, wrapped in a tarp, looked like a humpbacked pig on the floor, and when Charlie and I picked it up, it felt as heavy as a slaughtered hog.

'Good God,' I grunted as I followed Charlie out of the pawnshop. Simmons took my end from me and nearly fell with the weight.

'Old Ephram,' Charlie said, 'carries one big skin. Where's your car?'

'Over there. Why?'

'You just bought yourself a grizzly hide,' he said. 'Best job of mounting and tanning I've ever done, but Brother Bear is yours now, dad, and I'm damned glad to be rid of his spirit sitting on my medicine.'

'But I – ah . . .'

'Don't even say thanks, dad,' Charlie said as he and Simmons lowered the bundle gently into the bed of my pickup.

'Hey, how can I be sure this is the same bear that you and – '

'Sleep on it,' Charlie said happily, 'sing to the spirit of Brother Silvertip. You'll know.' Then he hoofed back toward the bar. He stopped at the door, opened his arms wide to the clean, windy sky, and shouted, 'Hey, brothers, can I buy you a drink?'

'I think I just went on the wagon,' I said, much as I hated the idea.

'What now, boss?' Simmons asked as we got back in the pickup.

'I'm tired of being dead,' I said. 'Let's get your rent car, check out of that crappy motel and into the Riverfront, and try to live up to our clothes.'

'You sure, boss?'

'Sure,' I said. 'Only Jesus Christ and Mark Twain ever made the evening news when it turned out that the reports of their deaths had been exaggerated.'

Simmons chewed on that until we were halfway back to Meriwether, then he said, 'I don't know what we're doing, boss, but I do know one thing.'

'What's that?'

'This shit's crazier than the war.'

11

In spite of my leanings to be among the living again, there were too many advantages to staying among the dead, so I let Simmons check us back into the Riverfront as Mr. Rodgers and Mr. Autry. It took four trips to pack our arsenal, luggage, and the bearskin up to the room the back way. We unrolled the hide, and it nearly covered the king-size bed, but the head looked too alive dangling off the foot of the bed, so we turned it around, propped the giant head on the pillows, and let the glass eye stare blankly at a terrible painting of a romantic mountain valley, waterfalls and crags, mists and dancing fawns.

'That son of a bitch weighs a ton,' Simmons sighed. 'What the hell are you going to do with it?'

'Sleep under it.'

He giggled nervously. 'Smother under it, more likely,' he said.

I gave him some money to buy gun-cleaning supplies, and while he was gone I considered the grizzly, wishing I had a drink. I ordered half a dozen stinking shots of peppermint schnapps from room service, but when they arrived I left them sitting on the table. 'I'd almost rather be sober,' I said to the hide. Brother Silvertip didn't give me any answers, just raised questions in my mind, stories, memories.

A friend of mine had been on the trail crew that found the bodies of the three girls killed by a grizzly at the Granite Park campground up in Glacier back in 1967. Over a bottle of Jack Daniel's one night, he told me about the body he had found. 'Nothing left but bones,' he kept saying softly, 'nothing but bones from hipbones to collarbones, nothing but bones.' And I talked to a park ranger once who had lost his tail bone and seven inches of his colon to a grizzly sow as he scrambled up a piss-fir. He had mastered an interesting sound effect to imitate the sound of her teeth on his bones, a sound he said he heard not with his ears, but through his bones. About the closest I had ever been to Lord Grizzly, though, was on my third honeymoon. My new wife and I sat on the porch of the Granite Park Chalet in Glacier, sipping unblended Scotch and watching, at the safe distance provided by our binoculars, a sow with two cubs cavorting by the side of a small lake down the mountainside. I wanted to get closer; she didn't; that marriage didn't make it back to town.

I didn't know how many grizzlies were left – six or eight hundred, at the most – and here was the dead hide of one of the last few, draped over my bed in a goddamned motel room.

'You deserve better accommodations than this, old man,' I said, then choked down one of the shots. It was a beautiful piece of work Charlie Two Moons had done, but I thought he perhaps deserved forty moons more of bad medicine. I didn't know, though, that poor Johnny deserved to fry the way he had. Maybe just beaten with a stick every day for the rest of his life. Except for the occasional poached cow elk or white-tailed doe, I hadn't hunted for years, and looking at the obscenity on my bed, I quit forever. I went into the other room, away from the hide, to use the telephone.

The woman at the Friends of the Dancing Bear Wilderness Area took my message for Carolyn politely enough, but she had trouble with my name. 'Mr. Grandfather Timberland,' I repeated slowly, 'it's an old Native American name.' She got so effusively apologetic that it drove me into a sulk. If the hunters and the Sierra Club ever went to war, I suspected I would like to sit on the sidelines and drop 81mm mortar rounds at random on the field.

I called Sarah's number, with no luck – with no hope, really. Somehow in all the confusion, I suppose I had resigned myself to the fact that I wasn't going to find the old woman or Gail. Not by myself. So I called the colonel. Since I was afraid the lines were still tapped, I wouldn't give the receptionist my name, and she wouldn't let me talk to the colonel without a name, so I gave her Jamison's name, and she put me through. When the colonel heard my voice, he said, 'It's okay, Milo. The taps are gone.'

'Dying helped, sir.'

'Jamison told me. Both of us are somewhat concerned, Milo, about the trouble you seem to be in. Very concerned, as a matter of fact.'

'I'm in so deep, sir, that if you reached out a hand for me, you'd go down too.'

'Please try to remember that I am not without resources, Milo.'

'Yes, sir,' I said, 'that's why I called. I want to hire the firm to mount a search for Mrs. Weddington and – '

'I already have some men on it,' he said, 'and I thought we had located them through the young girl's mother – or rather, through her telephone records; she had nothing to say to the operative who talked to her in Minot – located them at the Hilton in Seattle, but by the time we checked, they were no longer there. An older woman and a young girl had been registered under the name of Hildebrandt. The descriptions were too vague to make a positive identification. But they had paid cash, which is in itself suspicious . . .'

'The world has gone to shit, sir – '

'I beg your pardon.'

' – when cash is suspicious, sir.'

'It's not the world we made, Milo, just a world we have to live in.'

'Yes, sir,' I said. 'Thanks for taking this on yourself, Colonel Haliburton.'

'Please remember that it was *my* telephones they tapped, Milo,' he said tartly. 'But I would like to know – '

'I'll make a tape, sir, and mail it to myself at the office, and if I turn up dead, at least you'll know as much as I do.'

'Not a very pleasant thought.'

'What the hell, sir, I'm getting used to being dead, and I'll check back in every afternoon, sir.'

'You need any expense money, Milo?'

I told him no, thanked him again, and rang off. I sat there, running the whole number back through my mind one more time, the whole knotted string of events, as I held the receiver in my hand. The dial tone didn't have any answers either. I hung up the phone, and it rang before I could get my hand off it.

'Goddammit, I hate that,' I grumbled as I jerked it back up.

'Hate what, Mr. Grandfather Timberland?' Carolyn said over the wires.

'Everything.'

'I got your message,' she said. 'I'm glad you called, I've needed to talk to you . . .'

'Where are you?'

'At the office.'

'Why don't you meet me in my room?' I said, and she said she would within the hour. I went back into my bedroom, where the bearskin and the schnapps waited.

Simmons returned shortly, and when he sat down at the table in his room to clean the guns, I asked him if he wanted a drink. Since the two drinks in Stone City still sat uneasily on his stomach, he thought not, but he did wonder, shyly, if I really had done up all the cocaine.

'All of that,' I said, 'but there's this.' And I retrieved the packet from the briefcase and chopped two large lines of the heady shit from the trunk of poor Johnny's car. Two lines, too large, perhaps, then two more too quickly. By the time Carolyn knocked on my door, Simmons was cleaning arms in a frenzy and trying to tell me his life story at the same time. He had gotten as far as his second pre-adolescent sexual experience with his third cousin by his mother's second marriage, or second cousin by her third marriage . . . But when he heard the knocking, he picked up the .357 and cocked it.

'Easy,' I said, 'easy.'

'Maybe I'm too nervous for this shit, boss.'

'Maybe,' I said, 'but uncock that son of a bitch, Bob, and put it back on the table.' He did, carefully, and I released the breath I had been holding. 'Thanks.'

'Sorry.'

'No sweat.'

Since it was closer, I went to Simmons' hallway door, stuck my head out, and whistled at Carolyn.

'Cute,' she said, 'lover boy.'

'Lay off the lover-boy shit, okay?' I said as I stepped out of the way to let her in.

When she saw the guns scattered around the room, she stopped dead. 'Are you guys starting a war?' she asked, wide-eyed.

'Finishing one,' I said, then took her arm and led her into my room.

She liked the grizzly hide and head even less than she had the arsenal. I kicked the connecting door shut with my heel, and said, 'Now, before you give me your latent-homosexuality and hunting lecture, I want you to know that I didn't shoot that bear, I've never

657

shot a bear, never intend to, and it's not even my bearskin, it's a piece of evidence, in a – ah, very important case, and before you bother to ask what it's about, let me tell you that I can't tell you . . .'

She held up a finger to stop me, used it to tug down one of my lower eyelids, then walked over to the table and picked up my sunglasses, saying, as she handed them to me, 'It's about a quarter gram beyond reality, Milo, so put these on before your eyes start bleeding.'

'Huh? Right you are,' I said. 'Sorry.' I threw down a shot of schnapps and a glass of water, then opened the drapes and the sliding door to the balcony for a lungful of fresh air. 'Hey, it's goddamned dark, for Christ's sake.' And it was. Even after I took off the sunglasses.

'Busy day, huh?' she said, then took off her full-length down coat and lit a cigarette. 'Nice weather,' she added, 'but why don't you shut the door.'

'Of course,' I said. 'Anything for a lady. Why don't you sit down, make yourself comfortable. Can I get you a drink? Dinner? Anything?'

'You're in a good mood, aren't you?'

'Great,' I said. I shut the door and drapes, and held her chair for her at the table.

'Looking good, too,' she said. 'You should wear a suit more often, Milo.'

'Right,' I said, laughing as I took off the suit coat and draped it over a chair.

'And a shoulder holster less often.'

'You got it,' I said, unstrapping, and I took the Airweight into Simmons.

'Maybe I'll have that drink now, boss man,' he suggested. 'Either that, or clean all these goddamned guns again.'

'Sure. A pitcher of martinis for us, Beefeater, and whatever you want, lad – call room service.'

When I got back to Carolyn, she had already snubbed out her first cigarette and started another. 'I'm glad you called,' she said, tapping her long nails on the table. 'I've been trying to get in touch with you.'

'Me? Why? I'm supposed to get in touch with you.' I hadn't forgotten why I had called Carolyn – Cassandra Bogardus – but I just couldn't seem to keep it in my snowy mind long enough to mention the name. 'Why?'

'Well, you know that night we were here . . .' she began slowly. 'When we left, I sat in the parking lot downstairs while I let the motor warm up, and I heard about the fire, about your house, on the car radio, so I knew you were still alive. When I – ah, we left, you were lying on the bed, depleted but alive, and I wondered about the reports of your death . . . By the way, I am truly sorry about your house, Milo, I know what it must have meant to – '

'Don't mention it.'

'And I wanted to apologize for my behavior that – ah, night . . .'

'Behavior?'

'I just had a childish fit of jealousy,' she said, 'perhaps as much directed at Cassie as at you. She is – ah, an impressive-looking woman without her clothes.'

'Impressive?'

'Yes,' she said, 'but it's none of my business. My business is the proposed Dancing Bear Wilderness Area. A friend of mine in D.C. has gotten a line on the owners of the old C, C&K Railroad sections – some holding company out of Luxembourg – and he thinks they will go for a land swap, since most of the timber on their sections is third growth and on sidehills too steep to log economically under current regulations. And I've been working on your deal – '

'My deal?'

'My God, you really are out of it, aren't you!' she said. 'I've arranged for a plaque to be placed in Camas Meadows and come up with private monies to supplement the price we can offer, and I've also decided that those private things we talked about can be arranged.'

'Private things?'

'You know,' she said, snuffing out the cigarette butt, 'the weekend in Seattle, the night on your grandfather's grave . . .' Even in the fading light her dark hair glistened, and a blush rose from beneath the collar of her brown satin blouse, flushed across her neck and softened the rough planes of her face.

I leaned over, brushed her cheek with my lips, then whispered in her ear, 'You listen to me, lady . . .' She tried to move away but I pulled her closer. 'And listen good. I am about to go fucking insane, lady, my house has been burned down, people have been trying to

kill me, and I've seen enough dead bodies in the last week or so to
last a lifetime, and I'm in no mood to talk about some goddamned
wilderness area. If you don't tell me where the fuck Cassandra
Bogardus is, I'm going to rip this ear right off the side of your head.'
I took a sturdy grip on her ear with my teeth. From someplace so
deep in my chest that I couldn't imagine it, a low, rumbling growl
rattled.

Only Simmons saved me. He came in without knocking, the martini pitcher and two glasses in his hands.

'Oops! Sorry, boss,' he said, then unloaded the drinks on the table,
excused himself again, and rushed out of the room as I released
Carolyn's ear, straightened up, and stopped growling. At least I
couldn't hear it anymore, but I felt it down there waiting to be let
out again.

'Jesus Christ,' I sighed, 'I'm sorry, babe.' But when I put a hand
on her shoulder, Carolyn bolted for the bathroom, her face in her
hands.

When she came out, I sat slumped in a chair at the table, feeling
as small and tired as Charlie Two Moons had looked in the cab of
his pickup. I had poured a martini, but it sat untouched before me,
the crystal liquid still trembling in the dim light. Carolyn switched
on the hanging lamp over the table.

'I'm sorry,' I said, 'it's been – '

But she held up her hand to stop me. She gunned the martini I
had poured and wiped the tears off her tough face. Then she stood
across the table from me, saying, 'Don't interrupt me, Milo, please.
I do not know where Cassie is, I do not know what sort of trouble
she is in, and I do not think I can stand one more second of this
goddamned cowboy-and-Indian shit. It is just too crazy for me.' She
paused to take a deep breath. 'And now will you do me a favor?'

'Anything, love.'

'Will you please stand up and hold me?'

I did, standing up, then lying down in our clothes on the thick fur
of Brother Silvertip, held her until she finally went to sleep. I went
into Simmons' room to borrow a blanket. He was watching *Blood on
the Moon* with Robert Mitchum, a movie I hadn't seen since my
childhood. But I didn't have time to watch it now.

'Anything I can do, boss?' he asked.

'Watch this movie for me,' I said, then used his telephone to call the young lawyer, McMahon, at his home number in Seattle. He wasn't there, so I tried his office, even though it was late. He was there, but it sounded as if a party was going on around him. He had news, but not good news. Multitechtronics, Inc., was a wholly owned subsidiary of a Hong Kong import-export firm, which in turn was owned by a Bangkok holding company. A paper maze, he explained, that only more money could solve. I promised to send more money, then went back to cover up Carolyn's sleeping body.

I poured a martini and took it out to the balcony. The moon had waxed toward fullness since last I saw it, and in its quiet glow the rushing waters of the Meriwether looked like a sheet of black ice. Maybe if I took a steam bath, sweated the confusion and poison out of my bloodstream, then slept, I would know what to do tomorrow – a three-day steam bath and a long winter's nap, maybe. Sarah, Gail, poor Jimmy Rideout/Rausche with his saluting son and Sally with the cancer behind her eye, Korean nightmares in Elk City, a dawn full of guns and drugs, dead bodies and fire, that goddamned Cassandra Bogardus and her windy tale of poachers who acted like a Mafia family . . .

Maybe she had already called Goodpasture in Albuquerque to tell him where the fat lady sang, maybe she hadn't lied about that. But as I thought of the fat lady, I remembered the fat cocaine dealer on the Olympic Peninsula fingering the thick plastic wrapping, the odd pinkish-gray powder, and telling me I must have balls the size of a gorilla. And the brain of an addled chicken, lizards with feathers. She had seen the black plastic and the powder before. Maybe she knew where it came from. Whatever, at least it was a place to begin again, something to do besides watch the Meriwether run its rocky, cold course to the sea.

After Simmons and I had shed our rich duds and loaded all our goods, except the grizzly hide, into my pickup, I tried to wake Carolyn, but she had fallen so deeply asleep that she didn't even stir. I lifted her limp body off the bed as Simmons tugged the bear hide from beneath her, then I laid her back in the middle of the bed. We rolled up the skin and head in the tarp, and I got the keys to Carolyn's Mustang out of her purse.

As we struggled out the side door with the heavy bundle, a pair of drunks were coming in, faces red with whiskey and cold. One held the door for us, and the other laughed and said, 'Hey, buddy. Watcha got there? A dead body?' I guess the look I gave him wasn't exactly pleasant. 'It's a joke, buddy, a joke,' he added lamely.

'You're the fucking joke, jerk,' I said, but he acted as if he hadn't heard.

'Easy, boss,' Simmons huffed.

'Right.'

As soon as we managed to fit the hide into the small trunk and slammed the lid, I started to worry about it. What if it froze and cracked? Or the cold made the hair fall out? But, like Charlie Two Moons, I was glad to be rid of bad medicine, so I shoved the worries aside and went back up to leave Carolyn a note.

Love, you were sleeping hard, and we had to split. Sorry. Hope you wake from happy dreams. Brother Silvertip is in your trunk. Keep him for me, please, and if I don't come back – well, I trust you to do something appropriate to his spirit. Sorry we didn't meet in another world. Take care.

'What now, boss?' Simmons asked when I got back to the pickup.

'Listen, son, I'm sorry I don't ever tell you what we're doing until it's too late, and I appreciate your backing me up and not asking too many questions . . .'

'Shit, I trust you, Milo.'

'God knows why, Bob,' I said, 'but trust me now. If I can't work out this shit in Seattle this trip, I'm going to give it to the law dogs and run for Mexico – '

'I ain't never been to Mexico, boss,' he interrupted, grinning.

'You son of a bitch,' I said to his grin. 'Let's drop your rent car at the airport and head out into the sunset, Mr. Autry.'

'Mr. Rodgers,' he said, and we shook on it.

We made good time on the plowed and sanded interstate, kept our noses clean, stayed sober, and made Seattle by dawn, in time to catch the first ferry to Bremerton. We had breakfast in Poulsbo, then I called the number the fat girl had given me and left the message about Leroy and the basket of crabs. She called back in five minutes, suggested we meet on neutral ground on the Port Angeles–Victoria ferry that noon, no guns, no drugs because we would have to clear

662

Canadian customs going and American coming back. 'And no funny shit with hand grenades, okay?' she said with a laugh.

It took us longer to drive to Port Angeles than I had thought it would, so I had Simmons drop me at the dock, where I left him with my pickup, all the weapons and cocaine, told him to check into the Holiday Inn and wait for my call.

'Thanks, boss,' he said as I stepped out of the cab.

'Thanks?'

'For not thinking I'd run with all the goods.'

'Shit,' I said, 'it never crossed my mind.'

'So thanks,' he said, grinning.

Instead of searching for the fat girl, I went up to the bow to watch the ferry back away from the dock and turn into the Juan de Fuca Strait. A light mist mixed with an occasional snowflake, which melted as soon as it touched the deck, seemed to hang in the air between the lowering clouds and the gray sea as deep, heavy swells rolled down the Strait with a power that suggested they had risen in the middle of the Pacific with the sole purpose of washing down the rocky bluffs of this narrow neck of water. The fat girl came up beside me, slipped her hand into the pocket of my parka, and nestled her fingers in mine.

'Hello,' she said. Her hair had been curled, her face softly made up. Even in the electric-blue down parka she seemed slimmer somehow, and in her gold-rimmed granny glasses she might have been a schoolteacher playing hooky. 'No business for a while,' she said, then helped me stare at the mists as if we could see the far shore on Vancouver Island.

'I don't know your name,' I said.

'You can call me Monica. I've always thought of myself as a Monica. And yours, sir?'

'Carlos.'

'Have you ever been to Victoria, Carlos?'

'Only in the summertime.'

'Let's have lunch at the Oak Bay Hotel.'

'I've been drunk there,' I said. 'One of my favorite places.'

'I reserved a room, just in case.'

'Good idea, as long as we catch the last ferry back to Port Angeles.'

'No problem. We've got all the time in the world,' she whispered into the rain.

Over a slow lunch in a dining room that might have been brought over from England brick by brick, beam by beam in the hold of a clipper ship around the Horn, gazing out the wide windows into the light rain that seemed British in its damp stodginess, we got our stories straight. I had been a friend of her father's when she was growing up someplace dull, Cleveland or Pittsburgh, Des Moines or St. Paul, and she had always had a crush on me. We had happened upon each other in this English village of a city so far from home. Monica had been around a bit too much to suit herself, and I was once again between marriages, and as we walked hand in hand up the carpeted stairway we trembled like children.

We nearly missed the ferry back to the States, and stood again on the bow as the mist became snowflakes. When we could see the gray form of the Port Angeles dock, she shook her wet curly hair and said, 'What did you want to know?'

'The coke you bought from me,' I said, 'you'd seen that powder-coated plastic before, right?' She nodded carefully. 'Can I ask where?'

'If this comes back on me, man, I am not just dead,' she said softly, 'I am bad hurt before I get a chance to die. You understand that?'

'Monica . . .'

'Carlos,' she said, 'goddammit,' then gave me an address on West Marginal Way in Seattle, a pat on the cheek, a damp kiss. Behind her foggy glasses, her blue eyes turned dark-gray. 'Good luck.'

'Thanks,' I said, 'but I'm not afraid anymore. For the first time since all this started.'

'Maybe you should be,' she said and walked back toward the warm lights of the passenger lounge. Once she was safely inside, I turned back to face the black waters, the heavy, tolling swells.

It was past midnight by the time Simmons and I drove back to Seattle, but I was determined to get to the address anyway. Even though the dank air seemed to absorb the glow from the street lights, I could make out the small sign on the chain-link gate: ENVIRONMENTAL QUALITY CONTROL SERVICES, INC.

'What the hell does that mean?' Simmons asked.

'Garbage,' I said, 'fucking garbage.'

12

It took McMahon, the young lawyer, all day and a large jolt of cash, but by seven o'clock that evening in his office, he was able to hand me a fairly complete file on EQCS, Inc., and its president and founder, Richard Tewels.

During WWII, Tewels had served in the European theater as a supply sergeant for a motorized transport outfit. After he mustered out at Fort Lewis, and with money he said he had won in a crap game on the troop ship back to the States but which one reporter suggested had come from a black-market operation in gasoline and tires, he bought a junkyard south of Tacoma. From there on, Tewels was an American success story.

In less than five years he owned half-a-dozen junkyards, a small trucking outfit, and three sand-and-gravel pits. When the pits were exhausted, he turned them into private landfills. In 1964, outside Chicago, where he had been raised, he bought his first garbage-truck company from a small town that could no longer afford to operate it themselves. By 1972 he owned over three hundred garbage trucks and more than twenty landfills in small towns and medium-sized cities from coast to coast, and he incorporated as EQCS, Inc. He kept growing richer and richer on garbage and junk. Along with his fortune, he also collected a number of indictments, but no convictions, for possession of stolen automobile parts and illegal dumping. At the same time, he was cited for achievement by state environmentalists from sea to shining sea.

In 1976 he sold EQCS, Inc., to an international consortium, although he remained president and a major stockholder. The consortium, based in Luxembourg, held controlling interests in casinos in the Caribbean, oil tankers, wheat farms in eastern Washington, hog farms in Iowa, and the usual range of investments. In 1980 EQCS bought a small tanker ship from one of its sister corporations and converted it into a floating furnace for the disposal of liquid toxic waste. The onboard incinerators could achieve Fahrenheit temperatures above 2500 degrees, hot enough to dispose of even the dreaded chemical polychlorinated biphenyls, PCBs. The tanker operated out of Tacoma and burned waste in international waters, four or five hundred miles out in the Pacific.

Well, the information didn't cause me to see a burst of clear, absolute light, but it did give me some notion of whom I had been dealing with, running from. Starting at the lowest end, junkyards had always been perfect covers for chop shops that dealt in stolen automobile parts. Say, for instance, that you stole a Caddy worth twenty thousand; you might be able to fence it for a third of its value, but if it was cut up into body parts, you could sell it for two or three times the original value. Or say you wanted to ship some cocaine or stolen arms or hot money across the country. Why not hide it in a barrel of PCBs, a toxic liquid so deadly that some environmental experts considered even one part per million parts of water as carcinogenic? And say you had been at sea burning toxic wastes on board your own ship. What sort of customs agent would crawl around in the holds of your tanker searching for cocaine?

Here I thought I had been playing gunfire games with something as nice as a large drug ring, and it turns out that I am playing hardball with a multinational corporation with a gross profit larger than two thirds of the countries in the world. Suddenly I felt even worse than I could deal with. When the father of a friend of mine found out he was dying of cancer, he went to see all his old friends and greeted them with, 'Boys, you're looking at a dead man.' Well, I couldn't beat them, and running would be a waste of time, but at least for Sarah's sake, I could go out in a small match flare of glory, maybe make the bastards flinch.

Or so I thought, dead as I assumed I was, as I looked at the rest of the file.

Although Tewels never gave interviews, McMahon had enough contacts in Seattle to find out that he lived in a large house on Capitol Hill, had a ranch in the Sierras west of Tahoe, a midtown Manhattan apartment, and a seventy-five-foot yacht. He was a large contributor to Seattle social and artistic organizations. He had three children – a daughter who was an off-Broadway set designer, another who was an anesthesiologist in Santa Barbara, and a younger son from a second marriage who was a tight end for Stanford. At fifty-nine, Tewels was still a nationally ranked seniors squash player.

After I went through the notes one more time, I handed them back to McMahon, then told him to get out his tape recorder. When I finished telling him everything that had happened and everything that I suspected, he whistled, then stood up. 'I sure as hell hope I don't have to defend you, man,' he said.

'It'll never come to that,' I said. 'They've covered it too neatly. I just wanted somebody to have a record, if – ah, worst comes to worst . . .'

'Sure. What about your friend in the waiting room?'

'I'm going to try to fire him,' I said, 'and I want you to draw me a will.'

'Are you serious?'

'Damn right,' I said. 'There's an old woman I owe, seriously.'

While he got the forms, I went out to talk to Simmons. He lounged in a chair beside a stack of tattered *Field and Streams* thumbing through one carefully as if he planned a long fishing trip to some distant exotic land.

'Okay, Bob,' I said, 'you're fired. It's over. I'm paying you off, and you're walking.'

'You can pick your nose, boss, but you can't pick your friends,' he said quietly. 'No more of this thirteen-month-tour crap, man. I've signed up for the duration.'

'You got any family?'

'A little brother in a foster home in Denver,' he said, 'and two little girls living with my ex-wife down in Casper.'

'Give me their names and addresses,' I said.

After I noted them down, I went back into McMahon's office, where we wrote a new will that split my father's estate, half going to my son, half to the Rausche children and Simmons' little brother and his daughters.

'How about witnesses?' McMahon said, and I followed him down the hallway, where we found a legal secretary working late and a janitor. 'I'll file it in the morning,' he said as we went back to his office, 'first thing. Now what are you planning to do?'

'You know I can't tell you.'

667

'Right,' he said. 'Good luck, Mr. Milodragovitch.'

'You can read about it in the papers,' I said, 'the funny papers.'

Even though, and melodramatic as it sounded, we seemed to be on a suicide mission, I wanted to do some reconnaissance work on Tewels to see where to hit them. I had some vague notion that I could trade Tewels for Sarah and Gail if they were still alive, or use him to hurt the bad guys if they weren't. And I had to tell Simmons what was going on. He didn't say much, just 'Sure, boss,' and hit the cocaine a little harder. He wasn't alone. I tried to interest him in a couple of really high-priced hookers, one last touch of flesh before we went under, but like me, he seemed embarrassed by the idea.

For the next three days and nights Simmons and I put a twenty-four tag on Tewels, and he kept us busier than a one-legged man at an ass-kicking contest. The second day, I bought a couple of portable CB units and a base station and rented a camper so we would have a place to sleep and shower. I lost count of how many times we changed rental cars, how many hours of sleep we lost. And all for nothing. While we were standing tired in the constant rain or trying to stay awake as it softly drummed on the tops of the cars, Tewels maintained a busy work schedule and an even busier social life – a Broadway roadshow, a dinner party, a cocktail fund raiser for a local film society, which I crashed in my rich man's suit. I managed to stand three feet away from Tewels, sipping sparkling French water and lime and listening to him discuss the New Wave directors, whatever they might be. He was a tall, lean man, bald except for a silver fringe, and moved like an athlete.

Even as my vague notion of kidnapping Tewels evolved into a real idea, he had so many people around him that it looked as if we would have to mount a military operation to snatch him. A young man, who looked as if he had a steel lump under his arm, drove Tewels around in his Bentley. The driver lived in an apartment over the garage, but a butler, a cook, and a housekeeper lived in the house. Even the housekeeper looked as if she could climb off her broom and chop down a tree with her hard, angular face.

But about eight o'clock on the third night as I was sitting down the street from his house in an anonymous dog-turd-brown Champ, the driver came down the stairs in a gray three-quarter-length parka with a fur-trimmed hood. He opened the garage and backed out a Toyota Land Cruiser station wagon. Tewels, wearing a shearling coat, a watch cap, and heavy gloves, and carrying a briefcase, met him in the driveway, and they drove away like men with business in mind.

As I followed, I stuck the portable CB's antenna out the window and tried to wake up Simmons. 'Break two-seven for Spider Man,' I said several times. 'You got a copy on the Russian Bear?'

'You got the Spider Man,' he answered sleepily. 'Over.'

'Spider Man, Spider Man,' I said into the mike, shaking because this felt like the right time to take them down – they weren't dressed like that and driving the Land Cruiser to take in a show, 'the Garbage Man is on his way to the dump. I want the pickup, winter duds, and all the rest. Over.'

'The rest? Over.'

'Pineapples and them little things that play bush-time rock 'n' roll,' I said, 'Over.'

'That's a big ten-four,' he answered, laughing, 'from the Viet-Vet Spider Man. Over.'

'Heading east on I-Ninety,' I said, 'pedal to the metal, so shake it, bo. Russian Bear eastbound and down.'

'Spider Man back door and down.'

Simmons must have flown, because he came up behind me before we made Issaquah, flashed his lights once, then dropped back.

The traffic wasn't too heavy, and the Land Cruiser was easy to tag. We went on up Snoqualmie Pass into a light, blowing snow, then past the ski areas, which hadn't had time to groom the slopes and open the lifts yet; just before we reached Cle Elum they turned north on 903, heading toward Cle Elum Lake. I jammed the Champ into a snowbank at the exit, then dashed over and jumped into the cab of the pickup.

'Cut your headlights,' I said, 'and stay after that rig.'

'You're the boss!'

We could have used a real snowstorm, but the light flurries mixed with the blowing snow were enough to keep the pickup invisible. 'Watch his taillights,' I said, 'and stay off the brakes.' Then I changed into my snow pacs, checked the loads in the Browning and the M–11, stuffed two grenades into the pockets of the Kevlar-lined vest, and two extra clips for the Ingram in my hip pockets.

'Jesus, boss, what's happening?'

'I don't know, son,' I admitted, 'but they're going out here where it's dark and cold.' Already so excited that my breathing had shifted to rapid-fire, I added, 'This is it, lad.'

'It?'

'Showdown city.'

'Oh shit,' Simmons sighed as he fumbled for the cocaine vial, which we snorted sloppily off our fists.

Beyond Roslyn, the Toyota's brake lights flared, then disappeared as the rig turned left. Simmons down-shifted and slowed, coasted up to the place they had turned. I could see a sign by the road but couldn't read it. I climbed out, ran over to the sign. VARNER AND ASSOCIATES, it said, REAL ESTATE. A number of four-wheel-drive vehicles had been up the snowy track recently. Through a gap in the storm, the brake lights blazed again about fifty yards up the hillside, and the headlight beams swung around a switchback behind the thick evergreen screen, and another fifty yards above that, I thought I could see the dim glow of house lights.

While Simmons put on his pacs, I drove the pickup on up the road until I found a place to pull off, then parked, dug through the parkas for woolen ear bands and sliced gaps in the palms of our mittens so we could get our trigger fingers out. Simmons' fingers were trembling so badly that when he checked the loads in the .357, he nearly dropped it in the snow.

'Easy,' I said. 'Let's see if we can't do this without blowing anybody's shit away, okay?'

'It's cold,' he said.

'You can still back out, son, stay with the pickup.'

'I'm scared of dying, you're scared of killing somebody,' he said. 'We make a great team – but we're a team, Milo.'

'Okay.'

We blackened our faces with muddy slush from the wheel wells, tried to grin in the freezing wind, then trotted back to the uphill track. Halfway there, we saw headlights and dove into the snowy ditch. A four-wheel-drive camper van turned up the road. We gave it a few minutes, then ran on.

After a short rest at the track while the storm seemed to intensify, we started up the frozen ruts of the road. At first we rested every twenty-five steps, trying to hold down the clouds of our breath, then every ten as we eased up the road. When the glow of the building showed up the last switchback, we stopped, walked more slowly, pushing our pacs into the snow before we shifted our weight forward. The tree trunks rubbed each other, moaning in the wind, and the branches rattled brittle and icy. When we reached the switchback, we went around it uphill, flat on our bellies, buried in the shadows of the snow-plowed berm. After another twenty-five yards we could see the front of the real estate office at the dead end of the road.

It was a wide, low log building with a parking lot cut into the slope on the side nearest us. Tewels' Land Cruiser, the camper, and a jeep station wagon were parked there. A porch with floodlights at either end stretched across the front of the building. In spite of his large, fluffy down parka, the man on the porch looked very cold as he walked back and forth, stamping his feet and slapping his gloved hands together. When he paused under the far flood, I could see his face. It was the dude in the Porsche who had wanted to get Western when I took his keys on the ferry dock. I was glad to see him again. Now we could have all the horse hit and gun smoke he wanted.

Simmons followed me as I bellied a long loop until we were in the shadows of the parked rigs and had a clear shot at the guy's feet and legs on the porch. I extended the wire stock of the Ingram, switched it to single fire, then handed it to Simmons.

'Cover me,' I whispered, 'but don't switch this little bastard to rock 'n' roll.'

'Gotcha, boss,' he said. Even in the darkness, I could see his lips, blue and trembling.

I slithered around the side of the parking lot to the building, stood up slowly and peeked through the corner of the window in the narrow gap that wasn't covered by frost. A long office took up the front half of the building, with three desks that looked little used spaced out along its length. Tewels' driver and the partner of the guy on the porch sat at the far desk, smoking and flipping the pages of a property album. Three doors were set into the back wall, but only one of them had light underneath it. The guy on the porch came in, complaining about the weather, and the driver cursed, zipped up his parka, flipped up the hood, and went outside.

I went on around to the back of the building, struggling in the deep, drifted snow, the Browning automatic freezing to my hand. The drapes were shut in the lighted office, but they didn't quite

671

reach the bottom of the sill. I couldn't see much – two sets of hands smoothing out a map, another set counting bundles of money – and couldn't hear anything but the rumble of their voices.

The odds didn't look good, but I heaved on through the drift to the far corner and peered around. The driver had stepped off the porch out of the wind to take a leak. From the wavering pattern of his smoking stream, it looked as if he were trying to write his name in the snowbank. That made the odds better. These guys might be tough in town, but this was my frozen turf. He was too busy melting snow and chuckling like a little boy in the wind to hear me as I crept up behind him. I jerked his hood back and laid the barrel of the Browning against the side of his head as hard as I could. His ear burst like a rotten plum and he fell into a snowbank, where I clubbed him again.

He had an S&W 9mm automatic on him, which I unloaded and pitched into the storm, then I took his parka, ripped out the draw-string, tied his wrists to his ankles, gagged him with his handkerchief, then buried him in the snow. I crawled around the porch and back to Simmons.

'Okay,' I whispered, putting on the driver's parka and tucking the fur-lined hood around my face. 'Are you ready to hit it?'

'One more toot, boss, okay?' he said. It was windy and imprecise, but we did the best we could. I couldn't tell if the tears in his eyes were from the cold or the fear. 'I'll be fine,' he said.

'It's not your war,' I whispered as I took the grenades out of my vest pockets.

'It's never anybody's war, boss,' he muttered through chattering teeth.

'Okay,' I said, trading him the grenades for the submachine gun, 'I'm going through the front door. You stand to the side, and if I shout "Bob," you pitch the grenades in on the right-hand side of the room.'

'What about you?'

'I'll get behind a desk,' I said as he straightened the pins. 'Let's do it.'

We crawled around the rigs onto the porch and across it under the front window to the door, where we stood up, Simmons with his back to the wall. He lifted one snow-covered eyebrow, and I turned the doorknob, stepped inside.

They let me get three steps into the office before the big guy raised his head to tell me to shut the door, but three steps was all I needed to get to the center of the narrow room. I thought they might give it up when they saw the ugly shape of the Ingram, but they didn't. They leapt to their feet, reaching for iron instead of the sky, and I chopped them down with two soft, sputtering bursts.

I tried to hold low, to wound instead of kill, and it worked for the smaller man – his right leg crumpled under him and he flopped to the floor – but I held the burst too long and the Ingram kicked up and away and stitched the big guy right up the middle, blood and goose feathers exploding up his chest. He would never get Western again. The silenced, subsonic .380 rounds hadn't made much noise at all, but the big guy crashed into a file cabinet and a large metal ashtray as he fell. I knelt to get the small wounded man's piece as the door to the rear office opened. I put a short burst under the chin of a man I had never seen before, blew him backward into the room. I was in the office before his body hit the floor, the blood-lust growl tickling my chest.

Four men sat on the far side of a long table, their faces and clothes splattered with blood and brain tissue, sat very still, their hands poised, their heads cocked, as if listening for something, perhaps the muffled drumming of the dead man's heels on the carpet. It was all I could do to keep from emptying the clip at them.

I stepped past the rattling heels – that soft, final sound that had echoed in my head since the night of my father's suicide – and got my back against the wall. The little guy in the front office still had a piece on him. 'Mr. Rodgers,' I shouted out the door. 'I want you to count to ten, and if you don't see two pieces on top of the desk, I want you to pitch the grenade in.'

'Holy shit,' he grunted, 'gimme a minute!'

'One,' Simmons said loudly, 'two . . .'

'There,' the wounded man said as he clunked his piece loudly on the desk top.

'Now the other guy's,' I said.

'Right, right!' He groaned with the effort, and I heard another clunk before Simmons got to seven.

'Mr. Rodgers,' I said, 'unload them and pitch them outside. And when you're done, drag the little guy in here where I can see him.'

After a moment Simmons backed through the doorway, dragging

673

the man by his collar. He clutched his thigh tightly above his bloody knee, and his right foot dangled off at an impossible angle. Simmons propped him against the wall of bookshelves in the back of the room.

'Now let's see what we've got,' I said.

Tewels sat at the far left, a scrap of gore stuck to his forehead, sweat and blood leaking between his eyebrows and down the side of his nose, where it dripped off his neat mustache and splattered on a Forest Service map. The man next to him looked like a Hollywood actor who once had hopes of playing leads but who had drunk himself into character roles that featured close-ups of his corrupt, bloated face, his mean, frightened eyes, and his silver thatch of hair. Beside him sat a very scared Oriental man, his slim frame draped in a silk suit, not a Japanese or a Chinese, but perhaps a Malaysian.

On the far right sat a pale blond man in his thirties with the weak chin and beady eyes of a bureaucrat, but except for a flicker of his pale eyelashes, he didn't look impressed. 'You were supposed to be dead, you fucking clown,' he said calmly, 'and now you are.'

'I've got a family,' the character actor said, his oddly high voice full of tremor, the whiskey sweat rolling off him.

'We can work something out,' Tewels offered quietly.

I put a short burst into the bookcase over the blond man's head, said, 'Shut up, gentlemen,' then watched the paper fragments drift down in the silence. 'Over here, Mr. Rodgers,' I said as I moved to the other side of the doorway, tripping over the feet of the dead man, just a brief stumble, but the blond man looked extremely amused. 'Get this piece of shit out of here,' I said to Simmons.

When Simmons got hold of his feet and tugged, the bloody back of his head popped softly loose from the carpet, like the sound of a top-feeding trout sucking down a May fly. The actor looked as if he was going to faint at the sound, and I had to struggle to hold my dinner down.

'You stupid drunken jerk,' the blond man said. 'Your nerves just aren't up to it anymore, Milodragovitch.'

'Would you please shut up,' Tewels said. He looked worried.

'Cover them,' I said to Simmons as I moved the Ingram to my left hand and drew the automatic with my right and handed it to him. 'If anybody moves,' I added, 'gut-shoot the albino.'

'Ain't got the heart for it, old man,' Blondie said as I put a fresh magazine in the submachine gun.

'Please,' Tewels pleaded, and the actor mouthed the word silently.

As I traded guns with Simmons again, Blondie said, 'You clowns juggle too?'

'Us old cowboys just don't seem to scare anybody anymore,' I said to Simmons, then shot a brass ashtray off the table beside the blond man. After all the stuttering pops of the Ingram, the roar of the 9mm automatic sounded like a major explosion in the office. And it was true – we didn't – except for the actor, whose eyes rolled back into his head as he buckled out of the chair in a dead faint.

Everybody wants to be a hero these days. When I glanced at the actor's fainting fit, the blond man's hand snaked under his coat while he dove for the corner. It was so easy it wasn't even funny – I shot him twice in the ribs in mid-dive, then once in the head when he hit the floor. But the little wounded guy, he was a pro; he came up with a hideout gun, a dinky .25 automatic, two tiny pops that bounced Simmons off the wall. God love him, though, he pulled his weight. Like good old Roy, he shot the gun out of the wounded man's hand, but unlike the movies, the fragments tore his gun hand to shreds and blew his face off. Simmons fell to his knees, lifted the Ingram, and took out the Oriental with a burst as closely spaced as a close-range shotgun blast, throwing him out of his chair and into the wall. Tewels had stood up, his hands raised as high as they would go, but Simmons started to pull down on him, too.

'Please, Bob, no,' I said as he pitched forward onto his face.

I did what I had to do, business as usual in my crappy line of work, made Tewels kneel, his fingers laced behind his head, his forehead leaning against the bookcase, then I made sure the dead were really dead. Nobody at home in Blondie's head, the little guy had swallowed his tongue, choked on his own blood, and the actor's buttocks jiggled like jelly when I shook them with my foot, unconscious. Then I went to check on Simmons.

The first round had flattened against his vest, but the second had caught him in the face, a black hole the size of a bee beside his nose, the flattened slug lodged somewhere beyond his brain pan. As I lifted him off the carpet and held him on my knees, the dark, echoing rattle had already begun. I said those empty words you give the dying – I'm sorry, I am a jerk, a fucking clown – but he didn't hear me, heard only that windy rush down the last highway. When he got

675

there, I closed his eyes, covered his face with his useless vest. Then went back to work.

Just so we got off on the right foot, I put a round two inches above his bald head. 'Just so we know where we stand,' I said, 'you're one nerve twitch from dead.'

'Yes, sir,' he said.

'Get up and take your clothes off, slow and easy,' I said, and he did. He might have looked athletic in his expensive clothes, but naked he was just another skinny old man. 'Tie Captain Faintheart's hands behind him with your belt.' When he finished that, I ordered, 'Outside.' Then we went out into the storm.

After I let him sit cross-legged in the snow with his hands behind his head for a few minutes, I lit a cigarette, and said, 'Answer quick, answer right. Maybe I won't blow your fucking head off, maybe we'll get through before you freeze to death.'

'Yes, sir,' he said, shivering, 'anything you want. We can work something out. I promise.'

'Maybe,' I said. 'Who's Captain Faintheart?'

'An EPA official from Denver, Sikes.'

'And the blond guy with the big mouth?'

'Head of security,' he said, 'an ex-CIA cowboy, Logan.'

'The Oriental gentleman?'

'A representative of the holding company that owns EQCS.'

'And what was supposed to go down up here tonight?'

'We give the EPA official twenty-five grand and a list of dump sites where we can't stand the heat,' he said, 'and he makes sure we don't get any.'

'Nice business,' I said, 'garbage. Who's John Rideout or Rausche?'

'Nobody. A driver. He picked up waste material on the East Coast, the Midwest, the South, hauled it out here.'

'Cassandra Bogardus?'

'She applied for a secretary's job at our downtown office, and when Logan's men checked her out, we discovered she wasn't who she said she was.'

'A reporter, huh?'

'Not even that,' he said, 'just a nosy rich girl who sometimes billed herself as a wildlife photographer, but when Logan found out her employment application was a fake, and that I had . . . ah – '

' – been taken in by a pretty face and big tits?' I said, and he nodded. Scared as he was, he wasn't generating enough body heat to melt the snow on his bald head. 'You're not the first,' I assured him. 'Why plant all the arms and drugs on Rideout before you killed him?'

'Logan killed him,' he said quickly, 'Logan. To discredit anything he might have told the Bogardus board. "Disinformation," he called it.'

'And why try me?'

'Nobody knew who you were at first, and Logan said he was just being tidy, but when we found out you were a security guard, I think he wanted to kill you out of contempt.'

'Nice people you have working for you.'

'They used to work for me,' he said sadly, 'but somewhere along the way I discovered that I really worked for them.'

'An innocent bystander?'

'Sort of . . .'

'You didn't mind killing people at long range with your goddamned toxic dumps,' I said, 'but when it got down to gunfire, you didn't like it?'

'Something like that,' he said, then added, 'I don't know how much more cold I can take.'

'I'll let you know,' I said. 'Where's Sarah Weddington?'

'Who?' he said, so confused and afraid that I knew he was telling the truth. As much as I hated it: the truth. 'Who?' he asked again, pleading.

'Nobody,' I said. 'Help me get your driver and let's go back inside.'

'I can't move,' he said, shaking so hard that the tiny drifts of snow scattered off his head and shoulders.

'You better figure out a way to make it,' I said, then went around the corner and dug the driver out of the snowbank. By the time I had dragged him onto the porch and up to the front door, Tewels had made the first step. I dumped the driver inside the door, then went back out for Tewels and carried him into the back office. As he struggled into his clothes, I collected all the weapons I could find, even the grenades out of the pockets of Simmons' vest, and made a sloppy pack out of the driver's parka.

'Any whiskey around?' I asked Tewels when he had his coat on. He reached behind the second shelf of books, ran his hand down it

677

until he came up with a half-pint of vodka. He had a quick snort, then offered it to me. I shook my head, and he hit it again.

'Guy that runs this place drinks,' Tewels explained.

'Do they actually sell real estate?' I asked, and he nodded, sucking on the bottle. 'They keep a camera in the office?'

'Probably,' he said.

I followed him as he checked the desks in the front office – he walked like a man who had played his last game of squash – where he found a Polaroid and three packs of film and a flash attachment. I took several pictures of Tewels and each of the dead bodies, with the maps and the lists and the money, with the sleeping face of the EPA official, used all the film. Then I cleaned up the table, rolling up the maps and the papers, checking the briefcase full of money. Tewels had fallen into a chair behind the table, still shivering, still sipping at the vodka.

'Can you get this place cleaned up and dispose of the bodies?' I asked, adding, 'Mister garbage man.'

'I've never done it before,' he said, 'but I know the drill.'

'Listen,' I said as I unholstered the Browning, 'I think you've been in the business from the beginning.'

'The business?' he said, looking at the pistol.

'Chop shops, stolen cars, the whole number, and when you saw a way to run drugs and arms and dump poison illegally, I think you jumped at the chance. The greed business. And if you try to pull this innocent-bystander shit on me again, I'm going to spend the next hour blowing chunks of you all over the room. Do you understand?'

'Whatever you say.'

'Let's go back to "Yes, sir," ' I said. 'I sort of like that.'

'Yes, sir,' he said, but didn't mean it. I should have left him in the snow a bit longer. 'Whatever you say.'

'Can you clean up this mess without involving the law?'

'No problem – sir.'

'You better hope there's no problem,' I said, 'because this is how it's going to be. These maps, these photos – they're my get-out-of-jail free card, okay? As long as I'm alive and healthy, untroubled by people on my tail, and as long as all my friends are, too, you guys can go on with business as usual . . .' Tewels looked surprised. 'What you do in your business, that's the government's problem, not mine. I got into this mess by accident, and tried to work it out to save my

678

ass. We could have made a cheaper trade a long time ago, but you bastards were too busy trying to be tidy by blowing me away – '

'Logan,' he said.

'Logan's ass,' I said. 'And there's one other thing – I'm taking the twenty-five grand and buying a contract on one of your children . . .'

'Leave my children out of this,' he said, alcohol-warm now, 'they don't know anything about this – ah, side of the business.'

'I'm buying a contract, and you better hope I live a long time, Tewels, and die in bed of natural causes because if I don't, your business life is over, and one of your kids turns to mincemeat,' I said. 'Understand?'

'Yes, sir.'

'Don't try to get in touch with me,' I said. 'I'll see you at the Stanford-Washington State game in Pullman a week from Saturday – wait by the main gate for me, alone – and let me know if you're having any trouble arranging the details.'

'Of course,' he said. 'Pullman. A week from Saturday.'

'Now I'm going to fix the telephones, and the transportation – I'll leave the rotor of your rig by the sign post at the bottom of the hill – if I were you, I'd wait for at least an hour, warm up, before I went down for it. Okay?'

'Yes, sir,' he said, but his eyes were as cold as his heart.

After I jerked the phone lines out of the wall and threw the sets into the snow, I loaded up the weapons and the briefcase. Tewels and I didn't bother to say goodbye. After I went out the front door, I paused long enough to give myself some insurance against insincerity. I pulled the pin from one of the grenades and left it leaning against the front door, planning to take ten or fifteen minutes of his hour buried in a snowbank across the road. If he stayed put – fine, I would put the pin back in. If he didn't – fine, too. After I lifted the distributor caps out of the rigs, I tucked myself into the snow across the parking lot.

He only waited five minutes and came out carrying a scoped hunting rifle – I should have checked the other office; I shouldn't have threatened his children – came out in such a hurry that he didn't even hear the handle pop off the grenade. Maybe I had seen too many dead people lately, maybe I didn't want it to end like this – whatever, I rose without thinking out of the snow, screaming 'Get down!' into the wind. But he made his choice, turned and fired from the hip, plowing snow at my feet, and he was working the rifle bolt when the grenade blew him off the porch. Even lying sodden and bloody in the snow, his hands searched for the rifle as I ran the twenty yards to him.

'No deal,' he whispered as I knelt beside him, 'no deal.'

'That's the trouble with your business,' I said, 'there's always somebody ready to make a deal.' But I don't think he heard me.

13

There is this little lake down in Wyoming, outside of Pinedale, Fremont Lake, and it is supposed to be nine hundred and some odd feet deep. After I called the night emergency number for EQCS and finally got hold of the assistant director of security and told him he'd better get a cleaning crew for a blood bath up to the real estate office, I headed home by way of Fremont Lake.

Two nights later, by the light of the waxing moon, I sat in the dark center of the lake in a small rubber raft dropping firearms over the side, dropped them all, then the ammo and the grenades, and the rest of the cocaine, and a half-full pint of schnapps into the cold black water.

I had heard once that a colleague of mine down in the Southwest, a private investigator by the name of Shepard, when asked by a journalist if he carried a gun in his work, replied, 'Hell, no. If somebody wants to shoot old Shepsy, they're gonna have to bring their own gun.'

Me too, Shepsy, me too.

Then I went back to the motel in Pinedale where I had been lying low watching television, the newspapers and an unopened half-gallon of vodka sitting on the dresser. Some of us had made the news, right, but only after the cleaning crew had dealt with the garbage. Tewels' yacht had been found floundered in the Juan de Fuca Strait, his body missing, supposedly lost at sea, along with the director of security and a distinguished Oriental businessman.

I waited a day, then called Sarah's number in Meriwether, but when Gail answered, I hung up. I didn't want to talk to them yet.

A few days later I saw the EPA official's picture in the Denver *Post* above his obituary. His heart had failed him, it seemed. None

681

of the other deaths had been reported, the bodies probably run through an automobile crusher, then ground into pellets and shipped to Japan. Or gone to sea in a floating incinerator. Simmons, God rest his soul, deserved better than that, to be treated like junk, then built into a Toyota or something. But I was going to have to live with that, and wonder if he might have lived if I hadn't been so far behind the cocaine.

Washington State and Stanford played their football game while I was in Pinedale, but it wasn't on television, so I didn't see it. According to the newspapers, though, my son had five tackles, sacked the quarterback twice, and blocked an extra point. The Tewels boy had caught three passes and scored the winning touchdown on a reverse. I wished the boys a better world than their fathers had made.

For another week or so, I wandered around Wyoming, Colorado, and Utah, leaving copies of the maps and papers, a few of the Polaroid prints, and detailed tapes in safe-deposit boxes and with small-town lawyers. Occasionally I called Goodpasture down in New Mexico to see if he knew where the fat lady sang, but she hadn't called. And I didn't open the vodka.

I found myself beginning to like motel rooms too much, spending too much time staring at my stubby gray beard in crooked mirrors. It was time to come out of the cold. When I called the new director of security at EQCS, I congratulated him on his promotion, then we made our deal, slightly different from the one I had made with Tewels, now that I had seen the dump sites marked on the maps, but business as usual. My untimely death wouldn't close them down, but it would cut into their profit margin.

A Mexican stand-off, as Charlie Two Moons had said.

Finally, the fourth or fifth time I called Goodpasture he had a number for me, an all too familiar number, so I headed north home with Mexico on my mind.

Back in town, I waited a few days until I could catch all of them at Sarah's at once. It was one of those gray, still afternoons when the light seemed filtered through old glacial ice, but I could see their shadows moving against the sheer drapes of the solarium. I slipped the front-door lock and eased up the stairs. Pausing at the top, I could smell the sweet stink of marijuana, herbal tea, and freshly baked cake, and could hear their laughter, that stoned laughter I knew too well myself, laughter without cause or purpose, and I guessed that on an afternoon much like this one, the ladies had gathered and come up with their insane plan. Somehow they would save America from toxic waste and corruption, and I would be their stooge, dance to their lies, dream of love in their arms. I didn't have the heart to be angry.

Without sunlight, the large room seemed adrift on some Arctic sea as I stood in the doorway. Carolyn saw me first, rose from the wicker couch, moved two steps toward me, then turned, her face in her hands, and went to the far corner of the room to stare at the weak light. Cassie suddenly became very interested in the pattern of the Oriental rug at her feet, and Gail busied herself picking up cake crumbs with her fingers and lifting them carefully to her mouth. Only Sarah Weddington had the guts to look at me, and even her eyes kept slipping away.

'Hello, Bud,' she said quietly. 'Would you like a drink?'

'No, ma'am,' I said.

'An explanation, darling?' Cassie asked lightly as she lifted her lovely face, one eyebrow arched.

'It's not necessary,' I said.

'Take off your coat and stay awhile,' Gail offered with false hospitality.

'I won't be here that long,' I said. 'I just came by to tell you ladies how it's going to be.' I walked over and tossed a list of names and addresses on the coffee table between Sarah and Cassie.

'What's this?' Cassie said. 'I don't know any of these people.'

'They're the innocent bystanders,' I said, 'the children. And you and Sarah have twenty-four hours to set up trust funds – don't be stingy – monthly payments until they're twenty-five, then the rest of the money goes to them. Okay?'

'Of course, Bud,' Sarah said, looking at the names.

'Now just a minute, darling,' Cassie said to Sarah. 'Who are these people, anyway?'

'A teenager in a foster home in Denver,' I said, 'two little girls in Casper, two little boys, and a little girl with a cancer behind her eye on Vashon Island . . .'

'Rideout's,' Cassie murmured. 'What is this – blackmail?'

'Let's just call it conscience money, okay?' I said. 'I've seen your Dun and Bradstreet rating, love – you can afford it.'

'Not if you don't explain, darling,' she said softly.

683

'If I do that,' I said, 'then you'll either have to go to the police or become an accessory after the fact to half a dozen assorted felonies.'

'Leave Cassie out of it,' Sarah said, almost weeping. 'I'll take care of it, Bud, for the memory of your father . . .'

'Just leave my father out of it,' I said more harshly than I meant. 'Please.'

'My conscience is clear,' Cassie said, almost laughing as she touched her smooth, lovely throat.

'I'll help however I can,' Carolyn said from the window. 'I wasn't in at the beginning, but I could have stopped it – should have stopped it.'

'Can you forgive us, Bud?' Sarah said weakly, her fingers kneading at her temples.

'I don't think so,' I said. 'You dug up my father's memory, old woman – '

'Oh, to goddamned hell with your father's precious memory!' Gail shouted as she stood up and kicked the corner of the coffee table, splashing tea out of the china cups. 'My father's dying . . . everybody dies, eventually. That's not the point.'

'What is?' I asked.

'Those bastards,' she said, 'they poison the air, pollute the ground water systems – thousands of children will die needlessly, horribly. Have you seen pictures of them? Their skin rots, their blood fails, they're born dying. Don't you care?'

'I guess so,' I said, 'but I do know that because of this dumb stunt you pulled, eight people died in front of me. Maybe a few of them deserved it. I don't know. That's not my decision to make. Or yours. You people made a terrible mess and now you have to clean it up.'

'Eight?' Cassie said thoughtfully, smiling. 'And how many did you personally blow away, Mr. Milodragovitch?' At the window, Carolyn turned as if to say something, but kept her mouth tightly shut. 'How many?' Cassie demanded sweetly.

'Enough to last me a lifetime,' I said.

'Eight!' Gail shouted, storming around the room, pounding floor-boards with her boots. 'Eight? What's eight against eight hundred thousand? Eight million? The whole goddamned planet Earth, huh?'

'You sound like an officer I knew in Korea,' I said.

'Well, by God, it is a war.'

'Right now,' I said, 'I'm having trouble choosing sides.'

'We chose you, darling,' Cassie said, 'because it's your war too, because – '

'Bullshit,' I said, 'you chose me because I was convenient, because you knew I could be manipulated. With your kind of money, you could have hired a battalion of lawyers and private detectives.'

'They did try,' Carolyn said from the far side of the room, 'but nobody was very interested in taking on a multinational corporation.'

'And how did you do, darling?' Cassie asked.

'Not very well,' I said. 'I got out alive. You people are still alive. Call it a draw.'

'A draw?' she said. 'Didn't you find out anything?'

I lied to keep from laughing. 'Hell, lady, I'm still not real sure what this was all about.'

'You want to know what it was all about?' she said. 'Well, let me get my coat and I'll show you what it was all about.'

'In a minute,' I said. 'I've got two other things to settle first.' I took out an envelope and tossed it into Sarah's lap. 'There's your credit cards, ma'am, my expense sheet, and your bill.'

'Her bill?' Cassie protested as she stood up. 'For what?'

'I did what I was hired to do,' I said. 'You're the bitch in the rented car, which is all she needs to know, and the guy in the yellow Toyota, his name is, or was, John Rausche. A long-haul trucker. An ex-con. He got blown to pieces over in Elk City, Idaho, then fried.' I turned to Cassandra Bogardus. 'And, sweetheart, you killed him with your little dumb-ass number in Seattle, you killed him the first time you let him touch that great body of yours . . .'

'Oh, for Christ's sake,' she murmured, 'that little worm.'

'You should be more careful where you put your mouth, lady,' I said, and Cassie shuddered. 'By the way, Mrs. Weddington, you'll also be getting a rather large bill from Haliburton Security. They spent some time looking for you after you and Gail pulled your cute little disappearing act.'

'I'll take care of it, Bud,' she said, her face so gray I hoped she'd live long enough to get it done. 'I'll take care of everything.'

'Well, are you quite through?' Cassie asked.

'One more thing,' I said. 'I want my bearskin back.'

'It's still in my trunk,' Carolyn said.

She came across the room, still not looking at me, and Cassie and I followed her to the door. Behind me I heard Sarah moan my name, the clatter of Gail's boots as she went to comfort the old lady. This foolishness had claimed enough victims, so I went back.

'It's okay, Sarah,' I said as I touched her wet cheek. Gail tried to shoulder me out of the way, but I didn't move. 'It's okay,' I repeated. 'What's done is done. In a couple of weeks, I'll call. We'll have tea and crumpets. Okay?'

'Please try to forgive me, Bud.'

'Ah, there's nothing to forgive,' I said. 'Your heart was in the right place. I just wish you hadn't chosen me.'

'Me too,' Gail complained. 'Nothing got done.'

'Hush,' Sarah said, her finger lifted, 'hush, child.'

When I got outside, Carolyn and Cassie were struggling angrily with the grizzly hide. I gave them a hand. We got it out and into the bed of my pickup.

'Well, are you ready now?' Cassie said sharply. 'To see what this is all about.' I nodded sadly. 'We'll need snowshoes,' she said.

'Nope.'

'Nope?' she said, her hand to her cheek.

'The illegal dump in the old mine above Camas Meadows,' I said, 'has been cleaned out.'

'Cleaned out? How do you know?'

'I went up yesterday,' I said.

'But why, what . . .'

'I had a list of their illegal dumps in seven Western states,' I said, 'and I made a deal.'

'A deal?'

'Right,' I said. 'I traded that list for cleaning up that one dump . . .'

'It wasn't yours to trade,' she said, her face pinched with anger.

'Sure as hell was,' I said, 'and I traded it for my life, Sarah's life, Gail's, even your pissant, rich-girl ass.'

'By why – '

'I had some notion I might like to see your goddamned face, lady, when you saw the empty mine galleries, but the truth is, it's not worth it.'

'What's not worth it?'

'Spending two hours in the same pickup with a piece of trash like you.'

'You son of a bitch!' She drew back and slapped me as hard as she could. I let her. It felt all right, washed the last bit of her out of me, the memory of her touch.

Carolyn turned around, pivoted neatly from the hips, and dropped Cassandra Bogardus in the snow with a perfect right cross. We laughed as we watched her scramble to her feet, moving backward, frightened by the small violence and the tiny trickle of blood out of the corner of her mouth, her green eyes gone gray, no glitter left.

'And you know, Cassie,' Carolyn huffed, 'if you don't do what Milo said about the children, I'm going to follow your ass around and knock you down every day for the rest of your stinking life.' Cassie nodded dumbly, then fled into the safety of the mansion. 'God, that felt good,' Carolyn said, her flat cheeks flushed. 'If only I had done that when I first found out what sort of crazy crap she had in mind.'

'I knew I was being taken for a ride,' I said, 'but I hoped she would be at the end of it.'

'Men,' she snorted. 'Ah, but what the hell, I was a fool too. Once you wouldn't turn loose of your – that is, your grandfather's – timberland, she convinced me that whatever happened to you was your fault. I'm sorry.'

'Not as sorry as I am, love.'

'What about it?' she said suddenly.

'What about what?'

'The deal I offered you the last time I saw you.'

'I've made my last deal,' I said, 'but I appreciate your persistence.'

'We'll get it eventually, you know,' she said. 'You can't get a draw with the government.'

'Over my dead body,' I said.

'God, I should have broken the rules,' she said, 'stayed at your house all night that night, fucked you to a frazzle, then gotten you to give your word at a weak moment. Isn't that the way it works out West? You can take a man's word to the bank?'

'Trigger's stuffed, love, and Gene Autry owns a baseball team,' I said. 'Now that the dump is gone, you people shouldn't have any trouble making a trade for the C, C&K sections, but you have my word on this – you'll never get my grandfather's land.'

'You're going to be bitter about all this, aren't you?' she said, reaching for my cheek with her cold hand. 'I like the beard.'

'You bet your sweet ass, lady, I'm going to be bitter.'

'How long?'

'As long as it takes.'

'So what now?'

'Chores,' I said, brushing her hand away, 'then I'm heading south, down to Mexico, try to grow old peacefully in the sunshine.'

'So it's all been for nothing?'

'Almost nothing,' I said. 'An EPA official down in Denver recently died, a fellow named Sikes. Get some of your hot-shot environmental lawyer buddies to check into his estate and his recent decisions. That should keep them busy for a few years, maybe even clean up some garbage in the process.'

'Sikes,' she said. 'Thanks.'

'For nothing, babe.'

'However you want it, Milo.'

'And, babe . . .'

'Yes?' she said, pulling the hood of her jacket up against the cold.

'Nothing,' I said, and we left it like that, went our separate ways, either because of or against our better judgment. You always hate to lose a good woman, one you might love for a long time, but she wanted to save the wilderness to look at it, and I wanted . . . well, I wasn't sure anymore what I wanted, maybe just an end to confusion.

When I knocked on Tante Marie's door in the fading, ashen dusk, she answered it wearing a long woolen robe with curlers in her hair. Over her shoulder, I could see the television set. A *Hawaii Five-O* rerun. She recognized me, saw me glance at the program, then said, 'One must study corruption to defeat it.'

'And take the occasional rest from the crusade,' I said.

She nodded without smiling. 'Can I help you?'

'You already have,' I said, handing her the deed to my grandfather's three thousand acres, 'and this is my end of the bargain.'

'What is it?'

'Camas Meadows,' I said, 'where the bears used to dance.'

'What?'

'That was the deal,' I said, 'Camas Meadows for Charlie Two Moons' name.'

'I'll be damned,' she said, digging her glasses out of her pocket.

'Sometimes even coyote tongue speaks without joking,' I said, 'and there's no need to thank me.'

'I hadn't planned on it,' she said, her eyes like wet black stones.

'Goddamn,' I said, 'you knew about the mine, didn't you?'

'The mine?' she said blandly.

'Jesus Christ, lady,' I said, amazed, 'when the gunfire starts, I want to be on your side.' But her small smile told me I hadn't bought a thing.

'Let me tell you a story,' she said. 'Once upon – '

'Lady,' I interrupted, 'I've heard enough stories lately to last me a lifetime.'

She was too busy rechecking the deed to pay much attention to my departure, but as I turned the pickup up the South Fork Road to spend one last night among my grandfather's ashes, I saw Tante Marie in my rear-view mirror. She still stood on the front porch, and at a distance it seemed as if she was dancing.

The road had been plowed over the divide and down to the old mine, but it was still hairy. I liked the idea of the crooked bastards out in the snow, putting tire chains on garbage trucks, but I suddenly realized that it was just some working stiffs out wrestling in the cold while the real bastards sat in warm offices on leather chairs. They hadn't done a great job at the mine, but at least the leaking drums had been removed and some of the toxic puddles shoveled up. Not a victory, not even a draw. God knows how much poison had already seeped into the ground water.

I parked at the mine and got out my snowshoes and pack. I set the grizzly hide on a pair of plastic saucers, then hiked like a coolie down the unplowed road to the edge of the meadow. There, I dug a great circular pit in the blue, glowing snow, then built as big a fire as I could find deadfall wood. I sat for several hours as the fire burned down, listening to the wilderness. The nearest wolf was probably in Canada, and the coyotes snuggled warm in their dens, so that night was silent except for the crackle of the fire. When it had burned down to embers, I shoveled them aside, then dug a shallow hole in the thawed earth and rolled the bearskin into it, then built another fire on top. When I had coals again, I baked a couple of potatoes in aluminum foil and grilled a large T-bone steak I had picked up in town. I didn't have much appetite, though, and threw most of the meal back into the fire, an American offering, a backyard barbecue.

689

I don't know what I planned to dream wrapped in my sleeping bag – sweet dancing, perhaps – but if I dreamed, I didn't remember the visions. When I woke, I felt as purified as I was ever going to feel, so I loaded up and hiked back to the truck.

The next week I finished my chores, sold my lot to the first cash buyer, and used some of Tewels' money to hire the best criminal lawyer in the Northwest for Billy Buffaloshoe and to take Abner and Yvonne out to dinner. They wanted to get married, but some goddamned Social Security regulation kept them from the altar, so they took up living in sin. I had a dull, sleepy tea with Sarah and a sullen Gail. Sarah showed me the trust-fund papers. They seemed fine. And she said Cassie was coming around, but as far as I knew she never did. Gail told me that next year there would be a government regulation to prevent the dumping of liquid toxic waste in landfills, but I just laughed at her, tried to explain that they would fight it in the courts until the government backed off. Then it was her turn to laugh, an unpleasant, naïve sound that brought tears to Sarah's eyes.

After that I put Meriwether in my rear-view mirror, heading south with something over forty thousand dollars in my kitty, planning to measure it out slowly in Mexico until I came into my father's estate.

I detoured through Seattle, though, with five thousand in an envelope for the former Mrs. Rausche. When I parked in front of her house on a dingy Sunday afternoon, John Paul, Jr., in a bright red parka that looked new, and Sally, with a white patch over her eye, were playing some game with rules only they knew, running from one edge of the sagging porch to the other, then freezing in place.

When he saw my pickup, the boy ran out to the driveway and gave me a crisp salute. Then he recognized me, even behind the beard. 'You're a private,' he said shyly, 'you're supposed to salute me.'

'Sorry,' I said and complied. 'Is your mother home?'

'She's gone to the store with Baby Luke,' he said as Sally crashed into his back.

'Will you give this to her?' I asked, and Sally peeked under his arm. 'It's from Captain Rausche's friends.'

He took the heavy envelope out of my hand, weighed it in his. 'Will you tell them "Thank you"?' he asked.

'I will,' I said, and we exchanged salutes again.

I went south like a gut-shot deer, breathing hard.

My intentions were the best, my reasons endless. My hometown had died inside me, and I craved sunshine and simplicity. I made it as far as Red Bluff, California, where I gave up, turned around, headed home, back into the heart of one of the worst Montana winters in years. Some things you can change, some you can't. A few months after the government put the regulation against liquid toxic waste in landfill into effect, they suspended it. For further study, or something.

I still have my beard, though, and haven't had a drink since the night Simmons died. When I see myself in a barroom mirror, I look like a ghost of my former self, and I see myself a lot as I tend bar at Arnie's across the street from the Deuce, work the day shift and swamp out the bar at night. Sometimes old Abner comes in for a short beer, but not too often because Yvonne gives him hell about it. Sometimes Raoul comes in for a laugh, sometimes the colonel to offer work, which I refuse. Carolyn even dropped by once. Her offer was harder to refuse, but I managed it. The poor postman, who somehow started all this, comes in occasionally, but he has lost his job and his wife, and doesn't have much to say after the third or fourth drink I turn down. I am not tempted. I live close to the grain, avoid even the appearance of evil, forgive all things, live alone in the tiny swamper's cubicle beside the alley, keep my nose clean.

I have learned some things. Modern life is warfare without end: take no prisoners, leave no wounded, eat the dead – that's environmentally sound.

Fifty-two draws closer every day, and with it, my father's ton of money. So I wait, survive the winters, and when the money comes, let the final dance begin.